REDEMPTION

LEON
A NOVEL
REDEMPTION
URIS

HarperCollins*Publishers*

For a map of Gallipoli, please write to: Trade Department, Box GJC, HarperCollins Publishers, Inc., 10 East 53rd Street, New York, NY 10022. Enclose a self-addressed stamped envelope.

HarperCollins books may be purchased for educational, business, or sales promotional use. For information please write: Special Markets Department, HarperCollins Publishers, Inc., 10 East 53rd Street, New York, NY 10022.

FIRST EDITION

Designed by Nancy Singer

ISBN 0-06-018333-0

95 96 97 98 99 ❖/RRD 10 9 8 7 6 5 4 3 2 1

For Rachael and Conor Uris
with love from Daddy

*Special thanks to my research associate
Jeanne Sillay Jacobson
and to my special assistant
Jeanne Randall*

FOOTSTEPS

PROLOGUE: THE YEAR OF 1894

It is apparent to me as I approach adulthood that I am destined to make a memorable impact on the political life of Great Britain. I must display sufficient qualities to assure England's subjects that I have the passion and courage for leadership.

Conversely, I must not appear too vain. Since my appetite as a writer is no less voracious than my will to ascend to power I shall keep copious notes.

Obviously, some of these notes must be secret and for my eyes alone. If one says what he is really thinking at all times he could advance no further in the rough and tumble of politics than a custodian in the House of Commons.

Therefore, *The Secret Files of Winston Churchill* shall remain under lock and key, for my eyes only, to remain unseen by friend and foe alike.

I have provided in my Will that upon my (untimely) death *The Secret Files of Winston Churchill* be held in Trust by His Majesty's National Archives until the year A.D. 2050.

At that time, when I am safely (and one would hope) ensconced among my countrymen of bygone centuries, the historians and academics may unseal these files and, perhaps, come in for a shock or two.

Winston S. Churchill

CHAPTER

1

1895

If the earth were flat, New Zealand would have fallen off it a long time ago, it's that far from Ireland.

Can ever a man be more stricken and disoriented than a penniless immigrant, out of steerage, upon arrival in a land so far removed?

The canvas cots in the passenger hold of the tramp steamer *Nova Scotia* were stacked so tight a man could not roll over or even sleep on his side. Heat from the adjoining boiler room often drove him on deck in any weather to keep from fainting. After he forced down the slop fed him in a zoolike manner, he'd head for the railing, often as not.

When the hills behind Lyttelton came into view ninety-two days after departure from Derry, Liam Larkin dropped to his knees and thanked the first thirty or forty saints who came to mind.

He wobbled down the gangplank, one of God's forgotten miseries, where he presented himself, pale and trembling, to his sponsor, Squire Bert Hargrove. A lot of the lads landed skinny and shaken from the long voyage, but as Bert looked Liam over, he thought he'd bought himself a bad nag. At least Liam Larkin and Bert Hargrove shared enough of a basic language so they could understand one another . . . barely.

Certain he was in for three years of Caribbean-like slave labor, the anxiety ebbed from Liam into a state that resembled euphoria.

Liam shared a clean bunkhouse with a wooden floor and a heating stove with six other station hands. Three of them were paddies like himself, contracted for forty months' labor to pay off their passage. In actual fact, Liam was replacing one who was about to strike out on his own. So, by God, maybe it wasn't going to be total slavery.

He knew he was going to be worked hard, but he had never known much more than hard work. Bert Hargrove was pleased. He'd bought himself a good horse.

Some of the changes dawned on Liam subtly while others crashed through. The vast and incredible difference was that this land was not fueled by anger . . . or fear . . . or hatred. Was this an actual place? he asked himself every night.

Take the scroggins. Indeed, the station house and the bunk house were fed from the very same kitchen and the food was served to the men by the three Hargrove daughters. And a man could eat all he could hold. Liam thought back. Maybe six times back in Ireland in his village of Ballyutogue he had left the table with his belly bulging. He ate here this way every single night. The cook knew fourteen ways to prepare mutton, which was a hell of a lot better than fourteen ways to cook potatoes. There were vegetables he had neither seen nor heard of.

Food was only one matter. In the beginning New Zealand reminded him of Ireland, it was that green and hilly, and likewise the weather was either dirty, going to be dirty, or had just been dirty.

The hills were grander than hills, they were wondrous white-haired old mountains. Where they sloped toward the sea, they plummeted as fjords so fearsome as to shock a man's breath away. Not only did this land run higher, it ran deeper with black earth.

New Zealanders were a stoic lot, not unlike the dour Ulstermen of County Donegal. Like the Ulstermen, loyalty here was to the Crown. Yet the tone of New Zealand patriotism was placid. Could it be such that he would never again have to hear the terrorizing rattle of the Lembeg drum and the hysterical rantings of the Orangemen and their preachers?

As with Ulster, New Zealand's union with Britain was the centerpiece of its existence. But how could two places, islands ... green ... with mountains and sea ... be so different and share the same planet? There were no whipping posts here, no hanging tree, no agony of the oppressed, poor little sheep rustling, smuggling, and moonshining, and he never saw an eviction, not one, not once.

Even the native Maori had apparently been subdued rather easily and were left with their culture and their dignity. Or so it seemed.

Aye, New Zealand was Protestant country, but an absence of game and fishing wardens in the bountiful streams told the whole story.

Fortunately, there were enough families, runholders, and miners around of the True Faith to hold Mass twice a month in one of Methven's three public houses, otherwise padlocked on Sundays due to stringent "blue laws."

Their priest, Father Gionelli of Eye-tallion extract, wended his way up from Christchurch on the second and fourth Sundays of the month in a three-donkey train. His arrival seemed so Joseph-and-Mary-like.

Confessions were dispensed with first, but there wasn't too much to sin about in the mountain stations of the South Island, except for the drinking of the previous night, impure thoughts, and occasional fornication between man and sheep, a practice that never appealed to Liam.

With the Mass and sacraments finished, Father Gionelli read and wrote letters to and from home and transferred funds and consoled homesickness. His fractured English and their fractured English developed a melody all its own.

Liam Larkin was never truly homesick, only pained and angry over his dismissal from Ballyutogue and Ireland. He liked it here, to the utmost.

The pastures of New Zealand's South Island gave a wonderful soft feel under his Wellington boots—in comparison to the back-breaking rocks and fragile topsoil and constant torment of wind, laws, weather, and omnipresent loathing of the oppressors that afforded the Irish hill farmer his marginal existence and life-long suffering.

Back in Ireland in Ballyutogue, high in the heather, Liam had dug alongside his daddy, Tomas Larkin, since he had been a chip of a lad, and when one carries seaweed up from the lough to make it into a crust of topsoil, he damned well better know what he is doing.

In the beginning Bert Hargrove thought Liam Larkin a dullard with a broad back. Given this kind of land in this kind of atmosphere, Liam Larkin, in his quiet manner, inched his way into acceptance as an extremely knowledgeable farmer and sheep man. His wise observations, keen suggestions for logical changes here and there, and the penchant for a long day's work caught the squire's eye.

At the end of the first season Liam was made assistant to the station foreman. Free at last from constraints, Liam blossomed, took on responsibility, organized and had no qualms in running a crew. Tilted shears invented by his brother Conor in the black-smith forge speeded the wool cropping by ten percent.

Things never stand still, not even in paradise.

Bert Hargrove was the most successful Catholic runholder hereabouts and was blessed with two fine young sons. On the minus side of the ledger, he was burdened with three daughters. As the inheritors, the squire's sons would be adequate. Women, as they always do, presented the problems that caused him sleep-lessness.

The Hargrove girls were a bovine lot, and endowed with the stout requirements for a future life as runholders' wives, they seemed to have excellent breeding possibilities. Bert's wife Edna made the mainstay of her life the future respectable and nearby placement of her daughters. She was bloody well determined that she would have a large family around her to comfort her during her declining years.

This was no simple matter. There were not enough eligible Catholic lads who fit into her scheme. By eligible, one would consider the inheritor of a station, an independent merchant of means, or perhaps a professional—a doctor or solicitor down in Christchurch. Beyond Christchurch was out of bounds.

The girls were off limits to the hands on the station. Edna Hargrove had the precision of a Prussian field marshal in her mind, knowing at every instant where each troop was. One pat on the rump and you were off the Hargrove Station, the debt for your passage auctioned to another runholder.

As an English-born lady, Edna was confronted with the fact that most Catholic lads in the region were Irish station hands, working off their passages or eking out a life on forty acres. She was reminded every second and fourth Sunday at the Mass when the paddies would stagger in, legless, shaking from a night's drinking and hell-raising, lying and slothful as they were.

Certain forces of nature were too powerful even for the steel of Edna Hargrove, as powerful as the waters atop the fjords plunging into Milford Straits.

Her oldest daughter, Mildred, was not what one would call a comely maiden, but pleasant from the inside and good and sturdy otherwise. It was most important that Mildred make a good match to serve as an example to her sisters. Edna's vulture eye picked up on the first glances exchanged by Mildred and Liam Larkin. One time they were looking at each other across the stable. Edna walked between them and could *feel* their vibrations going back and forth.

She suggested to Bert that Liam's contract be auctioned to another station, preferably one up on the North Island.

"He's too damned valuable," Bert responded. "And he still owes us more than two and a half years' work. Talk to Mildred and explain her about things."

"I've been explaining her about things since she was four years old, Bert. We simply can't risk some illiterate paddy to destroy all our lives."

"That paddy is a good investment, old girl. It's your job to keep them out of the breeding pens."

"Don't be vulgar, Bert. Two and a half years?"

It was a bit much. The Hargroves decided to make Liam sign

his name to a nonfornication oath. Although he could sign his name, he couldn't read a word on the paper, even though Bert explained its meaning, precisely.

Edna Hargrove should have known that a mere sheet of paper was not going to stop certain powerful natural forces. She had her work cut out for her.

It was at the district fair during the wool-shearing contest that what was apparent, was apparent. Stripped to the waist, Liam Larkin represented the Hargrove Station. Odds against him were delicious. No newcomer held a prayer, even with the saints on his side. Twenty-to-one odds against Larkin put him close to the bottom of the heap. Of course, no one at Hargrove spoke about Conor's newly designed shears.

Mildred could scarcely conceal her delight at the sight of Conor's upper body. The shears did the rest. After due deliberation by the judges, Liam's tilty, grindy-toothed instrument was declared legal in Liam's hands and the squire and all the squire's men went home with a hat full of silver.

In the beginning, when working out artful dodges from Edna, Liam could scarcely believe that a girl of English descent, schooled at a convent in Auckland, would consider him worthy. Liam didn't know all that much about birds. What he knew he found out back in Ballyutogue tagging along with his brother Conor.

What was there to say about Conor? Conor could get a shag any time he whistled. On such occasions Conor always sought out Protestant girls so he wouldn't have to get seriously involved afterward. A couple of times at fairs on the other side of Donegal or down in Derry, Liam had the opportunity to latch on to the extra girl, and he wasn't too awkward, so long as Conor was nearby. He figured that he would be equal to the occasion, should it occur.

The occasion occurred at the celebration of the Queen's birthday, no less, which also marked the first time Liam ever mouthed the "forbidden" words to "God Save the Queen" praying that certain ancestors were not beholding him from above.

No greater catastrophe could have befallen Edna Hargrove

than Mildred's pregnancy, which destroyed half a lifetime of delicate manipulation. Bert raged because something had been put over on him and there was a balance due on Liam's obligations. When the Hargrove cloudburst was dry of rage, Liam and Mildred were presented with a monstrous ultimatum.

The pair would be broken up permanently. Liam's labor indenture would be sold to a station elsewhere. Mildred would be slipped out of the country to Australia to a convent. Since abortion was unthinkable, the child would be put up for adoption in Australia.

The alternative was uglier. Bert Hargrove had legal recourse both on Liam's debt and a number of "sexual" offenses that could put him in prison for years.

Liam and Mildred had backed themselves to the edge of a cliff and seemed to have no choice but to submit or hurl themselves over the edge, when the hand of Providence stretched out clear from Ireland in the form of a cable. It was opened with shaky hands because a cable almost always announced a death. Mildred read it to him:

DEAR LIAM STOP I HAVE COLLECTED A SMALL FORTUNE IN ADVANCE ON A COMMISSION TO RESTORE THE GREAT SCREEN IN THE LONG HALL OF HUBBLE MANOR STOP I HAVE PAID OFF YOUR PASSAGE IN FULL STOP CERTIFICATE IS ON THE WAY STOP FURTHER FUNDS ARE BEING TRANSFERRED FOR YOU TO START A HOMESTEAD STOP DADDY UNAWARE STOP YOUR BROTHER CONOR

CHAPTER
2

Well, Conor's cable changed the manner of doing things. The couple departed the Hargrove acres with only the mutilated suitcase Liam had arrived with. Mildred left everything, every stitch of clothing, her hope chest, her show horses, and her private possessions.

However, since young womanhood she had been in control of a bank account of earnings. Much of the money she had acquired was by shrewd trading on the various agricultural markets. It would serve as a down payment on something.

Father Gionelli, who had heard both of their confessions over a period of time, had been expecting them. He agreed to marry them provided they agreed to invite Bert and Edna to the christening. They agreed, reluctantly. The Hargroves felt one-third betrayed, one-third guilty, and one-third enraged, and they declined to come. A bitter seed had been planted.

Liam chose a strange and oblique name for his son: Rory. No one in the Larkin line had been named such and to name the first born outside of family was rare and uneasy. Liam reckoned that Rory had been a great Irish king and that was sufficient.

Rory was christened immediately after birth and dubbed "wee" Rory to indicate he had probably been born premature. Rory was hardly "wee" but hardy and quite beautiful. It almost seemed impossible he was born out of the two of them. "Wee" Rory had been hung about his neck like an invisible pendant. It was not that he was born in disgrace but that "an unusual child should have an unusual name."

Bert Hargrove had always said that if Mildred had been a

boy she would have been the best runholder in the South Island, she was that certain of the skills she needed. Her leaving was another cruel blow for Bert, for she had kept the ledgers, the payroll, the taxes, the contracts for land purchases, and knew the buy-and-sell game of the wool market keenly.

With Mildred's head operating Liam's instinct and knowledge of farming, they made a team that went from humble homesteaders to important runholders in a few years. The government of New Zealand at the time was intent on building a cattle and wool industry able to trade with the world and become an important cog in Britain's wheel. Privileged terms on land and animal stock were backed by the government and the Larkins knew how to grab them.

There was additional support from Conor Larkin, who was faring well with his foundry in Derry. Mildred's whipsaw mind knew exactly what to do with the windfall funds from Conor. When the thousandth acre was acquired, mortgage free, Liam hung up a sign: BALLYUTOGUE STATION, LIAM LARKIN, ESQ. "Squire Liam, mind you, *a commoner of stature demanding respect by his achievement.*" Ballyutogue Station—Liam Larkin, Esq. How many times did he repeat it? Mildred knew. She knew that "Squire" look in his eyes and how she loved it.

Why did he name his station, Ballyutogue, after his village in Ireland? The word itself meant "a place of sorrow" and sorrow is what he had gotten from it. Sweet ... sweet revenge. "I'll show all of you Liam was not the bumbling fool of the Larkins. The Ballyutogue Station I created will remind me of my victory every time I enter its gates."

For a landless croppy it was far more than burgeoning boundaries of his land and far more than a country that wanted and accepted him. It was Mildred.

"My husband is not going to be an illiterate," she commanded, and taught him how to read and write far beyond ordinary requirements. He'd think to himself when he had solved a difficult passage in the Bible or one of Mildred's novels—What would Conor think if he saw me now! Aye, he remembered well how Conor always had his nose stuck in a book, taught by his little friend Seamus O'Neill. Someday, he'd read as well as Conor himself.

Oh, Mildred, what a dear! He loved every plump round feel of her. They may have been plain and rough hewn but there was nothing plain about the way they loved each other.

Mildred was the first thing that ever belonged to him, not counting the required love of certain family members. Mildred was the first person and the only person to love him alone.

Liam was the first person to love Mildred. The first person who belonged to her. They were the first to be tender to each other. They wallowed in each other, gloriously, never passing without a touch to make up for a lifetime of touches never before given or felt.

It took a third of a lifetime of misery and a journey halfway around the world, but his salvation from purgatory was felt every day of his life after he awakened to the realization that New Zealand was true.

Edna Hargrove's anger lasted only until the second child, Spring, was christened. A proper English mother forgives and Spring *was* named after her own mother. Certainly Mildred had sent a signal in naming Spring that she wanted Edna's forgiveness. At least things could be mixed around so no one really knew who was forgiving whom.

Bert held out for one more baby, Madge.

Through this ordeal Liam realized that a certain unplanned sense of exaltation was being awarded the victor. Continuing kindness to one's former crucifier can be the most delicious and artful form of revenge. Had he and Mildred become belligerent, the Hargroves would certainly have found justification for their obnoxious behavior.

By accepting them with open arms, Liam had laid guilt and shame everlasting on Mildred's parents. The terrible thing they had done was the Hargroves' subject of many hours with Father Gionelli, but they could never erase it fully. The Aussies had a saying about the evil hunter missing his prey and getting whacked with his own boomerang. The Bible was a catalogue of "what goes around comes around."

Of the other Hargrove boys, King Hargrove, their oldest son, grew into a first-rate lout with a penchant for gambling losses and the kind of irresponsibility that Bert Hargrove formerly attributed only to Irishmen. Bert was delighted when King stayed on in South Africa chasing a gold rush after serving in the Boer War.

Gilbert, the younger son, was a good bloke but he would not be dissuaded from being educated in England with aspirations of becoming an engineer.

There came a divine moment for Liam Larkin when Bert stood, hat in hand, and tolled off a litany of failures, bad investments, things on the turn with his sons, unforeseen sweeps of sickness through his flock and herd. None of this was Bert's fault. Land had been easy to get and greed was his undoing. Bert's overextension had no plan for a reserve in the event of failure. Hell, Liam knew when he was ten years old that a man doesn't try to plow a thousand acres without a tractor.

He smiled and shook his head sympathetically and did not say aloud but Bert could read the silence in Liam's face . . . What would you give for another stupid paddy like me to come off the ship and bail you out, you fuck-faced monster?

"Ah glory, Bert, let me and Millie sit down with you and see how we can get you through this little muddle of yours."

Goddamned! Liam's kindness damned near killed Bert Hargrove, but the terms, rather generous under the circumstances, saved the station, which would now be distributed on an equitable basis among his three daughters.

Actually, kindness as the ultimate revenge had begun to evolve in Liam's mind years earlier when he and Millie and the baby struggled through that first winter in their first home, a leaking, clapboard, one-room, windblown misery of a shack. It was like the nightmare of Ireland all over, but they endured until spring and from that moment on never looked back.

His careworn daddy, Tomas Larkin, had driven him out of Ireland instead of giving him the careworn Larkin acres, which were rightfully his and which he craved. With springtime came a letter from Tomas pleading for Liam to return to Ireland and take over.

After a first rush of joy, Liam realized what lay behind the letter. After four generations, the Larkin land would not have the Larkin name on it unless Liam came back.

Conor had left the village of Ballyutogue and had established himself as a great ironmaster. Dary, the younger brother, was on the way of fulfilling his mother, Finola's, dream of his becoming a priest. That left Brigid, who had given up her only love because he had no land and was forced to leave.

Brigid would now have to marry some old run-down bachelor because she was beyond the age of youth and loveliness and it was doubtful that she would ever bear a child.

"I treated you sorely," Tomas's letter pleaded, "but come home, the farm and all I have is yours."

Liam could imagine both the agony and hope in his father's pen. He could also imagine Tomas at Dooley McCloskey's public house waving the return letter that his boy, Liam, would soon be coming home.

Too bad, Daddy, too damned bad. Keep your hair on. Me and Millie were never part of anyone's plan because nobody ever loved either of us . . . except my brothers, Conor and Dary.

Liam was not yet literate enough to compose an answer and he did not want to introduce Mildred by way of the family brouhaha. He went to Father Gionelli and together they crafted a letter that oozed with compassion and concern. Between the compassion and concern he dropped little mouse turds . . . "Conor has paid off my passage . . . I've a lease with option to purchase of six hundred acres . . . the government is helping me with a thousand head of sheep . . . the land in New Zealand is rich and black . . . tell Ma I still say the rosary and Angelus. . . ."

Then Liam stroked a razor's edge of kindness across his daddy's throat. He wrote about Mildred. Liam did not mention that they were already married and had a son but . . . "Mildred is from an English family and convent-educated and we will marry soon and I'm not coming back to Ireland."

Liam held his tongue until the letter was mailed then went to the priest again. "Father, I feel no anger toward my daddy but I must confess that the letter filled me with a tremendous thrill of happiness, and I know that's wrong because I know how much I hurt him. I know the hurt because that is the way he hurt me. I'm sorry for my joy, but I cannot deny it."

"I comprehend you, Liam," Father Gionelli answered. "Your letter is the story of my own childhood."

"Have I sinned?"

"Sin? What is sin inside the dynamic of family relationships? It is a mystery that began with man. No one can solve it except through his own unique experience. How you feel is human. But do not think it will leave you alone. We are never free of our blood."

Tomas Larkin was struck down with the diabetes shortly after receiving Liam's letter. He passed on through as the sun inched up along the horizon of a new century. Tomas died, deep in consternation over the way he had treated his son.

January 1915

The benevolence of Squire Larkin grew along with his acres. He built a church for Father Gionelli at Methven and beautified it with stained-glass windows dedicated to his father, and later, his mother. He pondered as he had never pondered for almost six months but finally ended up calling the church St. Columba's, the same name his childhood church bore in Ballyutogue.

He was a benefactor of Father Gionelli's nonsectarian orphanage in Christchurch, which he thought was a noble idea worthy of the attitudes of New Zealand.

Although it was not the same as seeing the priest arrive at Methven with his donkey train, Liam was chief contributor for the purchase of a Model-T automobile from America to carry the Father up and down the mountain road.

And he had been a benefactor for the folks back in Ireland! He made sure his mother, Finola, lived like a queen in her village. The Larkin cottage roof had slates, a singular signature that one of the family over the water had made it big. Liam sent money for fine new tombstones for all the Larkins who'd gone on to their rewards.

For his brother, the priest Father Dary Larkin, there was a generous fund for Dary's good works.

Try though he might, Liam could not carry out his philanthropies without a measure of revenge still attached to it. He guessed he was a hard shot. As Father Gionelli had told him years before, "It just doesn't go away. We are never free of our blood."

Liam realized that there was only one way to find an accommodation with his childhood, and that was to be certain his own children would not suffer from him.

He and Mildred often spoke in terms of advanced thinking for his times. The daughters, Spring and Madge, were coming into courting age. Unfortunately, they were behind the door when good looks were passed out. Yet all was not lost: The girls were nice young ladies and not only inherited their mother's ampleness but her pleasant manner and keen mind as well.

Although, please God, they would never interfere or try to dictate the girls' lives, Millie was certain that with Squire Larkin's strong name they would be attractive beyond their physical liabilities. Liam and Mildred had come to a unique idea that there was nothing wrong with *daughters* inheriting land. It would mean marrying men with different names, but Ballyutogue Station would always be over the entry arch.

Liam even dared to take it one step further. If, God forbid, Madge and Spring fell in love with Protestants, and they were decent Protestants, they would be welcomed as sons-in-law. Of course the grandchildren would have to be raised in the True Faith.

He christened Tommy, proudly named after his daddy, Tomas Larkin. Alas, resemblances to his father were only name deep. Tommy seemed to have the bottom half of everyone's traits. He was a good lad, mind you, a strong and rough-hewn number. He had all of Liam's dull and awkward ways but none of his peasant's instincts.

Because unconsciously Tommy reminded Liam of himself, and because consciously Liam knew he had to put wisdom and field smarts into the boy's head, the two became plastered together indelibly. Liam's heart of hearts cried silently because Tommy had a hundred-acre limitation.

Tommy would be schooled and schooled hard. He had to be pushed through so he could live a life of quality. It would be a chore. If worse came to worst there would always be something for him at the station.

So there it was, Madge and Spring with good husbands who

would have shares in the station. So long as it was overseen by a Larkin, all would be in good order.

Yes, Mildred and Liam talked of it often. They would not manipulate the lives of their children the way they had been manipulated. They would not be played off one against the other for land. Wisdom and guidance, and all would be well.

Everything was in hand for Squire Larkin except for one small matter. The operation of the station would rightfully go to his oldest, Wee Rory, and Rory was a man equal to the task.

However, there were slight problems with Rory and his wild ways with the girls and his hell-raising and growing wanderlust. Ah, he'd calm down. He did love the land and from the junior lads on up to manhood, he was winner of every kind of shearing and riding and roping and breeding prize the South Island had to offer.

And, a rugby hero to boot.

Shyte, if truth be known, Liam had spent many an hour with Father Gionelli steeped in worry over Rory. On a turn of the ha'penny, Liam's worry turned to fear.

War had broken out in Europe. In that instant, remote and placid New Zealand changed. The seemingly tranquil lads in this faraway countryside were suddenly charged with war fever and were queuing up for blocks outside the recruiting stations.

It made no sense. New Zealand had no quarrel with Germans or Austrians and none had ever seen a Turk. Why in the name of Jesus and Mary should they rush off like a mob to die for the British Empire? What would they find out there that could hold a candle to the life in New Zealand?

Young men became restless and adventurous and convinced themselves that the liberation of Belgium—which was someplace or the other in Europe—was the noblest cause since the Crusades and they were hot to muck in and make a fist of it.

It made sense and Liam knew it. The British Empire was calling in its dues and debts. Without Britain there would have been no New Zealand. Without Britain they might well be speaking German and toasting the Kaiser.

For a thriving farmer on the South Island of New Zealand

the war had put words into their language. Squire Liam Larkin was now a "sheep baron." All the product the farmers could induce from this fertile soil was loaded aboard ships at prices never to be seen again and steamed away to try to fill the ultimate bottomless pit, war.

Sheep barons and their key personnel would be exempt from military or other war service. Every hand was desperately needed on the station. Surely, Liam could operate Ballyutogue Station himself, but if Rory had a sniff of the outside world it posed a danger to everyone's future.

Rory had indeed inherited his father's penchant for holding rage deep inside him. The fact of the matter being that father and son spoke an equitable station language to each other as far as sheep, cattle, and crops went, but were otherwise angry strangers.

Liam had deceived himself into believing that Rory loved Ballyutogue Station so much he would never consider leaving it, even if the two of them were never truly mates.

He wondered now if there were any way to catch up and reverse the past, even though he was not quite certain of what he had done wrong. What? When? How? Rory seemed angry, almost from birth. Why?

"I know when it started," Liam said one night to Mildred. "It started ten years ago when Conor came to visit us. The boy changed from that moment on."

It was another battle of silence between Rory and his father. The boy had gone up to Wellington to see the New Zealand All-Black rugby team defeat the Aussies, a game that ended in a piss-up to end all piss-ups.

When aroused, Rory was a battler of fierce proportions who could fight his way through almost anything with fist, foot, bite, or with any weapon available—chair, lamp, beer bottle.

Rank nationalistic remarks occurred from a bunch of Aussies crying in their cups. A Chinese brothel, permitted in this Christian land to service lonely seamen, was dismantled. Liam went north to pay the bill and get his son released. The rest was silence, utter silence.

In times like this Liam would go to the crown of his land, a high hill site by a trout stream, and communicate with himself, reliving his own epic.

Liam had laid claim to victory over Ireland by making his immigration a stunning success. Despite it, he was never free of hovering ghosts, the men who had created the Larkin legacy. Each, for generations back, was the big fellow in his own times. And he, Liam, lost and unheard among them. Every time he thought himself free, they reached out from their graves in the family plot in Ballyutogue.

His great-grandfather Ronen, beaten with the cat-o'-nine until the bones poked through his flesh during the Wolfe Tone rising of 1798. His grandda Kilty, who brought them through the great famine by fighting bare knuckles for pennies in the alleyways of London and later rode with the Fenian rebels. And his daddy, Tomas, the silent warrior, the man who made the Orangemen part like the Red Sea when they tried to block his way to the first vote given to the Catholic croppy.

Conor! He was the Larkin of them all. Conor had left Ireland after a tragic shirt factory fire in Derry and roved for five years. Ten years earlier he had stopped off in New Zealand. Liam tried to make him stay, but he returned to his life in dubious battle.

Conor joined the illegal Brotherhood and masterminded a gunrunning scheme, was caught, imprisoned, escaped, and now lived life on the run.

"Cripes," Liam mumbled to himself. "I'm going down and talk to Rory, this time without anger. This time we'll get to the bottom of what is hurting us. Oh God, I dare not think of it, but if Rory would stay in New Zealand out of newfound love for me, and maybe, me for him, then this unholy Trinity would be off me back. God help me hold my temper with the lad."

Liam could tell the instant he saw Mildred that something terrible had happened.

"Rory!"

"No, he's all right," Mildred assured. "In fact he's been mumbling to me about the curse of his temper. He feels badly about being such a nark."

He damned well should! Too bloody right! Liam thought. That latest little piss-up cost me three hundred fucking quid. Three hundred quid! You could buy half of County Donegal with that!

"Good," Liam said, "the other kids?"

"They're fine. Everyone is waiting in the parlor."

They were gathered about the fireplace as the squire was wont to do for a prayer and chat before supper. Rory's head hung low as he poked the fire.

Well, someone caught him a good one in the chops, Liam observed. I hope to hell it hurts down to his pisser.

Liam became aware of the silence. Then he saw it on the table. A cable envelope. What the hell! We get cables, lots of them. Ballyutogue Station in New Zealand must have gotten twenty cables last year. He lifted it. It bore a black star, indicating a death.

"We've been waiting for you to open it," Mildred said.

OUR BELOVED BROTHER CONOR IS DEAD STOP HE WAS KILLED LEADING A RAIDING PARTY WHICH DESTROYED AN ULSTER VOLUNTEER ARMY ARSENAL AT LETTER-SHAMBO CASTLE STOP WE ARE NEGOTIATING WITH THE BRITISH FOR THE RETURN OF HIS REMAINS STOP A LETTER OF DETAIL FOLLOWS STOP GOD REST HIS SOUL AND GOD BE WITH YOU IN YOUR MOMENT OF GRIEF STOP DARY LARKIN

CHAPTER

4

Liam afforded himself a quick glance at their distraught faces then left the wreckage for Millie to contend with.

Rory stopped his father on the stairs. "Da," he croaked.

What the hell, Liam thought, you loved Conor more than you loved me. "I need to be alone, boy," he said.

As he pushed open the bedroom door, Liam could hear the family weeping in the parlor, which was suddenly punctuated by a door slam, Rory's signature that he was going flat tack to get drunk.

Mildred made heavy-footed haste up the stairs to the bedroom where Liam was packing his kit. He was all Liam now, containing his grief. He reckoned he would head again to the high meadow for whatever delayed reaction might come. In went a bottle of poteen, a vile moonshine. He creaked the springs of the bed as he worked on a pair of hobnail boots.

"I need to be alone."

"There are others here with needs as well," she snapped.

"I'm no good at this, Millie. You'll have to do it for me."

"Let me come."

"No."

"At least have a word with Rory."

"Shyte, he's probably halfway down to the junction already. Damned kid can hold more booze than my old man could."

"Rory didn't leave," Millie persisted. "He's in the barn. He's weeping."

Rory weeping? Rory seldom cried, except in a rage. Sure,

he'd be weeping now. Conor was all to him. For ten years Rory has been trying to walk in Conor's footsteps. Just what Ireland needs, another fucking Larkin martyr. "Rory has never needed my comfort," Liam said.

"Liam. This house is shattered! Touch him! Just touch him and tell him we'll get through it together."

"I'm no good at this, Millie."

"One word of kindness could have saved a lot of tears."

"I . . . ugh . . . I'll try."

Liam entered the barn gingerly and turned up the lantern, mesmerized by the sobs coming from the far end. The flicker showed Rory on a hay bale, face in hands. Liam opened a stall, led his mare out and saddled her, as Rory watched in torment.

I know that look, Liam thought. I must have looked that grief-torn myself. Well, nothing can ever hurt me like that again. Nae, not even this news. So, what is it I'm supposed to say? he wondered. The damned fool corked it with no help from us. Daddy always said he'd end up from a hanging tree, one way or another. Fuck Ireland!

Liam cleared his throat. The two stared like startled deer caught in torchlight. Liam cleared his throat once more. Yes, Squire, he thought, you're just like your daddy. Old Tomas would not have shown the likes of Liam any sentiment. Liam lowered his eyes and led the horse from the barn. In a moment there was a whinny and the sound of pounding hooves, away to the hills.

Squire Larkin was soon on the crown of his land. Everything in view belonged to him. He blew on the fire until it flared and bit into the chill, then he reached into the tent and felt for the poteen, tossed one down and leaned against the great oak that he considered the personal altar and throne of his kingdom. A wind carried up faint bleatings and tinkling bells of the flock in the east pasture. The bells blended into a steady rising and falling tone as if the animals were having a natter with him.

"The beauty of Ireland lies slain! How the mighty have fallen! Ye mountains of Donegal, let there be no dew, neither let there be rain upon you, for the shield of the mighty is vilely cast away. He was lovely in his life. He was swifter than an eagle. He was stronger than a lion. How the mighty have fallen! Thou, Conor, thou hast been slain in thy high place! How the mighty ... how the mighty ... how the mighty ... my beloved brother ... has fallen."

Liam dropped to his knees. "Conor!" he shrieked and the echo returned on the tinkling bells ... CONOR ... Conor ... Conor ...

"Oh God, man! I loved ye so!" Liam beat at his breast and groveled and screamed as his pain and confusion convulsed him. Felled to his hands and knees, he crawled and gagged and vomited and grabbed the great tree, wailing softer and softer into exhaustion.

A time later, a beastly chill cut through him. Liam awakened to a cloud pawing its way through the top of the hill. The fire was down. Liam moved quickly into the tent and wrapped himself in the heavy bedroll until his shivering quelled into rhythmic grunts.

"God," he whispered, "punish me for that instant of elation that swept me when I read the cable. God, please punish me. I loved you, Conor lad, and that's the truth of it."

CHAPTER

5

As Liam went up to the hills, so Rory headed down to the sea by the path that his stallion RumRunner knew by rote.

Being in the saddle comforted him, even at such a grievous time as this. His most profound memory of his father's affection came on his third birthday in the form of his first pony.

Rory was seven and RumRunner four when they made their lifelong partnership. In short order Rory was a full-fledged drover. Moving RumRunner into the midst of a flock was like leaping up onto a cloud, a sky of wool below him and the border collies circling and yapping and nipping butt.

RumRunner knew the weight of his master was heavy this night. As Rory reached into the saddlebag and withdrew a bottle, the horse set himself on automatic; four hours and one fifth of whiskey would see them down to Christchurch.

New Zealand kids were filled with wanderlust these days. They now had justification and rationalization to scream out against the entrapment that closes in on most island youngsters. Had there been no war on, they'd have probably invented one.

From the time of Conor's visit, much of Rory's curiosity had been filled by a parade of books, which found their way to him through Uncle Wally. He became a prolific reader, but strange, his drive to get out of New Zealand seemed pacified.

Rory had not been caught up in the war fever, partly because it made no sense for him to go halfway around the world to fight for the freedom of Belgium.

You inherit this, that, and the other from your parents, sometimes reluctantly. He had found their sense of peace that told him he would do his roving at some future day, when he was entirely ready and sound of mind about it.

By sixteen he was among the best sheep- and cattlemen on the South Island and had talked his father into raising domesticated deer, which was turning into a profitable venture. He also imported a few mules from Cyprus, which turned out not so profitable.

Although the yen to leave was there, the yen to stay was also there. It was Liam's fears and suspicions that triggered Rory to look to the horizon. He loved the station, the country, his calling.

It had been years and years since he had heard from Conor. Only cryptic mentions of his uncle came in the letters from his other uncle, Father Dary.

But on this night of Conor's death, the past became the present again and the present took on a sudden urgency. He must follow in Conor's footsteps.

Even now he adored riding the station with his da, who was quiet and leathery and had wondrous ways with the soil and weather. They said that only pigs could see the wind, but Liam Larkin sure as hell could, he was that keen.

If containing one's emotions were a kingly value, his father was a great king. His early longings to buddy up with his da had been turned back by Liam's constant taciturn attitude toward him. Mom and Tommy, and occasionally the girls, got whatever there was of his father's outward shows of affection.

If being taciturn were truly his da's basic nature Rory felt he could find a rhythm to it, a good clean way that two quiet men can have respecting and caring for one another.

Rory had caught a drift as a child that the silence and later the snappishness toward him had a wrong rub to it. It was a special annoyance his da had for him from something that must have happened long ago and far away.

It was a dark night, but RumRunner knew the way. Rory dozed in the saddle knowing his horse would advise him if he were about to fall off. He jolted to wakefulness and snapped upright time and time again. Each time he did, he remembered his horror . . . UNCLE CONOR IS DEAD!

Rory, stop playing the game, he told himself. You've a rover's bone stuck in your throat and you know it and your da knows it. The sourness between them had set in almost ten years ago to the day, when Uncle Conor came to visit.

Liam Larkin understood his son's itch and he was unable to do the right thing about it. It boiled down to a single word, *Ireland*, and Rory had built his uncle into a deity. Liam's fear was that the same curse-laden bedevilment would take his son away.

A word of comfort to his da that his love of New Zealand would keep him here, and things would have changed between them in a flick.

Liam saw his son become more like his brother, and it was beyond his scope to do anything about it. As for Rory, he could never bring himself to comfort his da about Ireland.

So, the malice and cancer grew.

UNCLE CONOR IS DEAD!

Tears stung Rory's cheeks. His throat told him the bottle was empty. He tossed it and looked for the lights of Christchurch. They always seem to come up like the sound of a Protestant hymn. If New Zealand ever fell off the earth, Christchurch would be first to go. It was born dull and stayed that way without curiosity or anger, just a transplanted English garden in perpetual whispers and prayer. This was the Motherland once removed, the old royal and loyal outpost of empire. It was eleven o'clock and Christchurch drowsed. Christchurch always drowsed.

RumRunner trotted on through to the Lyttleton Harbour, where an oasis of levity from the outside world had filtered through the Christian ramparts.

Wally Ferguson's Sheepmen and Miners' Exchange was the lone sanctuary from all that goodness. Wally's operation centered around the sheep and cattle pens by the docks. There was a bunkhouse hotel, warehouse, auction barn, and the most active pub on the South Island.

Wally's greatest asset was an ability to size up men: good, bad, truthful, liar, fighter, coward . . . that one will fold up in one season . . . that one will make a go of it . . . that one's a right yahoo.

In the beginning, when Mildred and Liam had been evicted from Bert Hargrove's station, Wally had made an astute judgment and took the young and frightened couple in. What to buy, when to buy, how to buy, good land, bad land, safe ships, diseased ships, market up, market down, good ram, bad ram—all of this was shared with Liam Larkin, more so because he hated Bert Hargrove, but mostly because he knew a winning team when he saw one.

That kid, Rory Larkin, became a kind of alter ego, winning at the fairs, almost good enough to play rugby with the All-Blacks, and a fighter of devastating proportions.

Rory could hold his feelings in like his da, Liam. The lad was always much of a loner except for the girls who couldn't keep their hands off him and their legs crossed.

Likewise, there were many differences between father and son, but the greatest of these was Liam's ability to stuff in his rage, no matter what.

Rory was able to contain himself for only so long, and when he erupted it could be monumental and he could be dangerous.

 RumRunner stopped at the corral gate. Rory whistled. Old Glenn the stableman limped over from the bunkhouse and let them in. The journey ended, the whiskey hit with a delayed punch. Rory needed a hand to dismount and he leaned against the fence, blurry.

"My, my," the old man said, "get your ass to the bunkhouse, I'll sack you down as soon as I take care of your horse."

The intensity of pain was stronger than the effects of mere alcohol. Rory came together in a fuzzy sort of way. "I'm not after sleeping yet," he said. "Night's young and I'm wasting good drinking time."

"You've got enough in you to keep the House of Lords drunk for a month."

"Glenn, just take care of my fucking horse."

"All right, but mind your manners. There's a foursome of thugs down from the copper mine just dying to get into a piss-up. And see Wally before you go into the bar. He thought you might be coming down."

Rory heaved in a sigh to prove he was absolutely sober, thanked RumRunner, and started across the corral.

"Rory. We've heard about Conor Larkin. I'm sorry, man."

Rory stopped for a moment and surveyed a landscape of pens bulging with sheep and three ships at dockside. The bar would be full. A tinderbox.

Rory knocked and entered Wally Ferguson's office, slumped into the chair, and hung his head. The feel of Wally's two strong hands tightening hard on his shoulders helped so much.

"Glenn says they know about it here already. How did they get the news so quick?"

"I think your ma must have held the cable for a couple of days. I called her and told her it was in the newspaper today. Some of the republican journalists in Dublin must have put it on the wires before it could be censored."

Rory lifted his head to see a newspaper on the desk. He closed his eyes and bit his lip.

"You'll have to read it to me."

"'It is confirmed that the Ulster Volunteer Army arsenal and barracks of Lettershambo Castle in County Londonderry was destroyed by a raiding party of the Irish Republican Brotherhood, reversing an earlier report from His Majesty's Spokesman that the explosion was an accident.

"'Details now emerging seem to indicate that a small raiding party crossed Lough Foyle and was able to enter the castle by a series of hidden caves and tunnels.

"'The explosion which occurred at 4:22 A.M. was so great that it could be seen and heard from Scotland down to Londonderry City. No figures of casualties have been released but informed sources say that over a hundred officers and men in the garrison have not been accounted for. Damage has not been made public, but from the power of the blast it is believed that tons of dynamite stored within the Castle were ignited and that tens of thousands of weapons along with millions of rounds of ammunition were destroyed.

"'Only two bodies of the IRB raiding party have been recovered and identified. One was Daniel Hugh Sweeney known in the republican movement as "Long Dan" and believed to be in command of the illegal organization.

"'The second body was that of Conor Larkin, a longtime Brotherhood operator whose whereabouts had been unknown since a jailbreak from Portlaoise Prison almost six years ago. He had surfaced in America for a time then disappeared again. Larkin won national fame for an earlier gunrunning exploit that culminated in his capture at the well-known ambush at Sixmilecross.

"'Sweeney and Larkin were killed manning a machine gun, apparently covering the retreating raiding party . . .' and so forth and so forth," Wally said. "He sure went out in style, Rory. I guess you might consider me to be a royalist," he continued, "but if I were Irish I'd probably have another point of view. I met him when he was here ten years ago. He was a gentle man unable to escape the curse he was born into."

"Thanks, Wally."

"Now, what about the squire?"

"Oh God, my da's brains must really be unhinged now. We—he and I—are like one of his fine pieces of Waterford crystal. Ever see one of those things smash? It's not into chunks and slivers but a billion little flakes that can't be put together—not by the two of us, anyhow."

"Have you got the guts to stay in New Zealand?"

"Stay? Hell! Don't you understand, Wally? Conor was so tall he cast his shadow halfway around the world. Now it's settling like a black cloud. Ballyutogue and Ireland and Uncle Conor have been left unspoken through the years except in snippets of fear. The ghosts of Tomas and Kilty and Ireland have been rankling every corner of our land and every inch of our house. Uncle Conor's unseen presence can fairly choke you at times."

"Your da is a good man," Wally said.

"So am I," Rory answered. "Don't worry, between the squire and Mom Larkin that station will prosper till eternity."

"Ah, jumping Jesus," Wally moaned.

"Let's heist a couple," Rory said rising.

"There's a bunch of beasts in there from the mine including Oak Kelley."

"Good," Rory said, "Oak is just the ticket."

"Wait, I'm coming with you."

"'S'truth, Wally, take my word, I'm sober as the Virgin."

"That's not what I'm worried about. Your face isn't cleaned up from your last donnybrook up in Wellington. I don't want a homicide on your record as well."

The barroom had a certain raunchy stateliness to it. It was sturdy and its walls told of the hunting and fishing glories of the South Island in heads stuffed and fish embalmed in fighting poses. It was aged and sturdy and reeked lovely with a magnificent blend of ale, whiskey, tobacco, and various aromas from the pens outside.

Wally nodded to his big Maori bartender to be alert. Times like this were why Wally kept the furnishings simple. The lowering of all voices and the entry of tension was automatic as Rory found a space at the end of the bar and Wally stood slightly behind him.

The four mashers from the copper mine quickly positioned themselves on either side of Rory. The chief troublemaker quickly took charge of his role. They called him Oak and he was known as a terror around the mining camps. Oak won most of his fights without throwing a punch, he was that fearsome-looking, with pocked face, red beard, and hands the size of cannonballs.

"I hear some pigshit by the name of Conor Larkin attacked a British fort in Ulster," Oak said for openers.

"Bloody disgrace," a mate chimed in, "what with Irish boys in the trenches in France having dirty traitors stabbing us in the back."

"And I'm drinking to the man who blew Larkin's guts out," the third said.

"Yeah," said the fourth, completing the alliance. "Us fighting a war, our lads dying in France, and that murdering jailbird committing treachery."

"If you've spoken your piece," Wally said, "would you mind retiring to a table so as further commerce won't suffer interruption."

"I want to know how this Larkin boy here feels about the matter," Oak said.

"I'm very sad," Rory said softly.

Too softly. Wally knew what Wally knew. The big Maori bartender reached down and wrapped his hand around a staying pin.

"We'd like you to step outside so we can express our sorrow as well," Oak taunted, "but first, what say about a toast to our beloved King."

"Ah now, gentlemen," Wally said. "It's four against one. That's kind of unsporting, Oak."

"Aye," Rory agreed, "that's indeed cowardly. Isn't that cowardly!" he shouted to the room.

"Tell you what we'll do," Wally said quickly. "I'll put twenty on Rory here, but no four against one."

"Then I'll only have to fight them two at a time?" Rory asked.

"That's still cowardly, isn't it?" Wally asked the bartender. The big Maori nodded.

"Tell you what. Twenty on Rory Larkin and I'll give two-to-one odds he lays out the four of you. Even money on the side says that one or more will require hospitalization. Clear back a few tables there to give them room to fall."

"Bullshit, Ferguson," Oak roared and brought a punch up from his boot tops that caught Rory directly between the eyes. Rory fell back, shook his head, and stared at the giant who groped, bewildered.

"If that's the best punch you've got, Oak, you're fucked!" Rory's fists blazed fast into the miner, who was stunned long enough so that a knee to the groin, elbow to the Adam's apple, and hand chop behind the neck caused the entire room to shake as he thudded to the floor, clapped out.

"Gentlemen," Rory said to the others, "who wishes the honors?"

There was a total loss of enthusiasm among those burdened with dragging Oak's hulk from the place.

Rory banged his mug on the bar and glared at the room. "My name is Rory Larkin and I'm a New Zealander! I love my country! I loved my uncle and I think the Brits got what was coming to them!"

He snatched a bottle off the bar and barreled for the door. Wally caught him outside and spun him around.

"Jesus, I hate to see this thing happen in New Zealand. Two Irishmen fighting each other. This is not the place for it, Rory. Now, God rest your uncle's soul, but this is your country!"

Rory backed away fighting for breath, trying to unscramble the whirl of torment so that words could form off his lips, somehow. Wally backed up and there was fear involved. He had never seen such a blaze of eyes and Rory shaking from top to bottom.

"Can't you see," Rory screamed. The veins bulged from his neck and his forehead. "I'm haunted, man!"

"Jesus, boy, you're not yourself now. Come on, calm-like. It's me, Wally, talking. Go to my office and drink yourself to sleep." Wally reached out, but Rory swung his arm.

"You're scared of me, aren't you, Wally?"

"No."

In a time Rory's control returned and he told Wally he was really, painfully sorry. He turned to leave.

"Where the hell you going?"

"You know," Rory answered.

"All right, then. Stay with her till you're ready to come out and when you come out, you come straight to me. Will you shake hands on it?"

"I promise."

CHAPTER

6

Rory found himself wandering past the docks and along the base of Mount Pleasant, a hill that afforded a triple vista; Christchurch to the north and its omni-dim lights and whispering hymns, the Lyttleton Harbour below and Taylor's Mistake at land's end luring the ships to crash in the wrong inlet.

Rory crossed the road and sat on the grass and drank from the bottle. Who was Admiral Taylor to have such an insult heaped upon himself? How many ships piled up aground in that shallow treacherous cove?

That's good, Rory thought. God has a way of disconnecting a man's brain when it is too mashed up to contend with tragedy. When you can bear no more you can think of silly things like Taylor's Mistake. Why am I here sitting on the wet grass and drinking when the Sheepmen's Exchange is down there? Oh yeah . . . Oak Kelley. Bastard's jaw hurt my fist.

"Oh, Uncle Conor," Rory mumbled. "Since you left I've wanted nothing more in life than to see you again. God, the joy of it when I learned you'd busted out of prison! Over the years only precious letters, read till the words almost disappeared from the paper."

He lay back and fell into a stupor.

Ugly, gray, wet, windy, chilled dawn told Rory either to wake up or die frozen in the grass. His infallible youth and strength won out. He crawled up from hands and knees and stood wavering like a tall ship's mast in a hurricane.

Oh yes . . . that's it . . . Georgia. Sister Georgia Norman, Chief Matron of the Christchurch Presbyterian Hospital. Several months earlier Rory had been taken down to the hospital with ribs cracked in a fall during the cattle muster. The war had swept a great number of the physicians into the army, including Dr. Calvin Norman, who was now on the way from somewhere to somewhere else.

In five months of hostilities, Rory Larkin had, by serendipity, found an unexpected windfall of unfaithful wives. Even as he rendered them and himself pleasure he disdained them. Wives were supposed to hunker down and wait it out in abstinence. Well, Rory concluded, one had to accept one's fate. There were two kinds of women about. Those who were married and those who wanted to be. The married birds were in no position to complain too loudly about his lack of attention. He could come and go as he pleased and they were most grateful.

Except for Georgia Norman. She was more mature, at thirty, and a woman of accomplishment and experience. She was English-born, like his mom, and a bit plump like her as well. As a young woman she trained and spent more than eight years nursing in the Medical Corps, including outstanding service during the Boer War.

It seemed the war did her in. She ran to the farthest place not in permanent ice fields, where she met Dr. Norman, a physician probably better suited to be a law clerk. Georgia craved peace and lacked great beauty. Calvin Norman was an acceptable compromise with life. Her desire for motherhood was soon derailed as she learned of her husband's overly solicitous examinations of his female patients.

Then came the war that so many New Zealand men felt had arrived as a blessing. Dr. Norman saw it as an excellent job opportunity, an advancement. The war would be short, no doubt, and he would return with a shoulder full of pips, a chest with at least two rows of medals, and the command of any hospital or practice of his choosing.

Georgia was unlike any woman Rory had encountered, and for a man of his tender age his conquests numbered quite a few.

No weeping, no jealousy, no laying on of guilt. Her code with Rory was humor and lovemaking. As a lady who had been in the company of the military for nearly a decade and a highly informed nurse, Georgia was a most knowledgeable and creative lover. No questions asked, no demands made. Easy come, easy go. She had no other lovers but she was clever and patient. Rory would always find his way back to her. And she kept her secret from him.

Her cottage had a wild look to the sea around the bend from Taylor's Mistake. As she gazed at the windswept horizon, a loud knock sounded. She responded to the knock and saw before her a drenched, battered sot with sour breath.

"Cor, blimey, what a gorgeous sight you are. Are you begging for alms or do you want to come in?"

Rory staggered into the room, shrugged, and shook his head several times.

"I read about it in the newspapers," she said.

"Please," he cried, and opened her robe and buried his face in her bosom and they slowly slipped to the floor and she held him and rocked him, her breasts soon salty from his tears. There are needs a strong man can't speak of. A need like this from him had never been considered. He allowed himself for the first time in memory to completely cave in.

When at last he disengaged, his jerky loud breathing continued as she ran her fingers through his hair. "You're soaking wet."

"I didn't know it had been raining. My da is up in the hills. It's raining on him, too. I need a jar, Georgia."

"To hell you do," she answered, "you need to hold your head over the toilet and stick your finger down your throat. Now, in with you."

Her strong nurse's hands pulled him to his feet and he obeyed. She soaked him afterward in a hot tub and dried him and wrapped him in her husband's ponderous wool bathrobe. Tea, bitters, and a drop of cognac calmed his tummywobbles.

Having felt that great surge of compassion from her flesh to his, he was desperate for more.

"Georgia," he said in nearly a whimper, "would you just lie down with me and hold on to me, I mean, real tight like . . . just that."

"What a grand idea," she said.

7

Liam unglued his eyes to an unlikely tattoo of sun rays on the tent. His hand reached under the quilt and fished for the poteen bottle. It had died and gone to heaven hours ago. He berated himself for leaving the station in such haste that he had not thought to bring more.

The trashy taste in his mouth and the need to relieve himself overtook his dread of the morning chill. The stream brought him back to life in a hurry.

Liam puffed on the embers of the fire until they fanned, and when tea was made, he wrapped his hands around the cup and let the heat bake through to his leathery skin. The sun was winning its dawn skirmish with the elements. "Thanks God, for that," he said.

Hunger pacified, he strung up his fishing rod automatically and selected a likely fly from his hat, hoping not to hook up seriously. He had yet to contemplate, to mourn, to allow flashes of memory to run through. He could never do that down off this hill because there were people around and things to do. What he wanted to ponder was not for sharing, even with Millie.

Liam commenced a long conversation with himself. In these kinds of discussions he could argue his case with utter clarity and dazzle the nonpresent adversary with his infallible logic. These arguments he always won. The fellow on the receiving end was almost always Rory.

The goddamned problem was that whenever Liam attempted to argue the case with Rory present he botched it. Rory would never give him the answers he had so positively anticipated.

After a time Liam stopped holding these conversation with actual persons, particularly Rory. He held them with himself up on the hill against the oak. It seemed that life between Liam and his son became a long trail of conversations that never took place.

It was like that in the old country, Liam thought. If you're Irish enough, you can go an entire lifetime filled with conversations that never took place, like those between himself and his own father, Tomas.

Up here on the hill by the stream, Liam would even allow himself to journey inward deep enough to inflict upon himself the hurt of Ireland.

How many pricks must a man endure before he becomes numb? Liam knew early on his place in life was set. He learned the futility of trying to win his father over or to change his lot in life. Liam realized a short time after he was born that he was a small matter in a field of giants. NOT ANYMORE! Squire Liam Larkin was no small matter anymore.

"Dear Lord, must I go to me grave without Rory once having a taste and touch of my true feelings? All our conversations end in ruin. After a time, one stops even thinking about having them, it becomes that futile.

"What am I guilty of, son? Building this magnificent life here? What have I done wrong, Rory? Saved you from the blistering misery of Ireland and the hanging tree? Because of me you'll never know the terror of going up a gangplank and down into the second hold of a tramp steamer on a voyage in purgatory with less than a quid in your pocket. I saved you from fear, boy, from puking over the rail and praying God for the strength to throw yourself into the sea!"

Liam's face knotted as he recalled the ugliest incident between them that had taken place two years earlier. June MacPherson was sixteen, the daughter of Protestant farmers. They had a small but decent holding of about three hundred acres of crop with a few animals. June was a good-looking lass but in a state of perpetual heat with a reputation of being loose with her knickers.

Rory became the pot of gold at the end of her rainbow. Determined to become Mrs. Larkin, she seduced him without qualms on numerous occasions by methods that would have been considered rape, were she a man. Rory took responsibility for the pregnancy.

The Larkin household flooded with bitter memories. Unlike the acrimony shown them by Mildred's parents, the Larkins decided to be real Christians about it. Moreover, Junie-girl was an answer to Liam's prayers. With a wife and child, Rory's roving days would be cut off at the knees. Now, he would have to remain in New Zealand!

June and all four parents seemed to be reveling in the plot, but Rory threw a wrench into it. He liked June very much. So had many other boys. She was not precisely the Virgin, but many girls had married after affairs with other partners and their marriages worked. It was a plain, simple, unfettered matter that he did not love her. There was more of this going on than the pious of the South Island were willing to admit. To be precise, June's sister had been in the same condition a few years earlier and did not marry.

Rory seemed to have three choices: flee, marry, or go to prison. He did none of them. Thus the unthinkable came into play. June made the short trip to Wellington, as two other girls had done this particular year, and had an abortion.

Liam and Mildred had consented to the most hideous of all crimes and sins. The Squire now had to bear the added guilt of his son's wretched behavior.

Thank God he had his own shining behavior with Mildred to show himself as the loftiest of men while his son was a scum. Liam cozily sloughed off the pertinent fact that he loved Mildred, and Rory and Junie did not really care for each other.

In another year, June MacPherson became pregnant again, this time with a lesser character than Rory, a lunker who marched off peacefully to the altar.

"Aye," Liam sighed, "if I couldn't get through to Rory in a matter of such moral magnitude, how can I get through to him at all?"

That's the bitter twist, he thought. "If we only had one golden conversation, one in which he would understand everything I told him and probably I had to hear a few things myself.

"But nae, the silence goes into the churchyard and the truth, never heard, is shoveled over by the grave digger. And another generation takes up a life of unspoken anger."

Suppose, Liam thought, everyone in a family were priests three days a week. On Monday, Wednesday, and Friday half the family, the priests, would be sitting in the confessional box and the other half of the family had to confess to them. Then on Tuesday, Thursday, and Saturday the confessors would become the priests and the priests would be hearing the confessions from them. On Sunday, they'd all go to Mass together.

"I'll wager there are Irish family debating societies in heaven, hell, and purgatory, and the misunderstandings could be argued century after century."

Or was it that there were always too many children and not enough land in Ireland? That boys lived in fear of forced marriages or married as toothless old bachelors or emigrated? Was it the absence of gracious wealth, or was it the damnable British stranger among them? Was it the Holy Church who force-fed a fear of sin like it was mother's milk?

"All of the bloody things that made the Irish heap wreckage on one another had brought grief upon grief, departed sons and daughters, shut out shows of compassion and affections from us. . . . Never touching . . . made us great fighters in other men's armies."

Could any of this have been averted, Liam wondered, with that one golden conversation?

He contemplated where Rory might be. Here was a lad twenty years old bedding down half the grass widows in Christchurch. One of these days some soldier was going to come home on leave unexpected and blow his head off. Jaysus, Liam thought, that boy draws women to him like nails to a magnet.

He draws them like Conor used to. Every other bird in Ballyutogue had broken a wing from flying too hard at Conor. Mr. Lambe's forge, where his brother worked since his apprenticeship, always had girls hanging around, Protestant and Catholic alike . . . "just happening by."

Rory was not much different. He had cornered all the good looks of the Larkin family and left crumbs for the rest of us.

Down the trail he'd go, asleep on RumRunner, who knew the route to Wally's better than most drovers.

Jaysus, that boy could hold a tank of booze, like his grandfather Tomas. Ah, he could count on Wally to keep the peace, then spill Rory into a bunk when his tank overflowed. Good old Wally. He and Mildred owed Wally for taking them in in the beginning and helping them get started. Wally was the only one who Rory had really taken to and could keep the boy from going on a tear.

Liam switched images as his hand poked through his kit more in hope that some faerie may have slipped in another bottle of poteen.

His thoughts ran to the homestead, now fourteen rooms large with a big and little lorry and a Model T like the one he bought for Father Gionelli. The gem of the Ballyutogue Station was a family chapel, with its awesome silver candlesticks.

Maybe the worst hurt of all was that his mother and father never saw his Ballyutogue Station. Every time he added land or new heads of cattle and extended his fences, Liam would play over and over in his mind that he was showing Tomas around. "See there, Da, picked up that hundred acres because of phosphate content, a natural for growing potatoes and American corn." Huh! A hundred acres, just a wee corner of this spread . . . but larger than all the Larkin fields together. Old Tomas would squint as he looked over his son's "barony" and the cut would be deep. Tomas would know how wrong he had been. And there, Liam's own private trout stream, like a lord, and electricity in the house and new combines in the fields.

Probably the greatest part of his mourning when his da died was the fact he'd never see Ballyutogue Station in New Zealand. The game was on to get his mom, Finola, to take the trip to New Zealand and with damned better accommodations than had been the case with him. She'd swoon from the sight of the place and go back to Ireland and spend her life bragging about Squire Liam to the respectful and awed neighbors.

Getting Finola to move out of Ballyutogue, except for the occasional county fair or the pilgrimage up Mount Patrick, took some years of convincing. By the time she agreed to come for a visit, she had gotten too old and, like Tomas, never saw the place.

Somehow, this grated on Liam almost more than anything in this life, almost more than Rory's behavior.

It hurt too much so he once again shifted images to Mildred, Madge, and Spring in the chapel, on their knees lamenting the death of Conor with his photograph bathed in candlelight. Tommy was nowhere, doing nothing. Tommy was like Liam had been in Ireland, doing nothing but mending harnesses or pitching horseshoes.

In another day the women would have spent the first cannonburst of grief and he'd come down. There was no use going sooner, even for another bottle of poteen. Liam knew he'd be somewhat less than nothing around three wailing females.

Liam thought of Millie. "What a horrible time to think of my wife laying naked in bed," he blushed aloud. Back in Ireland when a girl went up the pole and the guilty young man was shuffled in shame to the altar, it signaled the end of his dreams, the ultimate life sentence, the closing of the door to the outside world, adventures, the rover's itchy feet. Passion that ended bachelorhood had its dire consequences. Thank God for Millie, he had said a million times, thank God she defied her parents and had guided him through killer turbulence to land, to a homestead, to acceptance as one of the mighty. . . . Sheep Baron. By God, aristocracy, in a manner of speaking. . . . All fears of inadequacies, either on the land or with his woman, were vanquished.

The deliberate predating of Rory's birth to make him seem months younger was done mostly to preserve Mildred's honor. There were snickers and whispers, probably emanating from Bert and Edna Hargrove, but time would take care of it.

Or would it?

Try as he might there was a flicker of guilt every time he looked at Wee Rory, a trait that seemed to continue on through Rory's boyhood. The first time he saw the baby at Mildred's breast, he felt the infant had invaded their love. He never had the same problem in sharing Spring, Madge, and, particularly, Tommy when they nursed.

Rory was his son, all right, but it was Tommy who solidified the Larkin name in New Zealand. Tommy was named after someone from the old country. In a strange way, Tommy had more legitimacy.

What the hell! Rory didn't know, even at this time! Or did he, and did he take his rage inward? At one point, Mildred suggested they tell Rory about his early birth and their dire situation at the time, but Liam would not hear of it. Too much honor was involved, too much of his deepest Catholic beliefs had been willfully ignored by his lust.

Rory sensed friction from the start. Liam always went out of his way to give the boy a paternal pat on the shoulder or even a rumple of the hair. Something about it was always forced.

Affection was mainly for Mildred and some for the girls. All a real man like Rory needed was a slap on the back and a "job well done."

Rory used me, Liam thought. Running to Mildred's lap for an embrace just to annoy him. Damned kids can play parent against parent before they can walk, and Rory was a master of it because attention from mom always brought a secondary attention from Liam. Other routes to his father were through bossing around his sisters. Liam gave him angry attention for that in short order.

At last came Tommy, the real Larkin. But alas, it became apparent that Tommy was not going to be very tall in the saddle. Tommy had no natural sense for ranching.

Liam needed Rory, and knowing he needed Rory intensified the spite and arid spirit between them.

Conor came, and when Conor departed the rift was permanent. Liam's son had become his brother. Liam was again contending with the great Conor Larkin and all the fears he attributed to Tomas were now being done by him to Rory. Memories, so carefully controlled, had gotten out of hand as he fell back in time.

Of the four Larkin kids back in Ireland, Tomas's arms were most readily open to embrace Conor. Liam had to annoy the hell out of Tomas to get even pale recognition.

Liam believed the angels had smiled on him when Conor went to work at Mr. Lambe's forge as an apprentice farrier and blacksmith. Now Liam alone could go up to the fields every day with his daddy, digging lazy beds, pulling rocks, planting, slaning turf, harvesting alongside.

From the age of nine he worked without complaint in fair or dirty weather until he was knackered, waiting only for that grand moment when Tomas would lay a hand on his shoulder and say, "There's a good lad, now." No boy worked for his reward more earnestly. "There's a good lad," and maybe even a rumple of the hair.

But his daddy's gesture of recognition was soon submerged by the love he showed for Conor. Each day he and his daddy would trudge down from the fields, and at the village crossroads Conor would be waiting in his blacksmith leathers. Conor would run up to Tomas, who would swoop him up in his arms and ride him home on his shoulder.

His older sister, Brigid, and Dary, the baby, were not in the struggle for Tomas's affection. As the sole daughter, Brigid belonged to her mother, who made her girl religious and acutely aware of sins of the flesh. Thus, Brigid was able to control those amorous moments with her sweetheart, Myles McCracken. Poor Myles had to bumble around, never being able to court Brigid properly because he was born with the gravest curse, no land to inherit. Finola was more than up to the task of keeping Brigid half daft with fear until Myles was forced from Ballyutogue to find work in Derry.

Whatever affection Brigid and Finola might have shown Liam was gone with the winds after Dary was born. The two women smothered Dary, fierce-like. Ma had the wee wane kneeling and making the sign before he could even walk properly, preening him for the priesthood from the day she popped him.

Tomas had one obsession and that was to keep Conor in Ballyutogue to inherit the Larkin acres as well as own the forge. Tomas raged against Conor's equal obsession to read and dream of the world beyond Ballyutogue.

Their grandda Kilty, a Fenian hero, enchanted young Conor with the fires of Irish republicanism.

Conor wanted to go and Liam wanted nothing else but to stay and inherit the farm, but Liam was in no one's plans. He was just an extra bowl at the table.

The Larkin house was divided in long-established Irish tradition. Conor alone loved everyone and fought everyone. He stood up for Brigid and Myles McCracken. He challenged Finola in making Dary a priest. And oh, the deep love between Conor and Tomas was as fierce as their never-ending warfare.

Aware of Liam's awkwardness and shortcomings, Conor became his brother's keeper, teaching him the ways of girls, playing football, drinking like a man, protecting him from unfair treatment by Finola and Tomas. Conor taught him how to use his fists. And Liam was awed how Conor stood up to everyone and more awed by his brilliance as a scholar.

"Oh, how I hated myself because I wasn't you," the Squire mumbled aloud.

All the early stuff with Rory were merely skirmishes. It broke into warfare the day that Conor left New Zealand and Rory began walking in his uncle's footsteps.

CHAPTER

8

Rory awakened to instant remembrance. As he connected the threads of events, his groan filled the room. The light was gray. He hated dead light.

"There's a lad," Georgia whispered.

"Georgia. Thanks to God."

He sat up on sheets wet from sweat and torn from clawing. It was difficult to hold his head straight, so he let it fall into his hands like a heavy boulder. "I never knew any kind of pain like this."

"It's called a broken heart, Rory."

She sat beside him and pulled his head down onto her lap with the stern gentleness of a nurse.

"What's going to happen to me? I don't know how much I can take."

"It's near impossible to die of grief, even though you might long for it. God has worked out a blissful fog to envelop you. In a month, when you have accepted your uncle's death, the fog will begin to lift, very slowly. Come each dawn, along with the stab of pain will come a new sliver of light. One morning you'll wake up and life is on again, the pain has become manageable."

"I can't forget him."

"No, but you'll transfer him into a memory chamber. For a time he will come out by night and invade your dreams. Then even your dreams come under control. I've seen men off the battlefield with the life force and men without it. You'll not go under."

Georgia moved him to the armchair, stripped the bed and put on clean linens, ordered him on his stomach, and massaged him with alcohol.

"Glory! No one should have a body like yours," she said slapping his bottom and ordering him to roll over. She set the bottle down and took him in hand and played with him until he responded.

"I'm in deep mourning. How can you be arousing me at a time like this?"

"Just checking to see if you're still alive and if a sense of humor existed. Grief transformed to lust is not a matter to be overlooked."

Rory suddenly got off the bed to curb his own rising passion and draped himself in a towel. Georgia fixed tea.

"Where do we start?" she asked.

"Hard to say. My da must have been squashed like a bug when he was a kid. He rarely talks of his past except for the occasional bitter reference. What drive he must have had to win the title of Squire and put the sign Ballyutogue Station over the arch of our gate. Powerful force, rage—but inside him, always inside him."

"We all seem to spend the second half of our lives getting over the first half. That's what the winners in this world lust for, to beat their parents' ears back," Georgia replied.

"My da can't accept his own victory over Ireland and his father. It's merciful that he's such a strong Catholic. He can only venture so far into his own mind. When it starts to hurt too much he lights the old candle and takes the 'mystery' route. Strongly religious that he is, there is one black mark on him he can't shake."

"What black mark?"

"Me," Rory answered. "My mother was four months' pregnant when they secretly married. I was christened immediately and the records were altered to prove I was actually born nine months and two seconds after they exchanged vows."

"But what's it about? He loves your mother. He wanted to marry her."

"My grandparents, the Hargroves, rained unmerciful damnation on them. I don't know how to say it, Georgia, but I always knew there was something wrong about me."

"Your father has never told you?"

"God no. He'd light a billion candles first."

"How did you find out? How old were you?"

"Hurled in my teeth from a so-called friend when I was about eight. I learned it in a way that made me hide in a closet. What does it matter? When your mother and father perpetuate a lie, somewhere, somehow, sometime there is going to be a slip, or maybe I knew anyhow, an innate feeling I was born with. From the time I realized he had always looked at me differently, the child who had dishonored his mother by being born and whose secret must be kept from those in Ireland at all costs. We got along after my sisters came, but from the minute I really knew the truth, everything between us took on a double meaning.

"Da tried doing the sporting things with me, training the dogs, fishing, riding. Somehow, whatever we did together turned into a contest. Jesus, Georgia, I had to deliberately lose to him at checkers. Well, when Tommy came, things seemed better for a time . . . the legitimate heir had been born . . . hallelujah. . . . The sin of Rory's birth was now buried . . . not atoned, but buried."

The screen door banged with the wind. Georgia went to the porch where an invigorating breeze passed through. "Come on out, Rory," she called. "It's a rare night. Stars are coming up."

They found the rockers. Rory put his feet on the rail and listened for a time to the sea and watched the breakers throw off sprinkling phosphorescence.

"My brother Tommy didn't solve the problem. Tommy only enhanced it when my da realized he wasn't much good for working anything larger than a potato patch."

"He was forced to come back to you?"

"Cursed, because he had to have me. He saw me every day becoming more and more like my Uncle Conor. . . . Why are you so good to me, Georgia?" he asked suddenly.

"I've a long career of healing warriors."

Rory took her hands. "I love you in a very strong way. I'd

do anything in the world for you. Sometimes, I wish we could go out together in the daylight and take a ride up in the hills."

"Ah, you wouldn't want to be seeing me in full daylight. I'm more than slightly your senior."

"You're my beautiful friend. I wish I were more comfortable with our situation."

"Those lady friends of yours. You want them to fall madly—madly and stomp out on them, like getting even with your parents?"

"Shyte, Georgia, you're too bloody smart. Truth be known, you're better than the lot of them combined. . . . I want to talk some more."

"As long as you need."

"My da was afraid Conor would infect me with Ireland, but Conor avoided telling me about it. He taught me about books and searching for love and the beauty of beauty. Your kind of beauty. You see, let me make myself clear . . . knowing that my uncle was such a splendiferous man I realized that if he was obsessed with Ireland, there must be something there that explains the mystery of life itself."

"What was the lesson?"

"In order to be the most total human you're capable of you must serve something other than yourself."

"He must have been a melancholy man, too, to have Ireland as his mistress. Rory, I felt that patriotic once. Glory is tin. When the band stops playing the shooting begins. Soldiering or playing the patriot's game is filthy and disgusting work, humiliating and boring, mutilating and inhuman. . . ." Her voice trailed off to another continent. "During the Boer War, Kitchener—I was on his staff—ordered tens of thousands of women and children behind barbed wire at Bloemfontein—he called it a concentration camp—and while he burned down the countryside he neglected untold thousands of kids and their mothers and let them die of starvation and disease."

"Like they did to us in Ireland."

"'Us'? Us?"

"I guess I said us, didn't I?"

"What is taking you to battle is the same thing that drove me out of it. It is easy to make fun of a black man and paint him as an inferior and, God help me, I went for it. I believed in the empire. But in the Transvaal, Afrikaaners were white Christians being murdered by the most civilized white Christians in the world."

"Like they're doing in Ireland. That's why Conor died."

"You've got to get there, don't you, Rory?"

"Aye."

"Enlisting?"

"Aye."

"What about your father? You're not quite of age. If he stops you now, it could be a problem for you to join later."

"I'm going up to the North Island. They say you don't even need proof of age. If it doesn't work there, I'll get aboard a ship to Australia. Light horse cavalry regiments are forming up both places."

"The way you ride you'll end up being their colonel."

"So long as it gets me on the road to Ireland. And yourself, Georgia?"

"No more war for me. I've seen too many young men never live to fill their promise. How many great men went, never knowing of their greatness? No more war for me. But I'm glad we passed each other by."

"So you're here, waiting for Dr. Norman. Or is that it?"

Georgia paled. "You're too damned smart as well, Rory."

"You weren't happy when we met. Not the way you are now," he said.

"Like all places of great beauty, when you see the South Island from a distance, you must say, this is the place. That's what I said. Peace is here. But up close, we all have pimples on our arses. Behind the hymn singers and pulpit thumpers of Christchurch are some sanctimonious savages. Knock on any door . . . but you know that, Rory. You've knocked on a few of them these days yourself."

"Don't tell me your old man played around on you. Not on you, Georgia."

"With a minister's wife, among others."

"Bleeding Jesus, a preacher's wife!"

"Tight-arsed and wearing a quivering potted plant on her head. The tip of her nose wiggled when she talked, like there was a fly on it."

"I don't understand it. Not to a woman like you. Georgia, you've forgotten more about loving a man than any woman knows. You were just too much for him to handle, that's what."

"He never found out what I could give him. And he was no Rory Larkin. Once I was collected and in place, loving him was like trying to love a preening peacock."

"But a woman like you . . ."

"Men like Calvin Norman are only interested in the head count. Numbers to stroke his vanity. Conquest of no-matter-who reassures his virility. Have any idea how many desperate women fling themselves on a doctor during an intimate examination? Well now, I'm asking the wrong lad. You're doing a bit of head hunting as well. All of you like it when the girl says, 'Let's go to it.' Few refuse."

"Now wait a minute. I'm generally faithful to you," Rory blurted. "That's not what I meant to say. I meant to say, if you were mine, I wouldn't be doing that. But you aren't mine and it's almost as if you want me to go out and find women so I won't think of you as a jealous sort. Right, love?"

"I'd never put pressure on you. I can't because I'm married. I wouldn't because I'd run you off."

Rory reached for her, but she backed up a bit, out of reach and their rocking chairs stopped.

"Anyhow," she went on, "he got his cheap thrills with a minister's wife. Afterward he used up all the hot water taking baths to clean the itch off his skin."

"Want him back?"

"When the war came I gave him amnesty," she lied, almost spilling the secret. "Stitching up men with their guts hanging out and cutting off arms and legs could have a positive effect on him about what really matters."

"Had your husband been straight with you, would we have happened?"

"No," she answered. "I've seen my share of glorious bodies. There was one boy I loved desperately who died in the Boer War. The few other lovers until Calvin were part of growing up in the colonial service. I've never been cynical. I've cared for them all. It was what it was, but I neither lied nor cheated."

"Were they all bad numbers in the end?"

"They were soldiers. I was a nurse. And boys will be boys. But, the fact of the matter was, it was I who wanted to be free. I settled on Calvin because he was part of the illusion of the South Island."

"Could you have loved me?" Rory asked suddenly.

"Don't be foolish. We're an odd couple."

"We're not that odd," Rory said. "Could you have loved me?"

Georgia shrugged. "It's a moot question. We are uncomplicated. I want it to stay that way."

"I've been thinking," Rory said, "of the three things I'll miss the most. I'll miss the Ballyutogue Station and I'll miss RumRunner, and yourself as well."

"I'm in fine company," she said. "Now, go find your wars."

Rory suddenly lifted her into his arms, and she was not precisely weightless. He edged the screen door open with his toe first, then his backside, and carried her to the bedroom. Georgia did not stop screaming and laughing and beating at his shoulders until he dumped her on the bed.

Then, he wrapped himself around her to still her like a calf he had just roped and they grabbed each other's hair and exploded into a new furious kind of lovemaking that told each they both had held back words, thoughts, commitments. The raw rush of man and woman answered it all.

PART TWO

THE VISIT

CHAPTER

9

County Galway, Ireland, 1881

The door on the tenant's cottage had been posted with a cholera notice. Atty held Jack Murphy's hand so hard it hurt as he gingerly shoved open the forbidden door. Atty was seven. Jack Murphy, the foreman's son, was fourteen.

Their eyes played over a misery. Four wanes, all under ten years of age, lay moaning or beyond the strength to moan in a fogged, then comatose, crawl toward death. A thin voice of desperate prayer from their mother was the only pointless tad of hope.

The entire village was stricken, as was much of the region. The mother's prayer was interrupted by her sharp hack from the tuberculosis. Atty knelt before the children laid out on a mattress of bog peat before the fire.

"God has abandoned us," the farmer's wife said. "You shouldn't be bringing her up here in the heather."

Atty turned loose from Jack and felt the children's faces, then smiled at the smallest wane, who managed a smile back. Atty held the child's hand until he passed on to death. She stood and went outside, her mouth in a vice grip as the sounds of sobs and wails mixed with prayers and preparations for yet another wake and burial.

Jack was about to say that they had better leave but was stunned speechless by the incredibly ferocious expression in Atty's eyes. He had not seen the likes of it, ever. The fires lit in Atty would burst in fury all her life, like sunspots flaring into space.

It became apparent in a few years that she would be the sole inheritor of the Barony of Lough Clara, a land-owning family institution of County Galway dating back nearly three centuries.

It was also apparent that she loved Jack Murphy and would love no one else, forever. As the foreman's son, Jack had a privileged social position among the Catholics on the enormous estate. He had fetched the doctor for Atty's birth and watched over her ever since.

Lord Charles Royce-Moore was not disconsolate at being unable to produce a proper male heir. Atty was as capable as any man and her willpower was of the stuff that made empires. She would do all right by Lough Clara.

His feelings for Atty ran deeper than any frantic efforts for continuity. In fact, somewhat the opposite. The summation of his family's generations in Ireland disturbed him: After three centuries, they were still strangers in a strange land.

The defining event of his own life had been the potato famine in the late 1840s and early 1850s. For the first few years of the crop failure he bore witness to the sweeping scythe of death littering the fields with starved corpses, their mouths green from eating grass . . . then came the typhoid and TB and the mass flights from Ireland, many on infamous death ships.

All of this was too harsh for a young lad of the gentry, so he and most of the family sat out the great hunger in the more hospitable atmosphere of England. In order to save the barony, Lord Charles's father shipped off every head of cattle to England rather than go on a plan to share food with the peasants.

Charles returned to Lough Clara eventually, but his innards were too soft to further invoke the harsh rule when he ascended to baron and lord of the manor.

Baron Royce-Moore did what most of the Anglo landed gentry did, let his estate drift into an unkempt and undirected holding. While many of his class went under, he was skillful enough to keep the lifestyle grand and the manor house stocked with vintage cognac, mainly through his horse-breeding operation. At the same time he socked away enough in London to be able to have that city as his eventual retreat, living out his days in the comfort of a plush leather chair in some fine club.

Shrewd consolidation of the barony would afford Atty and a husband of her choice a handsome way of life and the continuation of the aristocracy for at least another generation. Charles would be long gone and really didn't give a damn what happened after Atty took over. She could reinvoke the ugly edicts necessary for large profit or simply get rid of the estate, as she wished.

In 1884, when Atty was ten, she was whisked off to schools in Switzerland, then London, considerable continental travel, and a "rounding out" of a proper lady, often in the company of her mother. They occasioned themselves at Lough Clara only during the summers. At first Atty did not protest, but every time she returned she fell in love with Jack Murphy all over again. More and more Jack recognized the rage of sunspots flaring off her angry star, but he didn't recognize that some of her passion was aimed at him. Because Atty was very young and there was a substantial age difference between her and Jack, the relationship resembled older brother to little sister. They made many extended horse excursions into the lunarscape of Connemara and along the sea.

But there was more to it than Atty and Jack just enjoying themselves. What soon seemed deeper and more important than winning Jack's love was what she saw—the destitution of the peasants. Aye, her fury over their bottomless agony became stronger than any personal feeling toward another human being.

Atty simply leapt over the awkward years when one's teeth usually required straightening or the skin was sprinkled with spots. She left Lough Clara as a girl of ten and returned as a completed young lady of thirteen, erect, a full glorious body, and a face of chilled beauty. She made no attempt at the games of coquetry, for there was no nonsense in her, no time for the frivolous things that amused her mother and her mother's circle. The male hunt occupied them . . . the gossip . . . the next ball. The girl was an off-horse, too serious and too determined. Her mother wondered, to what end?

Atty chopped off the heads of the parade of suitors with a

belittling quick glare. Moreover, she was tall as most men and a specimen to intimidate them. She became comfortable with her ability to keep the eager lads in step and exercised that power without pity. There were no backside slappers and sneaky pinchers pursuing that one.

Atty's escapes from Mother's inane pursuits were her great escapades to Jack Murphy's cottage. Jack's father, as estate foreman, had been able to see to a fine education for all his children. Jack had been schooled by the Christian Brothers in Galway and he responded with a keen love and grasp of the classics. He would read to Atty or play the guitar with winged fingers and sing out phrases of poetry he had set to his own music. Jack was a dandy-looking lad, for sure, and never at a loss for female company. He loved them all a little but never too strongly, never so he might fall into the Irish mating trap. Not a lass could put the bell around his neck.

This was fine with Atty. It would give her time to blossom to that point where she would be noticed by him as something other than his little friend. Then she could end her long silence and make her feelings known. In Atty's sixteenth summer she studied herself in the mirror and declared herself ready. She seldom asked but often commanded. With Jack Murphy she knew she had to be clever. He was a full-grown man of twenty-three edging toward a life decision.

Over the years the two had developed a physical relationship, that of buddies, a pair of mates up for a little horseplay and "innocent" wrestling. Atty would always break it off and leave before her sighs and outright panting of passion gave her away. Now sixteen, she was satisfied she could elicit the same feelings from him. Setting the scene carefully, after a gallop, she jumped him in the hayloft of the barn.

"I'm still your master!" he roared.

Her legs parted and her pelvis rolled about searching for what had made her vastly curious to feel. She found it and rocked back and forth. Jack's trying to hide it failed, and it began to grow and search for her. Atty, sitting on him, loosened the buttons of her blouse. Jack held her off and crawled away.

"Jaysus," he said, "I think you've grown a bit too much for us to go on with our kid games."

Atty grabbed his hand as he came to his feet. "Or maybe I've blossomed enough to start a real game."

Jack knew that Atty would always be direct and he had learned never to be at a loss. This was different. He held out a hand for her to halt, then sat beside her. "If we rolled around in past summers it was all for the sport. I never meant to lure you into temptation."

"To hell with that, Jack. Let's let our feelings do what they may," she said.

"We can't, luv."

"I can do anything I want," she responded.

"You're a young woman now and all kinds of new sensations are churning up inside you. We're very good pals, the best ever, and I'm familiar to you. That makes you comfortable with me. However, I'm just not the lad you should be experimenting with. You'll easily find the young man you're meant to do these things with."

"I don't like any of them, Jack. You know that. I hate almost all of them and what their fathers and my father have done to this place."

"Well, now, just because you hate someone doesn't mean he isn't the right fellow. Besides, Atty, some of those young suitors are rather decent sorts. Only problem is, you don't give them half a chance. When you look at them in that blood-curdling manner you can put on, I can see them shrink down to midgets before my very eyes."

Atty pouted.

"You can have any of those fellows you want when the time comes."

She opened her blouse. Jack reddened and closed it. "I'm not your man, only a little girl's fantasy gone amok. Let us not go into all the reasons this isn't right. I've only got one suit, Atty, and that was passed to me by my da and I'll probably pass it to my son."

"That's not true," she snapped. "We are exactly suited. It is in every line of poetry you write and every song you sing. Jack, you and I together can do something about all this wretchedness here."

"But I see you as my sister and always will."

"I'm not leaving this barn as a virgin," she all but commanded.

"The only way you're going to lose your virginity here now is by a good spanking."

As the summer wore on, Atty measured the situation. To flirt? To set up an accidental injury from a fall off a horse far out in the hillsides with him? To pout and rant?

She concluded Jack meant his words and decided it was better to go on as loving friends than not go on at all.

At the summer's end, she returned to London and he caught a ship out of Galway, another son of Ireland who had to seek a life away from his country.

Ballyutogue, County Donegal, Ireland, 1885

"The dray is all loaded, Mr. Lambe," Conor said.

Josiah Lambe, the blacksmith of Ballyutogue, both upper village of the Catholics and lower village of the Protestants, checked the donkey cart his apprentice boy had loaded. "Is that charcoal box secure?"

"Aye. Why are we bringing our own coal?"

"The coal they use at Hubble Manor couldn't build up enough fire to light my pipe."

The cart sagged, a wheel going down in the mud. "Jaysus," Conor said, "looks like we got the entire forge on the dray."

"Aye, we'll be working at the manor for ten days."

"Hope we don't bust an axle."

Mr. Lambe surveyed, grunted, and took a few extra pieces off to lighten the load. That apprentice of his was a gift. And what a touch he had twisting iron at the anvil.

"Hitch up the team, Conor lad. Did you tell your ma you wouldn't be home till after dark?"

"Aye, I did."

Mr. Lambe pinned a note to the front door:

WORKING AT THE MANOR. LEAVE YOUR WORK OR A NOTE
FOR ME INSIDE. WE'LL OPEN AT FIVE TOMORROW MORN-
ING IF ANY OF YOUR NAGS NEED SHOES.

*   *   *

"Take off your filthy boots," the second assistant house-keeper of the manor commanded with all the authority vested in her. She led them into the Long Hall of Hubble Manor, a massive room well over a hundred feet long and half as tall. The place reverberated with activity: window cleaners washing the stained glass; painters, polishers, brick repairmen, carpenters in organized frenzy to prepare the pre-Cromwellian navelike space for some very important event.

The second assistant housekeeper led them toward a knot of people all trying to get the attention of a woman in their midst.

Conor Larkin's twelve-and-a-half-year-old eyes became locked on her powerfully. She was neither tall nor short, but quite erect . . . but not erect in a stiff aristocratic way . . . bouncy, like a very beautiful girl balancing a pail of milk on her head with ease. Her hair was the most silken golden shimmering mane he had ever seen, and it flew, just so, at half speed when she turned it. And Jaysus! The top of her dress was like nothing in the upper village. It was all open and showed rounded parts of the gorgeous things tucked under a line of lace . . . and a sweet smell from her almost put him in a trance.

"Excuse me, m'lady," the second assistant housekeeper said with the humility of her station. "Mr. Lambe has arrived."

"Mr. Lambe?"

"The blacksmith."

"Oh yes, how do you do, Mr. Lambe?"

He nodded in a semibow and elbowed Conor to stop gawking and bow likewise. "Me assistant, young Conor Larkin."

"You're staring at me, Master Larkin."

"Aye, you're very beautiful."

Mr. Lambe groaned and ordered Conor to unload the dray. "Sorry about that, Countess. Catholic lad, you know. Sometimes they're a bit short on manners up in the heather."

"Actually, I thought he was disarmingly charming. Isn't he rather young to be an apprentice boy?"

"They start 'em young. They have to. This lad has the magic of the faeries at the forge."

"Well now, Mr. Lambe. Lord Hubble and I were suddenly recalled from our honeymoon, no less."

"Oh now, that's a pity."

"One must get used to the ways of the west. It seems that politics hereabouts has number one priority . . . after an heir is produced. However, his lordship and myself have hardly had the time to accomplish that, so it's politics with a capital P."

Mr. Lambe liked her. No snot about her. She had a gist, a pleasant gist, a smart woman who would get you to work your arse off for her, he thought.

"We were returned from paradise because it seems like Charles Stewart Parnell's victory in the election has caused a panic. Lord Randolph Churchill is landing at Larne, perhaps at this very moment, to rally our loyal Protestant forces against the pending Irish Home Rule Bill. A final rally will take place here in the Long Hall. The great screen is very unsteady and my blacksmith is shorthanded."

The manor's blacksmith, Mr. Leland, was born shorthanded, Mr. Lambe thought.

Lady Caroline continued. "I trust you can help him shore it up so that it won't be a safety hazard."

Mr. Lambe studied it. Once it had been most likely the greatest single example of wrought iron in Ireland, if not the world. Fires, explosions, and all those things that came with the insurrections had taken its toll. He went over it with Mr. Leland and reckoned it could be made safe in a few weeks.

"Good, that is how long it is going to take Lord Churchill to talk his way across Ulster."

Each night when the workmen had cleared out, Lady Caroline inspected the day's progress. Often as not, Mr. Lambe's apprentice boy, the Harkin or O'Leary lad—whatever his name was—would still be there staring at the screen. He'd inspect it from a few inches' distance, running his fingertips over the more circuitous parts and speaking to himself. The boy was obviously taken by the work.

A fortnight went by and the lad's fascination had not waned.

"Master Harkin," she said one evening late.

"Larkin, ma'am, Conor Larkin."

"You always seem to be the last one to leave."

"I hope you don't mind, ma'am. Mr. Lambe leaves me one of his horses to ride home."

"What is it that you find so awesome in this tangle of iron?"

"It was the masterpiece of Jean Tijou, the greatest man who ever put a hammer on a hot piece of iron."

"You know about this screen? Its history?"

"Aye. It's legend. I mean, the legends are really old schanachie tales. Our schanachie, Daddo Friel, he's near blind now. . . . Anyhow, he told me about this screen for hours on end."

"That's fascinating. Care to share your secrets?"

"Oh, you know how it is. Most schanachie stories are pretty wild . . . they shoot them past you like comets. Just old stories."

"I insist."

"No, ma'am."

"I insist."

"Well, it might not be to your liking."

"I insist."

"It is an utter paradox," Conor said, "how the most beautiful work of its kind could be used for the most cruel . . . "

"Go on. I was born in Belfast. I do know my Irish history."

"During the insurrection of seventeen hundred and fifteen, a local rising, the earl at that time imprisoned three hundred and fifty women and children behind the screen as hostages. The rest is not too important."

"They died?"

"Something like that. Probably a faerie's tale."

"Yes," she said rather harshly, "the schanachies can be frightful liars. Anyhow, Londonderry seems to be filled with tales I'll need catching up on."

Conor's cheeks turned crimson. Daddo Friel does not lie, he thought angrily! And it's *not* Londonderry . . . it's *Derry*.

"Well, perhaps some day in the future, when you are older and have earned your ironmaster certification, you can work on a full restoration of the screen."

"Yes, ma'am," he replied without enthusiasm.

"Anyhow, just make certain it doesn't fall down on Lord Churchill's head."

Oh, if it would only collapse and squish Randolph Churchill like an ugly bug, Conor thought.

"You see," she said backing off a bit, "Lord Churchill is very important...."

"I know who he is. He's no friend of Charles Stewart Parnell."

Conor and Lady Caroline had nothing to say to each other after that. However, once or twice a day, and sometimes even more often, there was a direct look from one to the other and sometimes it lasted for several seconds.

Conor Larkin's dearest friend, Seamus O'Neill, was born as an afterthought, the scrapings of the pot. With a family of more than enough O'Neill men to work their fields, young Seamus had a childhood of exceptional leisure. For an Irish mother, no greater pleasure in life could come than spoiling the youngest son. To his credit, Seamus did not spend his time creating mischief as he might, but rather enriching his everlasting and deep and monumental friendship with Conor—who was also his hero, because Conor was destined to become a great republican fighter like all the Larkin men and particularly Conor's grandfather Kilty, God rest his soul.

When the new national school opened in Ballyutogue for the villages around, Seamus talked his parents into letting him enroll. Being one of three Catholics in a roomful of Protestants and being the runt of the litter had its disadvantages.

Although the teacher, Mr. Andrew Ingram, was a Scottish Presbyterian, he was an enlightened man who would tolerate no bigotry within his eyesight. Mr. Ingram was fast to realize that Seamus was his best student and supplied the boy with books that would otherwise be inaccessible. Moreover, he tutored Seamus to fill the boy's longing to become a writer.

Seamus had protection outside the schoolyard if he could make it to Mr. Lambe's forge close by. When chased, he would scurry to his eternal friend Conor for help.

Finally, the boys made a pact. Seamus would teach Conor to read and write and Conor would teach Seamus to fight. It was difficult going for both of them in the beginning, but when Seamus punched the school bully bloody and Conor conquered the first primer, their battle was won.

Conor now had access to books, and the worlds they told of that he never dreamed he would know. A magic planet burst open. Each school day Seamus ran to the forge and when Conor closed it down the two would go off to their secret place near the old Norman keep to explore their new world beyond Ballyutogue.

It was not only of places and things they read, but great ideas. Mr. Ingram exposed them to Thomas Paine and assured them that all the signers of the American Declaration of Independence were Presbyterians. They were sure as hell different than the Ulster Presbyterians, Seamus thought.

Conor was a wizard, soon caught up to and passing Seamus. Suddenly, something went haywire with Conor. After he and Mr. Lambe had worked at Hubble Manor fixing the screen, Conor seemed suddenly to lose interest in books and just about everything else. His mind drifted away from republican matters, which was very disconcerting to Seamus. After a week of it, Seamus rebelled.

"Your face looks like the potato mush at the bottom of me ma's crock, Conor. What's the matter with you!"

"Nothin'."

"Is your ma pregnant again?"

"Christ, no, praise Mary."

"Then what's wrong with you?"

"Ugh, forget it."

"Ah shyte, Conor, you're a blister, that's wot!"

"If it is that evident then maybe I'd better confide in you, but this is even more sacred a secret than the confessional, understand? If you ever breathe a word about what I am about to tell you, I'll really kill you."

"When," Seamus protested, "have I ever betrayed a confidence? Name me just one time!"

"Then hold up your right hand."

Seamus did, proudly.

"Do you swear on your republican honor that this is our eternal secret?"

"Aye, I do. Have you killed somebody?"

"Christ, no. I'm in love with Caroline Hubble."

"Caroline Hubble! You'll not live to see another harvest harboring thoughts like that! This one time, you'd better go to confession."

"That's the last place I'd tell."

"I mean, really in love with her?"

"Aye, deeply, fiercely, tenderly. I think about her all the time and these wonderful sensations just shoot through me. I think about her before I fall asleep and you know what happens down there."

"Jaysus!"

"I'll tell you something. I see her look at me, too. Now, maybe she's not in love with me or anything but I know that she wants to tell me something. I know that!"

"You ain't got nothing she's looking for."

"Yeah, it's crazy-like," Conor agreed. "I'll just have to get over it."

"And fast-like. Suppose the utterly worst thing happened. In a trance induced by the faeries, she was to fall in love with you, despite the vast difference in your ages. And suppose she took you into a secret room and you and her did it. I mean really did it and while you were doing it, the viscount walked in and caught youse! Oh boy! Protestants would be rioting all over the world! And they'd take her out to the Guildhall Square in Derry and march her up to the chopping block like Anne Boleyn and hoick off her head, or maybe they'd burn her at the stake like Joan of Arc . . . and as for you, croppy boy, they'd draw and quarter you with four horses and hang your head up on a pike and every Protestant would come for miles just to spit on it . . . and she'd haunt Hubble Manor walking around whooing with her head tucked under her arm and all the potatoes in the fields would rot again and there'd be another famine because of your foul lust!"

"All right, all right. I've forgotten about her!"

"You swear!"

"Aye, I swear. I've forgotten about her."

Seamus sighed in relief at having waylaid his best friend on a certain path to self-destruction. "I don't believe you," he said at last.

11

SECRET FILES OF WINSTON CHURCHILL,
COVERING 1885

General Recollections Regarding Ireland

I recall my introduction to Ireland with utter clarity. I was twelve at the time and one is not apt to forget when he first learns he was almost born out of wedlock. I have often pondered if the lifelong strangeness and standoffishness that existed between my father and myself had anything to do with his adventures with my mother before their marriage. And, his adventures with other women after their marriage until his untimely death due to syphilis.

The trauma of learning of my "premature" arrival and my trip to Ireland came at the same time, near my twelfth birthday. Ireland was England's quasi-bastard, and I had similar status in my own family.

Lord Randolph's journey over the Irish Sea to Ulster fit into his relentless drive to become prime minister. My father had an issue of great urgency and popularity to be exploited; namely, he was out to stop the Irish Home Rule legislation that had been introduced into Commons by Charles Stewart Parnell and his new Irish Party.

I was to accompany him, and I suspect I was a good stage prop because the Ulster Protestant family unit was considered a blessing, in contrast to the popular platitude that "the Catholic family unit was a curse."

If my father could generate enough support in Ulster to turn back the Irish Home Rule Bill, he calculated it might bring about the downfall of the Gladstone government. This would put him in line for a high-ranking cabinet ministry in the new government as well as making him the leader in Commons. Thus he would be first in line to become the next prime minister.

The Orange Order, a fanatical Protestant fraternal lodge, and my father's ally, the Unionist Party of Ulster, were there to greet us at Larne with a banner and band. We were to traverse Ulster in the private train of their leading industrialist, Sir Frederick Weed, a bluff bully of a chap but rather likable.

Onward we clickety-clacked over our loyal province ... Portadown ... Armagh ... Dungannon ... speaking to ever growing throngs of men wearing bowler hats and orange sashes, generally in a state of frenzy. It was at Lurgan that Lord Randolph pressed their nerve with the battle cry, "Ulster will fight and Ulster will be right."

Our finale was a great hall in a stately home outside Londonderry belonging to the Earl of Foyle and his son Roger Hubble, the Viscount Coleraine. Londonderry was the sacred city of the Protestants, a sort of Rome, Mecca, and Jerusalem rolled into one.

On this occasion at Hubble Manor my father went beyond himself. "You gallant comrades in Western Ulster stand on the forwardmost rampart of our great imperial adventure and you must not falter. I dare you to hold these walls as your ancestors held them three centuries ago. There are two Irelands in spirit, in religion, and in reality. The Ireland which is loyal to the Crown must remain in the Empire." And then it came ... Rudyard Kipling's latest ... "Sail on, oh ship of state, sail on, oh Union great ... Shall Ulster from Britain sever? By the God who made us, never!"

I shall remember this speech for gentler things. Roger Hubble was also the son-in-law of Sir Frederick Weed, having recently married his daughter, Caroline. Even at my young age, standing in short trousers and school cap, I felt my first understanding of male passion. I had never seen so exquisite a woman.

For myself, at the age of twelve, I was privy, for the first time, to the private dialogue and strategies of men of great influence. Hearing my father's words and watching their effect upon the crowd . . . playing with cadence and key phrases was a lesson long remembered.

This was my introduction to the private and public use of power.

Although I loved my father, we spent little time together. This trip to Ulster, where he played his famous "Orange card" was to be our longest visit. He was a stange and erratic aristocrat, driven to seek power. Most of the other times we shared as father and son were strange, yes bizarre, little tours through the flesh-pots of London where he seemed to receive deviant thrills watching freak shows, many of weird sexual content.

On our overnight trip from Belfast back to England he felt a strong desire to come to my cabin and explain to me the mean-ing of Ireland in the life of England. I was playing with my box of toy soldiers, which always accompanied me, setting up a tacti-cal exercise while Lord Randolph was in his usual posture of fin-ishing up his whiskey.

"The English people has made its mark on mankind as a great people. Through exploration, conquest, the plantation of loyal subjects in our colonies, trade and spreading our cultural bene-fits and legal superiority have made us the greatest nation in mankind's history."

There was nothing there to disagree with at the age of twelve.

"England is an island," he continued, "and in order to maintain our greatness we are dependent on our seafaring power, both commercially and militarily. Our sea lanes are our blood lines."

He asked me if I understood, and when put the way he stated it, it was quite clear to me.

"Ireland is a mass of destitute rocks. Its only importance is vis-à-vis England. Well then, we cannot allow a smaller or lesser people to threaten our position in the world.

"Winston," he said, turning blunt, "the Irish are a backward people with no right to deny England its destiny. It is England's right and England's duty to protect England's vital interests and thus, we must govern Ireland to protect ourselves."

He went on to say that the planting of a population loyal to the Crown in Ulster protected the Crown's interests.

Never failing to arouse himself on the subject, even after some fifty speeches over the Province of Ulster, he came to his feet.

"What we are dealing with is the fact that the Irish are hostile people who have rejected all overtures to unite with us, as have the Scots and Welsh. Ireland's only purpose for self-government is to bring disaster on us, and we cannot permit that to happen."

The rough sea sent my father back to his couch, emptying his bottle and mumbling a comment about Countess Caroline Hubble's bosom.

I returned to my toy soldiers, sharing my father's thoughts.

CHAPTER

12

1890

A lesser girl than Atty would have taken Jack Murphy's emigration as a personal rebuff. Atty refused to be humiliated. She came to her decisions only after great consideration and pondering. Once she made them, they remained fast. Her emotions, shaped by her own truths, were set in concrete.

Atty made two life decisions by the age of sixteen. She hated the injustice of the British rule and she loved Jack Murphy. Both decisions were logical to her and both inseparable.

Jack's departure was soothed somewhat by kindly letters from rare and exotic surrounding places . . . Tampico . . . Bora Bora . . . Christchurch . . . Monrovia . . . Montevideo.

"I do love you, Atty," Jack Murphy wrote, "but not in the mating way. Even if I had the right to love you with physical passion in mind, it still might not be possible. Too many things we came into the world with have frayed our tapestry from the beginning. We might as well have been born, you in India and me in Argentina, there are so many differences between us.

"To be utterly honest, there is you, Atty, who is the real difference. You are so soft and beautiful to look upon, yet so hard and frightening to know. You are bitter, Atty, determined to throw your life into changing an unchangeable world. The odds you have placed on reaching your goals are insurmountable. While I adore your courage and determination, I don't adore my own that much. I know I could never be a proper partner for you in such a venture. I seek much less from life. You are too strong for me, Atty, and I dare say you are too strong for almost any man, for he must be willing to subvert himself to your insatiable drive.

"Only myself sees that inner rage in you now, but soon all of Ireland will know about it. Nae, all the world. Do I make any sense to you at all? Now I close as I opened this letter. I love you, but not in that way."

Was Jack Murphy too weak for her or simply too wise? He knew her truths and said he could not match them. It was an elegant rebuff. He called himself a quitter. Nonetheless, Atty felt anger with her pain. Why couldn't Jack hold up? Or was it all just his way of saying he didn't really love her?

After her seventeenth birthday, Atty announced to her parents that she was not returning to London for further schooling but was off to Dublin instead.

"Is this an advisement or a consultation?" her father asked.

"I've made my decision, Father. Seek whatever justifications you need."

There was no call going into all that trash about disinheriting her, Charles Royce-Moore wisely concluded. It was a small miracle he was able to keep her close for seventeen years. "I suppose," he said, "that you are intent on joining this Gaelic mutiny going on in Dublin."

"I'm not all that certain."

"Well, since Parnell," he said, trying to manage not to make a mock spit, "the clans have been gathering to run the Anglo rascals out with a new birth of ancient Celtic tribalism. Gaelic sports, Gaelic literature, and all those bloody newspaper articles—how in the name of the Almighty did this one little place sprout so many writers? They're like mushrooms growing wild near a moldy swamp."

"Perhaps it is because you have made Ireland a moldy swamp," she answered.

"Can we negotiate?" her father said candidly.

"One does not negotiate with the English without getting buggered," she replied, only half joking.

"I've watched you wander among the lepers for years," he said. "I've had my moments of great consternation. More than once I've asked myself, what the hell are we doing here? Well, I was born here. My estate is out there. Things have been done a certain way for centuries and despite a pang of conscience now and then, I have always known I could not change things."

"That's a very pleasant line of justification for picking the Irish carcass clean in a most hideous way. Your class—"

"Our class, Atty."

"Your class," she continued, "has reduced these people to the most destitute in Western civilization. Their larder is empty," she said.

"That's a fact. The time of the estates is coming to an end. Although it is all beyond my reach, there must be a supplanting of new ideas, the kind that you are up to. Look here, my velvet collar has turned shiny. I'm not going to keep up the pretense, and I know you won't, either. This is a shabby place, growing shabbier."

"I will say, Father, that you have been better than some."

"I shall not turn against my class, Atty. The radical goings-on in Dublin are beyond me, yet I see a time coming when we will completely fade from the landscape. I suggest there will be very few Irish tears shed for us when we leave. Now, do you want to listen to my proposition or not?"

Atty loved her father almost as much as she despised his class. Is it more evil to be aware of his evil and not do anything about it? Most of his goodfellows accepted the fortunate circumstances of their inheritances without a ha'penny of guilt. Sneering down on the inferior croppy Irish justified the exploitation. At least her father did not do that.

"Here is my proposal. As you know by your study of the estate books, I have transferred a decent sum to London to see out your mother's and my days. I am quite provincial myself and am actually very fond of Ireland. Yet, I cannot bear the thought of doing my declining years in a townhouse in Dublin. Dublin is seedy. A few stone facades scarcely cover a shantytown soggy with all those pubs and their bad poets. I am going to retire to

the comfort of London. You have my major sins on the table—
my class loyalty, my inability to change the world.

"The estate is in rather decent order," he continued.
"Murphy and my land agents have done an admirable job in the
framework in which they've been allowed to operate. We have
tried not to inflict too much more pain on our tenants. I have set
aside a tidy little trust for you to conclude your education,
which you now reject. So, go to Dublin and use this money to
keep yourself. All I ask is that you indulge your mother now
and then and let her give a few parties a year so you can examine
and guillotine her newest collection of eligible suitors."

"No, Daddy, you want more. Now what is it?"

"Atty, for seventeen you are a monster. All right, then. By
the time you reach your twenty-first birthday, the barony will
be yours whether I survive or not. You have to promise me that
you'll keep things in balance with Murphy. Once Mother and I
die, you can do with it what you will."

"Why the wait, Father?"

"I want to live in London as a retired member of the gentry
and not as some sort of traitor."

Atty's answer would be quick—in five years she would be
able to make of Lough Clara what she had dreamed of doing
since she was a child.

"Meanwhile, join the bloody rising," he finished.

"I agree, Father. Lough Clara will still bear the family crest
until you and Mother die. I hope that won't be for a long time.
But understand what I'm doing in Dublin."

"Oh hell, we all know that. You see, Atty, I have known all
along what I am and cannot be otherwise or even pretend to be
otherwise. The potato famine turned me into a lump instead of a
crusader. I was happy when I was called off to do my naval duty
and did not want to return to Lough Clara. But I did, and I did
nothing new or stunning, only what was expected of me. I am an
Englishman and all that implies, good and bad. I'll stand aside
for you. Let me have my dignity."

Tender kisses from Atty had been hard to come by. He trea-
sured this one.

"And now, willful, wonderful, wise, angry Atty, allow me to offer you one piece of advice."

"Of course, Father."

"Forget about Jack Murphy."

"I can't and I won't."

"You're far too strong for him. Forgive me for saying this, Atty, but you're far too strong for any man I've met. But Jack Murphy will not be ground under and unless you can reach an accommodation with him, as you just have with me, then you *will* grind him under."

"And if he doesn't come back? No one else will have me?"

"No one else can hold you, Atty. Unless . . . and I find this highly unlikely . . . you fall in love so desperately that you completely lose yourself."

"What do you believe?"

"I told you. Find an accommodation with Jack or someone, a way you can live together without great passion or great desire to destroy each other. You see, my girl, the man who can make my Atty lose herself does not exist. Be British in this instance. Make an accommodation."

CHAPTER
13

1890

Lord Randolph Churchill had come. The Long Hall of Hubble Manor was packed. Every member of the landed gentry and aristocracy west of Westport and north of Athlone had come. All men of the cloth who were the inheritors of the Reformation had come. Every loyalmost of the loyalmost, the Orange Grandmasters, had come. Beribboned veterans of the Queen's loyal Ulster regiments had come. And their women.

Shivering from Charles Stewart Parnell's smashing victory and fearing for their continuation in isolated Londonderry, they heard the archconservative of England play his Orange card. His voice, couched in words to reach beyond the wall and over the sea to Parliament, took dead aim at intimidation of the Liberal Party.

His young son Winston sopped it up for future reference. His father had splayed the unsuspecting foe, broken their ranks, left them reeling.

It was also the first successful adventure of the partnership of Western Ulster, defended by Roger Hubble and the Belfast establishment controlled by Sir Frederick Weed. Between them now, they had a lock on the province's political direction. Their relationship was consummated by the marriage of Caroline Weed to Roger Hubble. Churchill at Long Hall became one of the most consequential events in the history of Ulster. The moment was a culmination of two different men with two different careers suddenly and daringly merged.

Weed was the bully Scotsman, an entrepreneur in an age of British entrepreneurship. The self-made magnate whose mighty industrial plant was now laying the hulls for steel ships of up to ten thousand tons. The rail king with his Red Hand Express engine and personal train, the envy of every South American dictator and Indian maharajah. Steel from his mills spun the rails that eighty percent of Ireland's trains ran on. He had accomplished it all, by God, with his great derring-do.

His bastion of Belfast, unfortunately, was the only place where the British had made substantial investments. It stood unique on an Irish landscape bereft of manufacturing. Manned with loyal Protestant workers, Belfast was the solitary enclave of enterprise.

Out on the land, the days of the great estates were ending. Since the potato famine, the gentry had been reduced to tattered curtains and mumbled their pledges to the Crown by rote.

Viscount Roger Hubble, the pending Earl of Foyle, proved an exception. He snatched the earldom from his bumbling father, pensioned him off with his mistress, and not only survived but created a new chapter to add to the horrors of the Industrial Revolution.

Roger Hubble was an ultimate master of creating a cradle-to-grave labor force, which was always in his debt. On the land, his tenant farmers cultivated the raw product he needed and he allowed them just enough acreage to farm food for a marginal existence. Hubble carefully nipped off the weaker farms, evicting the tenants, and converted the land into a growing cattle ranch, the prime export product to England.

He set the price for planting seeds and carried the peasant's debt, which was paid off at the next harvest with obscene interest. He then set the price of the flax that was harvested. Conversion of flax to linen was a slimy job, done mostly with labor provided by the younger children of the peasants, often to keep even with the family debts.

Evictions on the land assured a constant flow of desperate and jobless people into Londonderry and into their squalid neighborhood of Bogside. Thus, he always had a surplus of cheap labor. Unemployment of men ran around fifty percent, and those who worked had menial jobs.

The big profit-maker was his shirt factory, the largest in the British Isles, which used the linen produced by his peasants.

Roger Hubble's control of everything from seed to finished product, power over the political machinery, and labor force represented all that was deemed glorious in colonization and imperialism.

The decent positions in the municipality, in the shipyard, in the schools as well as the mercantile were locked in for those who swore loyalty to the Crown. This was Ulsterism.

Charles Stewart Parnell and his Irish Party dented the system and opened their own salvo for Home Rule. Londonderry both historically and geographically belonged in County Donegal, which would have been outside Ulster's boundaries. By shamefully gerrymandering the borders, Roger Hubble was able to shift Londonderry into Ulster.

In the beginning of the new political era, Sir Frederick Weed and the Belfast industrialists wanted to expend Londonderry as a liability. Roger Hubble, and later Randolph Churchill, threatened civil war if the sacred Protestant city was lost to the Catholics. The marriage of Roger and Caroline set the alliance in stone.

Caroline was an exciting lady with a recent past that included a marriage to a penniless gigolo, an Italian count. Her main purpose was to enrage her father, which she did. Many thousands of pounds sterling were spread around the Vatican, which ultimately came up with an annulment.

The heady lady smashed up a hotel suite filled with priceless antiques, bolted Rome, and took on Paris. Here she shared a garret with a struggling but extremely talented artist painting in the new Impressionistic style. When his garlic and gout and the climb to his attic no longer endeared him, she returned to Ulster, where she became the model of decorum, a queen of culture and charity, and awaited her fate, which appeared in the form of Roger Hubble.

They realized the power of their union. Titillated by whispers of Caroline's past, Roger's sexuality was unearthed and aroused to a point that he became an excellent lover. Roger adored her.

Caroline bore him two sons, one for the earldom and one for Weed Ship & Iron. Lord Jeremy, the elder and heir, seemed to be a throwback to Roger's own father, the dawdling Arthur Hubble, a boy too frivolous to do the stern stuff necessary to run the hard course.

Fortunately, Christopher, the younger son, showed all the ice of his father. So be it. Jeremy would be the ceremonial earl while Christopher would be schooled to run the machinery.

Caroline! Caroline the magnificent! She turned Londonderry from a cultural blob to a cultural way station. Every touring Shakespearean company, every second-rate troupe of operatic Italians, every lecturer, poet, musician, orchestra who touched Ireland made the now mandatory trip to Londonderry. Most were brought there through her cultural foundation. Caroline was the *grande dame* of Western Ulster.

Life was complete for Roger Hubble, except for one grating habit of Caroline's. She never stopped remodeling. Hubble Manor was a historic monstrosity with its dozens of fish and gun and knife rooms and ice houses and fowl rooms and stables and a Buckingham Palace–size kitchen, subkitchens, a poultry room, twenty linen closets, and workshops for the drapers, rug menders, upholsterers, painters, glazers, gardeners, and a boathouse on the Lough Foyle, and butlers, maids, carriage drivers, and footmen, all two hundred of them in their hideous mint green uniforms with vile lemon piping.

Roger played the role of woeful wounded husband opening the bills, but Caroline's seduction kept his sexual appetite always hungry enough for the marriage to work. Fortunately, when the bills came due, Caroline had an enormously wealthy daddy and funds of her own.

The place for any *great* event . . . Caruso singing, a world collection of scholars, the Queen's state visit . . . was always the Long Hall, which could house almost a thousand people at a seated dinner and more for a concert.

Having been repaired, remodeled, rebuilt, and added on with nonstop activity for a decade, Hubble Manor was transformed from a seedy weed-covered haunted house to a palace of legendary grandeur, the epitome of what the ultimate colonizer could do with his imperial appetite.

Another ultimate was Lord Hubble's shirt factory. Conditions within were filthy, numbing cold by winter, darkness, suffocating heat by summer, a void of human facilities, and a page-long list of miseries that were direct leftovers from the blackest days of the Industrial Revolution.

With all the new liberalism in the air, Roger Hubble became uneasy that industrial and labor reform might find its way into Londonderry and, particularly, his shirt factory, which was the chief supporter of Lady Caroline's excesses. To make matters worse, a Catholic peasants' and workers' rights solicitor had won the seat in Commons.

Having redone everything redoable, Caroline turned to the final great project, restoration of the great screen in the Long Hall. It was forty feet wide and forty feet high, forming a majestic entrance gate. It might have well been a copy of the gates of heaven, inspired by the Almighty.

Tradition had it that the screen was the work of Jean Tijou, a great French ironmaster who had been brought to England centuries earlier during the reign of William and Mary. Much of its history, as well as its twisted agony, remained hidden by legend.

Obviously, Lady Hubble searched out the foremost living ironmaster, one Joaquim Schmidt, the German. For two years Schmidt worked on what had become an enigma. As a good German would, Herr Schmidt believed things would happen if he commanded and hollered. His shouting dimmed to a disoriented mumble and he departed.

Then Caroline brought in the Italian, Tustini. At first he made some progress but he became torn emotionally between the screen and a number of the upstairs and downstairs maids. Ulster weather sent him into long depressions, followed by too much *vino*, and he sobbed all the way to Cork to catch his ship back to Italy.

Her failure gnawed at her every time an event was held in the Long Hall, as the great screen remained limp and disoriented.

CHAPTER

14

1895

Lady Atty Brooke Royce-Moore, the Baroness of Lough Clara, burst on the scene of the Gaelic revival as though she and Dublin had been waiting for one another for a century.

Her first act, which endeared her to the native Dubliners, was to dehyphenate and degentrify her name and titles to a simple Miss Atty Moore.

Atty's generous per annum allowance enabled her to purchase a four-story Georgian row house at 34 Garville Avenue in the suburb of Rathgar. It was neither an aristocrat's home nor a poor man's dwelling. A spacious drawing room hosted most of those who identified with and spearheaded the Gaelic revival. Spicy conversation rang from writers, journalists, pamphleteers, leafleteers, republicans, actors, playwrights, and new-breed politicians.

Atty's basic identification was with Arthur Griffith, whose newspaper the *United Irishman* was a growing force. Griffith had also formed a new political party, Sinn Fein, whose translation meant "Ourselves Alone." Sinn Fein was born to replace the Irish Party, whose spirit had died with the death of Parnell. Once a determined force, the Irish Party members became lackeys in the British Parliament, incapable of pushing the Home Rule agenda.

Atty kept quiet about her age. She was seventeen when she arrived in Dublin like a Celtic myth riding out of the west. Her physical stature, keen mind, and willful personality revealed a persona beyond her years. She was more than at home in this moment of Gaelic revival. She spoke the ancient language to perfection and soon discovered the speaker's platform at street corner rallies where she decried the evils of imperialism.

All of it was euphoric, the ringing cries for liberty by the pamphleteers, the circle of intellectuals, the old games of the Gaels on the sports fields, the spawning ground of awakening.

Shortly after her arrival, three of her closest friends, Lady Gregory, Edward Martyn, and William Butler Yeats declared the beginnings of an Irish National Theatre.

> We propose to have performed in Dublin, in the spring of every year, certain Celtic and Irish plays, which, whatever be their degrees of excellence, will be written with high ambition and so build up a Celtic and Irish school of dramatic literature.... We will show that Ireland is not the home of buffoonery and of easy sentiment, as it has been represented, but the home of an ancient idealism. We are confident of the support of all Irish people, who are weary of misrepresentation, in carrying out a work that is outside all the political questions that divide us.

Well, that was a marriage in heaven waiting to happen for Atty Moore. A permanent home was found in the rebuilt Mechanics' Theatre on Abbey Street. Atty followed her physical stature and commanding presence onto the stage. In the beginning her presence was so powerful, all she had to do was walk on and stare at the audience to chill them.

She was a star, but there was a problem. Atty's enthusiasm and her ability as an actress were not quite on the same page. With a blunderbuss cry from the dock or dying of TB from linen mill dust, she could overact to move any Irishman to tears.

Because her acceptance of a script assured a playwright a production, she was heavily courted by aspirants. One playwright who caught her fancy was a young journalist out of Donegal.

Atty sensed from the onset that, despite her power, Seamus O'Neill did not seem quite as awed as those in her court.

Seamus had written two ten-minute readings, the kind of lyrical prose that any actress would want as a part of her repertoire. She sensed that he was not happy that she merely took his writing for herself, when in fact she had been expecting Seamus to swoon over the honor.

They went to work, one-on-one, and he rolled his eyes to the heavens once too often. Down flung the script and off stomped the actress. Seamus picked up his pages and repaired to an always handy pub.

"Well?" she said, slipping alongside him at the bar twenty minutes later.

"You're not Joshua," Seamus said, "you aren't going to knock down the walls of Dublin Castle by blowing a trumpet."

Atty passed through several stages of fury. Well, she did ask him and the little bastard had the right to his opinion. What hurt was that he had hit the bull's-eye. Atty was going nowhere except as a big busted trumpet.

"Should I go out and buy a harp?"

"Keep Atty off the stage," Seamus said. "Bring on the stage the woman whom the playwright wrote. Otherwise, you're going to end up as a dog with one trick, shout your way through your roles. You don't trust the words."

"I'm trying to decide if I should spit on you or ask you to help me," she said.

"Theatre of this sort is new. I'm not a director. No one is yet in Ireland."

"I must act," she said as fiercely as she had ever spoken. "This is what I can do as a republican and I have never known an experience as tremendous, as exhilarating, as powerful as when I'm up there."

"Colonels and rugby players and women giving birth have the same experience. You've got to look inside you and ask God if you can play someone other than Atty."

"Can you give me a hand, sir?"

"How deep can you look into other people's joy and pain

without becoming frightened and locking them out?"

"I'm going to find out, Seamus, and you're going to help me."

Seamus wrote a half-dozen short readings for her, each demanding her to probe a different emotion. She was often asked to play someone she feared or loathed . . . to be devious, bigoted, hateful, of loose values. The game was to turn herself believably into the anti-Atty.

To go along with her dynamic stature and commanding voice, Atty added nuances and dimensions and range and a command of subtle moments and movements. All of this, to do the utmost with her talent.

Seamus had done wonders and Atty was pleased. However, both of them realized that she had only so much capacity to give. She always had to retain the ability to become Atty again, in the blink of an eye.

She was a good actress, now easy, now humorous, now filled with confidence . . . but always in control. She adored what she was doing as life itself. She adored the adoration that went with it and the centerstage world she occupied.

Yet, there was a locked vault inside her that held all of her demons, and she feared to enter it onstage or offstage. Maybe she might never open the door to the vault. Only if she chanced it would she ever ascend to immortality on the stage. It was the only dare she ever shied from.

Jack Murphy's dad, Darby Murphy, kept things well in hand aided by Atty's constant visits. A competent solicitor in Galway kept the operation profitable. Lord Charles and Lady Royce-Moore felt confident enough to make their long desired move to London.

His lordship had no sooner sunk into that deep leather chair of London's Standard Club than he snoozed off and never awakened. At the very same tick of the clock, Darby Murphy died of a heart attack as well.

When the grief and turmoil of the double deaths had eased, Atty had to make decisions. Lough Clara would not be hers for three more years, and trying to modernize without displacing the tenants was a tricky bit of business. It would mean that she would have to spend more time away from Dublin.

She closed the manor house and moved into Darby Murphy's lovely cottage, set in a rare stand of oaks near the stables and horse training grounds. No harm. The entire Murphy family was gone from Lough Clara forever and the cottage was far more to her liking than the big house.

She made it cozy and delicious, using it as her "western" office, where she could read far into the nights, receive wayward republicans passing through, and keep the estate on firm ground, working things out to allow her to go to Dublin often.

Six months into her new routine the postman handed her a cable along with the daily mail. She tore the envelope open and saw the signature ... Jack Murphy ... and she felt entirely weak with a thundering flush of passion.

MY FAMILY HAS ELECTED ME TO SETTLE MY FATHER'S AFFAIRS STOP RETURNING TO IRELAND SOONEST STOP CAN WE MEET AT LOUGH CLARA FEBRUARY 24 STOP PLEASE CABLE AFFIRMATION STOP LOOK FORWARD TO SEEING YOU STOP LOVE JACK MURPHY

Everything she had managed so meticulously and determinedly to suppress could no longer be suppressed. She knew by the cable that nothing had changed in the way she felt about him. Damned, Atty, she challenged, you will not fling yourself at him.

Nonetheless Atty dotted the final "i" and crossed the final "t" to make things ready, to make things perfect. Jack would be twenty-eight now. How would he look? She almost hoped, but at the same time did not hope, sight of him would do nothing to arouse her.

She studied herself with no less intensity than the lovelorn men in her audience had studied her up on the stage. How can he turn me down?

Or was he desperately in love with someone? Dear Lord. Atty realized that a totally new sensation was overwhelming her. It was fear.

The stately queen of the Dublin stage bit her nails and became teary over nothing several times a day . . . each day one day closer. She was flighty at the meetings with her solicitor and estate manager. She yelled needlessly at an actor or director, followed by yards of apology.

The day came. Yes, the ship arrived at Galway. She managed to remain calm as he came down the gangplank, smiled, set down his suitcase, and gave her an old-fashioned Jack-and-Atty hug. Jack held her at arm's length. "Jaysus, lass, all you need is a truly fine poet for immortalization. Sure, you're the most glorious creature in Ireland."

"Oh Jesus, Jack, if you'd have been one day longer I'd have wet my knickers," she cried in relief.

The cottage had a feel of a new inhabitant, a conversion to a mode of seriousness and resolve. Atty's papers and practicalities had replaced doilies. Important thoughts and conversations emanated from it now, no longer a loafer's and children's romping place, but one for study and future rebellion. Nonetheless she had softened it for his visit with flowers and fireplace glow and the best of wines and whiskey. Although Atty made little formal effort, she was a gorgeous piece of work.

Jack Murphy had turned out well. He was not the irresistible handsome lad of memories, but slight and intense and very much in command. Atty's apprehension melted. When he returned to Canada he would be on his way to Toronto to become the book editor of the country's largest newspaper, and an occasional critic of music and art.

"Ah, Dublin is the place for the journalist," Atty tweaked.

"It's far too fierce for me here," he replied.

"Really, Jack. Isn't there a mutated Orange crowd in Toronto, and don't the Brits and French go at it all the time?"

"Aye, but their warfare is fought with cannonballs of pudding. Irish politics is like the Islamic religion, an all-consuming way of life. In Dublin, the culture, the sports, the religion, the politics are one in the same. In Canada we have interests other than perpetual warfare."

As Jack talked on about his travels and his contentment in

Canada, Atty finally realized what she had known all along but would never admit—that Jack had no desire for battle. Did that make him less of a man?

By the end of the evening all the main details of his father's estate had been cleared up. Atty would have her solicitor prepare the necessary documents.

As evening fell on the lough and the fireplace smoldered alive with intoxicating turf aroma it became awkward time.

Atty commented that she didn't realize the Murphy library was so extensive. She told him to pull the books he wanted and she would ship them to Canada.

That would be lovely, just grand, he agreed. And what were Atty's plans for the estate? Hard to really say, she told him, for it wouldn't be hers legally for another three years. The horse-breeding operation had always done well and perhaps she'd focus on it. Would Jack be around long enough to look over a couple of applicants for the job?

"Do I know any of them?"

She rattled off a list of contenders. "None like Darby Murphy."

"Let me give it some thought," he suggested. "Well, my love, word has gotten all the way to Canada that a great star is rising on the Dublin stage."

"Truth, Jack? I am tall and rather full-bodied. I am profound in presenting my case, enunciating crisply, shouting in righteous protest, and all in all I make an ideal figure of Mother Ireland. One old priest who marveled at my cleavage looked directly down my front and told me I could have fed an entire village during the famine. Mother Ireland, yes; a great actress, hardly. But I love it up there. The Brits have the guns and we have the words, and now the stage to shout them from."

Jack caught sight of a guitar case on the bench under the bay window. He settled there and urged the instrument to give him a reasonable pitch. Atty watched, mesmerized.

His fingers did not stumble and his voice did not falter. He was well in practice. To whom did Jack sing his songs these days?

"Did you think of me often?" she asked with Atty-abruptness.

"Yes."

"How often?"

"Always."

"Did you ever feel that maybe you made a mistake about me?"

"All the time."

"But not enough to love me ... love me ... *love me!*"

"Maybe, but I'm wise enough about Jack Murphy to realize it would do me no good at all. I never let my thoughts of you get a foothold. You are where you ought to be and doing what you should be doing, Atty, in Dublin-town at the dawn of insurrection."

"Jack, you've always played it with me with too much constraint. Can't you let yourself go? You might even like it. Oh, Jack, I get so damned frustrated in Dublin. I need you as a partner. We could do so much together."

"What? Riding a tigress in constant prowl for the kill?"

"Do you indulge in much sex, Jack?"

"I think of it more in qualitative terms rather than numbers."

"Are you in love ... with a Canadian woman, then?"

"Truth?"

"I don't know if I want the truth. Well, are you?"

"Aye, I am."

"Desperately? Madly?"

"Deeply, committedly."

"Are you married?"

"No, but she is and she has two children."

"Oh, shyte, isn't that always the way? Is this person in Toronto?"

"Nearby."

"How sad for you."

"It's not sad at all. It's very joyous."

"How can it be joyous? Love, maybe ... but joyous love under those conditions?"

"We make it joyous. We are more grateful for the time together than we are mournful for the time apart."

"I suppose I see."

"No, you don't see, Atty. With you it's either possess him or send him packing. There are a million variations on the love theme, darlin'."

"Like subtleties that I don't have," she said, turning her back.

Jack gripped her softly and turned her around. She wished he had gripped her hard and spun her hard into him. Not Jack.

"Beloved little Atty," he began.

"I'm not so little."

"Beloved little Atty. Your great flirtation in life is your sporting for tragedy. As far as tragedy is concerned you've found the pot at the end of the rainbow here in Ireland, and it suits you fine. You don't have to look very far here . . . just down the road to the next village . . . into the Dublin Liberties with their open sewers. Death by cholera. Even your poor old dad finally found his plush chair and sat down and died in it. Tragedy is always at hand . . . open a letter and find it . . . or it may hit from the sky as lightning. Or you may be standing at the crossroads and some messenger will come up to you and tell you someone you love is desperately sick or that your house is burning down or that a ship has sunk in midocean. Tragedy, over which we have absolutely no control, is never far away. And it's the place you've chosen to live."

She put her hands over her ears. He brought them down.

"Now joy is another matter. We can create joy any time, any place. Joy comes from our inside, and it's ours if we've the will to find it. Tragedy is a human legacy. Joy is a human creation."

"Am I that grim?"

"Grim enough to have slammed a steel door and locked your joy in you so that it can't escape."

"I've never felt any joy like that," she whispered.

"I know."

"You'll be amused to know that I have had sex a number of times," she said suddenly.

"I'd be shocked if you hadn't," he replied.

"I mean, being in the theatre with all those mad actors and

writers. They die for my body. Well, actually it was four times . . . five if you count having it twice with the same fellow. It wasn't all that grand, Jack. In fact it was lousy. But I like men, you know. There seems to be a sticking point."

"Could it be that you can't memorize lines of a new play, run a rents strike, write an editorial, and make love at the same time between meals or acts of a play?"

"I'd like it better if you shouted at me, Jack, rather than slice me up with your bloody delicate razor."

"Sorry, Atty. But—"

"But what!"

"Your magnificent breasts and all the rest can sorely inhibit a poor fellow who is doing it by the numbers on command, probably too petrified to perform decently."

"I hate your ugly fucking mouth, Jack!" she yelled.

"So, don't ask me about sex. I didn't bring the subject up."

"Don't you even know how to curse! Get mad, Jack!"

"Atty, love, we both knew this conversation was going to come up. So let's finish it off and enjoy our few days together."

That was always the way that bloody Jack Murphy handled things, she thought. Unflustered! Thoughtful! Why doesn't he wilt like other men? No stutters, no awkward shifting of feet, no dropping of eyes. Just a dead-on answer and "If you don't like it, little girl, pack your butt out of here." Goddamn you, Jack Murphy.

She found herself slumped in old Darby's big armchair feeling stripped. "Jack," she whispered, "I'm always so damned alone."

"I know that, darlin'."

"Why can't I create joy? Why can't I feel it? Do you think I like it this way? Jack, good God, what's the matter with me?"

He knelt and took her hands. "You've the curse of being a great person, Atty Moore. You've been walking dead on into a storm since I've known ye and you've got no choice. There are very few who can walk alongside you and keep up. You just keep pressing forward and the storm drenches you and your hair is strung down like a wild banshee and the cloth of your dress is bolted against your body, but you keep shouting in rage, violent with anger when you are forced to take a half step back. You can't help yourself. You're Atty. That's what Atty is."

She slipped from the chair and let him hold her and rock her back and forth, and Atty wept. Atty weeping? Oh, what a hurtful sight.

Jack found the guitar and strummed above her.

She was torn by the cruel stones of Connemara,
And she wept for the dear peasant's plight,
So to hell with you Brits,
In your bright shiny castles,
I'll end the hard sorrows,
Of Ireland's long night.

He pulled her to her feet and saw tears, so strange on that magnificent face.

"I have a fear, Jack. I fear I might go to my grave without ever knowing the joy you speak of. And now having heard it so clearly from you, I fear it more because there is nothing I can do about myself."

"No, you'll find it," he lied.

"Jack, did you know you get a little tic on your right cheek when you lie? I've known that since I was ten. I deplore my loneliness almost as much as I deplore the men I've invited in."

"There's one out there for everybody."

"Not for me. I have no ability to give myself and I cannot be taken."

She made herself erect and cut off further weeping and blather.

"Jack, I have another fear. I want you to show me what it is like outside this prison I live in. I want only one short moment of your time and you're on your way. I do not want to go on for fifty more years and never know what it was like, even for a moment. Jack, I am terrified you'll turn and walk out on me now."

Jack Murphy's lips kissed her face and Atty's eyes lowered as they had never lowered and she let herself be drawn against him and felt something unearthly in the wrap of his arms.

"I really don't know what to do," she said softly. "I suppose I'm not good at this at all."

"Jack and Atty," he said, "are going to lie down beside each other. As the sun dies and the night grows we will stand up from the bed for a moment and I will undress you and you will undress me and we will look at each other. Then we will lie down again and spend the night only playing our fingers and our lips over one another, everywhere. There will be nothing more for now until we understand each soft warm path the other likes and each place that makes us thrill. In the morning I'll pack two saddlebags and we'll ride up to the fishing lodge and start again the same way. And then we'll make love. All your fire will turn into intense control. We will make love softly, perhaps many times, until we have finally driven each other mad, and then we'll let go, angry and abusive. And then we'll sleep and start again until we are too exhausted to go on. And we'll lie there with the tenderest and softest touching and we'll stay that way until you say it's all right for me to leave."

"Oh Jaysus, I've been waiting for you, man. Does it really work that way?"

"We'll find out. Aye, it works if we don't lose control. Unvarnished lust and orgasms really destroy quality lovemaking."

"You bastard! I'm shaking from head to foot."

How many days? Who cared? She knew she would not have to go to her grave without having known it. It was part of her now, the knowing that she was capable of it, the knowing that she could always think back to it . . . with joy.

Atty's back was to him and once more he wandered and wondered over the magnificence of the line from her shoulder to her perfect soft back without a bone poking to mar it and down the spine and over that line of hip.

"Jack Murphy . . . go you now," she said.

"Aye, lass."

"How can I tell you, man?"

"Well, you're anything but a sterile little bird. It may sleep but you'll know what to do when the time comes."

"God, I'm happy. Jack?"

"Aye."

"Can it keep on growing from a place like this?"

"Aye, it's never ending . . . and he's out there, Atty . . . and you'll find him."

CHAPTER
15

Ballyutogue, August 1885

On the third day of this fine month in 1873, Mairead O'Neill, the midwife of Ballyutogue, spanked life into the firstborn son of her next door neighbors, the Larkins. Wee Conor was drowsy and the story goes that he came into the world as a dreamer and never changed his ways.

One year later, almost to the hour, Finola Larkin returned the compliment by midwifing the birth of Seamus O'Neill, who needed no whap but made his entrance with flaming red hair and temper to match.

Seamus O'Neill and Conor Larkin could have been fraternal twins, they were that close. The boys spent as much time in each other's kitchens as their own, just as their daddies worked side by side high up in the heather farming their reluctant acres.

Seamus O'Neill came in short and would remain so. His brother Colm, the eldest, was heir-designate to the thirty-five O'Neill acres. The middle son, Eamonn, emigrated to America where he was a fireman in Baltimore.

Seamus was spoiled by his mom, and by his sisters until they married and left the cottage, and his intellectual curiosity soon surpassed his parents' and the village priest's ability to fill it. It was his deep and abiding friendship with Conor Larkin, who likewise had a boundless curiosity, that kept him on a quest for knowledge. A third party, a Scottish schoolmaster named Mr. Andrew Ingram, came to Ballyutogue when the new

National School opened, and Seamus was allowed to attend.

Conor Larkin had no such luck. The Larkin men were of a separate stripe, chieftains as far back as the Wolfe Tone Rising against the Crown in 1798.

Grandfather Kilty was a legendary legend. Of the twenty-some Larkins in three families who farmed in Ballyutogue in 1846 when the potato crop had failed for five straight years, only Kilty and his oldest son Tomas survived.

One family died on a death ship on the way to Canada. Another of the Larkins was killed by the British when they came to tumble his cottage and evict him, and his wife and wanes all croaked in the workhouse.

As Kilty fought bare knuckles in the London alleys for pennies and bets, young Tomas buried his own mother and sister and brothers and had dug his own grave when Kilty returned.

Later, Kilty went on to ride with the Fenians, and for his troubles was a guest of the Crown at Strangeways Prison, forced to eat on his hands and knees like a dog. He called the first hunger strike and otherwise immortalized himself to all of western Ireland.

Tomas Larkin was a chieftain of a different color. He was the master of the possible, in contrast to Kilty, who chased a wild Irish fantasy to his death.

With all his common sense, wit, and feel for the situation, Tomas came face-to-face with the most fearsome decision of them all. In 1885, the Catholic peasant, for the first time in five or six centuries of British rule, had won the right to vote.

Kevin O'Garvey, a Land League Catholic lawyer, decided to stand for Parliament against the Earl of Foyle's candidate.

After the Earl's man used every real or imagined threat possible, it all boiled down to Tomas Larkin. If Tomas voted, the croppies in the peninsula would follow him. If Tomas stayed away from the polls, the meaning was clear.

With a thick cloud of fear hovering, Tomas was given two messages. If he stayed away from the polls, his bread would be baked for life, by a cleverly conceived bribe. If he attempted to vote he was faced with a savage reprisal that would evict dozens of his neighbors. He didn't want to go near the fecking polls, and that's a fact. It was his son Conor who, but a young boy, half-shamed his father into it and walked into an Orange mob at the polls holding Tomas's hand.

Kevin O'Garvey won. Tomas became the reluctant chieftain and Conor Larkin, obviously, the chieftain apparent.

You'd think a couple of men who loved one another as fiercely as Conor and Tomas did would have shared a long life of mutual admiration. They were more like two comets on a collision course.

It started the year of a flax crop failure. A bad planting and worse harvest spelled debt. Conor, it seemed, had been hanging around Mr. Lambe's forge from the age of five or six. Mr. Lambe, though a Presbyterian and Orangeman, was affectionately regarded by all the croppies.

The Larkins sorely needed Conor's wages and Tomas let him apprentice. Liam, the middle son, was a farmer and utterly happy going up in the heather with his da and working alongside him. This arrangement, like all arrangements thereabouts, born of too many sons and too little land with hostile soil, opened the way to Larkin family intrigue and conspiracy.

As Conor clearly showed unusual talent at the forge, Tomas began to lie to himself. Conor had to have the land and Conor had to stop trying to educate himself about things beyond Ballyutogue. Liam was odd man out and foredoomed to emigrate.

The boyhood pals, Conor and Seamus, went into a few conspiracies of their own. When school was done for the day and as soon as Conor closed down the forge, the two repaired to a secret place where Seamus taught Conor to read and write.

The conspiracy widened when Conor met the teacher Andrew Ingram, who, although a Presbyterian, was a man of the likes of Mr. Lambe.

The conspiracy widened once more. Seamus wrote to his brother Eamonn in Baltimore and confided his longing for books which were unobtainable. Eamonn was a bachelor fellow with a great love for his baby brother and he began to pipe the forbidden books through Mr. Ingram.

Tomas Larkin wasn't behind the door when brains were passed out. Now it was books, books with ideas, books about places that would lure his son beyond the horizon.

Tomas suddenly sentenced Conor to spend the summer shepherding the flock in an isolated high meadow, without contact with the village for nearly three months.

Seamus O'Neill saw the way to convert disaster into good fortune. He talked his parents into letting him go up to the booley house, the shepherd's shelter, with Conor for the summer. When they agreed, the boys planned to hide two dozen books among the provisions and read the nights through by the midsummer's sun.

Tomas found the books and threatened to destroy them, when Conor swore he would run away. Tomas struck Conor a blow that would stay with him until his end, but he would not back down. Tomas was forced to relent. The battle lines were now drawn.

In the high meadows that summer a powerful bond was forged between the boys and Andrew Ingram. The teacher came up to the booley house with his sweetheart, Miss Enid Lockwood, also a teacher at another village. The kind of intimate relations Mr. Ingram had with Miss Enid could scarcely be accepted by the codes of the day. Yet, he knew his two croppy scholars would keep his secret as, indeed, they did. They were like four wild, wondrous scholars, alone on a mountaintop seeking out the puzzles of the human race.

Discovered by Caroline Hubble, Andrew Ingram gave her own sons, Jeremy and Christopher, early tutoring. His intellect and scholarship impressed her so that she became his patroness and, after Ingram's marriage to Enid Lockwood, sponsored him to the position of school superintendent of a large district that included Londonderry. His departure from Ballyutogue fell on the boys sorely.

The love and joy that once marked the Larkins no longer existed. Tomas and Finola had once enjoyed a grand old sex life, but because of her ailments following childbirth, the Church forced them to live as brother and sister rather than let them make love during safe times.

Young Dary, the last of the Larkins, was seized by his mother and earmarked for priesthood.

Liam became a sad boy, with only Conor's love keeping him from tearing apart.

Brigid was manipulated away from Myles McCracken, a boy she loved, because he would be landless.

Eamonn O'Neill, Seamus's and Conor's early conduit for forbidden books, died in a fire and left a small insurance policy with the proviso that it be used to further Seamus's education. Seamus moved down to Derry, where Enid and Andrew Ingram tutored him so he could take the entrance exams for Queens College in Belfast. Thus Seamus O'Neill became the first Catholic to attend college in Ballyutogue's long and anguished history.

Conor's happiness for Seamus was stifled by his own terrible loneliness. The intensity of the silent war under the Larkin roof became short-fused when Conor won his ironmaster's certificate. Conor's hunger for the world beyond was close to consuming him.

The hour, the moment, the second came. Through Kevin O'Garvey, now a member of Parliament, Liam arranged passage to New Zealand. When Conor learned of it, he was thrown into a frenzy of fear that Liam's departure would chain him to Ballyutogue.

Conor begged his father to let Liam inherit the land. Tomas refused. Both of the sons left Ballyutogue that night, Liam forever to New Zealand and Conor down to Derry's Bogside.

16

Dublin, 1895

Dublin was a he-man's world, new pubs lined three deep at the bar, the sporting scene, and the new volatile Gaelic politics of Griffith's Sinn Fein Party. Ladies of the Anglo-ascendancy—English-born but rising in Irish society—had their saloons, flower shows, and the theatre. Most Catholic girls learned their catechisms, bore the babies, and remained docile about all the worldly matters exploding around them.

Nonetheless, the Gaelic revival was giving birth to a number of extraordinary women cut from different cloth. Among the leaders were a group of Anglo-Protestants whose families had been in Ireland for generations and who finally came to a turn of conscience over British misrule.

None among them was more stunning or daring than Atty Moore, who, barely out of her teens, was fast turning into an Irish Joan of Arc.

On her twenty-first birthday Atty inherited the Barony of Lough Clara. No sooner had the ink dried on the documents than she renounced her title and canceled the debts of the tenant farmers. She sold the manor house and a few hundred acres that surrounded it to a retired British general.

Atty kept the cottage of Darby Murphy and the grounds of the horse-breeding operation, which had always been profitable.

The balance of the barony was given to the peasants along

with an office of agricultural experts to help modernize operations and increase yields.

She spent the bulk of her estate to set up scholarships to
Trinity College for worthy scholars among the peasants and vil-
lagers, and she established a unique girls' school in Galway to
teach job skills from which females had formerly been barred.

The last major grant was made for research into the scourge
of tuberculosis in western Ireland.

Atty was ever on the run. If a rent-and-rate strike had been
declared in Waterford, she was there. If an epidemic struck
Cork, she was there. If unjustified evictions surfaced, she was
there. She was there in the scummy cobblestones of Dublin's
Liberties to help abate hunger.

More and more she defied the Crown, speaking at rallies
where patience was short and anger was great. At last she was
jailed and it caused such an uproar she was released immediately
. . . only to lead another illegal march and be jailed again.

Each time she came through the bridewell gate, she did so
defiantly, as though it were her intention to be a guest of the
Crown in every prison in Ireland.

After months of nonstop skirmishes or a stretch in prison, Atty
would fall out of the scene, retreating to her cottage at Lough
Clara. She could lose the Gaelic revival for a time, riding far up
into the hills and bens, but the movement soon came after her.

In the cottage, often alone, she would allow herself memories
of Jack Murphy and a rereading of their correspondence. Jack
had been able to marry his lady after her divorce and he worked
his way into an editorship and daily column for his newspaper.
Sometimes he wrote columns about Atty, as her fame crossed the
waters. Their relationship continued until his end. Jack joined a
group of explorers on an expedition to Canada's Northwest
Territory. It turned into a disaster when an unexpected spring
blizzard struck above the Arctic Circle. Everyone died.
Although she and Jack were an ocean apart, there was a safety
net for her so long as he was alive. Her closest intimate contact,
her only real lover, was no longer to be dreamed about. With
that illusion gone, Atty felt mercilessly alone.

*   *   *

Dublin was a provincial place. The inner circle of the revival was counted in a few dozen who were constantly rubbing elbows with one another at meetings and saloons.

Atty had met Desmond Fitzpatrick, a formidable barrister who worked a great deal in London. It wasn't until he moved permanently to Dublin to take on a series of court cases and she took the lead in a long-running new play that they had a chance to extend their time together.

Desmond Fitzpatrick, an early follower of Parnell, was in his late twenties, the scion of an old Norman Catholic family from the genre who had conquered Ireland for the English in the twelfth century. After a time the Normans integrated to become "more Irish than the Irish." The Fitzgeralds, Barrys, Roches, Burkes, Joyces, and Plunketts became the mighty Earls of Ireland before they, too, were ground down under the Cromwellian heel. They had fared better than their poor Gaelic coreligionists, the croppies.

As the Catholics emerged from generations of darkness in the nineteenth century, those of Norman ancestry made up a large part of the Catholic middle and upper classes.

Desmond was a long fellow, some six foot four, and joked that he and Atty should be together more often because they were the only two who could see each other over the heads of a roomful of Irishmen.

He was deeply moved by her performance in the new play *Elvira the Hackler*. The drama decried the horrors of the linen mills of Belfast. Atty ranged from a gallant and spirited rebel to a wasted drunk with tuberculosis, made worse by the linen dust and slimy wet floors of the mills where the hacklers worked barefoot.

Atty owned this play and her audience. Nothing onstage could take the focus from her, she was that dominating. On that special night Desmond Fitzpatrick leapt to his feet leading the chorus of bravos as Atty, bowing low, and the curtain fell to the stage floor simultaneously.

Desmond fancied himself a bit of an actor, as did most barristers. They balanced one another marvelously as players offstage.

Atty had the raw rage and power of a warrior while Desmond Fitzpatrick had the wit and cunning of a Shakespearean conspirator.

His early career was as a Land League lawyer, defending the tenant farmer with notable success. Even when Desmond lost a case, he shook things up.

Then came a stint in Parliament as a member of Parnell's "Pope's Brass Band." When he returned to Dublin and the revival, he worked for years as the political liaison for the Irish Party until it became stagnant.

Dublin was it, now. Desmond reckoned he could take nips and bites out of the steel web of legal entanglement by which the British controlled the Irish.

He pressed a theory called "Victor's Validation," which claimed that one nation could not own another nation either under God's Law or, more appropriately, under British Common Law. Using British precedents and landmark cases of Common Law against the British proved a nightmare for the judges. Each time Desmond won a point, he weakened the British legal position just a mite but meanwhile laid monumental groundwork, not only for the Irish, but for all colonized peoples.

To repay Desmond's visit to *Elvira the Hackler* and pacify her own curiosity, Atty went to the Four Courts to watch his performance in a small but far-reaching case.

Using his robes like a toreador, his wig askew, Desmond played fox and hounds with Justice Lord Barwell until the judge was finally compelled to engage the young barrister on basic grounds of Common Law.

"Common Law," Barwell fumed, "was not in place nor was it recognized as the law of the land until centuries after the annexation of Ireland was a fact. I don't give a hoot, Mr. Fitzpatrick, if the conquest of a neighbor is even arguable. The joining of England and Ireland was accomplished prior to the acceptance of Common Law as the law of the land . . . period."

"But, m'lord," Desmond answered, as though he were watching Atty Moore from eyes in the back of his head, "the conquest of Ireland was illegal prior to Common Law."

"Nonsense," the judge retorted, aggravated that he had been baited into the discussion. "Ireland was ceded to England by the Vatican. *Your* Vatican."

"Indeed, m'lord," Desmond shot back before Barwell could close the subject, "history records that Nicholas Breakspear, the son of a priest, went on to become the *only* English pope in history. He took the name of Hadrian IV and gave the land of Ireland to Richard II in 1159 for the purpose of amassing kingdoms for his sons."

"I don't care who the devil gave Ireland to England, and it could have been to pay his gambling debts for all I'm concerned. A papal bull issued by Hadrian, whether he was English or Mongolian, legitimizes our presence here centuries before the adoption of Common Law."

"Exactly my point, m'lord."

"What point?"

"Hadrian could not give Ireland to England because he did not own it."

"I appreciate your attempt to revise history, Mr. Fitzpatrick, but we are at the point of wasting the court's time and patience. Popes have been giving lands away since time immemorial and what's done is done."

"I agree, m'lord," Desmond answered quickly and tenaciously. "But it has been proved . . . I repeat, *proved* . . . that all land grants during the reign of Hadrian IV, including granting Ireland, were forgeries. These grants have always been contested, and the Vatican itself—the *Vatican*—had declared these grants as forgeries and, therefore, invalid. May I go on, m'lord?" And he did so without waiting for an answer. "In 1440 the papal aide Lorenzo Valla proved, beyond doubt, that the document granting Ireland to England was a forgery."

The judge laughed. "Now just where did you get this stunning bit of information, Mr. Fitzpatrick? Perhaps an editorial by Griffith in the *United Irishman*, or maybe in some hidden vault under St. Peter's Cathedral?"

"No, m'lord. In the London Public Library. So you see, one can legally conclude that England never owned Ireland and conquered it under a forged document. Therefore, all laws passed against the Irish, as well as all attempts to force a union with the Irish, are illegal."

"Historical precedent, our centuries of presence here, outweighs any argument you have set forth. You are free to believe your fantasy, but not in my courtroom."

"But, m'lord, once science solves a mystery, an ancient mystery, it is no longer an ancient mystery but a new truth."

"Religion is a subjective force, not scientific law. It cannot be revised," Barwell concluded. "All right, Mr. Fitzpatrick, your arguments fail to present anything compelling regarding the case before us. The prisoner murdered one of Her Majesty's revenue collectors. In your petition you agree that the prisoner, one Mr. Fogarty, is indeed guilty of the aforementioned crime."

"Yes, m'lord. Mr. Fogarty has refused to wear prison clothing or adhere to prison regulations imposed on common criminals. He is a soldier and, thus, a prisoner of war. Mr. Fogarty bore arms against your revenue collector because he does not recognize your rule of his land and he bore them as a soldier of his own country against yours and is entitled—"

"That will be all, Mr. Fitzpatrick."

"Sir, I wish a ruling on the principle of Victor's Validation—that is, you have no rights in Ireland except those imposed upon us through use of arms."

"*Bravo!*" Atty shouted from the rear.

"Remove that personage," the judge said without looking up. The gavel banged. "Mr. Fogarty's petition is denied. He is a common murderer."

Desmond Fitzpatrick walked back to the table and lifted a thick bundle. "I have similar petitions for twenty clients who are now serving prison terms. None of these prisoners committed murders, but they do not wish to wear prison garb. I wish a ruling that the wearing of prison garb is restricted to murderers exclusively."

Wham! went the gavel. "See me in my chambers, Mr. Fitzpatrick."

"All rise," cried the tipstaff as Justice Barwell snarled his way from the courtroom. Lawyers for the Crown really wanted to avoid Fitzpatrick in the courtroom. This often made them settle civil matters in his favor out of court.

While the military and political and governmental and industrial powers of England held their own against the Irish, some bright young chaps like Desmond Fitzpatrick were making inroads through the use of the law.

Desmond and Atty entered Jury's dining room to a round of applause and wended their way through handshakes and congratulations until they were secluded in a backroom booth.

Des made a hasty dispatch of a double Irish whiskey and allowed the rumble of battle to subside. Atty had not realized until she saw with her own eyes what a brilliant man he was. Good Lord, setting up poor Barwell on nuances of a faked papal bull then striking home at the heart of the matter, prison uniforms.

"Des, why is the prison uniform fight so vital?"

"Because we are establishing that the common criminal and the Irishman who fights for Ireland's independence as a unique nation separate from England are two different men. By granting a republican prisoner-of-war status, the English would recognize that the Irish have a right to challenge their presence here."

A second drink done in, Des heated up to the subject. "The grand strategy which is emerging is that the revival of the old language, the old sports, the speeches, and the plays defines us as a people different from the British. Our first line of attack is that Irishmen are Irishmen are Irishmen are Irishmen.

"The second flank of the attack is the Irish Party in the House of Commons, which also says that the Irish are a separate people. Meanwhile," he said with finger pointing skyward, "we attack in the courts. We do this by turning their own law on them."

"We're not going to talk them out of Ireland, Des."

"Yes, but for the time being, our only ammunition consists of words. We have been able to fend them off from destroying us as Irish because of our way with words, deprecating them, laughing at ourselves. But as we know, sticks and stones may break their bones, but words will never hurt them. Soon, Atty, the third line of our attack will have to merge. Military action."

"The Irish Republican Brotherhood," she said.

"The Brotherhood. Armed warfare. You see, if we can establish that the Irish *are* different, then the Irish have a right to their own army. The Brotherhood will either be that army or lead that army." Desmond turned to the menu in his hand, looked up at Atty, and said, "Nothing looks good on the menu, but let's eat anyhow. Unless . . . you let me eat the icing off you. You look magnificent."

And so it went, two revolutionaries in a curtained booth. Both intense, handsome people with fires in their bellies and courage to waste. One was male, one female, and in that instant they recognized that difference, as England was different from Ireland, in a manner of comparison.

"Shouldn't we be a couple?" Des asked forthrightly. "That is to say, I detest short women, particularly ones who like to kick big men around. And your good self? I've watched you incinerate the chaps as though they had been struck by lightning."

"Well, I always thought that when the right lad came along there had to be more to it than my height," she said.

"We have much more than height," Des said. "We have Ireland."

"Good Lord, you are such a romantic, Des. What girl wouldn't tremble at your words."

Des took her hand softly. "I didn't think you cared for sentimental shenanigans."

"I suppose I don't," she agreed. "I once knew a romantic Irishman, but he had to find true love in Canada. The others only seem to get romantic when they are blasted."

Des kissed her hand and tilted his head so as to look into her eyes, not directly, but obliquely. "I'm blasted. I'm blasted from the trimming I gave his lordship today. I'm also blasted from four divine Bushmills. And, alas, I am blasted from the sight of you, Atty. You are ravishing beyond fantasy. Besides, everyone

in all branches of the movement think we make a smashing couple. So, what about it?"

"Why, Des," she cooed, "give me some time to think about it."

"How long? I'm very busy."

"That's long enough," she said.

"Settled. Then, we're a couple, or some such."

"Yes, I think that's what they call it."

"By Jaysus, that calls for champagne."

"How about a kiss, instead?"

"How about both?"

There was a kiss, a fine, stalwart kiss. Irishman to Irishwoman. In later days there would be lovemaking, Irishman to
Irishwoman.

Since Jack Murphy had gone, Atty had chatted up the occasional lad and left her bedroom door open. She knew it was not
fair to compare a new lover to those four days with Jack at the
fishing lodge. However, the experience did tell her what was
attainable. She had the range, the substance, and the daring, and
she tried to make the best of the man she had to work with. No
one could ever again take her like Jack Murphy, she believed, not
even Desmond Fitzpatrick.

Atty pondered why two people, otherwise so intelligent and
attractive, could reduce themselves to clods when it came to lovemaking. Was it an Irish affliction, the subject of barroom banter,
that an Irish lad would crawl over ten women to get to a bottle of
Guinness? What about intelligent people? How could a man like
Desmond Fitzpatrick, so utterly profound in a courtroom, so
literate, so worldly, reduce himself to perfunctory shallowness in
a bedroom? How could this aspect of life be so horribly misman-
aged in an entire society?

Atty also pondered Atty. Did she excite more than superfi-
ciality? Had she sniffed too much religious smoke of sin? What
were the forces that combatted nature itself, that made a man
and a woman who loved each other become strangers in that
moment?

Desmond and Atty did make a smashing couple. The apparent lack of a wild and wondrous sex life seemed to be compensated by what they really craved, the electric charge they set off that played from one to the other, that bucked up their resolve as they plunged into battle as Celtic warriors.

They were two self-contained gladiators, gamecocks, always at the ready. They did not want to be caught without their swords, shields, body armor, and helmets . . . not even in bed. Except on the odd occasion.

Had not Ireland disdained all things of a royal nature, surely Desmond and Atty Fitzpatrick would have been crowned the king and queen of the republicans.

They had a private sanctuary on the fourth story of their Georgian home at 34 Garville Avenue, a warm and even sensuous library with a turf stove where they spent endless time, often until daylight, speaking of the next day's tactics and long-term strategies.

There were, indeed, small affections, patting of hands, perfection of behavior in public, the occasional adoring stare. And the bed. Somehow the bed was a place to collect all the thoughts properly before falling off. He didn't like to hold her, and she never melted into him. Des sprawled, she wrapped up mummy-like. When they did meet, the touches were kind and automatic but from distant planets. Each could almost hear the other thinking of tomorrow, at times almost with a smell of smoke coming from their grinding minds.

There were times when Des needed her comfort, her mind, her words. Comfort didn't include her beautiful round, rich body.

To be sure there was a bit of lust. Quick and meaningful, but once done, never dwelt upon. A pause to release those stuffed-in mystery feelings. Once the compulsion was satisfied, they regrouped for the rent-and-rate strike in Cork or Kerry and the joust at Four Courts.

They seemed content. Their long talks in the library were at the heart of what really mattered. If either sensed something lacking, they did not seem overly concerned. Both gloried in each other's victories, shared each other's sorrows, enjoyed each other's stunning good looks, and supported the combined focus of their life's worth.

Atty had not met a man like Des. The memory of Jack Murphy remained vivid, often at the most unusual times and places. Maybe, she pondered, Jack Murphy didn't even really happen. As the passage of time defused reality, her memories became more misty. She realized that the simple experience with Jack would never be repeated. Life was nearly complete now, except for that one void, but it was overcome by the zeal of the mission. And God knows, Atty did adore Desmond Fitzpatrick.

CHAPTER

17

As there were legendary people in Derry and Donegal and also legendary mythological people, the mothers of Ballyutogue and all up and down Inishowen Peninsula and surrounding counties as well had a saying for their sons. "When you are old enough to support a beard, may you be half the man as Kevin O'Garvey."

During the famine, his da was caught stealing food and hanged, and the O'Garvey cottage tumbled. Kevin's ma, with five young wanes including himself as the oldest, tried to get into the workhouse in Derry, even though the workhouse terrified them. After the fourth straight potato crop failure, there was no room even at the workhouse.

The entire family, save Kevin O'Garvey, died in the fields with their mouths green from eating grass, and he became an orphan. It was said, not totally in jest, that you could count all the orphans who survived the great hunger on both hands and toes and have three fingers and a toe left over.

As fortune had it, Kevin O'Garvey was twelve and the Earl of Foyle's agents took him and a number of other orphan boys to a poor farm, integrated into the grand scheme of things.

The grand scheme, never spoken, was to turn the famine into a means of thinning out the Catholic population through emigration, disease, and hunger. Once a family was evicted, the cottage was destroyed by a team of eight horses dragging a huge tree trunk through it.

The boys on the poor farm were sent to clear rocks and prepare the old fields for cattle pasture. During the height of the famine, cattle and many crops poured out of Ireland from the large estates.

The boys on the poor farm were given ether to sniff so they could labor long hours in a state of euphoria. By age fourteen, Kevin O'Garvey was also familiar with the taste of poteen, and he was an accomplished thief and smuggler.

Toward the end of the famine, O'Garvey escaped to the misery of Bogside in Derry and became a crafty pickpocket, like a player in a Dickens novel.

He was in and out of the borstal a number of times and realized that his life would soon be over unless he educated himself out of trouble.

Mr. Henry, a keen Protestant solicitor and barrister, had to take his turn representing the young Catholic criminals and was impressed by Kevin's knowledge of law and his sharpness of mind. On a flyer, Mr. Henry convinced the court to allow him to take O'Garvey as his apprentice.

It was a brilliant move on Mr. Henry's part, because O'Garvey's wizardry lessened his own work. On the other hand, Mr. Henry lived to regret his apprentice's talent. Over time, Kevin O'Garvey became one of the few Catholic solicitors in the region and a festering splinter under the Crown's fingernail.

Kevin O'Garvey became a tireless battler for Catholic rights both on the land and in the city. He became head of the Land League in that part of Ulster and was instrumental in slowing down the indiscriminate evictions and some of the outrageous practices against the croppies—one hundred percent interest on loans . . . impounding the livestock of a debtor . . . inflated seed prices for planting. Aye, the peasants were hostage to a catalogue of injustices refined over a half-dozen centuries.

In his work in the Land League, O'Garvey saved God knows how many farms. He caught the eye of Charles Stewart Parnell, who was at the head of a rising new Irish Party bent on divorcing Ireland from England.

O'Garvey's urban base was the Bogside of Derry jammed with the overflow of those who had fled the land and were too weak to emigrate. Most of the large Anglo land owners had more decent pig sties than the Bogside.

Loaded to the gills with unemployed, Bogside fed cheap female labor into the shirt factories. Of these hellholes, none was more terrible than Witherspoon & McNab, owned by the Earldom of Foyle. This place and the linen mills of Belfast were the sewers of the Industrial Revolution.

In 1885, the great breakthrough came allowing the Catholic farmer to vote for the first time, and, with Parnell's prodding, O'Garvey stood for the House of Commons. This was a most dangerous time because Kilty Larkin, the old chieftain of the croppies on the peninsula, croaked right before the election. A last-second decision by Tomas Larkin to go to the polls with his boy Conor at his side gave O'Garvey the victory.

Over the years Kevin O'Garvey continued his wonderful work from his office in a rundown but proud Celtic Hall where a Gaelic revival was budding. As his power grew in the British Parliament, Kevin O'Garvey lived for a single moment . . . to be made chairman of a select committee that could investigate the Witherspoon & McNab shirt factory and blow its stench over the British Isles.

On the other side of town Andrew Ingram had an equally impressive rise until he finally ran a school district from Strabane to Dungiven, including Londonderry.

To the establishment, Ingram was a pain, with his Scottish Presbyterian liberalism. His daring selection of curriculum and books kept the preachermen in a righteous tizzy and the Orangemen gnashing their incisors. Ingram had the necessary ingredients going for him to spike their noise. He was courageous, moral, brilliant, and had the Countess Caroline Hubble as his chief supporter. On matters of culture and education, Caroline Hubble was a major force in the west. Many a time Roger Hubble was simply overruled by his wife in these matters.

Andrew Ingram's eye-opener came with nothing less than a compact with a superconservative churchman, Bishop Nugent, in charge of the diocese of Derry. The Bishop was embedded in concrete in the protection of his monopoly over Catholic education. Nor did the Bishop care much for Kevin O'Garvey. Nonetheless, people with dissimilar views had to get along with one another as a matter of mutual survival.

Ingram, with the support of O'Garvey and Caroline Hubble, convinced the Bishop to allow higher education to the brightest of the Catholic students. In the dim future, they hoped to be able to found a public college in the region and wanted it filled with as many Catholics as Protestants. It was so stunning an idea that Nugent put his toe in the water and gave it a try. It was the first viable move to give equal advantage to girls and to keep Bogside children in school before they became child labor in the factories, and soon Andrew Ingram had forty of the brightest youngsters in Bogside being trained for college.

School budgets and a raft of mutual interests brought Andrew Ingram and Kevin O'Garvey into an intimate and enlightened relationship, one enjoyed immensely by both men.

When Conor Larkin left Ballyutogue, he ended up in Derry and was taken in by Kevin who, among other things, was his godfather. When the ugly realities of Derry became apparent and Conor planned to move on, a desperate Kevin O'Garvey sought out Andrew Ingram.

CHAPTER

18

1895

The Londonderry Guildhall, a Neo-Gothic frosted cake of a building, lived in two worlds. It was set between the River Foyle and Foyle Street. From the south window in Andrew Ingram's office one could see two of the Earl of Foyle's principal enterprises, a distillery and the infamous Witherspoon & McNab shirt factory. From Andrew's rear window he saw the Earl's control over shipbuilding, repair, and ironwork, the Caw & Train Graving Yard.

Directly over Foyle Street from the Guildhall was Shipquay Gate leading into the old city, the most perfect example of a medieval fortified town in the British Isles. The wall was beautifully intact, complete with its double bastion holding the old Roaring Meg cannon. The walkway atop the wall was a veritable Reformation Via Dolorosa with platforms for pitching pennies down on the Catholics in Bogside.

The problem for Roger Hubble was that all this Foyle business and the city itself had a Catholic majority and lay in County Donegal.

Ulster started over the river in Protestant Waterside. Roger Hubble's most pressing political problem was either to finesse or crowbar the city into Ulster in any political settlement, and to do so he had to create utterly ridiculous boundaries.

That's how it was in the colonies. The majestic, jewel-walled city physically and by population in one country, the colonizer wanting it in another.

This was the strain of tug and haul that ran through every facet of life in Protestant Londonderry or Catholic Derry, which were one and the same.

Andrew Ingram welcomed Kevin O'Garvey into an office bending under the weight of loaded bookshelves. The two billowed up, Ingram with a blend in his pipe, a honeyed mixture whose aroma monogrammed his office, and O'Garvey with the Irish politician's trademark, a stout cigar.

Andrew knew right off that Kevin was on serious business. He gave himself away. When relaxed and jovial he turned his cigar slowly clockwise with his right hand. When it was serious stuff, Kevin's thumb reversed the direction. Kevin tried to form his thoughts carefully to his friendly adversary.

"Conor wants to up and leave Derry," Kevin blurted with a sudden absence of guile.

Andrew nodded his head and sighed. "What's it been, six months, seven months? He hasn't seen much of me since he's been here, fierce pride mostly. I offered him a room and whatever. It was natural that he stayed with you, of course. I'm still an oddity in his life; you are his godfather."

"You've a powerful sway over him, Andrew," Kevin said, slipping open a few buttons on his vest to allow his belly to rove a bit. O'Garvey dressed like a dandy, but of the tattered variety, frayed collar, all of it slightly ill-fitted and rumpled.

"The first time he ventured into my classroom after school in his smithy leathers, I never before or since witnessed such bottomless hunger for knowledge as when he stared at the books, unable to read. It was the hunger of five hundred years of Irish spiritual starvation determined to break free," Andrew remembered.

"When the blow-up came with Tomas, Conor wandered the countryside with a foggy mind and only came in to Derry when Liam's ship was due to sail," Kevin continued. "He pushed Liam up and cried, 'You're not the first Irishman to walk up the plank,' and looked about aching for the sight of Tomas to come and save the situation. So he bedded down over my stable and then a kind of a queer experience happened. Bit by bit he inched into the Bogside and began to change life there, despite the indignity of only being able to work making barrel rings and shoeing nags at the brewery. He began teaching people Gaelic in Celtic Hall, and young wanes after Mass would run to the place to hear our ancient legends. He mesmerized everyone with the tales of our history and our martyrs, producing every speech from the dock by heart. His talks were often behind drawn shades in candlelit rooms, with guards outside. Then he took to the football field, and you know that part—the old men pitching pennies at the base of the wall compared him to Ducey Malone, the greatest Gaelic footballer in Derry's history." Kevin knocked his fist on the desk sending ashes down his shirt.

"You see, Andrew, he is a light. I go off to Parliament these days without fear that something horrible may happen in my absence . . . because Conor is here. You see, when Parnell was alive, this disturbed us the most, always having to give up our brightest and most vital young people. It's an Irish curse worse than whiskey. Every time I see a brilliant young man or woman I just start counting the days till they leave. Andrew, I've got to draw the line with Conor."

"You know as well as I," Ingram said, "if he tries to rove the world, he'll never get far from Ireland. He is sealed into a life in dubious battle, we both know that. Trouble is, Kevin, he is a master of a great craft. Where can he go in Ireland?"

"Andrew, I know a thing or two about my visits to England and you know it as well. When Conor was in Ballyutogue at the wee village forge, the Anglos in two or three counties around were already seeking him out to do gilded ironwork. In Derry, they'd be coming from half the country. . . ."

"You're dreaming and you're desperate and I ache for you, Kevin, and I am pained for myself. But Conor cannot ever grow in stature in the Bogside without running head on to Roger Hubble's yard at Caw & Train."

Out came the bottle from the bottom drawer and two glasses

were glugged half full and clinked, for Andrew knew that O'Garvey was close to saying what he had come to say.

"Can't lose him, Andrew," Kevin said, with the whiskey and sincerity bringing water to his eyes. "I'm so bloody fucking tired of the agony of Bogside. I'm done in, man. I can't bear to see the wanes playing in the gutters all covered with sores, and husbands beating up wives, and old people dying of the cold in winter because the Bishop's fuel fund is empty, and the drunks without jobs from birth to death warming their hands over the fire at the base of the wall, and the factory girls, most of all, dragging home too tired to laugh, much less make love." His voice lowered to a weary rasp. "You know, Andrew, Conor has ethereal qualities about him. A light shines about him some-times, like he's the Holy Ghost, himself. You've a powerful sway over him, Andrew."

"And you want me to convince him to stay? Aren't we doing the same kind of manipulation that Tomas did?" Andrew asked.

"Fuck, no. They were a family filled with love until the rocks and debts and privation ground them down. What happens if a Conor Larkin is driven out of Ireland? I want to give him the place to follow his destiny and his dream." Kevin held up his hand as he brought himself under control and took another gulp with trembling hand. "Andrew, as you know, I'm a member of the Parliament and opportunities have shown up in the natural course of events . . . but I'm clean. I'll take and I'll deal, but only for Bogside. We've gone through a half-dozen schemes to try to get some enterprise started there, some male labor to create dig-nity. For one reason or another nothing has really ever come together. In the past several months I've been talking hard to a group of Irish-Americans who have scored big, some very fat cats. I've convinced them to set up a fund that can actually start changing things. We need everything, a decent livery stable, a girl's secretarial school, all kinds of stores, our own dairy. I can get together the money to put Conor into a first-class forge and foundry."

Andrew Ingram gnawed on his left forefinger, his thinking finger.

"I've got twenty enterprises in mind right off the bat, and more—the funds to buy fifty apprenticeships. I must have Conor lead off with a forge. If he can't make it, no one can."

"What is Roger Hubble going to say about all this?"

Kevin emptied the glass and leaned over the desk. "After all, Andrew, I also represent the Earl of Foyle in Parliament. We owe each other a lot of favors and, in actual fact, a word from you to Caroline Hubble wouldn't hurt a thing. What I mean is, I think I can work it out with Hubble to leave us alone."

"This American money . . . "

"It's in the bank in England."

"I want to see the names of your contributors," Andrew countered.

"I can't. I've gotten the money only on the condition of anonymity. Otherwise every member of the Irish Party will be after these fellows to do the same in every village in Ireland. I was able to convince them that Bogside was the most desperate situation in Ireland . . . and that's our pact."

"Is that it?" Andrew asked.

"No, there's something in it for you. I have the votes to pass a bill to open a new public college in your district."

Now it was Andrew Ingram's turn to lose his icy composure. A new college! Almighty! What a jewel in the Crown! "You're glinking yourself, Kevin. All Roger Hubble has to do is give a nod and the House of Lords will veto the bill."

"Not if you convince Lady Caroline to have her husband support it."

It came to pass that a fine new forge and foundry was opened in the Bogside by Conor Larkin. His quick success led to a number of new businesses taking root and that was followed by a flurry of apprenticeship purchases in a number of trades that were formerly unavailable to Catholics.

Conor had soon figured out that not only did Caw & Train have a monopoly on all ironwork in the region, but its municipal bids were corruptly inflated. With the daring that only the ignorant are blessed with, Conor entered a bid against the Earl's company. His forge was burned out shortly thereafter.

A new string of events came one after the other. Conor rebuilt and was actually subcontracted by Caw & Train to work on the restoration of Lettershambo Castle across the river.

Part of the Lettershambo reconstruction called for installation of a new central heating boiler. Sir Frederick Weed had sent a marine boiler from Belfast, which he used on his larger ships, and the engineers to set it up. Problem was the pipes were small because it needed to heat small spaces such as the ship's cabins, and these were done following meticulous blueprints.

The small pipes could not heat the great stone rooms of Lettershambo and the project staggered until Caw & Train came to Conor in desperation.

Conor knew the elements of whitesmithing, the use of thinner metals. No sooner had he opened his forge than he quickly filled a vacant market making pots, pans, and a variety of light tools for a hundred purposes.

Conor solved the problem at Lettershambo by making large pipes of thinner metals, more malleable to the quirks of the uneven walls, and lined them with asbestos. It threw out ten times more heat than the ship's small pipes.

Now on working terms with the establishment, Conor remained not only ignorant of the secret maneuverings that had taken place but unaware that he was deliberately being integrated into the Roger Hubble system in which Hubble controlled his competition.

CHAPTER
19

Conor Larkin had gained the fine measure of success that Kevin O'Garvey had prayed for. His line of wares from carpenter hammers to skillets were of such superior quality and design that the Protestant merchants of the region reluctantly trudged to the Bogside to place orders. Likewise a number of Protestant preachers came to the conclusion that the Lord did not take sides in matters of magnificent scrolled ironwork and small commissions came in for their churches. The forge survived its worst crisis, a burnout, when Conor bid against Caw & Train. After he rebuilt, Caw & Train called upon him for consultations and subcontracting so often he was accepted as somewhat of a left-handed member of the Protestant establishment.

Conor cared little for his own comforts, continuing to live in a small tidy flat over the forge, big enough to hold five or six mates to drink with, or bed down a willing lass, or spend his nights in luxurious reading. He saw to the needs of his family and particularly his brother Liam in New Zealand.

It was not as though Conor had not always loved the Ingrams, he simply would not and could not come to them until he felt he was on some kind of equal footing. The return to a close relationship was a glory.

Conor *was* Bogside. His second homes were in Celtic Hall and the football pitch. He also filled out a few dandy suits of clothing and ventured into the new cultural life of the city. Blessed with the kind of handsome and playful looks that made the ladies swarm to him, he always had a beauty on his arm, though he never became serious. He had created a perfect lady in his fruitful imagination, and until someone in real life could knock her off her pedestal and send himself crashingly into love ... well, then, he was always kind and gentle. Unable to bear such a grand-looking and happy bachelor, Enid Ingram put an entry into the derby, a lovely young school teacher whom Conor cared for very much, but not totally enough.

As Conor thrived and grew in stature, Andrew Ingram found himself suddenly in a springtime of discontent after he had agreed with Kevin O'Garvey to help keep Conor in Derry.

Conor had no idea that there had been maneuverings behind his back to put him into business. At first, like all lies, it seemed small and unimportant. After all, the deception had worked. Conor was not driven out of Derry, and his success had paved the way for others to succeed.

After another springtime of discontent, a brief announcement in the newspaper opened Andrew Ingram's mind with a sense of horror.

The announcement read that the Select Committee of Parliament chaired by Kevin O'Garvey was compelled to postpone his long-vowed investigation of the Witherspoon & McNab shirt factory.

Following logic, Andrew began to wonder about this anonymous group of Americans financing the ventures in Bogside. Trying to pin a master politician like O'Garvey down was like trying to close one's fist on a handful of mercury.

Was Andrew reading too much into O'Garvey's postponement? He questioned Kevin. Kevin came back with an unsatisfactory explanation about a parliamentary maze and a double cross by a couple of members of his Select Committee.

Well, there is only one way to get to the bottom of it, Andrew thought. He must demand to know who the financiers are. That would end all doubt. Kevin had shared many secrets with him prior to this. Kevin would have to lay it on the table.

A meeting had been set, but the night before Andrew Ingram found himself wandering along the promenade of the River Foyle, flushed and dazed. The simple demand he was going to make was not so simple at all. Andrew had wondered about Roger Hubble's passive reaction to Bogside's new run of progress. Except for the burnout of the forge, Hubble had accepted it . . . almost as though he endorsed it.

This was in keeping with Roger Hubble's overall strategy. When a challenge arose, Hubble calculated how much energy was going to be needed to crush it, and if the challenge succeeded, how much it was going to change things. In most cases it was easier to allow a competitor to take hold, then take control of him. What better way than to control your own competition?

Larkin's forge would be a perfect example, would it not? After allowing Conor to struggle to establish himself, Caw & Train would quietly draw him in by throwing him a bone.

What Andrew Ingram was revealing to himself was so crushing that, for the first time, he did not confide in his wife until it was too late.

The truth that was emerging was that there were no Americans involved in this. The money had come from Roger Hubble! Dear God! What did Kevin O'Garvey give him in exchange?

The springtime of discontent sunk into a gloomy autumn and winter and finally the news that the Select Committee had made a second postponement.

Kevin O'Garvey had called off the investigation of the Witherspoon & McNab factory in exchange for Hubble's financing of the new enterprises and apprenticeships.

Roger Hubble knew there might be a few successes, but in the end there would be one failure after another and Bogside would still be Bogside.

O'Garvey could no longer bear the destitution of Bogside and more failures of the croppies out on the land. He had tried to do something desperate to bring some light and hope to his people, but he had made a Faustian bargain!

But before you confront Kevin O'Garvey, you'd better think it over, man! Andrew told himself. Kevin had come to Andrew first and lured him into the scheme without his realization, using Conor Larkin as bait.

Once Andrew added his voice for Conor to remain in Derry, he was locked in, whether he knew it or not.

And now, what if he exposed the plot! This lie, the secret, the deceit would devastate Conor Larkin! Ingram, his mentor, and O'Garvey, his godfather and fighter for the people, had passed blessings by allowing child and female slave labor to continue at the shirt factory.

All those lofty flights of idealism he had flown with Conor Larkin and Seamus O'Neill ... worthless. Ingram, beloved teacher, just another ha'penny hack politician, eased into the system. O'Garvey had cried that "They always find out where you are hurting most and carve their deal." Yes, Bogside hurt the most and Roger Hubble knew how to protect the money machine that poured out of Witherspoon & McNab.

Andrew Ingram began to change. He pulled the blind on the window in his office that faced the factory. He could no longer hear the factory whistle without gritting his teeth and closing his eyes and finally clamping his hands over his ears.

He was a welcomed friend in Bogside. He had done more for Catholic students than three hundred years of Anglo ascendancy. He was coming close to establishing a college ... to what avail ... to what avail ... to allow the most indecent part of the system to continue unabated.

Andrew Ingram no longer went into the Bogside.

He had been a progressive and enlightened schoolmaster who feared no preacherman nor Orange ignorance nor Anglo arrogance.

But a Kevin O'Garvey, a devoted politician, a maker of events trying to penetrate the blackness of a Bogside, had to risk much more. Like a military general, Kevin O'Garvey had to risk other people's lives. Drawing Ingram in was a clever part of the tactic.

Andrew Ingram had always loathed his academic colleagues, who did their protesting from the safe bunker of a university. Ideas there were risk-free, till the moment when Kevin O'Garvey made him partner to a lie.

An educator counts his life by the achievements of a few

golden scholars. Andrew's were Seamus O'Neill and the ethereal Conor Larkin.

Had he made too much of Conor? He had failings. Wasn't Conor drifting away from the agony of Bogside? A few less hours at Celtic Hall as a starter? Was Conor now a Lothario, a clever seducer of women, some of them unhappy or adventurous married women on the prowl?

When all was said and done, the plain and utter truth, God, was that Andrew Ingram was unable to face the moment to tell his prodigy that he had surrendered his idealism in a dirty bargain.

Enid, a power of a supporting mate, became frightened watching her husband do himself in. In the deep of another sleepness night, Andrew caved in and blurted it out.

"I knew the minute Kevin walked in I was knowingly going into a deal, becoming the keeper of a lie. I had betrayed Conor by not demanding to know, immediately. Funny, how an ideal so nobly spun in the sunlight of a high meadow can become a web of total entanglement in reality. And what will Conor do? Try to blow open the stench of the deal? Destroy Conor by keeping him from ever believing again that the men he loves the most will not dishonor him?"

My Dear Lady Caroline,

It is with utmost sorrow that I pen you this note. After tormented hours of soul searching and with the concurrence of my beloved Enid, I have come to the decision that I am going to resign my position. The announcement will come at the conclusion of the present term and enable us to get things in order concerning the possibility of a new college.

I have accepted the position of Headmaster at Kirkmoor, a small but excellent private school near Edinburgh.

I'm afraid the decision is irrevocable and, for the present time, a highly confidential matter.

Your devoted friend,
Andrew Ingram

CHAPTER

20

"To hell!" Caroline cried, crumpling Andrew Ingram's note. Where have I been? she asked herself. Such a decision didn't happen between yesterday and today. Caroline was terribly close to the Ingrams, both in civic matters and socially. She chastised herself for not picking up on his duress.

Bloody hell! It was nigh on impossible to tell if Andrew was more somber or less somber behind that Scottish mask.

For Andrew Ingram, there was more than Conor to consider. There would be the heartbreak of Seamus O'Neill as well. A scandal whose bottom line read, "Hands off the shirt factory," would destroy Kevin O'Garvey, too, and try as Andrew might, he could not bring himself to totally blame Kevin for doing what he did.

What of Caroline? She was aware that both her father and husband were scoundrels, but there was no way she could have known about the shirt factory. If she found out now, what would happen to her own marriage?

When Enid let Caroline into Andrew's study she could see the pallor of his face. Enid excused herself as Caroline took a chair uncomfortably, then did the obvious foolish thing of trying to bait him with candy. She unrolled a map of the district on his desk.

"Roger has all but agreed to donate three hundred acres of land here for the college. O'Garvey says the minute Roger announces he's in favor, he'll start the bill through Commons."

Ingram looked at the map. "Lovely situation on the

Protestant side of the river, in Ulster, between Lettershambo, the largest arsenal in western Ireland and a military barracks two miles away."

"Let's get the damned thing built and worry about student riots later," she retorted.

"That will be for you and my successor to iron out."

"As the chairman of your board and as your friend, I have a right to know. Without you, Andrew, there are no woods or forests of learning in Londonderry, only an empty, rock-filled, windswept moor."

Andrew's eyes were misty. "I always held in disgust that my robed and hooded colleagues espoused the ideas of brave men, but from a position of no danger to them. That is why I left the campus. I have infused in a few extraordinary pupils the struggle required to have a grand ideal win out over evil. Yet, when I came to my own Rubicon, I slunk away."

"Just how vague do you intend to be, Andrew?"

"I knowingly let someone lead me into a game of deals and lies and compromise, pretending to myself that I had done the right thing and that I had let go of nothing sacred. Such mendacity has brought me to a conclusion that I have forgone five decades of idealism."

"I see a lovely man dreaming about being a perfect self in a perfect world who had to come face-to-face with the reality that he wasn't perfect."

"Caroline, I was party to a scheme. The price was to lie to myself by making myself believe there would be no price to pay. There is no such thing as a free lie. If I stay in Derry, those young people will turn acidly from idealists to cynics because I have betrayed them. Better that their beloved mentor simply disappear into the Scottish heather."

"Who the hell are you to believe that you are the only one who is going to get through this life without making your deals with the devil?" She looked at him as she had never looked at him before. "What do you think my marriage was?"

Andrew turned away, stung by her stab.

"When I was a wee lad," he whispered, "our family was

Scottish poor, which is about as terrible as being Irish poor. The one thing we had was a warm fireplace glowing at night and my daddy gathered us about to read the Bible. We all knew it so well that we'd only pretend to read, because actually we could recite it from memory . . . and I moved on to Burke's writings on the French Revolution . . . and *Gulliver's Travels* and Oliver Goldsmith . . . and Thomas Jefferson and Plato . . . and Mendoza and the great philosophers of the East. I was a fortress, Caroline, a fortress that could not be conquered. In my years as an educator, no man, no army could breach my fortress. Can you imagine my joy when I was able to secretly pass along the most passionate and stupendous of my books and their thoughts to a pair of yearning croppy boys from up in the heather?"

"You have told me that redemption is the greatest of all human qualities," she insisted.

"So it is. I must redeem myself in Scotland, lass, for here I will shake the walls down." For an instant he hovered on letting it all go. Soothing Caroline's curiosity would change her life, forever. She was stuck in Derry with a preordained existence.

Enid knocked and entered with a tray of tea, cognac, and Irish whiskey. The whiskey helped with Caroline's sense of numbness. Enid had also grown pallid, and Andrew's eyes were very weary.

"Why exile yourself to a nameless boarding school, Andrew?"

"I don't want to be around college teachers for the reasons previously stated. As for the students, each one reaches a level when he is certain he is infallible and doubly certain he knows more than his professor. No one is less wise and more stupid than a college student. No one is more strident in his beliefs. No one has better solutions. No, Caroline, I want fresh-faced young boys and to load them up with idealism before they have to make their first compromise with the devil."

As Caroline dabbed her eyes they became fixed on the most unusual piece of ironwork she had ever seen, a half-dozen delicately curled deep leaves, each of which was a holder of a live flower. There were iron threads so thin that one could scarcely see them above the leaves, and these held wrought-iron bees and birds so that the slightest zephyr would cause them to move as though they were hovering over the flowers. Between two of the leaves was a spider web, so fine it could not possibly be of iron ... but it was. The stand at the bottom was incredibly balanced. Caroline's fingertips whispered about it.

"I've never seen anything like this," Caroline said.

"A gift from one of Andrew's students," Enid said.

Andrew sipped his whiskey and appeared to be mesmerized by the multivase holder.

"One of your very prized students?"

"Aye," he said.

The moment had a strange quality to it. Caroline knew, without saying or asking, that this magnificent piece of work had something to do with his entire situation. Andrew was uncomfortable, as though he didn't want to share this with her.

"It's the work of a master, isn't it?" Caroline said.

"Yes," Enid answered.

"Who might he be?"

"His name is Conor Larkin. He has a forge in the Bogside."

Caroline was compelled by a surge of excitement. "You know how desperately I've wanted the great screen restored. Why haven't you told me about this chap?"

"That's not the way the system works, Caroline."

"To hell, you say. I should have met him. Does he know about the screen?"

"He's worked on it as a laborer for both your Italian and German masters. Caroline, he bid against Caw & Train and was burned out. His second home is in Celtic Hall, not your average manor house artisan." Suddenly Andrew's voice betrayed him and his words betrayed him further. "He's searching for the Holy Grail."

"And he is the reason you are leaving here. You feel you've betrayed him."

"It would kill Andrew if you told him!" Enid cried.

"Oh no. I love you both so dearly, so very dearly," Caroline assured. "It will never get past me."

"Strange how a little bloody lie takes on arms and legs and wings and heads. Anyway, Caroline, be very careful. I saw the fire flashing from your eyes," warned Andrew.

"Caroline, Conor Larkin is innocent of all the deals that have been made around him," Andrew continued. "He is fierce about what he believes of Ireland. I know you'll see him now, but I warn you, the great screen in the Long Hall has been a symbol of oppression to the Catholics. It was used as a prison and almost five hundred women and children died of torture and hunger behind it."

"That's in the long past."

"There is no long past in Ireland."

"It's a great work of art. Its creator never intended it to be a prison."

"I'll be brutally blunt, Caroline," Andrew said. "You're flirting with the one man in the world you can't handle. You'd better know that going in."

In that instant, Andrew knew he had said the exact opposite of what he wanted to say.

CHAPTER

21

Hands on her hips, Caroline stood before the great screen in the Long Hall considering the enormity its meaning was taking on. Every time she thought of the Ingrams' pending departure the ache renewed itself. Andrew was a kind of jewel of a man anywhere in the world one might find him. Few such passed the way through Londonderry. God, it was going to be so empty.

She came to realize that the failure of Andrew and Enid to confide in her was not due to a lack of trust, but for her own good. Caroline generally got what she wanted, but there was no keeping the Ingrams in Derry. Her enthusiasm for the college project all but halted. Instead of a crafty, witty ally, she would be dealing with unmovable concrete blocks of bureaucrats and, Satan save us, Bishop Nugent.

Caroline was a positive and assured woman whose soft touch moved the big house with lightness and gave Londonderry a taste of creative spirituality. At this moment, Caroline felt very down about Caroline and no shopping binge in Paris would rectify it.

The screen and its decade-long perplexity loomed before her. She could possibly throw herself into another restoration attempt but she knew she could only be building herself up for a fall.

Like the compromise of her marriage to Roger, the great screen was another aspect of her life that would never be whole or free.

What was that strange soul-stirring emotion that swept

through her when she saw the iron vase on Andrew's desk coming like a message from an unknown messenger?

As Andrew Ingram was closing the door behind himself, he wondered if he had unwittingly opened the door to something else? She admitted to herself that she had a schoolgirlish curiosity about this blacksmith in the Bogside, in a mild flirtation with herself. She had come to middle age with charm replacing dazzling beauty and she was an older woman . . . good Lord, how silly.

She had never felt the creeping of age until now. Was she not being ridiculous to dare even think this individual could restore the great screen?

Wasn't it all so odd how one thing seemed to be flowing into another? As she studied the screen, remembering her history with it, images telescoped backward. . . . She gasped and rang for Adam, the chief butler, a servant of three decades' standing.

"The Countess rang?" Adam asked.

"Adam, how many times has this screen been shored up before I came to the manor?"

"Oh, hard to say exactly, m'lady. Once or twice a year some bolts would fall out of the overhead beams. The manor house blacksmith shop always had it in on schedule for maintenance. There was an annual cleaning of the parts that could be dealt with."

"Do I recall correctly that the screen shifted and tilted rather ominously?"

"Oh m'lady, what an incredible memory. Yes, fourteen years ago it took a dangerous tilt."

"Lord Roger and I were on our honeymoon. My father recalled us because Randolph Churchill was going to make an appearance in the Long Hall to play his famous Orange card. We used outside help on the screen, did we not?"

"Astonishing you should remember, what with all the excitement and your own honeymoon cut short. Our late blacksmith, Mr. Leland, God rest his soul, was rather limited in his skills. He would generally call on Mr. Lambe, a very talented smith who served the area around Ballyutogue. Old chap is still alive."

"And this Mr. Lambe came and shored up the screen?"

"He did, m'lady, and just in time for Lord Churchill's address."

"I know this is going to stretch your memory, Adam, but did Mr. Lambe have an apprentice boy with him?"

Adam broke into an uncharacteristic smile.

"Don't tell me you know him, Adam?"

"Conor Larkin is the one lad most likely to be remembered. Catholic boy but from a very, how shall we say, special Catholic family. Rather famous footballer. Brought Donegal a regional championship."

"You don't say."

"I won a few bob on him. He now has his own forge down in Londonderry and is well considered."

"Thank you very much, Adam."

Well, that's Ulster, is it not? Caroline thought. Everyone mixed up with everyone . . . a young boy of twelve or fourteen had stared at her and she had asked him why and he had said because she was very beautiful and he went on to snap out the forbidden name of Charles Stewart Parnell. . . .

"Anything else, m'lady?"

"Yes. Send around a carriage. Immediately."

Having prepared himself for the playing out of his fairy tale in a decade and a half of daydreams, Conor Larkin was as cool as an autumn breeze off Lough Foyle when the Countess of Foyle's carriage came to a halt in the muddy Bogside lane before his shop.

A small crowd gathered about. It wasn't often they got a pair of white horses, driver, and footman in the Bogside unless it was a hearse or the paddy wagon.

Caroline swept into his shop. The game is most exciting when both players have a great capacity to show outwardly that no game is really being played, but then to perform a polite, subtle fiction filled with double meanings and all of it done with perfect demeanor, even indifference.

Conor let her know that he knew she was seeking him out as

the scrapings of the pot after a decade and a half of frustration
with all those European masters and Oxford dons. Having
pleasantly established a bit of comeuppance, he justified it by
letting her know that the great screen was not that much of a
mystery to him.

Andrew and Enid had issued fair warning. The paddy was a
stunning specimen, eloquent of speech and wit and sure of his
ground. A composite of a quintessential Irishman.

From Conor's view, she had aged lovely. So long as his heart
remained free there was no harm in the mystical feelings he bore
her. Only Conor's pal, Seamus, knew the whole gut-wrenching
fantasy beginning when they were kids. Conor had spotted her
now and again at the opera house and never failed to catch a
thrill from it.

When their stifled panting played out, they focused on the
screen. Conor's office was too small to hold the both of them so
he brought several books and rolled up drawings and blueprints
and they repaired to a back booth in Nick Blaney's public house.

The schanachie's tale, widely accepted until the Countess
sought out scholars, was that an original screen had been
destroyed during the Cromwell conquest of Ireland. In a later
war, which established Protestant rule, King William of Orange,
now the British monarch, wished to thank the Earl of Foyle for
his loyalty in arms.

Jean Tijou, a French Protestant, had come to the court of
William and Mary and executed a number of outstanding works
in England. Tijou, so the legend goes, was dispatched by the
King to Ulster to build a new screen as his gift to the third Earl
of Foyle. Alas, over the generations and centuries the screen
became mangled and partly ruined by fire and insurrection. A
bit more than a third of the original screen remained.

When Caroline Hubble redid the manor, she assembled the
best historians on the various periods and commissioned
research papers at Oxford. On the matter of the great screen, the
principal study declared that the Jean Tijou myth was no more
than that, a myth. Tijou, although a favorite of King William and

Queen Mary, had never traveled to Ireland, they contended, and the original portions of the screen were probably constructed seventy years before Tijou was born. Its creator was a mystery. Years of patchwork on the screen set down a crooked trail, impossible to follow.

To Caroline's surprise, Conor Larkin was familiar with all her research and dismissed it out of hand as academic claptrap, theories created in faraway places by men totally in love with their own conclusions.

It was now up to Conor to prove them wrong and substantiate his own beliefs. The two quit their flirting and went into a professional posture as Conor began to sway her with his dazzling reconstruction of history. She was both enthralled and bemused and cautioned herself to be on the alert for vast amounts of blarney from this incredibly charming paddy.

Rogue or brilliant scholar? Caroline sharpened her mind as he unfolded his story.

The first area of proof was never discovered by her researchers and most convincing: namely, the parish record books of St. Columba's Church of Ballyutogue, which dated back to the beginning of the fifteenth century.

Entries dealing with the great screen were in Gaelic and had been translated by Conor years before. The years between 1697 and 1701 described the arrival of "the Frenchman" and the construction of "grand ironwork at Castle Hubble." The men from the village who worked on it at various times were listed and included the ancestors of his dear friend and neighbor, Seamus O'Neill. There were intimate tidbits of daily life that could only be known by someone living in the village two hundred years earlier.

Moreover, Conor was able to quote from a number of published works on the history of Ulster by British historians, which matched perfectly with St. Columba's records, although none of these historians had ever seen the church records.

*   *   *

"What have we here, now?" Caroline, asked looking at Conor's open palm holding a small rusty black mass.

"Feel this."

She did.

"How does it feel?"

"Very satiny. What is it?"

Conor offered his shirt sleeve to wipe her hand clean. After an instant of hesitation, she did.

"Years ago, Mr. Lambe and I were both curious about the texture of the iron in this screen. He took a few scrapings and had it assayed at the royal assay offices in London. I took some samples on my first visit here with you. It was assayed in Belfast."

"Where in Belfast?"

"At Weed Ship & Iron. Best assay office in Ireland."

"What are you getting at, Mr. Larkin?"

"It took a long time for Mr. Lambe to ascertain its origin. All of the iron used in the original work here came from the Clanconcardy mine in Northern Wales. Once Tijou discovered it, it became his ore of choice. All of his later works are of the same base."

"Well, what is that supposed to prove?"

"This screen is the only work in Ireland made of Clanconcardy ore."

"What makes this ore so special?"

"Other ores can be pounded, brutalized into shape. Your Italian chap, Tustini, had a nice delicate touch, but the screen conquered him instead of the other way around. Had he discovered and used Clanconcardy, this," he said, pointing, "would look more like this."

"Just what does this ore mean to you?"

"It's angel's ore, actually difficult to express my feelings without offending you," Conor answered.

"Please go on."

"Aye, how to say it? I've worked with this ore whenever I can afford a few hundred pounds of it for very special commissions or gifts. It's . . . uh . . . "

"Mr. Larkin, just say it like you were speaking to one of the lads in your shop."

"Working with this ore is like a woman's flesh yielding in ecstasy to her lover. It's pure magic. You see," he quickly changed the subject, "the mine has been closed for decades for lack of yield. There are a few old-timers who will go in and flush some out, but at great expense. Twenty tons of this would be hard to come by."

So, Caroline thought, the clever lad has finally sprung his trap. A king's ransom in exchange for what might or might not even be the answer to the great riddle.

"Pardon my temerity, Lady Caroline, but you still have grave doubts about Tijou."

"I must say, you present a compelling case."

"Jaysus, madam," Conor erupted, "Tijou's case is right in front of you, here and here and here and here. No man before Tijou and few since have had the mastery to create lily pads floating on gossamer . . . this scroll, he used only once later, at Versailles . . . and here, this angel's flute. Why, the man's finger-prints are all over this screen. Your Oxford research cannot be correct. If this screen were built seventy years earlier, no clunker in those times could have ever dreamed these things could be done with iron."

Conor had been borderline impertinent, but having dealt with artists and artisans, she knew they demanded a certain headway if they were worth a damn. She made an abrupt decision.

"Why don't we go forward with a small section?"

"Oh no, ma'am. I think m'lady has understood me wrong. The Italian and German counterfeits shriek out in horror and should be removed. Some small work can be done on the original screen, but one third of a Tijou is worth a thousand Conor Larkins."

"Am I to understand you don't want to restore this?"

"Sometimes I think that God meant for certain things to be left alone."

*   *   *

Roger and Caroline had a cozy arrangement where they finished their late paperwork together in her boudoir at a partners' desk facing each other. The matter of the screen was a testy bit of business; they had spent tens of thousands on it with no results.

"After all our travels and searching, there just may be an ironmaster right in our own backyard, a Conor Larkin in the Bogside."

Roger knew full well of whom she spoke but played the act of stuttering memory. He had been O'Garvey's pet enterprise in Bogside and was quite good but had to be burned out after he entered a bid against Caw & Train. Later he was assimilated into the overall system and actually did some splendid work at Lettershambo.

"Hmmm," Roger said at last. "Oh yes, Larkin. The family has been here about a century, always mixed up in some sort of disobedience. His grandfather was imprisoned."

"Would that cancel him out?"

"Not really. We've managed to stay in business because we've learned we have to live and deal with these people. Actually, it's always a good show for the Catholics to have one of their people do this and that. Mind you, they can be frightful liars and clever with the language."

"Why don't you look over his credentials and this report he's prepared and give me your assessment," she said, sliding a folder over to him.

"Certainly, darling. Problem as I see it from the onset is that a restoration will take several years. You know how feckless they are. He'd probably sell his mother to get that commission and eventually leave things in a worse mess than we have now."

"Larkin doesn't want to do a restoration."

"Really?"

"No, just remove our so-called masters' work and do a bit of cleaning up."

"Maybe just a clever way of getting his foot in the door, don't you think, Caroline?"

"By the time he finishes that work, we'll have a damned good idea if he's the real thing or not."

"Good thinking, dear. I'll get on this directly."

"The folder here makes a lot of references to the screen. I've left everything on the refectory table in the Long Hall. You'll find the translations from St. Columba's, his own drawings, historical references, the whole kit and caboodle."

Roger had been tweaked. Well, the report was probably full of holes. He'd better find them. God knows how much she wanted the restoration, but another disappointment would go down hard.

Morning found Roger Hubble red-eyed from reading through the night. In a sense, he thought, completion of the screen would amount to a symbolic end to Caroline's monstrous spending on the manor. The place now matched some of the greatest stately homes and castles in England. Indeed, the great screen would be a suitable, if outlandish, gesture of their imperial existence.

"There you are, Roger," Caroline said, leading a tray-bearing servant.

"Fascinating," Roger said. "This part really intrigued me." He lay flat several sheets of drawings of some tiny detail work on the screen and the same work on other projects in England. "Well, I suppose it's all right for Tijou to steal from Tijou."

"Particularly if he is the only one who could execute it."

"And Larkin thinks he can copy them?"

"We won't get to that for months, until after he removes the counterfeit sections."

"This is also very interesting," Roger said showing the drawings of the masterworks before Tijou's time. They were of heavy-handed metal-pounders in comparison. It did show that Tijou lifted the entire craft.

"Shall we let him have a go at it?" she asked.

"Yes, but first a couple of precautions. I'd like to have a separate set of translations by our own people to make certain these Gaelic church records are authentic. Also, I'll have Swan run a security check on him, you know, anarchist activities. One thing does trouble me. Must he have this Clanconcardy ore?" He nodded to a plate of scrapings.

"Hmmm, like butter . . . or silk . . . "

Caroline smiled inwardly. Or, she thought, a woman's skin. She looked and saw no mangled mess but a fully restored screen soaring and swirling and interlocking in a grandeur unmatched. She saw a great velvet curtain the size of a mainsail on the largest ship afloat. The curtain was raised by a handful of servants on a pair of winches. It rose! And there was the great screen in all its splendor!

She and her father often wanted a number of things more than anything.

CHAPTER

22

1897

Tomas Larkin accepted the fates, one after the other.

He accepted that Dary was doing well in seminary and would actually become a fine priest, if there was any such thing.

He accepted that Brigid would either remain a spinster or marry some wizened specimen with some acreage. Her only love, Myles McCracken, had flown Ballyutogue. Myles worked for Conor in his forge and was taken with a factory girl, Maud Tully.

Tomas accepted that Mother Church always wins in the end. He had made a fierce piss-up at his father Kilty's wake on learning that his da had taken absolution.

On further consideration, he slowly came around to giving God the benefit of the doubt. Father Lynch, a blister of a man, had grown theologically acceptable. Maybe he owed absolution to his wife? Maybe he owed it to his neighbors? If he left them believing he had seen the light, it would give them something to cling to after he was gone.

So Tomas took absolution, as fate dictated.

What Tomas Larkin would not accept was that his beloved Conor would not return. Mr. Lambe came to retirement age at his forge and could no longer start up a new apprentice. The old man traveled to Derry to try to convince Conor to take the forge but returned empty-handed and broken-hearted.

Still, Tomas would not accept that fate. Only after a young

blacksmith arrived from Scotland and bought the forge, did
Tomas yield.

For month after month he woke up with a lump knowing
now Conor was not coming back. It wasn't until he finally
accepted that fate, that the terrible wrong he had done Liam
seeped into his mind and grew until it began to possess him.
He wrote to Liam to come back home and take the Larkin
farm.

Tomas had been feeling poorly of late. He knew without
consulting the doctor what was wrong with him. It was the diabetes. He had seen too much of it. He now counted the days
until he heard from Liam.

The return letter finally arrived, written for Liam by a priest.
Liam was already along his way to becoming a squire some day
and was not returning to Ireland. The moment Tomas received
the news, he quit fighting his illness and collapsed in the field.
Shortly thereafter, Tomas Larkin was on his deathbed.

The power of their love prevailed over stubborn pride as
Conor came to his father's bedside. Tomas had gone blind but
in the darkness of the room was able to pretend he could still
see.

At his end of the line, Tomas was able to reflect, with a measure of good humor, on his foolish mistakes. For the most part,
he was relatively at peace because his three sons were faring well.
Poor dear Brigid had made her own bed by not going to Derry
with Myles.

As for the end of the Larkin name on the land, Tomas was
most concerned for fear his neighbors would have to endure
with the last of the chieftains gone. His lordship was testing new
steam machines in his field that could do the work of twenty to
fifty men. Those machines, Tomas reckoned, would probably
end up doing what the British and the famine together were
unable to do, drive them off their land.

When Conor left his father's side for a spell, Tomas drank a
fatal bottle of poteen he had hidden beneath his pillow and soon
fell into a coma.

For sixteen days and nights the family held a death watch

while kneelers outside the cottage spoke prayers so thick with fright they were too heavy to ride the wind.

On the seventeenth day, the giant fell.

The death of his father was soon followed by the departure of Andrew Ingram. Conor's prolonged grief was worsened by a strange new brittle and angry behavior from Kevin O'Garvey. The time he spent in Celtic Hall also fell into lethargy.

What lifted Conor now was pouring his energy into the great screen. Each time he thought deeply of it and each time he touched it, his sorrows seemed to fade for the moment.

Conor worked in something of a trance in the weeks following Tomas's death, becoming more and more involved in the mystery of Jean Tijou. Conor's dreams did not know day from night. . . .

"Why have I been called to heaven?" he asked.

"Well, look at these gates, Conor lad. I've been meaning to repair them for five thousand years."

"Why me, St. Peter? I'm only a croppy from up in the heather, and you know how the system works."

"Ah sure," St. Peter answered, "but thanks to the Big Fellow we've installed a different system up here. I am commissioning you to repair heaven's gates on behalf of all the Irishmen who have been fucked over by the British."

"I can't stand in for all that many people."

"You fix it up, Conor lad. I want these gates to be Irish. . . ."

Dawn these days often as not found Conor Larkin treading along the Foyle Quay, thunderously deep in concentration, after having been awakened from his sleep by finding an answer to one of Tijou's mysteries. Like a good actor, he was going deeper and deeper into the role he was playing. As he and Tijou had mumbling conversations an incredible truth revealed itself to him. The great screen was beyond mere artisanship. It was a pure work of art to stand tall alongside Greek statuary and Lady Caroline's collection of Impressionists . . . and the great music. The screen was its own masterpiece.

Tijou, at a certain point, realized he was in some sort of state of divine creation, sailing on a sea no one had ever sailed before, and either knowingly or inadvertently set up traps all over the screen so it could never be duplicated.

An awesome answer came to Conor during a visit to Seamus O'Neill in Belfast during which they attended a concert that concluded with Beethoven's Fifth Symphony. As Conor listened, he likened himself to the conductor, attempting to interpret what the composer meant. This work was astonishing, clear, so perfect that the listener needed no other teacher than his ears.

What he heard was probably the greatest piece of music ever composed. It was well played by an orchestra entirely caught up in its majesty and soaring somewhere together.

What Conor Larkin learned that night was that art, be it music, a magnificent piece of literature, or a great painting or sculpture, followed an absolute line of logic, and no music composed before Beethoven was as logical as his Fifth Symphony.

A great artist starts with one line on canvas.

A great writer starts with one line on paper.

A great musician starts with a single, often simple phrase as Beethoven's four notes . . . and takes a flight of logic to its otherworldly conclusion.

But what of the Impressionists in Lady Caroline's museum? The line of logic was still there, only defused by the light or exaggerated by the tone and expression.

There was a great deal of art and music and occasional literature where the line of logic was broken or never existed, and the words or sounds or images that reached canvas were not art, but an anti-art of distortion. Conor suspected that the quasi-artists in those cases were men of lesser talent with no capacity, skill, patience—or genius—to take on the mind-breaking, gut-wrenching task of following logic to a conclusion. A man of genius, van Gogh, remained logical as he painted, even in his insanity.

Those who could not put down the simple line ended up making cacophonous sounds or pitifully distorted logic in the creation of anti-art.

These smaller, self-proclaimed artists who lived in the shadows of the few mighty, sold their discord, confusion, and warped lines to the critical element who were also small people. They, in turn, created an illogical language to describe illogical art and music.

Ironsmiths, stone masons, and men who carved on cave walls were simple sorts with ponderous metal and siege weapon tools. The early artisanship in wrought iron was crude, but it all started with a logical line, because it was honest.

A Jean Tijou comes along and elevates the line and logic to a Fifth Symphony in iron, a majestic march to the mountaintop, then beyond, the epitome of human genius.

When Conor returned from Belfast he found those single and simple lines and followed them on the screen into their exquisite cascades, and the mystery became less and less threatening.

Twice a week Conor arrived at the manor by horseback before daylight. A scaffold had been erected and a forge set up in a fireplace. Shortly after the great house drifted into its day, the Countess would make a morning appearance and they would talk through the upcoming work.

Their time together took on great anticipation as he unrolled drawings, tried different strengths of brushes, cleaning toxins, and explained what his incredible eye saw.

When Caroline was a little girl she wanted her daddy to take her into the shipyard. When Mommy died and it was herself and Daddy, she renewed that hope. It didn't happen. She turned to music and art. Everything she did was quite decent. She played a decent Chopin, she wrote well, her paintings were pleasant but without the gift from God. Daddy couldn't buy the gift, nor could she create it.

This, and the gender curse, propelled her to Paris eventually, to loll in the glow of creative geniuses, model for them, love one, collect scraps of their creativity. This was the company she adored. She might have stayed in Paris, but Freddie refused to take a second wife to try for a male heir. In the end, her love for her father brought her back to Belfast, the beginning of her exile to the colonies.

For a time, when she restored Hubble Manor, she was able to rub elbows and breathe the same air as the imported artisans, but they finished and left. Her lone satisfaction now was the pale infusion of drama and music she had brought to Londonderry.

The croppy lad was there, and it soon became apparent to her that she might have under her patronage a man of unusual talent. As he drew down Tustini and Schmidt from the great screen the project took her back to the most intense dreams of her life . . . to bear witness . . . to inspire . . . to catch the twinkling vibrations . . . to live in the afterglow of creativity.

Both Conor and Caroline realized they had to lock away, in their own secret rooms, their footloose imaginations. They proceeded properly, artisan and patron with lovely decorum, intimate on matters of the screen, free to laugh a lot together. When touching was necessary, in showing plans or climbing the scaffold, it was carried off so that a house that ran on gossip had nothing to gossip about.

Decades of scum fell to Conor's continuous experiments of compounds, acids, and gentle abrasives. Age and unskilled hands and fire and cannon shot had left twisted seaweedlike bunches of iron. Timbers above and the foundation below were in tentative condition. Magnificent filigrees of leaves and vegetation and animals and lily pads were mutilated or missing.

Little by little the counterfeits were removed. Off came the Valhalla-inspired, mercilessly weighted sections of Joaquim Schmidt. Down came the starbursts of a puzzled and overwhelmed Italian master.

The original sections were now scrutinized by magnifying glass, inch by inch, and began to grow back in time in a rebirth of beauty. Each session, as Conor gained confidence, the level of his artistry rose. Each time it rose, Caroline knew without words. The silent communication was a flow from master to screen to patroness.

A good thing was taking place and it could be felt throughout the manor house. Roger felt it and treated himself to long visits, highly impressed, as Conor explained the logic behind his moves.

Other than Caroline Hubble and his own assistants, Conor steered clear of the prattle of life in a stately home. In fair weather, he took his lunch outside beneath a century-old English oak. In the beginning he was granted solitude so he was able to stick his face into a book, but soon that wall was breached by Jeremy Hubble.

The teenage Lord Jeremy, Viscount Coleraine and eventual heir to the earldom, was totally taken by his first legitimate hero, the great Gaelic footballer. Jeremy, and later his mates from ascendancy families, buzzed around Conor and badgered him into kicking and passing the awkwardly shaped Irish football and organizing little get-up scrimmages.

Conor tried to shoo Jeremy off, to no avail. When the weather was foul, which was more often than when it was fair, Jeremy reckoned that the Long Hall itself would serve as a fine indoor playing field.

When Conor returned to work, Jeremy continued to hang around making himself uselessly useful. At first he fetched, brought things up the scaffold. Later, he wheedled Conor into helping him with his school lessons.

One day, Conor's apprentice boy was ill. The Viscount Coleraine leapt into the fold and pumped the bellows, reveling in the sooty job. Stripped to the waist, he proved he would not be defeated by the demand of the bellows and soon his fetching and pumping and other bits of work became helpful.

What is not to like about Jeremy, Conor thought. How nice that a kid could grow up in such expansiveness and carry on a rapport with the staff, speaking to them as he spoke to his mother. His grandfather had been and remained a ruffian and adored Jeremy. He's almost like a natural, normal Irish boy, Conor thought.

Conor told himself not to let a deep friendship take root. Their parting was inevitable and there could be little contact once he left. He did not want the boy to be broken-hearted.

After five months, Conor had completed what he set out to

do. The mood of the place changed noticeably as he wound down to pack up. A night before his departure Caroline came to him, whiskey in hand, poured two stiff ones, and asked him to be seated at their "office," the refectory table.

"I want you to stay and do a complete restoration," she said right off. "If you can't do it, it can't be done. I am expressing Lord Hubble's wishes as well, and certainly Jeremy agrees."

"I feel quite good about what we've done here, but in truth it has only been a repair job."

"Your modesty is only to be matched by the dazzling arguments you intend to make. How do we get twenty tons of Clanconcardy ore, you've got a forge to run in Londonder—er, Derry. You'll have to destroy twenty molds to find the right one, etcetera, etcetera, etcetera. It's your fate, Mr. Larkin," she said with a brogue. "Now, here is my problem. We are heading to the end of the century. I intend to have a series of celebrations unlike anything this part of Ireland has ever seen—"

"And you always get what you want and you want this more than anything in the world ... m'lady," Conor said coyly. "The whole thing would take on a different scant. To beat the end of the century, I'd have to put on a large crew, up to a dozen men, another master to carry out my basic plan, and myself to finish it."

"Oh, I see you've been thinking about it."

"Of course I've thought of it. Enough to know it's time I leave."

"It's time you stay. I've read your poetry, as you know, I know you have misgivings about some symbolism of the screen, and I've taken you away from Celtic Hall. Are you afraid of living in two worlds?"

"I know what I want to be when I grow up," Conor retorted.

"Three years here would not exactly make you an old man. You've all that insurrection before you. Or, are you afraid? Did you spend your bundle on the repairs?"

"Lady Caroline ... "

"This restoration will make you a man of renown. You know you'll never get another chance to work on anything like this again. If you walk out now, you'll regret it all your life. You probably know Tijou better than he knew himself. What would poor Mozart do if future musicians balked at playing his symphonies?"

"Will you shut up for a minute, woman!" Caroline did as she was told as he blushed at his outburst. "Listen to me very carefully . . . please," he said.

"I am."

"This is a very difficult thing to express, so bear with me now. Tijou must have fallen madly in love with Ireland. Maybe it was a woman. The church records say he was quite, quite a boy with . . . well . . . the joy stick. Perhaps he executed this in a religious fever. See, he didn't do this in Windsor Castle . . . or the Vatican . . . it was done in a remote place in a remote country. He didn't care if the throngs came to pay homage. He didn't care if it wasn't seen again. This screen was between Tijou and God. He might not fancy me trampling on his grave."

"I think Tijou would approve—no, adore it."

"You're not listening to my message precisely," Conor blurted. "Let's see now, how to express it. Most of your great religious works, and this is a religious work, are from the viewpoint of God looking down, approving or disapproving. God is challenging man. But in Beethoven's Fifth Symphony, it was the viewpoint of man telling God of the glory of man. This screen is man looking up to God and saying how glorious man is. It is not God looking down in judgment."

Oh, this magic lad, Caroline said to herself as Conor paced.

"But God is a clever fellow. He does not let man imitate him on the highest level unless he finds a Beethoven or a Michelangelo and allows them to play God."

"How does God do that, Conor?"

"In a very few people who have ever graced this earth, God has instilled the Holy Ghost in them, some for a fleeting moment, some for a Shakespearean moment. Jean Tijou was transcendent when he did this screen, knowing moments of sublime passion as well as moments of total insanity. Who the hell knows what goes on inside such a man's head?"

"Oh, Mr. Larkin, Conor lad, I'd give half my life to bear witness to such creativity as a silent partner."

"Your man Cézanne was one of these transcendent masters, but could he copy Renoir without flying off in his own direction?"

"Having been a model for both of them, I'd say your analogy is ingenuous. Of course, I was a bit more lithe in those days."

Conor's sincere presentation was broken by their laughter. She had him on the ropes.

"You once said that a third of a ruined Tijou is worth a thousand Conor Larkins. Unfortunately, along the way you have taught me you are not only too modest, but if you aren't Tijou's reincarnation, you possibly may have surpassed him."

"Oh, come now . . . "

"You have to capture this moment, Conor. You must follow your dream because it's not going to happen again."

"You're asking me to leap off the edge of the world into the unknown."

"Aye, have you the guts, mon?"

"I don't know."

"Well, find out if it drives you mad. Ride a banshee's broomstick, howl at the wind, break glass, sniff ether, fall drunk. I'll pick you up. But for God's sake, realize it's your fate to do this work."

That was it, then, the gauntlet to the face, the ultimate challenge. "I've a friend coming to Derry this weekend," Conor said quite softly. "It is not to say that I agree with him on all matters, but I don't remember so far back when I've disagreed."

CHAPTER
23

The referee's whistle sounded the end of the game, blessedly. The pitch looked like a battlefield. Conor Larkin had exhausted himself pushing his mates to catch up and overtake a decidedly inferior team from Sligo.

Facedown, Conor could scarcely move, the mud was that thick. He felt several strong arms gripping him, under him, and pulling him to his knees. As he tried to wipe the blood from his nose and unglue his eyes, he went down in the mud again under the leaping bodies of his mates in a victory wallow. The crowd rushed from the swaying stands and sidelines and raised their mucky warriors onto their shoulders.

At Nick Blaney's public house the Bogside doctor went about patching up the lads, dousing a poteen antiseptic on their wounds as beer was poured over their heads.

Bets changed hands. The losers from Sligo were consoled in the spirit of brotherhood, which would reign at least until the first insult was followed by the first punch, in a matter of time.

Conor proudly showed off his pal, Seamus O'Neill, now a full-fledged reporter on the *Belfast Telegraph*, an establishment newspaper. Off duty, Seamus was banging out republican essays, poetry, and trying a hand at writing plays.

This was their first get-together since Tomas Larkin got away. As Seamus suspected, his own da, Fergus, who had worked alongside Tomas since childhood, would soon be making his departure as well.

The pain of the game began to creep through the numbness.

The level of celebration had fallen to singing Irish ballads. The lads were too tired for a punch-up. Conor and Seamus slipped away.

Seamus poured hot water into Conor's tub in the forge as he scraped half the mud in the Bogside off him, groaning as he did, then limped up to his cozy flat over the forge and flopped on the settee while Seamus took up residence by the whiskey bottle.

"Hard fought, hard fought," Seamus said.

"They were a bunch of foul brutes. They've got too many goddamned Orangemen on that team. Look here, would you ever, bite marks on my leg and I've got one on my arse as well."

"You'd think it was the Dublin stadium at the all-Ireland finals."

Conor shoved some pillows under his back and one beneath his arm to elevate it tenderly. "That bottle isn't a Christmas present."

Seamus passed it over.

"High and mighty journalist, are you, now?"

"I can't write anything of a republican nature in the paper. For the time being it's weddings and funerals and I cover the Catholic side of the constabulary beat."

"So, how goes it with the birds? Found anyone short enough for yourself?"

"Being a journalist, even an apprentice, has its privileges. I've always got a big bird on my arm. I like them high enough so my eyes are tit level. I tell you, Conor, it's like I've gone to heaven these days. For four years the O'Neills and Belfast took turns housing and feeding me, sometimes three to a bed. Fortunately, I was short enough to be able to lie down when I had a private closet, otherwise I'd have had to sleep standing up. Can you imagine, my very own flat with an icebox and pump in me own kitchen with the outhouse just one step outside the door. Only problem is you've got to keep rotating the birds, particularly the Catholic ones. Soon as you take a new one in they start rearranging things and want to dress you like a dandy, parade you into church, and Jaysus, do they have families. Anyhow, I'm going trolling in Protestant waters. I'm getting sick of all the weeping and Hail Marys, confessing. And your good self?"

"Just drifting," Conor said.

"Miss your daddy?"

Conor shook his head and tears welled in his eyes, and the two friends were quiet for ever so long.

"I went up to Ballyutogue. Never figured my da would travel the road much further without Tomas. Fergus doesn't say so, but it's in his voice. He's lonely. Sixty years, side by side, they were. Ballyutogue has fallen into real sorrow."

And they were quiet again. Seamus nodded to the first play he had written sitting on the stand.

"The dialogue is beautiful," Conor said, "the characters work well as themselves and with each other."

"So, what's the fecking problem with it?" Seamus demanded.

"Christ, runt, I'm not a bloody critic."

"What's the fecking problem with it?" Seamus repeated.

Conor groaned as he shifted positions. Seamus's face lit up, like when they were in the booley house in the high meadow and Conor went into a dissertation. "Almost all plays and novels start out with a hell of an idea," Conor began.

"Aye."

"Say that the play is a journey you're taking and Dublin is Act One. Act Two is the middle of the journey, in the middle of the Irish Sea. That's always the problem."

"What problem?"

"When you left Dublin you didn't know whether you were heading to London, Paris, or Amsterdam, so you kept going in circles and you never reached your destination because you didn't know what the destination was when you left Dublin. Seamus, you've got to know your curtain line . . . you've got to set down a line from Dublin to Paris and then the play becomes logical. You might get blown off course, but when you *know* it's Paris, you'll get there in the end."

"Know your curtain line, know your curtain line, know your curtain line," Seamus berated himself. "Of course."

"Don't take it to heart. You'd be surprised how many novels and plays sink in the middle. Even Shakespeare had problems with it, sometimes he just upped and killed everyone on stage."

"I should have figured it out," Seamus said.

"What you said in Act Two, before you sunk, do you really think there's going to be a rising against the Brits in our lifetime?"

"Aye, I'm positive about it, Conor. It's moving out of the courts and the Parliament into an unmistakable drift. The move is toward the gun."

"The Irish people have been subjugated for too long," Conor said. "They accept misery. There is a revival, but it's very slow. An old generation must pass before a new one can spark anything."

"Maybe we're that generation," Seamus said.

"Did Andrew Ingram see the play?"

Seamus shook his head. "You know, I wanted me mentor to see it close to perfect. When I felt I was writing myself into a hole, I thought you'd better look it over first. When I looked up, Andrew was gone. It was a blow."

"Terrible blow," Conor agreed, "something deep and haunting. Something strange, like O'Garvey's behavior these days. Somehow Kevin and Andrew are connected. I wish I knew what it was."

"Maybe it's best you don't know. It will all be dumped on your doorstep one day. Hey, I saw Crawford from the Belfast Boilermakers watching you today. Anything up?"

"He scouts the west every year about this time. I've got a standing offer for a tryout."

"Frederick Weed's rugby team," Seamus grunted. "Wasn't that the Countess of Foyle's kid with the Bogside bench?"

"Aye, we're the only team in Ireland with a viscount as a water boy."

"You're getting pretty incestuous with that crowd."

"You know why I asked you to come today?" Conor said.

"Let me guess."

"She's asked me to complete the great screen. Tomas and I never got around to talking about it, but he smelled it and he sent me a message from the grave via Dary. Dary told me that I was flirting with five hundred years of oil and water that could not mix. I had been in Hubble Manor long enough to see a human face on the enemy. Tomas said, tell Conor boy, don't let his own soul fall from grace in his own eyes."

"You've been in love with her since you were twelve years old. Are you telling me you two are going to keep your hands off each other for three years?"

"You don't want to hear me!" Conor retorted angrily.

"That's why I came, to hear you. Three years on something like the great screen requires passion," Seamus said, "like writing three plays."

"You went to Queens for four years to come up with a profound thought like that?"

"So, go to the manor and torment yourself. And the more comfortable you get with them, the more you'll be tormented."

"You call that making sense?"

"Aye, I do. You'll be tormented because you can never forget who you are and where you came from and what you intend to do with your life. Each day with them, you'll grow further from us and that will bloody well torment you."

"You don't want to hear me," Conor said.

"I'm hearing you very well."

"See, this has got to do with the beginning of a reconciliation."

"With Roger Hubble?"

"Seamus, goddamnit ... it's about ... about ... Jean Tijou didn't create the screen as a prison. Half of me has to do with twisting metal. That half of me is pulling me to Hubble Manor. That hot piece of metal in my hand is what my life is about now."

"As long as the other hand is on Caroline Hubble's ass. Suppose the great screen was in Cork and there was no Caroline Hubble?"

"Shyte!"

"Can you really separate her from the screen?"

Conor groaned the groan of the man exposed. "Maybe the screen does express the way I feel about her. Maybe the only way I'll ever express my feeling is through the screen. I do know that an energy, a spirit has entered me—a desire, if you will, that can only be satisfied when I have done the restoration. I can't control what is driving me, Seamus."

"Then I approve," Seamus answered, "and I'll tell you what I approve of. I approve of you walking on a tightrope for three years over a boiling caldron of lust."

"Well now," Conor whispered, "that will take a bit of doing, won't it."

"Aye. And if you don't leave each other be, you can send up half of Ulster in flames."

CHAPTER

24

1899

The restoration now took an entirely different orientation. It was removed from the exclusive domain of Conor Larkin and Caroline Hubble. Another iron master was imported from England and a full crew was trained, much to the delight of the maids.

Grand strategy was agreed upon as well as the day-to-day tactical approach. The screen would be done in sections, the rough work by the second master and crew and then attached by block and tackle. Conor alone would work on attaching the sections and then do the finishing work.

As the right molds were found after trial and error, the crew gained confidence under the masters, and the masters gained confidence in themselves. One discovery after another fell to them. The screen grew, almost immeasurably, but in perfect harmony with the original.

The center of the screen came close to being a Larkin creation because nothing had been left of the original. Conor had not only to create but also to conform and respect.

It became apparent that Tijou had a grand presentation in mind, and the discovery of it evolved and was as important as the Clanconcardy ore.

The nave, or length, of the Long Hall faced east and west. The southern side of the hall allowed sun in east in the morning and to west at sundown through a row of clerestory windows at the very top.

The reconstructed Long Hall was lit by four gigantic chandeliers, one at each corner in perfect symmetry. Each held ten dozen candles. Conor had the chandeliers lowered by pulley and filled with tapers then raised back into place. He sat through several nights studying the light. Something was out of kilter.

During the day an enchanting, defused, bluish light filled the hall through the natural light coming from the clerestory windows. At night, with the candles on, the room and the screen faded. Conor cursed Tijou, the destroyer of masters! The night light glowered. The dawn light that took its place came in like ghosts through a fog. The Long Hall transformed from the nighttime might of clanking men in armor into a daylight drape of silken gauze that flowed off the deep dark paneling and pushed one's eyes toward the screen . . . always the screen. It was the transformation of coming from a night dungeon to a tantalizing cloud in the sky.

Conor prowled around fifty feet above the floor on those original beams that remained. Tijou's logic slowly came to him as he found plugged-up bolt holes. Conor reckoned that these held a number of smaller chandeliers in a curved line and at staggered heights that imitated the natural light of day.

He had his forge make up some smaller candle holders and set them on the original beams. Again, he sat through the nights. Yes, the light was now becoming more subtle.

Like most perplexing problems, it was solved by a simple solution that had been staring one in the face all the time. When Conor had done the repairs on the original part, he left the black paint and gilt alone. He now ordered it all removed down to the raw iron, leaving the final touch up to his own hand.

What emerged was the gunmetal blue of the Clanconcardy ore, giving off not only a tactile thrill but a visual one as well. All wrought iron was covered with paint and gilt for a striking, monarchlike appearance, and to prevent rust. The paint had obviously been put on long after Tijou's death. Tijou wanted the screen natural with some brushed-in highlight colors.

Glory! Glory! Glory! Glory!

In keeping with their agreement, Caroline and Roger let

Conor have his way when he slimmed down the crew and barred entrance to the Long Hall except to his men. This exclusion included everyone in the household, including Jeremy, and the Earl and Countess themselves.

Consumed by the fervor of his secret discovery, Conor ordered more of the simple stand-in chandeliers, a fifth the size of those originally in the Long Hall, to be struck at his forge.

For the next four months, Conor worked alone during the night. By day, the best men on his crew painstakingly sanded and removed the paint with toxins. Each new day Conor had the dozen small candle holders moved a few feet here and a few inches there.

Some of the smaller chandeliers were set behind the screen at the short end of the nave so light would be coming from both directions.

The old manor house had a thing or two to gossip about now, for a madman had locked himself away for nightly werewolf prowls and he only slept in fits and jerks during the day, beard growing wild and cheeks sinking under blackened eyes. Those few who saw him said that he was altogether detached.

Roger was in Belfast when Adam delivered a note to Caroline.

Dear Lord and Lady Hubble,

I appreciate your putting up with my nonsense. The screen will be ready tonight after dark for proper presentation.

Conor Larkin

And a good thing. Artisans or no, Caroline was coming to the end of her patience.

When she opened the door, all the electric lights were out and the place was bathed in the light of fifteen hundred candles from a dozen mock chandeliers staggered curiously.

"Dear God," Caroline whispered, "dear God."

Conor was in a niche, staring dazed and perspiring.

"Are you here, Mr. Larkin?"

"Here . . . see it from here. . . ."

That was it, then. His sweat and the perfume she now always dabbed on for their late meetings drifted together. She knew what went well on her skin, and he had told her without words he wanted his evening treat. Neither knew until this instant how his sweat made her scent even sweeter.

The Long Hall was swaying in a fluttering of waves . . . a ship sailing on a sea of cobalt light reflecting from the screen. An irresistible force compelled her to look at the screen, up and up . . . man to God.

"The rough chandeliers are only temporary. . . . I'll make decent ones," he mumbled. "See how it all climbs up. . . ."

Being Irish and a tenor of Irish inclination, Conor pumped his lungs and opened everything in a burst.

"You're singing the new Puccini!" she cried.

"Aye! Aye! Aye!"

Their duet, such as it was, was flamed in blue velvet, loud, uncaringly loud, sadly untrained for such a moment, but they could hear nothing, feel nothing, see nothing that did not create ecstasy. And then they stood and stared gasping for air. No sound now, but their gasps. Conor started weeping and she began weeping.

Arm's length apart, they had to hold hands. She spun away, reeling from the urge that had swept through her to throw herself on him.

"I'm so bloody tired I can barely stand up," he said, slumping into a chair.

"You are Jean Tijou's peer, and more," she said, and left the room as quickly as she could.

CHAPTER
25

Strange, high-strung days and restless nights followed the completion of the great screen for Conor in the Bogside and her ladyship at the manor. It would seem natural enough to be tossed around after a sudden halt to an intense routine of three years' running.

Caroline, always a pleasant person and mistress, became snappish. She wisely announced to Roger that she was exhausted and shouted herself to a few weeks with her father, who was roistering about in Monte Carlo.

Conor's return to the republican movement at Celtic Hall and a waiting assortment of ladies found both causes lacking. In the mellow light of his flat he scanned his books for words of comfort, but he knew the cause of his ailment. He was drained, done in, not only from his accomplishment but from the restraint he had exercised for a thousand and one days of seeing Caroline's skin and the flow of her lines and her hair and the scent of her and her voice, which had mastered an art with him of speaking in double meanings.

At his forge he banged out on the anvil mistakes he wouldn't allow an apprentice boy to make. On the football pitch he was no longer a terror. His concentration was shredded.

After a second month Conor received a hand-delivered note requesting him to make an appointment to come to the manor and look over the screen. Some touching up, of a minor nature, seemed in order.

The doors of the Long Hall were opened. They entered into

a place that now owned a luxurious aura belonging to mighty creations. The lacework of iron burst softly, striking them silent.

"Did I really do that?" he said at last.

"Surely you must miss it terribly."

"Like an amputation. I have gained serious respect for the writer who works three years on a novel."

"I should have realized what a loss this would be. Consider that you have visitation rights whenever you wish."

"I didn't count on being so exhausted. There are bums pushing me all over the football field."

Conor went over the touch-up work. "Bloody dampness in Ulster," he mumbled, "but it should last a few centuries. . . ."

"Barring insurrection," she said.

"I'm going to train a couple of your people to keep its sheen, and especially how to rub out any rust spots. I'll also put it on a regular inspection schedule. The weight is going to make shifts, what with the moisture, bolts, and all the interwoven faces, the parts. They all have to learn to live together."

"I'm having the same problem," Caroline said. "That is, the routine here has changed so drastically."

"Mine as well."

"Conor, Sir Frederick repeated the offer he made to you, through me. He is absolutely convinced he should be your patron. He likes the idea of being a Medici. He has some commissions in mind and God knows Belfast could use your sort of work. He is also laying hulls for super transatlantic passenger ships and thinks you could do wonders for the grand rooms."

"Long time ago, when I left Ballyutogue, I had thoughts of becoming a rover for a while. Somehow now it has become difficult for me to see beyond Derry."

"There's another reason," she said.

"Now what would that be?"

"As you know he owns the Boilermakers. He's had scouts at your games. They all think you'd make a great player."

Conor smiled and shrugged. There they go, taking you over, he thought. Some guilt about having neglected his people in

Bogside had rushed in. In fact, he had seen Dary and blurted out that he felt very ashamed of himself.

"I know what you're thinking," she said. "You're thinking, 'I'm not your house paddy.'"

"Where's Jeremy lad?" Conor turned the conversation. "He wasn't at practice last week. I thought I'd bring the news myself. He's made the Bogside junior team."

"You're joshing?"

"He's fast, very fast, and he loves crashing into people."

"That will shake the old house down to the timbers." She laughed. "Jeremy is in Kinsale with his father and Christopher doing a spot of sailing and shark fishing."

"Lucky lad."

"He detests both sports, but you know, the old father and son, stiff-upper-lip stuff. He really misses you, Conor. Your hand on his shoulder is one of the most powerful things that has happened to him."

"We'll remain good friends. He's a very open chap."

"Unlike Christopher and Lord Hubble. Jeremy will never run Weed Ship & Iron. Christopher is tailor-made for that job. Jeremy will be a ceremonial earl under tight supervision, he's too friendly, too plain, you know. Roger always thought that I had Jeremy to make my father happy," Caroline said sharply.

"Why are you telling me this?"

"Because you've become my dear friend and I don't want my son to lose you."

"We could end up hurting each other, you know."

"Well, that's the risk we've got to start taking if we're ever going to get things turned around in this crazy province. You have his respect and affection. If the two of you can't be friends, who can?"

With all the republican teachings that had crowded his years, Conor rarely heard of, and believed less, that the ascendancy would ever make an accommodation. Yet he had with Caroline and Jeremy. Was this another door to open . . . or was it a way to be eased into their system? Surely Caroline meant well, but would it stand with Roger Hubble and his class?

"There was another reason I asked you here today," Caroline went on. "I've a small job I want you to look into. We've a lodge up in the Urris hills, about an hour's horseback ride."

"Oh, I know that place, from afar. When I was a lad pasturing the sheep in the summer in the high meadows, my pal Seamus and I could see the lodge."

"I need some guards on the windows and a sturdier gate and fence. Are you up for a ride?"

Conor galloped behind her playing out the boyhood dream. She rode well, at first. Not up to the top ladies of her class, but decently. The looseness of her blouse and streaming hair and riding astride instead of sidesaddle began to add up to a presence. As they pored through woods and over the stream, she opened up.

The wild side of Caroline burst out! This was the hidden Caroline breaking the restraints. Conor refused to listen to his own warning bells. The call of the siren enveloped him as he opened the reins on his mount.

The lodge was small but perfected, with the elegance of an earldom stamped all over it. Once inside, Conor realized this was Caroline's private domain. The stuffed animal heads were gone in a transition from a man's place for killing deer to a sensual affair.

Caroline knew she was a small matter as artists went, but here she could get rid of her frustration. Her paintings followed bad lines but burst forth with unmistakable erotica. A tidy but well-chosen library spoke of gods making love and men and women imitating the gods in all sorts of ways. The room was softened by silk and the floor was laid with beckoning fur.

Conor became a bit nervous as his eyes played over the room. There had never been whispers of any kind about Caroline engaging in nefarious trysts or infidelity. This place was wild. Conor was not the only one who knew how to play with light and shadows. Certainly she had brought her husband here, and it suddenly disturbed him.

"Now, would you be wanting these windows barred to keep poachers out of here or to lock them in?"

"I have forbidden hunting within sight and sound of this lodge. As for the salmon, I don't care if the poachers steal the streams dry. I want to be left alone here and be as totally mad as you were three months ago. Yes, Roger comes here and sometimes we find lightning for an instant, but I always leave, wanting. Any questions?"

"I was very proud of myself the day I left Hubble Manor," Conor said. "I thought I had come through this free. I had practiced the restraint of a saint. But I climb the steps to my loft, turn down the lamp each night, and grip the bars of my headboard and shake. I'm still a prisoner as I have been since I was twelve. This past two months have been worse than the twelve years put together. And these last three years I must have been soothed by the mere sight of you."

"Well, croppy boy, you need wait no longer."

They fit into each other's arms as though their bodies had been molded in a master's workshop, to perfection, and he held her like a precious bird, not to crush her and not to let her go. They rocked gently and rocked and sighed and sighed more deeply and held a bit tighter.

"Tuesdays," she said, "you always worked late. I knew you would be alone at night and I would wait all day with my heart in my mouth till your crew left, then I'd slip out on the balcony and watch you wash up and put your shirt back on."

"I knew you were watching," he said.

"I knew you knew, and you took your time."

All of the fierceness came out in the most gentle kisses and exploration. Their hunger was vast and had to be fed slowly. Conor's arms were the steel and the velvet of the screen, power and tenderness. He was not the self-adoring Roman or self-flagellating Parisian. Conor Larkin was all new.

He was mysterious Ireland, so wanting and so needful of compassion. But this lad did not smother it in drink. He let it go in the sweet misty words of his poetry, the poems she had never seen.

They slipped into an easy melting and molding and tasted and teased.

Come, on croppy lad, I've a few things of my own to show you . . . and I'm going to . . .

She backed off.

Come and get it, she thought . . . slowly . . . to the brink . . .

She turned away, walked till the fireplace halted her, faced him and took her blouse apart, laying her breasts open for him to gaze upon. They were still gorgeous, almost like those of a young lass.

Now, take them, Conor, no gift will ever be so glorious . . . just reach . . . just take them now . . . they are pleading for your touch, Conor.

"We've been on fire from the moment you first stepped into my forge. I'm clear faint with passion, Caroline. We shouldn't have willed this to happen."

"I don't want to hear any bloody Catholic guilt now!" She took his hands and placed them on her. His thumbs and forefingers whispered over her nipples and they burst out . . . and he slipped down and tasted them as though they were the most precious of breasts, like from a perfect statue.

An exquisite nip shot sensation through her, which she felt in her teeth and down to her thighs. Now, it was her hand, curious and skilled, finding him and they tugged each other's hair and bit each other's knuckles. . . .

"Oh you're something, lad," she gasped, "I mean, you're something." He was trying to break loose softly, get back from her. "No, no, no, no . . . " Her fingernails played down his back, striking him defenseless. She split his shirt open and her mouth licked the beautiful muscles of his neck and shoulders.

Conor sunk to his knees. . . .

Caroline loosened her grasp and hovered above him. "All right, Conor boy, go if you can. You've your princess now . . . feel me . . . I'm wet all over. . . . I'm bursting inside over and over and over just from the sight and the touch of you."

Conor doubled over and shook. "What do you want from me, God!" he screamed.

Caroline fell to her knees before him, took his hands away from his eyes. He reached out softly and tried to close her blouse.

"You're afraid!"

"I have little to lose, Caroline, but I'm afraid of the havoc we'll wreak. If we cross this line we're on a one-way path to hell. If it were you and me alone, I'd cross it. This could end up killing hundreds of people we don't even know. What about your sons? Your father?"

"I don't care what happens!"

"All we can be is in each other's spirits, Caroline. See, the pity of us is that we are utterly star-crossed."

"The most intense experiences of my life have been the births of my sons. I have had that intensity for you, just looking at you for three years. We're not the first man and woman who have risked. To hell with what happens. I want you, man!"

"And you get everything you want!"

Caroline came to her feet. "Do I? Do I now? Do you believe my father's arrangement with Roger and fourteen years of fidelity is what I wanted? Do you think that being the clay queen of the west is what I want? Oh yes, they let me play with my drapes and banquets and concerts to keep their dirty alliance alive, and I carry disgust deep in me for doing their bidding. Once, Conor . . . now . . . now . . . "

"You're selfish, Caroline. It's a lie that will never go away."

"Conor."

"Don't you ever think of anyone but yourself?"

The lust had been scarred, tempered, and confusion and futility had set in. Conor made to the couch and slumped down, and she went to her knees and rested her head on his lap. He stroked her hair sweetly.

"This is more my fault than yours," he said. "I wanted you to fall madly in love with me for all the wrong reasons. To inflict the most heinous pain on Roger Hubble and all his breed. But you see, Caroline, I failed because I have fallen desperately in love with you. Look up at me."

She managed to.

"Funny part of it," she whispered, "all I would have to do is throw a tantrum, only to establish I could get what I wanted, not that I particularly wanted it. You are the only man I've ever really wanted."

"Thank God fantasy is perfection. Fantasy is pure. Reality between you and me spells disaster."

As Conor stood and snapped his toolbox closed, she stood as well, unsnapped her skirt and made herself naked, then sunk into a deep rug covered with silk pillows, beckoning him with her body. He looked upon her, this once, so it would be with him all his life, then he knelt beside her once more.

"It's wrong," he said firmly and covered her with a lap robe.

Caroline's hand grabbed his arm.

"Conor," she implored.

Firmly, surely, Conor released her grip.

"Get out, croppy boy!" she cried slapping his face and burying herself in the pillows.

He backed away and reached for the door.

"Conor!" she cried. "Don't go!"

Caroline heard the door shut softly and looked up. He had left.

"Conor," her voice screamed after him, "come back! Do you hear me! Conor! Damn you! Come back!"

26

The Century Turns

In full pregnancy Atty Fitzpatrick was as close to depicting "Mother Ireland" as a mortal could be. Carrying children in her womb and bearing them proved much simpler than juggling them on her hip at rallies, or rocking the cradle with the left hand while holding a script to read in the right.

Their first child, Theobald, was followed in eighteen months by Rachael. They were the "royal" republican family.

Ireland would never be at a loss of an issue to contend so long as a British soldier remained on her soil. The caseload for Desmond was full, but legal fees for republican causes were scarce to nonexistent. However, Des seemed oblivious of the necessity to collect them. It was up to Atty's acting and inherited income to keep the family larder full.

In those days he worked desperately to keep the Irish Party from going under after the crucifixion of Charles Stewart Parnell by political enemies, aided full-out by the Irish bishops. Parnell had the temerity to live with and have children by his beloved, Kitty O'Shea, who was unable to divorce her perfidious husband.

He continued to struggle for an Irish Home Rule bill that would liberate the country, even partly. Des was one of the forces behind the Irish Party's boycott of Queen Victoria's Diamond Jubilee.

*   *   *

The Irish affront to the old queen, who still slept under the painting of her late husband and had his clothing laid out thirty-five years after his death, should have sounded a sobering note in England. The message was apparent. England's first colony was neither integrated nor pacified after more than three centuries of occupation, hundreds of subversion laws, forced acts of union with the home island, a famine, and harsh measures reserved solely for the Irish.

Far from Ireland another, greater warning shot was fired, in the Transvaal of South Africa. Cecil Rhodes was the epitome of imperial man. In a bald-faced snatch at the Transvaal's gold fields, he tried to incorporate two territories inhabited by Dutch Boers into a now-accepted "union" with Great Britain. It was resisted by Boer arms.

The British woke up to the realization that they had not engaged a modern army in nearly a century, since Napoleon, and were compelled to call in units from all over the empire until they had amassed a half-million men.

Although the Boer field army was a fraction of the size of the British force, their hit-and-run and ambush tactics compelled Lord Kitchener to subdue them in a most brutal manner, applying scorched earth tactics. He ordered massive numbers of Boers, mostly women and children, into what he termed "concentration camps," where conditions were so deplorable that tens of thousands died of hunger and disease.

In Ireland, the plight of the Boers brought on vivid memories of the potato famine. In Dublin, Atty Fitzpatrick headed the country's anti-British Transvaal Committee.

Although fine old Irish imperial brigades fought for the Crown, there were the usual band of Irish volunteers on the other side.

Atty's journalist pal Seamus O'Neill went to the Transvaal, writing for a world press association of Irish weeklies and magazines. He gained great note when he exposed the horrors of the Bloomfontein concentration camp.

Then Atty got unexpected news when another pregnancy announced itself. She would be one hip short to juggle her family on. Theo and Rachael carried placards as soon as they were able to walk, and their first words were not of Ma and Dad, but of Irish martyrs. It had worked well enough until Emma made her appearance.

Three wanes notwithstanding, it was not time for Atty to slow down because the Gaelic revival was in full bloom, having the new cause of the Boers to espouse. *Words,* the most dynamic, penetrating, sarcastic, and damning of all Irish weapons, rained from her stages, leapt from her occasional columns and from the speakers' stands in torch-lit rallies.

As the British added the Transvaal to their empire, returning Irishmen reignited Ireland's own struggle with the British.

A journalist named Arthur Griffith formed a new and aggressive political party called Sinn Fein, meaning "Ourselves Alone," a first political step in disclaiming the inept Irish Party. They made their rallying cry, "HOME RULE!"

Desmond Fitzpatrick and the legal battle had been the first prong of the Irish assault. Arthur Griffith and the Sinn Fein Party became the second prong.

The third prong, armed insurrection, arrived in the form of Long Dan Sweeney being slipped back into the country. He was a minor folk hero, a relic of the disastrous Fenian risings and resident of a half-dozen British prisons, where he underwent every sort of humiliation.

Sweeney had worked the world wherever a handful of Irishmen of fighting persuasion would gather. He kept the fires of rebellion fanned, dim though they were. He was the bare bones of the eternal revolutionary, created of acid. He was sloganless and loveless. He had been denounced by the church by a crucifix always hung above the cot where he rested for the night.

With the courts already in battle with the British, the political WORD and the rebel's GUN had come back to Ireland in the form of Arthur Griffith and Long Dan Sweeney.

Into this scene Seamus O'Neill made his reentry with a fine reputation from the Boer War. He was immediately employed by the *Dublin Journal,* a large daily paper tilting toward the republican point of view but most interested in handicapping the horses.

Seamus took a flat at the edge of the Liberties with the Guinness Brewery on one side and the governing Dublin Castle on the other. He was an immediate and welcome addition to the revival, and Des and Atty Fitzpatrick picked up on the earlier contact they had established with him through the Transvaal Committee.

Sure, Seamus O'Neill out of Ballyutogue, a rare Catholic educated on scholarship at Queens College, a war journalist hero and a swordsman with words, was soon a real Dublin dandy.

In addition to covering his beat for the *Journal*, he poured out essays for Irish-American papers and periodicals and served notice to Atty Fitzpatrick that a play was in the writing.

Seamus O'Neill, man about town at the pubs, the track, and the theatre, lived another life. As soon as he was able he made contact with Long Dan Sweeney and became a secret member of the illegal Irish Republican Brotherhood.

Desmond came into the dining room for a quick hello to the family, then retreated up to the library with his plate. This was par for the course at the Fitzpatricks'. Atty gave the children an extra half-hour, then sent them up to have a good-night tussle with Des, then joined him, thankful the theatre was dark tonight.

It was not always quite so hectic. Both parents made the effort to give their children companionship and comfort. They had set up a program of reading and discussing events to create a closeness.

By the age of twelve Theobald was already doing apprentice clerking for his father, able to pick his way through the law library.

Rachael played through her childhood using her sister, Emma, as her live doll and found rich hours in her mother's theatrical wardrobe. She showed little inclination for much other than being a little girl who enjoyed being a little girl.

They were well behaved and moved in a crowd of adults

with ease in the salons of discussion, debates, and poetry readings.

Supreme times were the family trips to Lough Clara, and one was always on the schedule up ahead. Horseback riding with Mom and fishing with Daddy and getting to know each other again about the fire.

When Des came in pressed as he did this night, the children always feared a sudden cancellation of the journey to Lough Clara. Theo went up to the library and stoked the turf for them. Things seemed iffy these days. Theo could tell by the radiation of tension, the quickening of their speech, and the short duration of their toleration that something was amiss.

When Rachael led the children in, their parents gave them perfunctory kisses as Des gobbled down the contents of his plate and punctuated it with a strong shot of whiskey.

"Are we calling off next week's trip to Lough Clara?" Theo asked at the door.

"It's still on with me," Des said to his son's relief.

"We'll go," Atty assured.

When the door shut, they slowed obvious tension with another clout from the bottle.

"Will your trial spill over into our holiday time?"

"Oh, the mood around the Four Courts seems to be conciliatory these days. The second reading of the Home Rule Bill is ready for Commons. They always get polite. I suspect a deal might be in the making." Des took off his glasses and rubbed his eyes. He was done in.

"You really need the time in Lough Clara," she said. "If the trial goes long we'll just pull the children out of school and bring a tutor with us."

"That might be a little difficult for Emma," Des said. "She's just getting her teeth into school."

"It's never been a problem in the past," Atty answered. "Theo and Rachael are the smartest kids in Dublin."

Des looked at the bundle of briefs confronting him.

Atty looked grim.

"What's up?" he asked directly.

"I saw Seamus O'Neill today," she said.

"How's his play coming?"

"It wasn't about the play."

"So is it you, not me, reneging on Lough Clara?"

"Damn you, Des, let me work up to it in my own way."

His undivided attention had been attained.

"Des, would it be dreadful if you took the kids with a nanny and tutor? Maybe I can join you for a long weekend."

"I don't like it and the children won't like it."

"Obviously, I don't like it, either. There is something here in Dublin that has to have a decision."

"Aye?"

"Seamus O'Neill has become the personal liaison of Arthur Griffith on some supersensitive Sinn Fein matters."

"Isn't Arthur speaking to his friends anymore?"

"On certain particular matters, he feels that a liaison would be a better procedure."

Des smelled it immediately. "The Irish Republican Brotherhood, perchance?"

"Yes, the IRB."

"So it's true that Long Dan Sweeney is back in Ireland?"

"Yes. Obviously Arthur and Sinn Fein cannot be openly involved with an illegal organization, but he must have day-to-day contact with them."

Des understood full well.

"Sinn Fein and the Brotherhood must coordinate basic policy very quietly. Seamus O'Neill is on the Brotherhood's Supreme Council. He will be the go-between between Arthur and Dan Sweeney."

Des knew where Atty was taking this and he was leery. As the Brotherhood went into business, the inner circle had to be tight . . . reliable . . . ultra-careful or they would be squashed by the British before they got their feet wet.

"The Brotherhood feels it learned a lot from the Boer tactics and that a new kind of urban warfare can be devised so that a few dozen well-placed men can force the Brits to tie up hundreds, if not thousands, of troops."

"Shyte, Atty, that's republican barroom bravado."

"Dan Sweeney says that a city has too many vulnerable sites unless they're heavily guarded ... docks, government buildings, electric stations, bridges ... and mostly, his squads have a hundred and one homes to ditch their weapons and hide in."

"How much of the population will support this?"

"Enough."

"Well, if anyone can bring it off, Sweeney is the man."

"I believe so, too," Atty said. "With the momentum the revival is building up in the courts, through Sinn Fein, by well-trained lads coming out of the Boer War, the Brotherhood can advance its own timetable."

"Now, you're off. Where are the IRB going to find weapons? Where will men be trained?"

"Lord Louis," she said, referring to an eccentric aristocrat of republican leanings, "has opened part of his barony for training. As you know, it's so deeply hidden in the bens of Connemara that the wind has trouble finding its way in and out."

"Well, I'll be damned, I thought Louis de Lacy was no more than a salon dilettante."

"Des, there are two thousand misplaced Boer War rifles ditched in a coal mine near Bradford. Sweeney is formulating a plan to get them to Ireland."

"Mother of God. Are you joshing me, Atty?"

"Two thousand rifles from the Boer War, picked clean."

"Care to tell me what Messrs. Sweeney, O'Neill, and Griffith have in mind for my child bride?"

"Both Arthur and Long Dan want me to join the Brotherhood as a member of the Supreme Council."

"Well, now, this calls for a drink."

Des's mind hummed. Ultimately there would have to be warfare against the British. Long Dan Sweeney was certainly the man to put the Brotherhood back on its feet. Arthur Griffith had to coordinate closely but never allow the legal Sinn Fein to be caught in bed with the illegal Brotherhood. Seamus O'Neill was the perfect liaison. . . .

And then came the painful part of his logic. Atty Fitzpatrick on the Supreme Council of the Irish Republican Brotherhood was no less than a stroke of genius.

"What do you want me to say?" Des asked with unusual weakness. "What I've been doing in the legal field and with legislation and what all the orators and writers have been doing has been child's play, fun and games. No one really gets hurt. Ah, but the Brotherhood. The time has come, dear Ireland, to start spilling a bit of blood. What shall I say? My wife's role in all the rhetoric ends with a curtain call at the Mechanics' Theatre? It's been a blast, lads, but not with my wife, you don't. What arguments would you like to hear from me, Atty? We've shyte on our kids enough without having Mom swing from the gallows. Please, give me an argument to present."

"Christ, Des, you are trying to make me feel treacherous."

"When is enough, enough? Haven't we given enough to the movement without this?"

"Then say no."

"I'd rather give you plain unadulterated family reasons to back off."

"I never took you for a paper tiger, Des."

"Stop that. Trouble with us Irish is that we are too damned intoxicated by the way we've hit this century running. But this will be no Boer War. Those British bastards have owned us for seven centuries, and it won't be the first time we've tried to settle it with a fight. Every time we've staged a rising it's ended up in a disaster. What makes you think this will be any different? This country is infested with fanatical Englishmen and even more infested with lily-livered paddies who will continue to do the dirty bidding for the Brits at the drop of a quid and a government job."

"Thanks, Des, thanks awfully. I really needed to be primed up on this. I'd all but forgotten."

"Atty," he croaked, "have mercy. Up till now, with all our shenanigans we have been able to live without fear in our daily lives. As of the minute you put your hand on the gun and

Bible, fear is in. Fear for Theo, for Emma, for Rachael. Fear of who is looking at our house from over the road. Fear of who is stalking us."

"Then say no, Des."

"No to what? Exit the Fitzpatricks, finest fair weather soldiers Erin ever had. Soon as we tried to stuff a few pistols in Atty's brassiere, they cut and run ... live in London or some such, don't they?"

"Stop beating up on yourself. Both of us were heading for this from the day we were born."

"Stop ... think.... It boils down to one thing and one thing alone—is it worth our three children?"

"Shall we wake them up and ask them?"

"Well, why bother to ask me? Your mind is made up."

Atty burst into tears, a strange sight and sound. Des let her alone and paced. "The Irish Republican Brotherhood," he moaned. "Well, won't I be a busy old scut working out legal defenses for that crowd." He stopped and held the thick velvet drapes whose feline texture somehow managed to soothe him during his storms. "Two thousand rifles in a Bradford colliery pit. Good God, it's come to this, has it? And the illusions I've lured myself into, prancing about in the old courtroom, spitting out hemlock-laced words at those wigged clowns. One could almost talk himself into the feeling we'd be able to run the Brits out of Ireland without bloodshed."

Atty stopped her crying abruptly. "Well?"

"If I were Long Dan Sweeney, I'd sure as hell want you on the Supreme Council of the Irish Republican Brotherhood, and that's for a fact, now."

"Will you give me your blessings?"

"Of course," he said quietly. "But I have new doubts and new fear."

"So do I. Des, I'll tell you what I believe. If the children were to learn in later life that I turned down the Brotherhood out of concern for them, they'd never forgive me. We have raised them to stand for something."

"Aye," Des said, "so it is." Des then plunged darkly into his stack of briefs and Atty excused herself.

She lay awake torturously counting off the minutes, listening to Des mumble aloud in the adjoining room, scratching away on his legal pad. She wanted so strongly for him to sidle up next to her, put his arms about her, pet her a bit, and tell her everything was going to be grand. God, she wanted to be held!

That was not Des and Atty. He worked into exhaustion, filled to the brim with whiskey, and dropped into bed with a thud. Atty reached for him, but he was already turned away from her, and, in a moment, was dead asleep.

CHAPTER
27

When Conor Larkin first came down to Derry from his village of Ballyutogue, he took a fancy to Maud Tully. Maudie was a Bogside lass of generations' standing, determined to escape the "life sentence" at the shirt factory that had consumed her family and friends.

She became an early daughter of the Gaelic revival, learning the ancient language and spending hours she could scarcely spare in the uplifting environs of Celtic Hall.

The hall was long the office of Kevin O'Garvey as head of the Land League, people's solicitor, Member of Parliament, and political healer to an endless line of impoverished petitioners. With all his titles, Kevin O'Garvey never knew the surplus of a pound sterling. If he had tuppence in his jacket, he always found someone who needed it more than himself.

After factory hours and a quick meal, Maudie worked for Kevin as an unpaid assistant, secretary, or whatever help she could render to him.

Maudie, like the rest of Bogside, was enamored with Conor Larkin's arrival, as he became a saint without wings. A great lad on the football pitch, he lectured to turnaway crowds and lifted the hopes of the wanes of Bogside.

Conor and Maudie became truly fond of each other, but he was just putting his toe in the water and she was well launched on the mission to escape Bogside. Setting romantic fervor aside, they remained as "brother and sister."

It was an entirely different circumstance when Maudie laid eyes on the handsome Myles McCracken, who had the voice of a songbird, and gentle and honorable ways. Myles had followed Conor from the village of Ballyutogue and gone to work in Conor's forge as an apprentice. Maudie figured that with Myles she could follow her dreams out of Derry. Love, marriage, and pregnancy, not necessarily in that order, befell the devoted couple.

To pinch every penny so they might buy a forge in a few years, she contined to work at the shirt factory, and to save rent they moved into an already overcrowded wee house and slept on bedrolls in an alcove in the kitchen.

Brigid Larkin arrived to claim Myles too late.

Myles was a good lunker, but it was Maud, with her smarts born of Bogside, and her compassion that drove her to work for Kevin. She was there for Conor when he needed it most.

Maudie helped Conor work his way through the death of Tomas Larkin. She was there for him when the sudden departure of his boyhood hero, Andrew Ingram, left him puzzled and pained.

She was there when, in a fury of defiance, Conor's wee forge entered a bid against Caw & Train Graving for an array of ironwork around the country. Caw & Train belonged to the Earl of Foyle, and Conor Larkin was burned out.

Aye, the burnout. That was the moment of challenge and decision. Now, a strange thing happened. Conor's forge was rebuilt instantly with "secret funds from America" and, stranger still, subcontract work began to fall his way from Caw & Train.

Maudie counted the minutes until Conor would demand to know some of the smoky things happening behind him . . . but Conor never made the demand.

Instead, he was swept up with the restoration of the great screen in Hubble Manor, and a changed Conor Larkin began to emerge.

Although he still showed up on the football field and drank at Nick Blaney's with the lads and had a viscount as a water boy for the team, there was a definite drifting away from the hot spot of history, ideals, and ideas that emanated from Celtic Hall.

He complained from time to time that he was so consumed with the great screen that his mind was limp to everything else.

Yet he wooed and won a number of ladies, all without the power or ability to win him.

Maudie wondered, was Conor Larkin destined to remain a dreamer, or hadn't the woman showed up yet, or . . . was she there in Hubble Manor?

When the great screen was done and Conor eased back into Bogside life, it wasn't quite the same. Maudie saw him spending less time at Celtic Hall, growing acrimonious with Kevin O'Garvey, and otherwise haunted and ill at ease with himself. Had Derry itself grown too small for him? What was left to do there?

Then came the blow that shocked them all. Kevin O'Garvey indefinitely postponed his Commission of Inquiry into the tinderbox Witherspoon & McNab shirt factory.

Maudie was eight months pregnant and planning to leave the shirt factory in a week or two. Myles had sped up his apprenticeship so quickly working on the great screen that Conor felt Myles was ready to take over his own blacksmith shop, and one was coming up for sale.

Late one evening in Celtic Hall, Maudie was tidying up Kevin's office when Conor arrived and parked himself at Kevin's desk.

"We have to talk, luv," Conor said.

"Indeed, we do," she said locking his door and pulling down the shade and taking a seat. "The answer to your question, before you ask it, it that I don't know why Kevin is calling off the investigation of the shirt factory."

"Then let's try to think of a reason," Conor said. "There are questions I should have asked months, nae, years ago, but I stuck my conscience in a dark corner and said, 'Stay there, conscience, things are going too well for me and I don't want you hovering over me until I'm ready to come back and get you.' But my fecking conscience didn't listen. It refused to stay where I tried to hide it."

"Glory be, it's nice to know, Conor. I was wondering if you had become totally comfortable up at the manor."

Conor ignored the barb and banged at the question he had avoided.

"How come I was able to rebuild so fast after I was burned out? How come his Lordship starts sending me more work than my shop can turn out?"

"Well, the story goes that her Ladyship had already spotted you as the man to rebuild her screen and to get you into the system."

"That's a fecking lie, Maudie. Where did Kevin O'Garvey get the money? And the money for a dozen Bogside enterprises? Who are the Americans supporting him? Why haven't they even shown up quietly to see the results of their good works?"

"I don't know."

"Well, Kevin knows, and he's going to tell me the minute he's back from London. I should have fecking demanded to know from day one instead of allowing this conspiring behind my back."

"Are you all that innocent, Conor boy?"

"Maybe."

"Yeah, yeah," she said, "in a way you are. There was blood and heartbreak on the land and Kevin ran the Land League, but you only saw it in terms of the Fenian Rising and the hanging tree and glories of the past. Yes, even the famine had its romantic aspects. And here in Bogside, Conor lad, let's go into Celtic Hall and purge our pain with tales of Wolfe Tone and Emmet. You're a bloody dreamer . . . you see us behind the veil of republican words to die by rather than to touch the pain with your own hands. . . .

"And when you did get involved, you got a reprieve in Hubble and had something really heavenly, really ethereal, to keep republicanism tucked away in a fantasy corner."

"Am I that naive?"

"Perhaps your greatest charm, Conor."

"Unless you've twisted iron," he cried, "you cannot understand what it means to a self-made anvil thumper like me to have a chance to create something of greater glory. I was consumed, Maudie, consumed."

"And you wanted Caroline Hubble, plain and simple."

As the wind oozed from him, Maudie's eyes were on him, and not with a great deal of sympathy. No use trying to work around that girl.

"Aye, it was our work together. I didn't make love to her. . . . "

"But you loved her. And you used the grandeur of your commission to further your floating away from the real world."

"Aye."

"Welcome to Bogside, Conor. I don't know what Kevin did and I don't give a damn. Everything in Ireland is a deal. Our politicians have a monumental reputation for it. I do know I've taken him home night after night in agony from the pain of Bogside. He was burned out from looking at skinny kids filled with sores, old men and women by the age of ten, and drunks pitching pennies against the wall who never had a job from birth to death, and factory girls too tired to smile, much less make love. He was done in and you were his white knight . . . and you made your bloody deals by not demanding to know what you suspected because you wanted to stay in your dream with Caroline Hubble and with that screen."

"Is that why Kevin called off the investigation of the factory? Did Roger Hubble pay him to set me and the others up in business? Is that it?"

"I don't know," she croaked.

"Say what you will, I've been betrayed by Kevin O'Garvey and probably Andrew Ingram as well. Well . . . I'm not taking their path. Kevin will tell me, the minute he returns from London, if he made the deal with Roger Hubble. We are going to close that fecking factory down. As for you, Maudie, stop, quit. Don't go work there another day. I'm bloody sick of Conor Larkin!"

He felt her hand on his bowed head.

"That's the way they do it, mon. If a golden one like yourself or Garvey shows you mean to take them on, they merely ease you into their system."

"Maudie . . . Maudie . . . don't go back into that factory."

"Soon, Conor, soon."

28

What force, what combination of forces, could generate enough power to drive Conor Larkin out of Ireland?

Was it the fire at the Witherspoon & McNab shirt factory?

What was overdue to happen, happened. In the mining towns and out on sea you're struck numb with fright when the disaster whistle screams ugly. As the whistle pierces over and over and over you move into desperate action gravitating in a run toward the trouble, gasping prayer, heart close to a burst, the most vile of fears consuming yourself.

The first thin spirals of smoke eked through the cracks into the air. Then came the blasts like cannonades shattering glass for a mile around, felling the onrushers, covering their ears as a hundred tongues of fire leapt from the factory windows.

There! On the rooftop! Women and children had gathered screaming their terror, dropping to their knees in prayer.

Fire bells! Whinnying, frothing horses!

Neither ladders nor water horses could reach the roof.

"They're jumping!"

Conor and his mates pinned Myles McCracken to the ground as Maud leapt. Conor rushed over to pick her up. She broke in half. Myles and Maud's unborn child splattered like a broken egg on the paving stones.

A blue and orange ball billowed over the top floors in an all-consuming inferno. Within the building, the hollow cast-iron pillars splintered, cracked, then burst apart, and the factory gave up quickly and collapsed.

With the broken corpses laid out on a streetside morgue, another hour and another of water, pumping the River Foyle dry, poured in on the sizzling remains until the firemen could inch in.

Human fragments, skulls, a braid of hair, charred rosary beads, a shoe, bits, pieces, teeth, glasses, rings. Forty children under teen age ... sixty pregnant women ... a hundred and fifty-four, maybe more, maybe a few less ...

Hail Mary...

Two few positive identifications. A common grave. Perhaps God would recognize them.

What could drive a Conor Larkin from Ireland? Was it the sudden and unexplained disappearance of Kevin O'Garvey?

Where did Kevin go? Why? What did Kevin know? Did they do away with him? Did he flee? We have to have Kevin O'Garvey or there is no chance of justice in Bogside ... if there ever was, anyhow. Kevin man, where are you, now?

Would disgust over the cover-up have driven Conor Larkin out of Ireland?

Martin Mulligan, a vagrant, was picked up for arson. Mulligan had worked at the factory stables years earlier, had been fired, and had sworn he was going to wreak vengeance.

Mulligan signed a confession that several Catholic constables swore to at the inquiry. The next morning, after confessing, Mulligan was found hanged in his cell. It was deemed a suicide.

Twenty witnesses at the inquiry testified that Mulligan had made the threats. What never came up was that he was an illiterate and therefore could neither read nor sign the confession.

Another two dozen witnesses—municipal inspectors, architects, factory owners—testified to the safety of the building.

No mention was made of toilets that did not work for years or windows stuck shut with grime or sand buckets whose bottoms had rotted out or fire hoses that had not worked in a decade or that no fire drill had taken place in ten years because the stairs and landings were too crammed with bolts of linen to move past ... a building whose very design all but guaranteed a disaster. . . .

So, the Earl of Foyle went his jolly way and grieving families had a few quid tossed to them.

That's it! Myles McCracken was admitted to the insane asylum and killed himself. That might have driven a Conor Larkin from Ireland.

Or was it that night after Conor had finished his rounds trying to tend the broken men of Bogside?

Conor climbed up to his flat, a wave of deep sighs holding back some of the pain. Four months had passed, but still there came the rain of ashes after every wind, and it seemed that the smell of rotten corpses found a way out of the rubble. He sensed the presence of someone.

"Who's here?" he rasped.

"Caroline."

He lit the lamp and saw her huddled on the settee, cloaked in a monk's cloth hooded cape so as not to attract notice. On sight of Conor she saw the toll that had been taken on him. He slumped into his reading chair.

"I've written you a dozen letters," she said.

"I've not received them," he answered.

"I never sent them. I tore them up. They were all inadequate to set my feelings down. I don't feel very good about myself," she said voice trembling. "I have an overwhelming need to face you.

"Why?"

"I am torn by a terrible notion about us."

"Caroline, there is so much confusion and guilt about what happened. That factory did not burn down because you and I fell in love."

"Part of the reason it burned down was that I am the Countess of Foyle and part of the establishment that allowed it to happen."

"Good God, Caroline, if there was ever an aristocrat out here who made some efforts to better things, it was you. You couldn't have known."

"I didn't know because I didn't want to know. . . . I didn't know because I never went above the first floor of that wretched place. There was conspiracy on the wind and I made it a point not to find out."

It was all too far gone to play at games. "Nor did I," Conor said. He said what he had held in till this moment. "All right. I smelled something wrong the first time Kevin O'Garvey postponed the investigation. His whole life was pointed to bringing the Earl up before his committee and exposing that factory. When he called it off, I did not challenge him because . . . I didn't want to know, either! I didn't want to have to face my hero and have him confess to me that he had made a deal. Not hard to figure out what the deal was, is it? I had my forge. I was on the way. I didn't say a word when the second postponement came. And then," he croaked, "nothing was going to take me away from the great screen, and no one except you could understand that. So, we didn't want to know and we joined the conspiracy by our silence."

"Conor, hear me. I cannot rationalize this, but there is a reason for our behavior. No man has ever taken on a great work of art without paying a terrible price and creating terrible pain for those he loves the most. But nothing . . . nothing . . . nothing could have kept that building from collapsing after my husband and Kevin went into some kind of deal."

"I keep trying to tell myself that . . . "

"Hang on to that belief," she said. "We were both trapped by the system. I came here to plead forgiveness for my part and beg you not to hate me."

"I believe you. I never went above the first story, myself. God, woman, I could never hate you."

She arose and came to him and mussed his hair and kissed his forehead. "Take care," she whispered.

"Aye."

And she was gone, into a snowfall of ashes.

What was it that drove Conor Larkin out of Ireland? Was it the terminal lethargy of the men of Bogside? They were worse than dead for they were living dead with no spirit of rage, not even the instinct for survival.

They had accepted the system of birth-to-death unemployment, birth-to-death poverty, birth-to-death humiliation.

Where in the name of Jesus were the Kilty Larkins!

For a year and a day Conor took to the roads of Ireland seeking the old Fenians, men who had done battle, Gaelic warriors of old. He found them. One or two in wee villages sitting at the end of the bar stool. The living legends were glassy-eyed drunks repeating their imagined valor one more time for one more pint.

What few Irishmen remained worthy of a rising were away in South Africa fighting the Brits. Seamus O'Neill was among them. They were all gone, Tomas and Kilty and Seamus and Andrew Ingram and Kevin O'Garvey and, in the most heart-wrenching sense, Caroline Hubble.

The thin thread of keeping Conor Larkin fell to his younger brother Dary, a seminary novice. Dary was able to transfer to the diocese of Derry in temporary service to help contend with the tragedy of Bogside. Wee Dary became a rock, a healer, and man of God in the ultimate sense. And, he was his brother's keeper.

One more bombastic drunk, one more bombastic hangover. Conor sat dizzy in the middle of his forge, which had not seen the glow of the fire for over a year.

"I have to return to the seminary and my studies," Dary announced abruptly.

Conor anguished. "How can I do without you, wee Dary?"

"It's nigh on to springtime," Dary said. "I saw some daisies pushing through the rubble. Enough time has passed, Conor. You and I have to have our go at it, now."

"Ah, what do you want of me, Dary? I've prostrated myself before your throne. I'm awash in guilt! You know my dark secret. Maybe the Lord took vengeance on me for loving Caroline Hubble?"

"Stop babbling, you're wracked with pity."

"You want me in a monastery talking this over with Jesus, don't you?"

"Tell you what I want, Conor. I want you to get on the next ship out of Ireland."

Conor gnarled and tried to weep at the same time. But the tears were all long spent on poor dear Myles. That was the last time he'd cried. "Go to hell, Father Dary."

"Well then," Dary pressed, "you've a few choices. You've done your year and a day looking for stout-hearted fighting men to no avail. You can take on the British singlehanded or take a shortcut and rip Roger Hubble's Adam's apple out with your bare hands."

"You're a kid and you're talking like a Jesuit. Say what you mean and mean what you say."

"I'm also a Larkin," Dary said. "I've a drop or two of republican blood in my veins, but I'll not go the way of the gunman. I'm also an Irishman. What I am now most of all is your brother. I know you better than you know yourself. You're very fuzzy, and what I see clearly is a man who is fast becoming a danger to himself."

Conor stopped battling his brother long enough to allow Dary's words to make their way in. "You really want me out of Ireland, don't you, Dary?"

"Aye, I do, until you can get reacquainted with yourself."

Conor was always baffled by Dary. He grew up liking skirts and bosoms well enough. Had he taken a stand against the priesthood, Finola could never have forced him. He was his own lad and he chose the priesthood. He made a deliberate choice that there was something better in the world than what he saw around him. Who could argue? He alone, among the Larkins, was at peace with himself.

"Dary . . . "

"You're almost to the point where you'll go to the bottom of the wall in Bogside and pitch pennies and never draw a sober breath again. Or, you'll go killer. You're a promise that will never be fulfilled. Look at this forge—it's desolate. Myles and Maud are not coming back and you can't take on the British presence in Ireland by yourself.

"Sail the seas, Conor," Dary went on. "Take control of the

memories of Caroline Hubble and tuck them away. There is a woman somewhere who wants to come in to you, but you'll not find her until Caroline stops blocking her way. What you need is space. You'll know when it's time to come back."

"I know I have to fight."

"Aye, you'll have to fight. I know I won't be able to stop you. But fight, man, when you have your wits and mind keenly focused. What you seek now is revenge, and revenge for the sake of revenge. Revenge is not to one man. Kill Roger Hubble and the miseries of Ireland will still be there. Don't give your life away. Make it count."

The two brothers walked through the Bogside, then to the quay and the shipping office. A likely vessel was due in in a week.

Conor hitched up his livery horses to the small buckboard and rode out into the countryside, over the Burntollet Bridge and to the gates of the seminary. Somehow, it still burned Conor to see his brother disappear behind the wall. Dary smiled.

"I'm ready," Dary said.

"I'm ready as well," Conor said.

Dary soon vanished from his sight.

CHAPTER

29

1904

Conor Larkin slid shut the door of the wheelhouse behind him and set down a cup of tea for Bojo at the helm. He sipped on his own as Bojo gave him the headings for his watch.

The S.S. *Famagusta* moved flat out at twelve knots on a smooth tabletop of windless water and a big show taking place up in the sky.

"Christchurch tomorrow," Bojo said. "You got a brother there?"

"Aye, he has a station somewhere in the middle of the island up in the hills."

"A real spread?"

"Couple thousand acres, maybe more."

"That's a station, good enough. Setting down for a spell?"

"For a spell."

"How long you been roving, Larkin?"

"I've been out of Ireland for about five years."

"Well, I'm going to miss you as much as one can miss a paddy. How long's it been since you came aboard in Australia?"

"Year ago."

"That long already. Yeah, I'll miss you."

Conor took the wheel and adjusted his eyes. It was a night of nights out there. Bojo slurped at his tea. "Five years. That's a piece of time, all right. Woman?"

"Isn't there always a woman?"

Bojo gurgled a laugh and gave his mouth a swipe from the back of his hand. He'd forgotten. Yeah, there was a woman, or two. "This New Zealand is beautiful country. If I ever quit the sea, I'd give it my utmost consideration."

Flecks of gray had shown up on Conor's temples, starting when he crossed the line past thirty.

Bojo was glad he was off watch. "Hate it up here at nights," he said, making his departure. They all hated the night watch, Conor thought. During the daylight there was always someone moving about, someone to chat up.

There were those bad days and nights when you battled the wheel or were rocked silly up in the crow's nest and all you could think about was finishing your watch and getting a shot of rum in your belly.

Sailors hated the calm nights like tonight. It was with but a sliver of moon and the heavens filled with stars and mischief that the watch became painful. They had time to ponder all they had left behind, all they would never find, all that useless wandering. They would hurt for that one woman—abandoned, dead, waiting, unfaithful. They would wish for something beneath their feet that didn't roll, something long and green with a covering of spring flowers. All that was gone. All that they would never see again. All that they would never know haunted them on night watch on a calm sea.

Conor loved it at the helm on these nights. These were nights for himself and Caroline. New port, new girl. Some of the lassies were lovely creatures. After a time, they would look into his eyes and become frightened. He saw through them and they could never look in too deep. They became frightened of losing him because he demanded a power of love they did not possess. Some loved him well, but they could not come between him and that ever-tilted sword charging at some unknown foe, nor could they come between him and a love he had touched once long ago.

So Conor found a new ship. He saw the swill holes; black, brown, yellow, and white, living through motions of life in the humility of colonization.

He saw Bogsides of Irish scattered about the world.

For the better part of a year Conor took to Australia. It was a grand place, indeed. There was a girl and a moment he thought he might end his journey from nowhere to nowhere. He became a foreman in a steel mill and played a spot of professional rugby.

But the damned turf fires of Ballyutogue reached his nostrils from ten thousand miles gone and the beauty of the voices singing from Dooley McCloskey's public house, and he smelled the fresh high meadows above the heather and the fog and wind blasting in from Lough Foyle . . . and Bogside!

Think about it, Conor lad. That's when you wanted to stand the night watch. In that manner you wouldn't have to come startled out of a nightmare of the fire.

Why did Conor leave Australia, then? He wasn't certain. The lass was fetching and dear. She came to learn that Ireland whispered to him, reached out for him. He was helpless. He fell into a black spell after his mother departed . . . and he went back to the sea again.

After a time the visions of the fire and of Myles hanging from a rafter and of Maud on the pavement came under control. After a time he could go three or even five nights . . . then a week and a month without the nightmare. It never went away, fully.

Even Caroline became more vague. Sooner or later her spirit came onto the scene as he grew serious with another woman. The vision he kept was one of perfection. Then she dimmed, as Dary told him she would.

At long last he was on a ship heading toward New Zealand and Squire Liam Larkin and a family of Larkins he did not know. Conor was happy now that it was Christchurch ahead. Five years of roving had purged what needed to be purged. His mind was clear. He laughed again. He told himself he was open-minded about New Zealand. Perhaps, he even believed it.

God willing, he might find the peace and love his brother Liam had found.

Tomorrow . . .

*   *   *

When Eye-tallions or Jews or Greeks came down the gangplank to waiting families, there was always a lot of hugging and
screaming and weeping. Russians slam one another and wail.
Brits give formal little pecks, grins, and sturdy handshakes.

No matter how long the time, how far the journey, an Irish
Squire and his roving brother are apt to be plaintive and stiff, as
though an explosive greeting were not natural.

Family members didn't touch each other much in the old
country. The Larkins were known to be far more affectionate
than most . . . until the chill set in.

Conor and Liam stood for a long moment or two or three, as
though they had to let their lives pass by until they rendered
rugged handshakes.

To hell, Conor thought, to hell!

He embraced Liam like no man had embraced him since
they had won the Donegal football championship. With the
air out of him and a wide grin replacing his somberness, the
Squire introduced his family: Mildred, Spring, Madge, Tommy,
and Rory.

Each in turn got a thunderous hug and kiss and they walked
off chattering like Eye-tallions or Jews.

The awkwardness between the brothers passed in a moment.
Four kids wanted to see a rough-up, hear sea chanteys, gape as
he spun his yarns, for Conor was the uncle of uncles.

There were the sorrows that Liam and his brother had to
work through: the death of their parents, Myles's suicide, the
fire, the spinsterhood of their sister, Brigid.

They spoke of happy times. There were more of these than
Liam had remembered. To look at the girls during the wracking
season, gathering up seaweed, the bottoms of their skirts tucked
in at the waist baring their limbs and the wet of the sea causing
their blouses to cling to their breasts, and times at the fairs trying
to outwit the tinkers, and Kilty's wake. Oh, so very many things
that were both joyous and essential to one's very being.

Yet Liam clung to some consternation. In fact, he owed
Conor his stature of Squire, for Conor had paid his passage and

got him into land. Yet, the monster of youth brought back fears of living under the awesome shadow of Conor.

Mildred watched this carefully, leading her husband along the path brightly. This was Liam's land. He had made the battle here and won it. Conor would never steal his kids or make himself larger than their daddy. His tension eased as he felt certain that Conor was no longer a threat.

In actual fact, as Mildred pointed out to her husband in the sanctity of their bed, Liam no longer needed Conor but Conor needed Liam now, sorely.

The same kind of lightness swept over Ballyutogue Station as had taken hold in the manor house. Of Hubble Manor . . . well, then . . . the restoration was a memorable time, but nothing was said of Caroline or the intrigue of Kevin O'Garvey and Andrew Ingram.

From initial apprehension, his throne intact, Liam's tack now drifted toward keeping his brother in New Zealand. As the weeks passed, the idea evolved. Conor was so in place here that the opposite idea took hold—what would it be like when Conor left? What a void! What an utter void! See now, that aura of beauty that always surrounded Conor was theirs and everyone in the family felt it.

Loving Conor, Liam concluded, was not a danger. Liam was keen now and saw through his brother's melancholy and mystery, a man who could give off sunshine but keep his darkness in himself.

Three hundred acres of the most magnificent, lush, deep soiled bottom land in the southern Alps came on the market and Liam and Mildred made quiet inquiries and placed a holding deposit, and waited for the right moment to offer it. As for a forge, Liam told his wife, they'd come from all over the country to him.

The ladies of the stations and villages clear down to Christchurch began to circle the campfire with Mildred Larkin brokering the plotters.

Now that he had made peace with himself, Liam had to admit to things he knew of his brother. Conor was a different breed, who had always aspired differently from other people.

Wealth and stature meant nothing to him. Conor had always been after something Liam could not see or touch or describe.

This soured the milk a little. Was not Rory a lot like his brother? Yes, he and Conor were at peace for the moment, but what power did he hold over Rory? A wariness set in.

Conor and Rory teamed off naturally. Conor had worked with horses all his life, but none of the class that populated this station. Although but eleven years of age, Rory rode his stallion, RumRunner, with the skill of a man who had been in the saddle three times as long.

Liam fell into the ancient game. Rory adored his uncle and Liam feared his son would be itchy to follow if Conor left. Rory had never taken to anyone as he had to his uncle. . . .

And Liam pondered. How much of Ireland would Conor fill Rory's head with? Had Conor dinned his son with Irish martyrs and speeches from the dock?

Liam was convinced that Conor's departure would guarantee Rory's departure, in time. Liam had to have Rory, or Ballyutogue Station might vanish. Liam concocted a new plan— he would encourage the deepening relationship between uncle and nephew. If Conor came to love Rory and also understood Rory's value to the station, then Conor might remain.

Jaysus, Liam thought. He and Conor and Rory together could build an estate the likes of which had never been seen on the South Island. He'd end up with more land than the Earl of Foyle! On the other hand, the Squire's unspoken partners might not give a damn!

"Rest your head, Liam," Mildred warned. "Your father made plans. My father made plans. We didn't listen very much, luv."

"What will I do now, Millie?"

They flirted with answers . . . all kinds of answers except the right one—to show Rory they loved him.

With Rory riding alongside, Conor lost much of his melancholy and felt for a moment he was at the forge, twisting iron and all joyous inside. How wonderful to ride the perimeters of his brother's acres mustering the lambs and the beef.

When there was a fence to mend or an hour to spend, Rory and Conor drifted toward the shade and became pals in the utmost sense of the word. Conor was quizzed and was wondrously happy to open the boy's mind.

Conor had a rover's eye view of the entire world, a world unknown to Rory. When his uncle ventured beyond the horizon his words pulsated in the lad's daydreams . . .

. . . of a ship around the Horn . . .

. . . of a cattle raid . . .

. . . of the scents and danger of the waterfronts . . .

. . . of the rugby pitch . . .

. . . and a lot of man talk about the girls.

In the beginning Uncle Conor always had a couple of books tucked away in his saddlebag, but Rory's incessant questions made the reading break impossible. Besides, Conor preferred conversation with his nephew.

There was a second, quiet reason Conor put the books away. Rory's curiosity about what lay in the pages had apparently invoked a dour reaction from Liam. It came from nothing that was said, but certainly sensed. Liam didn't like Conor's books any more than their daddy had.

An old family theme was being played with a new player. Books had been slipped to Conor as a boy from a sympathetic Protestant schoolteacher and from his closest boyhood pal, Seamus O'Neill. Liam sorely recalled an almost nightly replay of Conor slipping books into the cottage and whisking them out of sight before Tomas arrived.

"Why are you reading all them books," Liam would taunt, miffed. "You're only going to be a blacksmith. Besides, Dary is the one who needs to read if he's going to be a priest."

Finola would quickly and automatically add, "Get those books out of sight of your daddy, Conor. You know how he feels about your nose being stuck in the pages all night."

Damned right, Conor knew! It led to the fiercest explosion of his boyhood. To punish Conor and wean him away from the forge and back to the land, Tomas exiled him to the booley house in the high meadows to shepherd the flock for the summer. Conor and his pal Seamus hid a summer's worth of reading in the bottom of a sack of provisions and Tomas discovered them. In the rage that followed, Conor dared his father by swearing he would run away if the books were taken from him. Tomas caved in.

It was all a puzzle to Liam, an illiterate. What mysteries stoked Conor's insatiable drive? Liam came to learn that the pages held ideas, and Tomas feared ideas because pursuit of them would take his beloved Conor out of Ballyutogue.

All during his voyage to New Zealand, Liam longed for the knowledge in Conor's books to ease his fears of tomorrow. As if Conor had always known something he did not know.

When Mildred took Liam in hand and taught him to read, it was a wonderment only second to the wonderment of Mildred herself. He conquered government forms and learned of animal diseases and occasioned himself of a roaring sea story or the cunning of the sleuths.

For the soul, one needed only one book, the Bible. One needed no further input on the human condition. After all, he was comfortable on his farm and cared little of the fecked-up world outside and all its misery.

When Conor arrived in New Zealand, Liam enacted something he had rehearsed in his mind a thousand times. He opened a book and read to his brother and Conor shed tears of happiness.

That was fine, indeed, if it had been left right there. Now Rory was becoming curious about books. Liam contained himself because he did not want to play out the angry role with Rory that Tomas had played out with Conor.

Conor sensed his brother's discomfort in short order and set his books aside. Likewise, he stifled conversation of Ireland's epic. He would not be the brother to bring trouble. Could Rory's eager enchantment for his uncle's knowledge be stilled? The lad glued himself to Conor in hero worship.

"Take a look at RumRunner's left front hoof."

"Looks sound to me."

"Thought I saw a wee split."

"No."

"Always liked this part of the station," Rory said. "My da has his place up on the crown and his God-given greatest trout stream in the South Island. I like the woods and the scent of it here."

"Myself as well," Conor said. "We didn't have much woodland in the old country."

"How come?"

"The Brits cut down our forests to build a fleet to defend against the Spanish Armada and whatever else one uses wood for."

"I didn't know that. How come you don't bring books in your saddlebag anymore?"

"You know very well why, Rory."

"Want me to show you how to use the long whip to muster cattle? You're very bad at it."

"I'm too old. All the nags I ever rode had bad breath from age and swaybacks from the lack of decent breeding. Although Ireland itself breeds some of the finest horses in the world. I was at the Dublin horse show once, working as a farrier—" He cut short. Conversation, out of bounds.

"I want to know more about Ireland ... about Ballyutogue ... "

"It's a sore point with your da. He knew a thousand tons of misery there."

"It's not his misery," Rory said abruptly. "It's his fear of me knowing. The same fear he has of books. There's a St. Patrick's Day celebration every year and quite a time ... except Daddy takes a deep breath in the morning and holds it all day. He hates it."

"He's your father, I'm only your uncle."

"You defied your da," Rory pressed.

It was so damned apparent that Liam was trying to make his son live in a vacuum, cut off physically and now spiritually from Ireland.

"What about me!" Rory cried suddenly.

"I'll tell you about you," Conor answered. "You have the world by the balls on a downhill pull, Rory. You rove because you're in pain. You need not bash your skull in to learn that the world is a filthy place. Your daddy has struggled for the things you were born into. This farm is a full-fledged station and will be a giant sheep station in a few years. So, what's the purpose of glinking yourself only to find out that New Zealand is one of God's perfect creations."

"The reason I don't like it up on the crown of the hill where my daddy goes is because I can see the ocean from there. The water is an evil jailer."

"Or the safest moat in the world, Rory. The wise ones figure that out before they have to suffer for it."

"The wise ones ... or the dull ones?" the boy answered. "Too much peace here seems to drive a lot of people to religion and drink."

"It's so strange, lad. You leave Ireland hating to go but forced to go. Here, you leave for no good reason at all, except misplaced curiosity."

"That's not true. Your books tell me why there is something more than we can find here."

"Oh, you'll go, Rory, because you must. But always keep your eye on this place and thank your parents who gave it to you."

"Maybe I would if my daddy loved me."

Conor's throat went dry. There would be no side-slipping this lad. Conor/Rory ... Rory/Conor and poor dear Liam confused about who was who and why. Maybe I shouldn't have come here, Conor thought. But why not? I did for my brother what I could. I righted my wrongs to him. Five years at sea brought me to a desperation of loneliness. Am I not entitled to my brother's hand? Yet, has my coming here set off another cycle of Larkin madness?

"Of course your daddy loves you," Conor finally said. "It's just that he doesn't have a way with words."

"He has a way with them, all right, when they're meant to bite," Rory answered.

"He does love you, but things move slowly inside him. It is you who must give him time to work it out."

"I was just about born a bastard," Rory snapped.

"Well, that sort of thing happens all the time. It's normal and natural. After all, they sat you down and told you about it. That's love."

"They never told me. It was shit on my head in the school-yard one day."

Oh Liam! You dumb son of a bitch, Conor thought. Letting your lad suffer the pains of the unwanted. Conor's arm went around Rory's shoulders and the boy rested his head on his uncle's chest. Rory never felt so protected, so cared for, so invincible as now.

"You're but fourteen, but you are wiser in many regards than your parents. It is you who must continue to be the understanding and patient one."

"I try, Uncle Conor. I keep it stuffed until the fits overtake me, and when they do, it is beyond my will to stop myself. Then, I have to break things apart. It keeps happening over and over, and it will until I break loose of them here."

"What is it you're sporting for, boy?"

"Ireland."

"But Jaysus, Rory . . . "

"Uncle Conor, this farm is Ireland, from morning to night. It carries an Irish name. The proprietor is Irish. These acres were misplaced in New Zealand. Every hour you and me have not talked about Ireland, Ireland was sitting up on the limb of that tree looking down and laughing at us. Why? Because Ireland holds my Uncle Conor in an iron fist. You can't run from it, because you've tried and failed. Ireland owns anyone with the name of Larkin. I've got to have my piece of it."

Oh Lord, Conor moaned to himself. How many damned Irish pubs on how many waterfronts in how many shanty ports on how many continents have the Irish rovers gathered to slop in their beer and pine for all that dirty rock and hardship and British rottenness. What is its cursed hold on men! The memories are so bitter you'd think you'd close it off, once you escape.

But no, it sneaks after you on the quiet watch in the crow's nest. What the hell is it you long for . . . you don't even know . . . you don't understand it.

And here sits a lad who envisions it through a mist. His craving for it is worse because it is denied him by a bitter man.

'Tis true that most men of ordinary cut have the wanderlust knocked out of them for fear of the unknown. But Rory lad is going to be no ordinary man. He will have to go after it.

What should I do? Conor wondered. It's better to get out of New Zealand before this family blows like a volcano. My coming here has just brought salt into Liam's open wound.

"I want to know about the sheilas," Rory said, bending the subject to something more compatible.

"Women?"

"Jeeze, Uncle Conor, I've been watching rams and bulls fornicating all my life. I've even stuck RumRunner's cock in a mare."

"Well, then. I'll talk to you, but only in generalities."

Rory lay back and looked at the sky as his uncle spoke.

"What in life that is sublime, above everything, comes down to a simple proposition—a bed, or a place where a man and a woman make love."

Rory began to line up the million and one questions about this most sublime subject.

"The thing you must remember about women is that you are holding a precious little bird in your hand. If you squeeze it too tightly, you'll crush it. If you hold it too loosely, it will fly away. What women crave is patience. You must learn that, Rory. RumRunner can't control himself. That's why he's a horse. The longer you can suspend time, the higher the flight. Find that lovely balance between strong arms on the one hand and a velvet touch on the other."

Huh, Rory thought, a bit different than he had reckoned, but surely Uncle Conor knew more about women than anyone, he was that handsome.

"Rule number one. It is always the woman's choice to do it or not to do it. You present yourself charmingly . . . never try to overwhelm her, and let her size you up. She'll let you know when she's ready."

"Sounds foxy to me."

"It is. It's fox and hounds. The more casual you are, the more interested they become. And once it's a go, make her feel like a queen . . . before, during, and afterward. It's called tenderness."

"You ever been in love?"

"Of course," Conor answered, "in a manner of speaking."

"Desperately?"

"Aye, once."

"With a queen?"

"Only a countess." As Conor drifted into a schanachie's tale of his unconsummated love, he found speaking of such things to the boy to be very easy. Conor had never spoken of his love of Lady Caroline to anyone but Seamus O'Neill. It seemed so wistful and lovely a memory that he wanted to share it with Rory.

As they horsed around, wrestling and boxing openhanded, Conor saw a bit of room for improvement. He had, after all, taught Liam the finer points of fisticuffs and his very prize pupil had been Seamus O'Neill.

"Your being left-handed gives you a distinct advantage. Now then, take your pose . . . always circle to your right, which takes away my right hand . . . that's it . . . that's it . . . to your right . . . I flick out my left jab . . . bob under it and throw a thunderous right hand to me ribs . . . aye, that's the lad . . . under the jab . . . move to your right . . . under the jab, unleash that right to the body . . . good lad . . . now get away and circle right.

"After five or six slams to the ribs, your unworthy opponent will start to paw with his jab, fearing your blow to the body. When he starts pawing, go over the top to his face . . . poor chap won't last long . . .

"The madder they become, the calmer you become . . . you've got a target now because his ribs are getting red . . . move right . . . under the jab . . . unleash, move out . . . fearsome, utterly fearsome."

"Don't I ever get to throw my left hand, Uncle Conor?"
"In due course, lad, in due course."

They spoke of wrought iron and Shakespeare.

They spoke of a kind of sound Rory did not know . . . music played by great orchestras of eighty or ninety men and of operas sung by women with voices of nightingales.

They spoke of the wonders of the new century, of electric power and moving film and another magic kind of film that could see into a person's body.

They spoke of great boxers and of artists and men who painted the ceilings of cathedrals.

And places with magic names . . . Damascus . . . Calgary . . . Ponte Vecchio . . . and Montenegro . . .

But never a mention of Ireland or the book *Rights of Man* by Thomas Paine. Rory hungered to know the thoughts behind Conor's silence. The yellow and brown and black Bogsides all over the world, wretched creations of the colonizers.

What he spoke of and what he did not speak of was everything denied this lad from the South Island of New Zealand. The catalogue of Rory's longings grew so obviously that Conor knew he had better leave.

CHAPTER
30

One night Conor announced to Liam and Millie that he would be going down to Christchurch and perhaps up to Wellington to inquire about a berth on a ship. There was always a need for blacksmiths afloat, so something suitable was bound to come along in short order.

After a sigh of relief, Liam suddenly was jolted by the other side of the coin. He remembered twelve years ago in Ballyutogue when he had broken the news of his own emigration to Conor. Conor had gone into a panic. Liam's darkest memory of all was the family's ugly scene over Conor's futile attempt to keep Liam in Ireland.

From his initial reaction of deliverance, Liam was seized with fear. Conor had filled Rory's head with taunting notions of the world beyond. Rory had made his mark on Ballyutogue Station. Rory had to keep the continuity.

Manipulation. Aye, that's the name of the game. Practiced by the family, the tribe, and the order of nations since man came down from the trees and moved into the caves.

Few practiced it with more precision than our dear Irish compatriots. You see, there is so infinitely little to manipulate, five acres of land, a ha'penny more on the price of flax, the fear of sex. . . . Manipulation at the family level was no less an Irish art than their poetry.

There was much more for Squire Liam at stake: Ireland against New Zealand—keeping his needed son, Rory, in the country to ensure continuity and a new generation of manipulators.

After all, Liam reasoned, he was *not* his father, Tomas, trying to lock Conor to his land. Could Conor, who had never been taken by a need for wealth or power, suddenly become smitten by the idea that the two brothers could build their holdings into something even larger than an earldom?

Perhaps the promise of peace could hold Conor? He had known poor little of it. A return to Ireland would only guarantee a life of battle.

Peace, plenty, family.

There was the magnificent parcel of land. If Conor took the new farm and built toward Ballyutogue Station, when the two merged it would be the largest spread on the South Island.

Yet, even as Liam offered the proposition, he could see that Conor had to go. His brother was inquiring after a ship. Liam railed against an Ireland that had brought them nothing but misery. He pleaded the case for New Zealand's greater offer of freedom and dignity.

"Funny," Conor answered, "how everyone loves the Irish once they leave Ireland."

A letter had been sent to Liam in care of Conor from Seamus O'Neill in the event Conor showed up in New Zealand. When Liam handed it over, he learned there could be no keeping his brother.

The letter spoke of Irish stirrings, a heightened revival, and more . . . the probable renewal of the Irish Republican Brotherhood with the return of the old Fenian Long Dan Sweeney.

"What's it gotten us but the raw end of a whip," Liam repeated, now speaking in a hollow chamber.

Conor tried to comfort his stricken brother. "Your sorrow is misplaced. It might appear to be the best for me to remain in New Zealand but the enigma of it would follow us here as, indeed, it already has. You'd soon get sick of your big brother hovering about. My obvious love for Rory could throw us into an ugly contest and only complicate matters. Of course, there's more. I wish I could explain this stranger who sits on my shoulder who will never leave me alone until I return. I can't get rid of him, Liam. Five years of roving and I can't get rid of him."

*   *   *

Well, now comes the summing up. How did all the confused manipulation work out? Liam wanted his brother to stay and to leave at the same time. Why then did he feel relief when Conor announced his departure? Was Conor again casting his giant shadow?

What of it with Conor gone? Rory adored his uncle in a fever that only an eleven-year-old can muster, unadulterated hero worship. Conor's departure seemed a guarantee for Rory to follow. However, Liam now had some years to play with to make Rory change his mind. But how? Liam thought of everything . . . except love.

Manipulation gave way to utter disarray.

"I think I'm sorry that I came," Conor whispered to his brother.

Liam damned near collapsed.

"Oh Conor, man, you alone stuck with me. You paid off my passage. You gave me the first money for land. I owe you and I want to make it right for you. Forget my games. I don't want to see you suffer no more."

"I'd say we are more than even," Conor replied. "I am sorry for the pain I caused you in Ireland. I should have been a better brother."

Liam was about to shout out, I LOVE YOU, MAN, AND THAT'S WHAT IT'S ABOUT. I LOVE YOU. But the words died in Liam somewhere on the way out and were never said or heard.

"Well, being brothers means saying you're sorry, all the time, eh?" Conor said. "You're on an irreversible march to becoming a powerful man and you've a grand family around you."

"Except for the boy who is going to follow in your footsteps," Liam said bitterly.

"All right, Liam, you're a big man now, so here it is. Try giving Rory some love and honesty. You did him a rotten turn by trying to live a lie with him. You know how it feels to be unloved. Why are you trying so bloody hard to repeat Daddy's mistake? How can you do this to your own boy after what you've gone through."

Liam recoiled, stricken, denuded.

"I hear you," he finally rasped.

"Liam, I've tried desperately to avoid what is unavoidable. You cannot shut your son in a dark room and close the door. Rory is a keen lad with a mind of a wizard and a heart full of life and inquiry. You'd better realize that whether I had come to New Zealand or not, you can't turn him into a sheep-herding vegetable. He's going to cut his own path. Don't try to stop him. Only if you let him know that he is loved will he come back to this place."

Well, brothers go through the act of making up when a gangplank is staring one of them in the face. Liam wanted to know how to weep in Conor's arms but every time he felt a surge to do it, an even stronger surge of stubbornness prevented him. Their farewell was all proper, in the Irish manner. Figures looking small down on the dock. Kids and Mom crying. Liam rigid as a steel rod.

Rory stood on deck with his uncle. Conor slipped him an envelope.

"What's this?"

"A list of books that talk about all the things we never got to talk about. They all say about the same thing. It's a human truth that man can never accept not being free."

"And do any of these books tell me about Ireland?"

"Aye."

"To what avail?" Rory asked. "There is no way I can get them."

"Sure you can. Your friend, Uncle Wally Ferguson, will be receiving them from me. Sorry to do this to your da, but what the hell, I did it to my own da."

"Will you write me, and can I write to you?"

"I will, but remember it could be a real problem, Rory."

"The Irish Republican Brotherhood?"

"Aye. But if you don't hear from me, it's not my choice, but necessity."

"I understand."

"And you must know, I love you very much, Rory."

Liam held up his hand and waved as Rory came down the gangplank. He realized that his brother was taking his son's heart with him back to Ireland and one day his son would go looking for it.

PART THREE

DWELLER ON THE THRESHOLD

CHAPTER

31

Dublin, 1908

Ah Rory lad,

The long way home is done.

Since we all must learn from each journey, I have made discoveries of the utmost importance. My thoughts are far from original, but the journey was new to me. To be homeward bound, no matter what tragic memories you have harbored, is unlike any voyage a man can ever make.

In a manner of speaking Ireland is no different than any other place except a few more sorrows and a few less joys, but Ireland is *my* life, *my* joys and *my* sorrows.

Why is it so, Rory lad? What is the terrible beauty of one's country? The fields are still wretched with rocks, its cities impoverished, its wards filled with cholera and tuberculosis, the justice from its overlords a folly . . . yet, my feet on Irish soil says my goodself and Ireland are one.

My dear cobber, Seamus O'Neill himself, was back from the Boer War to greet me. Himself is a noted journalist and remains an aspiring playwright and a dandy about Dublin.

I found myself now able to speak of the shirt factory fire without half destroying myself. Then came the most gripping of fears, my first trip back to Ballyutogue. One cannot divorce one's self from one's country, and his childhood is the soul of it. I walked through the old cottage and fields and forge in a highly emotional state, and I lingered for many hours at the family graves.

Dear Brigid has become the keeper of our ashes. Your aunt's loveliness has flown. For years my ma wanted to coor her land with our next door neighbor's, the O'Neills. Brigid seems likely to go into a loveless marriage with Seamus's older brother, Colm, a blister of a man, and they'll have acreage to brag over. He's a twit with a smelly old dog at his feet, a smelly old pipe in his mouth, and the smell of booze from his innards. Although there is yet time for Brigid, I'm certain their bed will be barren.

Brother Dary now studies at the big seminary at Maynooth. He will be a people's priest and be loved because he will reason and not oppress. I pray God there is room for him in the Church.

Dary and Seamus and I returned to our lives bittersweet. It has been four decades gone, but the famine still hovers over Ballyutogue.

Aye, the great hunger has made an eternal mark on our people, destroyed dreams, stripped us of our manhood, dispersed our seed. When I left Ireland I saw a broken people, shorn of the will to protest, subjugated, a down-spirited paddy.

But now Dublin bursts with the Gaelic revival. New political parties, parties truly representing Irish longings, have joined the cause.

The most terrifying of my fears are now laid to rest. I feared I would live out my time watching Ireland go from nowhere to nowhere, and the unwritten words as well.

See now, Rory, what I can't tell you about was my chilling meeting with Long Dan Sweeney, who has returned to revive the Irish Republican Brotherhood, of which I am now a secret member.

Ah Rory, Long Dan is the revolution that is! His old face is like candle wax, his skin an unhealthy pallor and his face in crags and slits as too much life on the run will do to a man. Time and

British justice have knocked him about to where he is a cynical eccentric.

I'm bursting to tell you what I can't tell you. Two thousand guns are hidden in England and aye . . . your Uncle Conor has been charged with the mission of smuggling them into Ireland!

Your first dozen books are on the way. Fill yourself with them.

Remember kindly the two major points of my visit. Namely: when your opponent paws with his left jab, you come under him and belt him to the ribs with a right, then duck out of the way always circling right.

Secondly, be tender to the girls. Always make them feel like a queen, particularly after you've made love.

> Your loving uncle,
> *Conor*

CHAPTER

32

If Atty was doing a play, the Wednesday matinee left her free for the evening. Wednesday became the designated family evening, early dinner at the Russell Hotel, a browse in the Trinity library, and a stroll to St. Stephen's Green past the shop windows.

On this Wednesday, Atty was in rehearsal, tense rehearsal. This play was the Abbey Theatre's most ambitious product to date, and as opening night grew near, everyone seemed on edge.

Rachael came in with Emma in tow, waved to their mother on the stage, and found seats. Rachael's seat was near the lobby, where she could sink into her homework. Emma found her place in the third row so as not to miss a syllable.

There was quibbling on the stage. The director tenderly allowed, in carefully couched words, that Atty had been a bitch all day and the leading man concurred. She had been fumbling her lines and had been otherwise unpleasant. Undoubtedly, she was about to begin her period, was having her period, or just getting over her period.

She spruced up at the sight of her girls, gave her leading man a friendly elbow to the ribs, her manner of apologizing, and the director called places.

Again she muffed lines. The director took her aside.

"You're not being very Atty-like," he soothed. "What's the matter, darlin'?"

"I don't know," Atty whispered. "'Twas like I saw a banshee last night. Someone's dead . . . I don't know."

"Want to quit for the day?"

"God, no. Give me five."

"Sure."

She took a chair and wiped a sudden flash of perspiration from her forehead and took a glass of water from a stage assistant. She was dry. The water felt good going down.

Come on, Atty, she prodded herself, you're acting like an old whore.

She came to her feet, but her legs were unsteady. At that instant Theo burst into the theatre gasping and disheveled from a short hard run from the Four Courts.

"It's Da!" he screamed running up to the stage. "It's Da!"

Desmond Fitzpatrick had collapsed of a massive heart attack in the courtroom. By the time the family reached the hospital, he had been pronounced dead. Desmond was a few days short of his thirty-ninth birthday.

The rush of moods that tore through Atty Fitzpatrick solidified into a tight-lipped silence. Bare whispers to friends, bare words to her children. Never had she stood so tall as at the graveside with her children and five thousand stunned Irishmen about her.

Oratory wailed like ancient Gaelic pipes. A kind of sudden loss that shocks, yes, and frightens when a hero has fallen. A subdued wake of the stunned followed at 34 Garville Avenue. Atty remained all but wordless at the outpouring of sympathy.

When it was done, she locked herself in the library on the top floor seeing only Theo, Rachael, and Emma. A fortnight after Des was set down, she returned to the Abbey stage and carried off a performance that threw all Ireland into tears of admiration. She had taken the moment without bravado. . . .

And then she collapsed and retired with the children to Lough Clara.

Had it all been worth it, Des? she begged.

And he answered what he had answered many times before: "We are innocent victims, you and I, of vast compulsions. Insatiable forces squander us. Aye, all men and women battle the forces that create evil, laziness, vanity, lust to conquer, greed to own, hurt others. And all men and women, save you and me, find an accommodation with our compulsions, come to control them, and try to live as normal people. With Des and Atty, it is consumption by a foul ferocity to either win or drop dead in the attempt. We know nothing else. Did we do the right thing by bringing innocent children into our maniacal kingdom?"

She sat with the elegance of a mourning queen before the fireplace and the magic came to her. Theo, Emma, and Rachael did not hunker back in fear. They rallied about, immediate and strong, showing the tough stuff and idealism of their raising. And Atty rallied to them.

Theo had already strolled a bit in his father's shoes and showed the legal claws and brain of his father. He gestured like Des, lashed out with Des's biting wit. He let Atty know that despite her own strength, there was still a man, albeit a young man, in their home. From the outset of Des's death, she knew she would soon have a new soul partner.

Little Rachael was average in size but seemed little when her petite and willowy body stood alongside her statuesque mother. At the moment of grief, Rachael took her mother's lap, not to be held but to comfort. They quickly became the best of friends— indeed, the girlfriend Atty had never known.

Of the three children, Emma presented a soft link. She never truly demonstrated the iron of the other four but played the game, allowing herself to fade in the background of this powerful family. Emma was dolls and girl things. Des's death hit her the hardest, for her adoration of her father was paramount. Mom had always been something beyond her comprehension. Emma dared not come too close for fear of deterring Atty from her resolute determinations. She was a child who always felt second to the movement, and not part of it.

Atty's mother, Lady Charlotte Royce-Moore, had not had a little girl to dote over since Atty had discovered Dublin as a teenager. She traveled immediately to Lough Clara and served as a loving and calming force, although her Anglo mentality had to be overlooked.

Lady Charlotte had been desperately lonely since the death

of her husband. Seeing the family alignment for herself, she suggested to Atty that grandmother and Emma do a tour of the continent with a view that Emma might consider schooling in London.

Reality? Emma was the odd man out. Would Emma benefit more with her grandmother than she would suffer from the loss of her brother and sister, and herself? Atty thought it a good idea because her daughter favored it as well.

Aye, Atty knew Charlotte would lavish on Emma what Atty could never give her. Most possibly the girl sorely longed for it herself. She could see Emma becoming a prim and proper young lady in a social scene that better fitted her.

As for herself and Theo and Rachael, they quickly regrouped. Atty plunged into her work, this time with a powerful and devoted family unit, all whistling the same tune.

CHAPTER

33

Ballyutogue Station
Kowi Junction
Christchurch
South Island
New Zealand

Dear Uncle Conor,

Your tragic departure turned Ballyutogue Station into a graveyard of the living dead. For the first weeks nobody smiled, much less laughed. Then your postal cards began to arrive from various ports of call.

The Squire has had the worst of it, mumbling that he should have tried harder to make you stay but at the same time mumbling that nothing could have kept you. Like six times a day I hear him say under his breath, "Fuck Ireland."

Da looks at me, though I'm just twelve, like I'm going to catch the next ship out of New Zealand. Without speaking, his eyes say to me, "You love your Uncle Conor better than me."

How can I tell him that it is not possible for anyone to love anyone more than they love their parents? I love you more than I knew I could love and I can say so without shame because you told me how grand it is to tell someone you love them. However, I can't love you more than my own father, even if he was an ax murderer. Why can't he realize that?

A fortnight back I was in Christchurch and Uncle Wally

gave me the incredible box of books you sent. He slipped them to me the same way Mr. Ingram slipped them to you. The Squire won't be fooled, but he won't dare take them away from me. I never realized that you can get an actual feeling in the pit of your stomach by just opening the cover of a book. As you suggested, I began with *The Adventures of Tom Sawyer* and *Huckleberry Finn*. What a fellow that Mark Twain is! At first I struggled with the pages, but almost like magic, my eyes started getting words faster and faster and they held me like I was in a grip, clear till I fell asleep reading.

The really wondrous thing about Mr. Twain is that he knows so many things about me and what I'm thinking even though he's never been near New Zealand. He was writing about my own family and particularly the Squire. He told me what you told me, that "if you see yourself in a book, you aren't alone anymore."

I followed your plan of battle on a fellow in school who has been the school bully. I seem to always have to defend the poor, like Robin Hood. Anyhow, he isn't the school bully anymore. Three thumps to the ribs and he left his chin wide open. It was glorious.

I was contemplating commencing sexual activity after my next birthday inasmuch as I'm big for my age and several of the older girls at school know more than their parents think they know. However, having been cautioned by you, I've decided to delay things for a time. But, I have the itch all the time.

Love,
Rory

Nor could Rory write:
I try to read between the lines of your letter and wonder what heroic action you are into. Frankly, I'm thinking very heavily of the day I can be in Ireland and swear allegiance to the Irish Republican Brotherhood.

*   *   *

My Dear Rory,

It fills my heart to know you are reading your ninth book.

Looking up old acquaintances, I was encouraged to try to make the Belfast Boilermaker rugby team. Thanks to that year I played in Australia, your old uncle still has the legs. I'm at the loose head prop position.

It means a fine job at Weed Ship & Iron, and a series of coincidences. Jeremy Hubble is working at his grandfather's yard and is also trying to make the team. He moves very fast and has good nerve.

It appears that he is behind in his studies and will have trouble getting into Trinity College in Dublin. So, I've got me a viscount to tutor on the Midlands rugby tour. I've always cared for this lad and taking him under my wing makes me feel, sometimes, that I've got you with me.

Aye, I saw Caroline. She has aged lovely. There is no denying a love still exists between us and always will. But, our love, from both sides, had always been dream stuff, mystical, untouchable, breakable, dangerous.

I don't know about herself, for women can linger forever in love flown.

She was ethereal, and so long as I was in her spell, I was never fit for a real, live woman. Rory, the moment I saw her I knew I was free for the first time in my life to seek, to fly, to hold without her hovering about me.

Ah, I guess I carried my childhood to extremes but I don't dream quite so much, anymore. Realism has settled in . . . utter realism for my life now demands it. And thank God, with it, I can love a real woman.

I know you're reading right through this, Rory lad. All the coincidences were manufactured by me to get into Weed Ship & Iron and use Sir Frederick Weed's private train, which takes his rugby team on the Midlands tour and might end up carrying Brotherhood guns into Ireland.

Realism! I am a bastard for using Caroline and Jeremy.

Realism! I am of the Irish Republican Brotherhood so that deci-sion became automatic. It came down to a simple logic that I can no longer love Caroline in that way and be a member of the Brotherhood.

A lot of the old dream here changed the day I took the Brotherhood oath. We're playing a rough game now, but as Long Dan Sweeney said, "Nothing we do to gain our freedom can be as evil as those who have denied us our freedom."

Dear Uncle Conor,

It is a good thing you explained to me that a natural and proper step into manhood is masturbation, because I do it quite often now. If you hadn't told me I'd be swimming in guilt and confessing all the time, even though there is nothing to confess. I'm so glad because I got the worst lecture of my life from Father Gionelli about sin and self-abuse. Your advice to me on this matter is the same kind of advice I will give my own son.

As you said, history comes back to haunt. The Squire found my books. He just glared and glared and glared. After glaring, he took his mare up to his bloody hilltop and talked to whoever he talks to up there. Anyhow, Uncle Conor, when he came down from his bloody hilltop he never said a word to me for three weeks.

So you know what I do? I bring a book into the parlor at night and read to myself right in his face. But it doesn't really help. Everyone gets real tense. Besides, I'd rather read in my room, anyhow.

As long as we're talking about books, I think I am ready to go past Jack London and Robert Louis Stevenson, as adventurous as they are. Maybe I'm ready to have a go at Dickens.

I get so knotted up. If only the Squire and me could talk things through. I don't read for the purpose of getting him mad. Anyhow, I store up the utter frustration and sometimes fight with kids I'm not even angry at. Mostly I go after big guys using my increasing left-handed skills. I guess I've got a bad reputation. It seems like only after I've had a fight can I calm down and then the station helps me to be quiet.

Someday, the Squire and I are going to really talk things over, calm-like. Other than that, life is fine, now, just fine.

Love,
Rory

How Rory longed to write what he could not.

Uncle Conor, I hurt to see you again. How I envy Lord Jeremy Hubble. Mind you, I hold him no jealous thoughts. I mean, what a life traveling with you as his tutor and rugby coach. In a manner of speaking, I'm glad you have a young fellow on your hands so you'll never forget me.

And Jaysus, Uncle Conor, all those "coincidences" you write about. Sounds like you're living a great adventure.

CHAPTER
34

SECRET FILES OF WINSTON CHURCHILL

By the time I renounced the Conservative Party I had come to loathe—no, hate men, methods, words, and deeds. These Tories, methinks, are a confederation of corrupted men using aggression abroad in the form of cheap labor for the English millionaire. Although born into this class, and with boundless admiration for my late father, I cannot and will not continue as an upper-class toad.

Within the year, we Liberals under Campbell-Bannerman had swept into Parliament and I accepted my first subcabinet post as Under Secretary for the Colonies.

Rumors of my engagement to the daughter of South African Prime Minister Louis Botha were highly exaggerated. True feelings for the lady were nonexistent.

It was incumbent upon me to find a new constituency to remain in Parliament, and I chose Manchester, which I won rather handily.

During my election campaign I had occasion to be guest of that rather gruff bully Ulsterman, Sir Frederick Weed, who was carting his rugby team about the Midlands. Despite his severe Unionist politics I rather liked this chap and suspected we would be doing business in the future. We recalled our earlier meeting in Hubble Manor, Londonderry, when I was a boy and my father played his now famous "Orange card."

The purpose of my rambling here was that his Boilermaker brutes went on to take our coveted Admiral's Cup back to Ireland, but not before dismantling a brothel in Bradford along the way. Weed's grandson, the Viscount Coleraine, created an enormous and affectionate reputation for his role in the melee. If we had more of the stripe of Weed and Lord Jeremy Hubble, their class would certainly be more palatable. The son-in-law, the Earl of Foyle, Roger Hubble, represents all I abhor.

In my new office I have traveled considerably to the colonies and am rather pleased with the friendship I have developed with my private secretary, Eddie Marsh.

On the other hand I have earmarked for political extinction Sir Frederick Hopwood, whose communication to my boss, Colonial Secretary Lord Elgin, reached my eyes. Among other dastardly remarks he says, "He (meaning me) is most tiresome to deal with and I fear may give trouble—as his father did—in any position to which he may be called. The restless energy, uncontrollable desire for notoriety, and lack of moral perception made him an anxiety, indeed!"

Indeed, indeed! We shall see.

Winston Churchill

Oh, yes, that Ulster-Bradford rugby game was best remembered by my sitting next to Countess Hubble who, somehow, has managed to remain lovely despite her dreary husband. Her scent on that day was divine.

WSC

CHAPTER

35

Rory O'Rory!

How best to tell you this, now? I have found the other half of my half-lived life. She is not what I expected. She sings off-key, which is an insult to my finely tuned sense of melody, she is definitely not redheaded enough, and she prays sitting down, if, indeed, she prays at all, at all. Yet, despite her numerous faults and me own perfection, I've fallen madly, madly in love with her.

Her name is Shelley. She is a Protestant lass from the Shankill district of Belfast, a place that has known hunger, cholera, and lingering destitution. Nowadays shipyard workers live here mostly in wee row houses.

Her brother is captain of the Boilermakers team and her father an old-timer at Weed Ship & Iron. Despite the difference of our persuasions, her family saw the happiness in Shelley's eyes and they accepted me as their son and brother.

Waiting so long has its special rewards. How long have I looked into sterile eyes, into sterile hearts? How shallow the possibilities have been! Now I looked and saw something different, a partner rich to the voice, to the touch, to the sight . . . so rich I cannot fill myself enough of her riches nor can I believe such riches are mine.

My love of Shelley did not come easily. I had to face the fiercest test of my life in learning from her that she had been the mistress of a married man for three years. I felt a monster called jealousy spit out of me. This monster is beyond your capacity to reason with. It consumes you.

Well, lad, I've done a bit of roving and I set me down and explored myself. I had to discard the Irish peasant pride, to overcome the years of the Virgin being pounded into my brain. Shelley told me before we made love that she would not start with a lie, that I must know that when she spoke I was always hearing truth.

She was a poor girl who fought her way to a decent station in life against all odds. In the end, there was nothing to forgive or forget. Why shouldn't two people have found love with each other to escape the misery of Belfast as she had done? So I grew up very fast, Rory, for the thought of losing her was so staggering I would not inflict it on myself and I am the most fortunate man alive.

We go through our nights intertwined. We are in sorrow when we part for the day and follow bliss when we sight one another after work. Happiness is always around us when we are in each other's aura.

I know now that Ireland can only own part of me. How we will contend with it is our mystery.

We are keenly aware we may be doomed from the onset. Can I live with one foot in the Brotherhood and one in a pretense of living a normal life with her? Can we ever know peace from the Orange fanatics? For the first time I also question my unalterable march from childhood to a life in the patriot's game. Can I hold two such loves?

In time I will have to go underground and live life on the run. Can I condemn her to desperate meetings in squalid hideaways with bedsprings poking through and bedbugs having a meal off our hides? Can I ask a woman to live in fear of every knock on the door?

Well, Rory lad, I'm off on the Midlands tour, but that's not the half of it. I have earmarked Sir Frederick Weed's private train and engine to smuggle guns back to Ireland. Once the tour

is over and the first batch moves out of Bradford, the door to any
life outside the Brotherhood is closed.

Meeting Shelley this late in the game has now put a serious
sting into my commitment. The thought pounds at me that
although I was unable to live outside Ireland before I met her, I
think I can live anywhere in the world with her at my side. This
taunts the life from me, day and night.

From the Midlands Tour

Dear Rory!

For the first time in Ireland's long and tormented history, we
have won the Admiral's Cup. Aye, the Belfast Boilermakers
cleaned out one hairy and foul bunch of ruggers after another
and your old uncle did right well by you. All that's left now
is for us to come "down under" and clean out the All-Blacks.
I hope you're on the team when I come!

By Jaysus, in city after city they fell to us like shallow-
rooted trees in a tropical hurricane.

Here's a story to warm your heart. Robin MacLeod,
Shelley's brother and captain of the team, was my roommate
and between us we kept a hold on Jeremy in an adjoining
room. As you know I was boning the lad up for his entrance
exams to Trinity College in Dublin. He played extremely
well and was a factor in us winning the cup. Not a stuffy hair
on his head. He could have been a miner's son for all anyone
knew and won the admiration of all the beasts he has for
teammates.

His grandfather, Sir Frederick Weed, the team owner,
traveled with us off and on, with much finer accommodations. So I let Jeremy spend the odd night with his grandda,
and the little devil ends up consorting with prostitutes and
thought he was in love with one of them.

After we sorted that out I put him under lock and key.
However, ,there was a celebration to end all celebrations
when we won the cup. Jeremy jumped ship on me, stuffing
his bed with pillows and shinnying three stories down on the

drain pipe. While I slept, the team ended up in a brothel when the losing squad, the Bradford Bulls, arrived on the scene. A rank nationalistic insult was made and a monumental piss-up followed.

Lord Jeremy and most of the Boilermakers were jailed and the press treated it as though it were the second passing of Queen Victoria.

Caroline, after initial fury, saw the humor in the situation, and Sir Frederick was rather proud that his grandson would be a hero on entering Trinity. However, Lord Roger didn't see it that way. He slapped the boy in a rage, humiliating him beyond reason. My own da, Tomas, struck me once over the books, as you know. That happened a quarter of a century ago and I can still feel the blow.

So, me lad, it seems that fathers and sons have their go, no matter what the circumstances of their birth or wealth or station. Younger brother, Christopher, is a snotty little prick, the apple of his father's eye.

Our relationship with our parents is the eternal devilment of the human race. There is no way that the new generation can really learn from the old. Each boy and girl must make his own unique and perplexing journey into a relationship that ends with its own unique solution. And oftentimes, we must spend the second half of our life getting over the first half.

Every time I see Jeremy Hubble I pretend also that I am with my nephew Rory a half-dozen years up the line, hoisting a few at the bar, keeping you from consorting with prostitutes, and scraping the mud and blood of the rugby pitch off ye.

So there we are, Rory lad. The Admiral's Cup and Lord Jeremy were the joy of it. Shelley came over for holiday and when she leaves the gunrunning starts. She does not know of the scheme. And now, the quandary. I love this woman so desperately that believing there could be a life of peace with her away from Ireland is driving me near insane. Before there was Shelley

*there was never really a thought of life for me that didn't end up
with the Brotherhood.*

Shelley MacLeod got one whiff of Conor's wild notion to
flee Ireland and in the instant of euphoria, she agreed. By daylight, her senses had returned. If they ran, the Conor Larkin she
loved would be no more. He would turn into a shallow shell of
himself and soon be overcome by self-hatred. She knew, in the
light of day, the world was too small for them to hide in. Even
their wonderment and their love could not come between an
Irishman and his dream.

What was once love would grow rancid in a year or two of
never mentioning Ireland. She would have to watch him die in
pieces.

Conor refused to take her into the suffering and dead-end
life needed of a rebel boy's woman.

They returned to Belfast separately, in misery.

Letters and books to Rory became less frequent. Rory, who
could all but feel Conor halfway around the world, was so keen
that he figured out what had probably taken place.

CHAPTER

36

1908

The gunrunning scheme moved along flawlessly, recording trip after trip to and from Belfast and Liverpool without a hitch. Something other than departed souls were being dug under in many a village graveyard.

Having set up the route, the English side of it no longer required Conor's presence. Claiming age and injuries, he resigned from the Boilermaker team.

At first Sir Frederick would not hear of it, but finally relented. In truth, he knew the Boilermakers would not win the Admiral's Cup again for many years. Moreover, Jeremy was now in Trinity College and no longer a player.

Conor's forge inside Weed Ship & Iron became a source of a great deal of information for the Brotherhood, most of it distressing. It appeared as though Weed and the Orange crowd were able to smuggle in a *hundred* guns for every one the Brotherhood managed. Moreover, regular British officers were training the Ulster Volunteers, while the government turned a blind eye.

Although it was a comfortable period, Long Dan Sweeney had an itch that would not go away. A standoff bitterness had set in between him and Conor, who now seemed to be in a permanent state of melancholy.

Dan knew that Conor no longer saw the Shelley MacLeod girl and wondered if and why a man's love could bite so deeply.

To Dan, nothing reached the innards except the movement. A blip of pain, certainly. But not a republican of Larkin's stature, groomed by grandfather and great-grandfather. Yes, there were fools who went down, but Conor Larkin was no fool. Why the hell couldn't he shake it!

Dan encouraged more visits north by Seamus O'Neill, who was Conor's only confidant. Each time Seamus returned from Belfast it was with the same general report.

"Your pal, Larkin, seems to have contracted an abiding case of the red ass," Dan growled at Seamus in a hideaway south of Dublin in the Wicklow foothills. "I don't look forward to seeing him up in Belfast anymore."

"I'll tell him you need to be treated with the respect due one's commander—you know, Dan, like you were a British Colonel in the Sudan."

"Something's gone wrong with him. He used to make me break up laughing."

"Ask him, then."

"Hell, I know why. He busted up with that girl. They came back from England separately. He's been in a dire mood ever since, isn't that right, Seamus? That's what it is, isn't it?"

"I don't rat on my pal."

"There are no secrets from me," Dan demanded.

Seamus shrugged and poured tea. "Jaysus, Dan, you'd be real easy to find. All you have to do is pick up your trail of dirty teacups. Just because you're a revolutionary doesn't mean you can't wash your teacups. You've dirty teacups in every hideaway house you've been in."

Dan calmed down before his unbowed soldier. "You see, lad, I went and made a basic mistake with Larkin. I let sentiment cloud my judgment. I have developed an unmistakable affection for the man, and that is a mistake. Once I developed a great affection for a man, Richie Leary. Turned out to be an informer. I had to shoot him myself, both kneecaps. Not that anything like that will ever happen with Conor ... it's just that you can't develop an affection."

"Sometimes you can't help it, can you, Dan?"

"Forget the fucking personality involvement. I need Conor Larkin, and you are going to need him when I'm gone. I see him as our future chief of staff. We can't have this vinegar between us."

"He broke up with this woman when they were in Blackpool," Seamus said.

"He almost didn't come back to Ireland, isn't that right, Seamus? I know how a man behaves after he's made plans to make a run for it."

"He came back, didn't he?"

"Half of him came back. I need all of him."

"It isn't always that easy. So, you figure it out. Conor's got a broken heart."

"I'd figured it out thirty years ago, Seamus. The movement is always a swim upstream against treacherous currents, without ever reaching your destination. Too swift to drag someone along with you . . . it will pull you both under. I've seen a hundred smart lads think they could handle both the Brotherhood and a life outside it. I warned him of that, Seamus. Christ, she's not even a Catholic girl. She hasn't a drop of the movement in her blood. She's from the Shankill and her old man and brother are drum-thumping Orangemen. Damnit, Seamus, I gave him a choice to leave the Brotherhood in peace. It was him who chose to stay."

Long Dan was reminiscing sharply. It was a hundred Conors and Shelleys. Maybe a hundred and one. "Conor playing something out of your own past, Dan?"

Dan reacted as though he had been struck. His old eyes turned teary, a weird sight. "Her name was Aileen. Aileen O'Dunne. I don't remember exactly what she looked like, but I'll never get over how she felt. The Brits stashed me away the first time when I was sixteen. I met her right after I got out. I was twenty-something. We all march through the same ten miles of shit . . . weeping at O'Connell's grave . . . reciting speeches from the dock as kids . . . even writing more bad poetry. . . . See, we all walk the same ten miles of shit."

"Weird breed, aren't we, Dan?"

"If you love a woman, you cannot take her into a life of her waiting with every tick of the clock to find out if your head's been blown off . . . then creeping through alleys to a room in a hideaway . . . smelling of the damp. And oh, the fucking tears you have to stuff inside until the next glorious meeting. It didn't work then and it won't work now. It's a decision we all have to come to. Later makes it that much more desperate. With the kind of commitment a Conor Larkin makes, keeping a girl he loves so much is a one-way dead-end road to tragedy."

"What can I say, Dan? He doesn't see her anymore."

"When the hell is he going to get over it? We all got to get over it, you know."

It was Seamus's turn to feel the grief. "You'd better know the man you're dealing with in Conor," he said softly.

"Who is this Larkin anyhow, Jesus?"

"He's no Jesus. He's used the Hubbles to a fare-thee-well, and he'll pull the trigger when he needs to. Don't question his steel."

"What then? Irishmen's poems to their colleens are a large load of bullshit. It's putrid, childish sentiment, that's what."

"You'd better know the man you're dealing with," Seamus repeated.

"There is obviously something I don't understand. Would you be after telling me about it, Seamus?"

"Conor and I go back forever," Seamus said. "And forever, nothing of beauty has ever escaped his eye. No leaf, no sound, no drop of rain, no sweet word, no scent. He finds beauty in thunderheads and raging seas, and never a woman has he seen or touched did he not find beauty in. Along with his ravenous craving for knowledge and his fury against injustice, this man has gathered in beauty more fully than any human being I know or have ever heard of. Aye, he'd match Jesus in that department.

"All his life he has held that beauty, giving some to everyone, but never finding the right woman to entirely lavish it on.

"Shelley MacLeod is a wonderment of her own. She has the capacity for this man. I suppose what the two of them discovered was something beyond our universe of comprehension. Don't you know, Dan, I'd chop off ten years of my life to know ten minutes of what they had for each other. It was so intense, it's small wonder the both of them didn't shatter like a smashed glass . . . that the man came back to us needs no further comment on his loyalty to the movement."

"Can a man really love so?" Dan pondered.

"Conor Larkin can, and I'd rather see them take their death vows and be together for whatever time is in it for them than kill each other this way."

"Is the lad ever going to come back to us, really?"

"Never fully. Never even partly until something fills some of the void in him."

Strange, Seamus thought, how delicately Long Dan holds his teacup when he is thinking deeply. Why, even his little finger is curled.

"Do you think it's time he was introduced to Atty?"

"In actual fact," Seamus said, "I've been pondering along the same lines. Atty Fitzpatrick can never replace Shelley. But, by God, there's a woman of his power, and perhaps, praise Mary, she can find the capacity to receive love. She never had it from Des, you know."

"I thought as much."

"Even if his void . . . and her void . . . can be partly filled it might be something awesome to behold."

"I never been much in this area," Dan said, "but it seems something like this has to work or we'll lose him. Even your man Conor, Jesus or no, can't keep going like this."

CHAPTER
37

For the greatest occasion of her life Brigid Larkin was garbed in store-bought clothes from Derry that might never come out of the closet again. Brigid and what she was wearing were strangers giving one another no comfort at all. She crossed the bridge from the old city to the train station arriving with a limp from the pinch of her new shoes.

This was to be her first train ride. Thoughts of going clear down to Dublin was enough to make even the most educated of travelers tremble.

She asked about the arrival of her train twice and then a third time to make absolutely certain. She could tell the stationmaster was a Protestant, but kindly to her situation, having seen a number of first-time riders come down from the hills over the years.

"Your first trip, now, is it?"

"Aye," she answered bashfully.

"I'll see you safely aboard, miss," the trainman said.

"That's very kind of ye, indeed."

"How far are you traveling?"

"Dublin."

"That's a few yards down the road."

"Actually I'm going to Maynooth. My brother is going to be ordained this Sunday."

Just what the fucking country needs, the stationmaster thought, another fucking R.C. collar. "Ah, that will be a big day for you. The Great Northern will be along in fifteen minutes. It's never late in or out of Londonderry."

Brigid sat gingerly on the genuine imitation leather suitcase loaned to her by the Widow Dougherty. Fifteen minutes passed. It was announced that the Great Northern for Dublin would be a half-hour late, more or less.

From the train platform in Protestant Waterside, Brigid could see across the River Foyle to Catholic Derry and its waterfront lined with piers and shirt factories.

The old Witherspoon & McNab factory destroyed in the fire was no longer on the skyline, leaving an ugly gap like an extracted tooth.

Brigid had been down to Derry twice before. Once, when the linen crop failed, she and hundreds of other farm girls had to hire themselves out as domestics to earn tuppence. They stood like herded cattle in the Guildhall Square with prospective employers feeling their muscles and examining their teeth as if they were horses.

"We expect you to put in an honest fourteen hours a day, Brigid. You don't steal, do you, Brigid? And no fornicating with the help, Brigid."

Bogside was the place where all dreams tarnished.

After a lifetime of conniving, her mother, Finola, had succeeded in breaking her up with her only true love, Myles McCracken. True, part of it was Brigid's own fear of leaving Ballyutogue to go with him to Derry.

As she had told him on that sorrowful day, "Once a lad leaves Ballyutogue, he never returns." Myles's family was so poor, they couldn't give you the dirt off their necks, they'd need it for topsoil. He was landless, and that wasn't in Finola's plans for her daughter.

Myles might have stayed because all the other Larkin boys were gone or going, but her daddy Tomas clung to the fantasy that Conor might return so there could be a Larkin name on the farm.

Myles followed Conor down to Derry and later worked for Conor in his forge. Brigid had come to fetch Conor when Daddy was taken to the sickbed.

Brigid lowered her eyes for an instant from the waterfront view. She recalled, as she arrived in Derry, how impure thoughts had entered her head. If Daddy died and she married Myles and he made her pregnant right away, Finola would have to accept them because there was no other Larkin to run the farm. Dary was now in the seminary, Conor in his forge in Derry, and Liam all the way gone to New Zealand. . . .

Brigid began to breathe unevenly as the door of memory was kicked open. . . . She had come for Myles McCracken too late. He had married and was on his way to fatherhood. Over there, across the river, was the gaping hole where the factory had stood. It was where Myles's wife, Maud, leapt from the burning roof and their unborn child and its mother were splattered all over the cobblestones. . . .

Myles degenerated into a Bogside drunk, and later Conor had to commit him to the asylum. Myles hanged himself in a moment of sanity when he clearly remembered Maud jumping from the roof. . . .

The trainmaster picked up the genuine imitation leather suitcase and led Brigid to a compartment much fancier than her ticket price. He slipped her an extra coupon.

"For your first ride, you should have the window view all the way, miss." He placed her suitcase in an overhead bin.

"Bless you, sir."

Every sound and movement of it was new as the Great Northern belched and grunted from the station into a smooth *clickety-clack . . . clickety-clack.*

A dozen deep sighs quelled her uneasiness and she became mesmerized by the sway of the train and the way the fields and cottages fleeted past her. Alone in the compartment, Brigid dared open the wicker basket, take a slice of soda bread, and nibble on it.

With Myles McCracken dead, her mother's crusade was half done. She had saved Brigid from a pauper's marriage to a landless boy. She would never live to see the second part of her conspiracy of having Brigid marry a man with land, even a widower with kids, or, mainly, Colm O'Neill with the adjoining farm.

Finola's deeply honed sense of sin crept up on her. When Dary had been born, her physical state for childbearing was wrecked. She obeyed the priest to live as "brother and sister" with Tomas, with no further fornication. This sense of sin was triggered again by the tragic fate of Myles McCracken. She hid her guilt from Brigid and only in the end did she confess to the priest, but the rest of her life was an attempt to atone for her sin of sending Myles off. Finola held on to her secret as she took her last breaths looking into Brigid's eyes.

Clickety-clack . . . clickety-clack . . . clickety-clack . . .

The door to her compartment was flung open. "Strabane!" the conductor called.

Brigid became caught up watching a family on the platform, obviously a mom and da trying to say good-bye to an awkward clod of a son. He seemed to be a bit like Liam. All three of them were ill at ease. Da was rigid. Ma was holding back tears. The clod shifted feet, and then good solid handshakes and a flashlike peck on the cheek from son to mother.

Two new passengers invaded her compartment diminishing her space. One of them was the clod, who seemed wanting to weep but not exactly knowing how. He roughly jammed his suitcase in the overhead next to hers. He'd better not mess up my ordination dress, Brigid growled to herself. It had been sewn with devotion for Dary.

The train bolted unevenly, tossing the clod into her. He said, "Sorry," and she said, "That's just fine" and later, "I'm going to Maynooth. My brother is going to be ordained." The clod was a Catholic and would know just how important that was. The clod had a brother who was a priest as well. That's all they said for the next several hours.

"Tickets, now. Next stop, Omagh."

God, Brigid thought, look at the land out there, would you! So smooth and rolling. So Protestant. Why, she might as well be halfway around the world it was so different from the hill farms of Ballyutogue. Liam probably had land of this sort. I hope the dress is not rumpled, she thought. Does it really matter?

✶   ✶   ✶

Brigid was never a beauty, but she had enough Larkin in her to be very pretty at times. And she had a spark, so long as Myles was around. When he left, she spent her remaining love on her baby brother Dary. But Dary left as well. Most men leave. After Dary she was alone in the cottage with Finola and the lovelessness of her life crashed down. She slipped into drabness. She hated herself for entertaining a persistent and nagging thought that life would be much better if her mother simply up and died. Brigid confessed to this time and again and after each admission, her rancor toward her mother deepened.

The cycle of wanting her mother dead, the guilt of it, the confession, and the penance became a treadmill of existence.

Clickety-clack . . . clickety-clack . . . clickety-clack . . .

"Omagh! Yer next stop is Omagh!"

The clod was replaced by a mom and two squawking wanes and a grinning old nun. Every time Brigid saw a nun, the notion passed through her that she might have missed her own calling. But she would have never felt how Myles made her feel . . . even though it always stopped short of total and absolute fornication.

After a time it became more and more difficult to remember what Myles even looked like. She all but forgot the sweet sensations that flooded through her when she dashed over the bridge into his arms at their secret meeting place by the Norman keep. As the years passed it was as though Myles never really existed, because the pain of his loss was gone as well. As Myles faded, hatred for her mother faded.

Brigid Larkin became resigned to spinsterhood, being able neither to love nor hate anymore with any notable passion.

At this very moment she felt a twinge as she remembered that Dary was going to be ordained Sunday!

Dary becoming a priest was the centerpiece of Finola's life since his birth. Now, Finola was being cheated from the great moment. Was it God's vindication? Brigid would be in her mother's place and her mother would be looking down with bitter envy.

*   *   *

Eight miles out of Derry where the bridge crossed the river Burntollet, a side road wound up onto a wooded crest to the walled confines of the Sacred Heart Seminary of the Holy Order of the Fathers of St. Columba.

"He's so tiny," Finola had wept, "so tiny and frail."

Dary Larkin was among eight novices passing through forbidden gates. For the most part they were smooth of cheek and soft of hand, indicating they had been lorded over by their adoring mothers. Some, like Dary, had come eagerly to begin a twelve-year road to priesthood.

Dary gave up all his possessions save his rosary beads and was assigned to an eight-by-eleven-foot cell in an isolated building that housed twenty other novices. It would be his home for the next four years: stone floor and musty odor, with only the crucifix on the wall and a faded picture of the Sacred Heart as his companions.

On the novices' first day they met the consecrated brothers who were teachers from the Christian Brothers Order. They were issued a terse command to genuflect as the wizened old monsignor entered the assembly room. In uninspired monotone, he told them why they were there and what would be expected of them, never really seeing the faces that held an august glow or were frozen with apprehension. Dogmas of poverty, chastity, and obedience were imparted, equally void of passion, stringent rules clipped out, and a chronicle of long hours and complete devotion tolled.

The machinery that moved the seminary operated on few spoken words, and these spoken in hushed tones. The nod and the beckon gave all movement in the place a sense of flotation.

The rosary was recited with fervent ejaculations; the menu varied by season, not much, always bad; the hours of classical education were an endurance battle and humility incarnate. God was beseeched in states of barefooted prostration with limitless prayer.

The young lieutenants of Christ were being exquisitely cloned and honed in ancient tradition. While traditional, accepted, and unchallenged knowledge was being poured in, at the same time the desire for inquiry beyond Church teachings was being masked off. Once the mind was completely trained to be obedient within the framework of the teachings, and curiosity outside the framework shut down, the image of the priest began to be created.

Evil thoughts are no less a sin than evil deeds. The good priest must know the line where dogma forbids questioning and never cross it. When approaching that line, the mind must automatically switch off further adventuring. Thought control imposed so that one controls one's own thoughts ... aye ... that's the game. ...

At first Dary Larkin's small size caused both novices and the Brothers to attempt intimidation. The lad had Larkin steel and was soon singled out as the strongest among them.

Dary had told Conor that he could never be a Conor, to wade through life's battles slashing and fighting the republican cause. Yet, he was a Larkin and had to find the way to help alleviate the misery of the people with his own kind of strength.

Why, Dary wondered, does part of the family consider it a tragedy when one enters the priesthood?

"There are no locks on the seminary gate," he told Conor. "I want to be here. I am at peace."

Dary, impassioned, told his beloved brother that he boiled just as much over the injustices of Ireland and intended to do something about it in his own way.

And Conor snarled, "Someday, Dary, you'll walk through Bogside with me and understand."

"Someday, God willing," Dary answered, "I'll be a Bogside priest."

Clickety-clack ... clickety-clack ... clickety-clack ...

Outside the train, the sun failed. It was always in a battle in Ireland and generally lost. Mists and shadows and dew framed the landscape like spider webs. The Great Northern engine shifted into a slowing mode, squealing and hissing, then inched into a lay-by and stood.

Beyond the lay-by was a village church and a graveyard. Brigid became transfixed by the tombstones. There was nothing there to compare with the Larkin plot in St. Columba's in Ballyutogue, always fresh with flowers and crowned with magnificent, highly polished stones she had bought with money sent from Liam and Conor. Why, everyone said that Brigid kept the finest family plot in Donegal. . . .

For years Brigid and Finola invoked a ghastly emptiness on the cottage as each went to their separate corners, as if each had taken monastic vows of silence. Later, Rinty Doyle became the hired hand and slept in the byre and made himself as inconspicuous as possible.

Brigid's heart pounded with a sudden rush from a westbound train, terrifying her with its abrupt appearance. Faces in the passing window blurred . . . then, quickly as it had arrived, passed . . . again revealing the village graveyard.

The Great Northern inched out of the lay-by, the tombstones seemed to remain reflected on the window.

Of the Larkin sons, only Dary was in Ireland and able to come up from Maynooth Seminary for his mother's funeral.

The cairn was over her mother's grave and the last prayer intoned and the last wail of the pipe faded. Brigid stood before the cottage door for an eternity before she opened it, ever so slowly. It was hers now. The farm was hers. After all the manipulation and hells and wars. It was hers now, every lace spread, every gleaming pot, every featherbed, creepie, jug, harness, and even the recollections.

Her eyes played over the room. The seat closest to the fire would be her own, and all the pans would be scrubbed to a shine they never owned before. The benches and crane in the fireplace and the churn and weaver's lightholders were her own. Tomorrow, she'd walk through the fields counting up all that was hers.

Brigid made from room to room, touching, fondling her possessions, patting down the quilts, brushing away specks of gathering dust, nipping off lint.

She came to her parents' bedroom and stood at the foot of the birth bed of herself and her brothers, edged onto the side of it, lay back, and buried herself in the softness of the great comforter and closed her eyes as tears filled them.

"Oh Myles," she whispered, "if only you'd have waited. . . ."

"Dublin, next stop Dublin, Aimens Street Station. Wake up, miss."

"What!"

"We've arrived in Dublin, darlin'. We'll be at the station in a blink."

CHAPTER
38

The mighty chapel of St. Patrick's in Maynooth was a hymn to Roman Catholic grandeur, crafted by thousands of hands over a half-century. The Stahluhut organ vibrated the grounds announcing the parade of young men in blinding white robes as five hundred voices of the choir crescendoed the omnipotence of the Almighty. The bishop enthroned called for the deacon to summon forth the candidates.

Brigid wrung her already soppy handkerchief, ill at ease so far from Ballyutogue, feeling insignificant in the majesty of the surroundings, yet filled with a sense of euphoria she had never known, not even with Myles McCracken. She had traveled far for this walk in God's splendor, and vengeance against her mother had not even entered her head on this day.

Seamus O'Neill, though a republican journalist and secret member of the Brotherhood, was not cynical. The O'Neill family had not suffered the wrath of the Church as had the Larkin men.

Seamus had an off-view of the Church, but like many who held an off-view, he remained a slave to childhood rote and superstitions— "Don't take God lightly, just to be on the safe side."

Whatever bitter views Seamus held, he bent to them. The voice of his mother, though long departed, continued to command him to Sunday Mass more than he cared to admit.

Although this moment hardly reflected the simplicity and humility of Jesus, a people's rabbi, Conor accepted the grandeur

as a needed carnival to brighten the drab lives of the parish of
Ireland. The cathedral was wrong and distasteful for the parish
of impoverished Ireland, but somehow the Irish scarcely
resented it.

Conor was satisfied that Dary had become a priest on his
own and would have chosen priesthood with or without his
mother's obsession. And Father Dary would be the best of what
priesthood had to offer, what with his gentle capacity to charm a
mockingbird from its limb onto his shoulder, yet a man of
Larkin steel, within.

At the altar the priests droned through the saints, A to Z,
and Conor felt a contentment that Dary had found a higher
value to life. Why not even envy Dary at this moment?

Conor's separation from Shelley had all but ground him to
dust.

As his brother was called forward and asked if he was ready
and Dary prostrated himself, Conor felt bittersweet but with no
reason to rail against the moment.

Brigid wept . . . Conor wondered. Seamus? Well, there were
good priests and not such good priests. Seamus hoped the
Church knew the value of the man giving his promise.

Things had been wobbly between Dary and his brother since
Conor returned to Ireland and joined the Brotherhood. From
his earliest days in the seminary, Dary was keen but cautious to
try to sway Conor from active republicanism, not because of the
rights and wrongs of it, but because Dary didn't want Conor to
end up reliving the Larkin legacy of misery or to end up hanging
from the end of a British rope.

By the time Conor returned to Ireland, Dary had been singled out during those five years as a very special prospect. Early
on, Dary had opted for a missionary order for life among the
lepers in those places that only an Irish priest would go. He was
among a half-dozen candidates chosen for special African studies
under the mentorship of a brilliant priest, Father George
Mooney, whose own health had been devoured in the tropics.

Father Mooney was suddenly named the new Bishop of

Derry. The previous bishop had been installed a decade earlier to stamp out a rise of liberalism among Derry's priests, but after the shirt factory fire, the place continued to wallow in despair.

It was believed that a bit of controlled liberalism might be in order again to get Derry and the Bogside back into the faith.

The loss of Father Mooney hit hard at Dary Larkin. The Father was a teacher painful to lose. Dary sulked a lot and, each time Conor visited him, took out his own frustration on his brother. On Conor's last visit, a few months before the ordination, the brothers went at each other with verbal bombast for the first time in their lives.

"What good has eight hundred years of risings and bloodshed accomplished?" Dary demanded.

"And what good has eight hundred years of prayer done?" Conor retorted. "I'll not have you passing judgments on what I've chosen for life any more than I'm passing judgments on you, Dary."

"If you stay in the Brotherhood and keep up the way of the gunman, I'll not be there for you," Dary said, astonished at the furious rage of his own words.

"Well," Conor had answered, "that's a good old Irish family for you."

The chilling Mass of Ordination was done. Brigid was off to see the sights of Dublin with Seamus O'Neill. Conor had been somewhat dazed throughout the whole ceremony, and now, his apprehension was clear.

Conor tilted his chair back as Dary packed his suitcases silently. Of course there was the faded photograph of their mother taken at some long forgotten county fair.

"She was sorely missed today," Conor said.

"She was there," Dary answered.

"Aye, so she was."

Both of them ground their teeth. There had never been friction between Dary and Conor, as there had been between other factions within the family. The two were always strongly together. They had no unspoken conversations, for they had set down their innermost secrets of each other and spoke openly and decently of their differences.

Now the chill of Irish family acrimony was about to settle unless they could head it off.

"How long before you're off to England to get your doctorate?"

"I'm not going to England," Dary answered.

"But your African studies, now?"

"That's all changed."

"When did this come about?"

"When George Mooney was named Bishop of Derry. I didn't need much convincing that there was enough misery in Bogside without going halfway around the world to find it."

"Aye, that's a fact. But, so sudden a turn?"

"Maybe it wasn't all that sudden. We all come back to Ireland, don't we, Conor? So why bother to go in the first place if I'm only coming back? Bishop Mooney needs me badly."

"You told me once a long time ago you were sporting to become a Bogside priest."

"Obviously I revere the man. Poor old dear is in wretched health. Anyhow, things have not been right in Derry for all those years since the fire. Some sort of eternal ugliness has fallen over the place."

The news hit Conor like a sudden rumble of thunder on the horizon. He shook his head. "If you're thinking of changing things," Conor said carefully, "you might be in for a bitter experience. If Bishop Mooney fosters any such notions, he could have a short reign."

"Bogside and Derry have bottomed out. They need a temporary liberal there now. They know Mooney's not going to last very long in his state of health."

"And you realize this, and you're still willing to go?"

"Let's talk, Conor," Dary said suddenly, and it meant what it meant. Dary's eyes were not those of an eager young novice ready and willing to be flailed and stuffed out there. Father Dary was a man, years ahead of his time.

"I was hoping to God we'd break our logjam, Dary."

"My big problem was that I had a big brother whose eagerness to fill his mind drove him so that he became no man's fool. I always wondered what you were reading, where you were hiding your books. But I also knew there was a fork in the road for us and I would not tempt myself.

"The first four years of seminary went diligently into the creation of the robot. But I came to Maynooth realizing that a huge void had formed in me as I became more and more disciplined. We make that transition from the child who can never be wrong about anything to the young man converted into blind obedience ... and then ... we come to a manhood of inquiry. This is a dangerous moment for the Church and the priest alike. We've a threshold, where a dweller lives and the dweller demands to know. Is the dweller a demon, a monster, or just a fine old fellow? And here we run into the mightiest of power, our teachers, who are watching each student's dweller to see to it the dweller does not cross the threshold."

"Why?"

"That something might have been lost in translation between God's lips and the Pope's ear. There are things that the Church knows but will not tell us. If our faith is so weak we cannot be trusted to know, then we will be weak priests. I believe I am strong enough to know any truth and become a better priest."

"For God's sake, Dary, you were just ordained today."

"Aye, Conor, aye. I must follow unanswered questions to their resolution and that will only make me stronger."

"Don't you know you can't beat the system?" Conor said.

"You're a fine one to be telling me that," Dary retorted. "I know the moral code God intended for man. I also know that things have been imposed to fit the human politics that have nothing to do with God's morality."

"Mooney taught you that?"

"What Mooney taught me was that when we go to Africa as missionaries we must give up the notion of being strangers imposing our civilization on theirs. Look what the British have tried to do—destroy our Celtic translation of Catholicism and superimpose their own version of it. Each Catholic society—

black, yellow, brown, white—has its own version of Catholicism, some of it a blatant blend of Christianity and paganism. It is not absolute, because it changes and bends and yields throughout history against a Vatican entrenched to maintain the status quo."

"Status quo." Conor laughed. "Now, there's a line our daddy used to describe the British plans for Ireland. And just what do you think you're going to do about it, wee Dary?"

"Oh, Rome is the largest and oldest and most powerful game the world has ever known, and my presence will not be remembered. But my people will love me as a wise and compassionate priest."

"You were so certain that the dogma was infallible, once. What changed you, Dary?"

"You changed me, Conor. The deeper I went into the priesthood, the louder your words called to me. The shirt factory fire changed me. I went to Derry as a novice to help after the carnage and I saw their private hells, but I was unable to do anything about it. For two years now, I've asked myself over and over, how can I give up earthly things without even knowing what they are ... what is it that I'm to be giving up? I must be able to confront earthly matters on the other side of the threshold. Isn't that really what God wants of me?"

Where would this awakening take him, Conor wondered. Would he become a paragon among his fellows or a pariah to be cast out? Once a priest takes the forbidden fork in the road, it is near impossible for him to retrace his steps. Few do.

"Conor, you must never forget the fact that I am a priest and I am not going to be involved in republican matters. I told you that if you did not leave the Brotherhood I would not be there for you. I've never rested well since those words. I am a Larkin and an Irishman and your brother. I'll be there for you."

"You don't know how much that means to me."

"You see, man, I do have faith. Our father and our grandfather needed to come to God in the end. I'm not counting on you. However, I'm not counting you out."

"I understand," Conor said, loving his brother more profoundly at this moment than ever.

"Well, now," Dary continued, "what about yourself? That Shelley girl still has her spell over you, hasn't she?"

"I forget about her more each day."

"To hell you do. If you could see the look on your face, they grew better-looking potatoes during the famine."

Conor leapt from the chair, jammed his hands in his pockets, and paced, turning abruptly at the confines of the small room as though it were a cage. Dary knew his brother was about to burst.

"We're a hell of a lot alike, you and me. We've both taken sacred vows to unyielding institutions where marching orders are to be obeyed. Our lives cannot be normal lives with normal aspirations. We'll spend them in barren little rooms like this trying to infuse a spark of hope in the hopeless. And we both travel farther and faster without human baggage. You see, the Irish Republican Brotherhood all but demands an army of celibates as well."

"This sounds like your decision, not hers."

"What decision was there to make? To have her follow me to her death?"

"It could be that that is all she desires from life. From the looks of you, life holds no hell worse than the two of you being apart. If she is as miserable as you are, and I suspect she is, then you'll both die early from longing for each other. You must take what pleasure there is for you and hold on to each other while it lasts."

Conor was stopped cold and for the first time he was the younger brother in need of Father Dary's strong hand.

"The way you're flirting with it, it could happen to you, Dary."

"No, it won't," Dary answered firmly. "I'm daring to venture because I am determined to know the difference between what God means and what man distorts. This much I believe entirely. Celibacy is a truth of the Church. I cannot serve a woman and divide my commitment to God. I know that."

"Aye, so you do, and you're strong enough to stop that temptation at the threshold."

CHAPTER
39

The big night had come and gone for Seamus O'Neill. His play, *The Night of the Pilgrim*, had not only made it to the Abbey Theatre but marked the return of Atty Fitzpatrick, in widowhood, to the stage.

The play was neither stop nor go, but it had some sparkling moments, including a stirring soliloquy near the final curtain, a speech from the dock, no less, that never failed to mist up every Irish eye that saw it.

Atty's return from mourning for Des was no less moving. In this time Seamus had the opportunity of working with her on the script and seeing her at Brotherhood Council meetings.

Each Council gathering continued to report another successful run of guns into Ireland. Atty could not help but become intrigued by the skill and daring of the now mysterious Conor Larkin.

The Night of the Pilgrim could be improved, and each free moment they had Seamus worked with Atty on her role. He tucked away the notes from a meeting and lit a long thin cigar.

"Up to the devil's weed now, are you?"

"I thought a cigar would make me look a little longer," he answered. "By the way, Conor Larkin is in Dublin. I invited him to see the play Thursday."

"The mystery man himself," she said, with unmistakable sudden interest.

"You'll find him as large as his reputation."

"Ah, Seamus, you've no objectivity whatsoever about your pal."

"You'll see for yourself. I took the liberty of inviting the three of us for a jar or two after the show."

"Isn't Dan a little fidgety about who meets who?"

"Oh, Dan . . . well, Dan thinks you and Conor might be working together on something soon."

"Does he now? I still feel rather uncomfortable, you know."

"You've been in mourning long enough, Atty."

"What makes you think I'm ready to give it up?"

Atty was trying to intimidate. She was no more successful at it with this lad than Dan Sweeney was. "I've seen you battle your way out of your grief. I've heard you venerate Desmond so as to bring tears."

"What are you meaning to say, Seamus?"

"Too much veneration. You're a hell of an actress, Atty."

She had worked too closely with the little bastard, she thought. Playwrights see through people. That's why they're playwrights. Ah, play it straight with Seamus, he's too crafty for you. "Is Conor back with his woman in Belfast?"

"Uh-uh."

Rachael raced in and Atty showed herself impatient with her daughter's jabbering, as if she wanted to continue the other subject.

"There's a custard in the icebox," Atty bribed.

Rachael knew she had interrupted something and made herself vanish.

"Is he tough?" she asked.

"Extremely gentle."

"What happened with this girl in Belfast?"

"Shankill girl. Not too hard to figure out, now, is it?"

"He loved her very much?"

"Sometime in your life you should be loved that powerfully."

Atty felt her stomach flutter. Awakenings! Well, now! "Wasn't there something between him and the Countess Hubble a long time back?"

Oh, Atty girl, why are you asking things like that of the poor wee man?

"Thursday, you say?"

"Thursday."

"Well, I'll try to remember my lines."

"Aye, the lines are glorious," Seamus teased, "so don't feck them up."

On Thursday, Atty Fitzpatrick transcended Seamus O'Neill's lines, character, and play itself with a sudden surge of virtuosity that every actress prays will happen to her, never knowing when the moment of glory will strike or, indeed, if it ever will. The theatre was rapt as Seamus O'Neill, minor Irish playwright, sounded like Shakespeare on this night.

As Atty heard the knock on her dressing room door two words leapt out of her past—Jack Murphy.

"Aye, Jaysus, Atty girl," Seamus said through tears, "you've gone and immortalized me. Oh God, you were great."

The man behind was a tall man, above Seamus's head. Seamus turned, "Me pal, Conor Larkin, meet Atty Fitzpatrick."

Within a ha'penny of their introduction, without hesitation, Atty knew how her side of this relationship would go. Conor did not come as a stranger. His name in the Brotherhood Council had a mystique. His prowess on the playing field, as well as his great restoration in Hubble Manor, had been covered in the press.

He was the long-awaited return of Jack Murphy, and then some. So modest and compassionate in his manner, another woman might have fainted at this moment.

Atty was a respected widow emerging from her period of mourning and Conor had been without his Belfast girl a long time. Therefore, Seamus, bless his heart, suddenly remembered he had a late-breaking news story to cover and said he would catch up with them later.

Two people, although always in a crowd, were desolately lonely and grievously hurt, instantly recognized a need to know each other. Sharing similar hells made them want to talk things out, things they had hidden from the world outside.

The next night the theatre was dark. Atty invited him to dinner at her home. Atty's proletariat identification stopped at her doorstep. The house was an attached, flat front, three-and-a-half-story Georgian affair, the uniform of Dublin's affluent. A wildly colored door with a fanned window atop and gleaming grass said, "I am a Dubliner." It was a lovely home, filled with graces. Her son Theo and daughter Rachael were delightful and showed the maturity of character to cope with their mother's fame and the movement.

What a great little bird, this Rachael, Conor thought. Her da must have worshiped her. Well, not so. Desmond Fitzpatrick probably would have worshiped her if she had been a rare law book. Conor watched with enchantment the way Rachael kept an eye on her mother. In quick time he realized that the girl was her mother's big sister.

And there was young Theo, face screwed up, ready to stab an immortal word from pen to paper. Legal posturing at the desk in the drawing room . . . oh my, he'll be a terror in the courtroom, Conor thought.

"What might you be pondering on so mightily?" Conor asked.

"Nothing," Theo answered.

"Nothing is sure eating up a lot of your energy, lad."

"As it should be," Theo said. "Nothing requires absolute dedication, as my essay proves."

"You wouldn't be having me on, would you, Theo?"

Theo dropped his pen. "Mom is paying good money to have me educated by the Christian Brothers. However, they know nothing. Therefore, I have become an expert on nothing, in nothing, about nothing, for nothing. As you see, the first page of the essay is blank. I start with nothing."

"You're glinking me."

"If my essay is Antichrist enough, perhaps the Christian Brothers will kick me out of their school so I can get properly educated by the wee folk in the forest."

Conor took the pages up. Indeed, the first one was blank. He read on.

"Nothing is my subject because it is the oldest thing in existence. Nothing was there before the universe was created and Nothing is greater than Nothing because Nothing is absolutely perfect.

"For a long time I have seriously thought of Nothing, read Nothing, and who will argue that I am perfectly qualified to discuss Nothing intelligently? I place high value on Nothing.

"Two gentlemen recently raced to get to the North Pole first but when they arrived, they found Nothing there. Likewise, Nothing is generally what prospectors find. Nothing is in the head of politicians.

"We must try to understand oft-misunderstood philosophers who actually do Nothing, think Nothing, and say Nothing, because he who does Nothing can do Nothing wrong. He who thinks of Nothing day and night plants no evil and Nothing offends no one."

"I want you to defend me if I need a lawyer," Conor said.

"On what charges?" Theo asked.

"Nothing," Conor said.

"I'll have you out in no time flat."

"The soup's not getting any warmer," Rachael announced. As if on cue, Atty made her appearance. She swept in so elegantly attired, so cleavaged, and with such a divine scent trailing her, that Theo knew Conor was something other than Nothing.

Mom had been nervous all day. The children realized, with great hope, that the new chap had nudged her from a year of hibernation. And after a second look, they thought Conor was a pretty fair specimen as well.

After dinner, which was a happy affair—good food, bright kids, and a family that was secure with itself—Theo and Rachael disappeared as if they knew Mom and the stranger had republican business. And, just maybe, some other business as well. Atty's poker face was overwhelmed by her most daring gown.

"Come along," Atty said, forgoing the formal salon of high debate, poetry, and wisdom. "There's something cozier than this."

She led Conor to the top floor and opened the door into the

front room. It was a combination intimate parlor, library, and office, and had been the private retreat with her late husband. It was now a memory room filled with his writings, law books, photographs, and other vestiges of the life they had lived for the movement. For a time after Desmond's death she scarcely left the room when she was home. Once she did, she had not reentered until this moment.

"Those are beautiful children you have," Conor said.

"Aye," she agreed. "I laid a lot of guilt on myself because I thought I had, well, not exactly neglected them, but brought them up too entirely on my own itinerary in life. I was given to wonder if their life had been dealt to them properly, in the right atmosphere. My most difficult decision was to join the Brotherhood."

"They're where they want to be, Atty. They hear the song you've sung them well. The other girl?"

"Emma hasn't a republican bone in her body. London and her grandmother suit her fine. In a strange way, it has made her closer to us because she was odd man out here, and now when we visit, it's very intense. She is going to be a lovely lady."

"Like her mother," Conor said, admiring the way Atty had handled this part of her life.

"I wanted you to meet the kids because if we do visit again, it shouldn't be here. I don't want them to know too much about who is Brotherhood. God forbid they are ever questioned about it one day."

"It will be my loss," Conor said.

"And theirs. Are you up for a fire?"

"That would be grand," he said.

Conor fixed the turf in the small grate below the marble mantel. He drifted back in time as the smell of it reached him. He was drawn to the books and stunned Atty as he dissected the innards of Keats and Shelley.

"Where'd you learn all that, now?" she asked.

"Self-taught candlelight scholar," he said.

"Like Abraham Lincoln?"

"Well, the Lincoln family did come out of County Donegal."

"Lincoln was Irish?"

"Don't take my word for it, Atty. I learned that from a friend whose opinion I rarely question. Actually, Seamus O'Neill taught me to read and write."

"Well, we've something in common. I love that fellow. Seems like he's the only one I can really talk to anymore. But it doesn't happen too often. Being on the Supreme Council, it's not good to have him over too often. Des and I would talk here sometimes through the night, and we'd be absolutely astonished to see the daylight come up on us. You know?"

And they talked. It was not like she and Des had talked. Not even as with Seamus. She had only spoken to one person this way, very long ago: Jack Murphy. With Conor, it was more so. In the end she had to recognize Jack was a weak man looking for a safe harbor, out of the line of fire.

The more gently Conor Larkin spoke, the more powerful he seemed. Conor fawned over some of her books and she offered him to take what he wanted.

"Might not be a good idea," he said. "They've your book-plates in them. Maxwell Swan's goons search my flat every so often. I don't think it wise to connect us."

"Do you have a hard time shaking them?" she asked.

"No, not really. They're very clumsy fellows. Last time they were on my tail I went to the museum and studied every painting for fifteen minutes. They nearly croaked."

The mantel clock tolled a late hour. Conor reckoned he'd better get back into Dublin to catch his morning train up to Belfast.

"The train makes a stop at Rathmines," Atty said. "I'll run you over in the morning. You can stay over in a spare room. Go on, put another brick on the fire."

Their eager minds grasped the opportunity for fine conversation, lightened by fine cognac. Bright and lonely people had much to talk about and as they did they sized each other up.

What came through to Conor was that Atty Fitzpatrick was an extraordinarily strong human being, strong as her reputation, and she loved her own strength. Belief in herself would get her through anything. Yet she had bulwarks of protection within . . . to ward off suffering . . . to discourage pursuit . . . to press for what she wanted against all winds.

The study spoke to him. It spoke of Desmond Fitzpatrick's peacockery, cocksureness, the courtroom matador. Oh, for sure, they made love in this room, he thought, but not to each other. They made love to Ireland.

With all her renown as a great beauty, Atty was ill at ease as a female, Conor thought. He sensed that Des needed her as a partner and she needed him, but not as man and woman . . . as compatriots.

Conor's charm drew her in. She felt as though he were undressing her with his mesmerizing manner. Little tiny flicks of conversation told her that he knew she and Des used one another as crutches. And what of this big fellow before her poking up the turf?

Conor Larkin was frightening, that's what. Here was a man, she knew from Seamus, who had waited his life for his love, and he possessed this Shelley girl. Only he could shine in his woman's eyes. God, Atty thought, Conor's grief over the loss of Shelley is as deep as my grief over the loss of a husband of sixteen years and three children.

Jack Murphy had owned her once, but only for a fleeting moment. She knew when she asked Jack to show her the hidden side of herself, he would soon be gone. That would not happen with Conor lad.

In a sudden flick, innocent and curious, Atty invited him to her bed. When the powerful blacksmith's arms enfolded her, she had never felt the likes of it.

Conor let her down, lovely. He still loved Shelley. He and Atty would have a long life together in the movement and she was not a woman he would take lightly.

Part of Atty was furious. Mainly, she was furious at her own shamelessness. She was also flabbergasted at his honesty, and she felt he spoke the truth about his respect for her. That was nice, very nice. Even at her moment of rejection, she had only good feelings toward him. She did not like seeing him hurt and even wanted him to find his Shelley girl again. Having never fostered such feelings before, Atty was rather pleased with herself. He told her he wouldn't take her lightly, and she damned well knew she could not take him lightly.

He continued to hold her softly, and in their quiet she had a moment of strange revelation. They lived life on the brink, a life filled with odd twists and turns. They were thrown together as comrades in arms and they would work in close contact, sooner or later.

Someday, Atty thought, Conor Larkin was going to be a free man, and when that time came, she was going to have him.

"I'm going in to Dublin," he said at last. "If I stay, I'll not sleep all night. If you think I don't want your breasts, you're daft. Atty . . . if Ireland had a queen, Atty would be her name. You are far too great a woman to be trivialized."

"Thank you, Conor," she whispered, "thank you, luv. There's a taxi rank just two blocks down. On your way before I rape you."

Rat-a-tat-tat-tattat-tattat!

The Lembeg drum put all other war drums to shame when it came to striking fear into the heart of the enemy, real or imagined. It rattled in the "marching season" as Protestant Ulster celebrated its annual rebirth. Beginning on the Fourth of July, a date to ennoble themselves with their American cousins, a month of parades and rallies recalled ancient victories over the papists in song and sermon. Multitudes of banners, partial to orange, fluffed and glorified King, Empire, the Reformation, and above all, Ulster's patented, eternal, holy, indivisible *loyalty* to the British.

The Orange Lodgemen, beribboned, sporting derby hats and rolled black umbrellas, marched hither and yon, to and fro and round and round.

> *Oh, it's old but it is beautiful,*
> *And its colors, they are fine,*
> *It was Derry, Augrim,*
> *Enniskillen and the Boyne*
> *My father wore it as a youth,*
> *In bygone days of yore,*
> *And on the Twelfth I love to wear,*
> *The sash my father wore.*

On the Twelfth of August the marchers converged on their sacred city of Londonderry where they marched once again atop Derry's walls for a last hurrah in memory of a siege won in 1690.

Sure I am an Ulsterman,
From Erin's Isle I came,
To see my British brethren
All of honor and of fame
And to tell them of my forefathers,
Who fought in days of yore,
That I might have the right to wear
The sash my father wore.

They rained pennies down on the Catholic Bogside to re-humiliate the unfortunate losers and went to the town diamond for a final exaltation of their savior, Oliver Cromwell. . . .

And lest we forget another battle, the Battle of the Boyne, of no less importance than Waterloo and Trafalgar, where their beloved William of Orange, on his alabaster steed, wounded in the right hand, took up a saber in his left hand to lead the charge. King James, the papist, cowering and quivering on a horse of another color, tucked tail and fled, thus liberating Ulster from Vatican venality forever! And ever!

Let us pray.

For the industrialists and other rulers of the province this was the time of year that their religious and political messengers were able to introduce new agendas as well as reiterate ancient fears.

Marched silly and harangued silly, the righteous were easily ignited into anti-Catholic mobs, after a bit of blood and arson.

Sir Frederick Weed's agenda this year was union busting and, with a captive mob within his yard, had them frothed into burning down the copper shop where most of the Catholics worked. It was, after all, an obsolete facility and well insured by Lloyd's.

Conor Larkin got wind of the scene and was able to get the Catholics out of the yard. He returned to save Duffy O'Hurley, the driver of Weed's Red Hand Express, and an essential man in the gunrunning scheme.

The mob caught Conor and nearly beat him to death. Only Robin MacLeod's last-moment intervention saved his life.

*   *   *

Morgan MacLeod cared deeply for Conor Larkin and in the early days of Conor's relationship with Shelley, he stood by them forthrightly.

Morgan was a man to be reckoned with: a leader of the Shankill tribe, a deacon in his church, foreman of Weed's largest dry dock, and an Orange Lodge Grandmaster whose son had captained Ireland's only Admiral's Cup team.

No one in the Shankill cared when Shelley became the mistress of a married man. After all, this David Kimberly was upper English, a high midlevel career diplomat. Truth be known, Kimberly had been somewhat of a coup for a Shankill lass.

Conor Larkin was another matter. Although an R.C., he was under the patronage of Sir Frederick himself and also a member of the Belfast Boilermakers. Well, let's say Larkin was one of the good ones.

Although Conor and Shelley represented a kind of tentative truce, Belfast, a final sludge hole of the Industrial Revolution, passed out its tender mercies grudgingly.

When Conor and Shelley broke up and returned from holiday in England separately, Morgan MacLeod could not help but sigh in relief and hope to God his daughter would fall in love with a good, decent, Protestant lad. But he saw his beloved Shelley grow wan and listless without Conor.

Conor quit the rugby club. Morgan's information had it that the Larkin was like a dead man.

Morgan MacLeod feared that something would make the two of them rush back together, and he did not know if he could continue to hold a peace in place.

Morgan's fears came to pass when Shelley returned to Conor after he was beaten in the riots and lived with him, openly nursing him back to health and at the same time defying the natural law of tribal Belfast.

In its tormented and violent history, the Belfast poor of Protestant stripe gave birth to a breed of clever churchmen whose arts were showmanship in Reformation frock and striking fear of the Vatican into their flocks. The cleverest among them often rocketed from tent preacher onto a glory road of wielding great power.

One of these was the Reverend Oliver Cromwell MacIvor, who had his own schools, seminary, churches, press, and a quasi-private armed brigade known as the Knights of Christ, with his women's auxiliaries dubbed Angels of Christ.

The harlotry of Shelley MacLeod presented MacIvor with a golden issue, particularly to his Angels of Christ.

MacIvor had long needed a cunning victory over Morgan MacLeod, the only man in the Shankill strong enough to offer a challenge.

The Wednesday Angels meetings were soon venomized by MacIvor drawing visions, for his ladies, of papist flesh devouring them and their own dear, sweet, innocent daughters.

After she returned to Conor, Morgan had forbidden mention of Shelley within the home and had forbidden the family to see her. All Morgan had to do now was step up to the pulpit and denounce her. MacIvor would show mercy and the neighborhood would be purified of its stigma and become whole and Christian again.

Morgan MacLeod refused. How he loved his strange child, withdrawn as a girl, she of the sad green eyes. Determined, Shelley taught herself to speak without a trace of the confusing Belfast accent and carry herself erect and display proper manners. He all but died when, at fifteen, Shelley fled Belfast and worked as a maid in a manor house in England to escape her real mother's growing madness.

Day by day now, the MacLeod family tasted the fruits of hatred: garbage at their doorstep, Robin's son beaten, ostracism at the pub and green grocer, litanies of hate from MacIvor's pulpit.

As Conor healed, he and Shelley exchanged souls. Any risk, any danger, any hardship was better to bear together than continue with the unbearable life of living apart. They knew, going into it, it could mean an unwritten death warrant, but they also knew that the greatest tragedy would have been to pass each other by and never to have met.

Morgan's grief became consummate. He knew when one of the family had seen Shelley behind his back, but he asked nothing, gave no word, no blessing, nothing. Yet, day after day he'd push open the door to her room and look in and sometimes sit on the stool before the mirror and stare at the photographs tucked in it.

By night he'd fumble through the Bible searching out the words that might render him some hope. After a time, he began to search out passages about death.

Seized by a fierce pain in his chest and unable to breathe, Morgan toppled from the scaffold at the Big Mabel dry dock, falling twenty feet to the pavement and breaking his back.

"Robin! It's your dad! He's fallen off the Big Mabel."

CHAPTER

41

The gunrunning scheme plodded on, a few hundred rifles at a time. It began to spring little warning leaks.

Duffy O'Hurley, the engineer of the Red Hand, was getting a bad, bad case of nerves. His drinking went to the hard stuff and now and again he dropped double-edged little thoughts at the bar. Conor put a watch on him, except for when Duffy was running the train.

As rifles were buried around the countryside, more and more people became involved. Each new man or woman with knowledge upped the risks.

The onloadings in England and offloadings in Irish waysides hit more and more unseen glitches . . . the odd constable straying by . . . wrong signals to complete a meeting . . . the sudden raid on a hiding place.

Long Dan Sweeney and Atty wanted to close down the operation and look for a new route to bring the weapons in. Unfortunately that called for leaving one thousand rifles in England. This thousand could mean the Brotherhood could quicken their recruiting of men and form units, perhaps two years earlier than previously planned.

Conor then came up with a wild scheme to doctor Sir Frederick's train from engine to caboose and make one last run carrying a thousand rifles. The plan took things to the edge of the cliff, but Conor prevailed.

Putting brackets under every car, fixing false floors and roofs, and cutting more space under the coal tender, the thousand rifles were loaded on at Liverpool and made the crossing to Ireland.

Then came the terror! Duffy O'Hurley was unable to take the train out by himself on a deadhead run. He was packing the guns all over Ireland, unable to dump them and slowly going mad.

At last the call came. Duffy was in Derry, at Hubble Manor and was making a deadhead to Belfast and Dublin. He could dump the rifles at a water stop halfway accross the province, a place called Sixmilecross.

Conor himself had come to within a hair of stopping the shipment in England, but once they got to Ireland, the Brotherhood had to get them unloaded. Until Duffy's call Conor had a growing suspicion that only a miracle could deliver the guns, but he kept it to himself.

All the last night he lay awake holding Shelley, not thinking of Sixmilecross the next night, but trying to remember each time he had loved her and how the miracle of it always sent them to a new and different place.

It did not matter whether or not they had had enough time together, for a hundred years would not have been enough.

Shelley, Shelley, Shelley, don't be foolish. I pray you don't be foolish. I don't want to come back from Sixmilecross if you aren't alive. There are those in Belfast who hate our love so, your life would be taken if you stay.

It is unbearable enough to realize I may not hold you for five or ten years or maybe never again. But if you die . . . oh God . . .

Dawn, never come, dawn!

I cannot let myself believe, Shelley thought, I may never know him again. I must make a good show for him. Conor, my beloved, realize that I was born only for one thing . . . the moments I have had with you . . . and none of the rest matters tuppence. How can I have asked more? How could anyone?

Don't you understand, Conor Larkin, your girl is filled and she is not afraid.

The power of their dawn was known implicitly and need not

be spoken. A few instructions; take the pistol, use it if your life is in danger, go to Dublin immediately, stay there.

No use saying the rest of it now, was there?

IRISH REPUBLICAN BROTHERHOOD GUNRUNNING
OPERATION SMASHED BY AMBUSH AT SIXMILECROSS—
1 KILLED, 4 WOUNDED, 7 IN CUSTODY, 1,000 RIFLES
RECOVERED FROM PRIVATE TRAIN OF ULSTER INDUSTRIALIST
SIR FREDERICK WEED. RINGLEADER CAPTURED

DUBLIN, AUGUST 10, REUTERS—Acting on inside information, troops from the Londonderry Barracks rode aboard the Red Hand Express, the famous private train of Belfast shipbuilder and steel magnate, Sir Frederick Weed.

Destined for a rendezvous to unload smuggled rifles, the train was heading to the quiet lay-by of Sixmilecross, County Tyrone, in mid-Ulster.

Arriving at three minutes past midnight, they ambushed a waiting party of eight members of the Irish Republican Brotherhood.

The train was filled with sharpshooters from the 22nd West Anglicans. In addition, Ulster Militia and Constabulary forces had surrounded the entire area. Overwhelmed, there was only light resistance from the smugglers.

D. E. Dunkerlee, spokesman for His Majesty's Press Office in Dublin Castle, issued the following statement:

"Additional arrests have been made in England of members of the ring. Taken into custody were Owen O'Sullivan and his sons Brian and Barry, proprietors of the O'Sullivan Bell and Foundry Works in Merseyside, Liverpool.

"Also arrested was Mr. Dudley Callaghan, a Bradford mortician and operator of a funeral home on Wild Boar Road. Callaghan is known to have run a business in shipping home Irish bodies for burial."

Details of the gunrunning operation were slow in coming out of Dublin Castle but by all appearances the rifles, standard British Army issued Enfields, originated in England and probably were smuggled aboard the Red Hand Express for trans-shipment to Belfast.

"This is obviously the work of a highly organized and highly skilled unit of the Irish Republican Brotherhood and, from all appearances, has been in effect for several months," Dunkerlee concluded.

DUBLIN CASTLE DENIES GUNRUNNERS WERE IRISH REPUBLICAN BROTHERHOOD—RINGLEADER, CONOR LARKIN, NOTED RUGBY HERO NAMED—SIR FREDERICK WEED ENRAGED

DUBLIN, AUGUST 11, REUTERS, ASSOCIATED PRESS—Dublin Castle today recanted yesterday's release that the Sixmilecross Gang "was a highly organized and highly skilled unit of the Irish Republican Brotherhood."

D. E. Dunkerlee, spokesman for His Majesty's Press Office in Dublin Castle, briefed reporters at a hurriedly arranged press conference this morning. "Yesterday's report of Irish Brotherhood involvement was premature. There is no evidence whatsoever of Brotherhood units of this nature, nor evidence of any organized IRB activity in Ireland. This was the work of a ring of common criminals."

This reversal was in keeping with Dublin Castle's refusal to admit the existence of the IRB, which it has steadfastly done over the past three years.

Conor Larkin, now identified as the leader of the operation, is being held incommunicado while other members of the gang have been remanded to Mountjoy Prison. (See adjoining box for background of Mr. Larkin and his long association with the Weed and Hubble families of Belfast and Londonderry.)

Making a brief statement before going into seclusion, Sir Frederick Weed appeared to be livid with rage. "Using my family and myself as innocent victims of Conor Larkin's perfidy amounts to the most venal treachery I have ever known. We were his trusting patrons and this behavior boldly illustrates the despicable character of this breed. I shall live to see him hanged and his fellow conspirators, crushed."

While humiliated by the failure of Sir Frederick's own considerable intelligence-gathering sources, Irish humor over the incident at Sixmilecross has resulted in a large amount of laughter from the pubs, to the salons, to the editorial pages, to the man in the street. Larkin's cheek and daring seems to have captured that odd quirk of irony in the Irish character.

DUBLIN CASTLE ADMITS SIXMILECROSS GANG WERE
MEMBERS OF THE IRISH REPUBLICAN BROTHERHOOD

DUBLIN, AUGUST 12, REUTERS, ASSOCIATED PRESS, UNITED PRESS INTERNATIONAL NEWS SERVICE, EUROPA PRESS— Reversing themselves three times in three days, Dublin Castle today admitted existence of the IRB and held them directly responsible for the gunrunning scheme.

Sir Frederick Weed remains in seclusion.

Committees forming throughout the country demanded justice for Conor Larkin and the Sixmilecross Gang.

D. E. Dunkerlee, spokesman for His Majesty's Press Office issued the following statement at 4 P.M.:

"Further investigation into the Sixmilecross incident has brought His Majesty's government to conclude that the Irish Republican Brotherhood has been secretly active for several months, and possibly years, and is directly responsible for the gunrunning scheme aboard Sir Frederick Weed's Red Hand Express.

"Experts from Scotland Yard and Army Intelligence have concluded that such an operation could not be possible without a fair-sized support system.

"The rifles have been traced to Dunby Depot in Cape Town, South Africa, and had apparently been shipped in 1901 for issue to troops in the Boer War. Experts are trying to determine if they had been returned to England after the conflict, uncrated."

"Meanwhile the country remains agog with Sixmilecross

fever. Informed sources state that the IRB is being sought out for enlistment by hundreds, if not thousands, of men throughout Ireland.

"By naming the IRB as the 'nonexistent' entity who carried out the gun smuggling, the British have become our greatest recruiter. We could not have gotten this kind of publicity on our own in ten years and we are grateful to Dublin Castle for its cooperation," said one high-ranking Brotherhood official on the condition of anonymity.

CHAPTER
42

Atty recognized Shelley MacLeod the instant she stepped from the train onto the platform. Shelley seemed neither cowed nor lost as she held her hand above her forehead to shade out the sunlight. Standing as she was, Shelley seemed nearly translucent, ethereal. It was plain for Atty to see why Conor loved her so profoundly.

Atty was frustrated with a natural wont to dislike her, but it seemed impossible to dislike her. Shelley wore a purple satin ribbon around her neck to identify herself as she continued to look about.

"Hello, Shelley, I'm Atty Fitzpatrick."

"Thanks for coming, Mrs. Fitzpatrick."

"Please call me Atty."

"Is there any news?"

"No, except that Conor is alive. How about yourself, how are you holding up?"

"I'm all right, I'm fine. You're certain he got through?"

"That much we know for sure."

They stood silently, staring at one another curiously, not knowing exactly how to continue the conversation . . . then, as naturally and gently as you please, they came together with both of them trembling. As Shelley felt Atty's arms come about her, she let go a bit in jerky sighs and sniffles.

"Sorry," Shelley murmured.

"It's a wonder we're not both insane with fear. God, you're a good strong girl, Shelley. I'm glad you're here in Dublin with us.

We'll see to you." And at that, Atty broke and both of them hung on to each other and sobbed.

This was how Seamus O'Neill came upon them. "I see the two of you have met," he said.

"You must be Seamus," Shelley said.

"I'm easy to miss, especially if you're not looking for me."

"Any news?" Atty asked.

Seamus shook his head. "Do you have any more luggage?"

"No, Conor told me to leave everything."

"Aye," he said. "Well, he is alive and that's a start. We've got everyone working on information, but the Brits have clamped a lid. They're trying to get their story straight. They're very confused."

"I can see that from the newspapers."

They made down the platform. "I wanted you to stay with me," Atty said, "but we decided it would be best, for the time being, if we put you in a hideaway with a guard."

"Just a precaution," Seamus added quickly. "We don't believe the British will be watching you, and as soon as things settle down, you'll be able to move about freely with no problem. The main thing ye must know is that you're among friends and you'll be completely safe in Dublin."

Shelley held herself together until she was safely ensconced in a tidy little flat just a few blocks from Atty's house. Only then did she allow herself the luxury of fainting.

In the weeks that followed, it was apparent that the Castle was not interested in Shelley MacLeod. Virtually no one in Dublin was aware of her role in Conor Larkin's life, and she posed no threat to the British.

Nonetheless, the Brotherhood continued to keep a watch on her to make certain that no fanatic from Belfast would come down and attempt harm. She was free to move about Dublin as she pleased.

Shelley stepped right into the dash and vigor of Dublin life. She had been superior in her position, working for Belfast's only upper-crust couturier, and was able to obtain placement in a fine Dublin salon.

Her life revolved around Atty Fitzpatrick, young Theobald, and Rachael, the most loving of children who seemed to sense the meaning of who was who and what was what without being told in so many words. Rachael watched her mother continue to soften toward Shelley, which was against her mother's basic nature. Rachael needed no band to blare out that Conor Larkin held great sway over both of them.

As Atty Fitzpatrick came to love Shelley MacLeod against her conscious will, she wondered why. Atty came to realize that Shelley had opened a door within her that had been bolted shut. Atty Fitzpatrick had never thought herself capable of selflessness, not even with her children. Rachael and Theo were there because they fit into her scheme. Emma was given up because she did not.

Atty questioned her flare of passion for Conor Larkin. She had not thrown herself on anyone except Jack Murphy, so long ago, and that was for a limited venture, and only to check out her curiosity.

Her desire for Conor continued strongly after his kind rebuff, and she knew she loved him even though he would command whatever. Without rancor, Atty realized that Shelley MacLeod was the right woman for him . . . not her . . . but Shelley. Atty as Atty was incapable of what Shelley as Shelley was.

This became a transcending experience, the knowing that she could love greatly and accept the possibility that it would be unrequited. This love she would carry quietly, for Conor Larkin made her pleased with herself just in the realization.

Once it became settled in Atty's mind, then loving Shelley as her own sister followed easily. It seemed the stuff of bad plays, Atty believed at first . . . an awful cliché—of two sisters mad for the same fellow.

To make matters even more serene and velvety was Shelley's realization of how deeply Atty Fitzpatrick loved her man. She felt great empathy for Atty, as well as great respect for Atty's dignity.

What an utterly mad triangle, Atty thought! I love them both and want them for each other! I must be coming unhinged! As she discovered the impossibility of disliking Shelley MacLeod, Atty sensed she had come to a new capability of loving. If, indeed, she was able to love so unselfishly, then there might be a love for her sometime, someplace.

Once married to Des, Atty believed that a Jack Murphy intensity of love would elude her for all of her life, until she set eyes on Conor Larkin. "I can love now, without reservation," and this gave her a new and lovely path she must explore someday.

There was no getting around Rachael with child's talk and, having no sister of her own, Shelley and the girl filled each other with laughter and hugs.

Poor Theo was burdened by being sixteen. Naturally, he had secretly fallen desperately and eternally in love with Shelley. All he could do was suck in his frustration and continually demonstrate how charming and witty he was.

"I have a new thesis," Theo opened one evening. "God, we all agree, transcends all creatures, plants, livestock, and inanimate objects. God may choose to be whatever the hell God wishes to be—a mountain, a shark, ten trees, a lighter-than-air balloon. God, God forbid, may even be a priest. The only thing God cannot do is transform himself into a female. God only knows why, but God must be a man and certainly a man of our color. But, let us say, for the sake of argument God decided to be a trout, a male trout, naturally, and in his own infinite way let the clergy and the masses alike know that henceforth he will not be known as God, but as Trout. This would make a ponderous difference in our lives."

Rachael, attuned to such gobbledygook, looked up from the desk and her homework. "We could never eat Trout again," she said.

"Goes much deeper than that, Rachael. Take the British

anthem, 'Trout save our noble king, Trout save our noble king, Trout save the king.'"

"For Trout's sake, Theo, you're being ridiculous," Shelley said.

"'Mine eyes have seen the glory of the coming of the Trout,'" Theo bellowed.

"What Trout has joined, let no man put asunder."

"Trout damned you, Rachael Fitzpatrick. Trout knows I try to be a kind and loving brother, but in the name of Trout I find it trying."

"Trout Almighty, Theo, Trout is on my side."

"No, Trout is on the Protestant side."

"Beware the wrath of Trout, you two," Shelley said, being drawn in against her will.

"This matter is in Trout's hands . . . rather fins . . . "

Atty came from the kitchen and announced dinner.

"What are we having, Mom?" Rachael asked.

"God. Do you want yours off the bone or on the bone?"

As the days wearied on with no word of Conor, the two became extremely close and extremely dependent. Shelley freed Atty to pursue her calling and her calling now was speaking out at mass meetings on behalf of the Sixmilecross men.

When their days were done, they would retire to the library and light a turf fire and talk the hours away with words that took root in a fierce attachment.

CHAPTER

43

"Free Conor Larkin! Free Conor Larkin!"

A small but boisterous clump of students marched with torchlights and placards, passing beneath the window of Lord Jeremy Hubble's flat on Merrion Square. Ad hoc groups of young people from Trinity College and central Dublin were merging for a rally at St. Stephen's Green.

It was unusual for Trinity College students to be involved, for the school had been the stronghold of the Anglo gentry from the time of Queen Elizabeth. It remained a gentrified Protestant institution. Sixmilecross had occasioned more than a hundred young people and a half-dozen teachers to a new and public awareness that they were Irish, if not precisely republicans.

Jeremy allowed the thick velvet drape to fall over the window, dulling the street noise.

"You'd think they'd be hanging him as a traitor," Jeremy mumbled, "instead of treating him like a national hero. No doubt that Fitzpatrick woman will be bellowing her lungs out at the Green. Beastly mouth, she has."

Molly O'Rafferty remained sadly silent, as she had tried to do since Sixmilecross. Jeremy swayed this way, then that way. He tossed in his sleep, awakened sweating. He cursed Conor Larkin for betraying him and making him a dupe. And he still loved Conor, confusingly.

"Latin has its way of turning the old mind about," Molly said. "Back to your studies and on with them."

Jeremy returned to his desk and once again questioned the value of Latin.

"Just think, when you've conquered Caesar, you get a go at Cicero."

"I'd rather dine on a pail of maggots."

Thank God, Molly was determined to tutor him. Thank God for Molly for everything. Jeremy's snarling dimmed as she soothed him with the chords of her guitar.

Jeremy glanced back at her and fell in love with her once again, as he always did every time he glanced at her or touched her or held her.

It had been that way from the very first eye contact. He and his mates went to the Lord Sarsfield, a student pub on the river Liffey quay, where Molly sang folk ballads on Saturday nights. The voice that reached him was more pure than the tinkle of any crystal or silver bell in Hubble Manor.

I spied a fair damsel far fairer than any,
Her cheeks like the red rose that none could excel,
Her skin like the lily that grows in yon valley,
She's my own bonnie Annie, my factory girl.

That was it, then, now, and forever, Jeremy lad. Molly O'Rafferty barely past sixteen, newly out of convent school, and an apprentice teacher.

The marchers outside had passed for the moment and Jeremy was lulled into his Latin. He went at it diligently. When she saw him tire, Molly set down her guitar and hovered behind him checking his work and at the same time keeping enough distance to duck her skirts out of the way of his constant reaching back for her.

Mal Palmer burst in! One knock and in! Mal discombobulated the atmosphere of serenity once again.

"Oh, if Napoleon had the breastworks of that Atty Fitzpatrick, he'd have won at Waterloo."

"For God's sake, Mal," Jeremy snapped.

"I just wanted to hear what the Fenian avengers had to say." Mal touched the Sixmilecross button on his jacket. "Oh, oh," he said slipping it quickly into a pocket.

There was no use insulting or dressing Mal down. He was uninsultable, undressdownable, and had little sensitivity to Jeremy's situation. Somehow, he remained a pal. He was a good rugby player and terribly humorous at times . . . otherwise useless.

"Well, it *is* Saturday night. Are we off to the Lord Sarsfield to hear our Molly girl's angel voice?"

"You take Molly over," Jeremy said, "I'll catch up with you."

"I was saving a surprise for you, Jeremy," Molly said. "Nell McCaffery is singing in my place tonight."

"Pity, what," Mal said. "I hope old Nell knows some frog songs to harmonize with her voice. Jeremy, this pains me, old chap, but can I ding you for a fiver? Damned allowance hasn't arrived."

"You shouldn't gamble, Mal, you're no good at it," Jeremy said.

"Well, I am pressed for a fiver so on with your sermon."

Jeremy gave him the money and Mal said he loved them both and was off to scour the square for other mates for additional fivers.

"Poor Mal," Molly said, "what an ugly game he and his father play. Mal deliberately runs up gambling debts and Daddy pays them in a rage. This proves to Mal that his daddy truly loves him, although his daddy truly despises him."

"Trinity College is the bottom of the toilet bowl for all us good Anglo chaps who have disappointed our fathers by failing to get into Oxford."

"That's enough Latin, Mal, and rallies for one evening," Molly said closing his books.

"You didn't tell me you weren't singing at the pub tonight."

"I wanted to surprise you before himself burst in. I'm planning to give you a private performance tonight, m'lord. Jeremy, I can stay the night and all day tomorrow."

"Oh, that's bully! How did you manage it?"

"I told my folks I had a singing engagement at the girls' school in Dun Laoghaire and that I'll be staying over with a friend."

He was out of his chair in a blink and seized her. "No profanity till after dinner," she managed between kisses and his fumbling with her buttons. "Or we'll starve . . . once we start up . . . and everything like that . . . you know . . . "

"Oh Molly, Molly, Molly."

They stood huffing in each other's faces, eyes drifting off to dream stuff. . . .

". . . you hungry?"

". . . not really."

". . . me, either."

". . . the translations?"

". . . tomorrow. . . . "

Thump, thump, thump, thump. Outside, a bloody drum! A blurred message from marchers whooping it up, "Free Conor Larkin! Free Conor Larkin!"

Jeremy went into a quiver of clenched fists and clenched teeth, nearly shutting off his own breath. "I love Conor so!" he blurted without meaning to do so. "Molly, we must have done something terrible to make a man like Conor turn on us. It was that bloody factory fire!"

Molly turned away in frustration. Everyone had warned that her affair with the Viscount Coleraine was doomed from the start. Every year gentrified college lads fell desperately in love with nice sorts like her, away from their parents' eyes. And one day their college was done and they were gone.

But did not she and Jeremy have something grander? Somewhere, somehow, someday the diverse peoples of Ireland would have to start getting along with one another. The cases in point would have to be strong, like her and Jeremy. If two people could love each other so and not make it, then the country could never make it.

Jeremy now roiled against Conor and the Brotherhood. Molly closed her eyes and moved from his view. She wanted to shout at him, "You'd better learn about the potato famine, Jeremy, and before that the penal laws, and before that, death by Oliver Cromwell!"

Why must two decent people find out that their love always has to be a defiance of history? It was not that Jeremy wasn't one of the lads. He'd done the Irishtowns of the Midlands. His hero was a Catholic rebel. Yet, when one is raised in Hubble Manor, no matter how liberal the countess was, privilege was divined into him so that below a certain line of compassion, Jeremy was unable to understand suffering, humiliation, and slavery.

Jeremy was like the "decent" slave owners of Alabama and the Caribbean. He could only delve so deeply into black men and women before his "natural" order of superiority took over. His love of Conor was the exception. His love of Molly, yet to be resolved.

Jeremy merrily rolled along thinking everyone a fine fellow. This worried his father and grandfather enormously as they worked him into a ceremonial role in life. For the Weed and Hubble Ulster scheme to work, the Catholics and Protestants needed to be pitted against one another.

Molly O'Rafferty awakened frightened many mornings, knowing that Ireland's tragic past had breezed by Jeremy. If he deeply felt the injustice, he'd have to do something about it, and he didn't have the mustard to buck his father.

His mother never went over the first floor of the factory because she didn't want to know the misery above. Jeremy's dilemma about Conor was of the same cloth. He didn't really want to know why Conor was Brotherhood.

Molly, sweet Molly, what had she gotten herself into? She loved this boy as only a bedrock virgin could love after giving him her treasure.

"You'll have to make your way to Conor Larkin. You know the people to let you into his prison. You're going to have to make peace with him, and perhaps Conor will enlighten you about the treacherous waters you and I are in."

"Mother will stand up for us."

"There's more to it than that, Jeremy."

"I'll not let anything happen between us."

"We're in Ireland, Jeremy, and you're an Ulsterman with a golden set of credentials which excludes me. If we are to come through this together, you're going to have to start making some strong decisions."

As she embraced her lad, Molly knew that this was not the time to bring up the possibility of her pregnancy.

CHAPTER
44

The house descended into a sadness, yet with a feeling that something majestic had come to them along with tragedy. A surge of wonderment and a sense of dignity as strong as their fears of death.

When only Shelley and Atty were left in the study they sat silently, held hands, and lowered the level of the whiskey bottle.

"I'm leaving for Belfast tomorrow," Shelley said, breaking the silence.

"Please," Atty said, "I need you, Shelley."

"My father needs me more," she said. "He's called for me. He wants me. My place is beside him now. We have to make our peace with each other."

"What's happening?"

"Robin phoned. Morgan's back is broken. He's in excruciating pain . . . just keeps calling for me."

"You'll let us give you protection?"

"Aye, for certain. Robin will be with me a great deal of the time. He's a very tough lad. Hey now, the MacLeods are not a weak family or strangers to each other."

"Aren't you frightened?"

"Of course I am," Shelley said. "So was Conor. If our lives have any meaning at all, there are some things we can't back away from. Who am I telling that to anyhow, Atty Fitzpatrick? You told me how terrible your fears were in joining the Brotherhood, but it didn't delay you for five minutes, did it?"

"Take the later afternoon train, Shelley. I need to spend the morning making some safe arrangements for you."

"I plan to. I have to be up early and say good-bye to Rachael and Theo before they're off to school."

"Theo may die of a broken heart," Atty said.

"Rachael is your power," Shelley said.

"You see that, now? She's been taking care of me for years. Seems like with this avocation of ours, we all come to a hard dead end. What should I do about those kids?"

"No different than you're doing now. They'll come to their own decisions. No matter how you try to lead them, they'll do as they damned please."

"Like you?"

"Aye. Robin followed his dad. I did as I pleased. Dublin's a good old place. I like it here. I plan on coming back when I've gotten my dad through this."

"Please come back," Atty said, breaking again. She got up and rushed from the room.

Shelley took a last look about the grand old study, so warm to know and share with the only truly close friend she had had in her life. As she closed the door behind her she could hear faint sobs from Atty's room. The door gave way. As she sat on the edge of the bed and stroked Atty's hair, Atty made no attempt to stifle her tears, but accepted Shelley's stroking in rhythm with them.

There were unspoken conversations between the two of them. Shelley did not think it fair to tempt Atty by telling her of the depth of her love for Conor or of their moments together. It would have been so unfair, for Atty loved him obviously and profoundly. There were times Shelley had shared little things with Seamus, but that was different.

Now came words unspoken so loudly, they did not have to be said but went from fiber of being to fiber of being.

"Slide over, old girl," Shelley said, then lay alongside Atty, turned her over and held her in her arms as though she were a little child. . . . "If I don't come back," Shelley didn't say, "I know you'll take care of him and that makes me glad."

CHAPTER

45

Jeremy was always called to the opulent manor library to be dressed down by his father. In that vaunted room with thousands of leathered volumes glaring down, the great decisions of the earldom had been made.

It was here that Jeremy's grandfather, Morris, the "Famine Earl," signed more eviction notices than any landlord in Ireland. It was a fitting setting for Roger to unload his cynical, biting, understated scorn on his son.

The venue, this time, had deliberately been changed to Dublin, away from Caroline's eyes and protection. The cast in Jeremy's parlor had greatly enlarged to include Brigadier Maxwell Swan who always gave the lad the willies. His younger brother, Christopher, had come over from Oxford. One of Swan's detectives, W. W. Herd, stood sallowly in the shadows.

Jeremy squirmed as Roger paced, lifted the report, and leafed through it for the twentieth time. "Now again," Roger said, "we see that you are not to be trusted, Jeremy. You dismissed your manservant, Donaldson, whom I assigned personally to look after you in this cow pasture college."

"Father, I dismissed Donaldson because I felt he was spying on me."

"If, after your previous escapades with prostitutes, I did not keep an eye on your activities, I would not be a proper father, would I?"

Will he ever get to the point? Jeremy wondered.

"Well, answer up! Would I be a proper father?"

"No, sir, I mean, yes, sir, I see why I was under scrutiny."

"But nevertheless you converted this flat into a brothel."

"Hardly, Father."

Roger scanned a page. "Did you or did you not hold frequent parties of mixed company during which voluminous amounts of whiskey were consumed?"

"Yes, sir, we had parties after the rugby games and for birthday occasions—"

"I'll bet they loved their host, good old Jeremy. Why not, with half the whores in Dublin dancing between the sheets of your bedrooms."

"Father, I did not have prostitutes. The ladies were . . . girl friends . . . true girl friends from ascendancy families for the most part . . . three of the lads were secretly married and—"

"And what?"

"Needed a place . . . F-F-F-Father."

"Don't stutter, Jeremy! For God's sake, don't stutter!"

Now came the blasts of icy air as Roger once more entailed the story of his own father, poor stuttering Arthur Hubble. Jeremy's grandfather had watched as his own father, the Famine Earl, signed the eviction notices and became too weak to run the earldom properly. Funny . . . so said Roger . . . how we always skip a generation. Roger had the intestinal fortitude to take over from his faltering father and run the estate when hardly more than a young man. Jeremy was the recurring curse of the Hubble line. Jeremy was stuttering Arthur, and Arthur was stuttering Jeremy.

"Are these accounts correct or not?" Roger said, shoving the report under Jeremy's nose. Jeremy saw a listing of dates and times that his mates had held trysts in the flat.

"I suppose so. I didn't realize the maids were on your payroll to take a dirty linen count."

Roger flung the report on the desk. "Cohabitation with one Molly O'Rafferty, illiterate street urchin from the Dublin Liberties."

"She is convent-educated, a novice schoolteacher, and a folk singer of public renown."

"She sings in a bar, Jeremy. Is she or is she not a Roman Catholic?"

"Great God!" brother Christopher cried. "How could you bring this on the family? Everything we hold sacred has been profaned. Two hundred and fifty years of honorable service to the Crown has been besmirched."

"Twelve generations of Earls of Foyle," Roger picked up, "are now being imperiled by a trollop!"

Jeremy leapt to his feet. "I demand you show her respect!"

"Respect for what, indeed, Jeremy, respect for what!"

Jeremy fell back into his chair. His father and brother hovered over him. A step behind he saw the cruel crystal eyes of Swan gleaming hatred. W. W. Herd, in the shadows, snickered as a detective is wont to do when he has nailed his prey.

"I shall not give her up," Jeremy croaked.

"The girl is pregnant," Roger said hard on.

It was as Jeremy had suspected, but how did they know? "Molly?" he whimpered.

"Yes, Molly. Molly O'Rafferty, the Catholic folk singer."

"How did you find this out, Father?"

There was a long silence.

"I don't believe you," Jeremy said, finding a bit of his ebbing anger.

"Her priest told us," Herd replied.

"Her priest cannot tell you that!"

"Oh, come on, Jeremy, they're all on the take. Besides, we're not going to allow a few ridiculous Vatican rules to prevent the truth."

Jeremy came to his feet. "I'm going to her," he said.

"You will sit down and you will hear the rest of it." Roger nodded for Herd to open the door. Two Belfast toughs whom Jeremy recognized as members of Swan's goon squad in the shipyard escorted his classmates Mal Palmer and Cliff Coleman into the study.

Jeremy was shocked into silence. He grew faint and pale, and his stomach began to seize up.

"Tell him what you told us, Mr. Palmer."

"Sorry about this, Jeremy, but Molly has been passing it around ever since you took up with her," Mal said.

"Liar!"

"Sorry, Jeremy . . . really sorry about this," Mal said breathing shakily.

"Liar!"

The two thugs sealed Jeremy off and pushed him back.

"Continue, Mr. Palmer."

"Molly and I did it a lot of times. Lot of times. I'd give her your schedule and when you were in class we'd slip up to your flat and . . . and did the shagging."

"Mr. Coleman," Swan said.

"Same here, Jeremy. At my place. Half the team's fucked her."

"You've been a laughingstock," his brother reminded.

Cliff Coleman started to go into detail when Jeremy went for the wastebasket and vomited until his eyes and nose ran and he coughed up lines of mucus.

Roger and Christopher went at him with heightened rage and outrage as the classmates were whisked out. Jeremy went hysterical until he collapsed and was dragged to his bed and went on until he deflated to quivering moans.

"You'll survive," Roger said, "but I've had my fill of your childish, disastrous behavior. I'm taking you over now, Jeremy. Do you understand!"

"Yes . . . F-F-F-Father."

"Christopher is returning to Oxford to finish his year. As for you, Donaldson has arrived to pack you up. You are out of Dublin, here and now. I see no further need to educate you. When Christopher's term is over, the two of you will do your service in the family regiment. Christopher will return to Oxford after he obtains proper rank. As for you, you will remain in the service until I see fit. Do we understand each other?"

"What do you want of me, Father!"

"Sons!"

"I'll see to everything, Father," Christopher said.

"I know you will, son, I know you will. You, Jeremy, will be in your brother's care. I'm off to the manor to see your mother. In order to avoid a scandal we will make a suitable arrangement with Miss O'Rafferty. In fact, after what she has done to you, we think it quite generous. You are not to see her again. Is that clear, Jeremy?"

The boy writhed on his bed in agony.

"Is that clear, Jeremy?"

46

Frederick Weed was at his draftsman's table on the far side of his office. It was good to see him there again. The Admiralty was pressing hard to develop underwater craft comparable to the German U-boats, and there was a lot of catching up to do.

His secretary entered. "The Red Hand has just passed through Portadown, Sir Frederick. She should be in the yard within the hour."

"Go down and meet the train. Bring Lady Caroline to my office directly."

"Very well, sir."

Weed left the drafting table and went back to his desk. There was a lot of catching up to do with Caroline as well. Bad seeds had bloomed after the Sixmilecross ambush. The humiliation by the Irish Republican Brotherhood gunrunning on his private train would go with him to his grave.

Sir Frederick had suffered a minor stroke in the aftermath of the uproar. Considering his advanced age and hard style of life, his recovery was rather amazing.

What hurt him more than the hazing in the press and the laughter from the pubs was the ambivalent behavior of both Caroline and Jeremy.

They had been gladly used by this Larkin—whose Machiavellian deceit had constituted the lowest form of treachery! He had used them! Instead of rallying to Weed, the two of them remained quiet. At times, Weed felt that Larkin had cast an evil spell over them. Oh, once or twice they referred to his treachery, but never very convincingly.

It came back to him once that Jeremy had tried to steal his way in to see Larkin in prison. Well, he bloody well put a stop to that! Caroline, her father suspected, may have been seriously emotionally involved with Larkin.

A strange family standoff ensued. Volumes of buried thoughts lay in volumes of unspoken words. Did indeed they forgive Larkin's dastardly behavior? Sir Frederick balked at putting the question to them directly. For the first time in his life, he feared the answer.

So, he had a quiet little stroke and Caroline and Jeremy patched things over with him, but the great bombast and love between them was now missing. From the raucous laughter over Jeremy's piss-up at the brothel in England it had been a polite and formal relationship with the family patriarch.

God in heaven, Freddie felt so alone. The two he held most dear, penning him proper notes these days. Horseshit!

Weed grunted to his feet, checked his pocket watch as the five o'clock whistle sounded. Soon his legions marched under his window toward the factory gate, doffing their caps as they passed.

Would that bloody train ever get in!

"Hello, Freddie, you're looking well."

"Hello, Caroline, I look like hell and so do you."

"Should you be smoking and drinking?"

"All I get to do with this cognac is swirl it in an elegant manner and sniff it. As for the cigar, I only feel it."

They were both shaken by his words. One of their life's pleasures was Caroline biting off the end of his cigar and lighting it, just so.

"Jeremy?" she asked.

"He's at Rathweed Hall in his apartment. He's locked himself in. We've scarcely exchanged a dozen words. Yourself?"

"Things between Roger and myself are extremely rocky. There could well be a separation."

"Oh dear."

"Roger has finally succeeded in breaking the boy. God only knows what transpired in Dublin, but Roger has what he wants, an obedient little pissant for a son. . . ."

Weed could not take the disdain in his daughter's eyes. He lowered his own.

"You and I have spoken about Jeremy for hours. We know he has limited capabilities. How in the name of God could you have joined in this barbaric scheme?" she demanded.

"Caroline—"

"How in the name of God did you permit this to happen!"

Weed closed his eyes and held his hands up in a manner of pleading for her to stop and listen to him.

"I am not going to claim virginity in this matter," he began, "but let's put it in its proper context. You know how many ongoing enterprises Roger and I have together. It is not, I repeat, *not* unusual for him to ask for Brigadier Swan a dozen times a year to check this out, check that out. After Jeremy's behavior in England and the estrangement I've felt from him since that . . . incident . . . when I was told he had taken up with a Catholic pub singer—and that's what they told me, a Catholic pub singer—I said fine, keep an eye on him. I swear to you I had no idea of the depth of his involvement nor the true picture of this young lady. I fully thought that Jeremy was on another of his ridiculous escapades. I'm guilty. I lent Roger the brigadier and I didn't follow through with an inquiry."

Caroline hardly seemed mollified. "This is a very, very lovely young lady and she is carrying my grandchild. I am making a stand about this."

"Marriage?"

"Absolutely."

"I see."

"You'd better see, Freddie, indeed you'd better see," she said, coming from her chair and walking away, dabbing her eyes and bringing under control the chills trembling her.

"Well . . . I . . . uh . . . it should be no problem to have her converted to the Anglican church, quietly. But how will Jeremy stand up to Roger if you're contemplating a separation?"

"I'll go back to Hubble Manor with them. It may take a year, it may take longer, but Roger is going to give up his medieval, Reformation mentality. They will have this child in Hubble Manor before he pushes Christopher to the altar to stud an heir."

"Aren't we playing Roger's game?"

"No, goddamnit, we're playing Caroline's game! My son is going to inherit the earldom and he is going to do something about the deplorable conditions out there."

Sir Frederick Weed contained all the winces and groans. If he objected, he'd lose Caroline. She already had a foot out the door. What would then be left? Christopher? Christopher was only slightly less despicable than Roger, and the only reason for that was that he hadn't lived long enough to pick up all of Roger's slime.

Roger, Christopher, and Sir Frederick? It had come down to this. The two of them ready to move in and carve him up at the first sign of another stroke.

"Caroline," he said shakily.

"Aye, Father."

"We've a lot of making up to do, don't we? I'm standing with you. That's a start."

"Do you know where Molly O'Rafferty is?" Caroline asked.

"Yes, she's left her house, she's living in . . . the Liberties . . . with friends."

"Shall we go see Jeremy?" she asked.

"I think you'd better do that by yourself. And let him know how distressed I am."

Caroline knocked, and knocked again, hard.

"Who is it?"

"It's your mother."

The door was unbolted and cracked open. Caroline entered Jeremy's sitting room, shut down by graying darkness. The boy was haggard and bearded and pitifully ashamed.

"Uh . . . don't really know where I was or what happened to

my ... head. But I woke up clear-minded at the end of the week and realized what had taken place. Donaldson had me packed and ready to move back to Hubble Manor. I ... uh ... escaped and it wasn't hard to pick up Mal's trail. ...

"What did you find out?"

"What I should have known from the beginning. Mal was lying ... he'd run up a gambling debt of over a hundred ... his father said he wouldn't pay it ... he was desperate. Brigadier Swan gave him two hundred, and the same to Cliff Coleman. They were paid to lie to me about Molly. ... I went to try to find her ... she was gone. ... I came here."

"I don't know how much you love Molly."

"I do, Mother. I love her. I love her!"

"That helps, then. In any event, you have a responsibility to that girl. We know where she is, Jeremy."

"Where, Mother, where!"

"She's with friends in Dublin, but in her situation, she could leave the country at any time."

"Tell me where she is!"

"Now you hold on, Jeremy, and you listen to me. First of all, in this matter, your grandfather is only guilty of ignorance."

"But he sent Swan!"

"Freddie was unaware of the true nature of things."

"He's lying."

"He doesn't lie to me, Jeremy. He's ready to stand with us. The question is, are you ready to do what needs being done?"

"Tell me, Mother."

"You are to go to Molly and you are to beg her forgiveness. You are to ask her to make a quiet conversion and the two of you will marry. There is not a damned thing your father can do about it." Caroline spoke on, extremely slowly and extremely deliberately.

"You are the Viscount Coleraine, the undisputed and undeniable heir to the Earldom of Foyle. Your father cannot disown you. He cannot disinherit you. You and Molly are to return to Hubble Manor. I shall be there with you."

"Mother, I'm frightened."

"You should be. But you have everything on your side, including myself and your grandfather."

Belief and terror clashed inside him.

"Jeremy," his mother said softly, "if you fail, you will lose Molly and you will lose me. What you will win is a life between your father and your brother in Hubble Manor. That's your alternative."

"I'll do it, Mother," Jeremy said stoutly.

"I'm not your coach exhorting you at halftime," she pressed, "this is going to take balls."

He sucked in a breath to assure himself. "You'll see," he said.

CHAPTER

47

The arrangement Maxwell Swan had proposed to Molly O'Rafferty called for her to make a quick trip to Switzerland to a clinic that specialized in dealing with illegitimate children of the aristocracy.

Molly could have an abortion performed. Afterward she would receive "comfort" money in the form of three hundred quid a year for five years provided she was not heard from again. This was an enormous sum that would enable her to establish herself somewhere other than the British Isles.

If she insisted on having the child because of religious reasons, she would remain in seclusion at the clinic. A well-situated blind adoption would be arranged and she would surrender the child upon delivery.

The monies plus a steamer ticket to anywhere in the world would then be doled out.

Upon sight of her, Jeremy was overcome with guilt and sorrow and begged forgiveness for believing the ugly lies about her and his mates.

The girl, not yet seventeen, gave Jeremy short shrift. She simply would not enter into a conspiracy with Jeremy to marry in defiance and then stand up to Roger Hubble. The entire scene and way of life of the earldom disgusted her. She would not live under the roof of a man who offered her money to destroy his own grandchild.

She had dishonored her own family and her faith. She would make her departure from Ireland and have her child and raise it

by teaching and by singing ballads and would not take a
ha'penny from the Hubbles.

But what of Jeremy? He was thrown into confusion. Molly
asked the unthinkable. To go off with her he would have to
renounce his title and be thrown into a world of working men
and women and this terrified him . . . utterly . . . completely.

If only Conor were there to give him counsel. If only Conor
were there to shake him and impose courage. If only Conor . . .

Life in a cold water flat with a baby? What could he do?
Really . . . all those things he was used to . . . Surely Jeremy had
played games with his father, letting Roger know he would never
measure up to responsibility because he liked life as it was. Life as
he had known it could not be taken from him. He was born at
the top of the ladder. No way that could be taken from him.

Molly was obstinate. She loathed his family, purely and simply. It was they who were the underclass and not herself.

Molly left Jeremy at the Liffey, a boy trying to be a man but
not able to make it. He pumped himself up into believing he had
done the proper thing. He was not put on earth to become part
of a faceless mass of strugglers. He had a duty of generations,
centuries standing, and this was more important!

Caroline and Sir Frederick held their collective breath as
Jeremy went down to Dublin on his mission. They knew what
had happened the instant he returned to Rathweed Hall, alone.

Jeremy was standing up, all right. He had made a decision
and he had made himself believe his decision was based on
honor.

"I think I'd like to speak to Mother, alone," he said after he
found them in the billiard room.

"I think not," Caroline said. "Your grandfather has doted
over you from the moment you were born."

"This is an intimate family matter," Jeremy retorted, swelling
up his own sense of righteousness.

"No," his mother snapped quickly.

"I have an enormous stake in you, Jeremy," his grandfather
said.

"Very well. I've come to a decision. I'm standing with Father."

"What do you mean?" Sir Frederick said in a voice that Jeremy had never heard before.

Jeremy flushed. There was welling fear to suppress, a dryness to make wet inside his mouth, a trembling to bring under control.

"Molly was cynical and insulting to our family and . . . our way of life. She refused to live in Hubble Manor. She portrayed us rather harshly."

"Well, bully for her," Caroline said. "It seems that the only people involved in this beloved land with any sense of honor are the croppies."

She looked to her father in a dare. Frederick wanted to jump in, in outrage, but he merely reddened. One false word and Caroline would be gone and his life would end in a disaster.

Mind the temper, he told himself, mind the temper. You're sweating, Freddie. Don't let another bloody stroke do you in, now.

"You let her go?" Caroline questioned.

"She refused, Mother. I had no choice."

"That girl is carrying your child in her belly, conceived in love. Do you love her?"

"I do, Mother, but my duty is greater than my folly."

"God! You sound like Christopher! You damned fool, Jeremy! What kind of a man are you! You should have taken her and gone anywhere . . . anywhere . . . "

"Caroline!" her father interceded.

"Shut up, Freddie. Jeremy, you should have taken her and fled. Can't you see how magnificent she is?"

"Now, just a minute, Mother!" Jeremy cried. "Don't you be so damned pious. You loved Conor Larkin! You loved him, did you not!"

The words, never to be spoken, were now uncaged into a room growing wild. After the fall . . . after the silence . . . Caroline looked to her father, wavering and ashen.

"I loved Conor Larkin," she said.

Freddie turned and sagged.

"Why didn't you up and run away with Conor? It's not all that easy, is it, Mother?"

"I loved him," she repeated, "but he was too decent to make love to me. He did not make me pregnant. So you see, there is a difference, my son."

"Really, Mother? You didn't go with him because you didn't want to abdicate your throne and live on the run. That's why. The same bloody reason you condemn me for."

"That's a reasonable point, Caroline," her father said harshly.

"I would have gone with him, anywhere," she said.

"But you didn't!" Jeremy cried.

"Conor would not take me because he cared for things other than himself. He did not want the blood of innocent people on his hands, from the riots your father and grandfather would have created. They would have turned his province into a pyre."

Suddenly Frederick Weed emitted a laugh, low at first, then rather hardy. "Well now, we've all said our little piece," he said. "Your mother is probably right. Well, Jeremy?"

"Poor, dear pitiful little Jeremy!" Jeremy screamed. "Poor, weak stuttering Arthur! Despicable Jeremy! Shitty Jeremy!"

"Jeremy, go to Molly O'Rafferty!"

"I am going to Hubble Manor and I shall soon join the family regiment!"

"You are a despicable coward," Caroline said very softly and firmly. "I am ashamed that you are my son. Now, get out of my sight."

"Grandfather!"

"Pack your things and leave, Jeremy," Frederick Weed said.

Frederick Weed led a pair of servants into Caroline's quarters, one carrying a tray of food and the other holding a pair of candelabra.

"Caroline?"

"I'm over here, Freddie, I'm not sleeping."

The food and soft light were arranged at a table. Caroline took off her lap robe and went from her chaise lounge.

"He's gone," her father said.

"I know."

"Well now," Freddie said, twirling his unlit cigar, "it's been quite a day. I guess we've both been lying to ourselves about Jeremy all his life."

"Isn't that a fact," she said. "I was so pleased when he made his entrance. Roger knew from the minute he was born that Jeremy belonged to you. Well, Jolly Roger has what he wants. Not one, but two young men in stud service."

"And we," he laughed, "are back to square one. To hell," he said, "I'm lighting this damned cigar."

"Freddie, you shouldn't. . . . Here, give it to me." Caroline went through the old ritual of softening it, biting off the end, and rolling the flame on, just so, and stuck it in his mouth.

"Caroline," he said contemplatively, "the damned stroke brought me face to face with the myth of my invincibility. One starts summing up. I'm an entrepreneur, a product of my times. The era has called for hard men. Along the way Ulster has become some kind of a mutation. It's too late for me to change. I have to go out the way I know."

"I realize that, but you don't act like you're history, Freddie."

"We face the most serious challenge of my life in Roger. He is intrinsically evil. Roger has those two boys under this thumb. They are his Orange card just as Londonderry was once his Orange card. But I still have the ace in the hole. I still have you, Caroline." He took his daughter's hand and held it to his lips and unlikely tears fell down his cheeks.

"The worst mistake in my life was engineering you into marriage with Roger Hubble. I have loved you more than anyone in my life, Caroline, including your dear mother."

"Freddie . . . "

"I should have known that a daughter like you was worth a half-dozen sons. It's not too late. You can manage my operation, blindfolded."

"Are you certain, Freddie?"

"Aye."

"Then I'm your girl."

"I intend to be around for some time. But since the stroke I have become obsessed with a fear of Roger taking over Weed Ship & Iron. His earldom is nonsense alongside of what I control. A great deal of prosperity comes from ventures I've brought him into. He'll jump us the minute I go down."

Candlelight enshadowed her hair, hanging below her shoulders as she wore it when she was a little girl. The chamber was scented and silk-walled with portraits of her by her Impressionist friends. Freddie sipped a nip of forbidden cognac.

"I have assembled a brilliant team of engineers, architects, scientists, foremen, and a work force second to none in Britain. My board of directors, save Roger, is totally clean. Your seat on the board until now has always been used by me as a proxy. I want you to activate it and learn. The team is loyal to me and they will be loyal to you."

"Roger is not going to disappear that easily, Freddie."

"Now don't interrupt me for a minute," he said. "Roger and I have been involved in a lot of very black business. I have a record book on him six inches thick. Give him the boundaries of his earldom and not one inch more."

"These records, Freddie. Won't they implicate you as well?"

"I'm an old man, Caroline. My lawyers are clever enough to put on an artful dodge for the rest of my days. I'll never see the inside of a courtroom. As for Roger, it's death incarnate. He'll never outlive the scandal."

"A long time ago I cared for Maxwell Swan. I have grown to hate him."

"Max sees the wisdom of taking early retirement. He was the trigger man on too many dirty jobs. Why are you staring at me like that, Caroline?"

She asked about the factory fire and he told her how Roger had been going into a cover-up as the building was burning. O'Garvey had indeed called off the investigation of the factory in exchange for Roger's putting money into the Bogside. When the building went up, they feared O'Garvey would blow the whistle on them and Swan had him assassinated.

For ever so long they remained quiet.

"Don't come in if you've not got the stomach for it," her father said. "There are some other disturbing things. The first is the worst of it. Do you hate me?"

"Do you hate me because of Conor Larkin?"

"I tried to get him hanged, of course," he answered. "In time the whole thing became rather amusing. Brilliant fellow, what? Pity he wasn't working our side of the game. Well, let's say I can certainly see the attraction. I can't hate you."

"And I love you, Freddie, and that's always been the fact of it."

Caroline lay on satin sheets and she felt sensuous to her own touch as well. She was astonished at her capacity to enter the forbidden rooms of Hubble Manor with such consummate ease ... even with their dirty secrets and foul play. She told herself she could and would make a lot of things better, but for the moment she luxuriated in the amazing sensation of her ascension to power. It was awesome. She was Frederick Weed's girl, the worth of six sons!

I've won! But what have I won? A dying father, the admission of a crumbled marriage that took half my life, the loss of my sons, the defection of an Andrew Ingram, a living death laid on Maxwell Swan, a hero of my childhood ... and the means to destroy my husband.

The satin on her face felt so good. She wrapped her arms around it. Now, what would she give for him?

"Oh, Conor lad, where are you now?" she wept.

THE MISSING YEARS

BY SEAMUS O'NEILL

INTERLUDE

I

What was plain to see was plain to see; namely, that my own path of glory in this life required me to hitch my wagon to a shooting star, and the life of Conor Larkin was going to be something to write about. His spirit was in my early ramblings at the students' center and from the debate stage at Queens College.

His passion for freedom was in my dispatches from the Boer War. He was the ghost crying for justice in my plays.

I have gathered copious notes of our childhood, of Ballyutogue life and our ventures in the high meadows, of the Larkins, of Mr. Andrew Ingram, and of Mr. Josiah Lambe and Conor's gift of the forge.

Everything else was compiled when Conor returned from roving; his years in Derry and the great screen and Caroline Hubble and his fierce renown on the football pitch. The ghastly factory fire and Conor's years at sea and the deep love he had for Rory. This love for Rory had a melancholy bent to it, as if Conor knew he would never have sons of his own and needed to leave Rory his legacy. Conor's final thoughts to me before we went on the big raid were about Rory, a veiled hope that Rory would follow him to Ireland.

It appears that I will never get to write his story. I will leave all my notes in the hands of Atty Fitzpatrick, who will no doubt succeed me by decades. She will find the author who will do the story justice.

＊　　＊　　＊

Conor was hit by three bullets at Sixmilecross, two in his back and one through the thigh. He was held incommunicado for weeks and tortured by clever methods so he would bear no visible signs.

For example: A pint of castor oil was forced into him. He was made to stand against a wall, spread-eagle in his bare feet. Jagged glass was laid all around him on the floor, so that if he moved so much as a centimeter he would be sliced up. Standing thusly, he was hooded and loud sirens and whistles were blown into his ears between questionings.

Conor told me that of all his accomplishments in life, none was greater than to be able to shyte standing up.

What happened after Sixmilecross was in nobody's plans. Serendipity of an unusual nature fell into the Brotherhood's lap. In reality, Sixmilecross was another of those famous Irish fuck-ups, a glorious tale of defeat, so prevalent in our history, but one that grows in grandeur from pub to pub.

Conor Larkin's audacity in using Sir Frederick Weed's personal train to run guns for the Brotherhood struck a nerve in the Irish funny bone. With public prodding by Atty Fitzpatrick and editorials by myself leading the free press, the country was soon awash in protest for the Sixmilecross "heroes" to receive justice.

England held a shifting balance of power in Ireland after the turn of the century. The Gaelic revival had been fanned into republican hot spots around the land. A sudden hope for freedom erupted.

Only Ulster, loyal Ulster, was safely in hand for the Crown.

On the European continent the Balkans were commencing nasty little neighborhood wars and it was only a matter of time until a monumental conflict between the great alliances would break out. Perhaps a year or two. Five years at the most.

Such eventuality caused England to consider closely her Irish situation. Ireland's unfortunate geographic position would be vital to England's sea lanes during any such conflict.

Moreover, England would need tens of thousands, nae, hundreds of thousands of Irishmen to fill in the fine old brigades and form new ones and otherwise provide Irish fodder for the Crown.

The obvious enemy in the coming war would plainly be Germany. Germany was thus in a position to supply arms to an Irish freedom movement and otherwise do what was necessary to destabilize Ireland.

The first impulse of the Crown was to take Conor Larkin and the Sixmilecross prisoners directly to the gallows and hang them. In one day the Parliament had passed "Larkin legislation" legalizing his seizure and allowing for secret trial and execution without so much as a lawyer to defend him.

However, the size and fury of the nationwide protest shocked the British into rethinking their position. To hang Larkin now could well ignite further riots.

The British deemed it too dangerous to rock the Irish boat and concocted a deal. In exchange for a halt to the protests and three years of silence by the Brotherhood, the Sixmilecross prisoners would plead guilty and receive a "benevolent" short prison term and then freedom.

Although it was a blow to Brotherhood ambitions and against stated policy, the thought of Conor Larkin's hanging or serving a life term was unbearable. The Council, including Atty, Long Dan Sweeney, and my good self all agreed to the deal.

I was the messenger to tell Conor to plead guilty.

I was taken to the Curragh military camp where he was being held secretly. Seven weeks had passed without anyone's seeing him. Manacled, limping, left arm slinged, eyes in deep bruised sockets . . . I brought him up to date and then delivered his orders of capitulation. Oh Jesus, it was the most wrong I had ever been in my life.

Conor replied, "After three hundred years of rubbing our faces in the mud and three hundred years of talking in circles, we have to draw a line. After a famine used deliberately to murder the Irish race, we have to test our mettle as a people, here and now. We may not have what it takes. As for me, I am Conor Larkin. I am an Irishman and I've had enough."

I was never so ashamed of myself. He had turned our childhood dreams into the terrible reality of taking Ireland upon his own two shoulders.

There was nothing of bravado in the way he told me his words. There were no cheering crowds. There was no hope of justice.

Yet he had now risen to the greatness I had always known was his, but feared for him to claim. I slunk away to Dublin.

The Parliament had legislated "Star Chamber" proceedings, straight out of the Spanish Inquisition.

By a miracle, Atty and I were privy to the first of the trials. The British did not know going in that Conor would not accept the deal, and we were there to assure they carried out the terms. Again, we were under the oath of silence as part of the bargain.

Conor Larkin, in chains, in a dungeon-turned-courtroom hidden in a military barracks in the Wicklow mountains, denounced England's presence in Ireland as a perverse, greedy corruption of England's own Common Law and God's will.

He denounced England's attempt to destroy the ancient Celtic culture and the Irish race.

He denounced the English contempt for the Irish people that made them appear inferior in British eyes and thus allowed England to go out into the world and likewise cast browns and blacks as inferiors ... grist for the colonial mill ... to be saved and redeemed by a superior English society.

He denounced the proceedings as a total mockery of British justice.

He predicted that before the century was out, the colonizers would pack their kits and be drummed out of every colony in the world where they had imposed their bloody repression.

He did what he did, not knowing if he'd ever see trees again or walk a single step in free air, much less live to see another day.

The British were outraged. In the end they owned the courts, the military, the press, the industry, the banks, the schools, the land.

You see, he made his protest from a dark and lonely place, but he made the British blink.

In the face of his condemnation they did not take his life.

Conor was remanded, instead, to thirty years in prison. For his hostile behavior, twenty lashes with the cat-o'-nine-tails was added to his sentence.

To us, British infallibility had been cracked ever so slightly. We were moved, inspired by one man who had had enough. A rebellion, some day faraway, had been born.

God and my beliefs had been going through a revolving turnstile all my life. I always knew he was there. Using my left-handed logic, I always tried to find a rationale for why he continued to abandon the Irish. The Irish, whose only crime was not being born English.

For the first time I questioned the wisdom, the compassion, the love from God and even the existence of God himself. Why does he demand that his finest sons have to suffer having the living shit kicked out of them?

So, let me tell you about the cat-o'-nine-tails. The whip is a braided leather tail three feet long. Not one tail—but nine of them—so each stroke is worth nine of the ordinary bull whip. In order to keep the ends of the tails from unraveling during a whipping, they are dipped in lead. An accomplished whipper can lay the nine tails across the victim's back . . . just so . . . so that the lead tips curl under his armpit and shred his flesh like cabbage for coleslaw.

From later reports I heard that Conor refused a stretcher and walked back to his cell.

At the same moment that Conor received his lashes, part of Shelley's body was found tied to a lamppost in the Shankill. Parts of her dismembered corpse were strewn about the alleyway . . . over fifty stab wounds . . . and at least that many hammer blows were struck.

On the wall behind her, written in her blood, the words, PAPIST WHORE.

The following months can only be imagined. Perhaps even Conor was unaware of what was happening. To my dismay I learned that one man cannot bear another man's pain. I wanted so desperately to be able to take some of his agony as my own. No matter how dear and willing the friend, the sufferer must suffer alone.

I have spoken to Warder Hugh Dalton on four occasions. Dalton was the senior Catholic guard at Portlaoise Prison. He inherited the task of keeping R.C. prisoners under control.

In order to carry out his job, he had long learned to inure himself to the pain of his charges. That all changed the first time he met Conor Larkin, who sang during his whipping.

Hugh Dalton told me that the human system shuts down on learning of the death of a loved one on the outside. Otherwise, the pain would not be bearable.

Conor sat on the edge of his cot in his dungeon cell in a torpid state, neither dead nor alive, giving off no signs of collapse or survival.

Hugh Dalton said that in this state the mind no longer makes conscious decisions. It is now that the inner truth of the man comes through. Either he has an unconscious will to live or an unconscious will to die. The body is comatose, the spirit decides.

For nearly four months Conor Larkin sat thus. Hugh Dalton suspected that Conor was going to survive simply because, by this time, those men who were bound to die were already dead.

In a sudden flash of sanity Conor spoke his first words. He cried for Dalton and told the warder to have him taken to the padded cell and chained so he would not destroy himself.

The dangerous moment had come with the lifting of the veil and the onrush of reality, of the vision of his beloved's slain and mutilated body.

The following weeks he was in and out of madness. Awakening to what had happened ... going crazy ... being restrained until he fell limp.

Slowly, he realized he would neither will himself to death nor take his own life and he had to bear the torment. Beginning then and for years to come he never went to sleep without praying that God would bring him death during the night.

As he returned to life, Conor made things hell for the governor of Portlaoise and for Warder Hugh Dalton.

First, he refused to wear prison clothing on the basis that he was not a criminal but a political prisoner. The Governor had his bed and all furnishings removed from his cell and left him with only a blanket. He ripped out a hole in the center for his head and slept on a stone floor for the three winter months.

Shortly after he won that round, he declared a hunger strike for books and the ceasing of all humiliating behavior toward him. This one nearly did him in. He lost so much flesh he was able to see through his own eyelids while they were shut. With fear of the consequences of Conor's death, the British ordered the Governor to submit once more.

God's meanings began to become apparent to me! Conor Larkin was not performing a role before an audience to promote and magnify his heroism. All that Conor Larkin ever was, was an extraordinary human, an Irishman, one Irishman who had had enough. God didn't make Conor a hero or any other man a hero because they bluffed their way to heroism.

God compelled the true and unvarnished heroes to undergo superhuman feats of heroism because God had instilled in them part of His own soul and spirit.

Only through the example of a hero can ordinary common men like me even realize the power of the extraordinary man. Only through such heroes can common men like me be moved to aspire and emulate.

His anguish and his triumph arose from truths he came into the world with. He won his ordeal. In the end, Conor Larkin was able to endure more punishment than the British could inflict. He laid upon them a moral and spiritual defeat. His spirit triumphed over their armies.

It made all of us in the Brotherhood examine ourselves and understand the sacrifice and dedication needed if we were to have any chance to declare our freedom against an enemy of immense power. Would we find enough men and women to follow in his footsteps?

Could we, always weaker in arms, eventually triumph by

sheer force of our righteousness? The nonrecognition of British institutions on Irish soil and acts of disobedience became a canon of faith for breaking the yoke of the colonizer.

Did we as a people have the stuff to pay the ultimate price?

First among those to be broken by Conor's valor was Warder Hugh Dalton who never got over the abuse poured on the republican prisoners. Conor forced him to consider his thirty years of kissing British ass . . . and to what avail . . . a small pension coming up and a life to live out, full of disgust with himself.

Knowing of my childhood connection to Conor and my republican leanings in my newspaper column, Dalton brought an outrageous escape plan to me.

I took it to Long Dan Sweeney and Atty. They were convinced of Dalton's desire for redemption.

Next, I went to Conor's dear brother, Father Dary Larkin. Dary was a Bogside priest and close confidant of the enlightened Bishop Mooney.

Dary did not hesitate a ha'penny's worth and threw his lot in with us. Did he have Mooney's blessing? Not to ask.

Hugh Dalton was up for retirement as we set up the plan. Conor was instructed to start serving the Mass so that it would appear natural after a time. This gave Dalton the needed time to get his pension and leave for civilian life where he would be above suspicion.

On certain Sundays the prison was made a sort of open house for visiting relatives. Usually two or three dozen priests came from around the country as well.

Father Dary entered Portlaoise under an assumed name among twenty other priests. Father Kyle, a willing victim, was "attacked" in the sacristy by Conor, who pretended to be robbing him. The "victim" was bound, gagged, and locked in a closet where he would later be discovered.

After the noon Mass, all the priests assembled near the chapel and, as a group, passed through the main gate. Conor Larkin in the disguise of a priest in Father Kyle's clothing . . . and I'm certain the Lord will understand . . . walked out to freedom.

INTERLUDE

II

Dunleer, the landed estate of the Baron Louis de Lacy, lay hauntingly in the lunarscape of Connemara in County Galway. His land stretched over thousands of acres, encompassing dozens of the hundreds of lakes that pocked the area. The barony drifted up to the Twelve Bens, small but respectable mountains of jagged naked stone hovering over a moorlike bog, and a fairy coast of hidden coves and strands and plunging fjords. Most of the mystic de Lacy domain was all but hidden to the eye. Once out of the foothills, a prolific archipelago peppered a water world from the bay out to the open sea.

The de Lacys were old Norman Catholic aristocracy of the legendary "Tribes of Galway" eccentricized by generations of Connemara wilderness. Dunleer demesne was part of the tragic heritage, the land to which Oliver Cromwell had condemned the Irish into exile and mass death.

The present Baron, affectionately called "Lord Louie," had recently closed out a distinguished career in the British Navy and consular service and had retreated to Dunleer to breed Connemara ponies and continue his mania as a Gaelic scholar.

Lord Louis was also an ardent republican and secretly a member of the Irish Republican Brotherhood, a close confidant of Long Dan Sweeney and Atty Fitzpatrick. Dunleer figured in Brotherhood plans early on, a safe place for men in hiding and a place to store arms.

From the day Conor Larkin made his escape, he was spirited into Dunleer and hidden so deeply, so far back in a lakeside cottage, it would be impossible to find him.

❈   ❈   ❈

Well now, we had the most hunted head with the greatest bounty on it in our keep. Dan wanted to get Conor out of the country and let a few years pass. Even I could see the rationale of having him leave Ireland, but I feared it, greatly. The man was in no state to take care of himself.

In prison he lived in a survival mode. In Dunleer Conor now had open spaces and time to think. The wound of Shelley's death would never fully heal, we all knew that. As the weeks passed he still was not able to function normally. He would show the four of us periods of clarity, but the longer he remained clear, the more her murder and his guilt were laid bare.

After a time he'd flare and plunge into a nether world. Conor had locked himself with higher walls than Portlaoise. He was a prisoner of himself. His escapes now were his distorted journeys into madness. He could only face his torment head-on for so long, then fall.

Dan's frustration had to be tempered by reality. Conor had to be taken out of the country. Only Atty held out now.

"We've got to lay it on the table, Atty," Dan argued to her. "Conor is never going to come out of this. He will never be reliable to the Brotherhood again and he is a danger to himself."

"Give me some time," Atty pleaded. "I'll go to Dunleer and stay with him. Dan, we owe him that much."

"Seamus, you know him best," Dan challenged, "will he ever come out of it? And you fucking better speak the fucking truth."

"Aye, I'll answer that, Dan," I said. "Conor has shown us his iron will has an iron will. He has borne the unbearable. Yes, he will find a framework to live in. Yes, he will return to the Brotherhood. But Dan, he can't do it in five minutes."

"I'd keep him in Dunleer forever," Dan said, "if I could. For the moment the Brits are looking in every monastery and church in the country. Sooner or later they will focus on other likely places. If they find him here it would be a disaster the Brotherhood might not overcome. The Brotherhood comes first ... over any man ... even Conor Larkin."

"Maybe he never will come out of it, Dan," Atty retorted, "but to exile him in his condition now might do to him what the Brits were unable to do. It would kill him."

"Aye, it might well kill him," I agreed.

"Give me some time, Dan, and I will work with you," Atty begged.

"All right, Atty, I'll give you time. It will take us a couple of months to work out a fail-proof escape. I will give you those sixty days."

Atty took each of our hands and looked at us, fiercely. "I'll not let him go down!" she swore.

The woman exhausted herself trying to bring him back. Her devotion tested her beyond the breaking point.

Conor would warn her that if she were wise she'd clear out. He saw nothing but death all around him. Well, one does not think of Atty Fitzpatrick crying herself to sleep night after night. Time began to grow short and Atty grew desperate.

At wit's end, one day, she shrieked at him.

"Damn you! Don't you think of anyone but yourself? What makes you think you're the only one who has grieved for Shelley! She was the sister I never had. I adored her!"

Conor blinked in disbelief. He dared emerge from his winter's cave.

"I let her down, Conor. I failed her! I was responsible for her guard in Belfast."

"Surely you can't take that on yourself," Conor said. "She went into the danger with eyes opened. You were in Dublin. You're not to blame."

"I am to blame," Atty cried, "and my sister is dead."

She felt Conor's hands on her arms and he shook her gently. "Why couldn't I see it? Why haven't I helped you, Atty . . . my own self-pity, that's what!"

Atty tore loose from him. "I'm done in with pain and guilt, man!"

This time the embrace was too powerful for her to run from and she let his power and his compassion wash over her.

*   *   *

And so it was . . . so it was. The two of them, both trauma-
tized by the brutal murder, made a discovery in each other's
arms. . . .

It was bound to be. Shelley MacLeod had left them a legacy
to care for one another.

I know, for actual fact, that no sexual stirrings overtook them
as they clung to each other night after night. Their hunger to
overcome the tragedy was now a hunger for continuation of life
itself.

Thanks to God for Atty Fitzpatrick. Conor returned to the
living in bits and pieces in their bittersweet wilderness. There
was no time left for them to discover their capacity to love again,
for as he healed and found the will to take charge of himself, the
time came for him to leave Ireland.

Lord Louis made a trip to London to see the German ambassador. Although the Germans were supplying weapons to both
the Brotherhood and the Protestant Ulster Volunteers, they had
reason to cooperate with us in the Larkin matter.

A few months later, Lord Louis and Conor Larkin made
their way out of the barony to the nearby fishing village of
Roundstone, where his yacht, *Gráinne Uáile*, was docked. They
sailed from the small harbor past Slyne Head where a meeting at
sea was kept with a small German freighter.

Two weeks later Conor crossed the Canadian border into the
United States and made secret connection with Joe Devoy, the
leader of the American Clan of the Gaels. Conor's mission was
to raise funds for arms and an underground newspaper, the two
most vital components of future insurrection.

1909

'Twas a beautiful spring day in County Galway. In actual fact, it was raining cannonballs and razor blades, but it was the day that Conor Larkin slipped back into Ireland. His mission in America had been a grand success, separating Irish-Americans who had made it big from substantial mounts of money by his charm and persuasion.

Lord Louis's Barony of Dunleer had become a small training base as well as the best place to hide men on the run in Ireland. Atty was stuck in a play in Dublin for several weeks and Dan Sweeney had been laid low by illness, so I was first to see him.

I held my breath, fearing the kind of Conor Larkin that might have emerged. My fears were for naught. He was in command of his work and in control of the past miseries. Life as a fugitive, moving by darkness from hiding place to hiding place across Canada and America, had exacted a price, and the "collector" had taken his toll. But thanks to God, he had not turned cynical.

"What about Atty? Are you aching to see her?" I said.

His brow furrowed in thought, showing his aging, but he spoke with a slightly different voice, one that had picked up keen wisdom through time and suffering.

"I've had a lot to wonder about."

"You're not ambivalent, are you, Conor?"

"I am about both of us. Nothing was promised when I left

and we have not been in contact with each other for a long time now."

"She's never had eyes for anyone but you, if that's your concern."

"I have to tell you, Seamus, I would wake up from a hundred nightmares drenched with sweat until I trained myself to control my own dreams. I clutched up a hundred times when I saw a slim strawberry blonde in the streets and she'd turn and her face would not be Shelley's."

"Atty will understand, but she will be devastated if you reject her again."

"I know that Shelley is dead and Atty is alive. I know, also, that Atty is the strongest person I've ever met. She saw me groveling in weakness, totally dependent on her to survive the night. I don't know what is left of me as a man for this woman. I don't know if I have the capacity to love, even a different kind of love. She's too valuable for me to keep dragging her down."

I heard him now. Shelley had an ethereal beauty. Atty was a fair-sized woman, but everything was in a perfect state and her beauty was a kind that belonged to nobility.

Atty did not have the lithe wispiness of Shelley but made up for it with bottomless inner strength.

Shelley wore her emotions close to the surface. Atty was dark with her real feelings . . .

Leaving a ponderous question. Can a man emerge from an ultimate tragedy with one love and find another love to walk the rest of the way with?

I did not leave Dunleer dejected. There was an unbreakable thread between them that had held them together for many years and through terrible ordeals. They'd either find it on sight of one another or shortly thereafter, for I felt they could not be in the same country and live their lives apart. Was I wrong?

At first I thought so. Their initial meetings were uneasy, in the midst of Brotherhood business. She came to me, at last, containing what I felt was a sense of desperation.

"Conor must have a final exorcism of guilt," I told her. "Shelley has left the two of you a legacy—each other. You'd better take what is rightfully yours, Atty, or walk away and mean it."

Atty Fitzpatrick, a glorious figure of a horsewoman, rode from the manor house to Conor's hidden den along Lough Ballynahinch, then into a natural draw at Lough Fadda. At sight of her his heart thumped and a marvelous glow rushed through him and drove him to silliness and he jumped into the icy lake naked and challenged her to follow.

Atty took the dare and threw off her clothing. On seeing that woman bare and coming toward him in the lake, Conor felt that wonderful stirring again, only slightly modified by the freezing water. He carried her from the lake and wrapped her tightly in a blanket and dried her.

The sky closed in, ugly, billowing down the bens and making the landscape all gray now. The cottage grew deadly silent with anxiety. As he knelt and pondered at the fire, Atty filed away the dinner dishes.

"Conor," she said calmly but with utter finality, "I'll wait no longer. My bedroom door will be open tonight. If you don't come to me, it will be closed forever."

Conor looked to the comfort of the bottle, but as the heavens burst apart he found himself wandering in the rain outside, screaming to the unkind gods and to Shelley to free him.

His soggy figure filled her door frame, the clothing lashed against his body, still fine of structure. Atty rose from her chair and stood beside the bed and took her blouse off and opened her breasts to his sight. Her skirt fell to the floor.

"I've waited so long," she managed to murmur.

Conor moved in slowly and kicked the door shut behind him leaving them both as giant figures dancing in the lamplight.

"You're glorious, Atty," he said, "and I'm going to love you with all of my soul."

I can vouch that their fears of the moment had melted by morning, when I made an unsaintly visit to their cottage. They came to the cottage door, arms about the other's waist, half-croaked from weariness and dazed by the wonderment of discovering one another. It was forever after. And this was the love that brought him peace for the first time in his life. Strange, that in the imminent danger of the Brotherhood they discovered a constant sense of bliss and serenity.

After that, when the two of them were together, their eyes always seemed to be tied to the other's. It became as right as anything could be between a man and a woman. They had arrived at a good place only after mutual grief and longing. But they had discovered their own fine high meadow and had great strength and compassion to draw upon. The unity of their life's work did not hang over them like a guillotine.

How's it all going to end, Atty girl? There was no normal life for them. He would never live another day as a free man. He would always be Ireland's most wanted fugitive. She knew in her innards that Conor would author his own demise before he turned into a musty wheezing number like Long Dan Sweeney, brain soaked with revolution and unaware of the gnarl of bare walls and sheetless cots and sunlessness. So long as Conor was walking through, she would walk with him.

They both confided in me that Shelley came to them individually, often at first, but always in such a manner as to bring a smile of sweet memory and never as a threat.

In the months and years that followed Conor's return, the Irish Republican Brotherhood took its first tottering steps, but it was developing two hearts and two heads.

In Dublin, the Supreme Council set the lofty philosophical canons, published the underground newspaper, arranged our scanty finances, and made a firm political alliance with the legal Sinn Fein Party led by Arthur Griffith. The Council was partly quite capable, greatly visionary, Irishly irresponsible, and always argumentative.

Conor Larkin became the big fellow outside of Dublin, refusing a seat on the Council that would compromise his growing independence. Constantly on the move, Conor trained a few hundred men and broke them into highly secret skilled units.

Using former soldiers of the Boer War as instructors, his elite squads drilled in countryside sabotage. Scattered all around Ireland, Conor picked out a dozen tempting targets for each unit, and each unit learned what there was to learn about these targets and conducted dummy exercise after dummy exercise for the day they would become operational.

Conor ran the arms-smuggling operation, manufactured some small arms at Dunleer, and established a dummy company in Belfast under the guise of an Ulster sporting club. The "club," fronted by Protestant sympathizers of the Brotherhood, was actually allowed to import weapons by a quasi-legal route used by the Ulster Volunteers.

I think Conor's masterwork was the Brotherhood's espionage network. Our lads in the constabulary and in Dublin Castle kept us informed that there was fine intelligence on every move the British made.

The bedrock rule of Conor's elite squads was not of things particularly appreciated in the Irish psyche: discipline, patience, silence, physical readiness, and moderation.

The loyalty of Conor's men to him made the Supreme Council nervous. There was constant grumbling over Conor's secrecy and fears that he was forming a personal army.

Louis, Atty, Dan, and I knew that Conor had no aspirations for personal power and so long as Dan Sweeney supported Conor there was little the Council could do, but the old man was slowing down and wearing out. So, the brilliant minds on the Council came up with a highly suspect tactic. With Dan's approval, they voted for Conor to succeed Dan as chief of staff. This move would compel Conor to have Council approval on his plans.

Like the great Caesar himself, Conor rejected the throne with the terse message, "An underground army is not a democratic institution and that goes double for an Irish underground army. If you can't live with that, fire me."

Conor's answer was very clear indeed.

However, that grand old war that England was going to engage in on the European continent was about to erupt, and this brought on a whole new set of circumstances.

Should the Brotherhood declare Irish independence in the event of war? Should the Brotherhood's elite units become operational? Would the Irish public look kindly on the Brotherhood's attacking the Crown while tens of thousands of Irish lads served in the British Army?

The Irish Party under John Redmond caved in in the mother of Parliaments, pledging Irish loyalty in any coming war and taking the Home Rule Bill off the table till such a war ended. It was repugnant to even the most simple-minded Irishman, the last hurrah of a party that had begun with such promise under the late Charles Stewart Parnell.

The Sinn Fein Party—"Ourselves Alone"—swiftly moved into the political vacuum created by the vanishing Irish Party.

As for Ulster, they had made themselves immovable on all matters. In a blood-curdling crescendo, the Protestants took an oath of covenant, swearing to fight to the last drop to keep Ulster British.

Back to the matter of naming Conor Larkin as chief of staff designate. It was apparent even to me, Conor's most ardent supporter, that the Brotherhood could not go north and south at the same time. I understood Conor's ethereal moods and his drifting off into his own universe better than anyone. He had established himself as a loner from the time we were lads up in the heather above Ballyutogue.

Before the British ambush at Sixmilecross, Conor had acted largely on his own in setting up the gunrunning scheme on the Red Hand engine.

After the ambush, he defied Brotherhood orders to enter a guilty plea.

From the moment Conor returned to Ireland after his escape, I realize, he had thought his way through the ideological swamps and had come up with his own plan of what was possible. He must have realized that he could not accomplish what he had planned under the burden of being chief of staff. Indeed, were there deeper and more dire reasons why he refused the Brotherhood's command? Perhaps it was something very simple

... that Conor had never given an order to have an informer kneecapped or executed. Part of him was still a poet, a gentle man. Did he lack the needed sense of "killer," and did he realize it?

I caught up with Conor at the hideaway over Sam Grady's Monument Works in Cork. I locked us in with a couple of bottles and a view down to the latest tombstones awaiting delivery from Sam's yard. He knew what I was up to and I knew he knew, so we slid into it gingerly.

"The organization can't keep going like it is."

"It can and it will," Conor said.

"I know your opinion of the Council but can you blame them for fearing a one-man rule?"

"So long as Dan Sweeney knows every move I make and approves it, the Council should be satisfied. The more they know about clandestine plans, the more vulnerable those plans become. We've a long and tormented history of informers, Seamus. It's the bane of Irish life."

"Then that's it?"

"What's it?"

"Everyone knows you are reluctant to give an execution order."

"That's part of it."

"Then we'll relieve you of the burden. All executions will have full Council approval in the future. You'll have nothing to do with giving the orders."

"That's a British kind of word game, Seamus. Informers must be put away if we are to exist."

"But you won't do it?"

"Aye, and I do not aspire to be chief of staff."

"But, Jaysus, you're running the show now."

"Then take my resignation back to the Council."

"Shit, man!"

"Control yourself, runt."

"Shit, Conor! Now you fucking listen to me. I'm Seamus O'Neill, the most loyal man you'll ever know. But you've had a wild hair up your ass driving you crazy since we were kids. Think I don't know you've dirty doubts? What are they, Conor?

Why won't you take command of the Brotherhood?"

"Because I'm not a liar," he snapped suddenly. "I won't command men I'm lying to."

"Well now, it's becoming interesting," I said.

"You'd better start emptying the bottle, Seamus, because you won't want to be sober after you hear what I've got to say."

I respectfully did as he suggested. His face, always glowing with kindness, grew dark and hard-edged. In these moments his years of agony pushed through and I saw the rebel boy's cynicism.

"Let me ask you a question, Seamus. Would the Catholics of Ireland ever, of their own free will, declare themselves a part of England?"

"That's pretty stupid, Conor."

"Is it? Let me ask it again. Would Catholic Ireland freely declare itself loyal to the Crown?"

"Of course not," I said fearing what was coming.

"Then what makes you think that Protestant Ulster will ever openly and willingly declare themselves part of Ireland?"

"We know all that, Conor," I replied angrily.

"And do you know that the Ulsterman is incapable of rising above self-imposed ignorance fired by raw fear? Their minds have become vacuums and under the total manipulation of preachers who have shut out the light and air of ideas and beauty. Ulster has enslaved itself. The only ecstasy they are capable of is to demonize themselves into religious fanatics and sorely mistake their unlimited capacity for hatred as some form of joy."

"Tell me something I don't know!" I demanded.

"The Irish Republican Brotherhood," he said softly, "is fostering a delusion of a united Ireland."

Conor was speaking blasphemy! He was attacking the very cornerstone of republicanism. I tried to wave him off, to hear no more. . . .

"What the hell does Ireland want with a million lunatics sworn to destroy us? They are the tragic orphans of this Irish calamity, His Majesty's Royal Ulster lepers," he continued, grabbing me by the arms and shaking me. "By God, Seamus O'Neill, we Irish are a civilized people. We cannot allow them to poison our wells with their hatred. I say, wall them off and let them bang their bloody Lembeg drums and sing their bloody Reformation hymns and fly their bloody Union Jacks ... but keep them out of our lives or we will end up diseased like they are. I say, give them their filthy province, for if we don't we will have condemned the Irish people to eternal damnation."

"God!" I screamed, "Who else have you told this to!"

"Ah, Seamus lad, I've not seen you so pale. What's the matter? Truth is truth."

"And treason is treason!"

"So be it. The truth is that there is as much chance of bringing reason, much less love, to these people up north as there is of trying to draw gold out of the winds. The truth is that I would have to destroy my own truths, and myself, in order to become a Long Dan Sweeney."

We were as quiet as the tombstones in Sam Grady's yard. Ah shyte, it was vintage Conor Larkin I heard. Who in the Irish Republican Brotherhood had not lied to himself about the same question? We would go on for generation after generation without the courage to face the truth that Irish unity was a myth.

Who but Conor Larkin would have the courage to stand up and speak truth in the face of a hurricane of hypocrisy? Conor alone refused to play the game. That is why he had remained a loner.

I was totally captured by what the man had concluded in finding a path through the swamp. I've been his follower since I messed my first diaper. Would he confide in me now?

"Seeing as how you're unloading your mind," I said gingerly, "would you mind telling me how you see our recent future?"

He stared at me rather strangely. "Don't even question that I trust you entirely," he said, "but do you want to be burdened with some highly inflammable secrets, even if you don't agree with me?"

"That's up to you, Conor. You're the one with the burden. Maybe you need to hear yourself say out loud what you've been thinking."

"Maybe I do, runt. I'll give you the simple version," he said slowly. "We have brought the Brotherhood to a capability to execute well-planned raids."

"Bridges, police stations?" I asked.

"Bigger. Our first priority is to make a monumental strike, keenly planned, using a maximum of men—say two dozen volunteers on a target that will stop the momentum of the Ulster Volunteers, hit the British in the stomach like a mule's kick, and be of such magnitude they will never fully recover from it."

"Surely we've never had a success like that against the British in five hundred years. All we seem to end up with are glorious defeats."

"Victory," he said, and it was a lovely-sounding word. "A giant raid is the priority."

"Why, what's your thinking?"

"To make the Brotherhood believe in itself as fighters. To have gained the knowledge that the British are not invincible. To know two dozen Irishmen can inflict a grievous defeat on them. But mainly, the Irish people will realize they are being led by men of skill and valor and not a bunch of blowhard barroom republicans."

"That all sounds lovely," I said, playing the devil's advocate, "but where are you going to find twenty-five Irishmen who won't fuck up the detail?"

"We already have them, Seamus. It's merely a matter of making them believe they can do it."

"How?"

"We pick our finest and urge them gently to volunteer. Then we sequester them and inflict brutal training, infinite execution, willingness to sacrifice. We make them believe in each other. We make them believe in their leaders. We tease them about a target that will change the name of Irish history. You see, that's why I can't have the Council muck it up. The Council is well meaning and they're talented, but we've no discipline and less faith in ourselves."

"How are you going to keep this secret from them?"

"Dan Sweeney will approve the raid and the Council will

accept his argument for absolute secrecy. If they don't trust Dan Sweeney, then we have no Brotherhood."

"And just when does this extraordinary event take place?"

"We go into training the minute the war starts on the European continent."

Jesus, Conor Larkin was dead serious. When the man thinks things out, he does it, indeed, indeed. I felt myself quivering and almost too dry to speak. "So, you remove a major target, then what? Do the British leave Ireland?"

"Are you going to continue to be hilarious or are you after listening?"

"I'm listening," I croaked.

"After the big raid we bend all our efforts to completing our infiltration of a home army and make it our nationwide tactical unit. This will give us three to four thousand men, maybe more, legally under arms."

"You're dreaming. The British will never allow us to have a home guard."

"At some time they're going to have to. The Ulster Militia is going to become so powerful they'll have to throw us a bone, and in a war they'll have to let us watch the coast and guard certain facilities."

"You're dreaming."

"I say there will be an Irish Home Army. A year or so into the war, at a time of the Brotherhood's choosing, we use the Home Army to stage a nationwide rising and declare Irish independence."

"Declare what?"

"Independence, man, independence!"

"So then the British leave Ireland?"

"The Brits will put the rising down ruthlessly. How dare the paddies jump us in the back when we're in the trenches in Europe! The very savagery of their reaction will further arouse the Irish people. I say, fuck them, Seamus, fuck them. Our freedom is not on *their* timetable, but *ours*. When they have squashed the rising, the Declaration of Independence will still stand."

A drink, that's the ticket. I started to get into the flow of what I was hearing. You see, that's what you have to like about Conor. He was speaking in terms of what could be done in reality.

"Now then," Conor continued, "they've put the rising down, but a lot of Irish people are pissed about it who didn't give a damn before the rising, and a lot of Irish soldiers in British uniform will start to thinking about a free Ireland. Then, we spring the trap."

"What trap? They've put us down," I said.

"The Sinn Fein trap," Conor said. "We get elections. The Irish Party gets its burial from the Irish people and Sinn Fein represents us . . . and . . . "

"And," I whispered, "Arthur Griffith forms a provisional government."

Conor smiled and winked at me.

I think I repeated the name of our Savior twenty times, and his fine mother another twenty. He had smelled the rhythm of history itself. He knew that Irish people could be outraged in this manner. But his plan was filled with blood . . . our blood. I feared the asking, but I managed. "What will the British do even if we have declared independence and have a provisional government? You know we can never beat them on the battlefield."

"I've been thinking about it," Conor said.

"So you have."

"Aye. How does a small native force deal with a large foreign army throughout history? First, we win the people over so that every house in the land is a hideaway and every pair of eyes is spying for us. In the countryside we ambush their convoys and disappear into the landscape. We splatter out rail bridges and power stations. We assassinate their constabulary in the villages and towns. This will force them into their barracks and we will own the countryside. Lock their soldiers in so they are no longer free to dance with our lassies at the Saturday ceilidhi. Keep them looking over their shoulders."

"Can that happen?"

"Once the ship of freedom sets sail, it cannot be deterred. Too many new leaders will emerge from the ranks, too many people willing to follow them. And in the cities we will destroy their infrastructure by hit-and-run raids on their vital installations and force them to tie up thousands of troops to guard them."

"Conor, the British are not going to stand by and let this happen."

"Yes," he agreed excitedly, "they will be faced with two distinct choices. They will come to the conference table . . . "

"Or?"

"Or start to burn Ireland to the ground, and the more they burn, the angrier the Irish people will become."

"But who will come to save us, Conor?"

"No one, Seamus, it's Sinn Fein, Ourselves Alone."

"You and I have always feared the resolve of the Irish people."

"Aye," he said, "and it's going to be sorely tested. But when in all of man's history has freedom been handed to a people as a present? The Irish will deserve their freedom if they are willing to bleed and sacrifice for it. We have to crave our freedom more than the other fellow wants to keep us in his fist."

Stop! Stop, Conor, stop! My head is dinnlin'. Was this the ultimate fantasy, the grandiose theory of a man who had spent too much time pondering alone, or had he captured the crest of a movement on Gaelic wings that had been swelling to this crescendo since before the turn of the century?

He made remarkable sense. Something had to give in Ireland. The republican Sinn Fein had already rushed in to fill the political vacuum being left by the failing Irish Party. The Brotherhood did have an operational capacity.

Conor spoke common sense. He spoke of attainable goals. I realized that he had already picked out the target for the first big strike, and I knew what it was.

"Now, just what is it that we're going to take out in this big old raid we're going to make?"

"*We* aren't going to raid anything. *You* are not invited. That is a definite absolute."

"Don't make me sneak in through the back door," I said.

"You're too small."

"Bullshit. The greatest raid in Irish history and you are going to close me out after all the miles of muddy road we've walked together?"

"I'm thinking we'll need a highly placed writer of your caliber to immortalize things."

"Bullshit, Ireland has too many bad writers and twice as many orators to fail to immortalize you. You think it's too dangerous."

"I don't know how dangerous it is, see," Conor lied. I always knew when he was lying to me. If he was sitting, he always scratched his knee, three times, quickly. If he was up and walking he'd quicklike bite his lower lip. He scratched his knee, stood, and bit his lip. "There are more than a dozen targets under consideration," he continued.

"Bullshit," I explained.

"Don't even think about the half of it, Seamus. The target is only going to be known by myself and Dan, so dismiss any wild guesses."

"I'll not make a wild guess. I'll tell you the target, directly and precisely."

Conor narrowed his eyes and glared at me.

"Now then," I began, "It's going to be a target in Ulster. So, we're talking about the naval base in Belfast or the British Army Command at Castle MacStewart or cut the cable to England and so forth and so forth. However, if I were a lad who grew up in Ballyutogue and summered the flock for two years at the derelict castle grounds of Lettershambo, and as kids me and my best pal had found a cave at low tide on the lough leading to a tunnel into the castle . . ."

Conor's eyes breathed lightning.

"And later I worked on the restoration of Lettershambo, and the Ulster Militia stored maybe a hundred thousands guns in it along with a million rounds of ammunition, then I might be considering such a target . . . if the tunnel is still intact."

"It's still intact," Conor whispered.

"Myles McCracken's brother Boyd is the best poacher on Lough Foyle. He stole enough fish from his lordship to feed the entire village when the crops went sour. And Boyd is a Brotherhood man who can get us over Lough Foyle."

"We carry a few hundred pounds of dynamite into the castle."

"Charlie Hackett," I said, naming the best dynamite man in Ireland.

"Charlie Hackett," Conor repeated.

"Well, what the hell are we going to do with a few hundred pounds of dynamite?" I asked. "Put our initials in the castle wall?"

"During the restoration, I helped install the central heating boiler. It is only twenty or thirty feet from where the tunnel enters the castle."

"I know . . . "

"From the boiler there are large pipes, a foot in diameter, going to every room and hall in the castle. Hot-air ducts, they're called. One of the rooms holds their dynamite stash, probably several hundred tons of it. If we can blow up the boiler it will shoot a fierce concussion through the ducts."

"And blow their dynamite stash," I whispered.

"Aye, take down Lettershambo with their own dynamite."

"W-w-will it work?"

"We'll know for sure when we push in the plunger."

For a moment I swooned, then looked at him, crazylike. Why, that would be like blowing up Gibraltar! I looked at him again. He was dead serious. Obviously, he had worked it out in his mind down to the most finite detail. I just must have fallen into a chair and mumbled.

In time, night took over Cork. After the magnitude of what was contemplated sunk in, we both thought of what Ireland would be like the day after Lettershambo was blown up. Suddenly the worth of my entire life was clear. Conor and I, two bumpkins out of Ballyutogue, had reached a moment of euphoria together, in fulfillment over what we had lived to try to accomplish.

Conor Larkin's face showed the wearies. What a fitting way to bow out, I thought. Bow out? Bow out! Of course. As I rethought it, I sensed his awesome journey of a great deal of joy, of tragedy, and of melancholy reaching a climax in a burst that would shake the British Isles. Larkin intended to put every drop of his energy and wisdom into the raid and then depart the scene.

This realization was not that difficult to come by. In a sense he was going to be the first casualty of his own convictions that north and south would never unite. His decision to dot the "i" and cross the "t" with the great raid had been meticulously, if unconsciously, calculated.

Conor was always the lone voice. He knew it would be drowned out in a nationwide Irish rising. He knew such a rising would be an Irish stew. He could control his raid, but he could not control events after that.

Was it not Conor at his purest? Here was a man in an underground army who had never once pulled the trigger, who had refused to take any command that demanded he give an execution order.

I'll tell you the heart of the matter. I knew what Dan and Atty suspected strongly, that Conor Larkin was not a killer. A well-defined raid, yes, but an insurrection with blood all over the cobblestones? He had no more stomach for it than he had for executing an informer. No matter how he had been brutalized, he could not command men to their death or order the cold-blooded murder of the enemy leaders.

Conor had looked down the rest of his road in life. Atty had brought him great comfort and peace, and he depended upon her as he had never depended upon anyone. And he loved her, profoundly, and was amazed that he could find love again. That was his problem, you see. Life for a fugitive was dead-ended. He knew he would never live another day as a free man. He knew he would never last long enough to even dream about an amnesty. To continue on, he would eventually be gunned down or jailed for life or hung.

More and more, Conor Larkin's eyes told me that he had studied his mirror and had seen Long Dan Sweeney.

He and Atty girl had spoken idly of a child between them,

both knowing the other was not exactly telling the truth but allowing the sweet thought to remain.

Conor had come to love Theo and Rachael, but to what avail? He could not watch them flower or partake in their daily ups and downs. Their visits were a few times a year and all too short, and when they left Dunleer, Conor was heartsick for days.

The shadow hovering over Conor was the same one that hovered over myself as well. Our great mutual failure was that there was no son after us. For him, the Larkin name would be done in Ballyutogue, forever.

We let the room stay dark, with only our voices touching. In a matter of minutes he would spirit away into the night to another room no better than this one, perhaps one with a cot and the agony of Jesus on the wall, and groan himself into sleep.

"What are you thinking of these days, Conor?"

"Rory Larkin," he said. "I was able to write to him often when I was in America. I'm afraid the last letter he got from Ireland was over a year ago."

"And you from him?"

"Not possible. When I have a chance to speak to Dary, there's always a coded message sending me a bit of love. Rory's to be of age shortly. Shyte now, I wonder why he's always on my mind."

"He's your boy, in a manner of speaking."

"Of course, I know that. Seamus, I don't want him playing the patriot's game. I'd die if he followed in my footsteps. But in a year or so, Irishmen and Irishwomen are going to declare themselves a free people. What a moment in time that will be. A Larkin ought to be there."

That one hit me like a shot. "You'll be there," I said harshly.

"Ah, you know. Can't totally count on it. Mind you, now. I've done all in my power to get the raiding party out alive and back across the lough. It's not a suicide mission."

"Except for yourself and Dan Sweeney. Maybe you've assigned yourselves to holding a rear guard?"

"You're too bloody smart. Don't tell anyone, runt."

"I'm afraid I understand. As for the rising, Rory Larkin will be there. I can almost sense him on the way."

"And how's that, now?"

"It's the Larkin fate," I said.

The knocks on the door of the hideaway house always jolted me. Two of our lads had arrived to escort and guard Conor to his next stop. The street below looked clear and calm. Conor laid his paw on my shoulder and smiled. "I love you, Seamus, and that's a fact. See you soon."

I could see the three of them in shadows moving with precaution as usual, into the dark. It was time for weeping, but I did not weep. I had a few drinks, instead. My man Larkin was done in. But, by Jesus, the poet-warrior would write his own amen.

PART FOUR

THAT WILD COLONIAL BOY

CHAPTER
48

Rory Larkin had confused himself grandly. When one contemplates the unknown and is about to set sail into it, he conjures up certain images accompanied by certain sensations. As the images became stripped by reality, Rory found himself dangling in a strange place. The unknown was not unfolding as his mind's eye had seen it.

After Conor's death at Lettershambo Castle in Ireland, Rory had a clean rationale for bolting New Zealand. He became so anxious to get off the South Island and enlist in the army, he could have run atop the water like Jesus.

Then came a jolt, an unexpected reaction. He was unable to say good-bye to Georgia Norman. He certainly had not expected the sudden fierce chill that all but immobilized him. His mind stumbled about trying to understand what was happening.

He stood at her cottage door, dumblike, and saw a peculiar look on her face as well, and he began shaking. When he tried to speak he found himself twisting back tears. He walked back into the parlor and slumped.

"I've an idea," Georgia said quickly. "Why don't you enlist in Auckland? I'll go with you on one of the coastal steamers. That way we can have a final fling at sea."

Smashing idea! Or maybe, commuting a sentence? At any rate, Uncle Wally Ferguson was the man. Wally knew all the captains and half the crews.

Rory pondered with Wally about the chances of the Squire chasing him down. He was still several months shy of twenty-one and a member of an essential wartime industry. No, Liam Larkin would not run after his son. It was a matter of stiff-spined pride. He'd not look for Rory to bring him back, nor would he wish him well.

This journey had been on Rory's mind long before the war. It would eventually find its way to Ireland. The name *Larkin* entering Ireland was bound to set off alarms.

Eight years back, a certain Horace Landers owned land adjacent to Liam Larkin's growing sheep station. When the price was right, the Squire acquired it and Landers retired in England. Rory had grown up with the Landers kids and knew their kitchen as his own. If and when there were future inquiries about Rory's origins, he felt he could easily deal with them by using the name of the departed Landers family.

The idea of the steamer to Auckland was filled with excitement and mystery and would give Rory some space to examine his conflicting sentiments.

The once small but opulent fleet of passenger boats only did an overnight to Wellington these days. When the Wellington-Auckland railroad opened in '09, most travelers opted for the speedier nineteen-hour overland route.

Uncle Wally did have just the boat. The *Taranaki* was a coastal freighter with special passenger accommodations for four nights at sea, and it just happened to be in port. The old triple-screw steam turbine held the Lord Nelson Suite, the finest high-Victorian accommodation afloat in these waters. Once a man left Christchurch booked into the Lord Nelson, it was not necessarily with his wife. As the sheepmen prospered, the Auckland run was made idyllic, anonymous, and pricey ... with service such that guests would not have to leave their staterooms. Privacy was assured so that those who wished were the first to board and the last to debark.

Mr. and Mrs. R. Landers were slipped onto the *Taranaki* several hours before general boarding and were whisked to and ensconced in the Lord Nelson Suite.

Even the strongest of lovers who love one another half of forever, like Rory's mom and dad, are overtaken by a repetition, a pattern of steady comfort, a constant value, a level of satisfaction. If they are smart enough, they can reignite when a drift starts.

For Rory Larkin, who was young but wise in the ways of women, some were more exciting than others, but each adventure had a sameness to it ... the hunt ... the victory ... the escape. If you stay too long, he learned, the very thing that brought you together starts to pull you apart. Better to spit it out early on and save a lot of grief down the line.

That held true until he met Georgia Norman. When Sister Georgia unbuttoned her starched uniform, his approach was a smile and an attitude of kind humor and a flip now and then into sheer madness.

Georgia Norman's difference did not take long to become apparent to Rory. It was not a contest of win or lose. Georgia enjoyed what she had going. She did not condemn herself because of her lamentable marriage or curse her husband or condemn herself for being so un-Christchurch-like. She was not awkward after lovemaking, like the usual refrains of "Now that you've seen me naked, please close your eyes while I dress." Georgia liked herself and whatever she had been given. She was on the lookout for constant discovery or letting him in on places she had already been. She made a guy feel glorious, that's what, as if he were the most wonderful chap she had ever seen.

And after—Rory liked the after. She'd simmer for a long time and whisper about pretty near anything and he found himself talking about God knows what and playing lightly at both the entrance and exit to lovemaking.

As the *Taranaki* lost contact with land, an unplanned and unknown phenomenon happened, triggered by the realization that these could be their last moments together, ever.

Whatever restraints there may have been, caused by age and circumstance, disintegrated in a violent implosion that burst open locked vaults in each of them, freeing a rush of exquisite realization. The intensity and desperate grasping for each other took them to somewhere new.

Daybreak found the *Taranaki* tied up at the Glasgow Pier

dead across from the Wellington Rail Station. The moonstruck lovers held hands tightly on their balcony and looked down to the gangway where a line of travelers debarked and marched with their porters to the waiting train. Rory and Georgia thanked the master of their fate for granting them three more nights together.

On the final night out, the sea was extremely kind to them. They were allowed the most exhilarating sight of a fellow steamer passing in the opposite direction with cabin lights ablaze and a zephyr dimly blowing dance music from the ship's lounge. Each vessel blew off fireworks of recognition, followed by the other ship's being swallowed up by utter silence and darkness. The allegory was not lost.

Georgia lay tossed and disheveled on the bed in a most alluring way. Sailors at Uncle Wally's always had something to sell from the Orient. Rory had bought her a forest green silk kimono, which now was flung askew so that the lyrical lines of her rounded body spoke a single word . . . woman. Aye, the robe had found itself to the right one.

Her rusty hair was kept at working lady's length and made her whiteness seem touched by a perfect master. The flash of emerald, the high linen sheets intertwined, all made her no less in his eyes than an ancient goddess. He studied her from across the cabin, unblinking, as time seemed suspended. He was exhausted but had utter clarity. Rory could no longer hold back the tide of questions.

What was it that changed so abruptly the instant he tried to say farewell to her? The idea of fear came to him. Conor had told him never to stifle fear but to realize it, examine it, and gain control of it. That makes the man.

The fool is the one who lies to himself that he has no fear. Rory believed his bouts of genuine fear were few, once he stopped being afraid of his father. Now, it was not a fear of a mean person or suddenly being smashed up, but another kind of fear altogether. As the South Island left his sight, he became weak and dizzy. Jesus, he told himself, I'm afraid. For all the passionate desires to leave New Zealand, the actual moment of cutting the bind had sent him into a sweat.

He hid his feelings from Georgia. She should not see him frightened. As he brought himself under control, he thought, God knows the idea of battle is thrilling, not frightening. This long dream of Ireland after the war was nothing less than Homeric.

So, what's to fear, lad? Fear of the unknown? Well, not fear, just anxiety . . . normal curiosity speeded up. Rory was an independent entity, he knew that.

Or . . . do all men know a kind of sorrow as the lights off-shore blink off? He had received letters from mates who had already left the country or joined the army. Some of these lads had left rotten lives in rotten homes, but they were homesick to a man.

So, maybe my fear isn't fear at all, he reckoned. The porthole let in a quick sliver of light, which fell over Georgia, and he felt a burst of lust from his throat down to his stomach. He started out of his chair but settled back under the weight of more questions.

I understand something now that I never could quite get before, he thought. I often wondered why Conor was so torn to return to an Ireland that had been like the raw end of a whip to him all his life. The soul is planted in your village and never leaves it. Even though it is the army and Ireland, I can never really leave New Zealand.

Thinking of Conor as he did, his uncle's death swept over him. He clamped down to head off an outpouring of sorrow. With each new deep and uttered sigh the hurt in his chest lessened. He stood quickly and shoved open the cabin door, hoping to see the passing ship. It was long gone. The water was smooth and the heavens put on a spectacular show. Conor had told him that standing the watch on the calm nights was the worst because you remembered all you had had and lost.

"I've lost her," Rory spouted.

Conor had ached for Countess Caroline. Oh Lord, how he ached for her. Maybe it all has to do with the way I now ache for Georgia Norman.

Time and again of late when he went to her cottage past

Taylor's Mistake, he had longed to ride with her up in the hills and thrill her with what his life meant.

He fantasized about coming back from the war and telling the Squire to shove it up a round hole in his middle. He'd start off with a few acres and he'd look down on it from a hillock with an arm about Georgia Norman ... Georgia Larkin. By Jaysus, I could take on the world with her. She's a rock, and oh, what she'd do for her man. The wisdom of her, the spirit, the courage. And they'd be laughing half the night through.

Well, there it is, Rory boy. My woman, Georgia Larkin. Oh, the sound of it! I'm in love with her. The war has only begun and the South Island and Georgia are already together as a single thought.

Does the realization that you need someone necessarily mean you're in love with her? he wondered. Isn't that rather crappy of me? I mean, he thought, selfish. To even think about asking a woman to give up a marriage with a man who might deserve a second chance. To ask a woman to wait half of forever while you make your rounds of combat. Christ, Rory, get off it. It's bloody awful selfish of you to think that way, and if you care that much for her you can't ask her to chuck her life for you.

Forget my needs, he thought. Forget my fears. Forget it all. There is still this terrible, terrible feeing that makes me want to fall down and cry. I hurt, man! I hurt! I know what the fucking pain is. The fucking pain is that I might never see her again. The pain is ... I'll never touch her again. I guess this is the bloody hell of what this goddamned sonofabitching thing of love is. The pain is no less than the pain of Conor's death.

All right, Rory, you've confessed to yourself. The situation is impossible. At daylight, when you say good-bye, act like a man. You be a good man to this woman. You do what is right.

Over the years, Georgia had mastered the abstruse art of controlling her nightmares. They were no longer the stuff of sweat and chills. When annoyance invaded, she'd wake up before the nightmare crossed into bedlam. As soon as she awakened, she quickly read the dream's message. Most of them were very anxious. There would be burning or collapsing buildings or a variation thereof, or a threatening monster or a variation thereof, a flight to the edge of an abyss or a high structure and the beginning of a plunge.

Many times in the past months she reached across the bed when ugliness came in her sleep and she felt something sublime, beyond any measure she had ever experienced. It was Rory Larkin. The inner message quickly let her know she was safe and the full message let her know that this man would protect her. She'd never been protected before, and she wondered why it was a wild colonial boy as unlikely as Rory Larkin who now offered it to her. This sense of great comfort he provided was no less puzzling than the first mesmerizing sight of him, months earlier, with a body full of cracked ribs.

On this last night before Auckland, Georgia's dream was a throwback past horror. She flung her arm to defend herself and it banged against the mattress and abruptly ended her sleep. When she had gotten her whereabouts, she sunk back on the pillow and whispered a gentle curse. The voyage was all but done.

Georgia felt the seductive softness of her kimono and she smiled. Oh, Rory boy, Jesus damned, what have you done to me? She swung her legs off the bed and went to the mirror to touch up. She never wanted the lad to see her as if she had just come out of a steam bath. In the mirror Georgia could see through a porthole to the promenade deck. Rory stood motionless and featureless in the shadows. She began to tie her robe, then let it stay open for him to see what he would be wanting to see. She fixed on him, unseen by him, and luxuriated in just watching him.

Well, Georgia girl, she told herself, you are the queen of fools. For over twenty-eight years you've built a wall that was breached in a single moment.

Georgia had watched the ladies of the Territorial Force Reserve—the erstwhile "Daughters of the Regiment"—stalk and snare. Nurses were of low and middle station and here was a ripe moment to bag an officer, a future innkeeper or, by God, a colonel with a rose garden.

Soldier boys of all ranks either detested women or were overly sentimental about them. It wasn't difficult to tell which was which. Her fellow Sisters chirped and giggled but seldom spoke of love. Love was the automatic marriage prize, was it not? Why did bright and capable women who had pulled themselves up by their bootstraps settle for clods or arrogant bores?

Well, who the hell are you to stick your nose up? Calvin Norman was a fine surgeon in the main military hospital in India. He was only in for one enlistment to secure a good reserve rank, gain some necessary military medical experience, and have excellent credentials when he returned to his native New Zealand.

Georgia became his chief assistant in the operating theatre and was duly impressed by the man's skill. He also showed himself to be caring to his patients, a trait not often displayed. Georgia made a deliberate decision. Calvin Norman was a safe settlement and offered a comfortable life as far away from England as the planet afforded, as well as the family she craved. He was seduced and incredibly taken with her. Not the flaming love of her life, because that love was an illusion, but a gentle man who would not hurt her.

Well, old Calvin fooled her good and right, he did. He turned out to be the deadliest in a line of vipers and louts, comparable only to her dear father, Oliver Merriman.

Back in Christchurch and reigning as chief surgeon in the South Island's premier hospital, Calvin had a lot of settling up to do. Bit by bit her husband's pimply, pale-faced, humiliating childhood eked out. He was buffeted by a weakling boyhood in a wild land filled with ruffians who demonized his most formative years.

His long and bitter haul to the physician's oath now afforded him authority. The bully boys all needed him, and their wives were payment on account for his past torment. He was consumed by an insatiable urge to conquest, to prove and reprove his manhood.

From the onset, with her becoming chief matron at the hospital, their union was in trouble. He was recalled to the Medical

Corps with the fine rank of major long before the war started, and this was good for him, to get a head start in a career that could well end up in London.

Because Christchurch kept its secrets locked, and open scandal meant ostracism, Norman pleaded with her to keep a lid on things and expressed the first regrets of his behavior. Georgia pledged silence until the war ended. He had only begun to realize the quality of woman he had married.

You've got the rest of your life, Georgia Norman, to dream about why you fell in love with this Larkin bloke ... but why the hell did you risk this trip to Auckland and start to turn loose everything you've so far been able to hold inside?

Rory lad had at last broken her cycles of fear. He inflicted no harm, only grace. She had ridden the wild stallion and she knew she'd never have that ride again. Hot and wet and wild and you're smarter than to put a collar on a young rover just as he begins his roving, she mused.

How many times, Georgia girl, have you sat on the edge of a wounded soldier boy's cot and cooed at his faded brown, cracked photograph of a girl whose looks you could hardly make out? The soldier boy had all but forgotten what she really looked like, just as you have forgotten what your dead soldier boy looked like.

Nice chipper lad, he was, Lieutenant Sidney ... Sidney ... Sidney Clarkeson. First man you weren't frightened of. Through his innocent ways you learned the splendid skill of controlling a man. Face it, Georgia, you weren't all that keen for the marriage. You were sorry he was blown up in battle and you wept sincerely over his remains. But the ache passed too quickly, and you realized it. It might not have been love at all, just a lack of fear.

As other chaps came along, four or five in all, you enjoyed the hell out of men, but the instant that look of possession came into their eyes you moved away quickly.

That look ... *that look* ... wasn't your tour of service all about *that look* of Oliver Merriman's? Your daddy had status, that's what, a clerk and manager for five barristers in Lincoln Inn ... as respectable as a middle-class Englishman could aspire to be.

Oh, that sotty bastard! In his cups, he had held her up by her long red hair when she was thirteen and spat on her and slapped her and hurled her against the wall screaming, "Whore!"

Her mom quivered nearby, saying nothing. Mom had taken Oliver Merriman's rage a hundred times saying nothing. Her two older sisters had fled with early pregnancies into marriages in hell.

Oh, Mr. Merriman, the pastor gooed and gushed, and his lovely ladies . . . if only his flock had the character of that exemplary family!

By the age of fifteen, appearing advanced for her years, Georgia found refuge in Queen Alexandra's Imperial Military Nursing Service and never looked back. She had strong hands, powerful drive, absolute nerve under bloody conditions, and a range of humor and kindness. Most of all, she was a model of perfect and absolute competence.

Despite Oliver Merriman's shadow and the sickening experiences of her mother and sisters, Georgia wanted her men—but no man's cock would reduce her to bondage. She kept firmly in control, never too emotionally involved, and determined to be self-sustaining. No one would control her, not for a blink.

Georgia buddied with them all, from beer with the enlisted lads to elite waltzes at the officers' club. And then she made her Faustian bargain with Calvin Norman.

Rory, still motionless, remained on the promenade deck. Like all captains and kings, colonels and maharajahs, sisters and sweethearts, wives and workwomen, Rory was going to spend the second half of his life trying to get over the first half. Some never do. Would she? How many elders had she met still battling their childhood and their parents? God Almighty, wait till the Irish lassies, let alone the girls of Paris and London, get their hands on that one.

If Georgia had one absolute answer, it was that she knew this night was the end between herself and Rory. Put it to him gently. He will soon forget what you look like, anyhow.

The *Taranaki* greeted a relentless dawn oozing through a permanent mist as she slid along the line of hills toward

Auckland, each crowned with an impossible Maori name generally beginning with a W.

Georgia made a sudden decision to remain on the ship and
return aboard her to Christchurch. Rory packed, dazed. The
ashen lovers now hated each chug and groan of the ship's engine,
bringing them closer to their parting. For an instant, Rory
wanted to be Rory and smash up things in frustration. He
snapped his satchel shut and looked about. The pair of them
were light-headed from the loss of sleep and functioning at whisper level from the final crazy hours of lovemaking.

Good nurse Georgia was now in complete control under
duress. "It's been a hell of a trip, all of it, Rory," she said. "Try
not to win the war by yourself."

"You'll write?"

"As long as our letters are good for a laugh or two. You're
not obligated."

"Let's fuck the nice talk, Georgia. Something's happened."

"I want you to listen to me, Rory."

"Don't talk me down, Sister Georgia. I'm not one of your
bleeding corporals in need of a chat-up."

"All right. We've been knocked gaga. There is something
powerful between us. War speeds up feelings in a cockeyed way,
you know."

"I'm going to say one thing, Georgia, and I mean it. I cannot
fathom how any woman is ever going to be like you again. Not
in one year or ten years. If you and Calvin Norman do not make
it, I'm coming back for you."

"Rory, people get very sentimental at moments like this and
make utterly sloppy promises."

He unbuttoned his shirt, took her wrist, and placed her hand
on his chest. Georgia fairly swooned. "Things may change," he
said, "and I'll not lie to you when it happens. But at this moment
I hope Calvin Norman never comes back.'

She winced and took her hand away.

"Wishing for a man's death who doesn't deserve to die is no
good, Georgia, but that's how much I want you."

She drew him to her and opened her own blouse and lay his

head against her breasts. "Close your eyes . . . listen . . . will you, now?"

"Aye."

"We were never really on, you and me. An old girl getting over the anger of a feckless husband has all kinds of venom in her. Trying to make more out of what this has really been will make us fall down attempting to keep promises made in an unreal moment of parting. As the promises are broken, we dodge with little lies at first and the guilt grows. All of what you say is well meaning now, Rory, but it can't hold over the long haul."

"Georgia . . . "

"The military," she continued, "has a number of agonies, you'll learn. There is the day-to-day agony of soldiering—working like a dog, brutal discipline, rotten food, boredom, mud, dysentery. There is the agony of battle. These agonies are very real. No soldier has ever been able to avoid them. Yet the most horrific of all agonies is the memory of home and the woman you left behind. This agony becomes a delusion, blown out of proportion. Although you won't die from it, it is no less agonizing than the other agonies of soldiering."

She felt his tears on her breast and took down her straps so he could smother himself freely.

"You can't control the road you've taken. God knows where it will lead you. And if you get to Ireland—and you *will* get there—it could be endless. It is utterly unfair for either of us to make any promises. Understand me, Rory?"

"Aye."

She let his kisses rove over what she had put before him until a steward called out that they would be in port soon.

From there on out it was stalwart stuff, wan smiles, misty eyes, stout embrace, and down the gangplank we go. He turned and waved and was gone.

Georgia held together until she was certain Rory was out of sight, then doubled over trying to get air to fight her nausea. The steward caught her wobbling and assisted her back to the suite and helped her onto the bed.

"Some tea, Mrs. Landers?" the steward offered.

"I'll go with the cognac. It's on the ship's desk."

As her color returned and she assured him she was better, he left.

Georgia was grateful she did not falter in the end. So now he was off to his war and she had done what life had brought her to do. The first of her secrets had been safely kept. The second of her secrets was more within her control.

CHAPTER
49

Caroline's departure from Hubble Manor had been preceded by a thunderclap of rage over Roger's brutal squashing of Jeremy's affair with Molly O'Rafferty. The manner in which he savaged the girl's reputation, then condemned her and her unborn child to the garbage heap, was matched only by the way he transformed Jeremy into babbling submission.

Caroline and Roger had managed a week-long silence before the tinderbox exploded, spewing out a quarter of a century of pent-up rage.

Caroline unloaded on Roger his rotten fathership of Jeremy, his use of human fodder in his fields and industries, his bigoted Reformation mentality, and his dirty secrets.

Roger had a thing or two to say about her hypocrisy, her coddling of Jeremy, her obscene spending, which had required the continuous running of the shirt factory. In the hammer blow, he renounced her giving birth to Jeremy for the sake of her father and not for the earldom.

When Caroline left for Belfast, Sir Frederick's private train carried so much of her luggage it indicated her plan to stay away from Londonderry for a long time.

Sir Frederick, recovering from his stroke, seeing his family structure going to a shambles, made a long overdue decision committing the future of Weed Ship & Iron to Caroline. Caroline's hand fit the glove to perfection. As for Sir Frederick, by Jaysus, Caroline would have to sort out the family quagmire.

The removal of Brigadier Maxwell Swan was a sticky proposition, but even Weed recognized that that way of doing business may have had its day. A close and loving relationship between Caroline and Uncle Max had faltered badly over the years and collapsed completely after the factory fire.

The bloody goons who beat off the unions and the Catholics, industrial spies who gleaned the future plans of steel mills and shipyards, and covert financial dealings all had an archaic bent.

The liberal wave could not be diverted and found its way over the Irish Sea to Ulster, bringing a greater consideration for the welfare of the working people. Union-busting was losing its urgency among the industrialists. Slowly, ever so slowly, it occurred to the upper class that happier working people were producing much finer products at far less cost.

It was nothing that would take place overnight, to be sure, but who better than Caroline Hubble to sense the changes and flow with them?

The problem at the yard was that Maxwell Swan and Frederick Weed were covered with enough of each other's fleas to send the other to the hangman's scaffold a hundred times over.

In the end the two old boys, scoundrels and killers though they were, were birds of a feather. Swan was of an age that he wanted to go off someplace faraway and do his sunset years in style. Weed's stroke had shaken him up considerably. As Sir Frederick aged, Swan feared that Roger Hubble would try to pull him into Hubble's personal service. Sir Frederick had always had a keen and jolly sense about him, what with his bouts with the bottle and the ballerinas and his rugby team and his bombastic energy for faster trains and ships.

Lord Roger, on the other hand, seemed keen to kill with a sense of satisfaction. Except for Caroline, the man would have been an utter monster. And the last bloody job ... spying on Lord Jeremy, promising to keep the results from Freddie and Caroline ... feeling Roger's hot breath on his neck to recruit him away from Belfast.

Sir Frederick Weed, in his most charming and generous manner, took it eye-to-eye with the Brigadier.

"Max," Freddie said, "we're going to have to trust each other."

A sumptuous estate in Jamaica and a hefty pension were laid on the table. Here, he could be among dozens of cronies retired from the military. He could dress formally three or four times a week, complete with medals, and banquet into inebriated unconsciousness ... and make those visits to certain well-maintained cabins.

Now here was where the trust came in. As part of the arrangement, Swan left a handwritten memoir of his black deals with Roger Hubble. The authorship was certified in the presence of an impeccable quorum of his peers who witnessed his signature but did not read the contents of the document.

The book was placed in the hands of Sir Frederick and Caroline Hubble. Swan's risk was not all that great. After all, if either Caroline or Weed exposed the contents, Swan had a few hundred other pages on his exploits for Sir Frederick.

Trusting thieves will out. Caroline had her little nest egg, the biggest of all Orange cards, to assure that she alone would draw the final boundaries and settle the accounts favorably. Swan rotted away early in his retirement and was set down with stunning military honors but left behind him his little book of horrors, as if to say his pervasive spirit was still rankling around.

The disengagement of the Weed-Hubble combine was not a simple matter. They were welded together all over the province. Roger sat on the Weed Ship & Iron board and the two had numerous joint investments and partnerships, supplied one another and, until Swan's departure, attended to a lot of covert affairs together.

While Roger's earldom was a thin ha'penny alongside Sir Frederick's worldwide enterprises, Roger's ancient title had a mystical hold on Weed. Roger was still the master of Londonderry, endemic to a British Ulster. Londonderry had been Roger's original Orange card. Now, he had two more of them, Christopher and Jeremy.

Jeremy was let go by his mother for his cowardly behavior toward Molly O'Rafferty and his unborn child. Although

Freddie adored Jeremy as a harmless playboy, he had become resigned to the fact that Jeremy would not amount to much in the future of Weed Ship & Iron.

Sir Frederick had ceded Jeremy to Londonderry, to Hubble Manor, and to the Earldom of Foyle, where he could acquit himself as a functionary at charities, horse shows, and snoozing in the House of Lords. Jeremy was to be a ceremonial figurehead much as had been his grandfather, poor stuttering Arthur.

For the moment Jeremy was not up to even these most menial duties. After he had caved in and let her go, his joy and raffish behavior fled him.

Roger issued Jeremy orders. Caroline scarcely spoke to him, and then only in a perfunctory manner on public occasions. His grandfather, while still having a soft spot, grew weary of Jeremy's lack of steel.

Roger tried energetically to push him into a marriage, but so long as Molly's disappearance remained a mystery, he refused as though he were hanging on to his last shred of manhood and decency. Jeremy drank heavily, attended the races and horse shows, played rugby with Catholic thugs in the lower counties, and haunted the areas of Dublin around Trinity College and the river Liffey.

Now, Christopher Hubble was quite another matter. It seems that his first steps were out of the marching manual of the Coldstream Guards. Roger bemoaned the bloody fate that would deny Christopher the earldom. Denied it by birth but showing exceptional business skills, one would have thought he was heading straight for the top at Weed Ship & Iron. Only problem was that Sir Frederick thought his second grandson was a stiff-assed bore.

No doubt, Weed thought, Christopher had the inclination to run the earldom's croppy labor with a whip hand in Londonderry's archaic industries. However, and this was a tremendous *however,* between Christopher and his grandfather, Christopher did not have the gist of the Belfast atmosphere and the latitude and smarts to deal with ten thousand working people.

During his apprenticeships at the yard, Christopher behaved

toward the proud shipwrights and steelmakers as an overlord to his serfs. Likewise, department managers and foremen found him frustratingly priggish and overbearing.

See now, the entrepreneurs of Belfast and particularly his grandfather were rough and tumble bully boys, not the fastidiously clipped, moustached, hands-behind-the-back, slapping-the-old-riding-crop-on-the-breeches guardians of the Crown.

So be it. Roger Hubble had both his sons.

As Roger felt the remoteness grow, he put on a few moves of his own. Jeremy was snatched off the racetrack and ordered into the family regiment. The Coleraine Rifles first went into business three centuries earlier hanging croppy heads on pikes for Oliver Cromwell.

Thus, the Viscount of Coleraine went into the Coleraines as a subaltern and would stay there until he agreed to take a wife. Jeremy, fearing his father's tirades less all the time, showed little interest in rising above subaltern or anything other than amusing himself and making his forays into Dublin. Because of Lord Roger's influence in the Rifles, Jeremy was kept in meaningless positions, lest he become an embarrassment.

Enter Christopher, his brother's keeper. When Chris joined the Coleraines, Roger and Colonel Brodhead, an old Ulster hand, connived to allow Christopher to keep an eye on Jeremy.

Roger feared that Jeremy might bring some sort of humiliation to the earldom in one of his drunken stupors. Not that he cared for Jeremy very much, but Roger feared that if anything happened to Jeremy, Caroline and Freddie would take him out of the Belfast industries forever.

This charming family had splintered into a human patchwork of who was speaking to whom, how loudly, who was speaking behind whose back, and who was wishing whom well or unwell.

There was an absurd molecule in the family mix as Caroline and Freddie aligned against Roger and Christopher, with Jeremy dangling in limbo.

From the very beginning, Sir Frederick and Lord Roger were cemented together to defeat Irish Home Rule, each anchoring a geographical corner of the province. With all the splintering of family fortunes, the two were still cemented together on the Home Rule issue and remained bedfellows in illegally importing tens of thousands of weapons to the Ulster Militia.

Roger saw himself eased out of the Weed Ship & Iron as Sir Frederick made a remarkable recovery from his stroke and tutored his daughter on the company's future. One always finds bits of undercurrents in Ulster. Everyone seems to get mixed up with everyone somehow—a Catholic midwife assists in the birth of an aristocrat, a Methodist deacon sits elbow-to-elbow at the pub with the paddies—so many signs of normalcy.

No matter who does what to whom, all good Protestants are utterly united on two matters: allegiance to the Crown and the belief that all good Catholics are republicans.

So Roger and Freddie, despite the crumbling of their houses, treated one another as blood brothers in Militia and Unionist party matters.

Roger was not blind to the way Caroline was taking dead aim at the helm of Weed Ship & Iron. Despite Jeremy's watery obedience to his father, Roger could not shake the young man into a new marriage. It was as though Jeremy was caught up in some sort of Irish faerie's web and could not let go of it. The echoed sound of "Molly" came to him twenty times a day. Sometimes it faded on its own. Sometimes it had to be cast out by drink. Whatever this last defiance be, Roger could not crack it, so Jeremy stayed out of everyone's way in the Coleraine Rifles.

Lieutenant Christopher Hubble, amenable to all things good for the earldom, took one step, front and center, and set forth, forthrightly, on a short but sweeping courtship of Hester Glyn Gobbins, daughter of Baron and Baroness Hugh Gobbins. Roger was delighted.

Brother Jeremy, on exemplary behavior, whipped the saber from his scabbard to lead an archway of swords for the couple to sweep through on their way to the altar.

Chris and Hester were extremely close replicas of a fine English aristocratic pair and Gweedloe House's hedges were as clipped, its roses aburst, bannered, and butlered, the show was as close to perfect as it would have been across the sea on the main island.

On the receiving line, Christopher's lips parted and teeth revealed a kind smile as Hester offered her cheek to be bussed and said a sincere, "Mmmmugh" to all who kissed her. "Mmmmugh" . . . "mmmmugh." The "mmmm" came on contact and the "ugh" on the break . . . "mmmmugh."

Because Weed and Roger continued to appear often in public there was very little prattle about Caroline's departure from Londonderry. Since neither lover nor mistress appeared, one was given to think that the Countess was taking particularly close care of her father.

After the lawn party, the crowd of guests dissolved and the lads of the brigade invaded the township's pubs. Caroline retired to her apartment at Gweedloe House only to find Roger already there.

"Sorry about this," Roger said, "there's a manservant's room behind the pantry. It will do me quite well."

"We'll manage," Caroline said. "Actually we have a number of things that have been on hold. This might be a good time for it."

"Except for the chance rally or dinner, it's been two years. I think you've done a remarkable job with old Freddie. I say, he appears to be pleased with the marriage."

"Chris and Hester appear to be well suited to what they were bred and cultivated to do, like good horses. I hope Hester has the hips for it," Caroline said.

Roger grunted. Humor, however dark, was welcomed. "Colonel Brodhead is very happy with Christopher's progress in the Rifles."

"Chris has been a splendid officer since he was three years old," she retorted.

Roger contained his ire. Caroline lifted the phone and was put through to her father's room. Good, he was taking his rest. For a moment she was afraid he might have tippled just a bit too much and could have been off to the races. "He's like a little boy," she said.

"Caroline," Roger blurted. "I feel terribly awkward. Might I relax?"

"Yes, of course."

He unbuttoned his vest, doffed his shoes, and settled into a chair near her. Roger was immersed in deep concern and his face showed some hurt, she thought. Or was Roger doing up a little game? They had waited for this encounter for a long time. It came suddenly, but certainly each had rehearsed the lines and also rehearsed the other's answers ... but the answers were never as one thought they ought to be.

"As soon as you realized," she said, "that Jeremy was going to make Jeremy's Last Stand, you drew up a short list, blindfolded Chris, and let him pick a name from a hat—a Coleraine Rifle dress hat—and the winner is Hester Glyn Gobbins."

"Guilty," Roger answered.

"And in the next chapter we shall see how sweet and innocent Hester Glyn Gobbins deals with the ghosts of Hubble Manor."

"Hubble Manor is a tomb, not for its lack of magnificence, but for the lack of its mistress. I'm having Ballystorrs redone for them."

"Well, it's nice to know one is appreciated," Caroline said. "Did it ever occur to you that both a mistress and an heir might be alive and wandering about out there someplace?"

"Yes."

"I've never stopped looking for them," Caroline said abruptly.

Roger almost came to the point of making an inquiry. Was Molly yet alive? Did she have a son or daughter? Any clues as to where they may be? He did not ask and, in not asking, Roger answered all the questions she did not ask. Bedrock.

The oriel window with its aged thick beveled glass allowed in a sudden rainbow of elongated dots. She studied Roger in his slouch and for an instant seemed to be taken with pity.

"Old Jolly Roger is still old Jolly Roger," he said in monotone. "The monster of Foyle, installed in me at my birth, is still alive and well, thank you. You look surprised, Caroline."

"Actually, I am."

"I've known the monster was there from the beginning and it never performed so well as when I put my father on the dole and took what was mine. We've done right well together, the monster and I. When I came to realize that the monster was going to make all my decisions for me, I said to myself, 'Well, this is what good monsters do.' I never have to chose between right and wrong. Wrong is what is bad for the earldom. There is no evil; I'm powerless. What is right for the earldom are profits, power, and continuity. Oh yes, I have despised and wondered about my heartlessness all my life, but when one accepts that the monster knows best, one learns to live with it. I cannot control what controls me."

"What game are you playing, Roger? At the moment you appear to control all the functioning cocks in the family, although I wouldn't count old Freddie out. So, you want Jeremy to give up the ghost and sire a future earl ... but the monster tells you to cover your bet and have Chris and Hester get cracking on their duties. Then why don't you ask me for a divorce as well? I'd put my money on you making a couple of beautiful little monsters of your own."

"Your side of the table is the one that needs the heirs, Caroline."

"I'm sure you are aware that you have been cut back to the boundaries of the earldom. I love both my sons dearly. I would give what is left of my life to see Jeremy make amends for what he has done. Having said that, neither Chris nor Jeremy have any meaningful future in Weed Ship & Iron. They will inherit well, but they will never set foot in Belfast."

"I don't sail off into the sunset that easily, Caroline. No man, no matter how demented, gives his empire away to a daughter gone barren. Nor will you find that illegitimate child and bring him up as the Vatican's gift to Ulster."

"Good on you, Roger. You're sounding like your old self again."

"You and Freddie, no matter how powerful your seal, can't break the human order of family. Family is older than the earldom, older than the Celts, older than the Normans, older than the Angles and the Saxons ... older than mankind ... a hand-me-down from the apes and before them, family was stands of trees and dinosaurs—ever see two colonies of lichen on a rock moving toward each other? They don't join—the strong family devours the weak one. Freddie and I are up to here in some rather interesting deals with each other. We are going to work out an accommodation."

The moment had arrived. Yet Caroline saw no pleasure in it.

"Roger, kindly ask your monster if that was a blackmail threat."

"Try me," he hissed, coming to his feet.

"Sit down, Roger," she commanded.

"Are you telling me to—"

"Sit down and listen very, very carefully. The accommodation you seek has already been worked out. You are to resign from the board of Weed Ship & Iron. Freddie and I will put to you the choice of buying or selling all joint ventures. You will have your earldom and your sons."

"You are being ridiculous, Caroline. Try this and I'll bring Weed Ship & Iron down."

"You're interrupting me, Roger."

He blinked and narrowed his eyes ... so calm she was, so even.

"Sir Frederick Weed has passed ownership and control of Weed Ship & Iron to his barren daughter, Caroline. My father has borne the pain of forcing our marriage for decades. He absolutely despises you, despite your little joint gunrunning escapades. After his stroke Freddie wrote a diary and he initialed each page and signed it and it was certified before ten members of the House of Lords who, fortunately for you, do not know the rest of the book's content."

"That's blackmail! He can't bring me down without bringing himself down."

"Ah, you've never really known Freddie. He's a two-fisted gambler, my daddy. Freddie has had numerous small strokes since his first one. He's eighty-two years old now, and he and I decided jointly he goes out his way, at a big party. That is to say, Freddie doesn't give a big rat's ass if he is exposed or not. . . . However, Roger, that old monster in you has to be telling you to tread carefully, what?"

"You are a devil," he rasped.

"Father's diary has a companion volume detailing your dealings with Maxwell Swan—"

"Shit!"

"Uncle Max, just before he died toasting the king with a strychnine grin on his face, covered the volume in orange and presented it to me in exchange for his living out his life in piety and luxury in Jamaica."

Caroline broke, voice quivering, "It's all here, the murder of Kevin O'Garvey, the cover-up of the factory fire, and a few other murders and bribes and broken legs and riots."

"All right . . . all right, let's get ourselves together. The truth of the matter is, Caroline, that when Freddie goes, you can't continue Weed Ship & Iron beyond your own lifetime."

"That's being taken care of, Roger. We're going public on the London Stock Exchange."

"You're mad! Freddie is mad!"

"Please Roger, the guests are napping."

"My God! Public ownership! Tax collectors crawling over your books like maggots . . . every little pissant solicitor in the British Isles reading your contracts . . . conspiracies on your board of directors . . . bribes . . . corruption . . . unions. A business, an earldom, a nation must be run by a single leader!"

"We sense that imperial man may be on the wane."

"Gawd! Now you hear me, Caroline—publish those dirty little diaries if you dare and I dare expose you and your paddy boy, Conor Larkin. When the Orange mob learns about you fucking your croppy in the barn, they'll have your guts on the pavement of Shipquay Street! See, madam, you're not all that clean!"

"I am guilty of a lot of things, Roger, extravagance beyond that of Marie Antoinette, blindness to a slave labor operation, guilty of a despicable arrogance in treating decent human beings as if they were dogs—all that—but I am not a criminal. Sorry to disappoint you, but I *have* been faithful to you. I didn't want it that way, but Conor Larkin had too much decency, despite his low breeding, for the likes of us . . . just as Molly O'Rafferty has too much decency for the likes of us. As for infidelity, the Brigadier also supplied me with your little black book . . . some of whom you've been paying exorbitant amounts."

Roger made a few disjointed gestures, cried, croaked, mumbled a plea. He was boxed in on every side. He slumped in defeat.

"Is the old monster back in its cage, Roger?"

"Yes," he whispered.

"You will report to Freddie's office promptly at three tomorrow afternoon. The papers are drawn up. Take your fucking earldom and piss off. In the future, I pray that a redemption is possible between me and our sons and that I can help them in worthwhile enterprises."

A knock on the door was followed by a trio of maids. "May we draw a bath for the Countess?"

"Yes, that would be lovely. By the bye, his Lordship is running a slight fever. Do you suppose he might have his own room and a doctor?"

When they had gone, Caroline started for her bath, then turned.

"Freddie was right," she said. "He said you've got too much blue blood to duke it out with a street fighter. When it came down to eyeball-to-eyeball, you'd cave in."

50

SECRET FILES OF WINSTON CHURCHILL

October 3, 1911

I have reached the first major crisis of my career, requiring me to make the most serious decision imaginable.

No one, and I repeat, *no one* fought more vigorously for the *People's Budget* of 1910, a signature event denoting the beginning of the era of the common man's right to a higher standard of living.

To pass this budget I led the fight to threaten the dissolution of the House of Lords and fight off the Conservatives whose mentality is deadened with rigor mortis. They still live in the memory of an exploiting empire and massive military budgets.

I met the PM at 10 Downing today and he offered me the post of First Lord of the Admiralty. This not only means I must abandon my fight for more social reforms; it means a complete reversal of roles by becoming a leader in the arms race.

Asquith refused to take my "no" as an answer and was extremely compelling about the inevitability of a land war on the European continent.

As First Lord, I would be in charge of building a thousand-warship navy, the most powerful fleet the world has ever known.

I took a bundle of reports to study, written by our greatest experts in the military, intelligence, financial men, industrial wizards, scientists, and politicians and advised the PM I would give him an answer as soon as possible.

October 7, 1911

I am torn, utterly, horribly torn. There is no conclusion a sane and reasonable man can draw except that war will soon be upon us and there is no way we can finesse our way out of it. The German empire is in wretched shape and the Kaiser and General Staff feel that there is no way to prevent an internal collapse except to go to war against France and Russia.

What chills the marrow is the prediction of casualties. One million men from each of the major nations are predicted to be killed, a minimum of six million dead and God knows how many wounded.

All of my lovely dreams of the march of the common man with myself as their leader have now gone asunder. Although heavy of pain, I see no choice but to place myself at the pleasure of the Crown.

In addition to the gigantic task before me, this post is bound to make me leap forward toward the political goals I have set for myself.

My illustrious ancestor, John Churchill, the First Duke of Marlborough, never lost a battle or failed to capture a city under siege. I do not claim his mastery of field tactics and engagement, but I understand the grand strategy that England must employ against Germany.

When the time comes I shall set down this strategy and it will dazzle our War Council.

*　　*　　*

October 24, 1911

I have accepted the appointment of First Lord of the Admiralty at the age of thirty-four.

October 25, 1911

The Conservatives and a good part of the press are howling like mad dogs over my appointment.

Well, we shall see.

Predictions of Sir Frederick Weed's early demise failed to materialize. He stormed back, determined to get his empire in proper order. Weed went first into his own ranks, gleaning them for managers, executives, foremen able to think in twentieth-century terms. Those he could not find, he went out and stole from his competitors. A financial wizard from the Bank of England went on the board as did some of the foremost minds in the British Isles. The only thing Freddie questioned was why he hadn't done this years earlier.

At first there were a lot of bad jokes and snickers in the corridors of power. It was soon evident that Caroline Hubble had inherited her father's qualities of bossmanship. The snickering stopped cold as she took her seat at the opposite end of the long table from her father.

The day Caroline called to order and ran her first executive meeting, she showed an added dimension. Caroline obviously had the quality to extract the best a person had to offer. Had she not once helped create a masterpiece through a croppy blacksmith?

Naval shipbuilding was now going on at breakneck speed, beyond capacity. Belfast buzzed with full employment and high wages. With his new people making hard decisions, Weed was able to cut back his own role to an hour or two a day, often from Rathweed Hall.

The London office of Weed Ship & Iron, with its proximity to the heart of government and the financial world, became as vital as Belfast itself. Freddie had battled Caroline all her life to keep her in Ulster. Now, he could bestow on her the gift of London.

She took over the London end of the operation, cleared out three decades of rust, and yes, she thrived outside the landscape of Ireland, as one often does when one escapes captivity.

Caroline's London home was arty and elegant but did not shriek of wealth. The informality of it was assured by its Chelsea location in the midst of her closest friends—actors, writers, artists, scholars, and all sorts of off-horse, out of the ordinary, fun people. It was the home she never had in the marbled museum of Rathweed Hall or the ancient castle of the Foyles. She became a force in the arts and drifted heavily into Liberal Party politics.

Long steeped in the brutal and myopic politics of Ulster, the Liberals were yet another reprieve from the Belfast graveyard. Caroline's salon became a regular watering hole for their gatherings.

Her favorite was that odd fellow, Winston Churchill. The qualities Caroline had spotted in him from distant Londonderry were coming to fruition. She grew to be one of his very few confidantes, particularly on Irish matters. Indeed, Winston came to her with his dilemma before accepting the Admiralty post.

Frederick Weed knew that if he pouted too much about his daughter's house crawling with Liberals he could have a seizure. On the other hand, he'd also learned in his eighty-plus years that Caroline would not be deterred. There was no possibility whatsoever of changing her childlike, bohemian, bolshevik tendencies.

Caroline entered middle age lovely. What had been lost from her overpowering beauty had been replaced by a calm grace, wisdom, and aura of grandeur one usually wins only through tragedy. To supervise a powerful industrial complex and remain utterly feminine was perhaps her most endearing trait.

Her name in London became linked to Gorman Galloway, an untamed Anglo-Irishman of the other faith, who was saddled with an unfortunate and undivorceable marriage, as was Caroline. His wife lived in Dublin and his children, all Irish gems, were scattered about and in and out.

Galloway was mostly sane but occasionally pure mad Irish, always witty, an actor, producer, director, and a smashing writer. Mocking all political parties, he wrote magnificent, devastating social commentary, usually mercilessly jerking around the imperial union jackers.

Gorman was one hell of a fun fellow himself, with an adoring court at his feet and coattails. Though loosely tied, he and Caroline were looked upon as a rather committed couple despite the fact Gorman went off on outrageous binges that found him waking up in Cork or leading a suffragette rally in Bristol.

Caroline's meetings with Roger were mercifully minimal. She was now out from under any pretense of a successful or congenial marriage and too powerful in her own right to be brought down by titters and gossip. Free from her early struggle with Freddie for equality, free from the labored years with Roger, and finally at peace with her unrequited love of Conor Larkin, Caroline was open and joyous but always aware the joy could be gone in a wisp.

Hester, bloodless and all, made Christopher more acceptable. Caroline was compassionate to Hester and understood Hester's failure to become pregnant. Their visits were proper and of proper length and their conversation, noncontentious.

Gorman knew that when Caroline flashed that occasional look of terrible, terrible sadness it was for one of two men ... Conor Larkin or Jeremy Hubble. Jeremy was still a subaltern in the Coleraines and he'd gotten very Irish with his drinking and even worse with his self-pity.

Caroline had searched herself weary for Molly O'Rafferty, a search kept alive by the faintest of clues that always turned cold.

Caroline knew that she would need to make a first gesture to Jeremy sooner or later. What she really wanted was for him to join her search. She wanted Jeremy to finally be a man and demand to find that son or daughter of his. As long as he drank his way through it, she would not come to him.

✻ ✻ ✻

Caroline's Chelsea parlor became a whirlwind of exciting times as the Liberals rode the winds of change in trying to uproot the British class system. The bull's-eye of the target was the culpable hereditary powers vested in the House of Lords. Well, the House of Lords was not going to dismiss itself and abandon its privileges. At last the Liberals came up with a scheme. If Lords' powers were not curtailed, the Liberals would create hundreds of new Liberal peerages and double the size of Lords.

Faced with the dastardly specter of a slew of ordinary street people being named to the aristocracy, Lords yielded. Henceforth, if a bill passed Commons and was rejected by Lords, Commons had the right to pass it twice. If Lords rejected it a second time, then Commons could pass it a third time and it automatically became law.

Into this political grab bag came the dying gasps of John Redmond and his Irish Party. Prime Minister Asquith, Lloyd George, Winston Churchill, and the Liberal Party didn't really give a hoot in hell about Irish self-government. Nonetheless they needed the Irish Party in their coalition if they were to remain in power and so give their Home Rule Bill ambivalent sincerity.

The Third Irish Home Rule Bill was bloodless stuff. Under it the Irish could erect road signs, establish mental clinics, warden fishing streams, and trim hedges, but when it came to the hard stuff—defense, collection of taxes, loyalty to the Crown, and a place among the nations—England remained all. All, to the point that any legislation passed by a Dublin Parliament could be overruled by the House of Commons.

This legislation was the most meager of symbolic gestures, but Redmond desperately needed that gesture. Redmond's Irish Party was on its last legs and might well lose badly to the Sinn Fein in the next elections.

Despite the fact that the bill posed no real threat to the Unionists of Ulster, the mere words *Home Rule* were sufficient to open Pandora's box.

In early April of 1912, the Liberal and Irish Parties passed the Third Home Rule Bill in the House of Commons by 110 votes.

On April 14, the House of Lords rejected Irish Home Rule, 326 to 69.

The Liberals slated a second reading of the bill in Commons for later in the year, but across the sea Protestant Ulster was in a frenzy. Having earlier signed their Act of Covenant, often in blood, the province erupted in massive rallies from end to end. As the Protestant protest lapped up on England's shores, the Conservative Party leapt on the issue, sensing that any anti-Irish measure would gain popularity.

Protests, well financed from Ulster, swept England and Wales and Scotland. Conservatives fanned the fires with the goal of bringing down the Liberal government.

On cue, Rudyard Kipling penned a heroic new poem, soon memorized and recited with fervor by every Protestant school child in the British Isles.

> We know the war prepared
> On every peaceful home.
> We know the hells declared
> For such as serve not Rome.
> In terror, threats and dread,
> In market, hearth and field,
> We know when all is said
> We perish if we yield.
>
> Believe, we dare not boast.
> Believe we do not fear.
> We stand to pay the cost
> In all that men hold dear.
> What answer from the North?
> One Law, one Land, one Throne.
> If England drives us forth,
> We shall not fall alone.

Orange Ulster had declared war on anything within shooting range: Irish Catholics, Liberals, many of their own, and certainly everybody who disagreed with them.

For Roger Hubble, the Fourteenth Earl of Foyle, it was resurrection time. Armed with a wide-open mandate, Roger revived his Belfast connections. On matters of Unionism, Roger and Sir Frederick were still allies. Bringing in four of the most powerful Unionists in the province along with some high-ranking Ulster military, a series of attacks were concocted, each upping the ante against the British government.

The Ulster Militia, hitherto not quite legal, came out into the open for recruits after a public appeal by Sir Frederick himself.

No sooner were the words out of his mouth than a spokesman for 170 Unionist clubs and Orange lodges with a membership of 17,000 men of military age pledged to enlist their entire membership the minute the Militia's doors opened.

Lord Roberts, the leading general of India, tendered his resignation, presumably to assume command of the Militia.

Targeted retired British officers were contacted for hire to form a quasi-army with transportation, medical corps, intelligence units, communications, and whatever else the Militia required.

Sir Frederick was peppered with questions at a press conference that followed. Is this not a private army belonging to a political party? Is it loyal to the Crown? Is it legal?

"The Ulster Militia," Sir Frederick said cheekily, "may or may not be legal, depending on whose bull we are goring. We are only committed to the continued freedom of Ulster as part of the United Kingdom. That is legal! Furthermore, we will shoot anyone who denies us our British heritage."

"Does that mean the Militia will shoot British soldiers?" he was asked.

"Sir, no British soldier would shoot a kindred Ulsterman. Anyone who would order him to do so is a traitor!"

In England the Conservatives picked up on the word *traitor* . . . and the Liberals scrambled to organize themselves against the next assault, lest they go down as being incapable of governing the nation.

With the Liberals on the defensive, the Conservative-Unionist coalition pressed on audaciously.

*   *   *

What was amazing was the civility with which Sir Frederick could work with his loathed son-in-law on Unionist matters. Roger had concocted a scenario that, if successful, might well be the jugular blow to Asquith.

It was a conspiracy of lovely delicacy.

The now Brigadier Llewelyn Brodhead commanded Camp Bushy in the placid environs where the river Shannon opened into Lough Ree. Camp Bushy was the main garrison for Ulster. Brodhead was imperial Ulster incarnate. His breath, his flesh, all that was him and his, belonged to the empire.

The Brigadier and Lord Roger were longstanding pals of the sort who always owed one another a favor. Lettershambo Castle, the Militia arsenal of questionable legality, became out-and-out under Brodhead's protection with Brodhead's cooperation in the gunrunning.

Roger saw to it that the Brigadier was let in on a number of "good bets" with his insider information.

The principal troops at Bushy were the King's Midlanders, but the Coleraine Rifles were also included. When Roger exiled Jeremy to the Rifles, Brodhead assured him he'd keep the lad under control and out of trouble, which he did.

When Christopher went to the Rifles, he was earmarked for rapid promotion and became a close side to Brodhead. Chris was having a problem getting his wife pregnant and was given all the time off he needed to get the old job done.

With Brodhead and Captain Christopher Hubble in on the scheme, Lord Roger contacted Weed to set up a secret meeting and bring along three or four cronies who could deliver vast amounts of money.

When Roger unfolded the plan, tens of thousands of quid were laid in the center of the table. Their principal German arms dealer had purchased a shipload of heavy arms for the Militia, and two nine-hundred-ton vessels. It was done with the cooperation and assistance of the German government, keen on anything to disrupt Ireland or embarrass the British government.

The ship was in a Hamburg dock with her empty sister ship

in the next slip, to be used as a decoy. A story was circulated that the pair were bound for Mexico where the ousted dictator, Diaz, planned a coup.

Enter Captain Christopher Hubble, in civvies but blond, erect, correct, polished, moustached, the very model of empire man.

Christopher left with a German crew under a German flag, but instead of the usual North Sea route, swung into the English Channel and up the Irish Sea where the ship was shadowed by a British destroyer.

The sister ship trailed, then switched places with, the arms boat in the middle of the night. The captain of the British destroyer, a member of the plot, deliberately followed the wrong ship.

Christopher's boat slipped through the North Channel separating Ulster from Scotland. At the Rathlin Islands, the German crew was replaced by a crew of Ulster Militia. They raised the banner of the Militia and in broad daylight sailed down Lough Foyle to Londonderry.

Emergency inquiries from the Admiralty and War Office to Camp Bushy went unanswered as the arms boat unloaded into a waiting freight train, which whisked its cargo into the safety of Lettershambo Castle.

Christopher Hubble was spirited back to Camp Bushy to the winks and back slaps of knowing staff officers and a whispered chorus of "Well dones."

Asquith ordered a lid of secrecy clamped on the area as the cabinet went into emergency session. Brigadier Brodhead stiffened to take the blow. Two days after the landing, a personal message was delivered to Brigadier Brodhead by the Assistant Chief of Operations and signed by the Prime Minister.

Brodhead was ordered to place the King's Midlanders and all attached units, including the Coleraine Rifles, on twenty-four-hour alert. All leaves were canceled and all personnel restricted to base.

STAND BY TO ENTER ULSTER FOR THE PURPOSE OF MILITARY OCCUPATION AND DEFUSE A GROWING REVOLT BY THE ULSTER MILITIA. ALL PORTS, RAILWAY DEPOTS, ARSENALS INCLUDING LETTERSHAMBO CASTLE, FACTORIES ENGAGED IN ARMS MANUFACTURING, BRIDGES, UTILITY STATIONS, AND OTHER FACILITIES LISTED ARE TO BE SECURED IN COOPERATION WITH THE ROYAL IRISH CONSTABULARY. MAKE IMMEDI-ATE PLANS FOR DUSK-TO-DAWN CURFEWS IN ALL TOWNSHIPS.

ALL TROOPS ARE TO BE DEPLOYED IN COM-BAT-READY POSTURE. IF RESISTANCE IS OFFERED BY THE ULSTER MILITIA OR ANY OF ITS SUB-UNITS, TROOPS ARE RELEASED TO RESPOND WITH APPROPRIATE GUNFIRE.

The final act of the Weed-Hubble-Brodhead plot unfolded. Brigadier Llewelyn Brodhead tendered his resignation and sum-moned Captain Christopher Hubble to his office. Christopher, riding on hero's wings, affixed his signature below the Brigadier's. Within an hour every officer in the Coleraine Rifles, except for Subaltern Jeremy Hubble, had likewise resigned.

This was a gigantic relief. Now, at least, if the Brigadier and the Captain faced the firing squad, they'd have company.

By morning every officer in the King's Midlanders and else-where in Camp Bushy had resigned. Jeremy caved in as he had when he abandoned Molly.

For the moment secrecy held, but what the cabinet was look-ing at was open mutiny!

CHAPTER

52

Caroline's London office desk was neither slapdash with papers and trinkets nor wholly immaculate but for a single rose. It was cleared for action like a battleship deck, as she focused on a trio of thick reports, her nose balancing her specs in the manner of her father.

Chalmers, her chief financial adviser, and MacGregor, her father's top engineer, were both iffy about the bold stroke Caroline wanted to put on the boards for the future.

Like many facilities, Weed Ship & Iron was building at capacity and, to handle new bids, was leasing old facilities or patching up derelict ones.

Caroline was opting for an entire new shipyard north of Belfast. The vicinity around Larne would be perfect.

Caroline's vision was rooted in the fact that there would soon be a war. That war would end. When that war ended, the building of ships and other products of war would come to a screeching halt. While the other industrialists of the British Isles would go into retrenchment, Caroline would streak into the future.

Things grow obsolete during a war, things are destroyed during a war, shortages develop during a war, and war gives birth to all sorts of inventions that could be used in peacetime.

Caroline had a team working on how Weed Ship & Iron could make a swift postwar conversion. The Larne facility, if it were built, would be able to make an instant turnover into civilian product. The autobus would cut deeply into trains as a mode of passenger transportation. Thousands of flatbed rail cars would need replacement. Her product list ran from the smallest to the largest items.

Mostly, Caroline liked the future possibilities of the aircraft. Its growth potential as a means of transporting civilians was mind-boggling, as was the future construction of airdromes. Weed Ship & Iron, if the planning stayed targeted and acute, would have a jump on the entire British Isles.

Larne was the stuff of her old man, all right, but it had its usual Ulsterism negatives. The area was a pure Orange stronghold. At the moment, everyone had a job. If a Larne yard were opened now, it would invite an influx of Catholic job seekers and no doubt cause future friction.

Chalmers and MacGregor argued that the lads returning to Larne from the war would see it overrun with R.C.'s, who had all the jobs.

What galled Caroline was the realization that the loyal population had to be served first. There *had* to be a way to give the Catholics parity, or the cycles of fear and riots would never end. And she *knew* she was dead right about the future of aviation. Other sites were spoken of, but most of them were outside Ulster and that was the most sacred no of them all.

"I want County Down surveyed from end to end. The Newtonards Peninsula may have everything we need, including an absence of industry and a built-in unemployed Catholic population. I want it all laid out for me and ready in a month."

Chalmers and MacGregor exchanged "Oh Christ" expressions. She was as bad as the old man! As they gathered up their business from the desk, Caroline's secretary entered and waited at the door. He closed the door behind the two men as they left.

"What is it, Lawrence?" Caroline asked.

"Winston Churchill is here. I took him to the conference room."

"Fetch him, Larry, and I am not available to anyone for anything."

"Yes, m'lady."

Caroline got up from her plushy chair and insisted Churchill take it, while she seated herself at the end of the desk. Winston could play the poker face with the mightiest of them, but the color was gone from his cheeks and the man who seldom showed any tiredness seemed exhausted.

"Are you comfortable here, Winston?" she asked.

"Are we alone?" Caroline nodded. "Do you have a secure telephone line to Belfast to Sir Frederick?"

"I do."

"Can you reach him quickly?"

"We spoke this morning. He should be at Rathweed Hall all afternoon."

"Can he make a binding decision on Ulster Militia matters in which Lord Hubble, Lord Greystone, Sir Martin Bickford, and Henry Wallaby are also involved?"

"I'm rather certain he can, but I can't give you a hundred percent assurance."

"Instruct your man to have Sir Frederick on standby. He might try to reach the others in the interim, so have them stay put someplace he can get to them."

"Shouldn't Edward Carson be party to whatever you are about to dump on me?"

"No, Carson was deliberately left out of the entire operation in order to protect him. We'll never link Carson to this thing."

"Good Lord, what's going on, Winston?"

"A diabolical conspiracy is unfolding. A thousand-ton German vessel carrying heavy German weapons, artillery, shells, etcetera, etcetera, has made its way directly to Ulster. Our destroyer *Battersea* tailed as a decoy ship. We believe the commander of the *Battersea* is involved in the plot. At any rate, the ship holding the weaponry entered Lough Foyle flying an Ulster Militia flag and unloaded at your husband's dock in Londonderry. The weapons were transferred to a waiting line of freight cars and flatbeds, then moved into Lettershambo Castle in broad daylight."

Caroline rolled her eyes and blew a long breath. Oh, why did she love her daddy so fiercely? "Sounds like Roger and Freddie, all right. Bickford, Wallaby, Greystone, all charter members of the old boys' club. Yes, they could chunk in that kind of money. What the hell, Winston, they would not have done something this blatant unless they were dead certain they could get away with it. The way they've gotten the English people up in arms in the past three months and made no move to stop them, something like this was bound to happen."

Churchill drummed his finger elegantly on her desk top and looked down. "It is not totally clear yet, Caroline, but it seems that your son, Captain Christopher Hubble, ran the ship in."

After the first flash of terror came another wave and yet another. She sprung from her chair and muttered to unhearing gods. Once she got the thunder of it calmed, an off-scale tone poem of confusion and fear jumbled together.

"Is he under arrest?" she finally brought herself to ask.

"Well, certainly the boy's father and grandfather were going to see that he was covered . . . if indeed it was Christopher. The gunrunning was only one phase of the scheme."

Caroline realized it was going to be a very hard hour. She did what was necessary to gather her faculties and beckoned him to go on. Winston asked permission to light a cigar and she smiled.

"The object of this exercise is to put the Liberals into a trap. At my insistence, Asquith had an order issued that the forces at Camp Bushy, mainly the Midlanders and the Coleraines, go on standby to occupy vital facilities and declare Ulster under martial law."

"They're playing awfully rough," she said.

"Oh, yes. Brigadier Brodhead was obviously in on the whole thing from its inception."

"That follows. Roger and Freddie have made him wealthy on tips, to say nothing of the fact that he is pre-Neanderthal when it comes to empire."

"To go on," Churchill continued, "Brodhead not only refused to obey the order, but he tendered his resignation and obtained the resignations of all one hundred and fifty-some officers at Camp Bushy."

"That's an out-and-out mutiny."

"We have a little time to sort things out. Bushy is sealed off and thus far, no news of the resignations."

"And these are my people, the men of my life. They are not

normal when it comes to Ulsterism. If you and I held this conversation at the end of this century, they would still be marching around the same parade ground, thumping the same Lembeg drums and kissing the same Union Jack. You know your *King Lear*, Winston. Ulster is possessed. It has been too long on the path for them to ever turn back. They must keep going until victory or destruction. Even if both of my sons are involved, you have to put that entire bunch under arrest and court-martial them. Excuse my language, Winston, but that is the only fucking thing they'll ever understand."

They sat in silence for a time. Caroline's sense of outrage heightened. God, they'd even bring the empire down to save their filthy little province.

"Our reaction also was to throw them in jail, but nothing is quite that simple. Caroline, I have fought my entire political life to cut down on obscene military spending. Till now, the most difficult moment of my life was, as you know, when I became convinced there would be a war and I accepted the Admiralty post. But the War Office and the Admiralty have long memories and they loathe the Liberal Party for stopping the arms race and for trying to bring programs of social justice to the people to replace their imperial avarice."

His voice now quivered low. "Fact is, m'lady, probably most of the top generals and admirals are quietly applauding Brodhead. Using our best and most reliable sources, including the Staines group, between one-fourth and one-third of our entire officer corps will likely resign in protest if we arrest the Bushy crowd. How's that for blackmail on the eve of a war?"

Caroline laughed, compelled to see the humor in it. "What better time to blackmail you? What are our options?" she asked, casting her lot with his.

"If," he began, "we turn a blind eye and allow the Militia to become a private army, and if we allow ourselves to yield to blackmail by our own officer corps, then we are no longer fit to rule the country."

"That's exactly what the Conservatives are playing for," she said.

"It's even more dangerous than that, Caroline. Once the military knows they can bully the Commons and get away with anything, including mutiny and treason, we will witness a ravenous new colonialism after the war that will endanger our democracy. Once the generals have the notion we can be owned, we'll end up looking like a Latin American republic."

"The bloody Conservatives would like that, I fear."

"Let's 'if' some more," he said. "If we haul the mutineers in, take the deep cuts in our officer corps on the eve of war, we will lose the confidence of our allies. Those nations sitting on the fence, particularly the Italians, will surely go to the German side. When the German high command hears about this mutiny, they are going to go into an orgy of Valhallan ecstasy."

Caroline tilted her head back, closed her eyes, and tried to absorb the enormity of what was unfolding. Freddie's crowd had to be dancing on the clouds to be so heady, so brazen, so demonic.

"What do we do, Winston?"

"I have just met with the Conservatives. They are now considering our position, namely we will not be blown out of power by this trick, nor will we turn Britain over to a military junta. We Liberals intend, I advised them, that we shall remain in power and lead this nation when it goes to war."

Winston grunted the smallest of laughs as he recalled the meeting. "It was with Bonar, Law, and Balfour. I made it completely clear that their wild plot would blow up right in their faces. The Liberal Party has been voted into power by a majority of good, solid Englishmen. What could the Conservatives do? Blame over half the country for the loss of their officer corps? Indeed, I was quite willing to let the people decide who the villains in this play were. In the end. I resolutely believe they would have to take the blame for debilitating our military."

"That's carrying brinkmanship to a fine art."

"It can only be done if you believe in yourself. They chose to listen to a reasonable plan which will save their face and quiet the entire matter."

"And now you need the agreement of Freddie and his cronies."

"That's right."

"Do go on."

"We accept that the weapons in Lettershambo belong to the Militia and that the Militia will have some clear legal status. We will rescind the order for the Midlanders and Coleraines to occupy Ulster and there will be further action taken on the resignations."

Caroline jotted notes, wondering if it was not a total capitulation by some other name. No, it was only Winston spitting out the seeds of compromise's bitter fruit.

"To continue," he said, "we will remove the principal source of Unionist irritation, the Home Rule Bill. Redmond and the Irish Party have agreed to table the legislation during the crisis and, in the eventuality of war, to keep it tabled until such war is completed."

"What is John Redmond going to say to the Irish people?"

"Well, we'll throw him a bone. We will allow the Irish in the south to form a Home Army similar in legal structure to the Militia. Everyone in Ulster knows that the Irish could never muster a fiftieth of the strength of the Militia. It should not be a problem with your father."

"But isn't that the end of Redmond, giving up home rule for a few guardsmen?"

"I say, does it really matter, Caroline? Those hooligans from Sinn Fein are ready to rush in and fill any vacuum left by a defunct Irish Party. What matters for us is to postpone the entire Irish issue, get it off our backs, and allow us to conduct the war without a squabble in our kitchen ... to use Irish troops ... Ulster troops for our own battle purposes. We'll deal with the Irish after the war. That's what Redmond can assure us now."

Caroline took up the phone to call her father at Rathweed Hall, going over Churchill's points with care.

Weed digested it carefully. The only negative seemed to be the formation of a home army, but that was a fly speck. Bringing down the Liberals had been evaded and avoided.

"I don't think I can sell it," Freddie said. "It's Churchill's move, Caroline."

"Hold on, Father."

As Caroline laid out Freddie's ultimatum, Churchill smiled. He took a single-page order from his jacket and laid it on the desk before Caroline. As Caroline read it to her father she realized that the Liberals were not only going to quit but, furthermore, the Conservatives and Unionists would now have to share responsibility for the consequences. The Liberals were willing to risk the calamity, but it was one hour past brinkmanship and the Conservative Party would have to explain the loss of their officer corps to the people as well. Did they have the stomach for it? Or . . . was Churchill playing a dummy card?

The order she read to her father called for three divisions of troops to sail from England to Ireland immediately, this day, seize Camp Bushy, arrest all officers who had resigned, and charge them with mutiny and treason.

Furthermore, any British officers offering resignations in sympathy would likewise be treated as mutineers.

Thirdly, Ulster was to be placed under martial law with dawn-to-dusk curfew.

Caroline read it once more, slowly.

"He's bluffing," Weed said.

"Do I take that as a rejection, Freddie?"

"Hold on."

Silence . . . muffled background conversation . . . curses . . . silence.

"What do you think, Caroline?"

"Isn't there something in mythology or some such that says that I am only the messenger?"

"I'll call you back," Weed answered.

Churchill shook his head with a definite no, pocketed the order, and got up to leave.

"It won't wait," Caroline said quickly.

Silence . . . muffled curses.

"It's fucking blackmail!" Weed shouted.

"Freddie, Churchill has left my office."

"Well, grab the son of a bitch before he leaves the building and tell him he has a deal!"

"Lawrence! Get Mr. Churchill and bring him back, at once."

"Yes, m'lady. He's at the lift . . . Mr. Churchill! Mr. Churchill!"

As Winston reappeared Caroline held a thumbs-up. "Father, are you there?"

"Where the hell do you think I am!"

"I want you to remain calm, take your medication, and call for Dr. Symmons. I'll catch the overnight and be in Belfast in the morning."

"What the hell for! Damned if I want communists in my house!"

"I happen to love you, Father. Now, will you get yourself calmed down?"

A petulant pause. "It will be so good to see you," Weed said. "It's been a fortnight and I've missed you."

The Camp Bushy mutiny dissolved along with all records of the resignations, the Irish would get a home army, the Militia had an arsenal at Lettershambo Castle large enough to conquer a continent, the Home Rule Bill was put into a dead letter file, perhaps forever, and serenity ruled the land.

As war on the continent inched closer, the Balkans exploded in what was apparently a preamble to the big show. Churchill felt it might be a good time to go over to Ulster and smooth things over.

They did suffer a sense of isolation over there and Winston could promote the unity theme as his father had done thirty-four years earlier.

Astute politician that he was, Winston, as First Lord of the Admiralty, might follow up a successful Belfast rally with a speaking tour across the province.

Caroline Hubble, one of the few important Liberals in Ulster, became one of Churchill's sponsors, although she warned him not to make the trip. She told him once again that if they discussed the same thing at the end of the century, the Unionist position would not have changed one iota. Churchill, seeing too much future political coin to gain through a unity call, did not take her good advice.

As Churchill's ferry crossed the Irish Sea, Weed called in the press.

"It is lamentable," Sir Frederick said, "that this man, Churchill, deliberately comes to this loyal city to voice the line of the John Redmonds, to espouse treason, and defile the very same platform his beloved father, Randolph, spoke from so gloriously in behalf of our liberty."

Weed was asked by a reporter if the Liberal Party was or was not entitled to free speech in Belfast.

"Free speech," Freddie snapped back, "is not extended to turncoats. Winston Churchill has renounced his magnificent birthright and heritage and bolted the Conservative Party to consort with those radicals who would destroy the empire. Do not be taken in by his cunning. He is the most provocative orator in Britain and this visit is nothing more than an arrogant exercise at a time and in a place where the immortal words of his revered father still ring in our ears—'Ulster will fight and Ulster will be right.' In my frank opinion," Weed concluded, "Winston Churchill is no Englishman."

Landing at Larne, First Lord of the Admiralty Winston Churchill met with a far different reception than had been accorded Lord Randolph.

A great crowd had gathered and the mood was ugly. Churchill was booed along the route from the Midlands to the Grand Central Hotel. Effigies hung from lampposts and thousands of placards bearing the gravest insults were waved.

Churchill looked out at men edging to the brink of violence, shaking their fists, spitting, and screaming oaths at him. Rock throwing broke out and, at one juncture, two wheels of his vehicle were lifted off the ground and the auto shaken jarringly.

His welcome was only the beginning. After hasty consultations the Constabulary said it could not guarantee Churchill's safety if he spoke at Ulster Hall, the site of his father's triumphant speech.

At the last moment, Parnell Field, a rugby ground in the

Catholic Falls section, was used for the rally. The mission was a complete fizzle.

Churchill recrossed the Irish Sea needing no comfort from Caroline Hubble. They had played rough; he had played rough. The British people did not want a pussycat to lead their Admiralty. No grudges to be held, no scores to be settled. He might need them sometime in the future and they might need him. The main thing was that the Liberals were still in power, the Irish situation was on hold, and he could now concentrate full time on the coming war.

In August of 1914 the Great War began and the British Navy was ready.

A few months afterward the Ulster Militia's arsenal at Lettershambo Castle was destroyed by a small, swift raiding party of the Irish Republican Brotherhood.

The meaning of the destruction of Lettershambo Castle sent a number of messages to a complacent Ulster. All of the Protestant arms schemes, all of their illegal gunrunning, all of their flouting of the law had largely gone up in one big blast.

A shock wave of fear they had never known ran through the Protestant population. Always feeling safe and with the British Army at the beck and call, the Orange factions were suddenly faced with a new set of facts. The Irish Catholics, held in little esteem, had secretly developed a fighting capacity capable of inflicting great damage. There would be no more free riots, no more tossing pennies down on Bogside without reprisal.

The Brotherhood had won the respect of their enemy and at the same time won the respect of the Irish people. The most devastating of all their messages was that Ireland was not going to abide by a deal to "lay low" during the war. Lettershambo's destruction said that England's war and Ireland's struggle for freedom had nothing to do with each other.

Henceforth the Irish had to be reckoned with, and England in Ireland had to keep looking over its shoulder.

53

Christchurch, December 1914

Wally Ferguson halted his fist in midair, gulped uneasily, then rapped on the door of the Chief Matron of the hospital.

"Come in, please."

"Hello, Georgia," Wally said.

It was a familiar place for Wally. Sheepmen, cattlemen, timber men, miners, and sailors often checked into Wally's Exchange with something in need of repair or something busted up after an altercation on the premises. Georgia could make out someone standing behind Wally, as was often the case.

"Sister Georgia, this is Squire Liam Larkin."

"Yes, we've met. He brought his son in with some cracked ribs. Won't you have a seat, lads?"

Eyes danced among the three. All of them were in the business of sizing up people rapidly. Liam removed his hat, a gesture he performed profoundly since he was recognized as a squire. Outside it was a usual sunny day. Inside the atmosphere turned gray.

"I'm looking for my boy, Rory," Liam said directly.

"Are you here for consultation or confrontation?" Georgia asked.

"Liam came to me," Wally interceded quickly. "We go all the way back, as you might know. I was Rory's godfather. So he figured you would be the one to speak to and, knowing we are friends, you and me, I should introduce the two of you."

"What did you tell him, Wally?" Georgia asked coolly.

"I don't know where the hell Rory is or where he was going," Wally lied with the innocence of a lamb in one of his holding pens. "The boy was all shot down over the death of his uncle, Conor Larkin, and he said he needed a hundred quid which the Squire would repay. Hell, I figured he went on a tear or something. He made a mess out of Oak Kelley."

"Yes, we put Oak together here," she said. "I'm rather surprised Rory didn't confide in you, Wally."

"It's like this, Sister. I'm loyal to both these men. I'm sure Rory didn't want to put me in to an awkward position with his da. I'd like to know where he is as well."

Wally looked like a man standing over a trapdoor. "This is really between the two of you so I'll wait outside, Liam."

Liam had already started his reading on Georgia Norman. She wasn't a chief matron before the age of thirty because she could be easily bullied about. She was much more attractive than a head nurse ought to be, nicely curved and certainly able to hold her own with a man. He wasn't sure what to expect but was rather surprised at Rory's good taste.

"Do you know where he is?" Liam asked.

"I'm not sure, but it shouldn't be too hard to figure out," she answered.

"The recruiting people haven't given me much help."

Georgia shrugged. "I don't know if you know, but I did serve in the military."

"I heard about that."

"What I mean to say is that he could have easily used another name. In wartime the recruiters aren't going to let a specimen like Rory get away."

"I suppose you're right. Rory's a good enough liar to hoodwink anybody."

"Rory is not a liar," she said with eye contact to let him know he was starting his own war. "I was also underage when I went into combat zones during the Boer War. What's the difference now? He's not coming back."

Liam liked the lady's toughness. The army had made her

solid, like his own Mildred. She was damned well good-looking enough to stand alongside Rory. Hell of a lot more stature than the flippies he had waltzed around with. Did Rory see her as more than anything but an occasional romp between the sheets? To what avail, Liam caught himself. She was a married woman, married to a doctor and screwing around no sooner than he caught the boat to go to war.

Liam decided not to leave an adversary. The woman had character, some good, some bad, but on a level that you could talk pretty straight to. He stood to leave.

"I'm glad we had a few minutes, Sister. When you hear from him, you might mention that I was inquiring after him. His mother and sisters and brother would like to know how he's getting on."

"I'll do that. Anything else you want me to convey?"

"Like what?"

"Oh, I don't know. The farm will still be here if he ever decides to come back to New Zealand. No, that's family business. Besides, he's not coming back. We both know that, don't we?" Liam muttered.

"When I get his address, why don't I give it to you so you can write and ask him if he wants to come back?"

"All right, Sister, stop jerking my line."

"About what?"

"Write to him about what? The way he hurt his mom? His drinking and hell-raising? Sleeping around like a bull in heat?"

"With half the married women in Christchurch," she said.

"You said that, I didn't, Mrs. Norman."

"He just figured that married women were safer after what you put him through with June MacPherson's pregnancy. But Rory's not to blame because all of us whores wanted him."

Liam slammed his hat on as only a squire can do when a deal has soured and made for the door.

"I'll tell you what you can write him," Georgia said, her eyes now bubbling with anger. "You can tell him how grieved you are for the pain and anguish you've laid on him because you've looked down on him all your life as your bastard son."

"Who told him about that!"

"Certainly not his father and mother, the two people who should have."

"You are deliberately angering me to cover up your own filthy behavior, Mrs. Norman!"

"Dr. Norman and I were finished long before the war started. I filed for divorce over a year ago. I decided to keep it quiet so as not to hurt him professionally but with the understanding that our marriage was over. I was already divorced when Rory came into my life."

"Rory knew about this?"

"No, no one knows, not even Wally, just you and me. Rory has a bad view of things about women, starting with the way his mother hurt him by her silence. He liked getting women in bed because it helped him get even with you and his ma."

"You're lying! Why didn't you tell him you were divorced!"

"Because I love him. If he knew I was free I was afraid he'd flee from me."

Liam shook his head. Christ, the woman was a virtue. What unclean thoughts he'd held for months and months. Aye, there was a girl and a half, all right. She'd go right alongside any man, wouldn't she?

"Does he love you?" Liam asked at last.

"What does it matter? We had what we had and that is fine with me. I'm not making any more out of it than it is. It's a long way home for him, if he ever does come back, and I'll be just a featureless, brown, rumpled photo."

Liam wandered back to his chair and slumped into it. "Can I call you Georgia?"

"Yes."

"I'm Liam."

"Squire suits you," she said, almost friendly.

"How long has Rory known about me and Mildred's problems when he was born?"

"Since he was a kid. Since he was taunted in a schoolyard. Gave him a bit of an attitude growing up, you know."

Liam was bewildered and ashamed. His being felt soggy. "Oh Jesus," he wept.

"Want to hear about me and my family?" she said with irony.

"Why do we make the same fucking mistakes our da's made with us! Why the fuck don't we learn anything!"

"I think it's called life," she said.

"Is there anything I can do?" he cried.

"I'm not a Catholic," she answered quickly.

"Is there anything I can do!" he pleaded.

"God figured out when he separated us from the rest of the creatures that if we have the power to reason and justify and make decisions, then we are going to make a lot of mistakes passing through. Big, big, big mistakes. God understood that, then gave us the ultimate human power, the power of redemption."

Liam lay his head on his hands and down to the desk and let his anguish flow to softness.

"It's a shocking discovery that a deep wrong has to be righted and it might take the rest of your life to do it, so don't try to do it overnight."

"What can I do? What can I do?"

"Keep the fields of Ballyutogue Station green and let him know how the land longs for him. And, in time, it won't be all that hard to tell him you love him."

They were interrupted by an urgency in one of the wards.

"I have to go, Squire. I'm sorry about your brother, Conor."

CHAPTER

54

Camp Hobson, North Island, New Zealand, January 1915

Johnny Tarbox was an upscale artful dodger whose reputation for daring was as large as he could make it. He was a sometime independent drover, hired on for big sheep drives. If the station was moving a flock of several thousand, Tarbox would often be contracted to run a crew.

Likewise, he showed up at the Agricultural and Pastoral shows and was often the man to beat in the challenge horse races. For years he had been counted a Gun Shearer, one of the men who could shear a hundred sheep in an eight-hour stretch.

He boxed a little as well, at the A&P shows, demonstrating his dodger skills. In fact, Johnny Tarbox had droved at the Ballyutogue Station and did the A&P contests in their shows. That is, until Squire Larkin's punk kid Rory whipped him in the big race on RumRunner when the kid was only thirteen. When Rory was sixteen, he took Tarbox in a shearer contest, which he protested because the kid was using a new shear invented by his uncle.

Johnny made the final mistake of getting into the ring with eighteen-year-old Rory and never got past the first half of the first round.

Otherwise they were friends.

To hear Johnny Tarbox tell it, and he was never at a loss, he had done a lot of things: did a four-year hitch in the Royal

Marines when he was a kid, ran rum and other articles in the China Seas, prospected, and other endeavors that would come to mind at the moment.

Above all, Johnny Tarbox considered himself a sort of consummate lover and authority on female flesh. Marriage was something to be beaten off like the plague.

This was made even more so as Johnny Tarbox found the perfect niche in life. New Zealand was pretty far away from anything. It was not even on a way from place to place—you had to go out of your way to get there. Nonetheless, there were the half-dozen to dozen times a year some royalty or governmental mainstay or other notables landed at Wellington or Auckland.

They were greeted by a New Zealand Mounted Honor Guard led by none other than Serjeant Johnny Tarbox. Though the post was ceremonial, Johnny made the most of it with the ladies.

When the war broke out Johnny was a living recruiting poster, what with his smashing figure in uniform aboard his mount with the gorgeous broom moustache and a merry twinkle in his eye.

So, when a wee country gets involved as a wee participant in a very great war whose meaning is vague and whose battlefields are beyond the horizon and the equator, Tarbox was put to work enticing young men yearning for travel and adventure.

Johnny went from honorary serjeant to actual serjeant and was given the sweet job of going around the country giving tests and grading men for cavalry units. The war in France quickly settled into static lines and, by the time Johnny reached Camp Hobson outside Auckland, the cavalry was being put on hold in favor of infantry and artillery.

A last cavalry battalion, the Seventh Light Horse, was being put together up north. Five lads would be riding for each opening. When the complement was formed, Johnny Tarbox himself would become the battalion Serjeant Major.

Rory wasn't overly concerned, knowing he'd win himself a place, but he'd picked up this kid on the train from Auckland to Camp Hobson and seemed unable to disconnect himself.

It was like this. He'd boarded a trainload of recruits in

Auckland heading for Camp Hobson and found himself in a window seat.

"Seat open?" someone asked.

"Help yourself," Rory said to the kid, who eased down next to him and appeared to be a scared schoolboy. More like a drummer boy in Kyber Pass than a decapitating horseman.

"Chester Goodwood," the kid said.

"Rory Landers," Rory answered, laying his head against the window to indicate he'd prefer sleep to conversation.

"I'm trying for the Light Horse," the kid said.

"Yeah, good luck."

The recruiting serjeant was barking as the train filled up. A big roughneck goon looked about, saw no empty seats on the car, and informed Chester Goodwood, "You're in my seat."

"I don't think so," Chester answered with a verve that caused Rory to crack open one eye and have a look.

"Out!" the goon explained, grabbing Chester by the lapels and lifting him up. Chester responded by stomping hard on the foot of the bully, who angrily released him.

"I'm going to make you into a mutton chop, you little son of a bitch!"

As he reached for Chester once again, Rory's hands shot out and grabbed the goon's wrists. "No, no," Rory said, "this is my nephew, Chester Goodwood, and I promised his ma, me favorite auntie, that we'd sit together."

"Bullshit," the goon responded, freeing his wrists, balling his fists. "You got the seat I want," he said to Rory.

"Look, we're all in the old war together, right?" Rory said. "If I do get up, there's going to be one less Kiwi when we arrive at Camp Hobson. Is my meaning clear? Now, think again. Do you want me to stand up or not?"

The goon's cobber saved the moment. "Come on, Jed, there's seats up in the next car."

The altercation averted, the train soon oozed from the station for the three-hour jaunt to Camp Hobson, and Rory attempted to resume his nap.

"Thanks, awfully," Chester said.

Rory found himself longing to return to the misery of thinking of Georgia. In all the hustle of enlistment and going here and going there for physical examinations and uniforms and inoculations and questionnaires, he longed for a few moments alone so he could think of Georgia, and each time he did he lived another moment of their voyage on the *Taranaki*, realizing that this had now become the most powerful memory of his entire life.

Chester Goodwood wouldn't keep quiet. Rory was about to tell him to shut up, but the kid seemed very lost and particularly grateful for Rory's intervention . . . so Rory let him talk.

Chester Goodwood, like himself, was underage, but much more so. He was sixteen. As his story unfolded, Rory became engaged, then taken by it. . . .

Chester came from an aristocratic background. His father was a banker-businessman in Hong Kong. Everyone knew Sir Stanford Goodwood. He had connections in China that made him a power. Unfortunately, he also had four sons and Chester was the youngest. Following tradition, Chester grew up in English boarding schools, seeing his father perhaps a month each year.

Chester didn't tell Rory in so many words, but it was easy to get the drift from his own experience, that the lad was unwanted and his family let him know it in a most cavalier manner.

So, Chester managed to do one thing after another at the likes of Eton and Harrow to get himself expelled, which was one sure way of getting his father's attention.

Sir Stanford had brought the boy to Hong Kong a year earlier, as the boy's mother lay dying. It was then that Chester learned that his mother had been a nuisance, like himself. Father's keen interest centered on several nests of Chinese concubines . . . thus, all the trips into China.

At his mother's death, Chester was faced with a return to England. When war was declared, he made a dash for freedom. Chester stowed on a New Zealand–bound freighter, where the captain and crew favored him and slipped him ashore.

Chester had befriended some of the clerks in his father's bank, one of whom forged sufficient papers for him to enlist, although his age of twenty-one seemed to be stretching things.

"Can you ride?" Rory asked.

"I jumped at Harrow and I've actually played a spot of polo for a club in Hong Kong."

Impressive, Rory thought. The kid had spunk and there was a likable manner to him. Surely, if anyone in the world was lonelier than he, it had to be Chester.

When they pulled into Camp Hobson and Rory looked from the windows to see the goon squads of serjeants barking all at once, he thought Chester was never going to make it, and the confused look on Chester's face confirmed it.

"All right, you stick with me," Rory said.

"Thank you, I'm sure."

"But don't get on my nerves. You know what I mean. Don't get on my nerves, Chester."

Chester did get on his nerves. However, Rory was the only recruit at Camp Hobson who had his own batsman, shoe shiner, placeholder in the mess hall line, and roll call answerer so he could get an extra hour's sleep.

Within the week, while the army was trying to untie all the bureaucratic knots they had tied themselves into, Rory began to see further virtue in Chester Goodwood. The relationship was more than the satisfaction of a son of an aristocrat serving a sheepman's son. Chester had his own gall.

Although, according to Chester, three schools had dumped him, he apparently had picked up some education at each of them. The kid was a bloody wizard with figures and calculations. He must have inherited it from his daddy, the banker, Rory figured. On a practical basis, nobody could beat Chester Goodwood in any game of chance or skill. He was hands down the best in chess, checkers, dominos, cards, or whatever bored men pass their time with in the barracks.

On considering the rest of the lads in his unit, Rory decided Chester was a good one to hook up with and, as happens in times of war, an odd friendship was born.

Rory's stomach was in delicate condition and his head not much better. The Camp Hobson pub featured some god-awful rum and underaged ale, a combination potent enough to remove the varnish from the deck of a ship. Chester Goodwood came running into the tent, elated.

"Rory! They just posted it! Our group has its trials in an hour!"

"Jesus! Jesus! This bloody army's got some sense of humor. We've been lying around for a week and they pick this bloody minute." Rory came off the cot slowly. "I'm dying, Chester."

"I wish I could ride for you," Chester said.

Rory grabbed him. "Maybe you can! No, it would never work. Oh Jesus." He sat down then started to lie back.

"Get up!" Chester demanded. "We've been waiting for this!"

Rory turned his back on him. Chester dumped the cot. Rory crawled to his feet and looked for someone to punch.

"Now, you're on your feet," Chester said, "start walking and keep taking deep breaths."

Daylight erupted in Rory's face as he left the tent. "Gawd! . . . it's ugly!"

"What's ugly?"

"Life."

"It won't be so ugly once you relieve yourself. Now, we're heading for the latrine. Get on your knees over the hole, place your finger down your throat, and eject."

"Chester, get out of my life! And take your fucking hands off me. I can walk."

"Easy does it, cobber, easy does it."

Rory longed to fall to the ground where Georgia would be waiting with her sweet, gorgeous, warm bosom. . . . Chester held him upright and guided him toward the latrine.

Rory entered the assembly area of the barn with a plan formulated in his fuzzy mind. A hundred candidates were in line biting their fingernails. Good! Excellent! He elbowed Chester in up close to the front of the line so he could ride early. After Chester rode he could return and brief Rory on the layout of the course and possibly the best horse, if there was a choice. The line was moving fairly slowly . . . excellent . . . it would afford him another hour to recover.

Rory sat on a bench, his back to the wall, then slid to a sitting position.

He thought he had barely closed his eyes, when . . .

"You!" a voice boomed over his head.

Rory lifted his head off his chest. It was like a rock being pounded by an angry sea.

"You!" the ugly bass voice repeated. "Are you Rory Landers?"

"Aye," he moaned.

"Where the fuck you been! Get your ass up. You're last man to ride. I think it's a waste of time but the regulations say you can ride. Come on, prawn, I've had a long day and I'm in an unpleasant mood."

"Hey, Sarj," Rory moaned, "give us an old hand."

The serjeant snarled and jerked Rory to his feet and they stood eyeball to eyeball.

"Johnny Tarbox!"

"Aw, for Christ's sake, Rory Larkin!"

"Shhh," Rory said, putting his finger to his lips. "My name is not Larkin."

Tarbox looked at his clipboard. "What's this Landers shit? Getting away from the Squire, are you?"

"I'll be of age by Christmas," Rory said. "It's the bloody essential agricultural industry. The old man can freeze me."

"I don't know about this," Tarbox said with a sly grin. "You've shown me up in one too many A&P shows. See this. Stitches from our encounter." The grin opened to a smile as Tarbox threw his arms about Rory. "Oh Jaysus, you've been drinking that rotten canteen rum and green beer," he noted. "Not to worry. Half the kids here are underage."

"You know, I heard you were doing some kind of recruiting," Rory said. "Well, let's get on with it. Give me an old horse, will you?"

"You don't have to ride. I'm putting you right into headquarters company with myself. Want to hear the best? I'm Serjeant Major of the Seventh."

"No!"

"Indeed, and the ladies better watch their knickers. Hey, Rory, you all right?"

"Yeah, sure."

"You don't look all right."

"I'm not all right. I never had this set of feelings before. I don't understand what they are. I don't know how to manage them. I ... ugh ... got myself a little more involved than I figured on."

"You're not on the run, are you? You didn't knock her up?"

"No, just ... "

"Love?"

"Maybe."

"Good. Keep it at 'maybe.' Listen, happens to the best of us what those little girls can shake at you, but just don't let them get the collar around your neck. Anyhow, in the direction we're heading there's going to be a lot of ass out there to ease your pain ... French ass."

Johnny called over to a squad and told them the trials were done for the day and to get the horses settled.

"Johnny," Rory said on impulse, "I'm going to need a big favor. You know how the old wheel spins around. I'll owe you one soon enough."

"What do you need?"

"Being as you're helping judge these lads, there's a kid I'd like to see get assigned to our company."

"Our company, is it? I'm not a colonel. The officers make the final decision."

"Well, you can jiggle the grades a little and kind of let the Colonel or whoever he is know you've a special wish or two ... like with me."

Tarbox gnashed his discomfort. "Who?"

"Terrific kid."

"Who?"

"I teamed up with a kid named Chester Goodwood."

Johnny flipped through the pages on the clipboard, then squinted. "The little fucker?"

"He is a bit short."

My notation says he should be leading ponies for blind kids at the A&P shows."

"He didn't ride that bad, did he? I mean, he's a polo player . . . jumped horses at Harrow."

Tarbox shrugged.

"He *is* a good rider," Rory pressed.

"He rides good enough, but Jaysus, five will get you fifty he's a real underage runaway."

"Take him, he's a steal," Rory said.

"I know you sheepmen are queer, but that shit doesn't go in the army."

"Cut it out, Tarbox, He's a kid who needs a break. I just needed a break . . . you needed a break when the Squire gave you your first big muster . . . we all need a break. This kid is a wizard with the books and numbers."

"Numbers! Books! What the hell has that got to do with the Light Horse?"

"You're glinking me, Johnny Tarbox. You weren't in the crater of a volcano when the old man upstairs passed out the brains. Did you or did you not tell me you're going to be the battalion Serjeant Major? My mother does that job on the ranch and she spends half her life at it. Think! Muster rolls, pay rolls, sick reports, quartermaster reports . . . and the HORSES—you know how much ledgering and numbering and bookkeeping one fucking horse takes? You're going to have five hundred of them and, I shit you not, you're going to need Chester Goodwood."

Johnny was confused by the sudden waterfall. God! Johnny hated doing the books. To him it was an extension of marriage, itself.

"As soon as we board ship, I'm assigning Chester to me. If this little fuckhead fucks up, I'll throw his fucking ass to the sharks and you won't live long enough to shovel all the horseshit I have in mind for you."

"Good man, John Tarbox," Rory said, elated.

"Just this once, Larkin!"

"Johnny, the name is *Landers,* for Christ sake—*Rory Landers.*"

With the onset of hostilities in Europe, Brigadier Llewelyn Brodhead trained his Midlanders and Coleraine Rifles at Camp Bushy to a fighting edge.

The standing army of Fusiliers and Hussars of old standing brigades emptied out of England and crossed the Channel. For the moment the German thrust into Belgium and France had been halted.

Brodhead was at the ready, anticipating the order to move out. Then, Lettershambo Castle was destroyed and his troops were frozen in Ireland, lest an insurrection break out.

When his orders came, it was not at all what he expected. After a few hard nights of chewing on the pros and cons, Brodhead concluded that it was not some sort of vengeance from the Liberals, but a fair and equitable decision. He sorted things out and actually found himself in an interesting situation.

Captain Christopher Hubble, the best known junior officer at Bushy, was the Brigadier's man. He was the first to be called in.

Chris found the Brigadier in his usual military posture, pacing from desk to window and puffing out a smokestackful from his pipe. For a moment the Brigadier stopped and stared out to the neat barracks and grounds near the river, then spun about and shot a hard look at the younger man.

"Orders have come."

"That's a relief. We were getting a bit on edge."

"They're not what you think, Chris. Bang on. Both the Coleraine Rifles and the Midlanders are being broken up, reduced to one-fifth size. The other four-fifths—officers, warrant officers, and enlisted men—are to be transferred, one-fifth each to form the nucleus of four new brigades. That is, the War Office is making us a victim of our own success."

"Sounds to me, sir, like someone is punishing us for the resignations incident."

"That's what struck me at first. Our units, Chris, top to bottom, have the best people in the army. Hundreds of thousands of civilians are enlisting. Tens of dozens of new brigades have to be formed from scratch. The new forces simply have to have what experienced men we can provide."

"Yes, that makes sense."

"The Coleraine Rifles will be brought up to original strength again. Taking note that it is your family's regiment, I'd like to put a proposition to you. I'm odd man out. I've been given a new assignment. Bang on, Chris, you and I have gone through a tremendous experience together, and I personally see you as one of the finest junior officers anywhere. I know what it means to you to remain with the Coleraines, so I realize the sacrifice I am about to ask you to make, and mind you, it's not an order, it's a request."

"I'm grateful for your consideration in times like these," Chris said.

"I did something a bit out of school. I had a chat with your father. As you know, we're very thick. He expressed some dismay, of course, but gives his blessings to me. I'm taking on a very interesting command. I want you aboard with me."

"I rather fancy the idea of fighting the war with you, sir."

"Good man. Now then, assuming you will join me, I have obtained top secret clearance for you on any matter I think is a need to know situation. You will be privy to a lot of totally hush-hush information."

"I'm very flattered, Brigadier Brodhead."

Brodhead leaned on his desk showing white knuckles. "At this moment there is a huge convergence of Australian and New Zealand volunteers forming up into a convoy. Neither country has many standing peacetime troops so they are also breaking up the experienced units and using them to form the skeleton of new units. Same situation as ours."

"I follow you."

"I'm speaking of forty to fifty thousand of them. When we get the ships and escorts to them, their convoy will rendezvous near India to be joined by a few old Indian brigades and thence proceed through the Red Sea and Suez Canal for training in Egypt. The Aussies and New Zealanders have only one-third of the officers they require. Some, I suppose, will come right up through their ranks. We are to supply the rest. I have been kicked upstairs, Chris. I am to assume command of the joint Australian–New Zealand Expeditionary Force as their Major General."

"Congratulations . . . Brigadier . . . well, have to get used to saying, General Brodhead."

"Has a rather nice sound," Brodhead agreed. "My first task is to put together a cadre of two hundred officers from a pool of a thousand men. I got first crack and I think I've got the best unassigned officers in the entire army. We shall be on the way to Egypt shortly and hopefully we'll arrive before the advance contingent of Aussies."

Major General Brodhead sat and weighed his coming words with all the added responsibility of the new rank. "While we admire and honor the fighting skills of our colonials, it has been the unwritten law that the top commanders and key staff officers remain British."

"One can certainly understand the need for London to control the war," Chris said.

"Yes, down to the battalion level, whenever possible. I think that one of the reasons I was selected was that I was a light colonel and commanded a battalion of Aussies during the nasty business with the Boers. Now I see the New Zealand chaps as Englishmen, once removed. The Aussies, however, are wild colonial boys, their ranks filled with Irish of the wrong persuasion, and they behave as one might expect from the great-grandchildren of a penal colony. But properly disciplined and trained, they are bully in combat, smashing fighters."

"So, I take it we are to establish just who is running the show at once."

"Yes, and we don't have enough time to train them properly.

We're going to have to push them right up to the edge and then over it. Now, Chris, comes the interesting part of our little discussion."

"I thought it was pretty damned interesting up till now, General."

"I have a particular mission for you that I feel is absolutely essential to the success of the coming campaign. I can't give you the details now, but I've been cleared to unseal your orders aboard ship, en route to Egypt.

"When I say that win or lose depends on what you make of your assignment, I mean it," Brodhead continued. "I can also assure you you will absolutely hate the command and probably loathe me."

Chris knew he had been boxed in. Father, General, urgency and importance—and really no way out. "Well, sir," Chris said with a sort of smile, "seems like you and I are destined to be stuck with one another. I'm at your service."

Brodhead unleashed a half-wicked smile, opened his drawer, and tossed a pair of crown insignia on the desk.

"I wore these when I was a major. They're yours now."

Chris took the crowns with some ambivalence. What a show at his tender age. On the other hand, the General must have something really nasty up his sleeve.

"This is war, Chris. Do this job for me, without question, and I'll do everything in my power to skip you right over light colonel to full colonel. That could mean commanding your own regiment and, if the war goes on a year or two, a full brigade."

Heady stuff!

"Is Jeremy on the list?" Chris asked.

"Yes, he's been doing a fair job of late. I'm promoting him to lieutenant, but for reasons we both know, he's your responsibility, and if he fucks up, I'll not spare him. Lord Roger knows that as well."

"Actually, he's eased up on his drinking a bit. Maybe Egypt will do him some good."

When Major Hubble was dismissed, the General heaved a

great sigh of relief. He knew, in his guts, that Chris Hubble could do the job. It was key stuff.

"What till the poor chap finds out what I have in mind for him," he mumbled under his breath.

"Your son Christopher is on the secure line, m'lady," Lawrence, her secretary, said.

"Hello, Chris," Caroline said as Lawrence left and closed the door behind him.

"Major Chris," he corrected.

"My goodness! Congratulations! When did all this come about?"

"Yesterday, Mother. I'm up at the manor with Father and Hester. Mum, sorry, but Hester and I won't be able to come to London this weekend as we planned. Darned sorry."

"Oh, how disappointing. Hester did so want to see the Drury Lane production and she was chomping to do some shopping."

"Well you see, Mum, Hester might just dash over by herself, maybe visit with you for a week or so, if you can see clear. She's rather disconsolate about the latest miscarriage and you've been her biggest comfort."

"Poor darling. Please have her phone me later. I left my diary at the house. And you will join us later?"

"No, Mother."

No matter how one tries to prepare for the news, no matter how marginal the relationship might be, no matter the inevitability . . . when the message comes through that your son is going to war, the numbness and dryness of mouth and wetness of forehead and hand bursts in from its hidden pores. Although they were on a secure line, there were no more questions that could be asked and no more answers that could be told.

"Will you be seeing much of your brother in the coming days?"

"Yes."

The shock wave hit her again.

"He's got a couple of pips, First Lieutenant now. I must say,

Mother, he's been starting to show some good stuff lately."

"Ask him to call me, Chris . . . please ask him to call me."

"Of course."

"God bless, Chris."

"Cheerio, Mum."

The earldom was immense and everyone had developed a sense of where everyone else might be, in case of business. Chris knew Jeremy's most likely watering holes, and on this night was certain he'd find his brother at the Dooley McCloskey public house at the crossroads in the upper village of Ballyutogue.

Dooley and the old-timers were gone, but the new faces were quite similar to those of the Protestant boys who slipped up to escape their wives. However, no one from the Protestant town came to the Heather since the Lettershambo raid, with tonight's exception of Lord Jeremy.

Lord Jeremy had been a Gaelic footballer down in the Bogside and a longtime intimate of Conor Larkin. It could be said with some certainty that Lord Jeremy was probably the only Viscount Coleraine in the earldom's history who was actually welcome there.

Life between the brothers was a little less acid these days. Their long childhood of yapping and snapping was followed by years of separation due to education and indifference and due to values and who was loyal to whom.

Then came the terrible events with Molly O'Rafferty. Jeremy had surrendered the girl under the concerted assault of his father, his brother, and Maxwell Swan. It was Chris's voice that wounded him the most. It was sharp, biting, injuring his mind, slicing up his insides. Jeremy realized that he'd never escape his father, for Chris would take up when his father signed off.

In those morose months when Jeremy was first sent into the Coleraines, he tried to drink Ireland dry, a venture unsuccessful by many men with far greater capacities. In those days Chris offered him neither pity nor comfort, but used his superior situation to consolidate his own position.

Later, when the officers of Camp Bushy resigned, Jeremy

went through certain motions that he was going to defy them all and refuse to join the mutiny.

On this occasion it was Jeremy and Chris alone, and Chris caved in and sent Jeremy blabbering back to his bottle with no more than a whimper. *Who was who* in the *real* hierarchy was established.

Jeremy haunted the pubs of Dublin around the Liffey like a Dickensian ghost listening for the sweet drift of ballad from the angel's voice of his Molly.

Self-pity was honed to an art and became a wise fool's manner of justifying his weak spine.

Then things took a change. Not a sudden eruption of throwing off of shackles, but a dawning of realization. The day Lettershambo Castle was taken down and Conor Larkin went to his death, Jeremy began to come out of his fog.

Memory began to make him smile again at the childhood wonderment of being stripped to the waist, black with soot, pumping the bellows in the Long Hall, and of those magnificent hundreds of hours being tutored by the big fellow, and how Conor gleaned from every poem and historical event meanings that no one else could see, and of his hero's pulling him out of the mud on the rugby patch and dragging him back to scrum and the smell of ale in the shanty town pubs . . .

And the tragic realization that his own mother and Conor had a love far more desperate than he had on with Molly O'Rafferty. Conor Larkin walked away from it like a man.

A man, that's the game. Being a man.

Dooley McCloskey's establishment was quiet for the lack of Protestant drinkers. Major Christopher Hubble entered and looked about with a crawling feeling that assassins were all around, ready to close in and stab. They tipped their hats and resumed drinking, smiling inwardly over the raid.

Jeremy was parked in a corner in a reverie. He looked up, saw his brother, and winced, wondering what savage news brought him into the enemy lair on this night.

The chair opposite Jeremy needed cleaning. "Sit down,"

Jeremy said. "I've never known the chairs to give anyone a rare disease."

Jeremy found an extra glass and poured Chris a drink and Chris took it quickly. Good, Jeremy thought, better to have him a little mellow. "Are those crowns on your shoulders, Major?"

"You've a pair of pips awaiting yourself."

"First Lieutenant Lord Viscount Jeremy Hubble emerges from the family dungeon. Ye gods, the empire must have run out of subalterns to promote," Jeremy said. "Chris, I'm really sorry about Hester's miscarriage. Is she all right?"

Chris nodded, mumbled that she was fine, and lowered his eyes as though the whole business was a mark against his masculinity.

"We're to report to camp tomorrow by ten hundred hours," Chris said.

"I thought as much," Jeremy said. "I had to say my good-byes to Conor and promise him I'd start doing right about what I've been doing wrong so he'd be proud of me. I need him to be proud of me. Understand? I need that now. The best times of my life when I wasn't with Molly were when I was walking in his shadow . . ."

Chris grumbled in irritation.

"You're pissed because he went and scattered all your pretty little guns clear all over County Londonderry. Well, that's Ulster. Here we are, all drinking together in a fine old pub. See, nobody's mad at anybody. We can get along."

"You're leaving with me now," Chris snapped an order. "The way you're going you'll never make it back to camp."

"I'll leave when I am ready to leave and that is when I'll leave."

"God, you even speak like them when you're up here." Chris came to his feet. "You might phone Mother. She's in London. I spoke to her and she rather pleaded for you to call her. I think enough is enough, as well. Call her."

"Jesus," Jeremy said, "what a fucking family . . . what a fucking country. Tell Mother, should the occasion arise, that I'll contact her some day when I've finished my penance."

Port Albany, S.W. Australia, New Year's 1915

Convoys of various sizes and shapes began to form into an enormous armada from Perth on down to Port Albany. Modern ships came in to replace old ones, the Japanese Navy escorted the Kiwi warriors from New Zealand, and contingent after contingent of Aussies arrived by rail.

As thousands upon thousands of recruits flooded in, it seemed there was a rumor for each soldier boy.

"The German raider *Emden* is creating havoc in the Indian ocean."

"The Aussie-Kiwi expedition will be shipped to South Africa to put down a growing insurrection by the Boers."

"The Expeditionary Force is heading directly for France. A week's leave in Paris will be given all troops before training behind the lines."

"The Expeditionary Force is heading directly to England and, after a week's leave in London, will go to a training camp."

"German U-boats are hovering in a wolf pack in the Arabian Sea just waiting for the convoy."

"It is straight to South Africa to train for a campaign against German East Africa."

"A Canadian Expeditionary Force of forty thousand has reached England."

"Light Horse and other Cavalry will receive their horses in England or in *Ireland* or *ARABIA*."

And variations thereof.

A camp town sprang up around the racetrack, along with sports and other recreation encouraged to alleviate boredom and the tension that always follows boredom. A string of new pubs was well attended. The Kiwis and Aussies faced off in mostly friendly competitions.

Kiwis had their go at boxing the Aussies' pet kangaroos, and a fair few rugby matches kicked up clouds of dust on the grassless fields.

The best attended were the daily boxing matches, competitions to determine the champions of each weight class of the Expeditionary Force.

There was no doubt who was the heavyweight champion. Serjeant Baker, affectionately named Butcher Boy Baker, a tattooed giant weighing over seventeen stone and standing a bit over six feet and five inches. He had accrued every title through the Pacific and Asian commands to which his artillery unit was attached. There were no known or willing survivors to challenge him in this entire gathering.

Serjeant Baker and his entourage, therefore, put on daily challenge exhibitions, wagering on how long someone might last. His backers had to give enormous odds to find fresh fodder, but they were a greedy lot, and even laying fifteen to win one on their man, Baker never let them down.

At those odds there was a man or two a day willing to get into the ring to make his fortune, but they all met with uniform failure.

Rory and Johnny Tarbox were drawn inevitably to the delicious odds the Baker followers were giving. Each day they huddled ringside to study the man, but generally his victim was dispatched before the Butcher Boy gave away very many of his secrets.

Rory and Johnny observed closely to see if foul means were employed. Chester was sent up to him to shake his hands when his gloves were off in the event they had been dipped in plaster. Johnny snatched one of his gloves, but it was not sliced or nicked nor did it contain any metal objects. Rory got a taste of his water, straight gin, but no enhancing drugs. They all watched Baker's corner men to see if they were slipping pepper on his gloves or any other foreign substance to temporarily blind an opponent.

No, Butcher Baker had no need to fight too dirty.

He was slow and cumbersome, but no punch to his face fazed him. He'd stalk, corner, and wrap one arm around his opponent—then, good night, Clarinda. He could sink a destroyer with either hand. If, indeed, an opponent seemed troublesome, the Butcher Boy could become wicked and employ liberal use of elbows, forearms, head butts, low blows.

Neither Rory nor Johnny Tarbox even considered stepping in the ring with the big fellow until the Seventh New Zealand Light Horse Battalion was taken off the old coal burner that had brought them to Australia and transferred to a newly converted troopship, the *Wagga Wagga*. Rumor had it that they were not long for Port Albany.

Butcher Boy Baker was taking on three Kiwis on this day. After the first of them went out in the first round, the Serjeant Major and his cobber repaired to one of the pubs and left Chester to witness the rest.

Johnny was bemoaning the fact that they only got to stay in Melbourne for a quick visit. He had met his true love, it seemed, and would have pretty much jumped ship for one more night in paradise. After all these years, it was the real thing!

Chester wiggled his way to the bar.

"What happened?" Johnny asked.

"The three of them together lasted five rounds."

"What a foul brute," Johnny said.

"What were the odds?" Rory asked.

"Baker's bookmaker had to give fourteen to make one."

"Jaysus," Rory moaned, "we'll never live to see odds like that again."

The three were silent in an otherwise very noisy room.

"How much money you got, Johnny?" Rory asked at last.

"I know what you're thinking, Rory, and the answer is no."

"I'm asking for other reasons," Rory said.

"Maybe seven, eight quid."

"Chester?"

A shrug was answer enough.

"Let's see. I borrowed a hundred from Wally Ferguson," Rory said, pulling his money out and counting it. "About thirty left. We've got thirty-eight quid between us and it won't be much better after we get paid. The issue I am addressing is comfort. You served in the Royal Marines, Tarbox. What comforts did you enjoy?"

"You've got to be joking. They gave us steel wool to wipe our arses with."

"What comforts have we had since we've been aboard ship?" Rory went on. "Slave ships had better ventilation and food. Slaves had a market value. We are expendable."

"That's enough," Tarbox barked. "You're trying to weave a spell on us."

"I'm speaking of comfort. We're going to land somewhere sometime. They've got to issue us our horses. We've got to train somewhere. The minute I leave the camp gate I want the kind of comfort a thousand quid or two can buy because the army isn't going to give us comfort—however, Butcher Baker can supply it."

"You'll get your bloody comfort, fair enough. I've never seen a dead man who wasn't comfortable."

"We fan out, the three of us, and borrow as much as we can. Say, we put together a hundred quid and Baker's mates cover us with fifteen hundred quid. All we can lose is our hundred ... but we stand to make FIFTEEN HUNDRED QUID."

It was enough to cause a little transition in Johnny's thinking. He recollected Rory in a few fights at the A&P's, in and out of the ring, often with blokes half again his size. Once, he had been foolish enough to get into the ring with Rory and didn't last a round. Rory was a terror, all right, but this Butcher Baker ate terrors and monsters and alligators for breakfast. He had maybe three stone weight on Rory . . . at least over fifty pounds.

"A noble idea," Johnny lamented, "but I'll not let you do it."

"Johnny, you and I have studied this fucker. He moves like an ox. He lifts his left heel and slides his left leg and pushes his jab only to keep you at bay until he can grab you. When he pushes that left jab out he is so off balance that, for an instant, his right hand is useless. Follow me, Chester?"

"Sure."

"But somehow this awkward manure pile takes his opponents out with either hand," Johnny reminded them.

"Chester, put your hands up," Rory said, "let me show you the moves. Aye, that's it. Now throw your left hand out and lean forward as you do it. That opens the whole left side of your body . . . right, Chester?"

"I suppose so, if you say so."

"So what if you park a few left hooks to his body," Johnny said.

"No, no," Rory said earnestly. "He doesn't like getting hit in the ribs. He goes berserk, like a mad rhino. He's got to get rid of his man because he doesn't like getting hit in the ribs."

"In theory that's magnificent," Tarbox mocked.

"Know what I remember about being in the ring with you, Johnny?"

Tarbox began to pale.

"I remember that left hook you put in my belly. I can still feel it. That's why I was so desperate to stop you as fast as I could."

"Oh no, I'm not getting in the ring with that sonofabitch," Johnny said. "End of discussion."

"I'm not asking you to get busted up, am I? I'm asking you to get about four or five of your dynamite left hooks to his side. Then I come in."

"It is totally inappropriate for a warrant officer such as myself to be indulging in fisticuffs with enlisted personnel. I shouldn't even be drinking beer with you."

"You're right," Rory said, "I'll speak no more except, well, maybe it just might have been a beautiful apartment in Paris overlooking the Champs de ... you know, and the Arch of Triumph and all those big-titted French birds just sashaying up and down the old boulevard looking for their very own Johnny Tarbox, the big spending handsome Kiwi Serjeant Major."

The three of them managed to scratch up a hundred and seventeen pounds and Chester Goodwood was dispatched from the *Wagga Wagga* to the HMAS *Thunderhead* where Serjeant Baker held court. It was frightening to look at the Butcher Boy up close. Knowing the convoy would be off soon, this greedy lot agreed to the bouts, particularly when Chester assured them neither opponent weighed over fourteen stone.

Only one thing Chester asked for—a chaplain to referee and hold the bets.

Rory spent half the night in brotherly love, alternating images for Johnny of French birds and the open left side of Baker's body. Punctuated with a bottle of gin, Johnny fell into a restless sleep, only partially terrorized.

It was a moody day as Rory and Chester and the Catholic chaplain led a semi-paralyzed Johnny Tarbox into the ring, where rules of engagement were gone over. Tarbox would go first and Landers second. A small matter of the bets was discussed. Chester Goodwood put up a hundred and fifteen, which was covered by the Baker bunch's sixteen hundred and fifty quid.

The mainly Aussie crowd was seething for Kiwi blood and gave their champion a most rousing hurrah.

"Time, lads," the chaplain said.

There comes a moment to the life of every man when fear locks his every joint into an immovable frozen mass, or sees him go wild and frantic with fright, or the very same man comes to a golden acre on a golden plateau where an eternity of courage is condensed into a single fraction of a second with utter clarity.

Was it the thought of French breasts and nipples and white thighs above black stockings? Was it a life as a roustabout who had felt the whack of a mighty blow and survived? No one will ever really know, but as the referee called "Time, lads," Johnny Tarbox was immaculately, divinely, focused on the left side of Butcher Boy Baker's body whereon was tattooed a heart inside a map of Australia undersigned with the single word *Mother*.

Tarbox had transcended mortal fear and was some higher form of being, as if in a dream state. As Rory lad had predicted, when Serjeant Baker lifted his left heel to slide his foot forward in conjunction with a pawing jab, Mother-Heart-Australia opened up like the golden gates.

The din was so tremendous the whack went unheard. Johnny's left arm vibrated as though it had been hit by an electric shock. The huge Aussie blinked, confused by the unseemly tactic, then reacted with a wild swing that Johnny was able to duck, giving him another clear view of Baker's art work. The blow struck right around Perth.

Serjeant Baker, who had found himself in this situation every once in a while, collected himself and moved forward in a stalk. Knowing he had gained a measure of respect, Johnny's terrible fear vanished and he put on a show of boxmanship by making himself elusive.

However, Butcher Baker knew the art of cutting down the ring size for he spent half his time in there chasing and cornering his opponent. Feeling as if he had conquered Gibraltar now, Johnny leaned in with a head fake and damned if the Aussie didn't go for it! AUSTRALIA! *POW!*

"Don't get reckless!" Rory screamed.

That is the last that Johnny Tarbox remembered until the blurred face of Rory came into focus. The smelling salts whizzed through Johnny's head and brought him back to where he was.

"You did good," Rory assured him.

"I never saw it coming. It was like a fourteen-inch artillery shell, but Jaysus, Rory, I heard him wince out loud the last time I hooked him."

Butcher Boy remained standing in his corner favoring some

pain in his side, perhaps only a cracked rib. His erstwhile second and manager came to the center of the ring.

"We'll settle for fifty quid of theirs. My man is getting indigestion eating all these raw Kiwis. We'll let the other kid live as a gesture of expeditionary unity."

"Jaysus!" Rory screamed.

The announcer called for quiet through his loud hailer. "As an act of kindness and mercy, Serjeant Baker will allow the final boxer to be free of his commitment in that he is showing such terrible fear."

Rory was in the ring and snatched the loud hailer.

"I demand to fight! Baker's a liar!"

Baker gave a wave of disgust. As he started to climb through the ropes, Rory reached him, pushed him in the face, and walked around the ring with his hands raised in victory. When the confusion was settled, the match commenced.

Rory, the natural left-hander, came dancing out fighting right-handed. He's fancy on his feet but he's got nothing to hit me with, Baker preached to himself.

Fighting from this stance in the center of the ring, Rory showed very little. The big fellow's arms were too long and he was just too high.

"Time."

"How's he breathing, Chester?"

"Not quite heavy enough."

"Shyte. In order to corner me he has to throw that left jab."

"Maybe he learned better," Johnny said.

"Time."

Suddenly, in the middle of the second round, Rory Landers switched from right-handed to left-handed, made a feint, and damned if the Aussie didn't throw an instinctive jab. Rory ducked under it and slammed two fast right hands into Baker's reddening ribs.

Rory skipped out, now fighting right-handed again, and faked a hook to the body. Baker lowered his arm to protect his aching side and got blasted on the jaw.

In that moment, Butcher Boy Baker became indecisive and

Rory swarmed all over him ... and Jaysus Almighty, Baker began backing up!

"Time! Time! Time!"

"He's puffing now!" Chester yelled.

"Keep your eye on the chaplain," Rory puffed. "He's holding the money."

"Be careful, Rory, " Johnny cried, "he's going to get dirty."

"Time."

Baker blew across the room like a typhoon and sent a punch from hallelujah-land that whistled past Rory's face so close it nipped his eyelashes.

Rory suddenly became a bit mushy from all his maneuvering. They were a soggy pair squirting and oozing blood from various incisions.

But look! Baker was no longer using his left hand at all, at all. His arm was tucked in against his side to keep his body from taking any more blows. Rory leapt in with a glorious right hand to the jaw. Butcher Boy Baker scarcely acknowledged the blow, but Rory's right hand felt broken.

"Time!"

"You sonofabitch, you called time early!" Tarbox screamed. Rory was all but done in, getting small comfort from the welts rising on Baker's map of Australia as if they were new settlements, and the fact that he was puffing and wheezing.

"Time!"

The racetrack danced like an earth rumble from the noise.

Baker held his hands over his face and body in peek-a-boo manner and backed into a corner to lure Rory into range. Rory was moving in and out quickly, but his legs were very rubbery at the knees. Feeling himself evaporating, he did the foolish thing and tried to break through Butcher Boy's guard. . . .

Baker wrapped his hairy arms around Rory, turned him into the corner, and lay all over him like a side of beef, pinning his arms so he could not punch. Baker led with a knee to the groin and an elbow to the face.

Baker was on his way!

Rory was able to land one more desperation blow on Mother-

Heart-Australia and this only enraged the big fellow, who pinned his man again and butted him between the eyes. Rory sunk to one knee and Baker unloaded his infamous right hand.

The place went completely wild!

"Throw in the towel, Johnny!" Chester begged.

There was Rory taking a count on one knee . . . blood gushing from his nose and mouth . . . and three more rounds to go. Johnny reached around for a towel, Rory leapt to his feet, and as the Butcher grabbed him, Rory bit his ear.

The Australian giant screamed so loud you could hear it clear up to Perth. He covered himself, and as he tried to protect his ear, Rory hit his side, and as he tried to cover his side, Rory hit his ear . . . ear . . . side . . . ear . . . side . . .

Butcher Boy Baker fell into the ropes and down came the ropes with Rory falling atop him.

Rory staggered to his feet first. "We don't need a fucking ring! Get up and fight!"

Baker crawled around on hands and knees like a three-legged dog, then looked up as Goliath must have. "I shouldn't have butted him."

"Time!" screamed Baker's corner, one minute and fourteen seconds early as a half-dozen of his entourage rushed into the ring. Baker tipped over on his face before being dragged to his stool.

Rory was in Butcher's corner, above him, bleeding and sweating all over him.

"Fuck it," Baker blubbered, disgorging a mouthful of blood of his own.

"Quit!" Rory demanded.

"Fuck it!"

Rory smashed him and Baker and stool went at the same time.

"Enough!" Baker said, and just lay there and cried like a baby.

COMMANDER OF FLEET, INDIAN THEATRE OF OPERATIONS. COMMANDER OF LAND FORCES ANZAC CONVOY

PERTH–ALBANY. GERMAN RAIDER EMDEN SUNK BY RAN BATTLESHIP SYDNEY THIS DATE OFF SUMATRA. PROCEED ACCORDING TO COURSE, SPEED AND FORMATION IN ATTACHED ORDERS AT 0430-JANUARY 28 TO GULF OF ADAN, THENCE RED SEA TO SUEZ CANAL. TROOP TRAINS WILL BE ON HAND TO TRANSFER ANZAC AND INDIAN FORCES TO ENCAMPMENTS IN CAIRO VICINITY.

WINSTON S. CHURCHILL
FIRST LORD OF THE ADMIRALTY

CHAPTER
57

SECRET FILES OF WINSTON CHURCHILL, LATE 1914

I am unflinchingly prepared to present my "grand strategy"to the War Council, earliest. Reviewing the war to date, I draw the following conclusion:

1. *The Navy was ready!* We successfully shipped the British Expeditionary Force across the Channel to France and Belgium without casualty.

2. Waters and lanes around the British Isles are impervious to attack. The Channel Fleet guards us with twenty super-dreadnoughts. Our shipping lanes are open despite the prowl of German U-boats.

3. The German fleet is bottled up, is hiding in their own canals, pens, and inlets.

The Western Front

Having halted the German advance, a stationary front has developed, anchored by the English Channel in the north and running for hundreds of miles to the Alps.

A series of layered trenches are manned by millions of men, fronted by mine fields and barbed wire, and backed by tens of thousands of artillery pieces and machine guns.

It appears only too obvious to me that in the coming year of 1915, little will change on the Western Front, as neither side will be able to dislodge the other.

The Eastern Front

The situation is fluid. Our Russian allies though not modern or of high morale are engaging dozens of German divisions. Russia is a vast land and German supply lines have dangerously stretched.

Thus far the Russians have given a good accounting against the Germans and Turks and I further believe 1915 will show the Eastern Front holding firm.

The Pacific Theatre

A decade ago the Japanese ministered an horrendous defeat on Russia, the first time an Oriental power prevailed over the West since Genghis Khan and the Mongol invasions.

Now, England and Russia are allies of the Japanese. I greet this with ambivalence. Japanese annexation of Korea clearly delineates their ambition to establish an empire on mainland Asia.

Their entry into the war was an opportunistic measure to grab off German-held Pacific Islands. We must reiterate our agreement with Japan that they be allowed to take over islands north of the equator only. Everything below the equator is to remain in the British sphere.

What I write now is what I believe to be the British course of action for the year of 1915:

1. England seeks no geographic gain on the European continent.

2. For Britain, the grand prize of war is the Ottoman Empire. To ensure British control over Egypt and the Suez Canal, we must extend our sphere by taking con-

trol of the Sinai Peninsula, establish a mandate to govern Palestine, create a British-controlled territory in the Trans-Jordan region, and assume control of Iraq.

3. Our French allies will extend their sphere to control Syria, including Lebanon.

4. Russia will control Armenia and the Caucasus region and Iran. They shall occupy and control Constantinople and ensure for all times warm water ports and access to the Mediterranean.

5. With the Canadian Expeditionary Force training in England and our national draft supplying fresh troops to Europe ... *1915 sees us with a surplus of naval vessels, British Divisions, and a major new army, the Australian and New Zealand Corps, about to set sail.*

I contend that we divert the Aussie/N.Z. Corps to Egypt and join them with British and French units for training to *conquer the Gallipoli Peninsula, and march on Constantinople, forcing open the Dardanelles.*

Once we have conquered Constantinople, uncommitted Balkan nations, sitting on the fence, will rush to our side and enable us to make a campaign up the Danube Valley and cut the German forces in half.

Moreover, opening of the Dardenelles will allow us to supply Russia with ammunition, of which they are becoming desperately short.

And finally, it will free up Ukrainian wheat for shipment to France and England.

Greece will join us whenever we wish, but Greek troops cannot enter Constantinople, which must go to our Russian ally. Italy, sitting on the fence as well, will be compelled to become our ally once we open the Dardanelles.

The Turks have been beaten in the Near East, North Africa, and ejected from Europe by the Balkan coalition. They are presently using all their remaining power against Russia.

Germany can ill afford to send troops to Turkey, although they may have some German staff. By any definition, the Ottoman Empire is ripe for collapse.

Although the Gallipoli Peninsula is a wild region of cliffs and valleys and with scant military intelligence I feel that our naval power will reduce their hilltop fortress. Many of our old battleships, ready to be scrapped, can still be used against Gallipoli as floating gun platforms.

Whilst a landing from the sea would be unique in modern warfare I envision our destuctive naval power breaking the morale of the Turkish defenders.

The Aussie/N.Z. units are woefully short of officers. I am pushing Kitchener (who likes the idea of the Dardanelles campaign) to get a cadre of British officers to Egypt to take over the Aussie/N.Z. Corps. I understand the Aussies are a wild lot, as one might expect from the descendants of a penal colony.

So there it is. The Dardanelles and Gallipoli, Constantinople and the Danube Valley, and the end of the Ottoman Empire in 1915.

WSC

CHAPTER
58

January 1915

Shunk-rooomshunk ... shunk-rooomshunk ... shunk-rooomshunk ... SHUNK-ROOOMSHUNK ... SHUNK-ROOOMSHUNK!

Daddy! Don't cry! Daddy!

SHUNK-ROOOMSHUNK!

Daddy! Run, man!

Rory sat up quickly. His head batted the canvas of the bunk above him.

"Jesus Christ!" the soldier over him complained.

Rory fell back. "Sorry, cobber," he apologized.

"Jesus Christ," the man mumbled again and was snoring in a moment.

Shunk-rooomshunk, the ship's engine repeated, never ending, and the *Wagga Wagga* groaned. Rory blew out deep sighs as though he could blow out the bad dream from his body. Why the hell was Squire Liam invading the nights he had reserved for weeping for his Uncle Conor or longing for Georgia Norman?

Why his daddy? Why?

He propped himself on an elbow, carefully so as not to bump the bunkmate atop him, and peered out the porthole. The convoy seemed to be moving at one-third speed on the sizzling waters near the equator. There was enough moon out there to have vanquished the stars. He squinted hard for the silhouettes of ships.

Chester would be sleeping on the bottom bunk, six tiers down. He and Chester switched off every several hours to give each other a breather at the porthole. Rory's head throbbed from the nightmare. It must be suffocating down on the bottom row, he thought. Rory slid out carefully as he was able to into the clutter of hanging kits, rifles, clanging mess gear, and helmets in the dimly lit hold.

He buttoned up his trousers, tied on his life vest, then fished about the bottom bunk for Chester. It was empty. Rory felt his way along the narrow passage cluttered with gear, arms and legs of dangling sweaty bodies stacked seven high, and inched toward the engine room.

Shunk-rooomshunk . . . shunk-rooomshunk . . .

He fished his way through a triple set of blackout curtains until he passed into the turbine room. The playing field was a far corner under a light bulb. One of the Aussie sailors of the crew had served a hitch in the American Navy and brought with him the advanced American cultural attainments of craps and black-jack.

Chester Goodwood observed the games for the first three days afloat, figured out the dice odds, and learned to read the deck in the second sport. He looked so inconspicuous and inno-cent, he was always welcomed into a game. Both Rory and Johnny Tarbox had to warn him not to get greedy and even to drop a few bob now and then, for appearance's sake. Otherwise, he always won.

Rory reached the game and stood over Chester, waiting until he got the dice and made his run. The lad was a gem. Can you imagine, a banker's son! He'll be able to open his own bank, Rory thought.

"Porthole bunk is open," Rory said. "I'm going topside."

"Goodo," Chester said.

The *shunk-rooomshunk* and the click of the dice and the groan of the *Wagga Wagga* fell into perfect harmony as Rory left the turbine room and was plunged into darkness as he worked his way to the ladder.

Topside, the hatches and any decent deck space looked like a

bin of silvery fish—it was covered with half-naked bodies, slimy
with sweat.

Rory went up the ladder until he reached a chain-bearing
sign: OFFICER'S COUNTRY; NO ENLISTED PERSONNEL. He slipped
on his MESSAGE CENTER armband provided by Johnny and was
passed through, then made it to the top deck where Johnny and
the other warrant officers had small quarters.

There was a single lifeboat lashed up and hanging from a
davit for the top-deck people, away from the other boats that
lined the lower decks. Johnny had deftly loosened the knots of
the canvas cover so it could easily be slipped off and recovered.
He had filled the boat from bow to stern with a mattress of life
vests, which he shared with Chester and Rory.

Johnny had ingested his fill of soggy hot air and was in a
fuzzed state as Rory crawled in. They traded remarks as to how
bloomin' hot it was.

"Well, we've crossed the equator and we're moving north,"
Rory said. "That tells me that South Africa is out."

"Got an uncoded message today at the center. We're making
a rendezvous around Ceylon with some Indian troops," Johnny
said.

"So, we're heading for the Mediterranean and maybe on up
to England."

"Sounds right to me."

"And just maybe we'll stop at Aden and the empty ships will
take on our Arabian horses."

"I'd like to take on a few Arab women ... first they come
out and do their belly dance and then start twirling their
tits. . . ."

They were quiet for a time. Tarbox was faraway, in an arched
room filled with belly dancers.

Rory had made a discipline of keeping Georgia Norman out
of his mind. The hours were better spent crying inside for his
Uncle Conor than longing for her. Conor was dead and in time
the hurt would fade. Georgia had told him that his pain would
be tucked away.

But Georgia! She came bursting through to him at the oddest

places and the oddest times. Mostly he thought of her lying on the bed with her green silk kimono opened to her whiteness. It never failed to create a sensation of sheer wanting, and it flowed all about him. He trained himself to let her in for only a few minutes or he'd get restless and moody.

Both Conor and Georgia strangely dimmed as Liam Larkin made his stand. Why the Squire! Something about the sea, the bloody convoy that was throwing him together with his father.

"Where's Chester?" Johnny asked.

"In the engine room giving dice lessons."

"I'll bet he learned it in Hong Kong in one of those gambling palaces with his old man, don't you think?" Johnny asked.

"Maybe, but he's a natural with numbers. He showed me the odds on every combination on the dice. As for blackjack, all he has to do is hold the deck. I'm only letting him have five quid a day. I don't want the whole ship in debt to him."

"It was brilliant of me," Johnny said, "to see the great merit of this lad and slip him into the Light Horse."

"You son of a bitch."

They were quiet again, now awake, and propped up so they could see out of the lifeboat down to the decks and out to the lightless convoy. Uncle Conor had told Rory that on the smooth seas and heaven-filled nights, the sailors dreaded the watch because they had time to think about everything they had left behind, everything they coveted . . . to become a rover.

"What's bothering you, Rory?"

"Nothing."

"Shit, I can hear your brains buzzing clear across the boat. Smoke is coming out of your ears."

"Hell, it must be crossing the equator. I can't seem to be keeping my old man off my mind. I feel like we're sharing a strange passage, him going down to New Zealand and us to wherever. Somehow, I wake up, like I was him in the darkness of steerage all alone without two shillings to rub against each other. He must have been scared shitless, Johnny. He always talked about that trip, but I never much listened."

"The Squire is something, all right," Johnny said.

"You liked him, didn't you?" Rory asked.

"I wasn't his son," Johnny said quickly.

"What'd you like about him?" Rory pressed.

"What he made out of nothing but his two hands. That was respect. I liked him as well. All my crew liked him. He cared about us. Our food was from your mother's kitchen and any hurt man was taken care of. He did a lot of quiet favors. He was so proud of Ballyutogue Station. And . . . he was fun to stand up to the bar and drink with and a joy to fish alongside of up at that trout stream of his. Like I said, I wasn't his son so I don't know why you two didn't get on, but it's mostly the same in every family."

That was the case, all right. Everybody wanted to deal with Squire Larkin. Drovers, shearing crews, the church, the auctioneers . . . everybody liked the Squire.

"Did you get along with your old man?" Rory asked.

"We had a rough life together, Rory. My father was never much more than a roustabout, the wandering prospector looking for that one lucky strike. Me and my sister spent our whole childhood living in a caravan, prospecting the South Island with him. We never had our own home."

"How'd you learn to read and write? Mother?"

"No!" Johnny said abruptly. Then he softened. "I picked up my schooling on my own. There was always someone in the mining camps teaching the kids. You know, those guys who get sick of civilization and run off looking for the bonanza. We had some smart people around."

Johnny had gone off like an alarm at mention of his mother. Rory knew the woman was off bounds, from then on.

"My mother," Tarbox said with another voice, "was an actress . . . like a music hall song-and-dance girl, and New Zealand was too small for her. She was a great theatrical success in the west of America in the gold and silver rush towns."

The quiet fell again. A long time quiet.

"You asleep?" Rory asked.

"Not anymore."

"Why is my father rattling around on this ship, now?"

Tarbox laughed. "What better place to think about your old man than on a troopship?"

"You liked the Squire?" Rory asked.

"Yeah, he is right out of the earth," Johnny said.

"But you didn't like prospecting with your old man."

"I hated it, Rory. I hated him for what he gave me. I hated watching my sister grow into a mining camp girl. So, I quit when I was able and did my hitch in the Royal Marines. You know what? For four years I grew hungry for my old man. I realized that he was doing what he was doing because it would have killed him to sit in one place and be without a dream, and I realized he had put a lot of good things into me. Every soldier on this ship is pissed off at his parents for screwing up their lives, and every soldier who lives through the war is going to spend the second half of his life getting over the first half. That's the way it goes down. We all blame our parents, all of us . . . then we never seem to see ourselves doing the same things to our own kids."

Johnny was annoying him. He didn't know what the hell Squire Larkin had done to him!

"So, I came back from the Marines," Johnny said, "and I saw my old man for what he was. A sweet man who did the best he could. But, you see, he always accepted me as a kid and I was pretty rotten. I never accepted him for what he was. After the Marines, we saw each other for what we were and not what we wanted the other to be. So, he started riding with me as one of my drovers and those four years were the happiest of my life."

It sounded like his Uncle Conor and the grandda he never knew, Tomas Larkin. Conor and Tomas gave each other bad, bad turns in the beginning, but in the end, there was love.

Oh Jaysus, Rory thought, there are too many mountains to cross with the Squire and the valleys are too deep. He never knew how to quit picking on me. He never stopped making me feel unwanted.

Could I have done something about it? Rory asked himself for the first time. . . . I knew he was proud of the way I rode but I rode reckless instead to piss him off and show him how much better I was than poor Tommy. I hated fishing with him because I didn't like him forcing me to come and I hated his joy in hooking the big one.

Every time I did something that could have made the Squire proud, I threw it at his feet like a pile of shit. I liked pissing him off. I loved his rage at me and knowing he had to have me.

Damnit! HE did it to ME, him and my Virgin Mary mother made me ashamed I was born.

Maybe ... maybe ... I could have made the right gestures. Maybe, here and there. No, the mountains are too high with that man, and the valleys too deep.

Shunk-rooomshunk ... shunk-rooomshunk ...

Rory remembered seeing Johnny Tarbox and his old man after they drove into Uncle Wally's pens in Christchurch. Old Johnny was so caring, took care of cooling down his da's horse, and then they headed into the bar, arms about the other's shoulder.

Steerage in a rusted freighter with an empty pocket and fear ahead. Christ! Get him off my back already!

... Maybe ... I should have made a gesture ...

Shunk-rooomshunk ...

As the Anzac convoy sweltered northward toward the Red Sea, a second convoy from England sweltered southward through the Straits of Gibraltar for a rendezvous in Egypt.

The British home armada carried forward echelons of a pair of veteran army divisions and a host of attached elements to establish a large permanent base camp and training facility.

Berthed on several of the southbound warships was a cadre of two hundred regular British officers to take over the Anzac units, bringing them up to strength and assuring British control.

Major General Sir Llewelyn Brodhead and his staff sailed aboard the cruiser, HMS *Foxhampton*. He set up a secure command center where he spent most of the day and half of the night.

Brodhead had expressed his concerns on a military venture he was not completely in tune with. Once the War Council made the decision, he got aboard in a positive manner, as one might expect of a fine field commander. When they passed Gibraltar he began briefing his senior officers on a need to know basis and made his presentation with very much of a can-do attitude.

Yet, can there be a man lonelier than one of high rank about to embark on a venture he held grave doubts about and who had to hold these doubts within himself?

Before the battle there was so damned much to be done. Brodhead would be assuming command of tens of thousands of untamed raw colonials. He and his officers had to get them into combat shape in three to four months. Beastly short time, that.

Training would be a merciless grind, worsened by the heat.

The trick here was to gain confidence. These Anzacs were apt to grow to hate their British overseers. Building a spirit of the corps was as important as their fighting skills.

If Sir Llewelyn had a soft spot, a sentimental button, it was Ulster. He intensely disliked what he was about to lay on young Major Hubble, but Hubble was his hand-picked gamble. Although Chris had a modest rank, the General felt close and at ease with his junior confidant, and he would most likely open up and tell more to impress Hubble with the importance of his mission.

"Sir! Major Hubble!" the General's botsman ripped off.

"Yes, show him in. No interruptions of any sort unless it's from Fleet Command."

"Sir!"

"Major Hubble, at your service!" Chris said, flashing a smart salute. The two were locked in with a clang. Chris's heart was a-thump. No one with the lowly rank of major had been privy to the command room. The whir of a powerful overhead fan and the sucking out of dead air was heard as Brodhead looked up with the eyes of a sorrowful bloodhound.

"Sit easy, Chris. Stop me for questions as you wish and prepare yourself for a real boot in the ass."

Chris laid his crop and hat aside and followed the General's lead in loosening his Sam Browne belt and field scarf.

"We're in top secret country now," the General began.

"Yes, sir."

Brodhead stood and rolled down a map like a large window shade, showing the eastern Mediterranean and bordering environs.

"It's a bang-on proposition, Chris. The Turks have closed the Dardanelles Straits and we have to open them. It is a brilliant concept designed to knock the Turks out of the war with a single blow and move up the Danube Valley to split the Germans in half. However, and I'm going to fill you up with howevers, it is more of a political decision than a military decision. Winston Churchill is its most forceful advocate."

Brodhead picked one of his pipes off the desk to use as a pointer. "This is it. This cock of land dangling into the Mediterranean. The Gallipoli Peninsula, forty miles long and varying in width up to four to ten miles. The Dardanelles Straits run along the eastern side into the Sea of Marmara, Constantinople, and the Black Sea. On the western side of the peninsula is the Aegean Sea."

Chris nearly shivered with excitement. Rumors and being a small man in a large staff are one thing. But to sit before a general and become a part of it was an ethereal experience.

"The Gallipoli Peninsula is a wild place, sparsely inhabited, with primitive trails, sheer cliffs, mountains, deep valleys. It is filled with caves and ravines and ridge tops and gorges that can house hundreds of machine-gun nests, mines, barbed wire. But these fellows up here," he said, tapping a series of hilltop positions, "are the key. Turks have forts with coastal guns capable of shooting down onto both sides."

"Yes, sir," Chris said in a whisper.

"It is also a political and not a military decision for us not to ally yourselves with the armies of the Balkan union. The thinking is that the Serbs, Bosnians, and Bulgarians are too unstable politically and too volatile to be dependable. I personally would like to see the Greeks drive across Thrace, but our Russian ally objects to that.

"What this means is," Brodhead went on, "it will be a British show with some French support. Churchill argues that we have an abundance of naval power to subject Gallipoli to the most devastating bombardment in history. Frankly, I expect that Churchill thinks he is going to sink the peninsula.... Questions up to now?"

"Yes, sir. This naval assault. I take it, it must knock out the Turkish hilltop forts and otherwise disrupt and disorient the other Turkish positions so they will be soft objectives later on."

"That's the thinking."

"You have reservations, sir?"

How much to confide, Brodhead pondered. "Yes," he said. "Naval guns fire in a flat trajectory. They are meant to hit other warships riding above the water. Will they be that effective against dug-in land positions? Damned fact is, nobody knows! Never been done! There are other parts of this operation that have never been done, namely, the landing and supplying from the sea of an army of this size. Never been done!

"Now," he went on, "come some other intangibles. What if we don't force the Dardanelles open? That means we will not be able to land on the eastern side of the peninsula. We will have to land from the Aegean side with very little beach, and immediately fight uphill."

The room, so splendid in its mythology a few moments earlier, now began to appear as a deadly vault to Chris.

"The plan is one, two, three," General Brodhead went on. "The French land on the opposite side of the straits in Anatolia—ancient Troy, as a matter of fact. They secure a perimeter, and hold. The Turks haven't much to send against them, nor do the French have to drive inland . . . just hold their side of the Dardanelles.

"The main British force will land on the tip of Gallipoli here at Cape Helles and drive up the peninsula. Their first major objective will be the hilltop of Achi Baba, about six miles upland.

"We," Brodhead said deliberately, "have very little room for deception. The navy will be pounding them for weeks so they'll know we're coming. The Anzacs will land farther up the peninsula, take Chunuk Bair hilltop, and cut off the entire place from Turkish reinforcements and eventually be joined by the British driving up to meet us."

"Would it be fair to say," Chris interrupted, "that the Turks have shown very little against the Balkan union and the Italians in Africa?"

"The grand scheme is that our navy clears the Dardanelles Straits, steams up to Constantinople, and opens a naval bombardment while we drive up and lay siege."

Suddenly Brodhead's eyes watered and he leaned over the desk and planted his fists in a manner that Chris had come to understand as the man's dead serious mode.

"IF the navy does not clean out the straits . . . IF the Turks are properly commanded by a German staff and their high ground is intact . . . IF we are forced to land on the Aegean side and start straight uphill . . . IF the Turks can force us into a stagnant situation, we may be fucked four ways from Sunday. God help you if what I said ever leaves this room."

Chris pleaded with himself not to turn pale and faint before the General, yet he knew that his legs would not hold him at that moment. Brodhead broke into a sweat of his own and felt like a naughty boy for betraying his doubts to a junior officer.

"What do you need me to do, sir?" Christ asked stoutly. Then, as an afterthought, he said, "One would suppose there will be no cavalry involved?"

Brodhead was relieved to be able to crack a smile followed by a laugh. He drummed his fingers on the table. "Well, here is what you've been waiting for, lad. Transport, in the event we are stalemated and hung up on the wrong side of the hills."

"I see," Chris said, realizing the enormity of it.

"The French have a relatively easy supply situation requiring no special transport capacity. Now, with the main British force down here at the tip of Cape Helles, there is a fluid front and difficult terrain to negotiate."

Chris nodded.

"There are Jews in Palestine, you know . . . pioneers . . . reclaiming land, that sort of thing. Life has been made difficult for them by the Ottomans. When the war started, the Turks rounded up many of the men and inflicted rather nasty punishment on them, claiming they were British spies and sympathizers. A large number of them, several hundred, escaped to Egypt and petitioned to form a unit of the British Army. It was decided, for political reasons, not to have them officially in the army per se but to allow them to form a unit we will use for transport at Cape Helles. The Zion Mule Corps."

"I say," Chris said.

"When I went over preliminary plans back at the War Office, a mule unit was the only way to go with my Anzacs. Damnedest thing, Chris, we discovered that neither New Zealand nor

Australia knows anything about mules. Never had them in either place, can you imagine?"

Chris looked as though he was going to burst into tears.

"Bang on, Chris. If the attack stalls and we have to go to the trenches, we are doomed without mule transport. There is no other way we can get food, ammunition, water, and medical supplies up the mountainside, and there is no way we can remove our wounded. What I told you back at Camp Bushy is the absolute truth. We are doomed without mules, should the battle go wrong. From this moment, the Seventh New Zealand Light Horse is the mule transportation battalion for the Anzacs. You must build it from the ground up. I will give you every priority within my power. Do this, and I repeat my promise, you'll jump directly to colonel at the end of the campaign . . . you have my word. . . . Well?"

"Mules," Chris said, "rather degrading, sir."

"So is war," Brodhead answered.

CHAPTER
60

The mail boat made a welcome round of the convoy at Gibraltar and, as they got under way again, the officers and men were given a fill of letters to be read and read again until the words themselves grew war-weary.

Jeremy reached his quarters and saw a packet of letters on the small ship's desk. He thumbed the envelopes, stopped on one that caught his eye, and opened it.

My Dear Jeremy,

How often in life it is a truth that we have no time for our friends but all the time in the world for our enemies. I write to you as the enemy, so kindly indulge me.

My name is Gorman Galloway. Most generally I fit the accepted descriptions of a "feckless Irishman." I am also the constant companion and dearest friend of your mother; therefore, your enemy.

I am risking your wrath for I can no longer bear witness to a magnificent rose withering and dying for want of a kind word from her son.

I believe in neither heaven nor hell, except for what we make for ourselves here on earth. You have created your private hell in the manner you handled Molly O'Rafferty. You have done a wretched deed and have then gone and branded yourself with a white-hot iron, flayed your flesh with whips, soaked your bereavement in gin—thank God, decent gin.

Your brother, Christopher, who I think is an ass, has

written that you have begun to show a spark of life. That means you are starting to forgive yourself. The ability of a man to atone, here on earth, has always been the most remarkable of human features. No sin, and certainly not even one as grave as yours, cannot be redeemed. It appears to all here, you have punished yourself sufficiently.

Had you read Caroline's letters, you would realize that she has forgiven her father and cares for him deeply and tenderly. She has likewise forgiven her husband to the point of being civil with him.

My dear Jeremy, she has forgiven you and longs for you with a longing that will surely kill her if you continue to punish her and yourself with your silence.

Life hinges on many factors we cannot control. Two of the most important factors, we can control. We can manage our relationships—and what is life but a series of relationships?—and we can correct our mistakes, here on earth within our life span. Bad relationships and mistakes are all a normal part of the game of life. Who are you, who has been forgiven, to continue to inflict pain upon a woman who adores you and grieves for your smile, your touch, your word?

Do you want to lay on Caroline what you have laid on Molly? Will that make things right? If you go into battle and, God forbid, are numbered with the slain, you must take her to a far more bitter death.

Her eyes well with tears when she speaks of your beauty, your sweetness, and of the absence of meanness that probably pushed you into your mistake.

Please, Jeremy, if there be any manliness in you at all, then you must make a gesture that you and she are on the mend.

> Your devoted enemy,
> *Gorman Galloway*

Jeremy opened the lid of his chest and took out the bundle of letters that lay on the top, tied with a ribbon and softly scented of his mother's perfume. He had agonized for the courage to take the moment to answer her. The time had come.

Mother dearest,

Please tell Gorman Galloway he is not the enemy. But you already know how fortunate you are to have one such beloved friend. I once had one and have recently gone to his grave to find guidance.

Gorman Galloway repeated to me what Conor Larkin tried to teach me: Mistakes are part of life and they need not be fatal to the moral man. Mistakes are crutches for cowards and I have used mine to further inflict pain on the people dear to me.

Mother dearest, I've swilled the bottle dry and I've wallowed at the bottom of a greasy pit of shame and guilt and self-pity and self-hatred for enough years.

It is time for Jeremy to quit his whimpering. As we gained distance from Ireland, the air itself took on a different scent and taste. It no longer suffocated me when I breathed.

I am going to get well, Mother. Perhaps, I'll be well for the first time in my infamous life as a rotten and useless peer. I am going to spend the balance of my days as a good and decent man.

The sorrow of Molly O'Rafferty will never leave me, nor do I want it to, nor will I let it pull me under, any longer. I shall follow every trail that might find her and our child.

If I fail to find her, if she has made a new and good life, if she is no longer alive, I will never go back to what I once was.

The rage of my father will also never leave me. I am disgusted with my cowardice in yielding to him and am in disgust of him for what he will do to keep his cursed kingdom.

What was once so important in my life, what I so dreaded losing, is now strangely unimportant. I intend to renounce my title when the war is over, but I want to do it standing in front of him.

When I think about my early days, I recall my terror of

him. Fond memories of Father are few. There was a time for many summers I adored going off with him to our summer home at Daars in Kinsale.

Father and I would go shark fishing. He picked mean weather and the seas lashed us cruelly, but what a master sailor he was! And when we pulled in those ugly gray monsters, the bigger the shark, the more daggerlike his teeth, the more we'd celebrate in unabashed joy.

I came to learn that my excitement was from destroying something evil and his came because I think he was trying to exorcise his own evil.

Then, we'd land and the instant his foot touched the pier, he was angry with me.

Come what may ahead, Mother, I shall not go under again. Come what may, I shall carry on to the end as a kind and decent man.

I have saved your letters for the precious day I would open them. The time has come and I pray that more are on the way from you and your dear friend, Gorman.

Your loving son,
Jeremy

CHAPTER
61

Camp Anzac, Mena, Egypt, February 1915

The sudden eruption of the Anzacs from their entombment on the troopships was a wonderment for men and for boys becoming men taking their first steps beyond home.

Miracles, photographs from their geography textbooks, took life in the form of the Sphinx and pyramids all around them. Camels! Cloth-headed tops on the men ... true and actual Arabs! Veiled women! It was the amusement park outside Sydney, wot!

To the Egyptians, this most recent onslaught, albeit peaceful, of another foreign army was absorbed with a shrug and the all encompassing allusion that it was "Allah's will." Unwelcome visitors had been the gist of their ancient and recent history, and soon the latest visitors would be absorbed in the bazaar that was Cairo.

These Anzacs were soldiers of great wealth receiving pay of ten, fifteen, twenty English pounds a month, which would serve as a balm for the hell-raising they intended to impose.

Within hours of the Anzac arrival, a full brigade of vendors had established stalls at the camp gates, backed by a battalion of hawkers. Hundreds of young boys, whom the Anzacs called Terriers, hustled a variety of services. The lads from down under soon realized they were princes in a land of poverty.

Mena was a haphazard site that housed an old Ottoman barracks. When the British relieved the Turks of Egypt, there were additions for a permanent base. While some of the camp was in ready condition, a feverish building program was under way by swarms of laborers from the city.

Camp Anzac became a flash flood of men and equipment with temporary two-man tent areas, jerry-built structures for supplies, hospitals, and hospital and command centers.

The day laborers—vendors and Terriers, the native Egyptians—were at the bottom of the social rung, picturesque and not entirely to be trusted. These men and boys represented the sole piece of imperialism, the living proof that some people are not fit to do anything in their own country other than serve the colonizer.

Until an orderly camp and training regimen were established, Cairo was out of bounds, and the only recreation was to hire a Terrier for a night climb up one of the pyramids. Even though there were quite a few broken bones and some deaths, pyramid climbing continued until the British officers took firm control.

The pommy officers all arrived tapping the same brand of riding crop against their riding britches above their riding boots. There were several cavalry units at Mena, but even the pommy infantry and artillery officers carried the riding crop as some sort of scepter of office.

The Aussies and New Zealanders whose lives had been relatively free of caste were nonplussed by the unfriendliness, formality, and vain arrogance of their new commanders. It came from the very tone of their ever so British voices and the look of their ever so British eyes. For the first time they were given a definite feeling of not being seen as good as the other fellow. An unseen line had been drawn, unseen but quite deep, indeed.

Yet, two volcanic questions burned brightly as the camp shaped up; namely, when do we get liberty into Cairo and *when do we get our horses?*

Serjeant Major John Tarbox stomped his boots and snapped off a beautiful salute, as befitted his new C.O.

"Sir, Serjeant Major Tarbox, at your service!"

"At ease, Tarbox," Christopher Hubble said. Chris neither rose nor extended a hand and seemed to be looking through and past the serjeant. Another officer, First Lieutenant Jeremy Hubble, sat nearby quite relaxed and smiled a friendly smile.

"I'm Major Hubble, battalion commander. The gentleman here is Lieutenant Hubble, coincidentally my brother."

Jeremy came to his feet, extended his hand and shook Johnny's warmly, to Christopher's annoyance.

"Let us get to the point," Chris interrupted. He leaned forward in much the same menacing manner his tutor General Brodhead did when he was dead serious. "There will be no cavalry in this expeditionary force. You understand what I'm saying?"

"I suppose so, Major."

"All horse battalions are to be reconstituted into infantry, heavy weapons, sappers, howitzer artillery, etcetera, etcetera."

"Yes, sir."

"Except," Christopher continued on, "for our Seventh New Zealand Light Horse, here. I have informed my officers as of this morning. The reason will become apparent."

Johnny found a weak smile and managed to get it on his face.

"The Seventh Light Horse is now a transportation battalion, a mule transportation battalion."

"Beg pardon, Major Hubble, but I don't know a fucking thing about mules."

Jeremy laughed aloud.

"Nor, may I add, does anyone else around here," Christopher snarled. "I strongly advise you to take this news in stride and demonstrate that I have your full and unstinting cooperation."

"Unstinting, sir."

"Unstinting," Chris repeated through clenched teeth. It had gone down hard as hell with the officers earlier. It would be a shock right straight down the line. Chris lifted the Tarbox records and plopped them in the center of the desk and went through them with agonizing deliberateness.

"Now then, Tarbox, you are one of the battalion elders, what?"

"I suppose so, sir, I'm uh . . . thirty-four."

"Thirty-six," Hubble corrected.

"If you count various contingencies."

"What contingencies?"

"I lied about my age when I ran off to do a hitch in the Royal Marines."

"And you rose to the rank of lance corporal in five years."

"I was a full corporal, sir, and except for a misunderstanding when I failed to catch the last liberty boat—"

"Because you were locked up in the Singapore jail for, shall we say, a barroom brawl, after which you received punishment in the form of thirty days of bread and water, and reduction in rank to lance corporal."

It was not my fault, Johnny thought, the goddamn prostitute's pimps jumped me. He was about to make his case but thought better of it.

"So, you're not really a proper serjeant major, are you?"

Oh Jaysus, Johnny thought, here it comes! "I certainly am, sir, in a manner of speaking."

"Oh, really? Kindly explain yourself."

"We don't have many standing units in New Zealand and because of my superior horsemanship and devotion, I commanded the Royal Color and Honor Guard, itself."

"That would be a half-dozen horses for ceremonial occasions, right?"

"Well, sir . . . "

"So, you really weren't a proper serjeant major?"

"If I may say so, sir, everybody in North Island and South Island knew Johnny Tarbox. Dads used to say to their kids, 'May you only grow up to ride like Johnny Tarbox. He does the King's colors proud.' The instant the war broke out, knowing my fame, I was asked to travel from one end of the country to the other and, pretty much single-handed, I signed up enough lads for four entire Light Horse battalions."

"And you consider yourself quite the horseman?"

"There may be a few men better, but you'll have to look damned hard to find them. I've done everything with a horse except fuck them and eat horseshit."

Jeremy broke up as Christopher went sallow, then stared, glazed blue eyes continuing to look through his man almost with hatred.

"I appreciate the differences between our cultures, but in the future, I shall consider obscene language before an officer as a punishable offense."

Johnny reddened and his mouth went dry.

"Have you ever been in charge of men?" Jeremy asked.

"Yes, sir, half my life, Lieutenant. I ran the big droving crews for the sheep and cattle stations all over the country. I've handled up to twenty men on some jobs."

Christopher shrugged. "Do you want this chap, Lieutenant?" he asked his brother.

"I do. Serjeant Tarbox is just what the doctor ordered for me."

Christopher rubbed his chin with his hand, as though Johnny were a head of cattle to be judged. Then he flipped through the report again.

"Well, you're not a proper serjeant major," Christopher repeated. "I'll have to find a proper serjeant major elsewhere. I'm certain I can requisition one from a British unit. Well, your Kiwi countrymen saw fit to swear you in as a serjeant major and I am going to allow you to retain the rank if you do your job flawlessly and unstintingly. Am I clear?"

"Exactly what is my job, sir?"

"The men in this battalion are all creditable horsemen, are they not?"

"They're the greatest, sir."

"Well, then, you convert them into the greatest mule hustlers, packers, and trail men."

"I am forming a gaffer squad," Jeremy said.

"A gaffer squad?"

"A small unit of mule specialists. It will be up to us to write a simplified manual, obtain the proper gear, work out miles of logistics and training, and be central to the task of indoctrinating the men and building this battalion from the hooves up," Jeremy said.

"I don't know how many mule men we're apt to find here, Lieutenant."

"We'll probably get some from other units as they arrive in Egypt. Meanwhile, your lads filled out questionnaires en route, aboard ship. Go through these and find me the most likely prospects."

As Jeremy handed Johnny two boxes of questionnaires, he nodded and smiled. "Look forward to working with you," he said.

"This is absolutely hush-hush," Chris interrupted. "Not a living, breathing soul, until we are ready."

"Yes, sir."

"Captain Ellsworth, the chief veterinarian with the British Corps, will come to Mena in three days—on Wednesday—to question any men who have mule knowledge," Jeremy said, patting the man on the shoulder.

"You are dismissed. Now remember, hush-hush," Chris said.

As the serjeant closed the door, Jeremy thought, oh Christ. Christopher spent a good part of his life irritated with him, and he wore that irritated expression now.

"We've got a good man there," Jeremy said, hoping to divert Chris's course. "All right, you're about to piss petrol."

Chris snorted until he was contained. "I believe you and I had better clear a few things up before we are involved with another enlisted man. I am saddled with a rather difficult situation of being your brother, and if you indeed take this gaffer squad, we will be working extremely closely."

"I don't see why you went out of your way to humiliate Serjeant Tarbox, and I seriously wonder if intimidation is the way to build a battalion," Jeremy answered.

"Oh, dear old Jeremy must be Mister Good Chap, one of the lads."

"What the hell did I do so horrible, shake his hand?"

"First a handshake, then, do sit down for tea . . . or let's make that gin and tonic. Jeremy, we are not dealing with proper manners, and the first job is to teach them discipline. We must never loosen the leash on them. I intend to turn this battalion into a proper British battalion, like the Coleraines."

"They aren't the Coleraines, Christopher. They don't shed the old tear when they hear 'God Save the King,' nor would they gladly die in battle for the Earl of Foyle. Look at these men. They're half again as big as your scrawny Englishmen. They live in the open and they eat beef and they don't know from blue blood. What the hell is this all about? We are three men in a peeling room halfway around the world barfing about mules and mule shit and you act like we're changing the guard at Buckingham Palace. Please, Chris, loosen up on the table manners. We're talking about very tough men and mules."

"Jeremy, you are not rolling around in the mud with these men the way you did on the rugby pitch, and you're not standing elbow-to-elbow drinking cheap ale in their pubs, showing off your tattoos."

"Tattoos," Jeremy said, "now there's a thought. Suppose any of the Earls had tattoos?"

"I have ordered my officers to lay down the law from day one. As for us, in the first instance, I'll no longer overlook your insubordination because of family circumstances and, in the second instance, we do not carry the same rank. This is my battalion, Lieutenant, and I was given this command because of the severity of its mission."

"You and General Brodhead are pretty cozy. I'm sure he'll honor my request for a transfer."

"Shall we speak calmly and without rancor?" Christopher said quickly.

"Why not?"

"I have made vows to both Mother and Father that I will do all in my power to see that you return home in one piece—"

"And without disgracing the family honor. Well, Chris, you are no longer the keeper of a self-pitying drunk."

"Your request will go no further than my desk."

"You know why? I'll tell you. These colonials are not patsies, and you don't know a fiddler's fart about how to deal with men. You want me to run the gaffer squad and be at your side in case you start to muck up."

"You think rather fondly of yourself," Chris said. "Let me say this clearly and calmly. Do not tinker with a system of order which has been keenly developed over the span of a thousand years and has resulted in the greatest nation mankind has ever known. Officers of my stripe have made the British Army a magnificent institution."

God Almighty, Jeremy cringed, trying to hold himself together . . . it was Apprentice Boys' Day on Derry's Walls all over again, raining pennies down on the Catholics in Bogside.

"We are the most fortunate people on earth," Chris continued coolly. "Our station was fixed at birth and privilege is our birthright. That's the way the universe spins, that's the way the world operates, that's how the British Army works, that's why we have an empire. Rip everything apart and exchange the have-nots with the privileged, and in ten years it will return to the way it was in the beginning. Jeremy Hubble is not going to change the natural order of things, and Jeremy Hubble better realize he is here on earth to protect his privilege."

Jeremy laid his hands on his brother's shoulders softly and looked at him pleadingly. God, if he could only get through somehow.

"Chris, when will you ever learn what father never learned, what grandfather never learned. You can't get the loyalty of men through intimidation."

"I'd say they did rather well."

"They got wealthy. In a battalion like this there has to be respect for their dignity. You cannot own a man's soul. Molly O'Rafferty left me because she would not surrender her soul."

Chris removed his brother's unwanted hands from him. "Give unto Caesar what is Caesar's," he said. "Let Jesus and Mary take care of their souls. I want their obedience, their unstinting obedience."

CHAPTER

62

Rory came to attention before a long table covered by green felt behind which a Captain Ellsworth was seated, flanked by Jeremy Hubble and Johnny Tarbox.

"Private Rory Landers reporting."

"I'm Captain Ellsworth. Please have a seat."

"And I am Lieutenant Hubble," Jeremy said extending his hand. "I believe you know Serjeant Major Tarbox."

"Yes, sir."

"According to the questionnaire you filled out aboard ship, you may have some special qualifications for us," Jeremy said.

"Certainly hope so, sir."

"I'm to be in charge of a small gaffer unit," Jeremy continued.

"Gaffer, sir?"

"It's a Johnny-on-the-spot squad, problem solvers, men with various expertise. We are in need of an updated and simplified transportation manual."

"You may have the wrong man, sir. I don't know anything about military transport."

"Mules, mule transport," Jeremy said.

"May I ask the Lieutenant a question?" Rory asked.

"Certainly, and please consider this to be informal chitchat."

"We are horse cavalry?"

"Indeed, horse cavalry," Jeremy lied. "Appears that we may be fighting in some dicey terrain and command feels that mules will be better suited to pack in our supplies. Although the

Seventh Light Horse are all magnificent riders, I understand, it seems there is a total lack of experience with mules. So, it's a gaffer squad problem to set it up properly. Don't worry, Landers, with any luck you may have several horses shot out from under you."

The Captain picked up Rory's questionnaire. "You say here you've had three years' experience with mules."

"That was a long time back. My da has a fair-sized sheep station on the South Island. He bought a large adjoining parcel of woodland, not ripe for sheep grazing or farming, so I talked him into importing a flock of deer for breeding and market."

"Now, how did that go?"

"Too well," Rory answered. "Trouble was, the deer raised hell with the forage and kicked up some fairly fragile topsoil. They needed a lot more space or we'd have to feed them entirely from stores. It raises the risk when you have to buy all their feed. We sold them out, at a very tidy profit. Sorry, I'm rambling on."

"Actually quite interesting," Ellsworth said, "carry on."

"The section wasn't ready for either planting or pasture, so I came up with another scheme. I thought we ought to breed mules."

"What was behind your reasoning, Landers?"

Rory shrugged. "Seemed logical. There are hundreds of small farms, and common sense tells me that a mule can do half again the work of the best draft horse on the same amount of feed. The mule is even more economical in hilly terrain. In addition to agriculture, there are a lot of mining and timber operations which could be better served by mules."

Seeing that Rory was on the new side of twenty, Captain Ellsworth asked, "How old were you when this took place?"

"I was eleven when I got the idea of importing reindeer and fourteen when I started breeding mules."

"Your father must have had a great deal of confidence in you."

Rory thought about that. Yes, the Squire gave him free reign when it came to anything about the farm. Maybe that was because Liam had trained him well.

"I know Squire, er . . . Landers," Johnny Tarbox said. "He was the smartest farmer I ever met. He could look at a virgin piece of land and sense the winds, read the contours and smell and taste the soil and tell you within the bushel of what it would yield."

"That's right," Rory whispered.

"What happened with the mule operation?" Captain Ellsworth asked.

"When you lose, there are all kinds of excuses. The reindeer bred naturally, too damned naturally," Rory said. "Putting a stud donkey up to a mare is a real mess. We didn't have a tradition of mule breeding so everything was trial and error. I'm not passing the blame, but I think the rock bottom cause of the failure was that the farmers and prospectors had formed notions about mules and didn't know how to handle them."

"You mean their stubbornness?"

"No, stubborn is the wrong label. Mules are very smart and when they appear to be stubborn it is usually from bad handling. Then, the owner gets the idea he can whip the work out of them, but a mule never forgets his whipping."

"Well," Ellsworth challenged, "if that isn't stubborn, I don't know what is."

"It's like this, Captain," Rory said, not having the slightest notion he was speaking to a veterinarian of nearly twenty years, "there are stubborn mules and there are wild mules. These mules are born wild, can be very dangerous, and you have no more chance of domesticating them than taming a hyena. There's no choice but to destroy them. It turns out we were breeding a pretty high percentage of wild ones."

"I see," Ellsworth said. "So you shot them in the forehead, right between the eyes."

Rory grimaced. "No, their skulls are very thick and sometimes you don't kill them. They can be in agony for hours. The sure way to destroy a wild mule is shoot through the eye, pointing up to the brain. They die instantly without suffering. One of the reasons I gave up on mules was that I found it too hard to kill them."

"Well, you certainly can't coddle a mule," Ellsworth prodded. "How do you discipline them?"

"First, you give him his dignity. Make pals. Let him know you are in this together. Sir, I tame horses the same way. I don't believe in breaking an animal. You talk to the mule by his name, give him the good word, always have some oats in your pocket. He'll work himself to death for you, if he loves you."

"You don't break horses?" Ellsworth said very puzzled.

"Rory Landers talks a saddle onto a horse," Tarbox said.

"Must take forever," Jeremy said.

"A few hours, most of the time. All you really have to do is get across the idea he shouldn't be afraid of you . . . that's all they want to know."

There was a silent time to digest this incredible idea from the officers, who had been rough riders most of their lives.

"I'm interested in your comment that the handlers, not the mules, are generally the ones at fault."

"Yes, sir. Mules are a lot smarter than horses. If the mule feels something isn't right, he'll stand fast. He's trying to tell you something. A lot of people take that for stubbornness."

"For example?"

"If the mule doesn't feel he is properly loaded, he may not budge until you fix up his pack. Or, if he's going over shifty ground, a mountain trail or a swaying bridge, he'll stop and poke his way around till he feels secure. Horse gets his foot caught in barbed wire, he'll jerk it out and likely rip himself. A mule will ease his foot free, carefully."

"Fascinating," Jeremy said.

"For the military they must be way better than a horse when it comes to transport," Rory said.

"How's that?"

"I've had them up in the mountains at night. They don't spook at fire or noises. Ever watch their ears turn in the direction of sound? I'd wager they are excellent sentries."

"How high is your average mule?"

"Our bucks ran around thirteen hands, jennies a hand shorter."

"How much did you feed them a day?"

"Oh, I'd say twenty pounds of mix."

"What will they carry?"

"About three hundred pounds, including their pack."

Ellsworth went into the art of packing, knots, ties, halters, common ailments, care, sanitation. In the ensuing hours the Captain did not elicit a wrong or unsure answer. If this Landers chap didn't know, he'd just say so.

At last Captain Ellsworth held up his hands and looked to Lieutenant Hubble to see if there were any further questions. "Thank you, Private Landers," Jeremy said. "If you'll wait outside we'll call you back, shortly. Oh, bye the bye, Tarbox tells me you knocked out the Aussie heavyweight champion."

"Big target, sir. He was wide open."

When the door was closed, Captain Ellsworth nodded in the affirmative and Serjeant Major Tarbox grinned widely. "Hubble, if you don't want him, I'll take him," the Captain said.

"I pray to God he writes well enough to put together a simplified manual."

"I've just the man to actually write the manual, sir," Tarbox said quickly.

"Who is he?"

"Private Chester Goodwood. Actual fact, he's English."

"Does he know anything about mules?"

"He knows about writing. He wrote the love letters for half the lads aboard the *Wagga Wagga*. I mean he used words like 'jasmine blooming in the spring.'"

"And he's a pal of yours?"

"Sir, this kid's old man is Sir Stanford Goodwood, a big-time banker in Hong Kong. He'll be of unspeakable value when it comes time to work out the logistics."

"Very well, we'll interview him later," Jeremy said. "So, you wouldn't hesitate to give Landers a go as paddock master?" Jeremy confirmed with the Captain.

"I'd wager on him," Ellsworth retorted.

"I have a good feeling, too," Jeremy said. "He's not a wild man, is he, Tarbox?"

"We're Kiwis, sir. We're not like that Aussie crowd, no sir. Rory Landers has a very sweet disposition."

"We still need several more key men, Captain, and I don't see them here," Jeremy worried.

"Let me look over some of the people at my base," the Captain offered. "We've a couple of groups arriving with mule experience. There's a Punjab battalion of mule-packed mountain howitzers. I'll find you a good packer and trail boss. Sikhs, you know, fierce fighters."

"The turbaned chaps?"

"Yes, and they all speak English. You will need a veterinarian. A lot of the horse care and mule care is the same but, nonetheless, mules have their special problems. Hummm, see here. We've gotten in a group of Palestinian Jews who we will be training for our transport. Some of these chaps ran mules for the Russian Army, I'm told, and used mules for farming in Palestine. There's bound to be several vets among them or, at least, someone with enough background to do the job. . . . Let me jot a note here . . . Punjab packer . . . Jew vet, English-speaking . . . "

Rory was once again welcomed to be seated.

"Landers, we've had to diddle you about for reasons of military security. What I tell you now is still hush-hush for several days. Kindly hold your breath before you scream."

Rory closed his eyes and braced himself.

"Captain Ellsworth here is the chief veterinarian for the British divisions stationed in the south."

"I figured the Captain to be a vet," Rory said. "You're shipping me to the mules, aren't you?"

"No, we're shipping the mules to you. All cavalry units have been disbanded and are being recommissioned as infantry, mostly. The Seventh New Zealand Light Horse is now the mule transportation battalion for the Anzac forces."

"No cavalry, sir?"

"No cavalry. One does not question command decisions and orders. It is apparent, is it not, that there will be no need for cavalry in the upcoming campaign. I want you on the gaffer squad as a troubleshooter for anything and everything as we make this transformation. Your main assignment now is to write a manual, and after that you will be the battalion's paddock master in charge of the four to five hundred mules we are expecting. And, to ease any pain and put you in the proper mood, there are first serjeant's chevrons to go with the job."

"Congratulations, Landers," Captain Ellsworth said.

"Captain, let us be off to the mess. I'll see you gentlemen in two hours. Bring along this, uh, Good . . . ?"

"Goodwood, Chester Goodwood."

Rory was a knot of intertwining bulging muscles, jaws clamped, fists clenched, neck veins distended. He turned to Johnny Tarbox with "killer" written all over him.

"You dirty no good son of a bitch!" Rory commented. "You knew about this yesterday. You fed me to these fucking mules when you went through my questionnaire. You could have torn up the fucking questionnaire. They'd have never known! You rotten son of a bitch!"

"Oh, I betrayed you, that it?"

"You son of a bitch!"

"All right, so I dispose of your questionnaire, then what? You end up shoveling shit in the paddock as a fucking private. Want a transfer! Fuck yes, I'll get you a fucking transfer to the fucking infantry and you'll march in the fucking desert in the fucking sun till you fucking drop! You! You ought to be kissing my feet, you asshole. First Serjeant chevrons! Five fucking years in the Royal Marines and I'm a fucking lance corporal and ten minutes and you're a first serjeant! You dumb shit! There is no cavalry! And they didn't consult me on the matter!"

Rory fell into a chair and blinked. As the enormity of Johnny's recommendation sank in, Rory put his face in his hands. "I'm sorry, Johnny," he sniffled.

"And me, going into the ring with that fucking Butcher monster and letting him rain blows on me."

"I said I'm sorry. I really mean I'm sorry."

"And know something?" Tarbox said standing over Rory. "You should kiss my feet for getting you into the gaffers with the only decent pommy officer in Camp Anzac."

"You going to keep ragging on me, now? I said I'm sorry."

"Lookit these pommies," Tarbox went on, "and remember how lucky we are to have Lieutenant Hubble. What's more, he's a genuine blue blood, a viscount. Fucking son of a fucking earl, that's what!"

Rory looked up to Johnny and Johnny became worried. "What's the matter with you, Rory?"

"They're Ulstermen. Is he ... is he the son of the Earl of Foyle?" Rory rasped.

"Something like that."

"Jeremy and Christopher Hubble," Rory whispered. "Jeremy Hubble."

CHAPTER
63

After several individual forays into Cairo, Serjeant Major Tarbox and Rory Landers, sporting his new first serjeant chevrons, got the distinct impression that Cairo was not Paris.

Rory had come from the stillness of Christchurch into the bombast of an untidy swarm of crowds, shrill sounds, impatient horns, wild aromas, glaring sun, strangely hidden women in black, unkempt streets—all a confused bazaar that was the ancient system of order the Cairenes thrived in.

The city was now host to a new army, and every vendor and every beggar, bar, brothel, omnibus tour, cameleer, and merchant reacted. Thousands of newly minted and carved genuine ancient artifacts, as well as a brigade of guaranteed virgin prostitutes, suddenly appeared.

The influx of soldiers' cash and their enormous thirsts produced foul vetches of native wines and beer leaving a trail of upchucks and near blindness.

The greed of the sellers was boundless. It was not as though they had invited this foreign army to their city.

In short order the Anzacs and the British despised Cairo, and the feeling was mutual except for the Pound Sterling. Coming from a land where a handshake was a man's honor, the Aussies felt taken in. As a result, in their flamboyant campaign hats they led a number of rowdy retributions. The Cairo police were a bit timid, so the military patrols were cleaning up messes from dawn to dusk and back to dawn.

Rory, Johnny, and Chester had a priority: to find an oasis of solitude in the maniacal mélange.

Due to a visit in Cairo years earlier as a Royal Marine, Johnny Tarbox boasted he could better cut through the maze of grubs, gooks, and geeks. Johnny hunted down the boss of the Terrier pack outside the camp gate and came up with a full-blown thug named Walid.

The Terriers performed all manner of duties in the camp, from polishing shoes to running errands to escorting new arrivals up the pyramids.

Walid operated the employment center, assigning the better jobs to members of his extended family, friends, and those who kicked back the most baksheesh.

Figuring he was playing the system, Johnny offered a goodly sum of five quid to put him in touch with the right man in the old city.

Walid's promises were extravagant and, for another two quid, Johnny could be connected with the "protector" for the lively Aguza District.

Tarbox knew that somewhere in those dark and twisting lanes with all that hollering and those delicious and non-delicious smells, there had to be a jewel of a hideaway ... with belly dancers to the right and belly dancers to the left ... and *decent* booze.

"We *have* to have decent booze."

"My man will take care of you, first class," Walid promised, and Johnny felt pleased with himself for cutting through all that chasing around and Oriental red tape.

First Serjeant Rory Landers took on the center of Cairo on the east side of the river and the Buluq District. A string of two- and three-star hotels lined the river bank. Rory felt a rooftop apartment with three bedrooms would be definitely in the realm of possibility.

As for Chester, they were worried about sending him into the morass of the marketplace. He was doing a bang-up job working on the mule manual. In fact, he was doing all three of their jobs.

However, when Rory and Johnny returned to camp a bit down in the mouth, Chester reckoned that Cairo had certain similarities to Hong Kong. Johnny and Rory agreed to let him join the search but ordered him to cruise only in the safer areas.

It was their fourth trip in, an overnighter, to stage the all-out hunt. They synchronized watches and fanned out. They would return to the bar across from their hotel near the railroad station at two-thirty the following day.

The clock in the rail tower tolled three, which actually meant it was two o'clock because the clock was an hour off. The city shuttered itself for the midday respite from the debilitating wet heat fuming up off the Nile.

Rory was the first to return. He fended off the foul brew they attempted to foist on him and, after a lengthy discussion, won the debate with a bottle of uncut, unopened, brand-name gin.

Rory watched as the swirl of Terriers ground to a listless few, except for the kids still hustling Muslim worry beads, Catholic rosaries, kaffias, and trinkets they couldn't mail to the girls back home.

Johnny Tarbox appeared like a mirage with steam shimmering up around him. He fell into a chair, limp.

"Nothin'."

"Nothin'."

"Fucking roaches had pet rats."

"Wouldn't put a pommy officer up in them."

"The Casbah has eyes and ears," Johnny said nipping the gin with an "ah." "We'd be paying off half the gangsters in the old city to keep from getting our throats cut. They're all sweaty and hairy and dirty in there, and the men are even worse."

Rory was unable to resist a beggar kid leading a blind and hideously warped old man. His coin brought on a swarm. He settled for a wooden crucifix carved from the true cross and shouted them away.

Johnny jerked a thumb in the direction of the island in the middle of the river. "There's where it's at, Rory. When the Brits take over running a country, they make it comfortable for themselves at a cheap price. The Zamalek District has got the only beds in town without fleas."

"Are you sure it's off bounds?"

"Not officially, but they've got military police on every bridge, and patrols sweep up anything that looks like an enlisted man. We're scum, cobber."

"Makes you really want to fight for them."

"Yeah," Johnny muttered, "officers' country deluxe ... staff officers' country. Nobody under a light colonel better blow his bugle over there. We got a tour of the gardens once when I was here. Like hotels you see in moving pictures ... villas ... gardens."

A number of egalitarian plans began rotating in Rory's mind.

"I hear you thinking, cobber, forget it. Anyhow, I found the best whorehouse in the old city—semi-exclusive—some real nice lookers in there. I think it's a cold tub for me and then I'll go fall in love," Johnny said.

The clock in the train tower rolled half past three. It was two-thirty.

"Jesus!" Rory cried.

"Wot!"

"Chester! He's been gone since we arrived yesterday."

"Goddamnit! I told that little bugger to stay in camp and work on the manual. We'd better start looking."

"Where?"

"The police, the morgue!"

"Calm down," Rory said. "Any kid who could stow away to New Zealand from Hong Kong ... "

"I'll never forgive myself if anything happens to that kid," Tarbox said. "I gave him over a hundred pounds out of our stash from the battalion safe. Ah Jaysus, he's been robbed and murdered. What do we do, Rory?"

"I say, for now, we sit tight and wait. If you have to visit a lady, I'll wait."

"No, no, I'll stay here with you. Oh Chester, boy."

Private Chester Goodwood spent the first day walking along Ramses Road admiring the exquisite shops and, as it turned dark, worked his way through a host of bars and hotel lobbies collecting information. Like a good detective on the scent, he did not return to his hotel but grabbed a nap at the train station so he could start again at the crack of dawn.

Chester zeroed in on a petite but well turned-out travel agency and studied the clientele. A pair of big-time Arabs entered. A high-fashion European lady came and left. Several officers went in, none under the rank of major.

Chester was greeted with a very uppity sneer at the main desk, but the agent did catch a glimpse of Chester's hand on the counter with the corner of a five-pound note visible.

"I'm making some inquiries on behalf of my commanding officer," the private said.

"Please"—arms open, invited behind the counter into the seat and, chop-chop, coffee for the gentleman.

"I want the name of the concierge with the best connections in Cairo. Phone him and tell him I'm coming on behalf of my general. Please speak in English and you have earned yourself another five."

The magic name of Mr. Hamdoon Sira came up for the first time.

Chester then worked his way to the bell captains of several of the better hotels, confirming Sira's credentials. He finally found himself in the office of a solicitor who, for ten, would recommend Chester highly to his very good friend Hamdoon Sira.

Chester took a taxi across the 14th of October Bridge onto the forbidden island and stopped at the most magnificent hotel in the Near East, the Memphis Palace.

All the dinginess and noise of the other Cairo was muffled by banks of defending hedges and flowers. Arched and marbled, the hotel boasted legions of white-gloved attendants who seemed to walk slightly off the ground. It was genteel, good stuff. More like it, Chester thought. Moreover, Chester seemed quite at ease in the midst of all that *rank*. And tea music.

"I am Private Chester Goodwood, I believe Mr. Sira is expecting me," he said, slapping the old pound sterling into the assistant's hand. Chester knew that a pound on the rich man's side of the bridge went farther than a fiver on the poor man's side. It was a singular accomplishment of the wealthy and powerful not to overpay for things.

"Mr. Sira is with a guest. He will be with you directly."

A pommy colonel locked in on Chester, annoyed by the soldier's familiarity. He looked the lad up and down and assumed by his New Zealand patch that he was unaware of the custom. Enlisted personnel serving and waiting for their officers at the Memphis Palace had their own waiting area, out of sight of the main lobby.

"Soldier," the colonel said gruffly, "are you quite certain you are in the proper place?"

"Quite, sir. I am waiting to see Mr. Sira on behalf of Lieutenant General Mulesworthy."

"Oh ... hmmm ... carry on."

"Sir!" Chester said, cracking off a salute fit for the King himself.

Mr. Sira and Chester Goodwood sized one another up. Mr. Sira was, as anticipated, the Egyptian version of the Chinese concierge in the Peninsula Hotel. Sira appeared to be a man who had come up through the ranks and survived—and in Cairo that spoke loudly.

Chester was simply baffling—smooth cheeks, innocent smile, and mild manner.

Now, Chester thought, we can go into an Egyptian tango and start endless word games and play dodge, or he could shoot the old arrow straight to the heart.

"You have been passing out large amounts of money to gain contact with me," Hamdoon Sira said, utterly certain the private had to be fronting for some senior officer. Sira knew his name was not passed around lightly.

"Mr. Sira," Chester said, "here's the situation. I'm a Brit from Hong Kong and I've got two pals, New Zealanders. We're part of a special squad and we have a great deal of camp leave. Two or three more men might be assigned to us, no more."

"You are representing the commander?"

"No, sir."

"Just what is it you think I can assist you with?"

"Camp Anzac is shit city incarnate. Over the river it's a real sleazy scene for enlisted personnel. We happen to be well financed and all we want is a quiet place where we can find some respite from our duties. As I said, we have ample funds."

Hamdoon Sira smiled. Well, now, the plot thickens ... this child before him is certainly fronting for a prostitution ring, perhaps hashish smuggling, black market liquor, British army weapons ... some such.

Chester read Hamdoon's smile. "We are not after running a whorehouse, drugs, or playing with dirty money. We are all proper people from proper homes and we don't wreck furniture."

Ah ... Hamdoon Sira liked Chester Goodwood. "I like you. I admire candor. We see so little of it. I am totally sympathetic but I am afraid there is nothing—" Hamdoon halted as he looked directly into the face of a fifty-pound bank note.

Hamdoon had been in the hotel scene since childhood. Before the war the new, rich oil sheiks from the peninsula gave out lavish gratuities, but they were no longer able to come here due to the war. Otherwise, he had never seen anything larger than five pounds from a British officer, and then only rarely.

"If you will come back tomorrow," Sira said.

"No," Chester retorted. "We're soldiers and we've no time to play the game. I'm buying. We move directly or forget it."

By my father's beard, Hamdoon thought, this is one clever individual.

"I plead with you, Mr. Goodwood, you cannot change basic nature. We must do things in a traditional way. For what you want will take some time. . . . Just what are your requirements?"

"Garden, parlor, veranda, three bedrooms, roach-free, access to Memphis Palace–type liquor, police protection, and ladies on call."

"Hmmm," Sira pondered as he rubbed his thumb and forefinger together as though he were caressing the fifty-pound note. It would be no problem to obtain this for a staff officer, but none of them could pay the passage. With the sheiks in Turkish

territory and ordinary travelers scarce, a number of villas sat
empty. I go one step further, he decided, once I ascertain if . . .
"Will there be a continuing way I could serve the situation?"

"You mean further commissions, somewhat more than a
shilling from a Brit officer, damp with the sweat of his palm?"

A toothy smile and an innocent holding apart of Hamdoon's
hands was followed by holding his heart.

"Absolutely," Chester said.

One does not come to decisions so quickly. What if this is a
trap? What kind of trap? No, it was not a trap but one must discuss this with other parties, there must be conversation . . . the
fifty-pound note was still before him. How much more was in
stock? A hundred? A half-year's wages, maybe more! Does one
reveal his sources so easily? After all, Hamdoon, he told himself,
you are a great concierge in a cheap land. You know where
everything is. . . .

DO IT!

Hamdoon picked up the phone, waited, then went into a
passionate discussion and, after a time, set the phone down. "I
believe I can do you some good. I have arranged an immediate
appointment with a prominent gentleman of great honor and
impeccable connections. Usually, it takes days to see him. He has
made such arrangements for ministers, generals, great sheiks.
BUT! Do not waste his time. You must be prepared to pay a
great sum, at least sixty to seventy-five pounds a week, exclusive
of the women and drink."

"I'll tell you what. I'll go ninety a week for the right place.
You, Mr. Sira, make the deal for me. Anything you can get it for,
under ninety, goes into your pocket plus another five a week."

"You must be prepared to pay in advance."

"Afraid not. We'll pay half a week in advance and the balance
at the end of each week."

Hamdoon Sira was standing before a cask of gold. Only
Allah knew what else he could provide these men. If only all the
English were as forthright as Mr. Goodwood. He jotted the
name of Farouk el Farouk. "I'll have the hotel limousine
brought around for you."

Chester ripped the fifty-pound note in two and gave a half to Mr. Sira. "The rest when you close the deal."

The bell tower clock tolled eight-thirty, which meant it was seven-thirty. As dusk fell, the calls of the muezzins floated from the minaret tops. Rory and Johnny were on the verge of panic envisioning the dear innocent face of Chester lying in a slimy, cobblestoned gutter with his ears and tongue missing.

Bong ... clang ... burrrrr ... bong ... tolled the bells.

"Ah Jaysus! Chester! Johnny, it's Chester!"

"You dirty little sonofabitch, where have you been? We've been going crazy!"

"Ought to break your fuckin' neck, that's wot!"

Chester sighed. "I almost found us a place."

"Almost, what do you mean, almost!"

Chester recounted the day, up to the meeting with Farouk el Farouk.

"He had a real obscure office on the second floor of a building on Sheik el Bustan. Pleasant fellow. I cut through the red tape and laid out our purpose and requirements."

"Including the women?" Johnny wanted to know.

"Including the women," Chester assured him.

"Ah, good lad."

"There's some villas in the Zamalek. Most of his regular clients got caught in Switzerland or otherwise by the war. The pommy officers haven't got the money or are too cheap to take them off his hands. At first he didn't even want to show them to me."

"What happened?"

"We got into a backgammon game. You know, he had centuries of tradition behind him. When I had him down over two hundred I told him I'd call it even if he showed me one of the villas."

"How was it?"

"Arabian nights ... Scheherazade ... on the Nile ... open courtyard with a fountain, big balcony overlooking the river, numerous arched rooms built around the center square. It was in our budget with a case of whiskey and two cases of beer a week thrown in."

"I'll kill for it!" Tarbox cried.

"Maybe I shouldn't have told you about it, guys. I think if it was up to Farouk, he'd go for it . . . but he can't sell police protection to enlisted men in such thick officers' country, and secondly, if the British command got wind of it, they'd close him down."

"I don't want to hear any more!" Rory snapped.

"Jesus, the dirty bastards."

"And we're supposed to fight a fucking war with these guys!"

"Unless," Chester said, "and this is clear crazy—"

"Unless what?"

"Unless we got somebody of the rank of colonel or above to sign the paper, and he means an in-person colonel . . . no forgeries."

Cairo jumped back to life around them once again.

CHAPTER
64

There was no aspect of soldiering minuscule enough to be overlooked in the basic training that ensued at Camp Anzac. Eager young broadbacks from down under, many of whom had envisioned themselves in the thunder of a cavalry charge, were rudely introduced to the fundamentals of soldiering.

Basic training brought them to a point of physical hardness, to where they could drill in unison, salute their pommies with proper pomp, prepare themselves, their weapons, and their quarters for white-glove inspection, become intimate with their rifles, and fire them accurately.

No battalion was going to be snappier, shine brighter, shoot straighter, follow regulations better, or exercise harder than Major Christopher Hubble's.

His group quickly earned the reputation as one where survival till the end of the day was considered a personal triumph. He demanded of his officers that they not spare the sweat box, an upright coffin with two small air holes, for the man who did not salute sharply enough or have the corners of his bedding tucked immaculately. Aloof from his men, the major seemed to thrive on their loathing of him.

Once the basic training was completed, Jeremy breathed a sigh of relief. While the other battalions would now convert to infantry, artillery, engineers, and other support units of a brigade and division, the Seventh Light Horse could get on with its special training on mules.

No specialized course could be established for them because

they did not have a guiding manual and could not complete the manual until certain experts arrived. Moreover, there was no packing equipment and, mostly . . . there were no mules.

While the four-man gaffer squad struggled with writing the manual and awaited the vet and packer to complete it, Major Hubble put his men into infantry training.

Llewelyn Brodhead was a marching general. No Anzac unit outmarched the Seventh Light Horse. They sprinted the short marches with light combat packs; they marched full-speed with field packs; they force-marched in full strength up to fifty miles over the sands. They marched in boot-top-covering, ankle-deep-sucking sand, dehydrating and blistering and getting double vision from the brutal sun, only to then be pelted and blinded by slicing sandstorms.

They crawled through sand, through and under barbed wire, with live gunfire, keeping bellies and asses flat. They attacked with grenades and mortars over the dunes.

Night marches in the sudden chill of the desert turned into night patrols. Either they were ambushed or they ambushed others. They stormed through defenses at fixed bayonets in games real enough to tell them that exhaustion can be blessed, if a mental fog enshrouds them, so long as they do not drop out of formation. The gunfire and explosions were tight enough around them to let them realize the fears of combat.

Those big Aussie and New Zealand beef-and-mutton eaters no longer poked fun at the scrawny limeys in the English units who knew the ways of soldiering.

When they weren't marching or participating in battle exercises, they dug trenches and latrines and trimmed up their areas. Throughout the Anzac Corps, many officers were lax and allowed the soldiers to use Terriers to do a lot of the cleanup work.

Major Hubble forbade the use of Terriers by his men. Major Hubble's punishments were double that of the rest of the corps. Major Hubble's battalion area was impeccable.

Even the stoutest Aussie desert rat buckled under the Egyptian sun, and what the sun didn't get, the sand did. Sand, sand, sand, sand. Clean the tent and it was filled with sand again in minutes. Sand in the mess kits. Sand in their teeth and hair. Sand in their clothing, up their rectums.

Yes, they would become good troops, given enough time. But as tough as they were, the Anzacs had a flaw. Almost all of them had come from rural settings free from exposure to the bacterias of urban "civilization." For the first time in their lives they were in total close quarters with crowds of humanity: crammed aboard troop ships, packed in the narrow streets of Cairo, at Camp Anzac. Their immune systems had not been built to handle the onslaught of typhoid and dysentery, stomach parasites, and killer influenza. A third of them were down at all times from illness.

Respite meant leave in Cairo, and soon venereal disease added to the infirmities.

Cairo had centuries of experience in swaying to the whims of the conqueror, occupier, and tourist. They all wanted the same thing—bargains, booze, and women ... preferably the illusion of a virgin. The soldier boys at the bottom of the ranks were young men. Nearly all of them were short on experience and felt they had to have a notch or two of girl-o in their belts to make memories before battle and to know they had joined the ranks of real men.

Cairo was having a reverse effect. The situation went from bad to rotten. Tempers grew shorter. The men, particularly of the Seventh Light Horse, returned to camp in a state of agitation, after which Major Hubble drilled it out of them.

As for Rory lad, his dream of that oasis—that Champs Elysée apartment—was blown away with the desert sands.

In a compound close to battalion headquarters, there was a large stable with indoor riding rings that was in decent condition and mostly unused, except to house polo ponies for the ranking officers. Jeremy talked Chris into allowing him to have the building and supplying him with laborers to convert it into housing and office space for his gaffers. Each man had a private sleeping cubicle and a small office. Most activity centered around a conference room, which was a feet-on-the-desk, nonmilitary, friendly spot.

Christopher did not like the gaffers' privileged setup or their independence. He considered himself a top-notch officer and justified special treatment to the squad. A fine officer knew when to yield slightly ... particularly when the gains would more than offset his "largesse." If Major Hubble learned one thing, it was that Jeremy's squad was the make-or-break of the battalion's unique commission. So long as they were out of sight and Chris did not have to buck heads with his brother, he yielded here and there.

One of the indoor riding rings had a grandstand that could hold two hundred men, or about a fourth of the battalion, at one time. In planning ahead, this would become a rotating classroom.

In Pig Island, a conference room walled with charts, the lieutenant and his three gaffers went as far as they could go on writing a workable mule manual, but the battalion desperately needed the expertise of the key men, a chief packer and a veterinarian.

Rory reckoned these missing chapters should be written substituting horses for mules. After all, the skeletons were the same and there were a whole range of similarities between the two animals. It stood to shorten the finishing time of the manual simply by replacing mules for horses and making whatever corrections were required.

The three gaffers awaited the arrival of the veterinarian in Pig Island with more than usual anticipation.

Rory had met only one Jew in his life, a nondescript general merchant in Christchurch who was generally well liked for his generosity in extending credit to prospectors and folks who had had a bad season.

Chester knew of two or three Jews in Hong Kong, bankers and money people. Actually he did not really *know* them, but had met them.

Johnny Tarbox did not know if he knew any Jews. He had seen some in his travels as a Royal Marine and actually suspected a member of his platoon was one.

Lieutenant Jeremy had known a few Jews here and there and found them to be decent sorts if treated decently.

They had a number of discussions and sought information about the Jews and everything they came up with was slimy ... unsavory ... crooked ... and altogether enough to make one very uneasy.

They were trying to look at the person behind Lieutenant Jeremy when he entered Pig Island. Rory was first to see an accordion among the man's possessions, which he took to be a positive sign. He was a good-sized fellow, rough-hewn. Obviously he did physical work, which belied the rumor to the contrary.

"Lads," Jeremy said, "this gentleman is our vet, assigned to us on detached duty from the Zion Mule Corps. We've been chatting for the past hour and I know he's going to fit right in with the gaffer squad. Mordechai Pearlman ... right to left, meet Serjeant Major Johnny Tarbox, First Serjeant Rory Landers, and Private Chester Goodwood."

Behind a wild beard came a split-tooth smile and a hand-shake capable of breaking bricks.

"Well, lads," Jeremy said to the three who gawked, "take care of our man here and show him the ropes. Now, let's get cracking on rewriting the chapters on ills, ails, and sanitation."

When Jeremy departed the awkward silence continued.

"Well now, Doctor, how's your English, sir?" Johnny ventured.

"Fine, how's yours?" Pearlman answered.

That helped.

"I have not been knighted so I am not a sir, and my doctor's diploma is somewhere in Minsk and not accredited by the British Army. Matter of fact, I'm not even a member of the army. I am an attached specialist ... however ... I know mules like you know women, Tarbox."

That loosened things up. "Now that's saying a mouthful," Johnny said, beaming.

Quiet again.

"So, maybe we better be talking *tocklus*," Pearlman said. "You are thinking, what is this Jew. No?"

"Aw, you know, we were sort of wondering, never having

met anyone of your religious persuasion person-to-person," Johnny said.

"Sure, we're curious," Rory said. "Like, New Zealand isn't in the middle of Moscow."

"I think I like all of you," Pearlman said, "and I think you will all like me. I come filled with peace and love. Good?"

"Good."

"Good."

"Goodo."

"But no Jew jokes, good? Who of you beat the Australian heavyweight?"

"Guilty," Rory said.

"After I softened him up," Johnny added.

"No doubt you can also beat me up. But let me say and I guarantee you, absolutely, with saber in my hand, I can peel you into delicate slices, so thin, like smoked salmon. And I think we should understand this—"

"Because you've taken enough shit," Johnny finished his sentence. "Take off your worries and stand at ease, you're among cobbers."

"Cobblers? You are shoemakers?"

"We've a small squad. It's us and the Lieutenant, and you're most welcome here."

Pearlman's bear hug on Johnny clanged. Chester was all but crushed by it. Rory feinted a couple of punches and embraced him.

Everyone sighed in relief a number of times and then broke into laughter.

"So, what do we call you? Doctor?"

"They call me Modi back in Palestine."

"Modi?"

"Modi, short for Mordechai."

"Modi, aye, that's a fine name, indeed."

Late into the night the lads were praising Allah for Modi's arrival. Not only had he given the corrections on "Ills, Ails, and Sanitation," but he had edited the entire manual.

"You boys have done a fantastic job, working in the dark like this," Modi complimented.

"I want to tell you, the Brit manual might as well have been written in Russian," Chester said. "I bent my mind trying to translate it—untwist it, that is."

"This is just what's needed. Very simple. And you tell me everyone in the battalion is a horseman."

"That's right."

"Very, very many things the same. But mainly, the men are comfortable around a big animal. . . . That will cut out weeks and weeks of mule feeling out the soldier and soldier feeling out the mule."

Mordechai Pearlman's mind leapt ahead. He had been told bluntly by Lieutenant Jeremy that the sand was running through the clock a lot faster than they wanted it to.

"You have classroom, I saw."

They walked over to the ring where the stadium seats had been built. One company at a time for each lecture. Four lectures a day. Give me a month, he thought. Thank God they know horses.

"Each company should have give men with special veterinary training. They will be used the same way you use medics. We have an aid station. We have them on the trail with mule trains."

"I'll talk to the Lieutenant tomorrow," Johnny said.

"I want to pick these boys myself," Modi asserted. "I train them, they'll be great."

Jesus! They'd come upon a work monster. They returned to Pig Island and kept going on the manual for four hours after the midnight oil was burned out. Modi stretched and produced a bottle of vodka.

"I know it's not regulations, but I'm unregulated," Modi said. "Besides, it's the last bottle of Russian vodka in Palestine and I think we should finish it."

Rory locked them in and Mordechai Pearlman opened wide his accordion and introduced them to the first of his repertoire of Russian-Yiddish-Hebrew-Arabic-and-Greek songs. It was a golden kind of moment. They were dead tired and tipsy, and Modi's voice was filled with passion and soul. Not even knowing what the words meant, one could be brought to tears. Jesus!

"Got a wife, Modi?"

"What makes you think?"

"You're an old fart, like Johnny. Past thirty."

"Past forty," Modi answered, "almost fifty. No, no wife."

Modi turned over the vodka bottle and grimaced. Empty. "Only thing good to come out of Russia," he said setting the bottle aside.

"Did I hear once that Jews don't drink?" Johnny asked.

"They don't," Modi answered, "so I have to drink for all of them that don't drink." He scratched his beard in thought. "We're all comrades, right?"

They agreed.

"I have something to tell you three men. It is something the rest of the battalion is not to know until combat. Obviously we will rotate our mule trains so each animal works the same and rests the same number of hours. It appears we will be working very tough terrain, and if we develop a static front we will have very little room to maneuver. *Fahrstaht?* Understand?"

"Aye."

"We will have no room ... no pasture to rehabilitate an injured animal and rest him up till he can return to the trains. Any animal too sick or lame, who can't go back to duty in two or three days, is to be destroyed. New mules will be fed in to us."

Rory fell back in his chair and closed his eyes.

"Rory, you are paddock master?"

"Aye."

"And yourself, Johnny?"

"I've got a title, I'm not sure what it means or how to do it. Apparently there is nothing in the books on my kind of duty."

"What is it?" Modi asked.

"I'm to be the beach master. Indicates we'll be landing from ships, I'd say."

"That answers a lot of questions about destroying the animals. We're probably to be supplied from the sea. Well, Rory, you and I will have to make the decisions to destroy ... and when we get the pack master, he can also do it."

Rory led a silence in which he came close to fainting. He felt Pearlman pat his shoulder over and over. "That's war. It's worse to see men die."

"At least they had a choice," Rory mumbled.

"I don't think so," Modi answered, with a knowing of wars past.

Two days later Serjeant Yurlob Singh, Third Sikh Mountain Howitzers, was brought to Pig Island. He was slender but military-ramrod, turbaned, his beard meticulously groomed hair by hair. From a sect of legendary fighters, Yurlob was annoyed to be transferred, yet totally proper and totally unfriendly as he snapped out his answers. He gave off an air that anyone who asked him a question was to be answered as though he were an idiot for asking.

For the next several days Yurlob tortured Chester Goodwood, demanding letter-perfect instructions on the very intricate art of packing.

"Yurlob is driving us nutty," Rory complained to Johnny Tarbox. "You can't get near the bugger."

"We're lucky to have him," Johnny retorted.

"He treats us like we're monkeys."

"We are, according to him."

"What's going on, John? You on that raghead's side?"

"Hey, Rory. Yurlob has had to work a hundred times harder to earn his respect and get his chevrons than we did. His dignity is his entire life ... but don't you know, he's a man. He's away from his own cobbers and he's a little bit scared inside. Remember, he's covering his fears. You know what I mean?"

"Yeah," Rory said, "I know. It's only, I wish, maybe a smile. Maybe some trust?"

"That will come," Johnny said. "Meanwhile, he'll teach this battalion packing like they were loading fine porcelain on the backs of those animals."

Rory had become more and more amazed by Johnny Tarbox and the way he sized up men. Christ, if men could only admit fear without being ashamed.

As the mule manual slugged to conclusion, a large shipment of equipment arrived, including saddles, blinds, shoes, ribbings, lines, canvas, leather, coronas, and a blacksmith shop.

This allowed a detailed training schedule to be laid out, including daily lectures by Yurlob Singh, Modi, and Rory. Everything was falling into place. They had a hardened battalion of nearly seven hundred men with animal experience, enough equipment to train with, and a manual.

They had everything now. Everything except mules.

CHAPTER
65

Rory had been emotionally wracked since learning that Lieutenant Jeremy was the very same Jeremy Hubble, the Viscount Coleraine whom Conor had befriended as a child. Jeremy apparently held Conor in the same high esteem he did. He had worked alongside Conor on the great screen at Hubble Manor and learned and played Gaelic football as a member of the Bogside team.

But more than Jeremy, his mother was the fabled Countess Caroline, Conor's childhood longing and later his patron and unfulfilled love.

After Conor left New Zealand his first letters to Rory told of a joyous reunion with Jeremy and Caroline and later of the tour of the English Midlands. He chaperoned, trained, and tutored Jeremy, and the Boilermakers had won the Admiral's Cup.

Rory now reckoned that Jeremy must have lost personal contact with Conor after Sixmilecross. In all likelihood Jeremy and Conor never spoke or wrote to one another again.

Why, Rory wondered, couldn't he just go to Jeremy straightforward and say, "Landers isn't my real name. I am Rory Larkin and Conor was my uncle?"

This was Rory's frustration. His secret about Conor being his uncle was so deep he could not even share it with Chester.

There was a final dark reason. Rory eventually had to find his way to Ireland. Once Jeremy knew that Rory was a "once removed" Irish republican with the Larkin name it stood to sour their relationship. Moreover, if the men of the battalion learned, it would change his standing. Men whose trust he had gained would have an attitude of apprehension.

Maybe someday he and Jeremy might be close enough to share the secret and share Conor, but it hardly seemed likely. The bottom line of it all was to keep on playing Rory Landers.

Being Landers was not all that bad. He was with some lively cobbers and included Lieutenant Jeremy as a kind of friend. He wore an armful of British chevrons and was doing a job to his liking.

Then came the shock of Georgia's letter and the earth beneath him opened up and he plunged into a bottomless hole and the earth swallowed him up.

He read the cruel words he already knew from memory, as though one more reading might change them on her pages.

My Dear Rory,

We know you are in Egypt. It is in all the newspapers. An Aussie journalist, Keith Murdock, has proclaimed himself as protector and defender of the Anzacs, feeling as all colonials do, that you are not getting a fair shake from the British. I've done a short tour of duty in Alexandria, as you know, and fairly well imagine what a day's work must be like.

I've all your darlin' letters and I only wished I was as gorgeous as you remember me. For the lonely soldier, any girl back home becomes a goddess over time. I'm not what you describe and I'm not apt to become any better looking.

The dream of your home can also be blown out of proportion. Mixed among the hills and woods and fields is a deep hurt and anger against your father and his utter confusion of being able to do anything about it.

I find Christchurch massively dull without you knocking at my door. As much as I originally craved the peace I found here, I feel a more urgent need to get involved in this war. War always brings on shortages of nurses, and with my background there are a dozen offers I can choose from. I will be leaving here quite soon.

From the moment you left I began receiving letters

almost daily from Calvin. He swears he has seen the light and mended his ways and he begs for a second chance. I can't play it any way but straight with you, Rory, and God only knows what it's like when soldiers read this kind of letter.

This is good-bye. I'll not be writing to you again.

For us even to continue writing would be to foster illusions. Affairs are only chapters of a long life and no matter how deep they run, one eventually goes back to reality. Affairs are not reality.

I do not fear writing you because I know what you're made of and I know you will sail through this and open wide the full and extraordinary life that lies ahead of you. I say this with a lump in my throat, but I also know that the right woman is waiting for you out there and that you'll find her before long.

Whether I love you or Calvin the most is not the issue. I married him. I made vows. He broke his vows. But ... I broke mine as well. All human beings, ourselves included, do our share of sin and ill deeds. But marriage is still marriage. For me not to forgive a husband facing battle who pleads for forgiveness, is beyond my capacity.

I loved every minute of it with you, but it is over.

Georgia

Rory toughed it out, determined not to let it take him down. Bad news from home was killer stuff. He made himself believe he'd weather it. Hell, Georgia was right. He knew how she loved him, but as she had told him on that final morning, "It was never on between us."

The initial pain was dulled by a climb to the top of a pyramid by moonlight and a bottle of deplorable Egyptian wine.

For morning after morning he awoke to remembering the letter, reading it again, bullying through the day, and turning fierce energy into the mule manual. One morning, he just plain knew he was going to keep on living.

There were a few corrections to make in the manual. Rory marked them carefully and jotted a requisition.

MAKE CORRECTIONS INDICATED AND PRINT THREE
COPIES ONLY. RETURN THEM TO PIG ISLAND AND GET SIG-
NATURE.

FIRST SJT. RORY LANDERS, 7TH NZLIGHTHORSE.

He put it in the message center basket, looked about the
office and secured it, flicked off the light, and locked the door.

There was a light down the hall coming from Lieutenant
Hubble's office. "Probably forgot to turn it off," Rory mumbled. He stepped in to see Lieutenant Jeremy with his face
buried in his folded arms on the desk. Rory turned to go, then
decided not to and cleared his throat.

Jeremy lifted his head. He looked awful. Rory closed the
door behind him. "You all right, sir?"

"Hell, no," Jeremy answered.

Rory saw a letter on the desk, apparently the object of
Lieutenant Jeremy's discomfort.

"Shall I go, sir?"

"No, no, no, sit down, Serjeant. Anything going on?"

"I made a final check of the manual. Looks fine. I ordered
three copies printed, one for us, one for the Major, and one to
submit to Dr. Ellsworth at Corps. Should I hold that one up?"

"Major Hubble is at staff school. He won't be back for several days, much to the battalion's sorrow, I'm sure. No, we can't
lose any more time. Send a copy through to Corps, I'll explain it
to the Major."

"Yes, sir."

"So it's really finished. Great job, Serjeant."

"We've got a super little squad, even . . . well, never mind."

"That asshole Yurlob?" Jeremy said.

"Well, let's put it this way. He's good. The soldiers in this
battalion will still be packing mules in their sleep when they are
old men."

It was apparent that Lieutenant Jeremy was in need of a
friend at this moment. He didn't seem to hang around with the
officers and certainly didn't hide his feelings about his brother.
Yet, despite the closeness of the gaffer squad, non-fraternization

rules between officer and enlisted men made intimate conversation extremely difficult.

"What happened, Lieutenant?" Rory dared ask.

Jeremy wanted to dump the centuries of ancient military tradition but merely shook his head.

"You're hurting, sir," Rory continued boldly. "We all feel very strongly about you, Lieutenant. You can trust us with your life. If we didn't have you between us and the Major, we couldn't have gotten our work done."

"I'm flattered, but you are exaggerating."

"May I say something that will never leave this room?"

"Go ahead."

"That's a real fine battalion the Major has built out there . . . but . . . enough is enough. If he pushes them any further he may be asking for trouble. Well, thank God the gaffers didn't have to deal with him. He would have fucked up our squad to a point where the entire battalion's training would be in trouble. We pushed through this manual and training schedule because of your protection."

"That's treason, you know. Mutiny," Jeremy said, smiling. "Let me tell you something, Serjeant. The last time I felt so good was when I was with men like you playing on the Boilermaker rugby squad. If I could have only held that moment of life, captured it, and put it in a bottle. Only time in my life I really felt like a . . . man . . . was with those mates. One of them in particular was my mentor, a big brother . . . even more."

Rory's heart raced.

"We do have a magical group of men: you—Tarbox, Chester, Modi . . . I really like Modi. Yurlob will come around. Bloody crime we just can't all go into Cairo and get pissed together."

"That would be a blast. You can count on us, Lieutenant, on duty or off. We're here for you. Excuse me, sir."

"Serjeant."

"Sir?"

"Don't go. I feel very comfortable and very strongly about the friendship you and I have developed. Jesus, I've got to unload."

Rory slipped into a chair and Jeremy soon closed his eyes

and spoke as if in a trance. The silent friendship had already begun by Jeremy's censoring Rory's letters. He was in on Rory's life. It was not difficult at all to suddenly find himself speaking about his own past.

Jeremy slowly wove the talk of his love affair with Molly O'Rafferty, his betrayal of her, his betrayal by mates of his own class, his years of drunken remorse. He spoke of the loss of his mother's love and the regaining of it. Time and again Conor Larkin's name came up, but in vain. Conor had already gone into an underground life when Jeremy and Molly ended their affair.

Jeremy then realized that this was the first time he had ever spoken the story aloud to anyone.

"This came today," Jeremy said, sliding the letter over the desk. "Please read it."

> My Dearest Son,
>
> Life for me has been a new morning fresh with dew cob-webbed on the rose trellis and a feeling of loveliness all about. Our peace and your devilish and charming letters have helped me emerge from Grandfather's second stroke (he still does his cognac and cigars) and the never-ending sadness of my failed marriage.
>
> Life is grand again. I am a busy lass these days trying to build and launch a ship or two, tending your growling grandfather, and much more laughter with Gorman, a mad Irishman who gives me the peace and warmth I've craved.

"She writes beautifully," Rory said.

"She writes as she is," Jeremy said. "She's a glorious woman, Rory." On hearing his first name spoken by the officer, Rory knew their relationship would not be as officer to enlisted man, except when on duty. "Call me Jeremy."

"I'd like that, but Jaysus, if I slip up in front of anyone."

"Fuck it, call me Jeremy."

"All right, cobber, Jeremy it is."

"Please read on."

. . . As you know we have searched for Molly. I did not want to write to you about slim clues and hopes that would turn out to be false. However, we got on to something solid. A trail was warm but lost because of the war.

I have agonized over whether or not to share information bound to bring you untold suffering. Neither Gorman nor myself nor any wise man I know can come to a sound judgment of the right or wrong of it. I do know our family became prisoners of lies and I'll hold back nothing from you.

Jeremy, your son is dead. He was stillborn in a workhouse in Glasgow. Apparently Molly was down with fever and the baby came early and poorly.

We were able to find that Molly entered a convent in Belgium and there our search comes to an end for the time being. The war blocks further inquiry.

There are more questions than answers. We cannot find the baby's grave. The Catholic Church is also very secretive about Molly's disappearance. We do not know if she joined an order as a novice or merely cloistered herself to work through her grief. There was a wisp of information that she may have gone to work in Belgium or France as an English teacher.

For all their perfidy, Freddie and your father have been devastated by the news. With you and Chris at war and Hester barren, the loss has affected them deeply.

Dear God, hang on, Jeremy. Tell me you are going to make it! No matter how this ultimately ends there is still richness and value to life for you if you dare live it.

If I could only hold you now, I'd give a kingdom. If only Conor Larkin could put his arm about your shoulder and speak his Irish magic to you.

I did not know how crushed I would be on learning of Conor's death. But, I have survived, as you must survive. Even laughter has returned and loving a new and wonderful man. Keep living, life is just too damned good.

Your loving,
Mother

Rory laid the letter down. "Sometimes I wish the fucking mail boat would sink before it gets here," he said. "Are you going to be all right?"

"I feel better just having talked about it. Yes, I'm going to tough it out. My days of rolling over and dying are done with."

The letter in Rory's breast pocket suddenly burned. He reached up, unbuttoned his pocket and withdrew it. Jeremy took it from his hand.

"From Georgia?"

Rory looked at him quizzically.

"I don't get any pleasure out of snooping, but I have to censor the outgoing mail. The married lady, heavy with lousy husband?"

"Aye," Rory grunted.

"After I read what goes out, I often wonder what comes back in," Jeremy said. "She writes beautifully as well." When he finished reading, the two letters lay touching, two more of war's uncounted casualties. The two men sat silent and motionless for a long, long spell.

"I guess this makes us pals to the death," Jeremy said at last. "I need a girl," he went on suddenly. "I need to close my eyes and maybe pretend. No, I've done enough pretending. I won't see Molly for five years, if ever, if she's alive . . . if . . . if . . . if. . . . Am I being a rotter for needing a woman?"

"We're soldiers heading for battle. We've nothing to come back to. Who's to pass judgment?"

"Hell, my family is a cascade, a landslide of judgments. Now Christopher, there's the king of judgments. He can do it because he is sexless. He's got a wife who is sexless. They can't procreate. Nothing excites him, nothing puts him into despair. He feels no moral pain or moral joy. Anger is his mother's milk, as though he were weaned from a pit bull. Well, once he terrified me, and my father terrified me, and the earldom terrified me. That's why I gave up Molly. No . . . the thought of poverty terrified me."

On speaking that truth, a season of hell burst out of him! He was free!

"If Molly is to be found, I'll find her."

"Ah, and the moment you do, you get on a ship and come to New Zealand." Rory saw that green gown of Georgia's lying in the ship's cabin. New Zealand green. "When it's over, I'm going back and start up my own acres."

"Molly sang for me all the time and the pure unvarnished Irish sentiment of it would bring me to tears. You danced for Georgia. She said so in one of your letters."

"Bare-butt naked while she was on bended knee."

"That's smashing! Molly and I . . . well . . . we did a lot of quiet holding."

"Nothing the matter with that. I've had more than my share of luck with the sheilas," Rory sent on. "Started in when I was fourteen. If I were to describe my idea of the absolute ideal woman she would look nothing like Georgia. But don't you know there is a particular feeling you get from only one person that makes her touch and words and mind and flesh and soul different from anything in the world? It pours into you and you suddenly know everything you didn't realize you needed."

He stopped suddenly. "I must forget Georgia," he whispered, "but I know what I know and I know my spiritual fulfillment will be on South Island, on my horse, riding in to some girl."

"New Zealand must be a hell of a place," Jeremy said. "I read it in every letter the lads write home. And I thought the ultimate love of loves was Ireland."

Ireland . . . New Zealand . . . Ireland . . . New Zealand . . . "Christ," Rory said, "let's consider our situation. In no way would either of us be practicing infidelity if we rehumanize ourselves. Only damned problem is, Cairo is a sewer."

"Yes," Jeremy agreed, "if we could only find our own oasis."

"God help me," Rory said, "but I know one, Jeremy!"

"Where?"

"On Zamalek Island between the Anglican cathedral and the Swedish Embassy. It's a very smart rental. The Villa Valhalla. You see—Chester, Johnny, and I came here loaded with money from bets on my fight in Fort Albany. Only problem . . . "

"What?"

"They won't rent it to enlisted personnel, or even an officer below the rank of colonel."

"You mean it's available by the week or month?"

"Yes, but if you even try something like that it could ruin your army career and put us behind bars."

"Jesus, Landers, I thought you had balls."

"There's balls and there's balls. The three of us are ready to go home in chains, but you're the son of an earl."

"What about Modi? Is he in?"

"Absolutely. He's our musician."

"Yurlob?"

"I wouldn't bring him in for a while. You know with the Sikhs it's no smoking and liquor and . . . he's real British Army. Wait now, Jeremy."

"Give me the details and swear the other lads to secrecy."

"You sure about this, Jeremy?"

"Yeah," he answered with an infectious smile that had won him many miles in the past.

Jeremy welcomed himself into Farouk el Farouk's office and, as coffee was ordered, he put on his father's most deliciously nauseous attitude. Farouk el Farouk was impressed with Chester Goodwood, and now the Lieutenant, for their persistence. His mind raced through his listings on what else he could possibly sell these people . . . in their own allowed environment . . . in place of the Villa Valhalla.

"My cards," Jeremy said laying a pair of them before the Egyptian. Farouk el Farouk squinted through his glasses and stared at the first one.

FIRST LIEUTENANT JEREMY HUBBLE
SEVENTH NEW ZEALAND LIGHT HORSE

He was about to reject Jeremy when the second card caught his attention massively and his eyes became nailed to it.

LORD JEREMY HUBBLE
THE VISCOUNT OF COLERAINE

"I have other credentials," Jeremy said, gazing out of the window. "I am a vice president and member of the board of directors of Weed Ship & Iron in Belfast, and my father is the Earl of Foyle."

Farouk el Farouk had to peer around gingerly to ascertain if this was real or a joke. Jeremy took it away from him by sliding a Cook's Travel draft over the desk made out for three hundred sterling.

"My expression of gratitude for your future services. Mr. Garfield, the manager, has cleared me and is expecting you to cash it."

Hand to heart, free arm extended like a baritone in mid-aria—"Lord Hubble, forgive me, but you know I must be extremely careful . . . I didn't realize . . . we will get Villa Valhalla prepared immediately. Do you have any special desires?"

"Hummm," Jeremy said nasally. "I want a tiptop hush-hush housekeeper, one who understands service to aristocracy."

"Sonya runs the villa for exceptional clients. She is requested constantly. She is a delight. Very well connected for *anything* you desire . . . dancers and more intimate company. I give you also George."

"Who the devil is George?"

"Only the best Terrier in Cairo. He is Christian, seventeen, and, I assure you, very well connected for *anything*."

"Yes, I don't want you to accept too much money from my lads. They may want to favor their girls but the food and beverage is on my account."

"We are well connected with only the best markets and alcohols."

"And, no problem with the police."

"I am very well connected with the police."

"I will pay you a hundred and fifty a week. I will pay half the week in advance and the other half at the end of the week, provided we continue to be satisfied."

"I am very well connected and I am your humble servant."

"Yes, so you are."

FIELD MANUAL FOR MULE TRANSPORTATION

Foreword

The Golden Mule Rule: LOVE THY MULE AS THYSELF

The mule's back is as of much value as your ass.

Each chapter will explain to you a simplified lesson on each phase in your relationship with your animal.

Before we get into individual chapters, here are a number of random facts and rules. You soldiers are about to partner up with the finest four-legged warrior the world has ever known.

The MULE has known combat for three thousand years.

The MULE was used by the Roman Legion.

Fourteen thousand MULES were used by the Spaniards in the Battle of Granada, which stopped the heathen Moslems from overrunning Christian Europe.

The MULE is the crown prince of mountain artillery.

Napoleon, himself, proudly rode a MULE.

Mules vs. Horses

Because the Seventh New Zealand Light Horse was formed as cavalry, you might believe you lost the beauty contest by becoming a MULE transport battalion. Consider these *facts* before you ask for a transfer to the infantry.

A MULE is more intelligent than a horse.

A MULE is stronger than a horse.

A MULE is more sure-footed than a horse.

In difficult terrain you can depend on the MULE's judgment to feel his way, whereas a horse in the same situation might just plunge over the edge.

A MULE has better eyesight than a horse.

A MULE does not panic anywhere near as quickly or as often as a horse in the same situation.

A MULE has far greater stamina than a horse. The pack-horse may cover more miles in a single day but the pack MULE will go on day after day long after the horse has quit. The MULE will not quit until he/she is dead.

The MULE carries loads in terrain you can't take a horse.

A MULE carries more load than a horse.

A MULE does not spook under gunfire or brush fire.

Some MULES are as fast as horses.

A MULE can endure heat better than a horse.

A Few Tips on You and Your Mule

Dispense with all MULE jokes. MULE jokes are not funny.

Treat your MULE with kindness.

Always have oats in your pocket for your MULE as a reward.

Water your MULE from your hat so he/she will not over-drink.

See to the comfort of your MULE before you sleep. Spread hay for your MULE, tell him/her you are grateful for the day's work he/she put in.

Tell your MULE you love him/her often.

Your MULE likes to be tickled under his/her eye with your fingers.

Your MULE is a dainty drinker. Do not let your MULE

become a greedy drinker or it will unhinge his/her bowels.

If you must punish your MULE, your displeasure is usually enough. *NEVER ABUSE YOUR MULE.*

We LEAD our MULES. You do not drive them, unless you must drive yourself.

Do not use rope to shackle your MULE. Your MULE will chew the ropes. Use short chains. Your MULE will also chew wood. Do not tie your MULE so he/she can chew wood.

MULES drown if their load is not centered and it pulls them to one side or another. *NEVER TOPLOAD YOUR MULE IN A WATER-CROSSING SITUATION.*

The MULE is not a fastidious eater. In times of utmost shortages, the MULE will eat almost anything and survive. A horse would die from the same diet.

THE MULE IS A GREAT SENTRY, DAY AND NIGHT. YOU WILL BE QUITE SAFE FROM SURPRISE ATTACK OR AMBUSH BECAUSE YOUR MULE WILL GIVE YOU WARNING.

Random Little Doodads

Consider your MULE as a true cobber and partner. MULES seldom fret or scare. If only our mates had the same lovely temperaments.

MULES are not vicious. They are made that way by stupid handlers. (Wild mules which cannot be tamed are usually destroyed shortly after birth.)

Give your Jack or Janet a pleasant name that he/she will enjoy and not a name of derision.

Because you are all people with backgrounds with horses, you will find many facts in the ensuing chapters are things you already know. As well as the differences between the two animals, there are numerous similarities.

Chapter One: Getting to Know Your Animal

Chapter Two: The Pack Equipment
Chap . . .

"*Oh my God!*" Major Christopher Hubble shrieked. "Oh my God!" he repeated, beating his fists on the desk top, wild-eyed. "Oh my God!" He pulled at his hair.

A clerk from the next office tumbled in. "Are you all right, sir?"

"Get my fucking brother . . . get Lieutenant Hubble in here. *Immediately!*"

By the time Jeremy arrived, Chris had calmed to a light simmer. gurgling under his breath. "You sent this ludicrous travesty to Corps?" he rumbled low.

"I wasn't going to leave it sitting here and lose six days while you were at staff school."

"Charming, charming, bloody fucking charming."

"Something wrong?" Jeremy asked.

"It reads," he gnashed out, "as though it were written by some low comic in a sleazy song and dance hall in Soho." Chris tore it in half. "You're bloody mad trying to pass this shit off as a British military manual."

"I turned pages in to you every night. You were too damned busy to read it because of your mania that everyone ate, slept, marched, saluted, and shit by the numbers."

"My clear intention was to read it in one sitting when it was completed and go over it with the gaffers. I did not instruct you to send it to Corps!"

"You told me that this book was entirely my responsibility."

"I did NOT, NOT, NOT tell you to send it to Corps!"

The Major's phone interrupted. Chris lifted the receiver and jumped to attention, swooning as he listened. "That was General Brodhead's office. He wants me, now."

"I'll go along with you and explain him what happened."

"You've done enough. You stay right here. Don't you move. Your gaffer squad is under barrack arrest." He paused. "Executive Officer! Captain North!"

"Coming, sir."

"Captain North, write up an order for the battalion to prepare and stand by for a route march tonight to the Wadi Muzzam and get it over to Corps for approval, at once."

"Fifty miles in the sand!" Jeremy cried.

Chris slammed the door and was on his way.

"Be seated, Chris," General Brodhead said.

Oh Lord, the manual was on the General's desk.

Brodhead held up the instruction book. "Who wrote this?" he asked.

"The gaffer squad, sir. I can explain."

"Explain? Yes, go ahead and explain."

"The ultimate responsibility is squarely mine. I should like to say that there was a real bollix in communications. You see, sir, I have been drilling my battalion as a first priority to whip them into fighting shape before their mules arrived and left the manual up to the gaffers with full intention of reviewing it personally. It was finished and sent to Corps without my approval when I was at staff school."

The farther from the green fields of Ulster and the closer to battle, the saltier Llewelyn Brodhead became. He banged his fist on the table several times and Chris blinked in unison.

"Give these gaffers some time away."

"You mean put them in the stockade before court-martial?"

Brodhead roared with laughter. "Well, you do have a sense of humor after all, Chris."

"I'm not quite certain . . . "

"Give them four-day leave. Best damned manual I've read in thirty-two years! Cuts through all the shit. Just the kind of thing you need to get to the point out in the field. Clear, explicit, humorous—that's what these fucking manuals need, humor. Too bad some twat in the War Office will assign some prig to rewrite it with a corkscrew. Captain Ellsworth has ordered seven hundred copies for the Zion Mule Corps."

"Well," Chris said, breathing more freely as he removed the noose from his neck, "I do admit I was just a tad nervous."

"God, these boys must have really burned the midnight oil. Old Jeremy has come through for us, big!"

In a cheerful mood and with his favorite young officer before him, Brodhead wanted to lift his own loneliness and apprehensions. Say a few things aloud. Things that had brought on insomnia. Things that . . . oh, better stuff it in, he thought.

"How soon will your battalion be ready?"

"Two or three weeks of intense schooling. A month to two months when we get our mules."

"Good," Brodhead said, not containing what he had just tried to contain. "The opening naval salvo on Gallipoli is a matter of a few weeks away. The *Queen Mary*, our top new superdreadnought, has completed its shakedown cruise and will be en route shortly to join our fleet. The French are forming up at Toulon."

"Does give one a bit of a start, doesn't it, sir?"

"Our troops are not ready, Chris. My Anzacs in particular could use a solid three or four more months of training. Fortunately, Darlington—"

"I understand your feelings about Darlington."

"Fortunately, General Darlington insists he will not invade until the 29th Division arrives from England. It's a veteran division, one of our best. Is Darlington playing it safe or is Darlington timid?" he wondered aloud. "Truth is, we haven't faced a modern white army since Napoleon. Darlington may be too old school for this kind of operation, too many new wrinkles in this landing from the sea. You've been in on many of the planning sessions."

"Yes, sir."

"You see how he hedges. We haven't much beach, particularly if we have to land from the Adriatic side. A lot of our thinking is based on the fact that the Turks are exhausted from the Balkan War and that their main army is tied up on the Russian front. But bear in mind—the Balkan union broke its skull trying to capture Gallipoli and lost a number of warships to the Turkish coastal guns."

"Shouldn't our naval bombardment pretty well reduce the Turkish guns, sir?"

"Too fucking much is being made of naval gunfire. The Germans have put one of their top men, General von Limon, in command of the Dardanelles defense. The Turks have opened an ammunition factory south of Constantinople. There are red hot radicals full of fight in the Turkish officers corps. From what little intelligence we can glean out of that Gallipoli wilderness, von Limon is going to stuff five or six divisions in there.

"As for the coastal guns," he continued to unload, "von Limon will replace them with mobile howitzer batteries. The coastal guns are meant to play pitty-pat with warships. Howitzers can loop fire down on troops and keep changing locations."

After a consideration, Brodhead dropped the bombshell. "We have to hit the beach running. The British must take the Achi Baba hilltop five miles inland and we must take Chunuk Bair, also five miles inland, in the first week. If Darlington dawdles we are in for one long hot summer. Chris, when the history of this war is writ, I absolutely guarantee you that more men will be killed and wounded by the machine gun than by all other weapons combined. The Gallipoli Peninsula has more places to hide machine guns than any piece of ground the British Empire has ever tried to capture."

"We'll take those hills, sir."

Proper stuff coming from a proper officer, Brodhead thought. *We'll take those hills, sir.* Shit! He did not share his final thought with the young major that if he were defending Gallipoli with his Anzacs, he could hold out forever.

The general's aide knocked and entered, then laid an order on the desk for his signature.

"I thought that as long as Major Hubble was here you might as well approve this for him."

"Let's see here," Brodhead said adjusting his glasses. "Forced night march exercise, battalion strength, to ... Jesus Christ ... Wadi Muzzam ... hummm." He dismissed his aide with a wave of the hand.

"Bit drastic, what?" Brodhead said. "Shouldn't your lads be concentrating on their mule training?"

"We don't have any mules, sir. Until we do there is only so much schooling we can give them. Otherwise, I intend to have the Seventh the most battle-ready battalion in the Corps."

"This wouldn't be entailing some kind of collective punishment, would it, Chris?"

Chris held tight so as not to fumble his thoughts. He had laid them out as his lullaby night after night for just this moment.

"This is a cavalry battalion, sir, and not a very refined one. They are roughnecks. They were furious to be turned into muleteers. There has not been a single morning that I haven't had to go to the stockade and collect dozens of them from their punch-ups in Cairo."

"Maybe you're caught in a vicious cycle. After a night march to Wadi Muzzam, aren't they going to try to dismantle Cairo? Chris, before you answer, I was going to speak to you on this matter. You have invoked twice as many punishments as any other battalion commander in the Corps."

"I daresay, sir, my battalion is twice as good as any in the Anzacs."

"Chris, one of the reasons we held the staff seminar was to clarify our traditional role with the colonials. God knows there isn't a more imperial man than myself, but we have to realize that each Commonwealth has its own system of social order. Indeed, we cannot go strictly by the book as we do with our British soldiers. Isn't that your understanding?"

"I'd rather not say, sir."

"I'd rather you do."

Llewelyn Brodhead watched Chris turn into Roger Hubble right before his eyes. The words were the same, the look was even the same.

"My grandfather, Sir Frederick, was a Victorian entrepreneur . . . always proud of his humble beginnings . . . playing the game with the Orange lodges, marching alongside the lads on the Twelfth of August . . . made an art of knowing his workers by first name, pretended to share their sorrows. Well, he's ended up with a public company and unions in his yards."

"I think probably a new era has overtaken him, Chris. No one in his right mind would consider Sir Frederick Weed a soft man."

"Perhaps," Chris agreed reluctantly.

"Do go on."

"I rather liken the Army to my father's earldom. The people tilling his fields and operating his factories are his soldiers, in a manner of speaking. They are there to fulfill the mission of the earldom, to continue our way of life. We cannot get involved with sentimentality over the hard luck of this worker or that farmer and his family. If we were to cave in to sentimentality, we would have lost the earldom during the great famine. If we here now in the Anzac Corps cave in to sentimentality, we will lose the empire."

Brodhead had always thought he had a hard man in Christopher Hubble. Now he knew exactly how hard. He was one of those few officers who seem to thrive on the hatred of his men and in return builds an awesome battalion. Yet, almost all these officers go one step too far.

"I agree we must have their utmost respect," Brodhead said, "but we must also respect them. I'm setting aside this night march. We don't want these boys to get a feeling they are out there fighting for nothing. I am instructing you to get on with your mule transport."

"It would be simpler if we had mules to work with. The Zion Mule Corps has already received a hundred animals."

"You'll learn that we colonials get the leftovers."

"I daresay, the Jews are not exactly British."

"But they are serving British divisions. Speaking of Jews, one of my brigade commanders is a Jew. Quite competent."

"Really, sir? A Jewish brigade commander? Which one?"

"Colonel Monash, the Aussie."

"Well, that's empire."

Brodhead gave the nod for Chris to leave.

"Oh Chris, who did the actual writing of your instruction

manual? I mean, the chap who put the words down. Very clever."

"Private Chester Goodwood. He's a member of the gaffer squad."

"Put a couple of chevrons on him. Corporal, for now."

"Yes, sir. He is equally good with numbers. He's the son of Sir Stanford Goodwood, a banker in Hong Kong."

"Sir Stanford Goodwood?"

"Yes, sir."

"Lord, I knew him years ago. I thought he was rather nelly queer, you know. At that time it was rumored he had a penchant for young boys. So he has a son? Well, probably has something to do with continuity and all that."

CHAPTER
67

Cairo, February 1915

Despite the flood of warriors into Cairo, Sonya Kulkarian's preferred, classical, elite, and lavish entertainments were not much in demand. No longer were the great sheikhs and princes of the Arabian peninsula able to gain easy access to Cairo because of the war, and when they did manage to come, it was long on business and short on bombastic orgies. Everything was business. The wealthy of Cairo, a staple for her enterprise, no longer established their little oases of relaxation in their headlong rush for war money.

British officials and generals had mostly been too tightfisted to avail themselves. Now and again, an off-horse Englishman liked and could afford her entertainers, but British pickings were lean.

But what did it matter? At the age of forty-one Sonya Kulkarian had packed in her fortune and was independently independent.

Did it matter that the royal palace had only called once since hostilities began? No! Truth be known, service to royalty was only good as a credential. Otherwise, they were impossible to serve. Their credit was hardly a thing of beauty. You cannot demand payment in advance from royalty.

So it did not matter. Moreover, the madams who had once been competitors jumped aboard the war wagon and cheapened their parties and their services.

Sonya, of course, kept in contact with the best of her girls, for contact was everything.

She was very happy, in fact, to receive Farouk el Farouk. He asked her to set up the Villa Valhalla for a small group of only five from the military who would be in Egypt for two, three, four months. It sounded perfect until he told her it was being leased by a corporal, two serjeants, a low-ranking officer, and a Palestinian Jew without rank.

"You ask this of Sonya? I have served the King's nephews and cousins and uncles!"

"And complained every minute of the time," he reminded her. "Do I come to Sonya Kulkarian to embarrass her? No. I assure you, my treasure, what they lack in rank, they make up in ... " He twittered the thumb against his third finger and his forefinger. "The lieutenant is of aristocratic nobility. He is heir to half of Ireland and has a most generous hand with the cheque."

"I don't deal with trash."

That may have been a harsh conclusion for a woman of her calling but Sonya Kulkarian was a Circassian. The Circassians were known to be particularly brutal to their women. The men obsessed that they had royal blood. In fact, some still kept slaves in the countryside.

The Circassian colony had been in Cairo for seventy years, though aloof from fellow Moslems, and had grown successful.

They had originated from the mountain regions of the Caucasus in southern Russia. After making the Haj to Mecca, many of them remained in the region. In the middle of the last century there had been a mass migration rather than accept a new political boundary and a ruler from outside their borders. If nothing else, they were the ultimate fierce fighters.

Oh, we know Sikhs are fierce, Turks are fierce, Serbs are fierce, Berbers are fierce, Cossacks are fierce, but one had better believe that the Circassians were the fiercest of the fierce. Their uniforms spoke of glorious soldiers, from their short boots to their high fur hats and great swatches of gold braid and flowing moustaches.

Because of their reputations, their riding skills, and their colorful attire, many Arab kings and princes used them as personal palace guards, which further enhanced their legend.

Sonya's business was for the elite and her associates were impeccable in manners and performance. It was the clients who were the pigs.

Having gained a sufficient fortune by her early thirties, Sonya managed properties leased for a month or more for those who could pay the high passage.

At forty-one, Sonya Kulkarian had lost some of her incredible native beauty but had the wisdom of the years in the movement of her hips and, what was more, she spoke English.

"So, try it for a month," Farouk el Farouk pleaded. "Their money is outrageous."

"I do not want five soldier desert rats who will smash furniture!"

"They can't be any worse than royalty," he said.

It was not wise to reject Farouk el Farouk's entreaties. Not that she needed him any longer, but one did have to keep one's connections. After the war, believe me, she had said, retirement to Italy . . . or France . . . or Spain.

After all, a party was still a party if it was a good one. And she missed the parties. Sonya agreed to a trial at the Villa Valhalla. She had the tiles shined, the rooms filled with flowers, the liquor cabinets packed, the crystal bowls laden with fruits and melons, the central fountain turned on, new silk coverings purchased, and pillows made, laid in the most sensual of incense and candles and lounging robes and oils and great towels. . . .

For what? A corporal, two serjeants, a low-ranking officer, and a Jew? She did not know what to expect except the worst.

Serjeant Major Johnny was the first to arrive. He threw off his clothing, jumped in the fountain, and just lay there for almost an hour after which he dragged himself up to one of the bedrooms and slept for the next five hours.

The Jew arrived later in the evening. He did not even bother to take off his clothing but plunged into the pool and groaned in ecstasy and found a second bedroom and slept until midnight.

Both of them were extremely courteous and made funny jokes. The Jew spoke some Arabic and, pointing to his accordion, warned her he had the voice of a god. Sonya was now puzzled.

The next day the young aristocratic officer came. He merely dangled his feet in the pool until she assured him it was all right to strip and enjoy.

Jeremy was completely out of the ordinary for an aristocratic nobleman. He was sweet, altogether different from any titled man she had ever known. He commanded no one, ordered no one about, did not shout, exhibited magnificent manners, cursed no one, and meditated half the night through on the veranda.

Little sweet Chester, a pet mouse. Why, his face was not manly enough to carry a beard. Such a nice boy. She had to almost force him into a tub and washed him herself before she let him slumber. He played backgammon with her. What a sweet boy. He played the game very, very well.

So far, so good. She would know better after the first party how it would go.

Rory did not arrive until the fourth morning, when the others had returned to camp.

"You are the world-famous Sonya," Rory said.

"And you are the missing Serjeant Rory."

"Sonya, show me that fountain, I'm dying."

When his shirt came off revealing his torso, she gawked. As the rest of him sank into the fountain, there was a stirring, no, a jolt that had not been expected. In manner of truth, Sonya Kulkarian's only feeling toward men for many years was hatred. For herself personally there were her women friends, though women were not entirely satisfactory. With women, she most loved the dancing and rolling about, the oils and the songs. Although her hatred of men was genuine, lesbianism was not one of her true desires.

Every so often a man would jolt her such. Not only was his body incredible, but this lad also had good mischief in his manner.

With her anxiety for the safety of her girls and the villa

calmed, she immediately liked them, despite herself. For the first two visits she believed all they wanted was sleep.

Although he was not of the highest rank, Serjeant Rory took charge because of his leadership tendencies. He went through the villa with her, telling her of this and that for the comfort of the men and he spoke with great familiarity, as though he and she had known each other for ten thousand lifetimes. He spoke about the women and seemed to know what kind of girl each man would want.

"Not different girls? But all men want different girls," Sonya said.

"Johnny Tarbox will want many women and he may get difficult, but he is not going to hurt anyone. I think the other three might want to settle with one girl. Peace and comfort and a sense of humor."

Sonya smiled as her mind flashed on several women. How much fun it would be not to have to battle with angry drunks.

"Sonya, love, I want you to try to find someone very special for Chester."

"The little corporal? He is only a child."

"Yeah, but don't get into a backgammon game with him."

"I already have."

"He's close to a genius," Serjeant Rory said. "But we may have a virgin on our hands."

"I know just the experienced woman who will bring him along properly."

"No. I want someone with a young girl's face and body. Someone who looks sweet and innocent. Maybe bring her into the kitchen to work and let Chester think he's made her on his own."

"Yes . . . of course . . . they start young here. But why do you want him deceived? He will know she is a prostitute sooner or later."

"Chester wants to be deceived. Let him believe he's in love before he goes to war."

"Why?"

"Because he's never received a letter from home or anywhere

else. He's sixteen. Maybe you know a girl who wants to be in love with a soldier boy as well."

"You are more than a brother," Sonya said. "He will meet Shaara."

"I love you, Sonya Clipclopian."

"You worry over everyone to make certain they are happy. You said, 'Find someone for Jeremy to keep him from being sad.' I find her. But what about yourself, Serjeant Rory?"

"I'm healing," he said making the mistake of looking into Sonya's eyes. Jaysus, what Egyptian women can do with their eyes! It must have been all those centuries of working behind a veil. They thought with their eyes, flirted, sang, danced, spoke, flashed anger. . . . No missing the meaning in Sonya's eyes. She was voluptuous and she knew the art of hips and cleavage and how to show just enough belly . . . just to him . . . and those eyes.

"I'm healing," he muttered.

"I am healer," she said.

"Not yet," Rory said.

In a few weeks Sonya had come to think of them as her boys. Not a single one of them pissed or defecated on the floor. What was so utterly amazing was the way they cared for each other dearly without being perverts . . . and the way Serjeant Rory saw to their peace and comfort.

Only Johnny Tarbox showed irritation now and then, and always after lovemaking. When he was there, Rory was on him quickly and finally Johnny quit acting out.

They arrived either in the morning or evening, from one to four of them. Once in every week or so all five were together overnight and it was party time.

There was abundance of laughter, such that Sonya could not believe. Realizing they were going to be respectful to the villa and not wreck it, she introduced them to the water pipe. Unknown to the gaffers, she mixed in reasonable amounts of the finest hashish, a brand of Lebanon #1 called Seventh Heaven.

The weekly parties became joyhouses of abandon . . . men and women belly dancing and teasing, oil wrestling, and above it all the highly emotional voice of Modi singing tragic Russian songs, which often brought on bouts of tears.

Three whole days and four whole nights with all of them at the Villa Valhalla! Each except Rory with someone to hold on to through the night that gave relief from all that sand and heat and of all they had given up to be in Egypt.

Some nights! No need to hurry the party this night. A seduction of peace fell over them. Chester had learned the tambour and played wildly during the belly dances. Now, in this state of subdued euphoria he beat the drum softly. Shaara's eyes were glazed.

Modi took a deep puff of the water pipe and picked up his accordion. One of the girls, Neva, knew how to play the flute. It was all very serene.

"How did you manage to get liberty passes for us all, Lieutenant Jeremy?" the Serjeant Major asked.

"Research, we're researching."

"You know, cobbers," Rory said, "I'm getting a little guilt on about the Serj, old Yurlob."

"I don't know," Modi said. "I think he might not be comfortable here."

"What the hell, we're all from different places," Rory argued.

"No, we're all from the same place," Johnny said. "Yurlob is from a different place. I've certainly tried to befriend him."

"Me, too," Chester said, waving as he tapped the tambour. He was next on the pipe. "He's got a real thing with the inferior/superior business."

"I think they've got a pretty vicious caste system," Jeremy said.

"He isn't a Hindu," Chester said, "so you'd think he might be more open with us."

"The Punjabs are Sikhs," Johnny said, "half-Hindu, half-Moslem or something. They still have a caste system. It's in his blood."

"How do you know?" Rory asked.

"Someone in the Marines told me about them. He served up in the Northwest Territory of India. They're fierce fighters."

"What is life without secrets?" she asked.

"You got secrets?" Chester asked Shaara. Shaara giggled.

"No secrets."

"Yeah, I'll bet."

"Do we have secrets from each other?" Jeremy asked. "I mean the five of us?"

The discussion slowed as the pipe went around one more time and everyone had got the notion he was in a dream in this place. How many hours on the battle line would be spent with memories of this? Too bad all the poor blokes drinking that rat poison in the old city couldn't have just a scent of this. They had it because the five of them cared for one another enough to keep the secret. Indeed, Villa Valhalla was a great secret the gaffer squad hid from the entire Anzac corps.

"We're all secret people," Johnny said. "There is the Johnny Tarbox who wants to be your friend and opens up enough to let you in. But the friendship only rises so high or falls so deep. Johnny lets you know what he wants you to know and hides what he doesn't want you to know. And Johnny tries to make you think he is what he isn't. We all put on a show, don't we? God, what did you put in this pipe tonight, Sonya? I'm really floating. Where did those damned words come from?"

"Deep inside," Modi said. "Yes, we all have secrets."

They looked from one to the other, not with suspicion but faced with a sudden fact that they knew each other and loved each other for a certain reason, because they had to take on a war together, but there was so very much one would never confide with the others. Trust? Good lord, no question that each trusted the other with his life, but not his secrets.

They all reclined on the pillows and felt what they needed to feel, a woman who pretended she cared for him. She had her secrets as well, but each man was adrift in his own buried thoughts.

The center court was afloat with scented fumes and quivering lights and one could hear the wail of the muezzin from the minarets calling the faithful to prayer, or suddenly smell the aromas from the cargoes of coffee and spices from the single sail feluccas ... and the singsong of a hundred thousand far-off voices ...

And soft silk pillows and wispy curtains and a woman to hold . . . a woman to hold . . . a woman to hold . . .

Either Chester and Shaara fell in love or were gob-smacked with exotica. They both knew they were playing but knew of nothing happier to play.

Mirror, mirror, on the wall, who holds the secret of us all? The doors inside the men were steel, clanged shut where secrets remain secrets.

Each man, no matter how floaty and brotherly he was of the moment, understood he must hang on to his secrets. He must never tell them about the ugly side that would change him in their eyes.

All of them had declared to the others their braveries, conquests, strengths, and all that was necessary to make them seem tall. They were reluctant to spell out their evils. Some of their evils were unknown even to themselves. No matter how potent Sonya's drug, they could never admit cowardice or moments of humiliation.

Yet they held a five-man confessional . . . all of it unspoken, unadmitted, the conversation that never took place.

You know, mates, I've bragged about my mother being this beautiful actress and song-and-dance queen, famous in her own right. Well, that's a fucking lie. My mother was a mining-camp whore. She damn near killed my father, first with her pussy, then she stabbed him with a knife when she was caught. She ran off with a pimp to the mining fields of Nevada. I got one Christmas card and one birthday card from her in my life. So, old Johnny Tarbox became the dandy, the Serjeant Major of the New Zealand Honor Guard. It was a fast and easy way to get the sheilas to spread their legs. I wanted the married ones, that's what. When I pumped them and they'd scream with passion, I wanted to choke them . . . to break their necks. I saw my mother twenty times, creeping in to our caravan when some hunky snuck in behind her and I could see her fucking him through cracks in the blinds. They're all whores . . . all of them . . .

*   *   *

The candle flames did great things off the white archways. Mordechai Pearlman became mesmerized by the fire. FIRE! He always got trapped into staring at fire. A thousand nightmares of fire. Will I ever be free from the fire?

My father slaughtered animals ritually and it disgusted me. That is why I went through the Veterinarian College in Kiev despite what it was for a Jew. For two years I slept with the animals in the college because I was too poor to have a room.

I was a good veterinarian. I traveled from shtetl to shtetl, all the little Jewish villages in my part of the Pale. You ask, what is the Pale? It is invisible borders in which all Jews must live. No Moscow, no professions, no merchants, no crafts that will compete with the Gentiles. Except I am a veterinarian much too good for my own good. The Ukrainians (and I spit) use me for their animals, I am so good.

When I married it was an arranged marriage because that was the custom, meeting my wife on our wedding day, and I came to love her. Malka. An ordinary good woman. She gave me a daughter. My baby was the dearest treasure of my life . . . I can't even speak her name to this day . . . I am several villages away when I learn that the Cossacks are going to make a pogrom in my village. I rush back. Everything is burning.

Was this the moment of my great cowardice? The Cossacks were still riding through the village. All I could do was watch the fire and hide in the outskirts.

Malka had been raped several times and my daughter decapitated. Should I have not rushed into the flames to save them?

I fled but was picked up by the police and impressed into the Czar's army. I am a prime find because I can treat horses and livestock. I know what is going to happen . . . shipment to Siberia to a remote post and then they'd beat on me day and night to make me convert. It happened to many from my village. They took Christian names and married and were never heard from again.

Once more I fled, to Palestine. Don't ask how. It was two years of agony as well as a miracle to reach Palestine. I go to

*work on the projects for the Baron Rothschild in Jewish fields
and later I become a founding member of a communal settlement
in Galilee.*

*I am a notable veterinarian for settlements in the area and I
take care of the Arab animals as well. We Jews of Palestine had a
rotten life under the Turks and were very much for the English
when the war broke out. The Turks rounded up dozens of my
comrades and tortured them as spies, beat them on the soles of
their feet . . . some were crippled. So I fled again, to Egypt along
with hundreds of other Jews, and soon we volunteered to make
up the Zion Mule Corps, although the British would not let us be
official members of the army. GOD! WHY DO THE FLAMES
LEAP SO WHEN THE CANDLES BECOME LOWER!
FUCKING FIRES!*

Modi's woman was large because, like an Arab, he liked
large! Her name? Not Malka . . . her name? She is Maat. She is
hushing me and wiping my brow. I will melt into her. . . .

*God in heaven, I can never let go of my secret. The gaffers
will despise me. These are my cobbers . . . the only people . . .
except for Uncle Ned Thornberry . . . who ever cared tuppence
for me.*

*Chester Goodwood was the name the Chinese forger put on
my documents so it would appear that I was a relative of Sir
Stanford Goodwood.*

*My name is Stanley Thornberry. I'm a bastard born in
London. My ma died from the consumption when I was six. I
fled the orphanage when I was seven, preferring to work the
streets. That didn't last too long. I ended up in the borstal, a
thief, before my ninth birthday.*

*My one relative was Ned Thornberry, but he lived in Hong
Kong. Uncle Ned ran the stables for the show horses and the polo
horses of Sir Stanford Goodwood.*

*Ned promised the court he'd give me a good home, and Sir
Stanford signed a letter for me, so I was shipped to Hong Kong.
Working for Uncle Ned is how I became a horseman.*

I thought what Sir Stanford was doing was pure kindness. He sent me to a proper school where I learned to speak correct English. Everyone was stunned at my mathematics skills. Sir Stanford provided me with a private tutor to learn banking and accounting and by the age of fourteen I was mastering all the ledgers.

. . . Kindness, was it, now? He had long-range plans for me. Uncle Ned passed away just after my fifteenth birthday and Sir Stanford invited me to move into the mansion . . . and I realized what he had been planning all those years.

. . . I was like a prisoner, kept on the grounds until he was sure I wouldn't run away. He came to my bed night after night making me do all the pansy things. Threatening my life if I made trouble, he also promised me I'd go far in the banking business if I became his nancy boy. I pretended to be going along with it until I could run for freedom.

My chance came just as the war was about to begin. I got this Chinaman to make false documents and I stowed away. I thank God every night for Rory and Johnny. How can I ever tell them what Sir Stanford and I did? I would become lower than shit in their eyes.

I know Rory fixed me up with Shaara and I know Shaara really makes believe also. I am going to become rich after the war. I'll give all my friends here a great deal of money so life will be easier for them. I know I won't see Shaara again but if I do I'll see that she gets a great deal of money, as well.

Leilah's heavy lips fell down to Jeremy's neck and she kissed him and he groaned and she whispered to go away and to the bedroom. Although the kisses were pleasing, she knew his mind was in a place far away. . . .

My secret, which only Rory knows, was my cowardice and my terror of poverty. My secret of secrets which I cannot share with even Rory is that I should like to kill my father.

Before I did I would make him recite every pain he has imposed on his peasants and his workers and make him beg for mercy for every foul deed he has ever done in his life. After I shot him, I'd burn Hubble Manor down, except for the Long Hall and the Great Screen.

Then I would renounce my title. I'd give away the lands of the earldom to those who deserved it, those who had toiled on it. Like other Irish Protestant patriots, like Theobald Wolfe Tone, Robert Emmet, and Charles Stewart Parnell, I would become a republican. What I mean is . . . I want to be an Irish Irishman.

Jaysus, Rory thought, the party has turned grim. Or has it? Is it not better to tell truths to yourself in the presence of friends, even though it is done in silence? Look at them. Each is in his own milky way.

I knew from the moment I wrote my first letters to my sisters and Tommy that I had always been their master and made them live somewhere beneath me. I've been a real prick to my brother Tommy. It wasn't Tommy's fault he was anointed by the Squire as the favorite son. It wasn't Tommy's fault he wasn't the brightest kid in South Island. I've gone out of my way to make certain he felt like a dunce when I might have helped him and taken care of him, as a decent brother should.

I see now, as I read the letters of my brothers and sisters and even my mom, I should have been a far better brother to them.

I was too damned busy establishing my prowess.

My da did me wrong, but even so there were a thousand times he fished around for a smile or a kind word from me and all I did was twist the knife or get his kind attention by wrecking something, by showing how tough I was. Maybe, if I had tried, he might have started trying, and things would have become lighter between us.

Secret? I'm scared of going to Ireland with the name of Larkin. What can any man do with the shadow of Conor Larkin hovering over him? But I'm going, and I'll do what is expected of a Larkin. That is the only way I can earn my passage back to New Zealand.

Secret? I'll hate myself if my prayer really comes true. I'll

*hate myself for the rest of my life, but the TRUTH is, I hope that
Dr. Calvin Norman gets killed in the war . . .*

"Hey!" Modi called through the creamy mist. "Everyone is
so passionately sad. What have I here? A room full of Russians?
I have a favorite idea."

"Is your idea about your public life, your private life, or
your secret life?"

"Definitely, a secret. Chester, stop playing the tambour so I
can tell everyone my secret idea."

Chester was in a trance. He continued playing.

Leilah became passionate. Jeremy gently admonished her.
"Please, Leilah, Modi has an idea."

"Yeah," Rory said, "let's hear your idea because I don't like
my own ideas right now."

"Are we not exceptional comrades?" Modi asked, then
answered, "Yes, we are, and in this sacred temple of paradise we
. . . let me think . . . oh yes, I know—we should desecrate our
brotherhood."

"You mean consecrate, old chap," Jeremy said.

Modi scratched his head. "I mean we should take a vow of
eternal brotherhood because we are eternal brothers."

"That's a bang-up idea," Johnny said.

"Chester? Hey, Chester."

"Eh?"

"Stop playing that fucking thing. Are you prepared to vow
an emotional desecration?"

"Absolutely."

"Aye," Rory said, "let's consecrate."

"How?" Jeremy asked.

"Let's cut our palms and mix blood," Johnny said.

"Tarbox, you are a real peasant," Modi said. "I say, we all get
a brotherhood tattoo."

"Done!" Jeremy said. "Nothing will piss my father off more,
although grandfather is apt to be delighted."

"That's very, very beautiful, Modi," Johnny said, starting
into tears.

"I have already spoke to our sister, dear Sonya. There is here nearby a tattoo artist who specializes in tattooing the dates of the Haj to Mecca, but he also does other things."

Sonya bared a breast. It held a tattoo of a pomegranate.

"Jaysus, that's magnificent," Rory said.

"It took long enough for you to make notice," Sonya retorted.

"Send for the bugger!" Johnny cried.

"Although he is Armenian, he is honest. I will also join and have a tattoo," Sonya said.

Chester puffed up. A tattoo! Goddamn! Bully!

"We don't just want to put on a date," Modi said. "What shall we tattoo?"

"I think something in Latin might be appropriate, a motto," Jeremy said.

"Oh shit," Johnny reacted. "Let's be warriors, let's get into battle. A fierce Maori to signify New Zealand."

"New Zealand?" Modi protested.

They tried to think. It was difficult for them to think.

Chester kept his rhythm going on the tambour. "A mule's head," he said, and kept on beating.

"Of course, I was just about to say a mule's head," Modi said.

"With gigantic ears so he won't be mistaken for a horse," Rory added.

And so it came to pass that the gaffer squad, headquarters company, Seventh New Zealand Light Horse Battalion, and three of the ladies of the evening had magnificent mules tattooed by Mr. Suhollanian, an Armenian artist, on their left buttocks.

CHAPTER
68

SECRET FILES OF WINSTON CHURCHILL,
FEBRUARY 1915

Nay to the Nay-sayers!

February 19

A glorious day in the history of the British Navy is commenced.

One hundred and seventy-eight guns ranging from five to fifteen inches, mounted on a dozen warships, opened fire on the four other forts at Cape Helles on the southernmost tip of the Gallipoli Peninsula.

What a magnificent sight we and our French allies must have evoked with our invincible vessels erupting in salvo after salvo. I shall regret not having been a personal witness to the Union Jack being raised to the staff of our mightiest dreadnought—HMS *QUEEN ELIZABETH.*

The attack fleet consisted of three divisions. The first squadron carried the heavy guns of the *ELIZABETH, AGAMEMNON,* and *INFLEXIBLE.*

The second division bore the names of *VENGEANCE, ALBION, CORNWALLIS, IRRESISTIBLE,* and *TRIUMPH.*

I salute the French squadron; *SEFFREN, BOUVET, CHARLE-MAGNE,* and *GAULOIS.*

We opened fire from a distance of fifteen thousand yards, beyond the range of the Turkish guns. Using the new technique of a spotter sea plane directing our guns and photographing the damage, Admiral Harmon concluded the long-range bombardment was having mixed success.

Admiral Harmon then ordered the fleet ever closer. We heard nothing from the Turks until *SEFFREN, VENGEANCE,* and *CORNWALLIS* came to within five thousand yards of Cape Helles.

Blast the luck, foul weather set in. Harmon had no choice but to order a withdrawal at the end of the day with victory still in abeyance.

February 25

Five days of foul weather has canceled our operations. Today we resumed the attack concentrating on the heavy Turkish guns all over the peninsula from a range of 12,000 yards. When we moved closer to Cape Helles, we received no return fire from their big guns. One must conclude that we knocked out the Turkish coastal guns without even having forced the Dardanelles Straits. The long-range barrage may have weakened them significantly.

Our expenditure of 31 fifteen-inch shells, 81 twelve-inch shells, and the French expenditure of 50 twelve-inch shells seems well spent.

February 26

Moving with caution, three of our destroyers sailed into very close range covering landing parties of 60 to 100 Marines and sappers. They found and disabled forty-eight smaller Turkish guns. The Marines probed up into the hills until they were engaged by the Turks. We immediately withdrew, drawing casualties of nine killed and wounded.

As we study these results it appears that the outermost Turkish forts on Cape Helles are out of commission. Further, many other heavy guns up the Gallipoli Peninsula appear to have been silenced from the long-range shellings.

Interesting bit of business, now. Do the Turks think our bombardment of Gallipoli is merely a feint? Do they believe our real objective is to mount an offensive over the Suez Canal into the Sinai, Palestine, and the oil states of Syria and Iraq? It would appear so.

The Turks sent an infantry brigade across the Sinai toward the Suez Canal, knowing full well of our overwhelming number of troops in Egypt.

We pushed them back into the Sinai but, of course, did not follow up. Therefore, they probably concluded that the invasion of Gallipoli is a reality.

Given the initial success we have had, I firmly believe that our naval might will carry the day. In a matter of a few weeks we shall force the Straits of the Dardanelles and, once again, our ships will punish the Turks on the peninsula into submission. I cannot help but feel that our forces will land and engage in a mop-up operation.

Meanwhile, the Navy will enter the Sea of Marmara and anchor outside of Constantinople as our troops drive from the Gallipoli to Constantinople's outskirts and the Turks shall sue for peace.

As these historic events unfold, I do harbor a secret apprehension.

If the Turks put up a fight on the peninsula, we should have a few more infantry divisions in reserve to get the job done. Kitchener will not release any new divisions to this campaign, save the 29th, which is en route.

I do not fear our ability to take Gallipoli with the forces at hand, and then march on Constantinople, except that General

Darlington may be a bit of old school as a tactician. I do not see him making the daring decisions and executing the swift movements to overwhelm the enemy.

I would feel more comfortable if Kitchener would let us have three or four more divisions.

WSC

CHAPTER
69

"Why must we have two paddocks?" Modi asked his students, and answered himself before anyone could speak. "I'll tell you. One major problem is more major than any other problem. That problem is biting flies. Add in mosquitoes and vermin, and we are dealing with a pot full of bloodsuckers."

Modi's students had quickly gotten the drift that Dr. Mordechai Pearlman, late of the Czar's army, knew his animals. The men he had selected from the battalion for the Mule Medic Platoon would own corporal's chevrons, if they cut it. The next day he would test them. If a soldier failed he was immediately dismissed from the medics and replaced. They hung on his every word and engaged in no horseplay unless he instigated it.

"So, we are two paddocks and our big problem is flies. Each night we will have confined several hundred mules eating twenty pounds of feed that day. Gentlemen, that is a lot of mule shit."

Controlled laughter.

"So," he went on, "each night we bring our trains into Paddock A, which has been spotless cleaned and has new hay spread for the animals.

"Alternative," Modi said. "The mule comes to a dirty paddock. The mules must stand in muleshit. Millions of biting flies attack. They attack ears, the genital areas, and open sores. I have seen jacks and janets attacked so bad, half their ears are chewed off. I have seen mules attacked so viciously, they go insane and have to be destroyed. The mule does not want to stand up all night. It uses his strength. But he cannot lie down and sleep in muleshit. What you will have the next morning is a weak animal, half-crazy, with not enough stamina to go on the trail. In this battalion the mule comes home to a clean paddock. We have been collecting bacon grease from the mess halls. Each night you will rub ears, sores, and genital areas with grease. It will give animals some relief from bites. Questions?"

"Is there anything we can use to drive off flies?" he was asked.

"Pine tar," Modi answered. "No trees in Egypt, no pine tar. I am trying mixtures, citronella, petrol torches, and such. Pine tar is best if we can find any.

"So," Modi went on, "when trains leave Paddock A for trail, it is then cleaned. However, Paddock B is already clean and mules return to Paddock B. Get it?"

They got it.

"Anybody don't get it?"

"We've got it!"

"How do we get rid of the muleshit, Dr. Modi?"

"With shovel. With luck, we can capture prisoners. Is good healthy work for prisoners. Better to guard prisoners than clean muleshit yourself. Otherwise, anyone in battalion who fucks off goes to muleshit detail.

"As soon as you muleteers return for day, you will go over every animal with his packers. You check for rope burns, skin bunches, watery places, swellings, sore withers, sore loins. You must check for constipation. A constipated mule is an unhappy mule. Later, you will check piss for kidney problems and muleshit for stomach parasites. Check for screw worms . . . use crysilic ointment. Look for snake bites. Ammonia is in everyone's kit. Every man in battalion will get some lecture, but you are specialist. I depend on you. You are my corporals."

First Serjeant Landers spoke to Company C in the stadium ring.

"If your animal needs new shoes, take him to the blacksmith the night before. After you have seen to the welfare of your mule and have bedded him down with praise, you may then get yourselves cleaned up and fed. No one goes to sleep, however, before cleaning and repairing your mule's leather, lashes, slings, and liar ropes. You will clean down your animal's saddle and reins, and polish all brass. I will personally inspect all mules and their equipment before they go to load. In this battalion, mules will not be pulled out of the line because of sloppy equipment. Sloppy equipment breaks and puts an added burden on your animal. Now, you think about it . . . suppose your mule is pulled out of the train and some ammunition doesn't reach the front lines because of it . . . "

Serjeant Yurlob Singh stood in a circle of fifty sawhorses representing fifty mules. He was speaking to fifty men he had selected as lead packers and trail masters, who would be promoted to corporals and serjeants when . . . and if . . . they could pass the bloody raghead's course.

His eyes were forever reflecting some sort of disdain. Before and after every lecture, Yurlob repeated the same invocation.

"The basic reason for a mule's failure is almost always the packer's stupidity in preparing and loading his animal."

Yurlob described the mixture of mud and straw that was blended into a featherbed blanket to lay over the mule's back. As it hardened, it retained a claylike consistency to protect the peculiar bone structure of the individual animal, a jell-like shock absorber between skin and saddle.

He held up wooden crossbars. "These are ribbings. Likewise, they must fit the contours of the mule's body to perfection. You must work these ribbings, bending them, carving them until they form perfectly."

Yurlob had examples of each type box and load the mule would pack to the front lines, ammunition boxes of all sizes and weights, rifle ammo, light and heavy machine-gun ammo, mortars, water cans, ration boxes, medical packs, communications gear, dynamite, grenades, barbed wire, and all those things that sustained the horror of life on the edge.

Hands behind his back, Yurlob walked up and down beside a long table where his students sat. He made terse comments as they struggled with the square knot, the double sling, the diamond hitch, the double diamond hitch, cross sling, clove hitch, short splice, long splice, liar knot, overhand granny, single and double sheet bend, fisherman's bend, timber hitch towline, barrel sling horizontal, barrel sling vertical, sheepshank, and cat's paw.

"You must get this right because you will be given a test blindfolded.

"Each mule must be prepared to carry down a stretcher on each trip from the front lines. First will come the most seriously wounded, then the more lightly wounded, and finally, the dead. The litter rides high on the cross of the ribbings making the journey perilous in hilly terrain. This is your most important cargo. You will not be stupid."

Serjeant Major Johnny Tarbox and Corporal Chester Goodwood spent their days in Pig Island making up tactical tables.

How many mules will it take to supply five thousand troops three miles from base camp on a line stretching three thousand yards using two quarts of water, fifty rounds of rifle ammo, five hundred rounds of light machine gun, fifty flares, two daily #14 ration . . . ?

How many hours of daylight are required to make a round trip of the above to the front line, and carry down one casualty on return trip . . . ?

What is the minimum-sized paddock required to house two hundred mules . . . ?

. . . three hundred mules . . . ?

. . . four hundred and fifty mules . . . ?

How much time is lost for each degree of uphill climb per mule over a six-mile route?

How many tons of hay will four hundred mules require for a two-week period?

In preparing for an offensive how much time will be required to have ready 100,000 rounds of rifle ammo, 300,000 rounds light machine-gun ammo, 1,000 80-mm mortar shells, 5-gallon cans of water at the rate of 2 quarts a day for 6,000 troops . . . ?

Modi: "Today we speak of calluses. If not softened and removed, they will ulcerate to cancer."

Yurlob: "You are stupid."

Chester Goodwood to Johnny Tarbox: "On a static front, how many mules can supply basic requirements as in table B, four miles from base camp on a line 2,000 yards long containing two companies of infantry and a heavy weapon squad in 3-to-8 terrain?"

Yurlob: "All correctly made ties will release by pulling two ropes, freeing the pack."

Rory: "It is forbidden to park your mule before a public house."
Jaysus! We have to be coming to the end.

It was dark before dawn, still an hour before reveille. Chester Goodwood ran down the hallway of the gaffers' quarters pounding on every door. "Mules have arrived! They're bringing twenty mules into the paddock!"

"Get the lieutenant!"

They dressed like firemen answering an alarm but with a little less grace, pitching, stumbling, and falling as they did.

In ten minutes Lieutenant Jeremy joined them at the hitching rail as the first crack of light shone on the mules. There stood, or wavered, mules in various degrees of infirmity—cowed, swayed, broken, bony, beaten, ears chewed, teeth missing, hooves split, sore-covered.

They could not believe what they saw.

"Jaysus."

"Good God."

"Who sent us these poor beasts?" Modi asked. "I was visiting yesterday comrades in Zion Mule Corps. They got some decent animals."

"The Zion Mule Corps got the best animals because they are servicing British troops," Jeremy said angrily. "I told the Major to let me send a couple of you people to the auction. Colonel Sattersfield at quartermaster buggered me."

"Every peasant in Egypt is trying to pass off his dying mule to the British Army."

They looked for some sort of salvation as Serjeant Yurlob entered the scene. Yurlob studied the animals and maintained an uncommitted expression. Urged, he refused to join the cries of dismay.

Well, here we have it, Jeremy thought. The good servant. These animals were British Army issue so they must be accepted according to the Yurlobs in the colonials.

"For Christ sake, or Buddha's sake," Johnny snapped, "try to put three hundred pounds on any of these creatures and they will collapse."

Yurlob said nothing.

"Damnit, which one can we use for training?" Johnny continued. "Just one . . . one."

Yurlob, always ramrod straight, became straighter.

Modi threw up his hands in futility. Mordechai Pearlman was officially a non-vet, non-soldier, non-person, and if he wasn't a person, he couldn't object. It looked to him like a cruel prank but he knew British officers were not into playing pranks.

"I don't see how we can accept these animals," Johnny said.

"You're the beach master," said Rory protectively. "It's out of your bailiwick. Modi can't say anything, and our bold, fierce, and loyal Sikh friend here wouldn't break the fucking code under torture. I reject these animals as unfit," Rory said shakily.

"I'll support your rejection," Jeremy said.

"Stay out of it, Lieutenant. You don't know doodly-shit about mules."

"I said, Serjeant Landers, that I'll support your rejection. I know a crippled mule when I see one."

"Fuck regulations," Modi said, "I also object to this business gone crazy!"

"And—" Chester said.

"Shut up, Chester," Rory commanded. "You keep out of it."

"I have my—"

"Shut up, Chester," Rory repeated. He turned to Jeremy. "Do you want me to go in to see the Major with you, Lieutenant?"

Jeremy looked to the offices. Good, the lights were on. Christopher usually came before reveille so he could go over just who needed shaping up at roll call, and to be certain he looked shiny and bright, even at this devil's hour.

"He's in. You lads stand fast."

Christopher had heard the commotion outside and opened the big wooden shutters. He could see the Jew laughing and everyone else either scratching or shaking their heads. Ah there, here comes Jeremy at a trot.

"What's going on out there?" Chris snapped as Jeremy entered.

"Colonel Sattersfield sent you twenty dead mules who don't even have the strength to fall down. I warned you to send a couple of my gaffers to the auction."

"I'm afraid," Christopher answered, "all the best mules went to the Jews."

"To the British troops as in contrast to the Anzac troops. Those mules out there are not acceptable."

"Who says they are unacceptable?"

"I do."

"You are not qualified to make that judgment. Who else said so? Tarbox? Corporal Goodwood? The Jew? Yurlob? Did Serjeant Yurlob say they were unacceptable?"

"No."

"So it was Landers."

"Instead of taking this out on your men, why don't you climb all over Sattersfield's ass!"

"This is the British Army. We take what we are issued. Now get the devil out of my way," Chris said, bolting past his brother to the outside. He took a shortcut through the paddock, storming up behind the picket line of mules.

"Ten-shun!" Yurlob cracked out upon sighting the major.

The men froze at attention as he continued toward them in a rage. "Damnit! Serjeant Yurlob! Call up your trail leaders! We are loading and marching within the hour!"

"Major! Stop!" Rory shouted. "Stop, goddamnit, freeze!"

"Who the hell do you think you're talking to, Landers!"

"Major, stop! Hit the dirt!"

As Christopher reached the back of the mule line, Rory leapt over the hitching rail, tackled the major, and sent him down with a thud, lay atop him till he was immobile ... then dragged him back.

The others ran over and untangled them. Christopher Hubble brushed off his uniform, too livid to speak.

Rory came to his feet clutching a shoulder and reeling from a mule kick. Half a dozen of the animals were lashing out with their hind legs.

"Quickly, get back to Pig Island before anyone gets wind of this. Modi, calm these mules down. Go on, lads. I'll take the Major back to his office." Jeremy jerked Chris to his feet and ran him back to the headquarters building and closed them in.

"Blast! That does it! Landers will not get away with the sweatbox. He struck an officer! It is going to be the whipping post. I'll see to it he has lashes."

"Shut up, you asshole!"

"How dare you, Jeremy. You ... you can put in your request for a transfer, immediately. As for Landers, it is within my purview to issue him five lashes before battalion parade." Chris cranked his phone handle. "Put me through to military police."

Jeremy snatched the phone. "Cancel that. The request was made in error."

"All right, let's have at it, Jeremy. This gaffer squad of yours think they command this battalion. They take leave every night in Cairo. They have their own quarters. And your fraternization with them is nothing short of disgusting. Where are you on your free hours? Whoring around with enlisted men? Landers has just been waiting like a snake in the grass for an opportunity to strike me. I'm certain he's planning to kill me in battle."

Christopher stood. Jeremy slapped him in the face and shoved him back into the chair. "Shut your fucking mouth. If you put Serjeant Landers to the whipping post I'm going to beat the shit out of you right in front of the entire battalion."

Christopher blinked, unable to totally fathom what he was hearing.

"In addition to the total collapse of a very beautiful battalion, with small thanks to your cheap brow-beating, you will have failed General Brodhead and disgraced your father for life," Jeremy said firmly.

Jeremy poked around Chris's desk, found a copy of the mule manual, and shoved it into his hands. "Open it to chapter two and read."

Reveille was being blown outside. It would be another half-hour to roll call and longer yet before anyone else arrived at the headquarters building. Chris was trapped by a madman and felt an intensity from his brother he had never before known. Better to play along with him for now, Chris thought. He'd settle Jeremy's number for good later in the day.

"Read!" Jeremy demanded.

Chris cleared his throat. His hands trembled and his voice was wavy. "'Establishing a bond with your animal. The mule is a keenly alert beast, more so than a horse or donkey. His ears serve almost as a second pair of eyes. Note your mule's ears always turn in the direction of sound. The mule will lay his ears back when contented but pop them up within a state of alert ...'" Looking up from the manual, Chris pleaded, "Must I go on with this nonsense?"

"Read!"

"Very well."

"'Never, and we repeat the word NEVER, approach a mule from the ... from the ...'"

"Read!"

"'Never approach a mule from the rear if there is another choice. If you must approach from the rear, remember that he is hitched and cannot see behind him, only hear. Call the mule by name softly to assure him of who you are and that there is no danger. Ask him how he feels today . . .'"

Chris sagged, looked up to Jeremy, and continued, "'Ask him how he feels today. Then go around to the front, give him a handful of oats (which you will always keep in your pocket). Then give him a tickle under his eye.'"

Christopher sighed resignedly. The next passage was underlined. "'If you come up behind a mule shouting or otherwise expressing distress or displeasure, it is an absolute certainty the mule will become alarmed and kick out with its hind legs. This can be extremely dangerous. The battalion vet has seen injuries resulting from mule kicks of cracked ribs, separated shoulders, broken arms, and more than one fractured skull.'"

Chris set the manual back on his desk.

"Now then," Jeremy said with normal voice, "these mules have no value to the British Army. They have been horrendously maltreated and all of them have one infirmity or another from overwork, underfeeding, neglect, and beatings. I suggest you send them back to Colonel Sattersfield and stand behind your men."

"Have the Jew . . . "

"He has a name."

"Have Mr. Pearlman confirm their condition in a written memorandum. I shall reject them. However, Jeremy, what you threatened here was mutiny. I want you out of here."

"You shouldn't be so surprised. You know all about mutiny, don't you?"

"I will not have you take command of my battalion."

"Christ sake, Chris, I don't want your battalion."

Christopher verged on a hard decision. He knew he'd better make it calmly. He had to set aside the unpleasantness that had taken place. The gaffers and his brother would swear that Landers had saved him from his own stupidity and probably a terrible injury. But, what if he did get rid of Jeremy . . . or was able to go through with a punishment of Landers . . . what then?

His battalion was fit. Jeremy whined that they had been pushed too hard, but they were fit.

Damned gaffer squad was good, too, best special squad in the corps. They had done the impossible task of teaching men as much as they could possibly know about mules without most of them having ever seen a mule.

Christopher dearly wanted to exact a stern punishment, to let them know who was who. Yet, to be overtaken by a desire for vengeance could exact a price too high to risk.

"Stay with your bloody gaffers," Chris said. "The book is closed on this incident. You have your job, Jeremy, and I want you to keep your nose out of my command."

"That's fine with me," Jeremy said, "but remember one thing. If you lay a finger on any one of my boys, I'll break your neck."

CHAPTER

70

The River Jordan
Flows down the mountainside
The earth is still
My Galilee
Her haunting valleys
Ancient olive trees
Her sun worn rocks
Her mystic sea
Oh how I love you
How I long for you
My Galilee
My Galilee
I see soft winds
Bending my fields
I hear a cry
A lamb at its birth
Oh how I love you
How I long for you
My Galilee
My Galilee . . .

Modi's song faded and his accordion shut down. Villa Valhalla dimmed for a rest. March groaned on and a restlessness tensed the gaffers, a sense of movement would soon begin as warships continued to pound the Gallipoli.

Even paradise had its limitations. The squad had tasted euphoria. Valhalla would become the centerpiece of grand remembrance for all their lives. For now, though, they were ready for war.

Johnny Tarbox was more highly keyed than the others. Rory knew it was something about a long lost mother now taking form in woman after woman. Rory was always able to calm him down. Good thing. Johnny sometimes didn't realize he was going on a tear.

The Lieutenant and First Serjeant Landers sat on the veranda looking over to the spires across the river that marked a great Moslem city. Sonya's pipe had the magic elixir that made conversation free . . . except for that locked chamber.

Sonya stood in the doorway.

"Johnny all right?" Rory asked.

She nodded he was asleep. Tarbox hates women, I hate men. Yet we love them as well. How torturous, she thought.

"You would like some fruit or drinks?" she asked, working her eyes on Rory's. They waved no and she retreated, but the power of her eyes remained.

"She's been so good to us," Jeremy said. "But she longs for her unrequited love. For God's sake, don't go into battle without making an effort to forget Georgia."

Rory did not answer.

"Did I ever tell you I was in love with a prostitute once, desperately, eternally."

"In actual fact?" Rory asked.

"In actual fact," Jeremy said. "It was on the Midlands Tour with the rugby team. I was being tutored for Trinity by Conor and he kept an indecent watch on me. Locked me in my room if my studies weren't up to snuff. I figured a foolproof way to get around him."

Rory thrived on Jeremy's tales of Conor. He settled back, happily.

"Her name was Felicia or something . . . Christ, this stuff destroys your mind. My grandfather traveled with the team but believe me he stayed in a better hotel. So, I fell desperately in love with this . . . Marcia . . . that's it, Marcia. Grandfather covered for me. I'd tell Conor I was going over to see Sir Frederick and spend the night. He checked up by phone a couple of times and there I was . . . and there was Marcia right in bed with me. Freddie even slipped her from one town to another until Conor paid me an unexpected visit. I only slipped past him one more time, after the Bradford game."

"That's when you won the Admiral's Cup?"

"Aye, first Irish team ever to do so. Grandfather threw a victory party to end all parties. When it moved from his hotel to a very, very fashionable brothel, Conor locked me in my room. I stuffed pillows in my bed and shinnied down the drain pipe, four stories, damn near killed myself. Smoke?"

"Thanks."

"This brothel was strictly for nobility. As beautiful as Villa Valhalla . . . until those foul brutes from the Bradford Bulls came in . . . we were willing to share, but you know how it goes . . . everybody wanted the same two or three ladies and one thing led to another and someone made a rank anti-Irish remark . . . mind you, Conor wasn't there."

"And the shit hit the fan."

"In diamonds. Rory, it was the punch-up of all times. Girls screaming, bodies flying, glass smashing, and then came the police. A few lads escaped, but I was hauled away in the paddy wagon, minus two teeth, along with most of our lads. You should have seen the headlines next morning . . . 'Lord Jeremy loses teeth for mates' . . . 'Future Earl of Foyle arrested in brothel brawl' . . . 'Midnight escapades of future member of Lords' . . . "

"And Conor was clean?"

"He didn't have a clue. So, next day I'm on the carpet in Grandfather's suite with my mother roasting my ass and Freddie trying to crawl under the couch. Conor is called into the room. Mother starts grilling him, not buying that he was innocent. He said—God, I'll never forget it—'What do you want for a son, the Christmas fairy?' Mother hauls off to slap him, but he catches her hand in midair and tells her he'd paddle her butt right before her father and son."

Rory laughed aloud. His envy was silent.

"The three of us fellows were doubled up, hysterical, even me with my missing teeth. Mother smashed up a few vases, then joined us, laughing hardest of us all. That's when my father came in."

Jeremy suddenly went silent and wore an expression of hurt that Rory had come to know.

"He slapped me in the face and walked out."

"That must have hurt real bad," Rory said.

"It still does," Jeremy said.

He patted Jeremy's shoulder. "The Squire never got around to hitting me, but the way he looked at me, I sometimes wished he had beaten me instead. I got into brawls to get his attention. Maybe it was to win his love ... or have him respect me for being a tough guy ... then after a while, just to piss him off. That was the one that worked, pissing him off. I did plenty of that."

The sadness flowed away. "Along with the Villa here, the Midlands trip has been it for me. Trinity, although there was Molly, I only remember in betrayals. Father, I expected to pound on me ... and Swan, that was his vocation. But, Chris. Anyhow ... I didn't know at the time Conor was already involved in gunrunning for the Irish Republican Brotherhood."

Rory held tight.

"I went on to Trinity in Dublin, met Molly. I saw Conor in Dublin only a few times. He was always in a hurry. I didn't realize why until Sixmilecross. I desperately tried to get to see him in prison. It was impossible. Things were caving in on Molly and me. Conor would have made me do what was right. Everyone around him drew strength from him. Maybe, if I'd seen him, I could have been motivated to behave like a man. . . . I miss him very much, Rory."

I do, too, Rory thought.

Leilah had been patient, just out of range. She softly made her presence known. Jeremy noted that he'd be in soon. She smiled and danced off.

"She's crazy about you," Rory said.

"She does her act well," Jeremy answered.

"It's more than that. You've treated them like ladies and made them feel beautiful. They can go a lifetime in Cairo without having felt that once. Sonya told me so."

Jeremy wove into the villa. Rory submitted to an onrush from the hashish. Where would it end with him and Jeremy? How could it end in Ireland without disaster?

Ireland, which had once been life's siren call now had ominous tones on its scale. Was he big enough to carry the Larkin name into Ireland? What could he do? Always be compared to Conor? No one was Conor. Sometimes it seemed that Conor wasn't even Conor. . . .

He stood gingerly and wove his way up the circular stair, balancing himself with his hand on the outside wall. A wind shift brought a din of street noises from across the Nile, high and shrill and flutelike. . . .

Conor! You're pissed at me for smoking hashish. Look at me. Don't you know me? I'm a man now. I've had women. I had a love and I don't want to think about her right now. . . . Jeremy talking on about you made me so sad I'll never see you again . . . they say Aunt Brigid keeps the Larkin plot the most beautiful in Ballyutogue . . . so, I'll see you there. CONOR! WHAT THE HELL DO YOU WANT FROM ME, NOW!

Rory aimed at his doorway and fell into kneeling position on the smooth, soft, sensuous pillows. Ah, dear old Sonya-lass. She's lit a candle. The breeze keeps blowing. The candlelight is going wild.

Sonya stood in the doorway naked to the waist, her body glistening with clove oil. She knelt before Rory, arched her back and undulated, and snapped her fingers, while her breasts rolled under large, rigid nipples.

Rory seized her in his arms. They hung on and swayed together on their knees, now keeping the long promise, now letting it all fly, now feeling the other's oils, now wild in kisses and her pleading, her groaning, now pulling each other's hair. She brought him down into softness and he let the Cairo night overcome him.

＊　　＊　　＊

At three o'clock in the morning everyone was abruptly awakened by a pounding on the door. It was an angry pounding. A voice shouted behind it.

The lads scrambled into some kind of covering—sheets, towels, Arab pantaloons—and made down the stairs. Chester slipped on all the oil and slid down. Sonya ran from room to room herding the girls and pushing them out of sight.

"Stop pounding, we're coming!"

Rory flung the door open and looked at Serjeant Yurlob Singh. He entered with George, the villa's Christian Terrier, whining that he had been taken by surprise. Rory ordered the boy upstairs with Sonya.

"What the hell's going on!" Jeremy managed.

"It's Major Hubble. He is being held hostage by the Egyptian police."

71

"Let me have the notes, Eddie," Churchill directed.

"They're rather loose, Winston. I haven't had a chance to tidy them up."

"Not to mind. I just want to see if I missed anything."

It was three o'clock in the morning, more or less the middle of the day for the First Lord of the Admiralty. Eddie poured a glass of Scotch for his boss and set a flame under Churchill's cigar.

Notes from the War Council Meeting—March 12, 1915

(Gathered and transcribed in the rough immediately after War Council meeting this day, adjourned 12:45 A.M. Eyes only for Churchill. Eddie Marsh.)

Foreign Minister—Sir Edward Grey
Grey continues to cling to the hope of obtaining a Balkan ally against the Turks.

First Lord of the Admiralty—Winston Churchill
Feels the Balkans are too risky and unstable except for the excellent Greek Army offered by the King, until British take Constantinople.

Prime Minister—Herbert Asquith
Adamant that Balkan issue is closed. Cites Bulgarians in recent union against Turks turning on their Romanian allies at end of conflict.

Use of Greek Army would only encourage former Balkan union to join war on side of Germans. Use of Greek Army would likewise anger our Russian ally.

Admiralty—Churchill
Expresses fears that naval gunfire may not be doing job as earlier believed.

At onset of war with Turks, British Naval Attaché in Constantinople, Admiral Limpus, warned that German General von Limon assuming command over Turks. Von Limon is apt to get the best out of his forces and will certainly defend Gallipoli more cleverly than Turkish staff.

Churchill agrees Balkans are too dicey but expresses strong feeling that Italy can be swayed to renounce its treaty with Germans and join Allies, thus giving us a reserve for the Dardanelles operation.

Believes that when we take Constantinople Balkans will fall in line with us for drive up Danube Valley.

Commander, British Forces—Field Marshal Lord Kitchener
When Italy is induced to join Allies, it is far more important that she open a major front against the Austrians.

Commander, British Forces in France—General Sir John French
The Western Front should have main priority. Dardanelles operation taking too much strength away. Against entire Dardanelles operation.

First Sea Admiral—John Fisher
Very much against Churchill. Continues to argue that oversized Mediterranean Fleet leaves British Isles and supply lanes too vulnerable. This is a flip-flop position. He favored it strongly.

Fisher points out that the new super-dreadnoughts such as *ELIZABETH* are required in Channel and Atlantic operations.

Fisher cites that there is activity detected in Turkish fleet in Black Sea and Sea of Marmara. Further argues that German U-boats will sooner than later pose a danger to British fleet anchored off Gallipoli.

Prime Minister
Overrules Admiral Fisher and General French. British interests in Ottoman Empire are too great. Dardanelles operation imperative.

Foreign Minister
Taking Turkey out of the war should be the 1915 priority.

Field Marshal Kitchener
Supports Dardanelles operation. However, agrees with General French that no more land troops can be assigned to the campaign.

Churchill
Time runs against us. The longer we delay the more opportunity Turks/Germans have to prepare defenses and the less likely it becomes to win peninsula quickly.

Suggests minesweepers force the straits at once, followed immediately by main battle fleet entering and using 2,000 Marines and 4,000 Anzacs to make coordinated landing.

Lord Kitchener
Churchill is asking the impossible. Admiral Harmon feels it will take at least two weeks to clear the mine fields.

Churchill
Admiral Harmon also has come to conclusion that naval gunfire alone will not subdue peninsula.

Lord Kitchener
Will not support an early troop landing.

Namely: Island of Lemnos has been commandeered as an advance base for the assault on Gallipoli. Troops must be moved over from Egypt in orderly fashion and supplies and other support built up.

Moreover, General Darlington, Chief of Mediterranean Operations, refuses to commit troops until British 29th Division has arrived in theatre and is battle-ready.

Churchill
Major General Brodhead, CC of Anzacs, complains that advance base at Lemnos is not being properly used.

Lord Kitchener
Rather disdainful of Churchill's poke at the Army. Lemnos is taking troops in order of battle priority. Namely: Marines, sappers, assault troops, artillery, in *that* order. Support troops: quartermaster, headquarters people, etc., will go to Lemnos last.

Churchill
Won't quit the argument. Brodhead argues strongly that special units such as mule transport are desperately in need of field training and must be given priority to go to Lemnos first.

Lord Kitchener
Darlington doesn't agree, but he will look into Brodhead's problem.

Prime Minister
Does not like the lack of unanimity. Outsiders such as Sir Edward Carson, the Ulster Unionist, are against the operation.

Asks Kitchener to name a date for troop landing so he can quiet growing opposition among party leaders and secret councils.

Lord Kitchener
Field Marshal Kitchener feels that late April/early May is more realistic date for landing of troops.

The War Council meeting was adjourned with no one truly satisfied. A terrible stress had now been placed on the Anzacs and British forces in Egypt. The clean stroke of the swift sword of victory was badly dulled. Darlington had no feel for bold movement. The growing outside political opposition was putting a negative whisper over the operation.

As he went over the notes, Churchill brooded. As Churchill brooded, Cairo was about to burn.

Sonya called to her girls to round up the squad's uniforms and bring soap and fresh towels to the fountain, where they had plunged in unison to cleanse their bodies of oil and clarify their minds. After they helped wipe the lads dry, Sonya sent the women from the villa and went off to make coffee—powerful coffee.

"From the beginning, Serjeant Yurlob."

"I was working in Pig Island on the requisition list. Upon leaving I saw that the Major's light was still burning and sought to get him to sign it. I knocked and upon entering saw that he was in a frightful state."

"What do you mean?"

"He had the eyes of a madman and was sweating all over."

"What in the name of God could it have been?"

"A letter was clutched in Major Hubble's fist. He thrust it into his pocket as though I would attempt to read it."

"I picked up the officers' mail," Johnny said. "The major had one letter. I personally took it to him."

"I received letters from both my parents today," Jeremy said. "There was nothing in mine to indicate any trouble."

"The Major ordered me to leave, brusquely," Yurlob went on, "but as I started out he said . . . 'Wait, do we have any transportation from the motor pool?' There was only a supply lorry, the one with the bad gears. The Major ordered me to bring it around."

As they dressed, Yurlob sniffed a scent known to him as militarily improper. He studied the luxury about him with a straight face.

"Keep talking, I'm listening," Jeremy said, lacing his boots.

"Fearing the Major was in no state of mind to drive the vehicle, and as the vehicle was not in such a good state to be driven, I offered to drive him. He tried to start the lorry alone but, after nearly stripping the gears, agreed to let me take him into Cairo."

Sonya arrived with the first of the coffee and went to make more.

"I raced to Cairo just as Major Hubble instructed."

"What did he say to you? Any orders? Any indication of what was disturbing him?"

"All he asked was to take him to an out-of-the-way hotel where no officers would be. There is a small Sikh club in the Shari el Haram District off Pyramid Road, but hardly a place one takes an officer of the British Army. However, he insisted."

"I know that area from before the war," Modi said. "It is a gangster place."

"I stopped at the Hotel Aida. I registered for him and quickly took him to the room number twenty-two, the best in the place but hardly proper for a man of his stature. He commanded me to leave. I feared for him so I walked around outside to see if I could see his room. I did so. On the top of a building, off a very narrow alley, one could crawl to the edge and just see into a part of his room. I waited as several hours passed. Then others came into his room, quickly and quietly. As I reached his room, I was apprehended by two policemen guarding his door."

"Didn't the police draw a crowd?"

"No, no. They came in quietly without causing a disturbance, and there were whispers, only whispers from his room."

"Are you smelling the same rat I'm smelling, Jeremy?" Rory asked.

"Yes, go on, Yurlob."

"Inside his room are four policemen, a police inspector, and a civilian. Major Hubble is on the bed without clothing and only barely conscious. I would think, drugged. I smell chloroform. On the floor they pull back a sheet over a woman who has been murdered. It appears she is a prostitute. The civilian tells me to find Lieutenant Jeremy Hubble and gives me this address. He warns me to remain secret or it will be the Major's life."

"Farouk el Farouk," Chester said.

"That's him," Jeremy agreed.

"Jaysus," Rory muttered, "a dead whore on the floor and a British officer in a blown-out state. It's a setup, Jeremy."

"Did they ask you about ransom?"

"No," Yurlob answered. "Only to bring you alone to the Hotel Aida at once."

"The Lieutenant has refused to let us pay for the villa, as you know," Rory said. "How have you been paying for it?"

"I set up a line of credit through Weed Ship & Iron in London. My mother runs the office. I've paid Farouk el Farouk through Cook's Travel cheques."

"Well, it looks like they're after a nice big one. If that's all there is to it, maybe we're in luck," Rory said. "They're always scratching around for something like this. How many ranking officers do you suppose have been blackmailed in this city? It's their game. Jeremy, why the hell would your brother want to go to such a dump?"

"Obviously, he got some terrible news. What makes you so optimistic we can get him back?"

"If it were cut and dried—officer goes to seedy hotel, gets a prostitute, murders her, is unconscious himself. Police arrive. What do they do in normal circumstances? They would take him in and book him on charges. But they didn't do that."

"I see it," Modi said. "A middle-ranking British officer and a murder would draw a crowd. There is no crowd. Cairo becomes a small town. The word gets to the right people that there is a live fish on the line at Hotel Aida."

"Ruddy bastards," Jeremy grunted.

"Thank God all they want is money. That gives us an opening," Rory said, moving into command.

"You're bloody right, cobber," Johnny said. "I say we pick up a couple dozen troops in some bars and rush the place."

"No, no brute tactics. We can't get anyone else involved.

They want to keep it hush-hush. We have to protect the Major."

"He's right, Johnny," Jeremy said.

"How'd you get here, Yurlob?" Rory asked.

"Taxi. He is waiting down the street."

"Where's the lorry?"

"About three blocks from the hotel."

"Shit, I hope it still has wheels on it."

"It is fine," Yurlob assured. "I put it in the yard of military police station. There is a small Sikh unit. My cousin is guarding it."

"Chester, can you drive it?"

"We'll find out," Chester answered.

"You say the lobby seems as if everything is normal?"

"Yes."

"Big lobby, little lobby?"

"Fair size. A very active hotel."

"Do you think, like, Modi and Johnny can just walk in and up the stairs to the Major's room?"

"Yes, but what about the police?"

"There are some short lengths of pipe left over from repairs on the fountain. Knee-cap the cops at the door and take their pistols."

Johnny and Modi nodded.

"I'll find the place on the roof where Yurlob watched. Can you reach the Major's room from there?"

"With a leap."

"Can you hear the railroad bell clock?"

"Clearly."

Rory looked at his watch. "When it strikes six, it means five o'clock. On the fifth bong ... Johnny and Modi hit the cops at the door. I'll come through the window. Yurlob, throw the Major under the bed and guard him."

"I want Farouk el Farouk," Jeremy hissed.

"I'll take the inspector," Rory said.

"But what of the other four armed policemen?" Yurlob asked.

"We'll think of something. We'll improvise. Jeremy, you and Yurlob take the taxi. We're five minutes behind you."

"Rory!" Sonya cried.

"Oh Christ, are they going to take this out on you?"

"Do not worry. I am halfway to Alexandria. You are wonderful boys. Please smash in Inspector Rawash's face. He has given me twenty years of misery."

The room was much as Serjeant Yurlob had described it. Christopher was strewn on a dirty, lumpy mattress with a dirtier sheet half covering him and he was mumbling incoherently.

"It's me, Jeremy!"

Christopher was glassy-eyed, but focused to some sort of recognition, then flopped back down.

"Where is his uniform?"

Inspector Rawash, who was very easy to identify, nodded to the closet door. Jeremy fished through the pockets and found what he was looking for—a vial and a letter. He lifted the cap on the vial and sniffed it.

"Cyanide," Rawash said.

"Yours or his?" Jeremy asked.

"His."

The letter was from Christopher's wife, Hester. It was but a page in length. She wrote that she had never really loved him and that life in the confines of the earldom was insufferable. She had fallen in love with an ordinary fellow, a musician. She had become pregnant and they had run off together, far away from Ireland and the British Isles.

Any malice, any anger Jeremy had ever known for the poor, limp, blubbering creature had flown.

"You're going to be all right, Chris," Jeremy said to his uncomprehending brother. "Yurlob, find some water and clean him up and get him into his uniform."

"There are some matters to be settled, Viscount, m'lord," Farouk el Farouk said. "May I introduce you to Chief Inspector Rawash who commands the eastern side of Cairo."

"I am honored," Rawash said.

"Sure, so am I." Jesus, a slithering pair of vipers out of some terrible novel, they were. What a dirty lousy game. Connections

... we've a live one ... praise Allah, his brother is Viscount Hubble, the Lieutenant of Villa Valhalla!

"We have a very serious situation. A woman is murdered in your brother's room and your brother at this moment does not do great honor to the British Army. If we take him in to the magistrate and prefer charges ... well, I have no further control over matters," Rawash recited.

"When the Inspector found your brother's papers, he came to me on the small chance I may know of this gentleman, in that I deal with dignitaries."

"And there's the matter of the Villa Valhalla," Rawash continued. "It is illegal that you are there and having illegal parties smoking hashish, a very serious crime in Cairo."

"You have a lot of serious criminals in Cairo. And, you don't have to smoke it. All you have to do is walk down the street and breathe," Jeremy said.

Farouk el Farouk gave a small smile at the humor. "I have convinced Chief Inspector Rawash that there is a better way than to imprison your brother and bring total disgrace to your family."

"I'm sure you have."

"My dear Viscount. We did not invite you to Cairo. But now that you have invited yourself, please do not try to change twenty-five centuries of custom."

"This city is going to be torn apart by the troops. You must know that," Jeremy said.

"Cairo has known five hundred riots and still stands. How will your father's earldom stand after this?"

"How much do you want?"

"We are prepared to keep this totally quiet, but a lot of people must be favored to ensure that it absolutely did not happen."

"How much?"

"You make it sound so rude!"

"How much?"

The Egyptians went to the corner of the room and put their heads together. Yurlob was busy assembling Chris to a reasonable state. Jeremy wanted to get him to the infirmary as quickly as possible.

"We must wait here until the Cook's Travel office opens at half past seven," Farouk el Farouk said. "I and you will go down there and clear a cheque for ten thousand."

"Ten thousand!"

"No bargaining, no bargaining. Believe me, by the time everyone is taken care of there won't be five quid in it for me."

"I can't make a cheque of that size."

"But of course you can. Everything of yours clears. If there is a problem, I have reserved a telephone line to London. You can explain it to the party at Weed Ship & Iron."

"You are garbage. All you live for is the slimy fucking deal. What a way to live!"

"And your father has not become the Earl over deals and dead bodies, m'lord? I am sorry you do not understand certain traditions. Opportunities such as we have at this moment only happen once in a lifetime. Your troops rape our city. We rape you."

"You murdered this woman and planted her here."

"She is of no consequence. No one forced your brother to this hotel. Are you prepared, yes or no, to go with me to Cook's? Do you wish him back, yes or no?"

"All right. You win," Jeremy said.

Large smiles from beaming faces. "Good, good." Farouk el Farouk glowed. "We have time till daybreak. Do you play backgammon, Lord Viscount?"

BONG rang the railroad tower clock.

"No, I don't play."

"Ah, too bad."

"I'll play with you," Rawash said.

BONG!

"First we had better send out for some food."

Yurlob placed himself before his Major as Jeremy looked down at the floor, appearing disconsolate, but staying within an arm's length of Farouk el Farouk.

BONG!

BONG!

"I set up the board at the table."

BONG!

Jeremy counted, a thousand one, a thousand two, a thousand three, oh Christ, a thousand . . .

"YOWWWW!"

"AHURRRGGG!"

The door blew off its hinges as Mordechai Pearlman and Johnny Tarbox crashed into the room brandishing a pair of pistols taken from the guards.

Rory flew through the window, bowling over two of the policemen. As they groped to their knees, he banged their heads together. Yurlob shoved Major Hubble under the bed, then dived himself as the other two police fired. Jeremy brought an uppercut into Farouk el Farouk's jaw, dropping him like a mummy.

There was a short but violent smashing of furniture amid screams and bursts of bright red blood. Inspector Rawash slid along the wall and was about to make it through the door when Rory caught him and got him in an armlock.

"Tell them to drop their pistols!" Rory commanded.

The inspector, screaming in pain, babbled orders to surrender, NOW!

AHUGAH! AHUGAH! The lorry horn sounded from the street.

"Modi! Johnny! Bring these two cops from the hall in here, quick."

AHUGAH! AHUGAH!

The six police were cuffed with their own handcuffs and stuffed into the closet. Rory had proudly remembered to bring the belt cords from their robes at Villa Valhalla. He shut the door.

"Come on, Rory, let's get the hell out of here."

"Give me just a minute." Rory was dancing on his toes throwing out his jab. He had not gotten his fill, not just yet.

AHUGAH! AHUGAH!

Rory walked to Inspector Rawash, who was too terrified to plead out loud. "I got into a fight with this big Aussie at Fort Albany, see . . . "

"Come on, Rory, we're clear," Johnny cried.

"Shut up!" Rory answered, near frothing. "Do you know what that fucking Aussie did to me?" Rory seized Rawash's lapels. "This is what he did to me," and promptly smashed his forehead between the Inspector's eyes. The bespattered man fell, crushed. Rory, nearly knocking himself out with his blow, wiped Rawash's blood from his own forehead, then focused on Farouk el Farouk. "So you know what I did to that son of a bitch?" Rory wrapped his arms about the Egyptian, lifted him off the ground, and squeezed him till the air was nearly gone from him, then bit his ear lobe so that it dangled by a thread. "That's what I did."

The two were quickly gagged and tied.

AHUGAH! AHUGAH! the horn cried desperately.

"Come on, Rory!"

Rory dragged Christopher Hubble from under the bed, tossed him over a shoulder, tucked a pair of pistols into his belt, and led them out.

An angry and threatening crowd had gathered at the bottom of the stairs.

AHUGAH! AHUGAH!

Rory took one of the pistols out, cocked it, and fired at the chandelier. The protesters scattered. He came down the stairs firing at the mirrors, the windows, the check-in desks. Emptying one pistol, he began firing the other.

"Move, you assholes! I'm coming through!"

CHAPTER
73

Jeremy shaved very carefully around assorted nicks, cuts, scrapes, and bruises on his face, recipient of stray blows in the Hotel Aida encounter. A knock.

"Come in, please."

Christopher, still in ragged condition, slumped in the easy chair and draped a leg over its arm.

"How's it?"

"I got a laboratory report. There were traces of, what the devil was it, chloral hydrate. I had ordered a number of drinks trying to find the wherewithal to write a glorious note of farewell and take that other stuff, the cyanide. You might say they saved my life by drugging me. I was either chloroformed first and they forced the drink down or vice versa. I was too drunk to know. Bad show," he whispered.

Jeremy dunked his face, patted on some bay rum carefully, grimaced at the sting and sat on the edge of his bed close to his brother.

"How's your mind holding up?"

"Not very well," Christopher said. "I know I owe an apology and expression of gratitude to the gaffers, but I'm not really certain if I ever learned how to apologize, at least with any sincerity. Not a notable Hubble trait. I've humiliated myself like a common beggar and I'm having difficulty managing that as well. Jeremy, I don't know if I can change. I don't know how to change or even if I want to change."

"No one really expects you to change."

"I do feel duty-bound to say I'm grateful."

"You don't have to tell them anything. You were in deep trouble and they didn't hesitate for a minute."

"They came because of you, Jeremy."

"We're all just a bunch of chaps from all over the place who have been thrown together to get through a war. We have to take care of each other."

"They hate me."

"They think you're a horse's ass. But these are good men. They understand wars can't be won without officers like you. They are also deeply pained and compassionate over what happened to you back home."

"I find that so difficult to comprehend."

"You should. You've never been there for anyone."

"That's not true, Jeremy. I've been there for Father, for General Brodhead."

"To cover yourself with glory. Or, you were there to protect your privilege. You were never there for love of anyone."

Christopher was stunned and tried to think back. It was cloudy in the past. When? Even once? Was his every profound act and gesture to someone encased in a hidden agenda to promote his own image and cause? Did he ever act selflessly without hope of recognition and reward? What maid in the manor house would speak up for him now? What butler? Did he not take the mule battalion in order to become a full colonel with his own brigade? Was he ever more than superficially considerate of anyone beneath his station?

Christopher had passed over the threshold. He'd bury his lie no longer. He was face-to-face with Christopher. He nearly gagged sorting out his words; they had to be untwisted carefully.

"I feel something now very deeply," he muttered. He now knew internal pain and the man had become bewildered by it. The discovery of buried passion suddenly tore him off the pedestal he had placed himself on and brought him down to common earth with common pain. Twenty-five years of building an armor of reserve attitude, of detaching himself from human misery was blown away, snatched from him and reduced him to dust in a sudden moment. Welcome to the human race, Major Hubble.

Christopher found his old steel. He looked directly at his brother. "When we took Molly from you, I was as evil as a brother could be. You writhed in agony and I kicked you and enjoyed it. I was above you, you see. When you became a drunk and I rose over you in rank, I delighted in humiliating you. When you were terrified to sign the resignations at Camp Bushy I adored tormenting you as a coward."

He stood and clasped his hands behind him. He was pleased that his words were direct and did not falter, for he had never ventured into such territory of the heart. "I never really understood the meaning of pain until I opened Hester's letter. Physical pain, yes. But one keeps a stiff upper lip when he is thrown from a horse and merely suffers a broken arm. This was pain of a horrible dimension. Oh, I admit I did not love Hester with any sort of bottomless fervor. Hester had to be collected by me along the way to fit into a niche. When I was unable to make her pregnant, I was concerned only that my manliness might be in question. I had no understanding why she seemed to be so distressed."

Christopher felt his brother's hand on his shoulder for the first time since they were kids. No touch of another person in his life had been so meaningful. He felt it all over, for the first time.

"I was foolish to block inside pain from my life, but I didn't consciously know I was doing it. Detachment from others seemed the normal way of being. To have learned it all in this single moment was too much for me to bear. I had betrayed Hester with my indifference. I never felt jealous of her, not once. She was not much to be jealous of, one would think. She existed only to serve my requirements, nothing more. I never understood that she was a tight rosebud who craved to bloom. She is happy now . . . truly in love . . . a baby in her belly and risking all. Only now do I realize what I did to you. God, you must despise me."

"I've never felt any sense of revenge. I wish I could take

some of your pain from you now. I can't. But I am your brother and I love you."

It was all too much for Christopher, to keep together, not to break down. Blast, he had his pride! "What can I do to make it right for those lads?" he asked softly.

"You have to put your head in a noose for them," Jeremy responded without hesitation.

"I'm listening."

"Camp Anzac is starting to fold its tents. The first battalions to move out are infantry, sappers, artillery. Apparently we are the tail end of the line."

"I've already spoken to General Brodhead about it. He said it is a typical army bureaucratic fuckup. We are officially a service unit. Service units have always brought up the rear. They made no provision for the fact that the Seventh Light Horse has extraordinary urgencies. The War Office and Darlington are on automatic. Brodhead has protested to London."

"We must leave Egypt first, Chris. If we don't have mules on Lemnos in a week or two and cram our training, we are going to fail in our mission, miserably," Jeremy said. "From what we can sniff out, there is going to be hell to pay, if the mules aren't working."

Chris became a bit sick to the stomach from a delayed wave of the effects of the past forty-eight hours.

"Chris," Jeremy continued, "we have been raised under the axiom that other people only existed for our use. We were taught they were faceless, without feelings, needed no compassion. The army is a brotherhood. What makes it go is your dedication to their lives, as human beings. They aren't mules to be worked until we have no more use for them and discarded. They are men to be brought through this and they trust you. You know what must be done."

Pig Island had been in a state of awful melancholy. Lieutenant Jeremy had been gone most of the day. The Major had been taken to the hospital over forty hours earlier. The blow fell on them in the first orders to break camp. Troop trains to

Alexandria and ships to Lemnos would be in motion in two more days. The schedule of battalion departures was set well into April. The Seventh Light Horse was not on the list.

No mules, no final training. Gallipoli seemed to be a well kept military secret that everyone knew, including the London newspapers. The squad had studied the maps. The landscape was treacherous. The job would be botched if they didn't get their animals at once.

Yurlob Singh entered and everyone cast their eyes down. They were in a state of communal guilt over having blackballed Yurlob from the Villa Valhalla.

"Listen, Yurlob," Rory said at last, "we feel shitty about the way you've been treated by us."

"Real shitty," Johnny added.

"Bad," Chester said.

Modi shook his head in shame.

"If you speak of the Villa Valhalla," the Sikh answered, "you made the proper decision. I would not have felt comfortable in that atmosphere and would have made you likewise not comfortable."

"I know," Rory said, "but at least we should have invited you and if it wasn't working, fine. But we should have asked you in."

"That would have been worse," Yurlob answered. "It would have imposed upon me to carry your secret. Your behavior was clearly in conflict with military code. I am glad I was not burdened with the secret."

"Are you sure you're not pissed off at us?" Rory asked.

"I was, but I am not. I feared you would not respond to the Major's dilemma. But you did, indeed, most gallantly."

"Actually it passed through my mind to let him fry," Modi said. "There are some people, like Major Hubble, who can let you know you're a dirty Jew without uttering a word."

"Or a Sikh houseboy," Yurlob answered. This sobered everyone. "The point is, we volunteered into this army and he is our commanding officer, so we must be loyal, if we are men."

"How is our beloved leader, anyhow," Rory asked. "Did they get him pumped out?"

"He was released from the hospital yesterday. Today, he met with Major General Brodhead and General Darlington."

"Darlington, the big man."

"Darlington!"

"Major Hubble and Major General Brodhead tried to get General Darlington to change the order of battalion departures and have the Seventh Light Horse arrive at Lemnos first."

"How the hell do you know this?" Johnny asked.

"Lieutenant Colonel Swaran Singh has been on General Darlington's staff since Darlington was CC of Punjab. He is my uncle, the brother of my father."

"What happened?" Chester asked shakily.

"I do not know. My uncle told me that in his twenty-two years of service in His Majesty's army, he had never heard a junior officer speak so forcefully to a general."

"Jaysus, what did he say?"

"I believe Major Hubble's most profound words were when he told the general, 'You're a fucking fool.' At that point Darlington removed his staff from the room. Only Major Hubble and Major General Brodhead remained."

"Yow."

"Mother of God."

"How long ago did this happen?"

"Over an hour ago."

"Oh Jaysus, they've jailed him."

They sat in fear-filled silence until Lieutenant Jeremy arrived. Jeremy knew nothing except that Christopher had a meeting at Corps.

"I wonder if those cops ever got out of the closet," Chester said.

"I wonder if Sonya made it out of Cairo."

"I hope she took Shaara with her. Shaara said Sonya promised to take her to Spain."

"I hear Cairo is ready to explode. They say that Corps has given leave to thirty thousand troops and let everyone know that no arrests for misconduct will be made."

"Yeah, I heard the same."

"So Cairo will burn."

"I wish we were going in."

"We made our own personal farewell."

"I hope Sonya made it out of town."

Silence.

"Although I am relieved I was not involved with Villa Valhalla, I should like to also have a tattoo. I have seen you in the showers with envy."

"Sure."

"Absolutely."

"You're going to have to wait awhile."

"I am honored."

Silence.

Mordechai left and returned with his accordion. He tried a happy song. It got baleful looks. He played a sad song. That was better.

"TEN-SHUN!"

Everyone scrambled to their feet as Major Hubble entered, appearing pale and weak.

"As you were," he said with a hoarse voice. As they went gingerly into their chairs, Christopher clasped his hands behind him and paced, groping for the language to express the emotions that overwhelmed him.

"What the devil," he finally managed. "Thank you." He went from man to man and offered his hand, and when that was done, he postured once more. "This does not mean I offer any apologies for the manner in which I have commanded this battalion. While some measures may have seemed excessive, we have a battalion second to none in this entire expeditionary force.... I'm afraid I have some bad news."

Everyone winced and turned their heads on cue as though to duck an oncoming punch.

"The bad news is that I offered my resignation to General Brodhead over my behavior and he refused it so I am to continue as your commanding officer." He snickered at his humor and was delighted to see broad smiles greet him. "I don't imagine I'm going to change all that much, although I have gained some new insight into my obligation to take care of you no less than you have taken care of me."

Jeremy's eyes brimmed near tears. Chris had made his first gesture to escape from a life-long prison imposed by privilege. It was about as much humility as his brother could muster.

"I say, I have other news. Shall we gather 'round the big table here? Do you suppose we might have some tea?"

"Yes, sir," Chester snapped, and went to the always ready pot.

"Nothing but tea for me for a while." Chris loosened his Sam Browne belt and put his jacket over the back of the chair. He could not help but feel a great deal of warmth coming to him from the men, a kind of sensation he had felt from his mother, long ago. Many times he had passed a room in a museum or missed an opera he should have attended or passed by some very special flowers at a show and he'd wished he had gone in. He was in that room now and it was a wonderful place to be.

"May I say, Major," Rory said, "that we are deeply sorry for your troubles."

"Thank you. It was quite a blow. I do censor a great deal of outgoing mail. It seems that this is a rather common occurrence for us chaps. . . . Shall we get to our business?"

After tea was served and properly balanced with condiments, Christopher wore a sly grin. "I was fortunate to be able to have a chat with Central Command today. I was able to convince General Darlington to reverse our order of departure. As of this moment, the Seventh Light Horse is breaking down to ship out immediately."

It was somewhat short of a formal hip-hip-hooray, but everyone shouted in delight and backs were pounded.

"The gaffer squad now takes on a very key position in the coming operations. You men will be dealing head-on with staff officers, battalion and company commanders, etcetera, etcetera. Commensurate with your duties and so that you will not be bullied about by rank, I have been authorized to issue field commissions. Goodwood, Yurlob, Tarbox, and Landers—you are now subalterns . . . second lieutenants."

The men that greeted the first news with such noise, greeted this with drop-jawed, stunned silence. When it sank in, they began to laugh and punch one another in the shoulders.

"Dr. Pearlman, as the vet of the Anzac Expeditionary Forces, you are commissioned as a first lieutenant."

"But how? I don't officially exist!"

"You are on detached duty from the Czar's Army. Russia is an ally."

"Lieutenant Pearlman?"

"Lieutenant Pearlman?"

"Hey, Lieutenant Pearlman."

"This puts us all on a first-name basis," Christopher said. "Landers ... Rory, you're off to Lemnos in twenty-four hours. Lieutenant Modi, you're off on a buying mission, at once. I'll explain in a moment. Tarbox and Goodwood will work with Jeremy on the logistics of breaking down the battalion and getting it moved. Jiggle things around to get maximum speed and efficiency."

"Yes, sir."

"Yurlob."

"Sir."

"You're in charge of all mule gear. Pick a work party from B Company."

He turned to Rory again. "You are to take a platoon from A Company to Lemnos and fence the paddocks, and what support buildings will be needed, blacksmith shop, medical shack, etcetera, etcetera. At the same time you will scout out the terrain of Lemnos and track out a three to five mile training run. Your orders state that the commanding officer on Lemnos is to give you top priority. After we break here, make up a rough plan of what you'll need and bring it to my office."

"I've got it."

"Doctor Modi. We have commandeered a cattle boat and have it on hold at Alexandria. You will locate four to five hundred tiptop mules and open up sources to keep reinforcements coming, as required. Get the first batch to Lemnos, yesterday."

"Questions, Major Chris. I am utterly beyond certain that I can come up with a couple hundred mules at once."

"Lord, where?"

"Cyprus. The Cyprus mules are renowned. They are even in Shakespeare."

"You don't say? Which play would that be?"

"*Othello.*"

"Bully. Well, we are in good fortune. Cyprus has been annexed and is directly under control of British forces."

"I know the mule dealers from my years in Palestine. Because of the urgency, I need a few things."

"Shoot."

"Greeks are Greeks. I'll have to bargain hard. If I know I can pay a premium, they will sell me all the mules we need and their daughters as well."

Chris stopped to consider. It flashed through his head that he didn't quite trust the Jew and was hesitant to give him carte blanche. What the hell. One had to trust.

"Can you work around the traders?"

"You don't change two thousand years of doing business. If a dealer can be worked with a bribe, then let him get us the mules. He'll find them in a minute."

"Rather hate doing business that way, but, considering the circumstances, pay what you must and get them to Lemnos."

"Good," Modi said. "In that case I would like to take the best negotiator with me, a man from the Zion Mule Corps. He speaks Greek. I have been on many trips with him. Cyprus has Greeks, Turks, and Arabs. He knows, first rate, how to deal with them."

"That sounds reasonable. What is this chap's name."

"Ben Gurion. David Ben Gurion. No rank like the rest of the Zion Mules."

"Odd name, what?"

"It is an ancient Hebrew name. Many Zionist settlers changed to such names. And, one more thing. I need Yurlob to come with me. I can verify the health and physical condition of the mules. However, I must have an expert to make judgments on habits and temperament. Even some of the best mules do not train well. I must have a man with the perfect eye."

"It's a good suggestion," Rory said.

"All right, then, it's the two of you ... and this Ben ... something fellow."

"Believe me," Yurlob said in agreement, "they will not sell us any three-legged mules."

March 18, 1915—Dispatched from Headquarters, Cyprus at 0530 from special mule purchasing commission to Major Christopher Hubble—Seventh New Zealand Light Horse Battalion—Camp Anzac—Mena Egypt Stop Decoded at Corps Message Center—Delivered okay.

Message as follows:

Three hundred twenty-eight magnificent mules purchased and en route to Lemnos. Two hundred more promised by end of week. Ship will round trip for them. Because of volume Ben Gurion was able to purchase lot well below market value. Subaltern Yurlob Singh properly tattooed in Nicosia. Shalom. Lieutenant Modi.

CHAPTER
74

March 16

To First Lord of the Admiralty Winston Churchill from Admiral HH Harmon *Commander, Naval Forces Mediterranean—*

At 0500 operations commenced to conclude minesweeping operations. Previous sweeps have looked extremely clean but intelligence cautions that Turks continually seeding new fields plus individual strays.

Our forces entered Narrows with forty-two class LM sweepers, 15 French sweepers plus following.

Eight Beagle class refitted for minesweeping.

Six River class.

Four torpedo boats as spotters with light sweeps.

One flotilla of picket boats with explosive creeps.

Marine sharpshooters aboard all vessels.

Operations will continue until 0900 March 18 when all-out assault into the Dardanelles will commence.

March 17

Seventy-four mines blown. No damage inflicted on our vessels.

We have ventured past Fort 20 with no fire from Turkish forces.

Ceased operations at dark, boats withdrawn.

March 18

0530: All minesweepers have entered Straits for a final go-round.

Attack on Dardanelles Narrows commenced

1045: *Queen Elizabeth, Inflexible, Lord Nelson, Triumph* and *Prince George* enter Straits.

1222: French vessels *Seffern, Gaulois, Charlemagne* and *Bouvet* now in Dardanelles and engaging Turkish forts.

1325: Turkish forts numbers seven, eight, eight A, thirteen, sixteen, seventeen, twenty and twenty-one appear to be silenced.

RED ALERT   RED ALERT   RED ALERT   RED ALERT

1354: French vessel *Bouvet* smoking—in distress.

1358: *Bouvet* has heeled and sunk in 36 fathoms before assistance could reach her.

1359: *Hull, Implacable, Lon Don* and *Prince of Wales* ordered into Strait to reinforce fleet.

1430: Relief ships enter Straits and engage ports. Minesweepers in reserve ordered in.

RED ALERT   RED ALERT   RED ALERT   RED ALERT

1604: *Irresistible* listing to starboard.

1614: *Inflexible* has struck mine, quitting line and proceeding out of Dardanelles.

RED ALERT   RED ALERT   RED ALERT   RED ALERT

1730: *Irresistible* abandoned under Turkish fire, sinking fast.

RED ALERT   RED ALERT   RED ALERT   RED ALERT

1850: *Ocean* has struck mine, listing, ordered abandoned, sinking fast.

1851: Roundup of smaller vessels indicates seven minesweepers of various classes sunk and ten more hit.

RED ALERT   RED ALERT   RED ALERT   RED ALERT

1900: *Gaulois* seriously damaged by gunfire, is sinking.

RED ALERT   RED ALERT   RED ALERT   RED ALERT

All vessels ordered to disengage and retire from Dardanelles immediately.

GALLIPOLI

BY RORY LARKIN

PART ONE: ANZAC COVE

Among the precious gifts my beloved uncle, Conor Larkin, bestowed upon me was knowing the luxury of bending my face into an open book and sopping up its pages until my eyes were more red than white.

Because of this, I have been able to attain a measure of coherent thought when I put words on paper. Conor taught me that the most ancient of human compulsions, one that sets man apart from all other creatures, is an insatiable desire to leave behind him the story of his times, from drawings on cave walls to the masterpieces of literature and, in this case, one soldier's memory of a battle that should never have taken place.

This urge to remember began the day the *Wagga Wagga* entered the ship-filled port of Mudros on the Greek Aegean island of Lemnos.

Some of the campaign returns to me in snatches. Some of the things I heard or learned. All is branded onto my soul. Events become intertwined, as the dead bodies of Turks and Anzacs lay intertwined in no-man's-land, each man's bayonet having done its stick and then they die together, falling to their knees, then sleeping forever in one another's arms.

Lemnos, a browned-out outcrop of some ancient volcano, arose from the sea sixty miles from Gallipoli and was to be our expedition's forward base.

In the Mudros harbor and on its beaches we went on constant maneuvers trying to refine the clunky business of getting down the ship's rope ladders and into landing boats, then rowing onto the beach.

The Seventh Light Horse was fortunate to get in three solid weeks of hard training with janets and jacks. Yurlob and Modi had purchased well. Like the final rehearsal of a scattered enterprise, everything fell into place at Mudros.

In the third week of April of 1915 we reboarded the *Wagga Wagga* feeling dreadful about Yurlob Singh's orders to remain on Lemnos, assigned to train new packers and mules and send them on to us as our losses required.

Yurlob Singh broke his life-long military posture and fell weeping into Modi's arms as we boarded ship. He had been the nonperson of the gaffers until the incident at the Hotel Aida. We had no realization of the deep, abiding bonds we had made. We now knew this venture would mean camaraderie for life. Well, that's longer than many marriages.

A magnificent armada of more than a hundred ships, led by a half-dozen powerful dreadnoughts, sailed forth resolutely to cross the sixty miles of sea to the Gallipoli Peninsula.

General Darlington's message was read to us, a rather schoolboyish charge, I thought.

ANZACS! WE SALLY FORTH ON NOBLE COMMISSION. I KNOW THAT YOU WILL PROVE YOURSELVES WORTHY SONS OF THE EMPIRE. ON BEHALF OF YOUR COMMANDERS AND HIS MAJESTY, I WISH YOU WELL. THREE CHEERS AND GOD SAVE THE KING!

DARLINGTON
COMMANDING GENERAL
ALLIED EXPEDITIONARY FORCES

Promoted to Lieutenant General, Sir Llewelyn Brodhead, the Anzac commander was a bit less zippy. He related his long-standing fondness for Australians and New Zealanders and vowed he considered us equal to the task ahead.

We received a third message from Major General Sir Alexander Godley, who commanded the New Zealand forces but had remained an enigma to us. Story goes that he was an Anglo-Irish opportunist leftover from the Boer War and hired by the New Zealand government to build up our armed forces. The glimpses I got of him conveyed something like an ice sculpture.

Johnny, Chester, and myself went into the wardroom a bit smugly for the officers' briefing. Maps were passed out and a larger one rolled down over a blackboard.

Gallipoli.

There was a smattering of laughter and applause.

"I see that no one here seems surprised," Major Chris said, continually testing his new penchant for humor. "First, the over-all scheme. A French division, mostly North African colonials, Moroccans and such, will land on the eastern, or Asian, side of the straits at Kum Kale. This is the site of ancient Troy, Homer, and the *Odyssey* and all that rot crammed into us by our wicked schoolmasters. There is not much of a Turkish military presence in the entire Anatolian province and not much is anticipated in the way of Turkish counteractivity. So, the French will hold open their half of the door.

"What is considered the main invasion thrust will take place at Cape Helles, here at the tip of the peninsula. A number of British brigades will land at Helles, principally to create a diversion for the British Twenty-ninth Division, which will drive inland up to this hill here, Achi Baba. So far so good?"

Everyone nodded.

"Anzacs," Chris went on. "As the British Twenty-ninth hits Cape Helles, the Aussies will simultaneously land ten miles north above this land protrusion called Gaba Tepe. Our site has been designated as Brighton Beach. As you can see, the Aussies will be landing in soft, gently rising hilly terrain."

"Resistance?" someone asked.

"Not too much, we think. The Turks will concentrate on Cape Helles and we believe our landing ten miles away is not going to give them time to organize. Considering everything, the Anzac should be on the Plain of Maidos, here, within an hour of landing. From there it should be clear sailing to drive to the Dardanelles just above the Narrows, keeping Turkish reinforcements from reaching Cape Helles.

"Second day," Chris went on. "The New Zealand Brigades, the Aucklands, Otagos, Wellingtons, will land at Brighton Beach and move up alongside the Aussie units in their push across the peninsula. Landers, Jeremy, Goodwood, Tarbox, and Subaltern Richards and your platoon will split into two boats. Jeremy, you will take half the platoon in your boat along with half the barbed wire. Unload and secure the supplies on the beach.

"Tarbox."

"Sir."

"You'll be in the second boat with Landers and Goodwood. You are to take over as beach master using the other half of the platoon. The Anzac assault troops will be carrying three to five days of ammunition, food, and water. New supplies will be landing right behind you. The beach will belong to you and Jeremy, get it organized."

"Yes, sir."

"Landers and Goodwood. Second wave, second day. You two find us our paddock area, stake it out, get back to the beach, and have Jeremy bring the platoon up to lay out barbed wire perimeters. Obviously, we want as much cover as we can for the paddock, and get it as close to the beach as is safely possible.

"I will land late on day two or early on day three and set up battalion headquarters. The mule barges will land on day five. Questions, gentlemen?"

"The British Twenty-ninth drives up from Cape Helles, while we drive across the peninsula," I said. "I take it we hook up."

"Yes, here, below Chunuk Bair Plateau. Chunuk Bair is the key bastion on Gallipoli. We hope to consolidate our forces by the sixth or seventh day, organize an attack, and take Chunuk Bair Plateau, say, on the eighth or ninth day. Once that strongpoint falls, the peninsula is ours and the way to Constantinople is open. So, in fact, the Anzac is to act as a diversion, a thorn in the Turk's side."

"What is north of Brighton Beach?" the Company C Captain asked. "The map is terribly vague."

"I agree we haven't gotten the best of intelligence. We've also tried to photograph from aircraft. I have a set of pictures here but find them hard to understand. I can say this much. North of Brighton Beach and inland to Chunuk Bair is very difficult terrain—ravines, gullies, cliffs, etcetera, etcetera. This is where the bulk of the Turkish defenses are expected. That is precisely why we are landing south, in relatively flat ground, to catch the Turks by surprise."

There were many questions, and most answers fell into the "We don't know for certain," "Our best estimates," "We feel confident." How many Turks? Perhaps four divisions. They are not considered to be first-rate troops.

I personally did not like the underestimation of the Turks. Maybe that's what they always say of one's enemy before battle. The Turks were experienced. Except for a few of our units, we were all untried, green, raw, without a day of combat. The Turks would be fighting on Turkish soil. They were up there and we would be down here and no matter . . . sooner or later Chunuk Bair Plateau had to be taken.

Maybe I worry too damned much, I don't know. I used to drive the Squire crazy with my mania for detail.

When I finally got to stretch out and think, the unreality of what we are about to do hit me. It would be easy enough for a Frenchman to say why he was in a trench on the Western Front, but why were people going wild with war fever in Auckland and Sydney? It was because of the Empire that we became enemies of the Turks, yet our kinship with Empire, our love of King, was mild stuff.

The big adventure, that's the ticket. Get off our wee islands and see the big world. There was a war to go to, so why not go while the going is good.

Georgia had had enough of war. She knew war. We only imagined war. Maybe you go to war just because it's there to go to and you haven't the slightest idea what it's really all about.

One thing was for certain. All of us—Jeremy, Johnny, Chester—had to show one another that we were capable of what might come. This became an ultimate goal—to come through clean for your mates. That's the mesh that makes the machine go, belief in the man on your right and your left.

Men had been caught up in this queer phenomenon in this very place three thousand years ago or some such. An armada launched by the face of a woman—but who owned the Trojan horse this time, us or the Turks?

I went over my coming day's work one more time. Maybe I

was overdoing it, but I put a pair of semaphore flags and a Very pistol and a pair of flares in my combat pack. Just a hunch that if I'm out alone scouting an area, I want the folks on the beach to know where I am. I felt good about Johnny and Jeremy, real good. I was a little worried about Chester. Chester had done everything we'd asked of him and a hell of a lot more, but something about him was so fragile. I'd get him through the first day and he'd be fine. I promised myself not to let him panic. . . .

I'm sleepy . . . and she is lying on the bed in the ship's cabin, all so white and rounded and the green silk shining and weaving in and out of her body, between her legs. . . . How's that now? With all that's on my mind, there's a stirring for her between my legs. Jesus, do you know how I loved you, Georgia. Oh Lord, why can I never tell you?

It seemed as though I had just closed my eyes when a predawn burst shook the *Wagga Wagga*. We rushed outside to see the warships cannonading. Orange bursts and flames were visible several miles off.

The light of day was so inundated with smoke from the gunfire we could not see the land.

The bos'n's whistle pierced the din.

"First wave assemble!"

A large lighter pulled up shipside. Reels of barbed wire, machine-gun ammo, water cans, were lowered and set in the boat.

Major Chris pulled us back away from the railing.

"The Aussies hit heavy resistance yesterday," he said. "We're pushing up our landing schedule. The Otagos and Wellingtons will hit shore at 0515. Move your time up to 0545."

"How far inland are our people?"

"Don't know. Keep your men as near to the beach as you can. Set up your own perimeter. Landers, Goodwood, you'd better take a light machine-gun squad with you when you go scouting. See you later."

"All right," Jeremy called twenty yards down the deck, "over the side."

"Webbing open! If anything falls off you, let it go."

My lighter signaled they had our gear stowed.

"Let's go, lads!" I called.

Oh Jesus! Two steps down the ladder I got my first true view of the water. It was foaming from shrapnel and bullets! The chop of the water slammed our lighter against the side of the *Wagga Wagga*. The man below me fell from the ladder and was crushed between the boat and the ship.

"Keep those fucking lines tight against the ship!"

I jumped into the boat, and began pulling men into the lighter and shoving them into their places. Johnny Tarbox was in last. We let go of the ropes and a wave hurled us away from the ship.

As the *Wagga Wagga* did a sweeping turn and retreated to rendezvous with the other troopships, a dozen destroyers bore down on us and tossed lines to our lighters, then maneuvered so that we were behind them. Our destroyer, HMS *Greenport*, was already towing a pair of pontoon piers. With a group of lighters hooked onto her stern, the *Greenport* waited for the remaining destroyers to ready their tows, and we all moved in a deliberate line for the shore.

The wake from the destroyers, the shells, and a sea gone angry rolled and pitched us without mercy. Vomiting broke out.

"Puke between your legs!"

Suddenly our line moved underneath the curtain of smoke and there she was, Gallipoli! My first reaction was, it was like New Zealand in a drought season. Rolling hills and . . .

Our boat went into shock as everybody dove to the bottom. As we inched toward land the racket grew. Now the *Greenport* and other destroyers dropped anchor and began slamming shells into the hills.

We needed to transfer one more time, from the lighters into lifeboat-size skiffs. Fortunately the lighter was higher than the boats and we could hurl ourselves over.

Johnny pointed. "That's the first wave, Rory. The Otagos. They're ashore!"

I saw Subaltern Richards, our platoon commander, working

his way to the back of our boat. Shrapnel had torn off his arm and part of his shoulder. How in the hell he remained conscious I don't know. There was no place to put a tourniquet on him. He'd be gone in a few minutes.

"Platoon Serjeant Amberson has my command," he said, and he went down fast, twitched, screamed, and was still.

"Take off his pips, half his identification tag. Get his wallet to send home," Johnny said in utter calm.

Chester did what Johnny ordered as I called for Platoon Serjeant Amberson to show his hand. He signaled back that he was in control up front.

"A couple of you grab his legs," Johnny said, reaching under Subaltern Richards's remaining shoulder. "All right, lads, heave him over the side."

I wiped Richards's blood off my field glasses. The Otago Battalion was moving inland! All morning all I could think of was getting on land, but now I was consumed with a vague notion that time might suddenly stand still and a voice from the sky might order us back to the *Wagga Wagga* and we would sail away. . . .

Time seemed to flee. 0542.

Johnny jabbed me in the ribs and smiled.

"Rowers! Man your oars!"

Our wave of some fifty boats grunted forward from a half-mile out. Oarsmen rotated, sweated, cursed. The racket of gunfire was so overwhelming we had to depend on hand signals. Come on, get this fucker on land!

"YOOOOWWWW!"

JESUS! SOMETHING LIKE TO TORE MY HEAD OFF! BLOOD AND OTHER STUFF SHOWERED ME! I instinctively felt myself frantically. Nothing hurt, nothing burned. I could move my arms and legs, but I was awash in blood and . . . and . . . BRAINS! My face! My face! It was all there. My chest, fine! *NO! NO!* The top of Johnny Tarbox's head was gone.

I don't know what happened to me then . . . I was almost blacked out . . . I heard vague distant voices.

"Cut off his pips . . . get his identification tag. . . ."

"Empty his pockets."

"All right, lads, heave him over the side."

I was hurtling down into a hole and very sleepy. Something hurt me. A sharp blow to my face! Someone was shaking me, screaming at me. My eyes crawled open.

Chester stood over me. He had me by the lapels and he came slowly into focus, slapping my face and jostling me with all his might.

"Snap out of it, Rory!" he screamed.

"What . . . what . . . ?"

"Goddamn you, Rory. Get yourself together. We've got work to do."

I groped for him and hung on to him for dear life, but he shoved me off. A soldier behind him handed him a bucket of seawater, which he poured on me, and then another.

"Johnny!" I screamed, "Johnny! Johnny! Johnny!"

"Johnny Tarbox is dead! What is my name? Tell me my name!"

"Johnny . . . "

"Fuck, I'm not Johnny. He's dead, Rory. Tell me my name, you son of a bitch!"

"Chester," I whimpered. "Chester Targood . . . "

"That's not my fucking name!"

I dropped my face into my hands, but he grabbed me by the hair. "What's my name, you no good asshole? Tell me my name."

"Subaltern Chester Goodwood, Seventh New Zealand Light Horse."

"Where are we?"

"Gallipoli."

"What's your job!"

"Soon as we get our people ashore and unloaded and join up with Jeremy . . . he'll secure a perimeter and we'll find a paddock and stake it out."

"Who's running this half of the platoon?"

"Platoon Serjeant . . . Amberson . . . up front . . . I'm all right now, Chester."

"Where are we?"

"Heading into Brighton Beach. Jeremy's boat is a little behind us. Send Johnny's pips and pistol up front to the Amberson lad."

"Look at me," he demanded.

I did and assured him I was on "go."

"Give me Johnny's pips and pistol. I'll take them up front," I said. "I'm going ashore first with a squad. You take the rest of the lads, unload, and hang out near the beach."

"Don't go too far inland," Chester said.

"Take the semaphore flags out of my pack," I said. "By the sounds of this racket, we're not too far from the front lines. You and Jeremy catch up to me as fast as you can."

I pushed to the front of the boat. Jesus, I was shaky. My head was working but my legs didn't want to mind. I found the Platoon Serjeant.

"What's your name, Serj?"

"Chipper Amberson. Call me Chipper. You're Rory Landers. I saw you destroy the Aussie at Port Albany."

"Well, he's on our side now. Chipper, you hang back on the beach with Chester back there, the kid with the glasses. Get the boat unloaded and hold. Now, I need the light machine gun with me. I'm going a little inland."

"Corporal O'Rourke!"

"Here."

"Bring your squad in with Lieutenant Landers."

"Righto."

The boat banged into land, throwing us awry.

"Over the side!"

Shit, we were waist-deep in water. I assembled O'Rourke and his three lads and looked back at the boat just in time to see Chipper Amberson ripped open by machine-gun bullets. He went under with the boat cracking him and then a blob of red pushing up from the sea. God Almighty. He was an officer for three minutes, maybe.

Chester was at my side and told me he had control. I waved for Corporal O'Rourke and his lads to follow.

I could see Chester turning command over to a warrant officer and then running down the beach waving Jeremy's boat in.

OH DEAR GOD IN HEAVEN!

For the first time in years, Mary's name came to my lips in prayer. Brighton Beach was littered with dead and dying men! There were only a few yards of beach to be had and then a steep uphill climb. The bodies were thick, thick like seagulls after a fishing trawler, dozens, hundreds, lying still or screaming or moaning while others were trying to put on iodine and wrap them up ... like ... I walked over the beach unable to step between them ... sorry, mate ... medics will be here soon ... sorry, mates ... shit, one of my squad went down.

We were in thick, prickly brush five and six feet high. It was no gentle slope, we were fucking going fucking uphill and the brush held dozens and dozens of dead men tangled in it.

I found a concave area big enough to hold the four of us and we huddled in.

"O'Rourke, I'm Rory. We've worked together at Lemnos." Turning to my left, I said, "What's your name, pal?" slapping a young Anzac on the shoulder.

"Happy Stevens from Palmerston North."

"Rory Landers. How many rounds have we got?"

"Two hundred."

"Not enough. Happy, get back to the beach. Find Chester Goodwood."

"Righto."

"We need a box of maybe three or four hundred more rounds. We'll stay right here."

"I'm gone," Happy said as he crouched and dashed for the beach.

"You read a map, O'Rourke?"

"They didn't make me corporal for nothing."

I opened my map. It was sticky with Johnny's blood. I looked uphill. Too steep. Something wrong. I studied the curve of the coastline. The jut of land called Gaba Tepe was nowhere to be seen to the south ... but north ... a large knob of landfall and then a long, long sweep of coast.

"If this is Brighton Beach I'll kiss your ass at battalion assembly," O'Rourke said.

"North?"

"North," he agreed, "we're north of our beach."

"Looks like they brought us ashore into the middle of the Turkish Army." I cleaned my field glasses. "Dead men as far uphill as I can see." I could make out Otagos pushing toward the Aussie line just beyond my sight. "There's a battle going on up there, maybe a little over a half-mile. The terrain is really dirty," I said, passing the binoculars to O'Rourke.

"Seems like the Turks are above our front line on higher ground and firing into the beach," he said.

"You've got it," I answered. "They're hitting us up here and down there with artillery. We're in a soft spot for now. Jesus, there goes a landing boat . . . blew it to hell."

I caught a semaphore flag just twenty yards away behind some brush.

"Over here!"

Happy Stevens of Palmerston North . . . why did I think of Palmerston North? . . . dashed up to us followed by a pair lugging an ammo box between them.

"Lieutenant Hubble is ashore and connected with Lieutenant Goodwood. They'll be up in a few moments, soon as they organize the beach party."

"You're Dan Elgin," I said.

He smiled. "Gisborne, Poverty Bay."

"I'd say we found poverty bay right here," O'Rourke said.

"And you're Spears," I said.

"By God, you remembered. Kaikoura, South Island."

"Sure, I remembered," I said, "Spears put the pack on your mule backward on Lemnos. Don't let him feed the ammo belts."

"Now, that's something to be remembered for," Spears said.

"Find yourselves cover. Don't go more than a few yards. Face the beach so any new troops heading uphill won't mistake you for Turks."

No sooner had I spoken than a new wave of men were quickly moving through us toward the front. I inquired. Things were no better on the beach. I could see why Stevens of Palmerston North was called Happy. He grinned as he caught sight of me and came in with Jeremy and Chester on his heels. They tucked in with me.

"My boat was a mess," Jeremy huffed. "We got caught on a sand spit, had to wade in from chest high. Lost three men and several reels of wire. Chester said Johnny Tarbox didn't make it."

"He's gone."

"Beach is under control," Jeremy said. "We've stacked the barbed-wire reels up against a little knoll. It should be safe. Rest of the platoon knows where to dig in. Right now, they're trying to get the wounded back to the hospital ship."

I nodded.

"Well so much for naval gunfire obliterating the Turks," Jeremy said. "I can't locate us on the map."

"Neither can I," I said, "and I don't see any place here to set up a paddock."

"Look!" O'Rourke cried, pointing uphill.

Coming over the rise above us, the walking wounded dragged their way back from the front. Litters holding the more seriously wounded were being hauled by two to four men, most of the walking wounded helping someone or trying to carry a part of the stretchers.

I flagged down a captain, arm shattered at the elbow.

"Give us a drink," he gasped.

"Can you talk?" Jeremy asked.

"Captain Huddleson, C Company, Otagos . . . what's left of it . . . over this ridge there's a deep gully, then a real high hill . . . it's not on the bloody map . . . can't see it from here . . . but you won't miss it. The Turks are dug in with a sweep of the entire field . . . they're kicking the shit out of us. . . ."

He began to tremble and his eyes rolled back in his head. Huddleson mumbled he had to get his men to safety. We tried to calm him, assure him they would make the beach safely. Up ahead, a dead man was rolled off a stretcher. O'Rourke brought the litter to us and we set the Captain on it.

About twenty yards uphill was a nice big boulder. The view

of things would be better from there. "Let's go upstairs and take a look. O'Rourke!"

"Here!"

"Come up to that rock with us! Happy Stevens of Palmerston North!"

"Yo!"

"You're in charge of the machine gun. Sit tight. Do not help with the wounded unless they fall on you!"

"Yo!"

One by one we made the sprint to the boulder and tucked in, our backs uphill to the front lines. The view to the coastline from here was better. While we studied it through our field glasses, wounded still poured down from the front and newly landed troops were passing through them on their way up.

"North," Jeremy said. "They've landed us north of Brighton Beach."

"North," Chester agreed. "We're more than a mile from where we should be. Down there is the Plain of Maidos. We're supposed to be crossing it."

"Jesus Christ," I muttered. "We're going right into the jaws of the Turkish defenses. We might be heading right into Chunuk Bair."

"Damn!" Jeremy cried. "First the naval gunfire draws a nil and now this. Isn't anybody talking to anybody in our command?"

"Hell, don't worry, it's only the first day," Chester said.

"Fucking funny."

"Well, I guess I'd better find us a paddock," I said. "Right off the beach over there starts up with gullies and ravines. Chester, want to keep me company?"

"I'm coming, too," Jeremy said.

"You're the one they sent to beach master school with Johnny. You better get back there and give some direction to the incoming boats and get those fucking piers lashed up."

"Are you giving me orders?" Jeremy demanded.

"Yes," Chester said. "It's your beach, Jeremy. We'll find the stables."

Jeremy grumbled acquiescence.

"We all want to go up the hill and fight Turks," I said, "but on the other hand, we seem to be the only ones here who know what the hell we're doing. I'm taking the machine-gun squad with us. If we can locate a paddock by, say, 0330, I'll send one of the men back to you. Get as many men and barbed-wire reels up to me as you can. If we go past 0400, we'll have to dig in for the night."

"Do you have flares?"

"I've got a pair. No time to look for more."

"There's a meltrami blowing," Chester said. "Look, a reverse wind. Everything in the sea is being pushed north. We'll be scouting that region over there." He pointed. "We'll try to stay within a couple of hundred yards of the beach."

"See you later or first thing in the morning," Jeremy said, and turned for the beach. A man with a leg wound was on his knees. Jeremy pulled him up and put an arm over his shoulder to help him.

I brought my lads together. "We're hunting for a gully or ravine north by east, say at twenty degrees to forty degrees, or like one o'clock if that knob of land is noon. I'll move in twenty-yard bursts, more or less. Chester is always in sight at my rear. You are twenty yards behind."

It was the most fucking miserable day of my life. No one had warned us that the sun shot the temperature up over a hundred degrees, even in the springtime. There wasn't much in the way of firefights, but the day was spent crawling on our bellies. We must have been in a line of fire from Chunuk Bair into what was supposed to be Brighton Beach. Shit! Had we landed on the true Brighton, we'd be beyond their fire.

I couldn't go too fast because the lads behind me were packing a fair load. I wanted to drop my jacket but the rock and underbrush would have ripped my flesh to pieces.

At one time or another we all came close to fainting from the heat. I had to keep telling them, "Easy on the water, lads, easy on the water."

Each gully was either in Turkish gun sights or had a ridge sticking up in the air exposing us to the skyline.

SHIT, NO! GODDAMN SONOFABITCH!

We were huddled in safe shade when our entire field started blowing apart! Our own destroyers were shooting us up. As we scattered for better cover I saw O'Rourke go . . . in God only knows how many pieces.

It seemed like a year before the assholes stepped their fire farther up the hill.

It was closing in on our witching hour. One more exposed hillside to crawl, our fourth gully. Either this would be the one or we'd have to call it a day.

Lord! It was almost like looking at the Promised Land from across the River Jordan. The gully below took a weird U-shaped turn with the end of it running down to the beach at an off-angle. We gathered up and counted shells landing in the area. Only one in five minutes, that was off the side walls. We could live with that.

"Happy."

"Yo."

"It's too late to set the barbed wire down, but get down to the beach and tell Hubble where we're at. He's to be here at the crack of."

It ran through my mind that we could all go back, but I didn't like the top of the ravine. It was too wide open. Hell . . . I don't know. I didn't like it that there were none of our troops above us here . . . the Turks could just maybe slip into the ravine. . . .

"Take off, Happy."

"Elgin, Spears, Chester. I like that indent about halfway up the ravine wall. Let's set up the machine gun there."

How in the hell with all those thousands of men shooting millions of rounds did anyone leave this ravine open? We set up the machine gun so that if anyone came into the middle of the ravine we'd catch them broadside.

I got a craving feeling in my stomach. I was hungry. We hadn't eaten for over twenty hours. I'd heard bitching about the rations, but on this very day nothing ever tasted so good. That would change over time.

As the firing went from dusk into darkness we moved to get a better look at the sea. There seemed to be more chaos than ever. I didn't like the looks of the water. It was filled with bobbing bodies.

Elgin and Spears were on the gun. Chester and I had our first minutes to reflect. I found a leaning rock, put my back against it, and directed abuse at myself. I hadn't made myself very proud this day.

"Forget it," Chester said, reading my mind.

"I didn't know myself," I whispered.

"And I didn't have Johnny Tarbox's brains and blood all over me. You were back in control within a minute."

"That's not what I mean, Chester. Not that I haven't been scared in my life. The worst fear I'd known before today was realizing I'd never see Georgia again. But I was totally frozen in terror when Johnny got hit. I couldn't move. I couldn't think. Jesus, I didn't know anything like this existed."

And I was going to take care of Chester today, make certain he didn't become freaky. He went through the day like a Sunday stroll in the botanical gardens.

"You've known the kind of fear I felt today, haven't you?" I asked.

"Yes."

"What happened to you?"

"It's just the way your life turns out, sometimes."

"What can you do about it, Chester?"

"Recognize that from this day on, the monster is sitting on our shoulder all the time. It can strike a hundred times, never twice the same way. It's worse when you pretend it's not there. Recognize it! Know it the instant that flush of terror paralyzes you and, at that same instant, say, 'Hello friend, it's you again . . . you sure scare the shit out of me but you can't stop me from thinking or moving.' You'll get plenty of practice."

I took Johnny's wallet. There was a picture of him and his old man. He loved his dad. Thought about him after. The photograph of his mother was so old and faded I couldn't make much of it. He never got a letter from her.

I'd made a basic mistake about Chester. Never judge courage from the size of a man. Won't make that mistake again. Bloody giant, that kid was.

We went to Spears and Elgin. "Two up and two down," I said. "You take the first watch. See if you can stay awake for two hours. If not, wake us up. If you have to talk, talk with your lips on each other's ear. No fucking noise, lads."

Chester and I found a bit of softer ground a few yards away. We were nearly asleep when some short rounds of artillery fell close to us. We could feel the heat and waves of the blast and a kick of dirt.

"Mind if I curl up with you?" Chester asked.

"My pleasure."

"If you feel an erection," he said, "don't take it personally. It only means I have to pee."

"Well, you'll get no hard-on from me this night," I retorted.

After a time.

"You know what?"

"What?"

"It's my birthday," Chester said.

"What the hell. I had mine a week ago. I turned twenty-one. My old man can't get me back now. How old are you anyhow, Chester?"

"Truth?"

"Doesn't make any difference out here."

"I'm turning seventeen."

I put my hand over Chester's mouth and watched his eyes open. What a kid! He wasn't even alarmed. I put my mouth around his ear. "Turks," I said. "They came over the ridge and are down in middle of the gully. Elgin's at the trigger. I'm putting up a flare in about thirty seconds."

I rolled away from him and put a flare into the Very pistol. There was almost no noise below. The Turks must be wearing rags over their shoes. There! A little snap of brush . . . I want them in just a little deeper . . . just a little . . .

I aimed for the opposite wall of the gully so we could light them up without being seen ourselves. The sound of the cartridge arcing out brought quick, loud whispers from the Turks. *THERE!* Night to day! They were caught and frozen in the white brilliance . . . trapped. The dummies were bunched up.

"Go!"

Elgin was lovely . . . a real machine-gunner . . . short bursts . . . picking up first on those who might make a charge at us . . . a scramble . . . they poured back toward the ridge and escaped. Elgin's tracers kept finding them. I don't know if any of their patrol got back over the ridge alive.

The light over the gully went from fierce white to dull bloody red and popped out . . .

"We'd better move to the opposite wall of the gully," I said, "in case they come back. Good go, lads."

"I didn't even use a half a belt of ammo," Elgin said, taking the carrying handle of the gun and draping it over his shoulder.

"I've got the ammo case," Spears said.

Chester Goodwood was frozen, then shivering and dried up. I slapped him and he grunted a nod. "Want me to carry you or can you hold on to the back of my shirt?"

"I can move," he assured me, wobbling to his feet.

I had studied the lines of the gully during the daylight hours and hoped that in near blackness I could find my way down the center and up the other side. Holding hands or shirts, we skidded and huffed into the gully bed. Something soft under my feet. Shit, a Turk!

He moaned and cried, begging for his life. I dared turn my torch on him for an instant. Poor bastard's stomach was out. His eyes screamed to me for mercy!

"I'd better finish him," I said, "or else he may call to another patrol."

"I'm sorry, Abdul," I said, and shot him.

Elgin and Spears were restless but dropped off to sleep, flinging themselves about and muttering. Chester said nothing. He was going through the same shit I had in the landing boat when I froze.

So, what did the day bring? I had lost much of the awe I had for men wearing admiral's stripes and the red collar of a general. They had done some fucking stupid things today.

As for Chester Goodwood, I suppose wars had been crafted for guys like us. He had become a very big man in my eyes.

All right, Rory, you've now known ultimate fear. You felt it again when the Turkish patrol entered the gully, but by God, the second time you had your head on.

Elgin . . . what a gunner . . . Happy Stevens from Palmerston North . . . where the hell was he? That's right, I sent him back to the beach. I hope he made it . . .

The Turk moaned . . . he refused to die. I couldn't get rid of that wild look he wore. Who would be crying tomorrow in Constantinople? A couple of little kids?

I never thought there would come the day I would wake up with sheer elation at the sight of Major Hubble. Happy had done his job. He had reached the beach. Just before dawn, the platoon and battalion company moved into the beach end of the gully with reels of barbed wire.

I saw them in the middle of the gully! Eight dead Turks! The wounded fellow had crawled halfway up to us when he gave out.

Jeremy handed me his canteen. Nothing ever felt as good going down . . . nothing.

"It was a good thing you were here," Christopher said. "This gully was wide open right down to the beach. The Turks could have come back with a battalion and attacked if you hadn't gotten their patrol."

"Shithouse luck," I mumbled.

Why did I put a Very pistol into my pack? Why did I call for a machine-gun squad even though I knew it would slow me down? Why did I select this ravine? Luck? Luck? Luck? How many lucks do you get before you are Johnny Tarbox? Why Johnny? Why not me? Chester told me that every soldier who ever experienced it probably wondered why he lived and the guy next to him died.

"I understand we lost Tarbox on the landing?" the Major asked.

"Yes, sir."

"Bad luck. Good fellow," Chris said. He scanned our area. "I see you've staked out the paddock. Good go. Jeremy, can you get it enclosed with wire?"

"Yes."

"Up at the top of the gully, don't spare the wire. Lay it down heavy. Major, I got a suspicion that there's a zigzag route into here. We'd better get a company of infantry up there with a couple of Vicker guns."

"I totally agree," Chris said. "You help Jeremy here. I'll take Goodwood back with me so he can explain this draw to General Brodhead."

"How goes the battle?" I asked.

"We're putting a lot of men ashore today," Christopher said. "We'll get everything tidied up."

When Christopher was gone, Jeremy sat alongside me. "Monumental fuckup," Jeremy said. "Naval gunfire, zero. Our landing, one mile north. The Anzacs are digging in for dear life a thousand to fifteen hundred yards uphill. Well, this looks like a fairly good spot."

It was. Not only did we have our paddock but also our battalion headquarters. Later Anzac Corps headquarters dug in in our general area.

With the paddock perimeter laid out and Major Hubble having more hands than needed to dig out battalion headquarters, I went back to the beach to help evacuate the wounded.

The day was all about men pouring onto the beach from the sea, rushing up to shore up our lines while we were getting our wounded into boats ... getting gear ... trying to anchor down the pontoon piers, which were being blown almost as fast as we could set them up.

I glimpsed a blur of faces ... Happy from somewhere ... Chester ... Dan Elgin, my machine-gunner last night, limped in with a leg wound ... whistling artillery, explosions, and the constant cries and moans of the wounded.

I stripped to the waist as the midday heat became insufferable and found myself in charge of one of the working piers, pulling in boat after boat unloading, then loading them with wounded. I filled them up until bodies totally covered the bottom of the craft. Most of them lay ankle deep in blood. As boats pulled off to the troop transport area, I could see the dead being dumped overboard.

By early evening I learned that there were no proper hospital facilities aboard the troopships. It seems that all the Red Cross transports were in service in the English Channel taking men back from the Western Front. We were using cattle boats here with virtually no medical personnel or equipment aboard. Some ships were making for Lemnos, others for Alexandria.

I don't know how many men I loaded that day . . . maybe fifty . . . maybe a hundred boatloads. I was so soggy with their blood, their bodies continually oozing and slipping through my hands.

Chester found me. A perimeter had been established at the head of what was now Mule Gully with two infantry companies digging in to protect it.

We found Jeremy on the beach, somehow managing to keep a line of order in the chaos.

"Let's take a bath," I said.

We couldn't take our boots off, the sea was too filled with sharp-edged bits of lava, and it was equally difficult to find a clean pool of water away from the blood and slime. We came out of the sea sticky. Then, my second delicious tin of bully beef and hard biscuits.

The Major had set up a fairly decent little cave for battalion headquarters in the hillside. "We've ten to twelve thousand more men ashore in this sector," he announced. "They're forming a line up there as best they can. Seems to be lots of open spots. How's the beach, Jeremy?"

"Reasonable. We have our boxes sorted out, more or less, and know about where to send the new units up."

"Rough paddock is ready," Chester said.

"The mules will be coming in another day," I said. "Right now we haven't got the slightest idea of where to dispatch them. I'd like to go out with a squad tomorrow and find our front lines and figure out the best route to each major post."

"Good."

Just like that, Major General Alexander Godley was standing over us in a semicircle of officers. We limped to our feet.

"What have we here?" Godley asked, not even knowing Major Hubble!

"Christopher Hubble, sir, Mule Transportation Battalion. We're making headquarters in this hill and we've set out a barbed wire fence for the paddock, right over there."

"You're the one who put those men stationed at the head of the gully?"

"Yes, sir . . . "

"Next time, get permission from me."

With no more, no less, he stomped off.

Captain Paul, the battalion executive officer, a ruddy farmer from Mataura, grunted his way in looking a bit shaky. "News from Cape Helles," Paul said. "The first wave landed and took up the left flank, meeting no resistance. Instead of pushing inland till they engaged the Turks, they sat on the beach and had tea."

"What!"

"The Twenty-ninth Division landed on the right flank. The Turks are cutting them to pieces."

PART TWO: QUINN'S POST

I learned that some officers submerged while other officers and enlisted men took charge. I knew clearly what my job and territory was and acted as though I had the authority. What I needed, I took. More and more folks thought me hard and I didn't bother to correct them.

I discovered that Happy Stevens of Palmerston North was a fabulous artist and confiscated him as well as Spears and Dan Elgin and the Vickers gun. I needed to lay out route maps from the beach to frontline posts in the next week or two and these men would make a sweet team.

Where were the goddamned mules? One day late and counting. I had told Modi to round up as many boats as he could with lowering ramps in the front to get the animals ashore more easily. Big sigh of relief as I saw a line of drop ramps heading into Anzac Cove.

Elgin, Happy, and Spears were standing by. As each boat unloaded they were to take the handlers and mules to Mule Gully and into the enclosure. Chester was at my side to go to the gully with Modi and show him where we were going to stash the gear and generally how the paddock was going to operate.

Shyte! We were at low tide and the first boat hit a sandbar twenty feet from the beach. The mules didn't want to go into the surf. As their packers wrestled with them I spotted Mordechai Pearlman. Beautiful sight!

"Modi! Over here, baby!"

"Rory! Chester! Comrades!"

A bear hug. A slobbery kiss. Chester got his as well.

"Noisy place," Modi said.

"Just wait."

"There's a real mess back on Lemnos. Not half enough beds for the wounded. We've been hearing bad stories."

"You've heard right. It's bad."

"How are the gaffers?"

"Johnny's dead," Chester said.

"Johnny! Johnny Tarbox is dead!"

"We'll talk about it later."

As the mules were coerced ashore, some fifty wounded men who had been in a holding gully limped to the beach. As the last mule hit land, the wounded began loading onto the boat.

"The boats are filthy," Modi protested. "They're full of shit."

"I told you it was bad. How many more boatloads do you have coming today?"

"A dozen. Four of them are barges. I thought we would be able to unload them on a pier."

"All the permanent piers are down. The pontoons bounce like kangaroos." I tried to sort it out. "We may have to beach the barges and smash them open, drive the animals out."

Elgin reported that the first load of mules and handlers was ready. I told him to take them to Mule Gully. "Modi, you go to the paddock with Chester and take a look, then better come back here and help me get the rest unloaded. Turn the paddock over to a warrant officer."

"Before I departure," Modi said, pulling me aside, "I have maybe a small surprise." He waved to a soldier standing almost hidden in waist-deep water at the rear of a landing craft. It was Yurlob Singh!

"Chester," I said, "where's Jeremy?"

"Second pier down."

"Get him. Get out of here, Modi."

Yurlob Singh waded in holding a ramrod posture as though he was determined to be soldierly to the bitter end, as if he were walking up the steps of the hangman's scaffold.

"Let me explain," Modi said.

"Wait over there for Chester!" I commanded, then turned to Mr. Singh. "Any fucking thing you want to say before we pay a visit to the brass?"

"Strictly according to regulations I am to use my judgment in being allowed to examine a forward position," he recited.

"Bullshit. Try again."

He stood at attention, as though to say, "No blindfold."

"It is not within the realm of my human capacity to remain on Lemnos. I am prepared for anything from the whipping post to the firing squad. Send me back to Lemnos and I will leave again."

"Oh, you big hero, you. You fucking raghead! You abandoned your post. How do we get replacement men and mules over here? Are the fucking mules going to walk on the fucking water!"

"If you will forgo your anger for a moment, I will explain."

"Explain! You better fucking pray to your fucking fat Buddha!"

"I do not think that remark was appropriate."

"Yurlob, you have no idea how many mules we are going to lose in a week."

"But there is no problem. My home battalion, the Sikh Mountain Howitzers, was training next to us on Lemnos, as you know. We always carry many extra packers. I have ordered two warrant officers, men of extremely high caliber, to be transferred into the Seventh Light Horse and run the operation in my absence."

"Yeah, I know, cousins from your home village."

"How did you know that? Actually, only one is a cousin. The other is a brother-in-law."

"You are in shit up to here," I said, pointing to his eyes.

I sat in the sand about to burst. He sat beside me and tapped my shoulder timidly.

"May I speak?"

"Yeah . . . sure . . . "

"During the landing I prayed for all my gaffer friends. For the entire day I went into profound meditation. A message transported itself over the water to me. I am badly needed here. I received the message that Johnny Tarbox was killed."

"Go charm a snake. Somebody told you."

"Johnny is dead, then?"

I looked at him. Tears ran down his cheeks. The first boat filled with wounded, their blood mingling with mule dung, was being muscled off the sand bar. Hell, who could argue with such a premonition . . . but how could I explain this to jolly Christopher Hubble? Christ.

"What the hell are you doing here?" Jeremy said on reaching us.

"Goddamned, Jeremy," I said getting to my feet and lending Yurlob a "friendly" hand. "I totally blew it. I told Yurlob to come in with the first load of mules so he would have a clear picture of our layout. I plain forgot to clear it with you and the Major."

Jeremy knew I was lying in my teeth.

"We'd better go see the Major," Jeremy said.

Christopher Hubble was pleased as punch, pacing to and fro before our battalion headquarters dug into the hillside. A work party was building permanent fencing at the paddock and pulling up the barbed wire. At least one outfit on Gallipoli knew what it was doing.

"Never thought I'd be glad to see a mule. Dr. Mordechai says we're getting in over a hundred today—Yurlob! What the devil are you doing here?" Christopher demanded.

"Totally my screwup," I said. "I had told Yurlob back on Lemnos to come ashore with the first batch of animals so he could get a fix on our situation. When we got aboard the *Wagga Wagga* I had so many things on my mind, I overlooked mentioning it to you. My responsibility, sir."

"Is your post covered, Yurlob?"

"Absolutely. By two of the best packers in Punjab."

"Do they speak English?"

"They are British troops, sir. They've trained half the Indian Army."

"Are you two people diddling me?" the Major asked.

"Yes, sir," I answered.

"Landers is covering for me, sir. It was my doing."

"And I suppose you want to stay, Yurlob?"

"Please, sir, you must let me stay."

"We do need him here," I said quickly. "I have to spend the next several days finding trails to the front lines. We really need him in the paddock . . . really. . . ."

"Really," Jeremy added.

We were utterly struck by the Major's next remark. "At least

you came ashore. That's a hell of a lot more than General
Darlington has done."

"Then I can remain, sir?"

"You chaps . . . you think . . . you're pressing . . . Oh, welcome to paradise."

How do I explain this thing? We were an Anzac nut inside of
a Turkish nutcracker.

The immediate objective was the stringing together of a
coherent front line. We had to push the Turks off this hill and
out of that ravine, take that ridge, hold this spur. We shoved
them far enough back so the Turk didn't have us squarely in his
gun sights and could not use us as free shooting gallery.

Colonel Monash, the Aussie, pushed his brigade forward by
a series of head-on-head bayonet charges until he created a series
of defensible positions.

The New Zealand Brigades were ostensibly led by Major
General Godley, but he never showed up during battle. Our
main frontline officer became Colonel Malone, a North Islander,
teacher, and farmer, who simply took over and crafted new units
out of what was left of the original ones.

The Anzac enclave was carved out by clawing at the ground,
turning rocks over with bayonets, using trenching tools, then
picks and shovels . . . filling sandbags, shoring the earth from
collapsing. . . .

As we burrowed in, the Turks made life hell. They sat above
us in defenses six and eight trench lines deep with sweeping
fields of fire. Behind them were batteries of mobile howitzers.

All ashore who were going ashore!

All ashore was everyone in the expeditionary force with a
weapon. I was at the bottom of the rung as an officer, but I knew
that an attacking force should hold a three-to-one superiority in
troops over the defending force, under ordinary circumstances.

Gallipoli held no ordinary circumstances. The Anzacs had
come in from the sea, a unique invasion in modern history. As
we hit land, we had an uphill push into brutal and forbidding
landscape against a well-entrenched, well-armed, well-led

enemy. Our ratio over the Turks should have been six or seven to one. My uneducated guess was that the Turks had as many men as we had, maybe more. Moreover, they had an unchallenged corridor from Constantinople to receive reinforcements and supplies.

The situation down at Cape Helles was no better. British and French forces inched inland and dug a line not much more than a mile up the peninsula and were under a constant rain of gunfire from the Turks on the high ground.

Our casualties were running in excess of fifty percent!

A horrendous blunder shook our trust in the officer corps down to the nubbins. With our advances at both Anzac Cove and Helles stopped cold, the southern height of Achi Baba no longer held strategic meaning.

Why? Why? Why? Why? It seemed that Major General Sir Alexander Godley thought Achi Baba should be captured as a show of resolve.

To even consider such an operation there should have been a Corps reserve of at least several divisions backing us up on Lemnos. There was no Corps reserve. All were ashore who were going ashore.

Godley pulled his New Zealanders off our lines at Anzac and transported them by boat down to Helles with orders to storm the heights of Achi Baba. This, apparently, was conceived by Godley to put himself up for hero status.

Using remnants of the Otagos, Wellingtons, and Aucklanders, they had to charge, in the open, across flat ground called the Poppy Field. It was a slaughter. No New Zealander reached the foothills of Achi Baba.

An enraged General Brodhead, who had been unaware of the debacle, recalled the survivors to Anzac Cove. From that time on, Colonel Malone disobeyed order after order from Godley to launch suicidal assaults. With Lieutenant General Brodhead obviously siding with Malone, Godley was all but stripped of authority.

Firing generals in the middle of a battle can have a debilitating effect on the troops' morale. Godley was kept around for ornamental purposes. He was a man who appeared to be looking at you through two glass eyes.

Here was now and this was what was what. From the minute we hit the beach at Anzac and Helles we had lost our offensive posture. All we could do was dig in and hang on by our rinny-chin-chins.

Anzac Cove was four hundred acres of ruptured and tormented land owned by the devil and under lease to the Turks. Four hundred bloody acres we had. Ballyutogue Station was over ten times larger. Fifty thousand of us were packed in, living in caves on the reverse side of the hills with a Turkish meat grinder in front of us and the sea to our backs.

May 1915—either end of the first week of May or beginning of the second, I'm not sure.

We were lucky Yurlob Singh had had the balls to stow away to Gallipoli. Between himself and Dr. Mordechai Pearlman, the mule operation was honed to a textbook study by future generations of muleteers. The animals were the best-fed, safest, cleanest, and most comfortable British troops on Gallipoli, and did they haul the tonnage uphill!

Unfortunately, we were losing the animals fast. In some areas the Turks had to change positions slightly to be able to hit our trains with gunfire. As luck would have it, a hundred mules from the Zion Battalion landed at Anzac by mistake and we also got some small mules from the Sikh Mountain Howitzers. Yurlob knew how to handle the Sikhs, and thank God, Modi was there to deal with the Palestinian Jews. They had no sense of military discipline. They argued about everything, although they worked like hell. I'm glad I wasn't at their paddock.

Anzac Cove grew even more colorful. We landed a couple battalions of Ghurka infantry of Nepalese origin. They were a lively bunch, the Yellow Aussies we called them, and the Aussies were called the White Ghurkas.

Some more New Zealanders arrived, a Maori battalion and troops that had been guarding the Suez Canal in Egypt. This was all well and good but these were not Corps reserves, just men to plug up the line and replace the steady stream of dead and wounded.

We were trying to play catchup because we had come ashore without a whole list of things a modern army carried. Because Australia and New Zealand had very little in the way of standing peacetime armies, we had no howitzer artillery, vital to this kind of fighting. We also came in without steel helmets, gas masks, with obsolete Boer War rifles and even makeshift uniforms. The Turks had hand-thrown bombs called grenades, something we'd never heard of.

Anzacs had achieved a standoff for the moment, but sooner or later the Turks were going to try to push us into the sea, and there seemed to be no movement from London to avert this.

Life around Mule Gully and battalion headquarters could have been worse. We were under constant fire, although Mule Gully itself proved to be quite safe. The Turks rarely let a night go by when they didn't probe the head of the gully just to make sure we were still on guard.

The real crappy part of soldiering was that there was never a moment when you could, of good conscience, not be working. Digging ... digging to make small safe areas for the wounded awaiting evacuation. Digging in pairs for personal rectangular dugouts straight into the hills, like to slide a coffin in. Troglodyte dwellings, as ancient cave men knew. Repairing the piers that the Turks hit daily with artillery fire.

Armies dig. Armies never stop digging.

We shored up the entrances to our troglodyte cave homes with sandbags and whatever timber we could locate. We covered the dirt floor with brush so it would not turn to mud on our bedrolls. It turned to mud anyhow. We wrapped the roofs and sides in isinglass and rubber sheets and canvas to cut down on leaking.

What the hell, it was home. It got a little bigger and fancier each day. Photographs we had purchased in Cairo went up on the walls, a few trinkets taken off the Turks, a little tea fire, piss pots, all made it homey.

Yurlob and Modi never left the paddock. Chester and Jeremy bunked in with me.

Jeremy Hubble and Chester Goodwood ran a good part of the beach operation. Jeremy proved himself to be an officer of quality. I'm not saying it because he's my cobber. What he gave, what every good officer gave, was a feeling that he knew what he was doing. He moved thousands of tons of war supplies to the men who needed them with very few screwups.

The wounded coming down from the lines were set into Widow's Gully for the night in a safe area Jeremy had carved out, and he had them evacuated, two, three, four hundred a day, gently and quickly.

Jeremy was responsible for keeping the piers operating. Repairs were done constantly under Turkish fire. He went through the heartbreaking exercise of getting big cannons ashore and into emplacements, only to have the Turks destroy them in three days.

Naval gunfire, you ask? Well, sometimes it was "go" and would pin the Turks down and cover an advance. Sometimes it didn't work. Too many of our men were taken down by our own guns.

If Jeremy was smart, Chester had to be credited for half the brains. Chester Goodwood knew where every box of gear was warehoused, which company was on the lines, what each post required on a daily basis, whether the mules had hay, and whether we had our foul stinking rations; he screamed for more water tankers, demanded clean boats to evacuate the wounded, sensed a shortage coming up, and headed it off. Can you imagine, a seventeen-year-old officer and a former drunken lord, beach-mastering such an operation!

I'd manage to see one or the other for a few minutes a day, and if we were lucky enough to go off duty together for a few hours, we'd hunker down in our bunker, review the world situation for a minute and a half, and fall dead asleep.

*   *   *

Yurlob's arrival freed me from the yard. I took on the most urgent detail. We had landed with maps so obsolete they must have been surplus from the Homeric period of Ancient Troy. Corps had a good team of cartographers correcting the maps and detailing every hill and gully, but what I had to do was NOW.

I needed to mark all our forward positions, number them, and draw a route map from Mule Gully to each post citing landscape peculiarities and Turkish hot spots.

Map #1—*Gully to Chatham's Post*—1¼ miles. Beach path as marked. Best time to dispatch is late afternoon (1530–1600) as sun is directly in Turks' eyes. Safe route to return after dark. *Danger points:* Turks on eastern ridge of Valley of Despair. There is a fifty-yard gap between Ryder's Post and Chatham's. Have covering fire laid down, enter post through Perry Draw for maximum cover. Chatham's is our southern anchor and a daily target for Turkish artillery fire. Expect to return with twelve to fifteen wounded on normal run.

Map #3—*Gully to Lone Pine—2 miles.* Beach south and into Victoria's Gully. This post is shit city . . .

Map #4—*Gully to Courtney's Post*—2 miles . . .

Map #5—*Rhododendron Spur*

Map #8—*The Apex*

Map #15—*Plugge Plateau*

Map #19—*Taylor's Hallow*

Map #25—*Beauchop Hill*

Map #31—*Guillotine Ridge*

For a tad of relief I put casual comments like, "This is your lucky day" or "Congratulations, you made it again" or "Spectacular view of sunset, a must" or "Make pee-pee before crossing open ground."

Major Chris admonished me to quit the editorials until Lieutenant General Brodhead found them amusing. You might get an idea now of how the battlefield ran. Starting at Mule Gully there were some thirty-five fingers or routes, each of different length and over different terrain, leading to our perimeter.

We did not have a solid front line. Some forward positions were heavily dug-in trenches, some were observation posts, some were along ridges, trenches, and others were nests to cover gaps in the line. The perimeter was zigzag, a disconnected labyrinth. My route maps became invaluable in pointing out hot spots, detours, cliffsides, dead ends.

Spears, Happy, Elgin, the machine gun and I were off at daylight and we became *the* team. Only trouble was, it never really stopped or started. As soon as we got back to battalion headquarters at night we'd have to work out two or three new route maps with the cartographers through part of the night. There was never a night that an extra hand wasn't needed at the paddock or with the wounded or something got crapped up with the boats in the cove or the Turks hit a dump of supplies.

I was getting down to the last of the trail maps when a new duty was added. I suppose my squad was doing its job too damned well, because General Brodhead took a liking to us, or possibly he thought we were charmed because we'd gotten through so far without a casualty. The General made daily sweeps of the front lines. Many of the places were simple to reach, so simple even his staff officers could find the way.

However, when it came to the "fun" places like Quinn's Post, we'd escort him. Quinn's was nightmare land. When Colonel Malone had taken it over, it was the most miserable shithole on the face of the earth.

He forced the troops to make the place livable, for as long as one remained alive. The no-man's-land in front of Quinn's Post ran from twelve to twenty yards from the Turkish lines. I do not lie—twelve to twenty yards. We and the Turks could hear each other complaining about rations.

My lads were feeling mighty haughty about the "honor" of taking Brodhead to worse places on the line. I felt it no great honor and I must have worn it on my face once too often.

"If you don't like the detail, Landers," he said to me, "we can assign you to General Godley."

That was the second time I realized Llewelyn Brodhead was more or less a human being, after all.

A little over two weeks into the campaign we'd had one of those really sorry days. We were drawing up our last map and what should have been an easy route map from Camel's Hump. The fucking Turks liked to dress themselves with brush, so they'd look like mulberry bushes. They sniped at us all day. We crawled on our bellies for at least seven hours.

As we entered our command area, our nightly salute from Farting Ferdinand, a big mobile Turkish gun, hit too close to make it funny.

The route to Camel's Hump was full of nuances, like that weird angle from which the Turks sniped at us today. I suppose all cartographers are humorless or they'd be something else. We finally finished our work and remembered we hadn't eaten all day.

Happy to draw rations we retreated to the squad's cave.

"What the hell's this?"

"New ration tonight. The regular bully beef ration had rotted in the sun. Half of headquarters has dysentery."

"I'll be. Chicken in aspic. Well, well."

"What's aspic?"

"Aspic is like a high-class jelly you float fancy dishes in, I think," I explained.

The label didn't quite explain that by chicken, they meant chicken feet. By feet, we got it with feather points, foot padding, tiny knuckle bones, and claws. It was Elgin's lucky day. He got crushed chicken neck.

Strangely, it occurred to me at this moment that I was one-fourth of a thing . . . a squad. We moved about in the hills with the deftness of ballet dancers, great lovers, movements of beauty through stony, ripping soil. A look into Spears' eyes told that he knew there was a sniper on our left. A quick hand signal and Elgin . . . the best gunner on Gallipoli . . . had his piece firing inside seven seconds. We'd go hours without passing a word, yet if one man was missing for a time . . . it was like the other three limped. We were a whole only when we were together.

Yet we didn't know a damned thing about each other. I knew their towns, professions. I knew they all hankered to get laid.

But I didn't know anything about them. Only that we were four New Zealanders drawing maps together in a very strange place.

Well, I'd arranged a surprise for them. A real surprise! No, not a woman, but the absolutely next best thing. It had taken some doing to put it together, but today was the final route map and it was time to celebrate.

Well, maybe we'd celebrate tomorrow, instead. I suppose we hadn't slept for ... maybe ... let me figure ... maybe like forty hours, and today was a real pisser.

"I'll run this map over to the Major," I said.

They were all asleep. Elgin was asleep sitting up, two chicken claws dangling from his mouth like upper fangs and oozing aspic.

"Map number 42-A," Major Chris said. "Good go, Landers. So, Abdul's set up a sniper's alley there. I'll get the information to the General. Think we can get them with one platoon?"

I propped my head in my hand and closed my eyes but continued the conversation. "No. They're shooting from over five hundred yards. They're not trying to hit anything, just make us miserable ... anyhow, I'm letting my lads sleep in tomorrow and then taking them to the beach to get cleaned up ... and I got a surprise for them."

The Major clenched his teeth together in just that particular way. Bad news was coming.

"Blast the luck," he said.

"Don't tell me."

"Afraid so. You and your imperial guards, myself included, are to report to command at 0500. The General wants you to take him up to Quinn's Post."

"That's a serious place."

"I'm only the messenger."

"Oh, I hate that position," I said.

"Colonel Malone also requested us."

I opened my eyes. How do I break this to my lads? "Fuck!" I cried, unbeknownst to myself. "I am not going up to Quinn's Post until I wash my feet."

My cave was right close to my squad. I took the surprise box and walked over to them guided by their snores. No matter how deeply they slept, the mere words "Quinn's Post" awakened them.

"On your feet," I commanded. "We're taking a swim . . . RIGHT NOW!"

There are flashes of golden moments in a lifetime. Suddenly you're in a situation of mind, taken wholly by surprise, and something is happening you never before knew existed. A moment like that was with Georgia on the boat to Auckland. Another night was at Villa Valhalla, just sitting and talking to Jeremy.

Now, in this bloody hole, I'm suddenly smitten by euphoria. The beach was fairly quiet this night with only an occasional shellburst, sort of like the fireworks on the King's birthday. Chester had told me of a place where the bottom was sandy and the water clean.

I gave my lads their surprise. "Take off your boots," I ordered. They gaped as though I were crazy. "Sincerely," I said. I picked up the box and opened it. Four new pair of boots, new socks, and three varieties of foot medication. Happy was the only one who carried a rifle and bayonet. I had told him to bring it to the beach. Fortunately, he had had it sharpened by the Maori lad who had the grindstone and was going to go home rich making the bayonets razor sharp.

You see, this was an enormous moment. We hadn't taken off our boots in over two weeks. Using extreme care, Happy sliced the laces, and from the tongues down to the toes, I pulled the boots apart.

Take the best instance of your entire existence . . . now triple it. That's what it felt like. We stripped down and waded into the water giggling like my sisters at a slumber party.

We sat in chest-high water with a sense of happiness never to be duplicated. I know we hadn't slept for two days and we had to report to command in a couple of hours, but we talked that night.

Dan Elgin, our gunner—hell, he was a farmer, you could tell that from a mile away. But do you know, his hobby was watching birds. He had drawn over a hundred varieties from the woods by his farm near the Rotorua Volcano. Well, there weren't many birds hanging around here except vultures, and we were thankful for them. They kept things tidy in no-man's-land.

Dan was worried that many species in the North Island were becoming extinct because of the logging. It was the first time I ever thought about the fact that New Zealand could run out of birds, although we'd nearly run out of our national bird, the kiwi, because it didn't have wings to escape its human predators.

Elgin had a wife and daughter, as well, but hardly mentioned them.

Happy Stevens of Palmerston North was a schoolteacher. Here, I thought he was more like Chester's age and all along he was an elder in his late twenties. The grin—that's what made Happy look young.

Spears didn't say much, never did. One would have the feeling he came from a background of poverty and hid whatever family life there might have been. To his credit, he didn't invent a nonexistent existence for himself, as many of the lonely do.

I was the only South Islander. God, I wanted to be able to talk about Ballyutogue Station. Anyhow, I laid it on thick about the beauty of the South Island.

It was a nice night, not from any secret revelations, but suddenly the four of us were New Zealanders, and somehow that meant terribly much to us.

We were nearly too tired to stand up but we got to wrestling in the water, then staggered back to our caves to catch the two hours and five minutes sleep due to us.

Quinn's Post. A piece of land in hell so nasty the devil exiled it to Gallipoli. It nubbed forward like the prow of a ship hanging out as a standing invitation to the Turks all around to pour in gunfire.

Quinn's Post was at the open end of Monash Valley, the most strategic position on our line. If, indeed, the Turks ever cracked it, they would be able to pour into Monash Valley to the sea and split our forces in half.

Abdul stacked his forces around Quinn's Post in a series of positions with ominous names: Bloody Angle, which gave them a view to the sea; the Chessboard, a brilliantly conceived series of square trench works that blocked us from every direction; Dead Man's Ridge (there must be one in every battle zone), which had a series of hidden gullies running off it toward Quinn's.

In a word, Quinn's Post probably faced the most heavily fortified acre of land in the world.

A trench line down from Quinn's Post ran for a quarter of a mile through our forward positions at Courtney's, Steele's, on down to Lone Pine. The Turkish trenches and ours in this quarter-mile stretch were pressed so close to one another that no-man's-land was a mere twelve and twenty yards wide. We could damn near use each other's latrines.

When Colonel Malone, a New Zealander of few words, took over the Quinn position, he had the shovels going twenty-four hours a day until our concentration and connection of trenches dulled the Turkish ambitions.

Every few feet at Quinn's Post there was an earthen step to a vertical niche so a rifleman or machine gunner could stand and have a field of fire.

By daylight nothing could move above the trench line without drawing a blizzard of gunfire from the Turks. By night, they had a weapon unknown to us, hand grenades. A couple of nights I had to lay over at Quinn's Post and the grenades never stopped.

I pulled up all the corrugated metal and heavy mesh I could find on the beach and took it to Quinn's and they roofed their trenches with it. The roof was set at an angle so that when a Turkish grenade landed, it rolled back down into no-man's-land, hopefully before it exploded.

At last we found a decent use for some of our rations. Empty jam tins were filled with bits of barbed wire and shrapnel. Powder, detonators, and fuses were added. These were very crude versions of the Turkish grenades, but Abdul was no longer going to get free throws.

Other innovations came about through necessity. We were able to scan the Turks through homemade periscopes. Other periscopes were rigged so they could be used to aim snipers' rifles. When we received new Enfield rifles, our sharpshooters, sighting in through periscopes, became so accurate they could shoot through the Turkish firing loopholes.

If the racket didn't get you at Quinn's, the smell would. When a man went down in the narrow waist of no-man's-land, it was impossible to get him back. The vultures became so fat they could hardly fly and began to leave the corpses to rot under a sun that shot the temperature up over a hundred degrees every day.

Our dead who went down in our trenches were stacked at a far end. We'd wait until the wind blew toward the Turkish lines, then pour on petrol and set the corpses afire.

At 0430 my squad gloried in our new socks and boots. Our party consisted of my lads, Major Chris, Lieutenant General Brodhead, and his right-hand strategist, Colonel Markham.

I took them up the eastern wall of Monash Valley where we passed less than two hundred yards from the German Officer's Trench, a major Turk stronghold.

Yurlob had carved out a mule track from where Monash Valley forked and one of the gullies led into the rear of Quinn's Post. Turks always had this spot under surveillance from Bloody Angle and the Chessboard.

Without mules we were able to crawl the last fifty yards without drawing fire. It amazed me how General Brodhead and Major Chris and Colonel Markham always looked like they had walked out of the tailor's shop, while me and my lads looked ravaged.

I was fascinated by the easy way Brodhead had as he moved through the trenches chatting up the troops, earnestly hearing their input and totally sympathetic about the trials of life at the Post. Brodhead went beyond the automatic stiff upper lip crap the senior Brits seemed compelled to dish out.

Brodhead and Markham went into Colonel Malone's headquarters dugout and after a few minutes I was called in.

"Landers, how far can you get us up the ridge toward Russell's Top?"

It hit me in the stomach. I wanted to say "About six inches" or "Depends on how anxious you are to die."

"How many in our party and what do we want to do?" I asked.

"Colonel Markham, Colonel Malone, and myself. We want to take a look at the Chessboard. Can you do it?"

"We can do an in and out," I said. We'd been running supplies to the outpost at Pope's Hill but came in from another direction.

"What we'd really like to get a look at are the four or five gullies falling off Bloody Angle," Markham said.

I looked at Malone's map table. "There's a ditch up Dead Man's that practically touches the Turkish lines, very close. I'm talking five, ten yards. I think we can see the gullies from there. I should tell you, sir, if the Turks engage us, we can't be rescued."

"Let's have a go at it, what?" Brodhead said.

Well, his uniform was going to get messed up on this one. I had learned from the time I was a kid that you can be standing five feet away from a lost lamb and not see it. If a man plays the brush and little bumps in the land correctly, he can hide his body almost anywhere.

The shallow ditch and deliberate slow movement could put us on a U-turn we wanted. A hundred yards . . . a hundred minutes . . . right near the end, I spotted a triangle of land mines and looked for trip wires . . . shit . . . I hate snipping trip wires. . . .

Click! Only pliers, but it sounded like a cannon.

Bloody Turks had the mines set so we couldn't get around them without waking up their army. We had to crawl through them . . . I hummed the Maori farewell song under my breath . . . "Now is the hour for us to say good-bye" . . . did they read my signals . . . three mines, go through them . . .

Close your mouth, Brodhead . . . the sun is going to bounce off your smiling teeth . . .

Wa . . . Wa . . . Wa . . . Wa! Lookee here! Whole fucking Chessboard, big curve at the top of Bloody Angle and one, two, three of the gullies . . . my, my, my.

Malone was beside me. He had that Quinn's Post perfume aura about him. Look at these sons of bitches ... they still haven't gotten their uniforms dirty.

I focused my binoculars as did the others. Shit! The Chessboard had grown by over a dozen squares ... an entire new trench area had been added on. The gullies off Bloody Angle were filled with troops ... lots and lots of them.

The four of us were packed tightly together. Our window to the Turks was only a few feet wide, the only possible place to have our look without exposing ourselves. I wanted to get back, even to Quinn's, but Brodhead seemed to be enamored with what he saw. It seemed like a year before he signaled me to take us back.

None too soon. I didn't see them, but after a time you sense a Turkish patrol and we'd been hanging out there for quite a time.

Okay, Rory, go back at exactly the same pace ... don't rush it ... breathe deep ... Maori farewell song ... now we go ... now we go ... through those fucking land mines.

I looked behind me. Got to say, the Brits were beautiful in the way they followed my line ... each pebble of recognition gave me an urge to stand up and run for it ... a hundred minutes out ... a hundred minutes back.

Oh God, it felt good when the hands in the trenches grabbed me and hauled me in.

"Come on, guys. You know, I always send extra rum up to this post. How about some now?"

"Here you go, chief," Dan Elgin said. "We owe them two bottles up here."

"In tomorrow morning's mail," I promised.

Damn the protocol. Malone, Markham, and the General saw the bottle and partook without ceremony or invitation.

"Nice work, Landers," Brodhead said. "Find Major Hubble and come with him to Colonel Malone's headquarters."

"Yes, sir."

I went through the tarp into the Colonel's quarters. All of them were on the bad side of grim.

"Malone?" Brodhead asked.

"Well, it's what my patrols suspected but never got to see. The Chessboard has increased in size by twenty percent."

"It feels like a full brigade in the gullies off Bloody Angle," Markham said.

"I'd say more," Malone suggested.

Brodhead posed with his teeth lurking through his lips. "Two brigades and we can identify them," Brodhead said. "One brigade is going to slide along the line between Quinn's on down to Lone Pine. Their attack will be to pin the line down. Their main assault will be directly on Quinn's Post with another brigade. They'll come over the gullies in waves right into your face, Malone. There's really no room to maneuver around with flanking tactics. They'll try to overrun us right down Monash Valley."

"Who's resting in Heavenly Spa Valley?" Malone asked of the place with the queer name where troops were rotated off the lines.

"Canterbury's," Colonel Markham said.

"Better get them up here," Brodhead ordered.

"Colonel Chapman's dead. They'll need a new commander."

"Who's the exec?"

"Lieutenant Colonel Hinshaw."

Malone held his tongue but showed visible uneasiness.

"I think not," Brodhead said.

"I'll take the Canterbury's," Colonel Markham said.

"Let me think about it," Brodhead said. "Well, we do have some decent news. Chris told me just as we pushed off this morning. A hundred Maxim guns were unloaded yesterday. How soon can you have them up here, Chris?"

"Depends how they're packed. Right away if they're not in grease."

"Just in light oil," I said. "I checked."

"Good. Landers, Chris . . . fifty of the Maxims go right here to Quinn's. I want another twenty-five down the line to Lone Pine. Twenty-five in reserve. We're going to need an ammunition dump up here."

"I don't like ammo on top of the trenches," Malone said strongly. "We almost had a catastrophe with that."

"It has to be within a few minutes' reach," Markham said.

"Landers?" Chris asked.

"I can set up a series of small dumps right behind the post, sir. If I stay up here with my squad, we'll create the space."

"All right with you, Hubble?" the General asked.

"Subaltern Yurlob has the transport completely under control. I think Landers up here is an excellent idea."

I knew Christopher Hubble had changed, but I could not help but be touched by the total trust he had placed in me since we landed. He knew I went crazy when Johnny Tarbox died but he saw past it.

Colonel John Monash, the Aussie commander of the line down to Lone Pine, entered.

"We've just drawn lottery dates at my headquarters," Monash said. "My date is ... let's see ... the Turks attack on May 18."

"Well, I hope they give us that much time," Brodhead retorted. He told Monash what we had seen today and his notion of the Turkish assault.

"I've lost over thirty men on patrols trying to get a look," Monash said. "So the Chessboard's pregnant. You're going to have to take the big hit," he said to Malone.

"All boils down to our little acre here," Brodhead said, "strength against strength. We either hold, die, or become prisoners of the Turks. The latter is out of the question for me. All right, gentlemen, 0200 at my command post tonight. We'll get a plan tidied up."

"Sir," Malone said, "is the wireless working to naval gunfire?"

"Yes, we're back in contact."

"General, we and the Turks are going to be on top of each other. I'd like to see the navy concentrate on the Chessboard and nothing but the Chessboard."

"Well, what about no-man's-land?"

"I have a notion, General," Malone went on. "We're too close to their trenches for naval gunfire. I say we keep a battalion on ready alert at all times. The minute the Turks attack, we send the battalion into no-man's-land and meet them with bayonets. They won't figure on that. I think it's a chance to confuse them."

That sobered the place up.

"Interesting," Markham agreed.

"I like it," Monash agreed. "But how do we get out of our trenches fast enough?"

"Have the battalion on alert lie behind the trenches and cross over the top of us by throwing down plank bridges."

"Let me think about it," Brodhead said. At that, the General dismissed everyone except Chris and myself. When they were gone, Brodhead stunned me with his sensitivity. "I know what you're going to ask me, Chris. The answer is no."

"Is this a private matter?" I asked.

"No, not at all. You have wheedled your way onto the front lines for the Turkish counterattack, Landers, and Major Hubble is about to suggest that so long as Colonel Chapman is dead, he should command the Canterbury's at Quinn's Post. Is that about it, Chris?"

"I'd say that is the gist of the matter."

"Not quite yet," Brodhead answered.

"Sir, I took on this mule detail out of deep loyalty to you. My brother Jeremy can run my battalion in his sleep with Subaltern Landers here as his exec."

"Sorry. I think Colonel Markham is better suited."

"You promised me, sir."

"So I did. Exactly what I promised is that if you got a mule transport working, I would skip you a rank at the end of the campaign and see that you got a regiment at that time. However, don't be too impatient. At the rate we are losing senior officers you may get your chance sooner than later, what?"

Anzac crammed as many men and as much ammo and water behind Quinn's and Courtney's Posts. Being the "professor" of the terrain, I helped find little pockets where one- and two-man observation posts could keep constant watch on the Turks. Phone lines were run to these.

Malone had me at his side a great deal of the time, dispensing our stores of material. The Colonel did a lot of his thinking out loud in rumble-mumbles and would then look at me curiously to see if I agreed with him. His richly endowed eyebrows covered his eyes like an English sheepdog to conceal surprise and unpleasant news. Each day I went with him on a sweep of his observation posts before he reported down to Brodhead at Corps.

By mid-May the late morning–early afternoon heat was so intense that hell up here and hell down there probably had little variance. Quinn's Post was always over 110 degrees. Everyone stripped off jackets, trousers, and leggings. We were down to underdrawers, shoes, our web belts, and some sort of head covering.

Between noon and 1500, men fainted from heat prostration all up and down the line. Water was only to drink; it had no secondary use and we were filthy and smelly. Lice and flies adored us.

On May 16, I'll never forget the day, I woke up to a revelation. It came through to me so clearly I bolted into Malone's quarters without invitation.

"Get up, Colonel," I suggested.

He pulled his naked butt off his cot, sat on its edge and got me into focus, quickly. At Quinn's Post a man could wake up within four seconds and be on the alert.

"I've got an utterly clear message about something," I said.

"Ummmm," he rumbled.

"I know when the Turks are going to attack."

"Sure you do."

"It came to me, just like that."

"Quinn's Post does this to people. It may be the heat, Landers."

"That's exactly what it is, Colonel, the heat."

Oh, that awful look of his. It's not fair looking at a man when you can't see through his eyebrows.

"The Turks are going to attack at midday."

"You nudged me out of my sleep for this? Go play with your

mules. They'll attack at dawn as any God-fearing Moslem or Christian or Buddhist army would. An attacking force wants all the daylight they can get. If they attack at midday they'll give away seven, eight hours of light."

"Colonel, look at our lads at midday. The lot of them are seeing double and hearing weird voices. They can barely move a limb." Thanking God I was talking to a New Zealander and not a pommy, I dared continue. "Suppose the Turks rest their men all morning in the shade, pump them up with water and a whiff or two of hashish. They'll be able to hit us like a thunderbolt, and ourselves with less than no energy."

Malone heard me.

The red-alert troops were put down in the trenches where it was apt to be twenty degrees cooler, but the observation posts were tripled and rotated so that our eyes never left the Turks. Observers were dead-on focused on the gullies running off Bloody Angle and the Chessboard, where we felt for sure the attack would begin.

"Watch for puffs of dust, particularly a line of dust. If the noise level drops, it could mean they are tensing up to make a charge."

Each morning Malone snapped, "Looks like you're right again, as far as today is concerned."

May 20, 1915—1150

Elgin, Spears, Stevens, and I were down to drawers again. In the trenches, the alert battalion waited bare-assed, sharpening their already razor-edged bayonets.

You know how you can sense . . . smell things . . . without a coherent reason? Yurlob Singh's yoga had rubbed off on me. I knew it was the day. I mean, I really knew. And I knew that when the Turks didn't hit us at dawn, it was going to be high noon. I knew it would be high noon because German and Turkish officers don't have any more imagination than British officers.

What I felt must have started running through our trenches.

Suddenly, the men who were going to lay up ladders to bridges over no-man's-land began to tense up. The alert battalion, Otagos, South Islanders like myself, were on their feet.

About three minutes to noon, my squad and I went to our own observation post.

Look! Fucking look!

Turk Gully #3 had a strung-out cloud of dust a hundred yards long and it was drifting. The high racket of the shells audibly fell and fell till it became quiet like we were on the moon.

Colonel Malone tore up a ladder, crouched, and looked.

A whistle went off from Pope's Hill Observation Post.

"Colonel. Pope thinks it seems Abdul ready to swarm."

A second whistle blasted from Dead Man's OP.

All noise from the Turkish lines stopped! Then, a droning sound rose on the air like a trillion bees buzzing.

"Let's go, lads!" Malone cried. A bridge was lifted up from the trench and laid over its top. Malone ran across it into no-man's-land but no one followed. I looked down in the trenches. The alert battalion was frozen. I grabbed my pistol and fired into the trench side.

"Get your asses up here!" I screamed.

Over the way, still out of sight, the buzzing swelled to a steady hum. Our men started up. I threw them bodily over the bridge.

"More bridges! More bridges! Follow the Colonel!"

The hum from the Turks exploded into "Allah Akbar!" Now our lads were coming . . . up, up, over, goddamnit, let's go, let's go!

I grabbed Elgin and shoved him at the bridge. He turned and hesitated and I kicked his ass over it, then snarled to Happy and Spears to follow me. All up and down the lines a haka battle cry arose as we surged into no-man's-land.

We were not greeted by gunfire from the Turkish trenches. Clearly, they were assaulting in waves from the gullies behind their trenches.

Just like so! The gullies were emptying thousands of Turks, coming at us at high port.

"Allah Akbar!"

We had beaten them onto no-man's-land by a full precious minute. Colonel Malone's outrageous gamble was working! We were at the edge of their trenches when Abdul tried to cross to us. They were shocked to see us greet them. I emptied my pistol, tossed it aside. A rifle and bayonet were not hard to find this day. We gutted their first line of attackers down into their own trenches. Their second line ran right up the backs of the first line.

The Turks were thrown from offense to defense. It was they who had to hold us off, then fight their way back onto no-man's-land where they thought they had free access.

In an attempt to achieve surprise, the Turks had not preceded their assault by cannon barrage so there was no clouding and smoke. The field was clear. As Abdul saw his comrades scream and sink, guts in hand, his nerve was shaken.

The second wave of Turks, boiling after their long dash from the gullies, threw off their jackets as well and it was naked Turk and naked Kiwi stabbing and slicing with their pointed razors.

Now I was filled with the antifear. In the insanity of no-man's-land, two things would get me out alive. I must not lock up my brains through maniacal rage. I must *think* about what I'm doing. My moves must be decisive and correctly drawn. I must also work like hell. This is harder than taking a barrage, harder than digging, harder than climbing a cliff. This is plain, bloody, hard work . . . think and work.

This was the gladiator's pit blown up by ten thousand! In the midst of fury and heat and confusion there came the blackest of black humor. Our uniforms—both Turks and Kiwis—were nearly the same color. Naked it was even more difficult to tell us apart. I went for men with swarthy color and big moustaches. An opening of flesh and in the point went . . . sometimes sticking tightly between his ribs . . . bring the rifle butt to the man's head, take him fast, pop him off balance, and pounce.

Was I still human? I was human in the speed my mind was working. I was not human in what I was doing. We were a bit bigger and stronger than the Turk with a great deal of bayonet training in Egypt, but the main thing was the tide . . . we had the tide with us, we had outfoxed them, and they were digging out of a hole.

By their sheer numbers we inched back.

Colonel Malone then unleashed a second battalion of bayonets—Maoris from our trenches, and their sudden fierce arrival was like a hard wave bashing.

Turks fell into disarray, which only made us press harder until finally they broke off the engagement and scrambled back beyond their trenches.

Another wave of Turks was arriving from the far gully stumbling over their own men in retreat.

Three sharp whistles, repeated and repeated, signaled us to return to our own trenches and take up firing positions. I found myself behind an empty Maxim gun and pressed a pair of lads into duty with me.

The new lines of Turks were confused. They did not know if we were going to come out again and meet them with bayonets. Perhaps we were going to counterassault and crack their trench lines.

Whatever, the storm and fury had been taken out of their assault. They came at us again, but rather gingerly, over the narrow no-man's-land filled with bodies, crying, moaning, still.

Colonel Malone had managed our maneuver brilliantly . . . maybe the Turks' steam was gone . . . we waited, waited, waited . . . then twenty Maxim guns went off at once.

Word from Colonel Monash's sector! It was brutally active beating back wave after wave of Turks who still had momentum. Monash called for every reserve machine-gun crew to fill in his line.

Again and again the Turks emptied the gullies. Now they came from another direction down from the Chessboard. Our troops, over the valley at Russell's Top, hit them in their flanks.

Now the Turk appeared like a herd of stampeding cattle over Dead Man's Ridge.

"*Allah Akbar!*"

Jesus, three bloody prongs coming at Quinn's. Were there

enough bullets in the British arsenal to halt them? Some were able to get within touching distance of our trench, some fell on the antigrenade sheeting and crashed down into us.

My field of fire took a queer change. At first it had been wide open. Now, it was filled with corpses that slowed down the advancing Turks. The Turks had to climb mounds of bodies, slipping in their own blood, then making targets of themselves as they stood erect. Their charge in front of me became very confused.

It was a big battle raging on a front two miles long but it was a tiny battle, as it is for every soldier. All I had to do was take care of what was in front of me and watch my comrades on my flanks. These are the grand minutiae of war, tiny windows. If my squad and I held our ground and our flanks and everyone else did, they'd not break us.

My machine gun began smoking and jammed. The water in the jackets had boiled. Shit! I picked up a rifle and fired until it burned the palms of my hands, then picked up another.

On the Turks came!

A breech in Monash's line! He called for a battalion at Angel's Haven Spa to come and plug it up. Runner in from the Aussies. Bayonet fight with the Turks at the breech. A second reserve battalion went up.

The Turks branched off and went after Pope's Hill, a small but vital observation post. How many guns at Pope's? Not enough. Malone dispatched a platoon to Pope's. Only half of them got through but the post held.

Abdul charged at us unabated for nearly seven hours until the sun began to fall into the Aegean. The night was flooded with flares. One more charge and the battle slowed to a trickle. . . .

Runner from Monash. Their line was straightened and held. They were bleeding with casualties. We had reached very deep into our reserves but Monash had to have them. His line was thin.

Quinn's Post had held! The cost was seventy-five percent casualties. Over half our weapons had burned out from overfiring.

Quick, Malone ordered, get new weapons and ammo out of the dumps behind the trenches.

Our dead had turned the trench floor into ankle-deep blood-mud. The night was amoan from the cries of thousands of wounded out in no-man's-land. We made a try to bring some lads in, but it was impossible. They were totally intertwined with corpses, ours and the Turks', and any illuminated movement in no-man's-land drew instant fire.

A few men managed to crawl back to our trench. We took them in—Kiwis, Aussies, Turks.

Yurlob and Modi brought mule trains as close as they dared, and throughout the night came up Monash Valley and carried the wounded down into Widow's Gully for daylight evacuation.

By midnight the dead had been removed from the trenches, reinforcements and supplies set in place, and we grabbed a quick, delicious meal of bully beef shit and hard biscuits, a fitting belly-warming dinner for the working lad.

My own anxiety level dropped to a point where I realized that my hands were blistering from burns from the gun barrels and I was bleeding from my sides. Christ, I had taken some bayonet cuts. No use using up a medic on me. They had their hands full. Can I tell you, I was aching so much all over I could hardly feel the pain of stitching myself up.

Happy Stevens, Dan Elgin, Spears, and I often got separated during the day up at Quinn's but always gathered near Malone's dugout come evening.

I could hear the Squire complaining to me . . . "Rory, you get into a punch-up just because there's a punch-up to get into, whether it's yours or not." I had no business on the line and I fucking threw away the lives of my friends.

"Colonel Malone wants to see you," a runner said.

Colonel Monash and Malone were ending a meeting as I came in. They both looked like ten-ton boulders had fallen on them, they'd got up, and been hit by beer wagons and then punched out in a pub.

"Did you get the machine-gun ammo distributed?"

"Yes, sir."

"How much?"

"Sixty boxes . . . sixty thousand rounds."

"Any in reserve?"

"Twenty thousand rounds up here. Some more is coming up from the beach tonight."

"Move the twenty thousand down to the north dump on Artillery Road."

"It's already been done, sir," I said. Maybe I was totally out of line or too tired to care or too hurt to care but it just came out. "Shall I send some more artillery shells up to Russell's?"

What I meant was clear. After the first Turkish charge, our howitzers were to turn loose on the gullies behind Bloody Angle where the enemy had massed. Not a single round was fired this day.

The Australian, Brodhead's "competent Jew" Monash, looked at the New Zealander, Colonel Malone. Either Godley or Brodhead at Corps had made a monumental fuckup.

The barrage might have severely slowed the subsequent Turkish charges. As it was, we held on by a hair.

"We have plenty of artillery ammo at Russell's," Malone appeased me. "As you know, none was fired today."

"Well, back to the office," Monash said. "They won't wait till midday to resume the attack tomorrow. Good night, Joshua . . . good night, Landers. You did a fair day's work, I'd say."

As Monash left, leaving the door ajar, the wind blew the moans of the wounded into the dugout. I suppose my legs must have wobbled. Malone told me to close the door and have a seat. What the hell do you talk about after a day like this? Colonel Malone . . . learned just now Joshua was his first name . . . seldom talked unless it was in the line of duty. He seemed to want to say just any damned thing.

"Think they'll come back tomorrow?" I asked.

"We killed an awful lot of Turks today. This must sound ridiculous, Landers, but is anything wrong?"

"One of my father's prophesies came true."

Malone laughed heartily. "Funny, in the middle of a punch-up we had today and we're thinking, 'Will my old da be proud of me when the day is over?'"

Out came the rum. We on the supplies always saw to it

Colonel Malone was taken care of. He was growing very tall in the Kiwis' eyes.

"Well, the lads did themselves proud, today. Jesus, for a minute I didn't think they were going to come out into no-man's-land after me."

"They always intended to do so, sir. They just had to stop for a few seconds and piss their pants."

"Well, damned if I pissed my pants," the Colonel said, "I shit mine."

"I lost my squad today, sir. I think due to my bad judgment."

"Well, this is the place to do it," Malone said, shocking me. "Hell, if every colonel and general had to account for the men he'd killed needlessly, nobody would take the damned jobs, and by golly, what would the human race do without the kind of thing that went on out there, today?"

"I pushed a man over the bridge who had no call to be pushed over the bridge," I said.

"And if you hadn't and he survived the day, his life would have been ruined. Hell, Landers, those three lads followed you over every hill in this wretched place, day after day. There's a problem. When someone survives a day like this, his cobber out in no-man's-land, he then finds himself wallowing in survivor's guilt syndrome."

"Yourself, sir?"

"No," he answered. "Soldiering is an honorable profession. I'm not speaking of Alexander and Caesar, but little soldiers who defend little nations. New Zealand is the smallest nation in this war and has come the longest way to fight. We owe the Brits and the Brits owe us. Unfortunately, no nation ever existed that didn't need soldiers. It's the order of things. Soldiering is an honorable profession that makes more mistakes over human life than any other."

"Does the guilt ever pass?"

"No," he answered. "But you have to learn to live with it."

"Why are you bothering with me after a day like this?"

"I admired the way you and Major Hubble and Jeremy and the Gaffers put your unit together in Egypt. I understand you had the best whorehouse in Cairo and pulled Hubble out of deep shit in the Hotel Aida. Besides, I won twenty quid on you when you torpedoed that Aussie in Port Albany. Get over today. You're going to make a great officer. I've got to make a round of the lines. You want to come with me?"

"Yes, sir."

"I think I lost my adjutant, my exec, and a couple battalion commanders today. Suppose Major Hubble could spare you for a few days?"

The Turks did not come at dawn.

The Turks never counterattacked again.

It would have been a lovely time for us to go after them but we had nothing to go after them with. Both sides were in shock, unable to follow up.

The bodies in no-man's-land were three and four deep around Quinn's Post. Two more days of rotting in the sun and ships could navigate their way into Anzac Cove by the smell. The stink kept us in a constant state of nausea. Then followed the world, international, universal, cosmic convention of flies, maggots, mosquitoes, and rats.

The flies were so thick that if you tried to take a spoon of bully beef, you'd have to place the spoon on your lips, shoo off the flies, and take a bite in a blink. It didn't help. You always had a half dozen flies to spit out.

Dysentery ran rampant, drawing yet more flies.

By the end of May, Quinn's Post and its environs was an unfit place for decent, civilized human beings to conduct a battle.

"Colonel, sir."

"Aye?"

"The Turks are waving a white flag."

I followed him down the trench where an officer pointed to the Turkish lines.

"Corporal Perkins," he said, knowing hundreds by name, "put a white cloth on your bayonet and wave above the trench."

We watched through periscopes as a Turkish and a German

officer rose out of their trench holding their hands up. Malone called for a loud hailer. The enemies walked a couple steps and halted.

"We are not armed!" the German said in commanding English.

"What do you want?" Malone shouted through the loud hailer.

"We wish to speak with an officer!"

Lieutenant Colonel Eastman put his hand on Malone's shoulder as Malone started to climb the ladder and, in a look that was all but an order, shook his head no. Three other officers, including myself, also gently eased the Colonel back down the ladder.

Malone had spoken to me too much in the past couple of days. He knew I had an insatiable urge to get into no-man's-land and look for my squad.

"I'll go," Eastman said.

"I'm coming with you," I said.

It was impossible to walk without pushing aside rotting and bloated bodies with your toe. All I could think of for the first minute was that I would not give the enemy the satisfaction of seeing me vomit. I thought Eastman, a very fine soldier, was going to pass out. The German and the Turk were in no better condition.

Damned if the German didn't click his heels and snap his head in a bow. "Major Krause."

"I am Captain Ramadam," the Turk said, extending his hand. Eastman nodded recognition, not offering his hand in return. Nor did I offer mine.

"I am representing General Limon von Sanders. We think, for reasons obvious to both sides, we should arrange a truce so each side can collect and bury its dead."

It took another two days to set up the rules, but this was the kind of good-fellow negotiations the British relished. Malone sent me out with the first fatigue party, hoping it would help me exorcise my demons.

Captain Ramadam had learned his English in London. What does one say? How are the wife and kids back in Constantinople? Or, try it again and we'll kick the shit out of you, again? Or, funny job we've got, Captain . . . well, let's get on with it?

We measured the distance from trench to trench and pegged down a string halfway down no-man's-land. Each work party could work either side, bringing their own men to their own side of the string.

I fashioned a primitive mask but the smell got through. Flies were almost as thick as concrete. We agreed to keep rotating the working parties as they could bear the stench for only a few minutes.

Captain Ramadam offered me a cigarette. It was so strange.

Nothing worked. Those men still wearing trousers had pretty much the same color uniform on both sides. The faces and flesh had been eaten off a goodly number. Many of the bodies were bloated and we had to stab them with bayonets to release the gas and whatever else blew out before we tried to move them, spewing all over us.

But the corpses had locked into one another with rigor mortis. We tried grappling hooks and ropes, but arms and legs and heads pulled off.

After another high-level meeting it was decided that a common grave be dug right down the center of no-man's-land and all bodies—Turk, Kiwi, Aussie, Ghurka, Maori, German—be put into a common grave and covered with lime.

We exchanged identification tags and personal possessions, both sides agreeing not to strip for souvenirs and wallets. Miraculously I got the tags of all three of my men and the wallet of Happy Stevens . . . of Palmerston North.

We and the Turks dug alongside each other, traded cigarettes, rations, mementos. Nobody seemed pissed at anyone, but more ashamed than anything else. I think a couple of the enemy even traded addresses . . . for after the war.

The diggers rotated every few moments, some going back to puke their guts out. When the lime was spread the predators were pissed off. Some of the smell went away. It would fade from our noses after they had turned to skeletons . . . it would never fade from our brains.

We had killed over five thousand Turks and there were a

couple thousand of our dead. Along with the wounded on both sides, the battle had cost nearly twenty-five thousand casualties.

When the dirt was thrown over the lime and the site patted down with shovel backs to clear new fields of fire, we shook hands with the Turks, returned to our trenches, and waited for 1800, when a flare from both sides signaled that it was all right to start shooting again.

I stayed with Colonel Malone for as long as I could. Through him. Through the incredible silence of his suffering I began to regain my own strength and sense of duty.

At last Jeremy came up to Quinn's to personally escort me back to Mule Gully. He and Chester and Modi took me to the beach, got me deloused and Jaysus, I got to take off my shoes again. No matter how much you are hurting, taking off the shoes and putting the feet in the water must have been what Jesus felt when he was baptized.

I slept for thirty hours.

When I awakened, Major Chris was sitting opposite me. "Well, you've vacationed at Quinn's resort long enough," he said.

"Colonel Malone said that if you could spare me, he'd like to have me as his aide."

"Sorry. Yurlob is quite ill."

"What's wrong with him?"

"Dysentery. I think it's starting to kill more of our people than the Turks."

"Yeah, I should stay here."

"Goodo. We've lost a lot of mules, as well."

"Maybe Yurlob will go back to Lemnos, now," I said.

"I ordered him back. I think sometimes you colonials don't believe you have to take our orders."

I know he meant that as black humor, but there was too much of the old Christopher Hubble twinkling in his voice.

"We've a long way to go here yet," he continued.

That got my attention and my clenched teeth got his attention.

"Why don't you just come out and say it, Landers?"

"Who am I to argue with the brilliant minds who put us on Gallipoli?"

"Llewelyn Brodhead was not one of them," Chris said, stunningly. "He protested this entire expedition. Generals do not get to choose their commands. He has fought tooth and nail for the Anzac and he has refused to leave Gallipoli because he believes he can do the best job for us."

Do I say it? Do I shut up? I do not doubt Brodhead's courage or his resolve or his standing with his troops. But something is fucked up in this command. A thousand men could have been saved by a simple howitzer barrage executed at the right moment. Fortunately for the general he has a cast-iron stomach when it comes to needlessly killing his men. That's part of the unique credentials a general has to have to be a general—to divorce himself from the consequences of his decisions over life and death. If you're wrong ... well, "Carry on, old chaps." Somewhere down the line, doesn't something catch up with these people? Maybe not ... so long as soldiering is an honorable profession.

"I'll get over to the paddock," I said.

Modi once had weight to spare. The Gallipoli diet took care of that. His embrace still had a good sharp bang to it. We went about the paddock. A gang of Turkish prisoners were chained together with ankle bracelets, shoveling up the dung into a big wagon to be dumped into a nearby pit with the executed animals. Not too bad. We had over four hundred mules in service and the replacement packers were excellent

Nasty green flies were getting the best of the mules' ears. Leather, hay, feed, medication, and water were all in good stead.

"They are a hell of a lot better off than the two-legged troops," I said.

"They've really held up under the heat. It can't get too hot for them," Modi said, "but we're still losing twenty to forty animals a week."

"Where's Yurlob?"

Modi shook his head. "He and a couple hundred other men sleep by the latrines. All most of them can do is pass their own blood and stomach linings. One lad fell into the trench and drowned before they could get to him."

Yurlob was inspecting a train. Whew! He was barely able to walk. He lit up when he saw me.

"I always thought English soldiers exaggerated when they said they shit their guts out. It is no exaggeration. I think, worse than cholera. To answer your questions. Modi keeps me stuffed with rice and tea. No, I will not go back to Lemnos. Did you have a good time at Quinn's?"

"Fantastic."

Yurlob broke off and became martial. "You, number four."

"Yes, sir."

"Your name?"

"Private Shannon, sir."

"You and your mate better work together. Line up the right side better or the pack will start sliding. Are both sides equal in weight?"

"I suppose not, sir."

"Wake up, Shannon."

"Yes, sir."

When the packer took the train out, Yurlob watched intently. "What I have tried to do is give the same train the same set of trails. The mules adapt quickly. Rotation was putting too many over the side in strange places. We're saving quite a few animals."

"How about Sikhs?" I said. "Let me explain something to you. You're going to be dead in a week if you don't get out of here. What I mean is, go to Lemnos and get off your feet for a fortnight. Deal? Just a fortnight?"

"Ah Rory, you are like a rapier with your words. I like you." He started to walk away. I turned him around.

We went into a staring contest which I lost. He put an extremely weak hand on my shoulder. I could not bear to look. The man was all but rotting away before my eyes.

"There are certain things in my culture more important. For me, things are in good order. With my years of service, my family will receive a fine pension. Landers, my old battalion is up in the hills here doing the real fighting. My family and the people of my village must know I died on Gallipoli and not in a hospital bed. Are we clear?"

"Clear," I said, "but off your feet. You schedule the loads at the office. I'll send the trains out. And, one more thing, you move in with Jeremy, Goodwood, and me."

"I prefer here . . . it's closer to the latrine. Be of good cheer, the Sikh religion makes all kinds of convenient delusions for the moment of death."

Days and night passed. Nothing got better. Wounded filled up Widow's Gully every night. We shelled, they shelled. Feints, patrols, small probes, ambushes, broken piers, trains going out, mules executed, bully beef, lice, flies, teeth falling out from the biscuits.

Jeremy came in early one evening. Lovely. We hadn't had much time to talk since I'd come down. He stared at his boots. "To take off or not to take off," he recited. "haven't had a swim for six nights."

"Let's go. We'll leave one shoe off and one shoe on."

"Isn't there an old nursery rhyme about that?"

Oh . . . the water felt good . . . oh, center of the universe . . .

"Ohhhhh."

"Ahhhhh."

"Ohhhhh."

"Ahhhhh."

Blast! The Turks were firing Farting Ferdinand. Good, Farting Ferdinand was firing way up to Taylor's Hollow.

We crawled into our hovel.

"Where's Chester?"

"Chewing some colonel's ass out. We're short on hay and .303 ammo."

I laughed. They were scared of little Chester. He exuded a hundred and thirty-five pounds of Tasmanian Devil authority.

Jeremy produced a bottle of rum from his kit.

"Jesus, should that be going to the lads on the line?" I asked.

"It's all right, I deducted it from Godley's personal stash."

We partook. Jesus, wouldn't it be great if old Sonya was

fixing us up a hash pipe? Wonder if she ever got to the continent.

"The Major greeted me like he had sand up his ass," I said.

"He's angry because you had all the fun during the Turkish counterattack."

"Men," I grunted, "are fucking crazy. Why would any sane human being want to get his stomach carved out?"

"*E gloribus bellum,*" Jeremy said.

"Why?" I asked again. "I wanted to be at Quinn's."

"I suppose we all want to prove something to Daddy, what? With Christopher, it's very important. Father came home from some doings in the Northwest Territory with a medal pinned on him. The lingering finger of family."

Swig.

Swig.

"Ahhhhh."

"Ahhhhh."

"Yurlob's gotten to me," I said.

"He got to me a long time ago," Jeremy answered. "This is his entire dignity, his Sikh mountain artillery. He sees the hour of his death clearly. It's difficult to retain dignity when dysentery is killing you. He's a beautiful man."

"Yeah ... all he wants is that his departure goes down honorably in the eyes of his battalion."

"Did you know he has four kids?" Jeremy asked.

"No."

"It came out at the odd moment. He has three sons and one of those other things. I don't think they treat their women too kindly. He prays that his sons will become Punjab fighters."

The contents of the bottle evaporated before our very eyes. Our conversation segued into Ireland and Conor Larkin because Jeremy wanted to talk about Conor and knew I wanted to hear. Jeremy wondered how Conor would have viewed these blood-soaked fields.

"Conor was the complete opposite of Imperial Man," Jeremy said. "He saw war only in terms of fighting for freedom. He viewed the American Revolution as man's foremost justification for war. I don't think he would view Gallipoli as a noble calling for New Zealanders and Aussies. He would have seen the greater war as stemming from Ireland's birthright to bear arms against the British. Namely, if Britain is in Turkey fighting for the freedom of Belgium, then Irishmen certainly had the right to fight for their own freedom."

Our tongues became gloriously loose.

"Something here must make sense," I said. "Gallipoli can't just go down as a forgotten page in history."

"I think all of us have to come through it with our own meaning. Wouldn't you say Christopher is evolving from something mucky to something fine?"

"Aye. I know the power I have to love a woman. Now I know I can love men."

"How about knowing the magnificence of being a New Zealander?" Jeremy asked. "Quinn's Post has defined the stuff of the men of your country."

"At what a fucking price."

"Everything comes with a price."

"What happened after your last contact with Conor?" I asked. "After he escaped prison? Was he in Ireland all the time?"

"The rumor was that he was in America for a few years, then slipped back to Ireland."

"Did he ever fall in love with another woman?"

"Very much so. It was a secret but quite an open secret."

"How was that, now?"

"Well, him living underground. There was a woman named Atty Fitzpatrick. She was Anglo-Protestant ascendancy. That means Irish-born, but with British ancestry. My family is the same. We are the generations of inheritors after our English ancestors divided up the country. Many Anglos became republican patriots. Atty Fitzpatrick was somewhat sainted in that she distributed her family barony among the tenants and gave virtually all her money for humane causes. Actually, I saw her several times. She was a great actress on the Dublin stage. Tall, glorious bosom, stately in a Joan-of-Arc way, very commanding. She was a widow with a family. When Conor was imprisoned she was a one-man army in his cause doing street rallies from one end of the country to the other."

Ah, that was my Uncle Conor with a woman like that, I thought.

"So, Conor was able to love again after the tragedy of Shelley?"

"We don't know for certain. He was a diamond with many facets. I think he had the capacity for many kinds of love. My mother never got over him. Yes, I think he could love again because he could trust again."

All I was hearing now made me very warm. No doubt he blamed himself for Shelley MacLeod's murder. It meant that I might get over Georgia some day.

"She went from Dublin all the way back to his village with his funeral cortege with crowds gathering and weeping at every town along the way. They say she lay on his grave for days. Hard to believe that this all happened just a few months ago."

Jeremy became terribly pensive and gave me a look to say, "We are brothers."

"You asked for a meaning about Gallipoli," he said slowly. "I think I've found my meaning."

"What did you find, Jeremy?"

"Maybe there are justifications for this war, that the other side is uglier in their intent than we are. But Gallipoli is wrong. Imperialism is wrong. Empire is wrong. It's Conor's voice saying to me that no one has the right to send men to places like this when the final objective is greed. Oh, we cloak ourselves in democracy, but the war here is not about democracy." He waited a long moment, never taking his eyes off me. "Rory, when I return to Ireland, I am going to join the republican cause."

"That's awesome," I whispered. Jeremy had gone from pitiful drunk to a man of worth onto a path of clarity.

"If I were Irish," I said, "I hope I'd come to the same conclusion."

"You're as Irish as I am," he said.

We stared at each other.

"I wanted you to know of my deepest secret because I want no further secrets between us."

"You know, don't you?" I asked.

"Rory Larkin, is it?" he said.

"God, I've wanted to hear the sound of my name for a long time. How did you learn?"

"From the first, I suppose. I knew there was a Rory Larkin in New Zealand. Conor had spoken to me about you. You have used the word Ballyutogue inadvertently a half dozen times. I didn't think it right to question you until you were ready to tell me and mostly, until I was ready to say out loud that I am going to be a republican."

"Gallipoli is filled with secret meanings," I mused.

"As my mother is wont to say, aye mon, indeed it is."

Chester Goodwood, the best of us all, entered. "Yurlob is gone," he said.

Modi followed in a moment, carrying Yurlob's body. He was not very heavy, anymore. "I didn't want to send him out on the boat," Modi said. "I thought, maybe, we'd like to bury him."

"Aye."

"Here, have a drink, first."

"I'm drunk already enough," Modi said.

"Don't they put their dead on pyres and burn them?" Jeremy asked.

"I don't know," I said, "but I think it's a good idea. That way the bloody flies won't get him."

We put on our shoes. Damn! I knew I shouldn't have taken the goddamn shoes off! Fuck it!

"You going to be all right, Rory?"

"No, I'm not all right. Let's send the lad off in a blaze. There's another bottle in my kit. Bring it."

I pushed into my boots but couldn't see to lace them. No matter. I lifted Yurlob Singh, fucking raghead Buddha-worshiping bastard . . . oh God . . . he doesn't weigh a thing now, does he . . . he doesn't weigh a thing.

PART THREE: THE SURGEON

I actually enjoyed my hangover. We had given Subaltern Yurlob Singh a send-off fit for the Maharajah of Lahore.

I was doing a hoof check at the railing when I saw a new officer, a light colonel, followed by an entourage of a half-dozen Ghurkas, leave Corps and go to battalion headquarters.

Chester came over with a list of the morning's shipments.

"Who's the new man?" I asked.

"Some mucky-mucky from Alexandria."

"Looks like he's traveling with his own private bodyguards. Maybe they're entertainers, sit on nails, charm snakes."

"You'll find out. You're to see him at Battalion HQ."

"Come with me will you, Chester?"

"Why?"

"Ah look, they're fixers. We're getting the greatest specialists in the world these days. They always need to know numbers." I wiped my hands and looked over the duty roster.

"Flynn."

"Yo."

"You're the big man here till further notice."

I nodded to the Ghurka convention outside the Major's office and entered.

"There you are, Landers," Chris said, standing behind his desk. The light colonel was a slender chap with a thin varnished moustache and slick black hair, as one would have if he were a dandy officer in Alexandria. Well, he'd get that uniform messed up if he hung around here long enough.

Next to him was a Ghurka captain.

"Subaltern Landers, I'd like you to meet a fellow New Zealander, Lieutenant Colonel Calvin Norman. His assistant, Captain Shurhum."

"Doctor will do fine," the colonel said. I clamored to get a grip on myself.

I winced aloud and maybe got to trembling.

"Damned stitches from the bayonet wound sort of cramp up on me at the damnedest times. Sorry, sir, pleased to meet you,

630

Doctor. I would say welcome aboard, but this place hardly warrants it."

Calvin Norman cracked a tenth of an inch smile at the corner of his lip, which lasted a second and a quarter. His steel-spring handshake told me he was a surgeon. My chest felt crushed. Air was hard to come by. I needed to settle down and regain my composure.

"Lift up your shirt," he commanded, and as I groped for it he pulled it up.

"Frightful, sloppy work. Who did that?"

"I sewed myself up. The medics were very busy."

"You're fortunate this didn't go septic on you."

"Oh, I poured a whole bottle of iodine into it," I said.

Doctor Norman winced. "See me later. I'll tidy it up."

"Landers has been recommended for a citation of valor during the Turkish counterattack. The legend goes that he chopped down nearly a hundred Turks with pistol, bayonet, rifle, and machine gun," Chris said in that fucking pommy way.

"You're embarrassing me now. How can I be of service to you, Doctor?"

"Too many men are dying between the evacuation and the time they arrive in Alexandria."

I wanted to shriek. Damned nice of you people to take notice.

Norman obviously caught my expression. "Let's understand something, shall we? As a New Zealander I am disgusted with what was probably the most inept evacuation plan in British military history. There are arms, legs, torsos, heads, and mules from Gallipoli floating across the entire Mediterranean and washing up by the hundreds on the beaches of Egypt and the coast of Africa. Let's see if something better can be done."

It was a sobering but clear moment for me. No matter what my personal animus, he was here on the most needed mission we had.

Chester knocked and entered. As I introduced him, Norman gazed at him as if to say, "Didn't realize we had little drummer boys here." That was . . . until Chester spoke up.

"Colonel Norman," Chester said.

"*Doctor* would be preferable."

"Doctor, I suggest the first thing we do is sit down and familiarize you with the big picture by map. I can also provide the average number of daily casualties from the major posts, types of wounds, and evacuation procedures."

"That will be helpful. I didn't realize you kept a ledger, what with all the chaos and casualties."

"I don't, sir. I carry it in my head," Chester said.

As we continued to the Corps map room, Norman introduced his Ghurka surgical teams, good fellows all. I could envision Dr. Shurhum trailing Norman as he walked through the hospital ward, hands clasped behind him, snipping out orders.

Norman's eyes played over the paddocks and the cave dwellings, a concentration of flies and stink and dung and filth, with bloody waters just beyond.

"We'll see if we can't start by instituting basic field sanitation."

Christopher took Norman by the arm and nodded for me to come with them. "Doctor, I respectfully submit that you don't break your skull trying to change what cannot be changed. We are in the most difficult military situation on the planet. I think your energies best be concentrated in your stated purpose of getting more men alive to Alexandria."

Calvin Norman's expression could break rocks, but Christopher Hubble was a British aristocrat speaking to a colonist.

"Major, I have fought my way through a bureaucratic nightmare to be able to come here and I have been given carte blanche. I do not quake before English generals."

"What the Major is trying to tell you," I jumped in quickly, "is that once you are familiar with conditions, a concentration on priorities might be the most rewarding path in the long run. In short, Doctor, no fucking way we're going to get rid of the flies, the smell of the corpses, the lice, the dysentery, the heat, and the Turks, so let's work on the wounded."

Calvin Norman did not tip off a yes, a no, or a go to hell.

I'm sorry some future military historian wasn't there to record Chester Goodwood's dissertation before the big map. From the northern reach opposite Turkish Hill #80 right down the line to Chatham's Post hinged to the beach, Chester explained the strength and reason of every post and trench. Calvin and his people followed the book of forty trail maps with their individual quirks and unseen dangers. As he spoke, members of Brodhead's staff, including Colonel Hugh Markham, listened as though it were Napoleon lecturing.

Chester's voice had not taken on its final tenor or baritone designation, but without saying it in so many words, blunders and communications of the general staff became apparent. He had to answer many questions with, "I'm afraid you'll have to ask Corps staff that, sir. I'd rather not speculate."

"There seems to be one overriding question," Norman said at the end. "Why in hell did anyone ever land you in this place?"

"That will be an interesting question for future military symposiums," Colonel Markham said from the rear, and departed.

Dr. Norman's air had gone from his balloon. He shifted about uncomfortably with the first smell of a reality that Anzac Cove was in Turkish jaws.

"How do you suppose we should carry on?" he asked Christopher. "I think, perhaps, I should make a round of the frontline positions."

The Major nodded. "Landers here is the man to take you around."

"Major, the paddock is quite hectic since Yurlob died," I said with a knee-jerk reaction.

"Jeremy can cover for you. Can you manage without him for a few days, Goodwood?"

Chester felt a sense of dread. "The beach is under control," he answered.

Speak of serendipity! I didn't like the sense of menace dripping into my thoughts. I didn't like the way my mind was working. When the others left I tried to justify what wanted to force its way out of me.

"Doctor, here's my suggestion," I said. "We can't run your

entire staff around the hills. I suggest, if they need familiariza-
tion, that they go out with the mule trains beginning tomorrow.
If we rotate them properly, they'll have a very good general picture in three days."

"Go on, Landers."

"There are all kinds of nuances on the terrain," I said. "The
two of us alone can give you a better detailed picture of things.
Now, I warn you, it is bloody hot and some of the climbing is
rough."

"I am perfectly fit," he snapped.

"Good," I said.

He was pretty much as Georgia had described him. A cold
number covering childhood pimples. What was his motive for
coming to Gallipoli? If he was looking for glory and colonel's
pips, he'd win them here. Whatever his motive, his objective was
humanitarian. So, why the hell should I care why he came? He's
probably a hell of a surgeon. Around Christchurch he sees a lot
of bashed-up cases: timbermen, miners, ranchers, sailors.

I felt annoyed that I had hoped for his death. I could see him,
all right, in a big-time London clinic putting his hands up the
ladies' thighs.

Each time I began to doze, I'd see him making love to
Georgia . . . MY Georgia. Prick, bastard!

It would be so easy in the hills with just the two of us.
Maybe I wouldn't have to do it myself. Maybe some Turkish
sniper would do it for me. Get a grip, Rory. The Anzacs' need
for Calvin Norman is greater than your desire to murder him. It
better be. What a queer world.

Odd moment, the first time I offered him my hand while we
were climbing our overlook at a rock formation called the
Sphinx. It protected the valley of Angel's Haven Spa, where men
tried to rest and delouse after being rotated off the lines.

He was not a frivolous man. His conversations with
Colonels Monash and Malone and other frontline commanders
were keen. He gave off no sympathy, but he got the gist that
merely living through a day of Turks, heat, lice, rations, dysen-

tery, and flies was about all a human being could manage.

At the end of a hard first day, he thanked me tersely and dismissed me, ordering me to continue at daybreak.

I was near daft. I wanted to tell Jeremy, but I dared not. I had not brought under control my compulsion to do away with him. If I confided in Jeremy and I killed the man, Jeremy would be stuck with a horrible secret.

On the second day we worked the northern end of the line. There were three ways back to the next post. I picked the most dangerous one, in Malone's Gully. God, I was serious. Could I ever look Georgia in the eyes again? I understood why she did not like this man. Why was she taking him back?

Bastard, it was hot today. Bloody rocks were melting. I knew the right bush in Malone's Gully that would give a speck of shade. He snapped at me for cautioning him not to drink too fast.

"I think I understand dehydration," he said.

"I found a couple of cans of hash. A man has to have a diverse diet," I said, "and some hard candies. Helps with the energy . . . as you well know."

He ate in silence, except for running his tongue over his teeth to clean them, then popped to his feet suddenly.

"What the hell are you doing!" I snapped automatically.

"I have to urinate, if you don't mind," he answered.

"Well, go in the other direction, Doctor. Ten feet in the direction you're heading and you'll be in the cross hairs of a Turkish sniper."

He blinked his eyes and peed where he was told.

"Thank you very much, indeed," he said, coming back to the shade by me. I wondered what instinct made me send him in the proper direction. Oh, Christ.

"South Islander?" he asked.

"Yes, sir."

"I'm from Christchurch myself. Trained in London, of course."

Of course.

"You're not related to Horace Landers from Kiwi Junction, by any chance?"

Maybe I was meant to kill him after all. . . .

"In fact, I am."

"I knew Horace off and on till he retired. Scotland, wasn't it?"

"Yes, sir."

"Didn't realize he had a son as young as you."

"Long story, Doctor. I'm an adopted member of the family through my dad's sister. Anyhow, I stayed on in the South Island. I worked the ranches."

"Small world. Give him my regards when you write."

"I certainly will."

Norman suddenly heaved for breath. His skin turned sallow and the sweat gushed from him. He was floating . . . light-headed. "What the devil . . . ?"

"Heat prostration. Lie back, Doctor."

He had nothing to protest with. I stretched him out and dampened a cloth, wiped his face and the back of his neck, and fanned him. He mumbled his embarrassment.

"Close your eyes and don't waste your breath," I said, "it will pass."

I opened his shirt and continued fanning him, cooling him down with his own sweat.

My own mouth went cotton-dry as I felt my hand unsnap my pistol holster. All that could be heard under the faraway gunfire was my breath and his breath, laboring. Oh, it was so simple now. Why in all this earth did I end up with him here if it was not a clear message to do away with him? What is one more dead man in this circus?

The pistol had dead aim at his temple.

"Your pain will be easier to bear if Calvin Norman is left alive. You know, Rory Larkin, if you kill him, he will destroy your soul day by day, year by year. Even in this savage land, a man cannot deliberately forsake his humanity."

Fuck! Just what I needed! Words of wisdom from Conor Larkin.

"How many other men are you going to kill by taking his life, Rory lad? Can you live with that one? Suppose it's Jeremy or Chester on the operating table . . . or yourself and no Calvin Norman to operate. Kill yourself, but don't kill a surgeon in a battlefield."

Norman groaned.

I replaced my pistol and sponged him again. He slowly became coherent.

There's an easy walk to the beach, but it's always covered by Turkish guns. The safe route was to make it to Walker's Ridge, but that was a hard climb. Norman was in no condition.

"Landers . . ."

"I laid a little more on you than I should have."

"I don't know if I can get back."

"Sure you can. Suck these candies and slowly sip both these canteens dry. That will set your mind right. We'll stay here till the sun is under us, then we'll make it up to Post #1 and hole in there for the night."

As the sun began to go for the sea, I helped him to his feet. He was a little better but didn't have much stamina.

"I'm carrying you piggyback," I said.

"I feel the fool."

"Just grab the ride. Up you go. Put your arms around my neck. There's my man. Not too far to go, down the gully two hundred yards and another two hundred up to Post #1."

"Can you manage?"

"You're light as . . . a fucking mule. . . ."

I'd done the right thing by not murdering the bastard, but I sure as hell didn't want to become his friend. I lost whatever little sleep was due me thinking about him and Georgia. Till now I had attained a measure of control over my longing for Georgia, but with this prick here, my hunger for her was constant.

Despite me staying out of his way, we had a lot of business to do. His Ghurkas doted on him, but otherwise he didn't have friends. Why the hell, out of all the troops in Anzac, did he want to be my cobber?

Even though I assured him that men save men on the battle-field all the time as a matter of fact, his gratitude was beyond the ordinary. He began leaning on me, knowing I could cut through red tape. I usually delivered. He liked me more and more. Every time I saw him, it felt like I was getting a punch in the mouth.

I did have to admire the way he snapped back. As fate would have it, I needed a favor from him. Modi got the dysentery bad and it scared the hell out of me. Fearing more for Modi's life than my own bitterness, I begged Dr. Norman that if there was any way to save Modi, he just had to do it for me.

You know how it is with doctors, they always carry a little something in their kit that generally isn't on the market. He gave me some kind of elixir for Modi, warning me that it contained diluted opium.

As Modi plugged up, I calculated that Calvin Norman and I were square. We owed each other nothing more.

I was helping unload some new leather about a week after Norman arrived and looked up to see him at the paddock. "Landers, I have to speak to you," he said seriously. Well, he was always serious, but today seemed a bit more so. "It's a personal matter, actually."

Calvin didn't have a full face like a jolly man. His grim personality had stretched the skin over his cheekbones tightly and whatever was annoying him now had him very taut. The first thing that came to mind was that Georgia had sent him a letter with my name in it.

I checked for Farting Ferdinand. The big bugger was shooting south.

"The beach looks quiet," I said. "Up for a dip?"

"Sounds excellent."

For obvious reasons I checked Norman out as he undressed. Well, Georgia got no great bargain with him in that department. We did the Anzac whore's bath, sitting deep enough to cover our shoulders.

"You warned me when we went out to tour the lines that there was no possibility of setting up a surgery closer to the trenches."

"Never can tell which post the Turks will hit or which one we will hit. We try to keep each other from sleeping during the night." I was relieved that this had nothing to do with his wife and me.

"So," he said, "back to your two original suggestions. I have to establish a surgery either in Widow's Gully or under the Red Cross tents. I had hoped to be able to give frontline treatment. Damned mule ride or the litter-bearers' run to Widow's can take up to two hours down from the lines. As you said, Gallipoli has certain built-in realities."

"It's a crying shame but we lose an awful lot of men bringing them down."

"Gallipoli," he said, "seems to be one long cry. A few more surgeons, a few more Ghurka teams will help. I hope they get here soon."

"I want to ask you a stupid question, Doctor. Most of the men we lose bleed to death. Isn't there some way we can pump new blood into them?"

"Good question, Landers. We've experimented with transferring blood. Sometimes it does work. Too many times it brings on instant death. It appears that there are different classifications of blood."

"By race?"

"No, not by race. By some set of ingredients which we cannot identify or group. Look, at least we have ether to work with, and morphine, iodine for infection. Wars of the last century didn't have much of anything—saws, knives, and stitches. Here, let me have a look at your stitches."

I stood in the water.

"How you escaped infection, I'll never know. So, the best I can do here is operate before we put them aboard ship for Alexandria . . . those who have a chance."

"Losing many wounded aboard ship?" I asked.

"Hundreds. I've demanded a pair of proper hospital ships. We'll see how far my carte blanche goes. Why I really asked you here was to get your opinion of where I should set the major surgery. At Widow's Gully we have a measure of safety from Turkish artillery, but it's very tight quarters with little possibility of assuring proper sanitation. However, if I set up in the Red

Cross tents, I'd be wide open to Turkish gunfire. What do you suggest, Landers?"

"Oh, for Christ's sake, I'm not Solomon."

"I'll make the decision," Norman said, "but I could use the benefit of your thinking."

I'll make the decision, he said. Phew! Both decisions could be wrong, but he didn't shirk. He'd make the decision fifty times a day about who had the chance to survive long enough to get to Alexandria . . . and who died here. . . . I could not help but feel deeply for this man. Without his mask of indifference, without his ability to accept the responsibility for many, many deaths . . . lives could not be saved. No wonder the bloke seemed to be made of cast-iron.

"Well, let me see. The Red Cross tents are preferable for you?"

"Yes."

"Up till now we've honored each other's Red Cross. Our tents are wide open. So far, so good, but the Turks are nobody's sweethearts. I wouldn't want to be their prisoner. Modi—Dr. Pearlman, the chap you gave me the dysentery medicine for—is from Palestine. The Turks beat him across the soles of his feet with a thick branch. Crippled a lot of his friends that way. The Turks also have a big thing about raping male prisoners. But even if they didn't fire on the Red Cross tents deliberately, mayhem and loss of fire control happens here all the time. A few shells can fall short or otherwise go awry. There's another major risk. Our own naval gunfire has killed hundreds of our men. Wouldn't there be added tension on the surgeons operating during a bombardment?"

"When in doubt, take cover," he said.

"I may be wrong but I think those tents are going to get hit."

"Well, thanks, Landers, you've helped awfully. You'd think the Turks would be running low on ammunition after a while."

"They've opened an ammunition factory south of Constantinople. It's about the only correct intelligence we've gotten."

The sappers and engineers created a mammoth cave in the east wall of Widow's Gully, roofed it with steel and piled up to twenty feet of sandbags and earth . . . too tough even for Farting Ferdinand.

As June wore on, the heat kicked up to 130 degrees at times. Down at Cape Helles the Brits made another futile attempt at Achi Baba. At terrible cost they advanced about a mile up the peninsula and never got another inch of this wretched ground. This offensive was utterly puzzling. As I was privy to official field reports I sorrowfully came to learn that not only could staff be monumentally incompetent, but they could also be monumental liars about the whys and wherefores. Disasters were being encased in the poetry of fantasy.

Of the original gaffers and Major Hubble, one man stood out as potentially the finest officer of us all, and that man was Chester Goodwood. Seemed like the entire Anzac depended on the way he ran the beach.

Chester had two assets. The first was an ability to sense requirements and future shortages and get the material in before the shortage occurred.

His second asset was a sensitivity that made him rail at incompetence, no matter what rank it carried on its shoulders. Chester tore into officers to get their asses moving and, at Lemnos, colonels froze in fear of his wrath.

In due course he demanded that Major General Godley fire his top-ranking quartermaster, a light colonel, and in the showdown, Godley meekly complied. I must say I could not have been more proud than when he become First Lieutenant Goodwood. Can you imagine? He still was not big enough to support his own beard.

Finally, Christopher Hubble got his long-held dream, a battalion to command under Colonel Malone. It was a mixed bag of troops, under the esoteric designation of First Kiwi.

Jeremy had done the beach long enough. He caught the fever and was transferred up to First Kiwi where he was given the scout platoon known as Reconn A.

To be factually honest, Modi could run the paddock in a yawn. Over time we had developed a couple dozen packers and trail masters who could handle the operation, including the Palestinian Jews and the Sikhs.

I therefore put in my own request to join the First Kiwi and used my weight with Brodhead to get the request directly to him. I was stunned when it was denied. I went to Colonel Markham, about as pommy as Christopher Hubble, and "requested" to know why.

At first Markham diddled with me, saying that as a man who was potentially going to be decorated, it would be better if I did not get shot up. Well, that's no reason, and I let him know it. He gave up and showed me my request for transfer. There was an attached sheet and notation. *Subaltern Landers would have utmost value to my unit in assisting with the wounded.* It was signed Lieutenant Colonel Calvin Norman.

What were the gods trying to tell me? Truth be known, as the paddock ran on automatic, I had become inexorably drawn to Widow's Gully, getting his surgery constructed, and doing a number of things requiring the common sense generally lacking among the staff officers.

Somehow I decided not to protest, knowing deep down I could make off to the front lines if I really cared to.

What I did was run the overall movement of the place . . . seeing that supplies got in for the surgery . . . carving out places where the wounded would be most safe and comfortable . . . using Turks around the clock to clean the area . . . keeping the floor of the surgery free of blood . . . moving amputated arms and legs to the garbage barge on a path that those waiting for surgery could not see them . . . working with Chester for extremely swift and smooth evacuations . . . sitting with the odd chap who particularly needed my hand as he was bleeding to death . . . keeping fresh uniforms supplied for Norman and his surgeons and teams. . . .

I can't even start to tell you, but there was a lot to do and I must say I found a real reason for being.

Every day Dr. Norman would select out fifty to a hundred most in need for surgery and divide them up among his surgeons. Down in the gully he would look them over, lying there like sides of beef in a slaughterhouse, and he'd tag them . . . some for death . . . some for evacuation without surgery . . . some for surgery.

He and the other doctors operated under beastly conditions, the floor under them always gone slippery from blood as the Turks mopped up bucketfuls under their feet as they operated.

The big room resembled a coal mine cave: badly lit, smelly, poorly ventilated, the fly netting constantly in need of repair ... bloody guns always banging nearby. . . .

It might sound diabolical but I learned more about humanity here than I knew existed. You see, here was the stuff of my people, the New Zealanders, and the Aussies as well. We tried to instill a single hard rule telling the wounded that we would all fare better if they could bear their pain in silence.

Screaming and yelling and thrashing about would only upset the other men and make it ten times more difficult for the surgeons. Maggots were put on rotting flesh to eat away the infection, rubber bits were clamped on the men's teeth. There was a steady moan of those suffering unmerciful agony ... but seldom a scream, and never mass screaming ... waiting on their litter or the floor for their turn on the operating table.

Calvin Norman sawed and stitched his way through most nights with scarcely time to clean himself and his tools between operations.

"Where are you from, lad? Auckland. Ah, I love those hills about Auckland."

"It's gone! My arm is gone!"

"Not to scream, lad, it will go hard on your mates."

About dawn Dr. Shurhum and Dr. Norman and the other chaps could scarcely stand up, but they continued on until their eyes blurred and their hands could no longer be controlled, making the instruments unsafe. Speech slurred. Dr. Norman could no longer give orders properly.

About that time I'd take him out to the beach and put him in the water. Chester always had a clean uniform laid out for him. As the light came up from behind Chunuk Bair I'd tuck Norman in away from the artillery and help empty Widow's Gully either for the evacuation boat or the ... you know ... burial at sea.

Bad news comes fast . . . good news takes its time drifting to Gallipoli. With a new hospital ship going into service, hundreds of men could be saved.

My nightmares had their own nightmares . . . a lot of blood and limbs . . . Dr. Norman's surgery all mixed up with me at Quinn's Post . . . and terribly strange dreams of Georgia. Chester hovered over me as if I was a cripple, as if he didn't have enough to do. See, I became afraid to sleep . . . but in this place, a man can learn to sleep standing up in twenty-second snatches.

Can you beat it! A day finally arrived, and none too soon, when Norman had no surgery to perform. We repaired to my troglodyte cave and feasted off some tins of staff officers' cream of potato soup, and, can you believe, salmon, vino, and custard! Well now, either Calvin Norman couldn't drink much or he was usually too dammed tired out to handle alcohol. I decided to get him pissed. He drank again and again and fell back against the wall and closed his eyes.

I knew I would have to listen to his worries and they were not long in coming.

"One of the problems here are the so-called healthy men," he said. "I'd estimate that in Anzac as a whole, man for man, each soldier is only operating at fifty percent of his strength. They are skin and bones and open to anything these bloody flies and lice are carrying in. How strong are you now, Landers?"

"Fifty percent."

"Well, I suppose the Turks are pretty weak as well, although they have access to wheat and meat."

"How do you feel when you operate on a Turk?" I asked.

"I feel I have to work twice as hard to save him."

"Aye. . . . Here, good fucking wine. French."

"I'm making some bad decisions every night," he babbled. "Sometimes, just before I put them under and their eyes plead to me, I already know he's gone and it comes to me that someone is going to get a cable the next day in Sydney or Wellington. . . ."

"Now, you listen to me, Doctor."

"You can call me Doctor. I don't scare you, do I, Landers?"

"How's a man standing on his feet for twenty hours saving lives going to scare anyone?"

"But that's the point, old man. I've spent an entire lifetime making myself *feared*," he growled. "I don't have any friends. I never did. Precision surgery was always my credential for respect. Alexandria was a puff of pastry. In a month I was the only surgeon there good enough to take out the plumbing of the officers' wives."

"Well, you're making up for lost time here."

"Here? I came to Gallipoli for the wrong reason. What are we eating? It's good."

"Some of the General's caviar. What's so good about this stuff?" I pondered.

"Well . . . let me think . . . it's better than bully beef."

"Shit is better than bully beef."

"Bully beef is shit," he said. "Speaking of shit. How are Dr. Modi's bowels these days?"

"He's chipper as a baby."

I was never that partial to wine, but I must say it was bestowing its benefits on both of us.

"Bet you can't wait to get back to Christchurch after the war," I said, knowing what I was leading into.

"Not going back," he said.

"London, then. A top-of-the-line clinic."

"I'm staying in the Army, Landers. I've done too many things for the wrong reasons in my life. We're going to come into a lot of new medicine before this thing is over. I'd like to do another tour of duty to help put some of these lads on their feet and make their lives more livable. How's that for the old hippopotamus oath?"

"A lot of thinking changes out here, doesn't it?"

"Thank God for that," he said.

I told myself, "Rory, get a grip. He's getting too drunk." What the hell, I've seen him either drunk or out on his feet and snap out of it in a blink and go on to operate on twenty more men without a mishap.

"You've no wife, Landers."

"No."

"But you've a sweetheart of a sweetheart."

"In actual fact, when I left home, the future was so far away I decided to leave New Zealand without commitments."

"I did, too," Norman said, "but it was the worst decision I ever made."

"But you've a wife," I blurted.

"Second wife. Brigadier Christian Holiday's widow. Decent sort."

"But you've no wife in New Zealand?"

"Noooo. I was divorced by the most lovely, quick-witted, capable woman any man could wish for. We were actually divorced six months before the war started. I knew I'd be heading back to the Army, what with my reserve commission. Georgia—that was her name—was decent enough to keep the divorce secret to protect my professional standing. I was a lecher, you see. She let me remain in our house until I went off to the Army . . . and I decided to make my mark in Alexandria . . . and I did. Brigadier Christian Holiday's widow is a decent sort, good career move for me. . . . I'm talking too much. . . ."

"Not at all, sir."

"Feels rather a relief to be able to speak about it. My Ghurka lads wouldn't understand, what? I was a rotter, Landers, driven to try to have sex with every woman I came upon."

"But . . . this Georgia woman . . . "

"Ah, Georgia."

"Didn't you ever write again to her?"

"I wrote once to ask for a chance and she wrote back inferring that she had found the love of her life and would probably be leaving New Zealand. Oh Landers, do keep this hush-hush. Bernice Holiday is a decent sort."

We were interrupted by a barrage that nearly shook us out of the shelter. From the sharpness of the explosions I guessed it was from mortar rounds.

"Cripes!" someone from outside called, "they got the Red Cross tent!"

My Beloved Georgia,

I pray that Wally knows where you are and gets this to you. I can scarce forgive myself for not declaring the enormity of the love I hold for you. I know you turned me loose because you thought it was a shallow fling of a wild boy, but it is not that way.

I have seen the trenches in a hard way and I write you not as a homesick lad, but as a man who has grown to know himself. If I do not find you, I will never get over it.

Your former husband, Calvin Norman, and I are in common cause here. He has become a giant, not only for the lives he has saved and for sacrificing himself physically and mentally . . . but because he has set lovely new values for his life.

He is a difficult man to know. I am the only one he speaks to in confidence. I'm sure you know, he gets pissed on two drinks and having taken to me, he's poured his guts out.

Calvin Norman has been good for me, Georgia. I have seen this nasty man become human and stand up under the cruel pressures of deciding life and death.

I also know that you did not tell me the truth when you told me he was writing to you every day and pleading with you. I know now you wanted to free me, to give me my own life. My only life is with you. I will not believe you don't love me until I hear it from your own lips.

Norman has married again, apparently the right marriage for him. She is the widow of a Brigadier. He confided that he is going to remain in the Army, but for the right reasons. A lot of men are going to need a lot of help after the war.

I don't know how to say this, but I've felt your love transcending time and space and it has reached me and told me we're still holding on to one another . . .

Please God, let's find each other.

We were sure glad as hell to see June over and done with, but July was no better. Until now, few among us believed we would get out of this alive.

Changes were happening that did not bode well. Our conditions continued to deteriorate. Calvin Norman's estimation that the individual soldiers were living at half-strength was a generous appraisal. So long as our spirit was there, we'd always find the strength for one more scrap.

I suppose it is standard when sending men into battle to berate the courage and capability of the enemy. Before we landed, our staff had downgraded the Turks. After all, the Turks spent years getting the bejesus kicked out of them, losing all of their empire in Europe.

Well, something woke Abdul up. Sometimes I believe that most battles are not won or lost by the tacticians or even the courage of the soldiers. I think it often comes down to a case of who has the most stamina. I'd wager my last quid that every battle in history was fought on two hours' sleep.

The Turks had stopped us cold, and although they were unable to throw us into the sea, there was a discernible shift in their spirit. We were no closer to Chunuk Bair than the first day we landed.

Word was that the Turks had defeated the Armenians and the Russians in the Caucasus and now had new divisions to shift down to Gallipoli.

There was also talk of a nationalistic rebellion by junior Turkish officers who had infused the troops with a real sense of nation.

The thought of a Turkish victory horrified London. It meant that the British would "lose face" in a part of the world where loss of face was the most catastrophic event in a nation's history.

So we hung on, not moving forward, not moving backward, not surrendering, and with no hope of winning.

Day after day it all came to roost in Calvin Norman's surgery. Anzac was slowly being sucked lifeless and bled to death.

At Corps, quandary begat quandary.

A series of tactical blunders and foolish assaults began to smell of desperation on the part of our generals. All during July, Widow's Gully was filled to capacity.

What keeps a group of men going? Each other, I suppose. We found ways of fending off despair, not letting each other sink. There was some despair but no thought of defeat, although our confidence fell concerning Generals Darlington and Brodhead. As for Godley—he may as well have been a Turk.

I had my own hope. Georgia was my hope. I could allow my mind to think of her again, every moment I was free to think. I could dream of her again, be tantalized by the thought of her.

I worried about Calvin Norman. He had cut off five hundred limbs in July. I feared for his sanity. More than once he blacked out at the operating table. His Ghurkas worshiped him. They'd lay him out in his shelter and call for me and he'd soon ask for rum. I didn't know what the fuck to do.

I stood outside the surgery netting and watched him when he'd been on his feet for hours. He became more and more irritated, but his hands remained steady and his mind was focused until he hit the wall.

At times I felt he was going crazy before my eyes. He disdained our entreaties to take a rest, his obsession to save lives turning maniacal and his frustration over losing too many men in the surgery destroying his innards.

There had been three bad days in a row at Lone Pine. Although we hadn't had rain for two weeks, Widow's Gully had turned muddy from blood.

A shell knocked out the surgery generator so they had to go on with torches and candlelight. I checked Norman. He was saturated with blood and brains and intestines. Rocking, he was like a pendulum on his feet. I went to argue with him, to get him out. He whacked me with his elbow.

I couldn't handle any more. I left and, after a quick dip, slunk into my bunker. My only connection with reality, as it had been many times lately, was Chester's voice.

"You can't live other people's lives, can you now, Rory?"

"No," I whimpered. "Sometimes I wonder if God isn't punishing me for all those married women I fucked."

"Jesus, have I got to hold a revival meeting for you? Sinners, assemble at Quinn's Post at 0530. Charge Bloody Angle and atone! Repent, Landers!"

"Ah, cut it out, Chester, it's no laughing matter."

"Then why are you smiling. . . . Look, you can't keep from laughing . . . look at me."

He got me settled down. He always did. Little bugger.

"What would you like? Godley's pâté, Godley's frog legs, or Godley's lamb curry?"

"Godley's rum."

Dr. Shurhum suddenly appeared in the opening, a calm number until this moment. I knew from his expression.

"We have the doctor outside. Please, may I bring him in?"

Two of the Ghurka operation assistants led a waxen, zombied Calvin Norman in and sat him on the floor. Dr. Shurhum looked uncomfortably at Chester.

"Lieutenant Goodwood can be trusted with this," I said quickly.

Shurhum ordered the Ghurkas to stand guard outside. He refused a drink and slowly brought himself under control.

"It had to happen," the little Nepalese said shakily. "He simply locked up, unable to move his hands, his mind shut off, not knowing us. We had to wrestle him down on the floor, tie his hands behind him, as you can see."

"We'd better turn him in," I said.

"No!" Shurhum said pointedly. "It will destroy Dr. Norman's career. We are fortunate that only he and I were together in the surgery without other physicians at the moment."

"The doctor is completely shut down," Chester said. "We can't hide him."

"No," Shurhum said, "I have seen this happen to other surgeons. He will recover after rest, but we cannot send him out as insane. Believe me, gentlemen, I know the Army . . . particularly when it comes to a colonial. He is a great doctor. This cannot happen to him. I studied under him in India."

"I've got the picture, Dr. Shurhum," I said.

"What the hell can we do?" Chester wondered.

"I brought him to you because I knew your decision would be the proper one. Please ... I tried ... every night when we tried to sleep he would go over his mistakes ... his sleep was one long scream to be able to transfuse blood."

"I said I have the picture. Please, give me some time to think."

"What he was doing was beyond any man's capacity."

"I know, Dr. Shurhum. Can you ... shut up!"

"He is the greatest surgeon in the Army. He is my teacher. He is my father."

"Anyone we can trust at Corps?" I asked. "What about Colonel Markham?"

"Markham is a prick," Chester said. "I don't see how we can cover this up."

Message, message, I need a message. Goddamnit, think, Rory ... wait a minute ... oh, you clever lad ... think, think, there we go ...

"I can hear you thinking, Rory," Chester said.

I looked at Norman. He was beyond and away from us all, oblivious.

"We're going to perform a little surgery on the doctor. Here's the program," I said. "He is hit by shrapnel on the beach. I rush him here and send for Dr. Shurhum. Dr. Shurhum certifies that Norman must be evacuated and he's out of here on the first boat in the morning."

"But when he arrives in Alexandria and they find no wound?"

"He's going to have one. You're going to put it on him right now."

"Me? How?"

"Cut him, then stitch him up. One across the forehead, one on the side, I don't know. Wrap his head up in bandages. Stick his arm in a sling ... I don't know. Do it, goddamnit, and we'll put him in the first boat out in the morning."

"Look at him. He has no stamina to survive!" Shurhum cried.

"Do it, asshole! And keep him unconscious until the boat

pulls out. Wait! Send one of the orderlies with him. We'll give him a wound, too. Do it!"

Shurhum nodded in accord and snapped an order to one of the Ghurkas outside. He returned in a few moments with the necessary surgical equipment.

I've got to say the rest of it went rather well. We put a neat cut on his cheek, like a German dueling scar, and Shurhum opened and closed a grand-looking hole in Norman's side, although it was hard to pull flesh away from his bones to make the cut. When we finished bandaging him up he looked like he had taken a direct hit from Farting Ferdinand.

Shurhum wrote a report citing the head wound and "a terrible loss of blood." I put on an addendum taking personal responsibility for the evacuation in lieu of going through regular channels, the norm for a ranking officer.

Poor bastard Shurhum had to return to the surgery.

I sat with Calvin Norman through the night, breaking into a sort of laughter from time to time at the paradox of it all. Two months ago I was a ha'penny away from murdering him.

Can you imagine?

PART FOUR: CHUNUK BAIR

August 1915

Major Christopher Hubble was happier than a hog wallowing in a ton of tailings. Oh, was the pommy boy in his element! He commanded a mixed bag of troops: a company of Aucklands, a company of Wellingtons, a company of Maoris, a battery of Sikh howitzers, six machine guns, heavy weapons platoon, and the pride of the battalion, Reconn A, a platoon of Canterbury Scouts commanded by his brother, Jeremy. The twelve hundred men of this reinforced battalion were known as the Kiwi All-Blacks in honor of our world championship rugby squad.

The Kiwis held the front line from the Apex to Rhododendron Spur about a half-mile beyond Quinn's on the other side of the Ravine. Across the Ravine was the Chunuk Bair Plateau, the illusive pot of gold of the entire campaign.

Between the Kiwi All-Blacks' line and Chunuk Bair, the Ravine lay several hundred feet below and several miles long, creating an impenetrable barrier to our prize of war.

Jeremy Hubble took command of Reconn A, fifty Canterbury Scouts with the most vital of missions. Each night and some days, part or all of Reconn A slipped into the Ravine, partly to contest its possession but mainly to look for some sort of hole or path up to Chunuk Bair Plateau.

The Canterbury Scouts were all South Islanders, like myself, born and raised in hill country. In actual fact, the terrain between the Apex and Chunuk Bair was so much like New Zealand you could barely tell one from the other, except that it was green back there and brown up here.

With Calvin Norman safely gone, Chester and Modi figured they could manage without me. Once more I went around Major General Godley, directly to Brodhead, requesting a transfer to the Kiwi All-Blacks.

"I see that Colonel Malone and Major Hubble have both countersigned this request, Landers. There is a chain of command here, you know. You chaps have been running your own private war ever since Egypt."

I put on my most sincere face, which Brodhead recognized as that of a confidence man.

"Well, you see, sir," I said, "if you live in hill country you come to realize that you can always find a hole to slip through. The Ravine has a thousand twists and turns in it through rising and valley ground. After all, sir, I did manage to plot out the trail maps."

"And you have a fanciful notion you're going to locate a back door to Chunuk Bair Plateau."

"If it's to be found, we'll find it."

"You're such a liar, I'd swear you were Irish," Brodhead said, approving my transfer. I took the paper with mixed emotions, never having heard that kind of remark from him.

Apparently I was just what Jeremy needed. Reconn A needed another officer, a trail man, like myself. We split the platoon in half, making a Reconn B unit and rotated leading patrols into the Ravine.

I spotted a clunky sort of lad, Lance Corporal Willumsen, who turned from human to vampire by night. Willumsen could see better in the dark than in daylight. I kept him on my right wing all the time.

The Turks weren't too frisky in the Ravine during the day. They didn't have to be. They had two positions that covered the Ravine floor—Beauchop Hill and the Farm.

By night, however, the Turk had to send in patrols to ward off sneak attacks by ourselves into the foothills of Chunuk Bair.

Willumsen was a fairly new replacement, not yet given to the "Gallipoli gallops" and other infirmities . . . he was healthy and with a brick-load of strength. We worked his ass off. Jeremy would take him into the Ravine one night and me, the next. Each time in, old snake eyes would wiggle his way closer to the bottom of the plateau.

At the end of a week, Willumsen, myself, and fifteen men from Reconn B had settled at the bottom of a steep hill that turned to a cliff directly under Chunuk Bair.

Oh Ma, do we do or do we don't!

"We'll go up, just a few yards at a time," I said into his ear. "If we hear any activity, freeze. We do not want to engage them. Got it?"

His idea of slow and steady and my idea of slow and steady were not at all the same. He scampered up like a jack rabbit. Jesus now ... I had no choice but to try to stay in his footsteps. ...

Just like that!

We were hauling each other up like Alpine climbers. Suddenly, out of the sheer crumbling dirt and lying there in the tall brown grass—Jesus, Mary, Mother of God ... we were on Chunuk Bair!

Willumsen slithered his slimy best so a mongoose would not find him and I kept watching his heel and tried to stay on it. We went in a hell of a-ways, maybe twenty-five yards, and the field opened.

The light was right fair. There were no visible fortifications such as the Turks had at the Chessboard, Bloody Angle, and the Nek, which made Quinn's Post so inhospitable. Nor was there the carnage of battle.

It was bloody simple. So long as the Turks had an impenetrable moat, the Ravine, protecting the plateau, they didn't have to keep much of a force on top and expose them to a pounding from the naval guns.

Let's get the hell out of here!

Next morning at Joshua Malone's bunker, the Major, Jeremy, and I watched as Willumsen's dirty fingernail traced a route through the Ravine to the spot he and I had gone up on the plateau.

"God," Malone whispered, "this is the top of the milk. What's your name, son?"

"Lance Corporal Willumsen, sir."

"You're not going to sell any secrets to the Turks, are you now?"

"Are you shitting me, Colonel?"

"Willumsen, you are now on a 'need to know' clearance. Lads, are we going to be able to take the Kiwi All-Black Battalion through the Ravine at night without detection?"

"The Turks don't like the Ravine at night," Chris said.

"I agree," Jeremy added. "Every time we engage them they pull out. I think they patrol the Ravine as a matter of routine."

"Problem as I see it," Chris said, "the Turks are watching the Apex down to Rhododendron Spur very closely."

"But suppose," Colonel Malone went on, "you withdraw Kiwi from the line at dark and are replaced, then Kiwi moves behind our own lines north, past Beauchop Hill. Keep moving up to Australia Valley and then come down the Ravine on the second night to the base of Chunuk Bair to attack on the third morning."

"That's a long walk with a thousand men without being seen," Chris said.

"The question we have to ask Lance Corporal Willumsen is whether or not he can lead us down the Ravine in the dark, and I've got to tell you, the climb up to Chunuk is a man-killer," I said.

"Just why are we going to try something like this, sir?" Jeremy asked. "We know the Turks keep several divisions of reserves behind Chunuk Bair."

Colonel Joshua Malone eyeballed us. "Grab your girdles, lads. In five days the British are landing a corps of four divisions at Suvla Bay."

"Four divisions!"

"About time!"

"Glory!"

"My Gawd!"

"I see that you heard me," Malone said, going back to the map and pointing to Suvla Bay, a few miles up the coast onto gently rising land leading up to a semicircle ring of ridges.

"The Turks do not keep much on Ridge 269, because there's been no need to, and their reserves are below. So ... the Suvla Corps lands, pushes quickly up to 269, while we launch a surprise assault on Chunuk Bair. Suvla Corps then connects with our left flank. Then, let the bloody Turks try to throw us off."

We studied Suvla Bay with its soft rise and salt lake to the easy height of Ridge 269.

"Suvla Bay," Malone said, thinking aloud, "is where the fuck we should have landed in the first place."

Our excitement sent us shivering with hope. If we could nail the Turks on this one, it would have all been worth it. The lot of us, including Lance Corporal Willumsen, went down to Corps where he detailed the prospective long march of the Kiwi All-Blacks to General Brodhead.

The final plan was so simple that it would be difficult for even the general staff to fuck up.

We'd do our night crawl down the Ravine to the foot of Chunuk Bair, gather the Kiwi All-Blacks at the base of the plateau, and wait.

Under dark, the ships of the Suvla Bay Corps would get into place and anchor.

At 0230 the Navy would hit the entire Turkish line including the Chunuk Bair Plateau. Whatever Turkish troops were up there were bound to drop behind the plateau until the shelling stopped. However, we would be climbing up at that point to beat them to the plateau at dawn.

At dawn, our entire line would attack. Aussies in the south would make their main attacks at the German Officers' Trench and across a narrow ridge called the Nek. These were diversionary attacks to pin down a large Turkish force and draw Turkish reserves to them.

The British Tenth, Eleventh, Fifty-third, and Fifty-fourth divisions, known as the Suvla Corps, would land *unopposed* at Suvla Bay and *immediately* push a mile or two inland and capture Ridge 269.

At the same time, the Kiwi All-Blacks would occupy Chunuk Bair Plateau, and Kiwi and the Suvla Bay Corps would connect lines.

Colonel Malone would then release several brigades of New Zealanders to cross the Ravine and reinforce us atop Chunuk Bair.

The Aussie would link up with our flank from the south.

We'd dig in by night.

On the second day, the Turks would counterattack, but troops from the Suvla Corps would continue to land and reinforce our lines.

We left Corps feeling exalted. It was your basic bread-and-butter plan. I was wondering whether or not we had enough stamina, guts, vinegar, and what have you to make the march, the climb, and then still be able to throw back the Turks.

Well, we'd soon find out.

No one knew the back of our lines better than my good self, so I led Reconn B down behind Rhododendron Spur. Colonel Malone kept Lance Corporal Willumsen alongside him as though he were a St. Christopher medal.

Although we should be out of sight of Turkish eyes, we traversed friendly terrain behind the lines with great caution. If we met an enemy patrol, Reconn B was to chase them off before they could get a look at the entire battalion. We played it tight, using this time to tape up anything rattling on the web belts and practice speaking through hand signals and semaphore. Reconn B moved a few yards at a time from safe point to safe point. Within an hour or two, it became like a dance. I was at the head of the line for this part of the journey. . . .

By afternoon you couldn't hear a sound. I watched at every stop to see that we weren't giving off telltale dust. Nothing. Lovely . . . lovely.

At dark we stopped briefly under Beauchop Hill where a store of water had been laid in. It was brought down to us and we refilled our canteens and kept moving.

I held up the line! Fucking Turks were creeping down a dry river bed . . . God, they could wake up a dead man . . . I called for us to lay low and only fire after I gave the first shot . . . and I didn't give the first shot until they were close enough to eat our lunch . . .

They never knew what hit them. We crept from body to body making certain they were dead. It had to be done by bayonet so as not to make any further noise.

I went back to Malone and suggested we hold up the line for forty minutes. Sometimes the Turks doubled up on their patrols, with the second one larger than the first. Nothing came.

We moved out, still in good time.

The colors of dawn found the Kiwi All-Blacks strung out on the banks of a dry river bed called Australia Valley. We were still behind our own lines but very observable.

Being a dry gulch, the river bed had good high brush on either side. The officers went up and down the line adjusting the men so we would have the day in cover and shade.

I gave Malone the best of the cover for his headquarters, a sort of temple of five boulders that had probably rolled down the hill a million years ago. He was an inspiring sight, indeed. After we made rounds we reported to him that we were satisfied Kiwi could not be seen by the enemy.

How can I say it? He was Wellington New Zealand–Auckland New Zealand–South Island–Milford Sound–Palmerston North. . . .

He was the kind of man, like Uncle Wally, who shook your hand and made you feel his grip and you knew his word was as strong as that grip. He was a man of straightforward values, but he also knew the inside cover of a fine book and the intricacies of battle.

We made one more run-through of the plan. I must have fallen asleep sitting up over the map because the next thing I knew, Jeremy was tapping my shoulder.

Jeez, I'd just gone to sleep and it was turning dark, already. I hefted my canteens and pondered if I could treat myself to a few sips, and did. We chewed on hardened chocolate bars, like pressed wood . . . supposed to give us energy.

Everything had a good feel to it. Although we were in a different location, it seemed like a normal night on Gallipoli. Farting Ferdinand started the party. Then came Turkish howitzers. Good. They were shooting from a different location than last night. This meant they were occupied during the day moving their guns and hadn't spotted Kiwi. Except for the brush along the banks, Australia Gully was not particularly sheltered.

If they knew we were there, they'd certainly be laying it on us now.

Lance Corporal Willumsen was the hairy man now. He took the point. Jeremy was behind him with half of Reconn A. I followed with the second part of the platoon, Reconn B.

"We're formed up, Colonel."

"Don't let the line get strung out. We assemble at the top of the Ravine."

Willumsen put on his night eyes as we crept from Anzac lines into Turkish Territory. The Kiwi All-Blacks were glorious. You couldn't hear voice nor rattle.

2015
Top of the Ravine

Reconn A and B held as the battalion tightened up.

Subaltern Higby brought up the First Platoon of the Auckland Company with an extra pair of machine guns. Our first target was to knock out a crucial Turkish position, an observation post called the Farm that guarded the opening to the Ravine from the western side.

As the raiding party took off, Subaltern Mellencamp brought the Fourth Platoon of the Wellingtons up, had them fix bayonets, and move into the Ravine to seek and destroy any Turkish patrols.

2125

The Ravine's echoes were voluminous. Mellencamp was hit by a Turkish ambush a few hundred yards in. Chris quickly moved in the Maori Company and they overwhelmed the Turks and abandoned the silence with a haka war cry.

. . . At the same time Higby had achieved total surprise at the Farm, knocking it out in one big burst.

. . . Higby in, Mellencamp and the Maoris back.

. . . Malone kept the Maoris right in back of Reconn, expecting the Turks to take a big look in the Ravine. Old Joshua was right! Wham! Fifty Turks! The Maoris, at fixed bayonets, plunged into them while the Wellington Company swung around the battle and got behind the Turks.

No Turks escaped.

We assembled, once more. It was 2350. Would the Turks come again or call it a night? When would they know for certain that the Farm had been taken? We had a small comfort in that the Turkish phones were even worse than ours were, so they might not become alarmed at the loss of contact. Activity in the Ravine? About normal for a heavy night.

"Well, let's get in there," Malone said. "We won't have to speculate long. They'll know in another hour and a half what we're up to when the Navy starts."

We moved a little more quickly now, and not so wary of maintaining silence. Abdul knew we were in the Ravine ... we only hoped he didn't know how many of us were there.

0130
There she is!

Steep, soft earth rivulets worn by centuries of water during the rainy season into perilous chimney-stack formations at the base of a dirty cliff.

Malone and Chris huddled with us for a big decision. Willumsen, Jeremy, and I could get Reconn up to the base of the cliff for certain, so we wouldn't have far to climb at dawn. This could give total surprise.

However, we stood more than a fair chance of getting hit by our own shells if they fell short, as they often did. However— and this is some bloody "however"—the closer we climbed to the plateau and waited, the shorter distance we'd have to go at dawn and the greater the chance of effecting surprise.

"Always in a case of not knowing whether to shit or go blind," Malone said, "I opt for closing one eye and farting. We're going to lose some men falling before you get to the base of the cliff."

We agreed.

"Keep Reconn in A and B sections. Jeremy take the left

wall. Rory, go to the right chimney. Stop at the base of the cliff and wait for naval gunfire. If they are shooting straight tonight, then creep the platoon as close to the plateau as possible and hit it at dawn. Push in no more than fifty yards and make a defensive perimeter to give us time to get the rest of the battalion up."

"Got it."

"Yes, sir."

"Who needs Willumsen most?" Jeremy asked me.

"You do," I lied.

"You take him. One of my squad leaders is a cat burglar."

0230

Maybe it was because this was the big push or maybe the Navy was throwing extra hurt at the Turks, but nothing was ever to compare with the orange balls that erupted offshore turning the entire front into bursts of flashing sunlight, waves of blinding heat, shaking the ground under us, nearly sweeping us off our feet. They were blasting Chunuk Bair Plateau dead-on.

"The Turks have got to pull back off the plateau," Malone said.

"Colonel, the shelling is giving us enough light to travel by," Willumsen said.

"Chris," Malone said.

"Sir."

"Start up Reconn A and B. Have the Maori Company on standby. Daybreak is 0455. Maori starts their ascent at 0400 and waits at the base of the cliff."

The Major gave two thumbs up, one to me and one to Jeremy. Up we started. Willumsen moved only by bursts of light, a few yards at a time. We were very good at picking out the next hand- and foothold. As the bombardment continued our confidence grew. Navy was absolutely saturating Chunuk Bair. If the Turks didn't back down, they'd be in a state of shock for certain or, at the very least, their communications would be knocked out. Easy Rory, I told myself, don't get cocky. You thought you had walk-overs before.

0400

We reached the bottom of the cliffs. Beneath us we could see the Maori Company begin their ascent.

I made the mistake of looking up at those last three hundred feet. I've got to share the last secret of my life. Even though I'm a South Island lad known for acts of derring-do, when I get beyond a certain height and I'm climbing upwards, I have to constantly gather myself. In other words, I was fucking frightened.

"Up we go, buddy system," Willumsen said. Good enough for him, he was a mountain goat with snake eyes. My bloody knees were knocking and weak. We wormed our way up ninety-degree crevices each time a shell-burst lit our way. It was the buddy system. The man above offered his hand to me and the man below pushed my ass up.

. . . *And don't look down anymore!*

. . . I wish I was in Dixie . . . hooray, hooray . . . Christ, man, your hand is sweating. None of that. Little wee hand and foot grips made for midgets and straining against gravity . . .

. . . Sorry, Georgia, not now. I've got to pay attention to what I'm doing. Some rock broke loose and skittered down under my feet. I felt Willumsen grab my shirt and hold me steady.

"Okay?" he asked.

"How much more?"

"We're about halfway up."

The other time Willumsen and I climbed this ascent, I was so exalted I almost ran to the top without thinking. The higher we got the more my legs ached and the ache began floating up my entire body. Gulps of air had to be fought for. My chest was too tight. . . .

Rory, you're aching and puffing because you're locking yourself up. The lads below are waiting. You're their leader. LEAD, DAMNIT, LEAD.

I stopped the line and told everyone to find something to sit on, and signaled Willumsen to come down to me.

"Do we hole up here or hit the top?" Willumsen said.

"You and me. We'll go up and have a look. Serjeant Duneen!" I called.

"Right below, I hear you, Landers!"

"I'm going to the top with Willumsen. I'll signal you by torch. Three dots repeated means stay put. One long flash of ten to twenty seconds and you come up!"

"Righto."

You know, the last fifty yards had so much work and urgency attached to them, I forgot to stay afraid. God in heaven, though, it did feel good when Willumsen grabbed my wrist and pulled me over the lip and onto Chunuk Bair Plateau. I allowed myself the pleasure of eight or ten gorgeous breaths and a sip of water, then rolled onto my belly and scanned the Plateau. Jesus! The shelling had done its mark, pocking the entire field and now they were hitting at the far end. I could see no Turkish activity of any sort.

"Abdul's gone," Willumsen said.

"Don't worry, he's waiting out of sight. Can you see Jeremy's lads?"

"I can. They're waiting about twenty-five yards down."

"Well, invite them up."

I went back to the edge. "Serjeant Duneen!"

I pressed my torch in the long signal to come up. As Duneen's head appeared, I grabbed him. "Call down to move the Maoris up. Tell the Major to come up and have a look. I think we may be able to position the battalion before daybreak."

Duneen slipped down easily.

Over the way I could see Jeremy's lads spilling over the top. Everyone tied rope around rock and thick brush anchors and began pulling men over the top.

Jeremy and Captain Matamata, the Maori commander, found me. "Matamata, give us a perimeter using Reconn as well. Don't go in any more than twenty-five yards."

"It's wide open," the captain said.

"Twenty-five fucking yards and not one fucking inch farther," I explained. "Abdul's just waiting for us to get stupid."

Deep breaths, deep breaths.

Oh God, it was good to see Joshua Malone and Christopher Hubble!

Malone looked at our perimeter. "Nice," he said, and checked his watch. Daybreak in fifty-two minutes.

"Willumsen," he called.

"Sir."

"Do you have a problem about going down to the bottom of the cliff now?"

"What kind of problem, sir?"

"Good lad. I want the machine guns from heavy weapons up here, next. Tell Captain Danielson to have Wellington and Auckland bring up the rear."

Willumsen was over the side. Malone turned to us. "My thinking is that we put all the big machine guns on the edge here, then have the infantry and Reconn creep over the plateau. If we have to withdraw, I want those big Vickers to be able to cover us."

It grew quiet as the naval shelling stopped. The sun rose from the direction of ancient Troy and spread its golden morning light over the Chunuk Bair Plateau! For the moment, it was ours!

In quick order a flare went up and we semaphored to the Apex. They acknowledged us. They knew where the Kiwi All-Blacks were. Malone and Chris danced quickly and firmly through our priorities.

. . . Have the Apex phone down to Corps and have Corps wireless to the Navy to cease shelling the Chunuk Bair Plateau area.

. . . Run a telephone line directly from the Apex up to Chunuk Bair.

Malone turned to the sea. Suvla Bay, a mile and a half up from Anzac Cove, was filled with landing boats and troops pouring ashore *without resistance!* The Suvla Corps bayonets beamed in the morning sun.

"Runner! Get Captain Matamata!"

"Yes, sir."

Another runner came back from the forward line. "Colonel! We can see the Dardanelles!"

"Jaysus!"

We took off at a trot over the field till we reached the Reconn perimeter. There! Below! We could see it all ... the Dardanelles into the Narrows and into the Sea of Marmara! There was no energy left to cheer. Behind us the Wellington and Auckland companies were coming over the top and fanning out.

Captain Matamata reported.

"Send two squads down to make contact with the Suvla Corps so we can seal off the Ravine."

"Right."

We relished the wonderment of seeing the Dardanelles before us, but this soon gave way to getting on with a lot of work. To our right and south the sounds of a major battle could be heard as the Aussies pushed for the German Officers' Trench and the Nek with the purpose of tying down the Turks and keeping reinforcements from going to Suvla Bay.

"Phone line in from the Apex, Colonel."

"Malone."

"Major Quigley at the Apex. I have three brigades in ready. Shall we cross to you?"

"No, not yet. We need to connect with the Suvla Corps first. What's going on down there from your point of view?"

"I don't know, Colonel. They seem to be regrouping."

"Come on, you bastards, up off that beach. Quigley, get back to me the moment they start moving inland."

"Yes, sir."

"And Quigley. What's going on with Monash?"

"Sorry to report that the Sixth Australian has been stopped cold at the German Officers' Trench."

Malone's expression gave off a sense of foreboding.

At Anzac Corps, Lieutenant General Brodhead was furious that the four divisions landed at Suvla Bay had not moved inland to the surrounding hills, but he seemed more concerned with finding shelter from the sun, locating a suitable area for officers' quarters, and settling on a safe place to set up their Corps command. General Stopford, chief of the Suvla Corps, remained aboard his command cruiser HMS *Helmsley*, relying on wireless to command his troops, although communications were very uneven.

Despite the lack of Turkish opposition at Suvla Bay, Stopford refused to order his divisions inland until he could build a line of trenches to ward off a Turkish counterattack. This was a direct countermand of the operational plan.

Stopford's commander ashore, Brigadier Dove, seemed glad to deliver the message to Stopford that there was no need for him to come ashore for a few days. Dove agreed that he would remain on the beach and make defensive precautions until at least twenty thousand men were landed.

. . . At Anzac Corps, Brodhead became frantic but was unable to reach Stopford's command ship. Finally, through wireless from a nearby destroyer, Stopford got the message to go on to the attack.

. . . After forty minutes of studying the map, Stopford sent a return message that he would not be pushed. He didn't like what he saw from the deck of the *Helmsley*.

. . . While the Tenth, Eleventh, Fifty-third and Fifty-fourth divisions made tea on the beach, Brodhead demanded they take the hills before the Turks got to them.

. . . "Not without sufficient artillery ashore," Stopford retorted.

As the Suvla Bay Corps dawdled to ineffectiveness, the Anzac line fell into perilous shape. The Kiwi All-Blacks were sitting alone on Chunuk Bair with twenty thousand Turks in the valley on their left flank and twenty thousand Turks in the valley on their right flank.

At the Nek, the guillotine had fallen!

Rather than calling off the attack until the Suvla Corps got moving, Brodhead made a horrendous error in judgment to capture the Nek at all costs, in order to keep the Turks guessing.

The Nek was in the heart of the Turkish defenses around Quinn's Post. It was a long ridge some thirty yards wide and two hundred yards long . . . and steep cliffs dropped off both sides. Anyone trying to cross the Nek would have to come straight down the boulevard with no cover.

The Eighth Australian Light Horse moved in four lines some twenty to thirty yards into the Nek and into the most concentrated enfilade of machine-gun fire the world had ever known.

With the Suvla Corps not moving inland, further attack over the Nek was suicidal. Monash tried desperately to call it to a halt, but Brodhead overrode him and ordered the assault continued.

With the Aussie Eighth Light Horse littering the field with their dead and wounded, the Third Australian Light Horse was butchered, and, after them, the Tenth Australian Light Horse was cut to pieces advancing into solid sheets of bullets. No soldier penetrated as much as fifty yards into the Nek, but on they came until there was no one left to come.

By early afternoon, the Turks had rendered the assaults on the German Officers' Trench and the Nek lifeless.

All that was left of the day was the Kiwi All-Blacks atop Chunuk Bair alone, the Ravine to their backs and some fifty thousand Turks ready to counterattack.

1530

Jeremy was out on a perimeter of shell holes with Reconn, the Maori, and the Auckland companies. The Wellington stayed in reserve. Captain Matamata came in with the chilling report that his patrol was unable to reach the Suvla Corps. They were still on the beach.

Colonel Markham, Brodhead's adjutant from Corps, found his way to Malone, where Chris and myself were working.

"Why aren't they moving off the beach?" Malone greeted Markham.

"We'd best not get excited," Markham responded in what was being set up as British-officer-speaking-to-colonial posture. "Communications got a bit slapdash between Suvla Corps and Anzac. We'll clear them up at a shipboard conference tonight."

"Tonight?"

"Tonight," Markham snapped back. "We'll get the Suvla Bay people moving off the beach by morning."

"Colonel Markham," Malone said, minding his temper. "The Turks have their reserves below, deciding where to send them. If the Suvla Corps does not take Ridge 269 in the next two hours, they will run into two Turkish Divisions who are going to—I guarantee—move in and occupy 269 tonight.

"I want to know what happened at the Nek," Malone finished.

Markham's mouth tightened. "The Nek is neither here nor there. I have come up with specific orders for you to release the New Zealand Brigades at the Apex and bring them over here, immediately."

"I'm not sure I hear you right," Malone said.

"We mean to hold Chunuk Bair. We'll sort Suvla out in good time."

"Colonel Markham, there has already been a massacre at the Nek."

"Who told you that!"

"Colonel Monash . . . and now you want me to put the entire New Zealand Corps in a trap up here. I will not—repeat, *not*—bring over my brigades until we hook up with the Suvla Corps."

"Major General Godley—"

"Fuck Godley."

Markham took the field phone, got the Apex, and told them to bring on General Brodhead at Corps. He reported he had Malone's refusal to send any more men over to Chunuk Bair.

"He wishes to speak to you," Markham said, giving Malone the phone.

"Malone."

"Brodhead here. Didn't you understand your order?"

"I did."

"Are you or are you not going to comply this instant?"

"Not until we have Suvla on our left flank and the Aussies on our right. Too breezy up here all by our lonesomes."

"Let me speak to Colonel Markham."

Markham listened and replaced the phone, then turned and looked about.

"Major Hubble," Markham said.

"Yes?"

"Place Colonel Malone under arrest and have him escorted back to Corps."

Well now, Christopher Hubble's life, as they say, flashed before his eyes in the next few seconds.

"Sorry, Colonel Markham, I refuse."

"Landers, place them both under arrest and remove them."

"No, sir," I said.

Colonel Joshua Malone put his big square timber-clearing hands on Colonel Markham's shoulders and looked at him squarely. "You and Brodhead and Churchill and Kitchener and Stopford and Godley and Darlington have betrayed the manhood of Australia and New Zealand. You have brought them to this place and you have butchered them with your collective, deplorable incompetence. The farce of Gallipoli was always beyond the capabilities of all the King's generals. I'm taking my people off Chunuk Bair. You've massacred enough men for one day."

He took the phone up again. "Quigley ... Malone here. Turks are out of the Ravine. Plug it up at both ends, I'll be bringing the Kiwi All-Blacks back in about an hour."

"Give me that phone!" Markham demanded.

"Get out of here, we have work to do. Major Chris. Go around our perimeter. We want an orderly withdrawal. Your people will be covered by the heavy machine guns. Donaldson, start moving Auckland down the hill. Make straight across the Ravine and up to the Apex. Apex is covering you."

"Indeed I shall, Colonel Malone."

"Willumsen."

"Sir."

"Better catch up with Major Chris. He's itching for a fight and I don't want him making any charges down the other side."

Ignoring the stunned Markham, Malone set up our tragic withdrawal. When Markham finally did get to the field phone, it wasn't working. I had disconnected it.

The Maori Company filtered back, waiting until the

Aucklands were on the way down, then went over the side themselves.

At that bloody instant came the final betrayal!

God knows who! God knows why! Naval gunfire opened up again. I reconnected the phone as the explosions tore into the plateau and called to the Apex to get the firing stopped.

Wellington drifted back and down into the Ravine. Jesus! No Chris or Jeremy!

"The Plateau looks clear," Malone said. "Retire the machine guns!"

The gunners broke down, tied their weapons to the lines, and lowered them. Colonel Markham continued to stand near Malone, confused as to what to do.

I went away from them with a growing feeling of fright as the last of the stragglers holding the rear guard went over the cliffside.

The Navy was really giving it to us. I went down, sensing a close hit. It splattered all about me. I looked up to see Markham being hurled off the cliff by concussion. Where the hell was . . . oh no . . . Malone was down. I took a couple of steps toward him, then saw it. The top of his head had been ripped off.

I can't be the last one up here! I can't be! Someone's late pulling back! No! Come on! Wait . . . Willumsen on the dead run.

"Let's go, Landers," he said. "Our lines are cleared."

"Where's the Major and Jeremy?"

"They won't be coming out," he said, grabbing me hard. "I found them in a shellhole. They're both dead."

I don't remember the march back. Nothing of it. Nor do I remember much of what happened for the next several days.

The first I recalled was hearing Chester's voice through a mist, and I do remember reaching out to find him. I felt his hand on my shoulder and his fingers stroking my head. I knew I had to push through the dense field that shrouded my mind. As memory started to filter in I realized that in a moment I would be faced with something terrible.

I remembered and wanted to crawl back into the fog but the sharpness of pain was too powerful. I could hide it no more.

"You remember now?" Chester asked.

I grunted.

"You've a decision to make, Rory. You cannot delay it," he said softly. "Rory, you have to tell me. Do you want to go on living?"

Oh Jeremy, Jeremy, my brother Jeremy!

Another voice, the sonorous sound of Modi. "If you will not accept that Jeremy is dead, then we must leave you alone with it," he said.

"Don't leave me alone," I rasped.

"Look at me and tell me that Jeremy is dead," Chester said.

"I can't do it."

"If you let it linger, it can put you into a serious black hole," Modi said.

I felt a rage well up in me. This is no time to hound me! I thought they were my friends. I wanted to destroy something, anything. Modi smelled my rage and blocked the entrance.

"If you go out and kill a thousand Turks, Jeremy will still be dead," Modi said.

"Get out of my way!"

"Sure," Modi said, stepping aside.

I stood but could not balance myself in my weakness, and I slumped down again.

Chester started in on me again. "Do you choose to go on living or not?"

"What the hell do you know? And you, Modi, what made you desert the Russian Army! Don't fucking preach to me! What do you know?"

Modi grabbed my hair and lifted my face so his beard was almost on me. "I'll tell you what I know. My village was burned before my eyes by Cossacks. My wife was raped by twenty of them and murdered. My baby daughter was decapitated. It's called a pogrom, Landers. Want me to sit and whimper with you! Yes? I live!"

Lord, I felt so low. I wrapped my arms about his knees and

whispered that I was never more sorry in my life. "Tell me what to do," I begged.

"In a place like this," Modi said, "despair is a greater enemy than the Turks. You'll rot as fast as a corpse in no-man's-land unless you take what happened face-on. Do you want to live as a cripple or as a man?"

"I hear you."

"Now tell us. Who died on Chunuk Bair?"

"Colonel Malone," I said with voice dry and croaky.

"And Major Chris?"

"Yes, Chris is dead."

"Who else?"

"Jeremy is dead."

Having opted for life and admitting to Jeremy's death was a very necessary first step. Either Chester or Modi was with me all the time, encouraging me to speak about Chunuk Bair and Jeremy.

Modi was right. Unless I took it on and fought it, I would be setting up a wreckage for a life. I needed power and wisdom from every source I could draw upon. . . .

I had to convince myself I was not trying to assign the battlefield as a distant memory. A man must carry such as this for all his days. The question was, how much of the battle do I let dictate how I will live from now on?

If the pain of it, the worthlessness of it, and aye, the godlessness of it consumes me for the rest of my days, as it will many men, then I have not honored the death of my beloved comrades.

Modi explained so clearly that he went to Palestine to honor the death of his wife and child by realizing their dreams for them.

And so I must honor my comrades' deaths by living a full life . . . live it with and for them . . . name children after them . . . see the green of New Zealand for them.

Modi and Chester told me to open my dreams up to finding Georgia. She was alive and real. She must be the hope.

Even with these two souls of compassion, the fight for my own survival was frightening and I asked Conor Larkin to help me.

I did not know Shelley MacLeod. I had learned of his love for her from his letters to me. The letters stopped after Sixmilecross. The news of Shelley's death came from Father Dary. Conor was in prison and had just taken a cat-o'-nine-tails lashing when he learned of her murder.

Knowing Conor, he must have blamed himself for her death or, at the very least, the two of them were certainly partners in a death vow.

And Conor's guilt? Now there's a man who must have suffered no less than the savior on the cross.

I asked him for some of his strength. Conor had survived the most foul and brutal of all human experiences. He came through it, God knows how, and he made a decent and important life, useful and worthy to his last breath.

More important than all else was that he found it within himself to be able to love again. This Atty Fitzpatrick must have been a wonderment to get through to him.

I clung to Conor ... and Modi ... and Chester ... and I demanded of myself not to let Gallipoli take me down.

Lieutenant General Brodhead kept me around Corps. His own shield had been pierced. He was in a sort of funk either over his mistakes or the heavy losses or both.

Why me? Brodhead had had a very special relationship with Christopher Hubble, older brother, father-son, what have you. Chris had done a lot of black work for the General from Ireland to Gallipoli. I think the General had come to depend on Chris enormously. Generalship is a lonely place. Confidants are golden nuggets. Had all gone well, Christopher Hubble was due to come out of the war as one of the youngest brigadiers in British history and, in a sense, Brodhead's legacy.

I certainly did not have that closeness of Ulster, the military tradition, the station that those two had, but he liked my ways and some of my fairly good results. I found him chatting me up about the promise of a bright future and felt that he was going to ask me to become his aide.

I did not harbor hatred for him. His terrible tactical and battlefield decisions were those of a general whose wars had been fought in the last century. He did not understand how to send men against machine guns. They marched in grenadier lines to be mowed down like wheat.

He was a personally courageous man, rather well liked by the troops, whose hardships he shared. He did the best he could for Anzac after being put into an impossible position, against his better judgment.

With myself at Corps, carrying top clearance and admission to the secured message center, I was able to pick up on the furor in the aftermath of the Suvla Bay landing.

Admiral Jack Fisher, the top naval officer of the Imperial Navy, had flipped and flopped several times over Gallipoli and finally resigned in protest.

Fisher's resignation forced Churchill to resign as First Lord of the Admiralty.

General Darlington, commander of the Mediterranean theatre, was relieved of his command.

General Stopford of Suvla Bay Corps was fired, as were his division commanders and staff.

The Asquith government fell and a coalition cabinet was formed to conduct the balance of the war.

Brodhead's probable fate was that he might well not be considered for another field command, a devastating blow to him.

As the shock and scandal of Gallipoli raged and the inquiries began, Keith Murdock, the Australian journalist, rocked the empire with his exposure of what had been done to the soldiers of Australia and New Zealand.

Despite an obvious defeat, the British continued to cling to their wretched acres on Gallipoli. They were confused as to what to do and desperate not to lose face.

August, September, and October came and passed. Gallipoli showed the other side of her ugly face as summer's inferno shifted into a cold and brittle autumn. We were less prepared for the great chill than we had been for the heat.

In mid-November a blizzard of near biblical proportions tormented the trenches. An Antarctic bluster of gale force winds and blinding snows found us with little shield against it.

The day after the blizzard passed, hundreds of men were found frozen to death or blackened with frostbite, requiring amputations of fingers and toes.

Through a night in late November, Chester, Modi, and I worked at the beach and paddock unloading and packing blankets, gloves, winter coats, scarves, and getting them to the front.

A most desperate situation existed at Chatham's Post and Ryder's Ridge. Because of their proximity to the sea, the sting was greater.

We were going 'round the clock and suddenly found ourselves short of trail men. Chester decided to make a night run to Chatham's and Ryder's. It had a bad scent to it because the Turks had set up a shooting gallery atop the Valley of Despair.

I made a run to a distribution point up Monash Gully, staggering home close to midnight. Chester's train had returned without him. Modi had been told that Chester had taken a light wound to the shoulder on the way to Chatham's and told the trailmaster he was walking back to Widow's Gully to get patched up.

Modi did not panic. The pair of us went to Widow's and uncovered the face of every man there dead or waiting for evacuation or surgery. No Chester.

In the hours before light, I did something I had not done in seven months of Gallipoli. I got on my knees and prayed.

We found him soon after daybreak on the side of the trail at Brighton Beach. He had frozen to death, curled up with his knees against his chest, not thinking to take a few of the blankets he was delivering to the post.

His wound was almost superficial. That was not what killed him. He had no strength or stamina left. He was so weakened that any hard blow was apt to do him in.

I did something else I had not done at Gallipoli.

I wept.

Late in November, secret plans came through for the evacuation of the Anzac Corps. Strangely, it was the best worked-out plan of the entire expedition. All heavy gear would be left so the men could travel unhindered. On the first night enough ships would appear to haul off as many men as possible and sail out of sight.

On the second night, the balance of the Corps would repeat the procedure. The problem was that on the second night, Farting Ferdinand and the other artillery might just light up the beach and the entire Turkish Army could pour down on us.

As fortune would have it, the main pair of eyes directing the Turkish artillery was an observation post called the Guillotine.

The Guillotine was in a freak position, so common at Anzac Cove. Mule's Gully on our side of the line continued upwards and narrowed, with numerous S-turns. To make the Guillotine almost invulnerable, a sudden rise of sheer cliffs stood on either side of the gully. The post was embedded in solid rock and could not be reached by climbing over it or trying to outflank it.

The only option was simply to rush at it. The gully was so narrow that only two or three men at a time could make the final S-turn and mount a charge. God only knows how many men we had lost in unsuccessful attempts to knock out the Guillotine.

A day after I had seen the secret evacuation plans, Corps advised me that all the mules were to be destroyed on the final night of the evacuation. We had gathered in nearly six hundred animals for the winter's siege.

I told command I did not want these orders to go beyond me. The reasons for their destruction were simple. There was no way on earth we could evacuate the animals. They would be left either to freeze or starve to death, or to be used against us later by the Turks, or to be slaughtered by the Turks for food.

I did not want Mordechai Pearlman to be involved in this final horror. Having prayed for Chester's life and wept for the death of my brothers, I saw no harm in asking God to grant me some sort of wisdom to help stave off a disaster on the second night of the evacuation.

After a staff meeting at Corps, Colonel Monash, of all people, came to my troglodyte to have a chat-up. We had come to care for each other as friends and I think he wanted some neutral ground to sit on and hear his voice aloud. He was a man with a large mind, somewhat like Conor.

"Sorry about the mules," he said.

As he spoke those very words, a plan came to me. It would be a hell of a lot better sending these mules to a soldier's death up Mule's Gully charging the Guillotine, than it was to send his soldiers over the Nek against his wishes.

"I'll cry a little for them as well," I said.

"The rains have washed away the shallow graves of no-man's-land," he said. "This land will be eternal valleys and hills of bones, theirs and ours, and you can't even tell the difference."

He looked at me knowingly.

"Was it worth it?" he asked. "No one will ever know the true figures, but there were no less than a half-million casualties, theirs and ours. Tens of thousands of them were New Zealanders and Australians. That's a vast number for countries so small as ours. We have to find something out of this that didn't make it an entire waste. What did you find out, Landers?"

"All men have a measure of cowardice in them. I learned that love of one's mates can overcome your fears. I learned that every survivor of this horror must try to live a good life because he lives for many men."

"That's very decent, Landers. I'll remember that."

"And you, sir?"

"We came to this field of battle, Landers, I from a former penal colony proud of its wild men and free ways. You came from a place of pioneers, woodsmen, sheepmen, and farmers. Neither of us were truly defined as a people. We leave as Australians and New Zealanders with a clear definition of who we are as men and as nations. In a manner of speaking, your country and mine were born at Gallipoli. We have shown our stuff to the world and ourselves, and only by such tragedy did we have this moment to show it."

I had orders cut for Mordechai Pearlman to go to Lemnos to survey our supplies of timothy hay, grain, blankets, and equipment for the balance of the winter. He still had no idea the mules were to be destroyed or an evacuation was to take place.

Even as I gave him the orders, I feigned complaining that it would be difficult to spare him, even for a few days. I believed I had duped him. He didn't realize he was not going to return ... or did he?

I took him to the dock, slapped him on the back and told him I'd see him back here in a couple of days, gave him a hand into the boat, and tossed his gear to him.

"Thanks, Rory," he said, "for everything. There'll never be another one like Cairo."

After his boat pulled away, I whispered, "I love you, man."

"You requested to see me, Landers," Brodhead said.

"Yes, sir. I believe I have an idea to knock out the Guillotine. If the Turks have to go without their eyes, we might be saved from artillery on the final night—"

"God, I wish we could. If the Turks get wind of us, it might mean a massacre, or at least they'll take thousands of our lads prisoner. I've been trying for six months to get the Guillotine. How the hell? We have to send men through the S-turns two or three at a time."

"How about stampeding the mules into the Guillotine?"

"My God," he whispered.

"We have to destroy the animals, anyhow."

"My God," he repeated, "it would certainly create a tremendous diversion. The Turks might either freeze in their positions or rush their reserves over there. It might just keep the beach clear for a few precious hours."

We set a line of fire blazing behind the mules and hustled them along, screaming and lashing at them, and they soon rampaged up Mule Gully through barbed wire, up and up into the S-turns, rolling over each other as the gully narrowed.

Flynn and I with two others tracked a path maybe used in ancient Greek history that roughly followed the gully line. We waited until the animals began hitting the final turns, hoping that our presence would go unnoticed.

The cries and screams of these beautiful soldiers was all but unbearable. As they hit the last turn, Flynn and myself and other lads, loaded down with Turkish grenades, stood on a wee narrow path ten feet over the top of the mules.

As they turned the bend, up went Turkish flares and the last fifty yards of the "charge" was illuminated. The Turks blazed gunfire from two weapons. Animals in front collapsed, while other mules behind them kept coming . . . coming . . . coming . . . piling up right in front of the Guillotine.

Oh God in heaven! One of the lads skidded down into the gully, and was mangled and crushed by the mules in an instant.

Now or never!

We hopped on a rock unseen, for the Turks had their hands full stopping the charge—one . . . two . . . three . . . four . . . ten . . . eleven—twelve grenades erupted right on their nest.

Get the hell out fast . . . fast . . . be careful now, don't slip into the gully. . . .

I felt very light-headed and warm. . . . What the hell does a man do on his knees and not able to stand up! What the hell! Blood was pouring down my front. . . .

Flynn jerked me to my feet.

"Hang on to me, Landers, we'll get you back, cobber, we'll get you back."

EPILOGUE

SECRET FILES OF WINSTON CHURCHILL,
CHRISTMAS 1915

The greatest generals appear to be the historians of future generations who had no decisions to make at the time the history was being made.

When all the commissions of inquiry are done, the finger-pointing and the cover-ups and the lying and the justifications are told and retold, I realize that one glaring fact shall remain, and that is that the name of Winston Churchill will forever be synonymous with one of the greatest disasters in military history.

What I say here is that the knowledgeable men of high station, men who created the world's greatest empire, favored the military and political strategy of attempting to open the Dardanelles. It was their judgment that Gallipoli was a naval and military probability, if not possibility.

What fell apart subsequently will fill hundreds of volumes yet unwrit. But to infer now that the plan was of evil or foolish intent or too much of a risk, or that it was undertaken to advance individual careers, or that we did not have compassion for the lives of our troops, is a damnable lie.

I could stand before the Parliament or any commission and argue my case. I could enlighten them on blunder upon blunder that was not my doing, but I choose not to spend the rest of my life pointing my finger at the competency of many generals, admirals, and ministers. No, I shall be the flogging boy for them all.

As First Lord of the Admiralty, I made my share of good decisions and my share of poor decisions. What is deplorable is the accusation that I did not care. It will not be remembered that many undertakings occurred after my resignation. It will be little remembered that most of the decisions were always beyond my control.

The War Council went into the venture with great confidence. After the failure of our naval firepower to produce the expected results, and after meeting unexpectedly fierce Turkish resistance on the landing, the entire venture began to cloud.

Resolve to win this campaign, and the means with which to win it, began to vanish in our highest councils.

The Suvla Bay landing was a disgrace to British arms. Field Marshal Kitchener was the man responsible for the appointment of General Darlington and General Stopford. Yet we do not hear Kitchener damned.

My most terrible personal moment came when I had to inform Lady Caroline Hubble that both her sons had been killed. Through my own sorrow I found majesty in the way this magnificent woman handled the most wrenching moment of her life. Her continued display of dignity and courage during the months of grief was incomparable.

Lord Roger Hubble was informed of the tragedy by cable, which reached him at his summer home, Daars, near Kinsale. The account is thus: Hubble, an aficionado of shark-fishing, ordered a small craft readied, although a terrible storm was sweeping in. Forewarned, he sailed deliberately into a fierce gale. Flotsam and jetsam of his boat later washed ashore, but his body was never found.

Thus, at the age of forty, my career stands on the threshold of disaster. Apparently I am still of sufficient value to His Majesty's

Government to have been recalled from my regiment in France to become Munitions Minister, although I no longer have a seat on the War Council.

Can I overcome a half-million casualties of Gallipoli, or must I die with its stigma engraved on my tomb? I am determined, because of this disaster, to continue to find a way to serve. I shall serve so well that in the end Gallipoli will be a footnote rather than the name of my volume.

I do not know how leaders must bear the result of having caused death in battle. There is no textbook written to give one guidance on the subject. Every king, every general, every minister, every president must deal in his own way with the deaths that result from his orders. May God have mercy on him who ends up with a Gallipoli.

I shall do my best, in future writings, to precisely explain my role and my thinking. Can I ever cleanse the gnaw in me? Perhaps some future day will allow me to make a cleansing gesture.

WSC

A
RETROSPECTIVE
ON THE EASTER
RISING OF 1916

BY THEOBALD FITZPATRICK

Part One: Conor's Wake

To refresh your memory, I am Theobald Fitzpatrick, the son of Atty and the late Desmond Fitzpatrick. I inherited enough of my father's legal skills to carry on his life's work as the barrister for the republican movement. His partner, Robert McAloon, is now my partner, though of an age where all motion is accompanied by a creak.

My mother had been Conor Larkin's lover for several years, since he returned to Ireland from America after his prison escape. He lived life on the run, the most wanted man in Ireland, and brought the Brotherhood up to a very respectful fighting level.

He was killed leading the raid on Lettershambo Castle. Some say, and not without a touch of wisdom and truth, that Conor saw a torturous road ahead, bound to end in life imprisonment or violent death. He also realized he could not continue his function as a loner in a Brotherhood growing large with a cumbersome Supreme Council.

Finally, he could never live a normal life for a single day with my mother. So, Conor wrote his own amen by blowing Lettershambo Castle halfway to Scotland.

The death of Conor Larkin at Lettershambo Castle spelled a loss of will and strength in my beloved mother, Atty Fitzpatrick.

When my own father, the late Desmond Fitzpatrick, died of the heart while arguing a republican cause in the Four Courts of Dublin, Mother mourned in measured tones of dignified dignity with never a display of public desolation.

Such was not the case for Conor Larkin.

The British returned the bodies of Conor and Long Dan Sweeney. What followed, in defiance of British law, was a public lying-in-state followed by graveside oratory over Long Dan Sweeney that ascended them to martyrdom.

My mother accompanied Conor's casket in a simple cortege over the breadth of Ireland all the way to Ballyutogue. At each crossroad, town, and village, a new honor guard of Home Army would accompany him to the next gathering. Children laid flowers on the roadway, women wept and prayed, and men were nudged by long dormant stirrings for freedom.

When, at last, Father Dary Larkin put his brother to rest alongside their father in St. Columba's churchyard in Ballyutogue, Mother flung herself on Conor's grave as a spontaneous keening erupted from mourners from Derry and Donegal and then, from all over the land.

Mother's lifelong posture of composure was flown as bitterthorn wailers purged their grief through uncontrolled leaps in and out of madness. They spilled from the Larkin cottage and clogged the wee paths, dancing and howling around Conor's cairn.

Mother stretched her distraught body upward like a banshee and joined the night keeners, rending her clothing and hair and flesh through ten hours of darkness until the damp-chilled dawn finally broke and she crumpled.

Aye, all of Ireland now knew that the whisperings about Atty Fitzpatrick's clandestine love with Conor Larkin were true. When my sister Rachael and I were able to pull her from his grave, she remained in the Larkin cottage until a week later, when the final revelers had exorcised themselves and drifted back to their own fields and villages.

During that week a disturbing scenario developed. To be direct, the mutual offerings of consolations between Rachael and Father Dary did not appear to be very ecumenical in nature to me.

As the waking week played out, I and others drank the public house and shabeen dry. Between hail-and-farewell toasts to the deceased, I did not know whether I should spend my time comforting Mother, who remained beyond my reach in any case, or to step in between an obviously budding forbidden romance.

Sorrow will out, and at last I was able to pack my two girls back to Dublin where Rachael went into a familiar role of becoming Mother's older sister. I thought this no time to offer Rachael unsolicited advice about the problems of falling in love with a priest.

Father Dary ... mind you, it is not possible to dislike this man ... had blazoned a light of hope in hopeless Derry. He fronted for an ailing Bishop with great compassion. Father Dary was much loved and far too liberal and, thus, in constant and deep trouble with the hierarchy.

He had been aloof from the Brotherhood. He took me aside during the funeral and allowed that he might be amenable to listen to us on special occasions. Was this due to his brother's death? Or, just possibly, my sister Rachael's beauty? After we left Ballyutogue, Father Dary did seem to find an inordinate amount of church business to bring him down to Dublin.

As for Mother, after a lifetime of hard sledding in the movement, she "hit the wall." The robustness that she carried off on the stage as "Mother Ireland" or that empowered her to blast her way through a meeting of the Brotherhood's Supreme Council was no longer there.

Her grief for Conor Larkin seemed consummate. She had worked with and supported two great, powerful, and daring men. With them both in their graves, her own energies were spent. She wisely withdrew from the Supreme Council of the Brotherhood but continued a significant, though lesser, role of elder statesman.

It is to be remembered that the raid on Lettershambo Castle gutted the upper echelons of the Supreme Council. Although not a member by choice, Conor was a spiritual leader as well as our most brilliant organizer and tactician in a land lamentable for the lack thereof.

Long Dan Sweeney was the revolution that was. His legendary glories going back to Fenian times irrevocably evolved into myth.

We lost our dear Lord Louis De Lacy, a mystical Gael who gave his barony to train our people. Loss of Dunleer was devastating to us.

And God love him, little Seamus O'Neill, the author of brilliant, stabbing, mocking, logical words, was dead in Lettershambo and, after all, words were one of Ireland's few weapons.

In the transition a tobacconist, a former bartender, a roving Irish soldier of fortune, an academic, a labor leader, and, depending on one's definition, one, two, or three poets took over the Supreme Council. It was an Irish stew without a single substantial military ingredient.

I, of course, carried on the role assigned me at birth, to do my stuff in the Four Courts. They did not name me Theobald for nothing.

Part Two: Of Nobler Causes

As the year 1916 came into view, dark clouds lifted from a number of issues.

The war in Europe was going to come down to a numbers game. The side that could absorb their casualties best would be declared the winner.

The big fellow in the numbers game was American manpower. America was still not committed. Ireland, therefore, had to supply its share of fodder until America could be lured in on the side of the Allies, but Ireland was a wee player in the numbers game.

American sentiment had always been strong for the Allies. France was America's first ally and vital to America's gaining her independence from England in 1776.

Britain represented America's principal heritage, her language and culture, and much of her original population.

On the other hand, America had to be concerned with her large German population, as well as a large Irish contingent, vocal and with republican leanings.

Wars are generally undertaken when a greedy nation or greedy alliance has a surplus of food and munitions and men. Men are the most expendable. Wheat is much more difficult to come by, as England learned when the Dardanelles was closed and Ukrainian wheat became unavailable.

Well now, no ambitious nation or alliance is going to admit to being *greedy*, is it? It is imperative for a nation embarking on a war to invent and superimpose a more noble reason than greed.

The American Revolution gives a clear and stunning example of changing cause in midstream. The Revolution began throughout the colonies as a series of disconnected and scattered forays protesting British inequities, mainly in taxation.

Difficult for one to blow a tax protest into a full-blown people's revolution. Thus the revolution elevated itself, donning the most magnificent mantle in human history by declaring it was really a war for independence and human dignity.

Take the American Civil War. This conflict came about to save the union as the result of two different economic, cultural, and moral entities trying to exist within a single nation.

Over a time, as the war developed, the brilliant Mr. Lincoln reinvented the far nobler cause that the abolition of slavery was what the war was really about.

This war now engulfing the European continent came about because two greedy alliances lusted for more of each other's empires. However, recruiting posters could hardly read: JOIN THE ARMY BECAUSE WE ARE VERY GREEDY.

The nobler cause had to be discovered, invented, or found under a rock, did it not? What emerged, heroically, from the Allied viewpoint, was that this was a "war to save democracy" for the world and affirmed the rights of small peoples to their freedom. Belgium, for example.

However, most nations burn the candle at both ends. The Allies, in addition to saving the world for democracy, fully intended to snatch for themselves the German, Turkish, and Austrian colonies.

A number of tiny nations took the Allies at their word and reserved a seat at the postwar peace conferences and treaty signings.

Among these small peoples were the Irish, who had surely earned at least a voice in the future of their country by the Irish blood now being spilled in defense of democracy.

Ireland represented a spearhead of discontent. If the Irish came to the peace table with their very own representatives, it could set off a chain reaction throughout all of Britain's colonies.

It became paramount to England's postwar strategy to keep

especially the Irish away from the peace table. Britain could not defend or justify this business of waging a war for democracy if the Irish dared to show up.

Thus, England launched a well-devised campaign against Irish independence:

"The British Parliament has already passed an Irish Home Rule Bill that was agreed to by the Irish Party."

"We have thousands of Irishmen, all volunteers, in British uniform. Obviously, they must have felt very British themselves to enlist."

"We have permitted the Irish to form their own Home Army to defend Irish soil."

"Certain Irish scoundrels are sleeping with the Hun."

To which I answer:

"The Irish Home Rule Bill demands Irish loyalty to the British Crown and allows the British Parliament to veto any legislation passed by an Irish government. The Irish Party is one election away from extinction."

"Thousands of Irish joined the British Army because it was the best job offer they had ever had."

"The Irish Home Army is of Gilbert & Sullivan caliber, its men armed with fierce broomsticks and century-old blunderbusses."

However, I never got to present my case to Woodrow Wilson. The British case sounded good to the American president because he wanted it to sound good. The big boys weren't going to let the little fellows screw things up, and alongside the British, the Irish were small potatoes, so to speak.

*   *   *

Although the Irish had come to America under the most abominable conditions, fleeing tyranny and deprivation, their support for the old country was boisterous but weak. Once the St. Patrick's Day Parade down Fifth Avenue broke up and the pubs were drunk dry, their net effect in Ireland didn't amount to much.

In Ireland itself, the nation had been beautifully divided by Dublin Castle's centuries of underhanded intrigue.

The cornerstone of British power in Ireland lay with an Anglo-Ascendancy awarded vast acreages of our land for the initial conquest and colonization of the country. These were the landed gentry, the bankers and factory owners, a privileged class intent on staying privileged through loyalty to England.

Ascendancy power was supported in one province: Ulster. By the importation of a Protestant population, it was likewise rewarded with privilege.

The Catholic middle class, such as it was, didn't want the boat rocked, and the Catholic hierarchy, protecting its own well-being, considered the Crown its benefactor. The Church did ugly work in purging generation after generation of Irishmen of their nationalistic aspirations.

Otherwise, Dublin Castle had set up a large Catholic constabulary and systems of briberies, small civil service jobs, spying, and whatever else was needed to keep the lid on the pot.

This left the Irish masses the most wretched in Europe, with more than three quarters of the population in a perpetual state of misery and subservience.

Once the Irish nation of her great Celtic chieftains had been shattered and scattered early in the 1600s, future risings from Theobald Wolfe Tone and Robert Emmet on through the Fenians were paltry affairs led by enormously courageous men, dreamers who ended up on the gallows with their necks hoicked in half after making a gallant speech from the dock.

These words became our mythology.

A Gaelic revival in recent times tried to connect that glorious past to our miserable present, but lost much of its zeal with the death of Charles Stewart Parnell.

Ireland had been committed to the war with England by a discredited John Redmond and a defunct Irish Party. Sinn Fein, the new republican political entity, was starting to win the minds of Irishmen, but elections were to be a long way off.

Indeed, the British felt so secure that they called for a draft of Irish youth into the Army in early 1916. What they were telling the Irish was ... "You aren't Irish and WE OWN YOU."

This jangled a nerve. It is one matter to volunteer for the Army, but it is quite another to be forced to serve. After centuries of trying, the British still could not understand that Irishmen did not consider it any great honor to be British.

Even though the British gingerly backed away from Irish conscription, the republican movement, led by the secret Brotherhood, knew that the Irish were being set up for yet another betrayal.

Conor Larkin had wondered if the Irish people could ever be awakened from their centuries of lethargy. Actions like Sixmilecross and Lettershambo said that there were a few good men left to keep the flame from flickering out.

What was desperately needed now was for the Irish people to make a smashing statement in the streets that our demands for freedom will no longer be deferred and that we are now ready to make the sacrifice and take the risk to win what is ours. WE WANT TO BE AT THE PEACE TABLE.

Otherwise the right of Irish freedom would again be passed over, and this time there could be a slide back into accepting underclass status in servitude to the Crown for another century or two.

Part Three: The Best Laid Plans of Mice and Men Were Not Made in Dublin

The Irish have always had a surplus of opinions. Several different volunteer defense groups cropped up. The one that we are keenly concerned with was a fairly well-knit group whom, for all practical purposes, we shall call the Irish Home Army.

Its founder, president, and chief of staff was Eoin MacNeill, an Ulsterman of mixed religious background. MacNeill was a straight-down-the-line Gaelic revivalist and republican. The extent of his military expertise was that he was a professor of history at Dublin University and an academic at the Royal Irish Academy.

In matters of a pending revolution, MacNeill steered a tenterhooks course with his Home Army, making certain it didn't get mixed up in anything with live ammunition. MacNeill did arch up his back to warn the British he would fight any attempt to conscript his men.

Otherwise he stayed aloof from intimate contact with the aggressive Irish Republican Brotherhood, although he certainly realized the Home Army was riddled with Brotherhood people.

Chief among the Brotherhood infiltrators into the Home Army was Padraic Pearse, who rose to second in command behind MacNeill. Pearse, who likewise had earned his military qualifications as headmaster of a secondary school, was a prominent force on the Supreme Council of the Brotherhood. The Brotherhood fully intended to use the Home Army as its instrument of a rebellion. The Supreme Council, therefore, secretly plotted the Rising without bothering to consult with Eoin MacNeill, Commander of the Home Army. They came to a decision that rebel Ireland would rise on Easter Sunday of 1916.

The gist of the plan was for Padraic Pearse to call up the Home Army for maneuvers on April 23, as was within his power to do. It was commonplace in Dublin these days to see the various volunteer groups holding maneuvers by storming buildings, throwing up barricades, and engaging in mock street battles, as well as marching through the town in close order drill.

Dublin Castle didn't put much coin in all this. The Home Army was held in quite shallow esteem.

*   *   *

A simultaneous rising of the countryside was also planned. Sir Roger Casement, a retired Anglo-Irish diplomat of Ulster Protestant origin, was a diehard Brotherhood man. He would travel first to America and thence to Germany to gain support. His plan was money from America and guns and possibly troops from Germany.

The German guns would be landed somewhere in the west of Ireland and put into the hands of republicans to support the Dublin Rising.

Many years ago Conor Larkin told me that this kind of coordinated operation was scarcely an Irish tradition. In utter confidence, he told me he felt it close to impossible to plan and execute a mission involving several thousand men—especially Irish men.

Sir Roger Casement learned bitterly that most Irish-Americans supported the Allies in the Great War, and a rebellion in Dublin would probably not sit well with them. Finding little support in America, he went on to Germany.

The German High Command was curious to learn how serious their involvement in Ireland should be. The wildest of scenarios might see German submarines using the waters off the west coast of Ireland, and possibly even some German troops or officers landing there. They offered Casement to form up an Irish Brigade out of their stockpile of Irish prisoners of war. When only fifty-two men volunteered, and most of them sleazy, German enthusiasm dimmed.

Nonetheless, Germany had to keep a hand in, should the rebels get lucky. Casement's plea for a hundred thousand rifles was reduced to one shipload of twenty thousand.

In the beginning of April, Padraic Pearse, as second in command and chief of operations, issued an order from Home Army Headquarters, Liberty Hall, the Dublin trade union building. He called on the Dublin Brigades to assemble with arms and ammunition for maneuvers on Easter Sunday, April 23.

The chief English representative at Dublin Castle, Lord Nathan, and his military commanders saw the document and did not seriously investigate the possibility of trouble.

In a stroke of something less than genius, Pearse issued a second order switching the maneuvers to Monday, April 24. He reasoned that because it was a bank holiday more men would show up at Liberty Hall. Also, the British officer corps would be out of Dublin for the opening of the horse races at the Fairyhouse Track.

The German ship *Aud*, disguised as a Norwegian freighter, was at sea with twenty thousand rifles while Casement himself was slipped back into Ireland by submarine.

The *Aud* finessed its way through the British blockade and made into Tralee Bay, awaiting the signal to unload. It never came. There had obviously—and predictably—been a communications foul-up and the *Aud* soon became as conspicuous as a lighthouse. A British naval patrol was dispatched to investigate and, with all escape routes closed, the crew of the *Aud* scuttled her, sending the ship and twenty thousand rifles to the bottom of Tralee Bay.

Sir Roger Casement, hiding in the fields, was betrayed by an informer who had landed with him as a member of the defunct Irish-German brigade.

Meanwhile, in Dublin, Eoin MacNeill got wind of the Brotherhood plot to use his Home Army and issued a countermanding order, which was published in newspapers over the country

With all this activity and more foul-ups building, Dublin Castle still failed to get overly concerned. As a matter of precautionary routine after the *Aud* incident, a sweep was made to round up "known republicans, Sinn Feiners, Brotherhood, and other known trouble makers" in the rural areas.

As for Dublin, not so much as an extra soldier or constable was put on duty.

Part Four: Easter Monday, 1916

It was a leisurely day. The Brits were off at the races. Despite the conflict of orders a number of men of the Home Army, by bicycle, foot, and tram, assembled at Liberty Hall, which bore a banner with the battle cry: WE SERVE NEITHER KING NOR KAISER, BUT IRELAND.

A terrible moment of decision was at hand. In order to put up a battle long enough to gain world attention, the Brotherhood felt that a minimum of three thousand men was needed. Only fifteen hundred showed up.

Padraic Pearse, a poet, scholar, and keeper of Gaelic mysticism, reckoned we should get on with it, knowing it was now a suicide mission. "If nothing else," he said, referring to Tom MacDonagh, Joseph Plunkett, and his good self, "Ireland would rid itself of three bad poets."

On that note, the Rising was committed.

My job, of course, would be to come in with my partner, Robert Emmet McAloon, after the fighting was over and see what we could legally do to save our people.

As for Mother and Rachael, I was glad they were not to be intimately involved in the fighting. They had a number of duties to carry out from the message center and hideaways. The woman of record was to be Countess Constance Markievicz, an Anglo aristocrat much like Mother, who would command a unit at St. Stephen's Green, a park in the center of the city.

So, off they went in their undermanned, underarmed little units to challenge the mighty lion who had come to their shores and taken their land almost a millennium earlier.

What follows will not particularly be told in the order it happened, but should give one a clear picture of the kind of battle that took place.

Countess Markievicz's total lack of military experience showed itself immediately as she planted her troops in the middle of St. Stephen's Green, a small square park surrounded by three- and four-story buildings. British troops grabbed the buildings surrounding her and poured in rifle and machine-gun fire compelling her unit to withdraw to the nearby College of Surgeons, where they dug in and made a splendid fight.

Edward Daly, a slight, pale, mustachioed twenty-five-year-old in command of a "battalion" of a hundred-odd men, seized the Four Courts, from which the British had dispensed black justice on the Irish. He needed five times the troops he had in order to face the nearby array of British barracks holding twenty times his number.

Four Courts was of special meaning to me, for my father dropped dead there of a heart attack at the feet of a British judge. Daly got all sorts of documentation that could be destroyed and cause immeasurable confusion to the English in later months.

A very dour chap, Eamon de Valera, an American-born schoolteacher with a house full of kids, commanded the third "battalion." He took over Boland's Flour Mill, which bisected a key route from the port of Kingstown into Dublin. It was expected that he could intercept British reinforcements only an overnight boat ride away.

In the few days of the Rising, two god-awful blunders occurred, which, if they had been successful, would have given us a momentary victory to emblazon our struggle to the world.

. . . In the first instance, a unit attacked the Magazine Fort in Phoenix Park containing a large British ammunition dump. Had it been blown, it would have become Lettershambo II. However, with no Conor Larkin or Dan Sweeney to lead them, the unit wired the wrong building for destruction and barely rattled the windows of the main storage dump.

. . . The second foul-up was far worse. Sean Connolly, a young actor who commanded a couple dozen men, had the key to the City Hall across the street from Dublin Castle.

Seeing the main gate to the Castle wide open and guarded by a single unarmed constable, he investigated. He entered, saw that it was undefended and his for the taking!

The entire history of British perfidy in Ireland lay within the Castle walls: all the intelligence, all the names of informers, all secret agents, records of secret trials, double-dealings, contracted murders, land steals ... all the symbolism was there! This was the Irish "Bastille"! What could be more daring and brazen than the capture of Dublin Castle! In a single moment, the Gaelic myth could be reinvented!

Moreover, the Viceroy, Lord Nathan, was sitting in his office, ripe for capture.

Alas, a confused rebel commander who had never before fired a shot was aghast at having killed the constable at the main gate and retired from the Castle.

The rest of the day was filled with many such incidents as confused discussion followed the seizing of a variety of pubs, a biscuit factory, and the nurses' quarters of the insane asylum because of its proximity to the Richmond Barracks. From Richmond Barracks one could hear the military band practicing. Among the things we failed to take was the telephone exchange, leaving the British with clear lines of communications. Another massive blunder.

The grand scheme was to storm the centerpiece of the rebellion, the great General Post Office building on the main boulevard, which the Irish called O'Connell Street and the British called Sackville.

A hundred and some Home Army in green uniforms and floppy hats, led by James Connolly the labor leader, were set into motion by the midday church bells.

His thin column was met by Padraic Pearse, Tom Clarke, a tobacconist and head of the Brotherhood, and Joe Plunkett, the chief of staff, a journalist.

This high command unit stormed the General Post Office, seized it, and barricaded themselves in. The moment of moments, reading a declaration of independence, was delayed when it was discovered that they had left the flag of the new republic back at Liberty Hall. The formality had to be delayed while one of the soldiers was sent by bicycle to retrieve and return the flag, which he carried in a brown paper bag.

The orange, white, and green banner was raised from the pediment alongside the traditional green flag with its golden harp and the words "The Irish Republic."

Padraic Pearse stepped outside to a curious and baffled crowd of strollers.

"Irishmen and Irishwomen!" Pearse cried over the chattering. "In the name of God and dead generations from which she receives her old tradition of nationhood, Ireland, through us, summons her children to her flag and strikes for her freedom.

"Having organized and trained her manhood through her secret revolutionary organization, the Irish Republican Brotherhood, and through her open military organizations ... having patiently perfected her discipline, having resolutely waited for the right moment to reveal herself, she now seizes the moment and, supported by her exiled children in America and by her gallant allies in Europe, but relying in the first on her own strength, she strikes in full confidence of victory.

"We declare the right of the people of Ireland to the ownership of Ireland and to the unfettered control of Irish destinies, to be sovereign and undefeatable. . . ."

Pearse continued to denounce the centuries of British misrule, six highly overstated Irish rebellions, and finally declared a republic and provisional government and, of course, petitioned God to our side. It was signed by Tom Clarke, Padraic Pearse, James Connolly, Eamonn Ceannt, and Joseph Plunkett.

Padraic Pearse was to be the provisional president and our various units renamed the Irish Republican Army.

I had looked over the declaration in advance for a legal opinion, which was neither wanted nor accepted. I certainly did not agree with the high state of readiness and skill of our forces, the support of America and, for God's sake, referring to the Germans as our gallant allies.

Nonetheless it was a most moving and powerful expression of human longing for justice and liberty, and it was clearly destined for immortality, providing the Rising succeeded.

Success meant holding out long enough to bring world opinion to our cause.

I was over the way on O'Connell Street barely able to hear Pearse, trying to calculate the impact on the gathering. They did not seem impressed. A few made hurrahs, others shrugged, some laughed, most thought it was part of Home Army maneuvers.

As the news spread, a hundred more Home Army made their way to the GPO, then a flash ran through the Liberties, whose long and tortured history made it Europe's most horrible slum. The Liberties erupted! Thousands of the wretched poured from its confines into O'Connell Street and engaged in a storm of looting and rioting that was an outburst of pent-up outrage and frustration.

In actual fact, it was Home Army lads who finally stopped the rampage of smashed windows and thefts.

It is said for future generations that everything was broken into *except for bookstores*. This was Irish pride saying, "We love the written word so much as to hold it sacred." In truth, most of the poor devils from the Liberties were illiterate and saw no value in lifting books.

Up to this point the British hadn't put two and two together. What brought out their first unit, a squadron of Lancers, was the rioting. When the Lancers trotted down O'Connell Street in a state of ignorance, they were hit by a fusillade from the rebel guns in the GPO.

Assembled hastily at Dublin Castle, Lord Nathan and his commanders were finally able to figure out that this was not a maneuver.

Assessing their own forces, the British had some five thousand troops in or within quick range of Dublin. Among these were Irish Fusiliers and Irish Rifles of the British Army. They were sent into battle immediately to demonstrate their loyalty to the Crown and infer that this was all about good British-Irish against bad Irish.

British reinforcements were only an overnight boat ride

away and they had something else . . . CANNONS. There were sufficient artillery, up to sixteen-pounders, to contain every building that was seized.

With our lack of knowledge of basic military tactics, we in the Home Army had closed ourselves into barricaded positions. We had no training or leadership to launch any kind of offensive. For the British it was a case of surrounding each of these buildings to cut off escape and then cannonading it.

By midnight the huge main floor of the GPO bounced eerily in a profusion of candlelight. Padraic Pearse went up to the roof and gazed at a flaming Dublin being battered by point-blank cannon fire.

The British occupied and fortified positions to engulf the rebels with rifle and machine-gun fire. . . .

Was it over before it began? Was our true destiny that of eternal subservience to the British Crown? All of my father's life and all of Conor Larkin's life was going up in flames! All of my mother's life seemed for naught! Dear God! Why have you made us so accursed as a race?

By morning it was all but done.

The British opted not to storm the rebel positions but simply to reduce them by shellfire. It was now a plain case of waiting until we ran out of food, ammunition, and water.

Only one skirmish of note occurred, when British reinforcements landed at Kingstown. These were young lads, scarcely trained, who bore the gallant name of Sherwood Forresters. They marched for Dublin right into de Valera's men at Boland's Flour Mill, and he did a right good job, stopping and capturing a number of them.

Otherwise it was an all-British mathematical reduction of some fine old buildings. Both sides had drawn a few hundred casualties, two minutes' worth on the Western Front in France.

With nothing left to eat and no ammunition left to shoot, Padraic Pearse offered to surrender in less than five days. In a rather sad attempt to display honor, he offered his sword to a British general, who simply passed it to an aide in disgust.

All prisons were jammed to the gunwales and the holding pens filled quickly.

Our top echelon was taken to the illustrious Kilmainham Prison in Dublin, in business to hold insurrectionists since the French Revolution. Its roll call included our hallowed martyrs from Theobald Wolfe Tone, my namesake, to Charles Stewart Parnell. My partner's namesake, Robert Emmet McAloon, had said in 1803, "When my country takes her place among the nations of the earth, then and not till then, shall my epitaph be written."

This time the British had made the catch of the centuries: scholars educated by Christian Brothers, some musicians, the omnipresent poets, and other such dangerous men.

My partner had been worn thin, as had my father, by a lifetime of defending pissed-off Irishmen. It fell to me to prepare a defense for several thousand men already incarcerated or being rounded up.

All of the traditional doors, as expected, were slammed in my face. The Four Courts had been badly damaged and *all law* for anyone connected with the Rising vanished. Ireland was under martial law, which meant the British could do anything they wanted without any accounting.

I appealed to John Redmond, but he and his Irish Party were impotent. Redmond was a defeated man.

I went to the Cardinal, but he had deftly removed the Church from the Irish struggle once again. While a number of priests, on their own, were republicans or silently applauded the Rising, the main body of bishops showed indifference.

Then came the most terrible moments of my life, when I realized that with tens of thousands of Irish lads in British uniform, the Irish public itself was overwhelmingly against us ... "for going to bed with the Germans."

With our meager resources, it was impossible to get our story across in the press. The truth of the Rising, that of Irish freedom after centuries of oppression, had nothing whatsoever to do with England's imperial war in France.

The Irish had been a subject people for so long that the spirit to protest had been dulled. Their souls no longer cried for freedom. They had been sanitized and pacified.

Then the other shoe dropped. America, herself born of a revolution against the British, supported the British in crushing the Rising. And by America, I mean the Irish-American community as well.

Eventually, all of us, no matter what our past dealings with God, find it necessary to kneel before the altar and pray; soldiers on the front, condemned men on death row, agnostic barristers . . .

So I prayed, "God have mercy on Ireland."

Part Five: The Worm Turns, Lovely

May 1916

I smelled a rat as soon as General Sir Llewelyn Brodhead was whisked into the country as special consultant to the Viceroy. Why would this particular officer be rushed to Dublin Castle as the dust settled on our pitiful little Rising? On the surface, it was chilling.

Brodhead, the Ulsterman, was out of a breed of super-officers spawned in that province whose imperial appetites were far greater than their military skills and whose inbred arrogance and sense of inherited privilege reduced their natures to subhuman status. Brodhead was a visceral Irish-hater.

He was also a lifelong crony of Roger Hubble. Brodhead used his military command at Camp Bushy in Ireland to covertly support gunrunning to the Ulster militia; he even sent his officers to train them. In fact, the Earl's youngest son, Christopher Hubble, had been used in a gunrunning venture from Germany, no less!

Shortly before the war, Protestant Ulster was so cocky it openly flaunted its military prowess and illegal activities. It came to a point where the English government felt compelled to order the troops up from Camp Bushy to occupy Ulster and declare martial law.

The Bushy commander, Llewelyn Brodhead, organized a document in which all the officers of his command refused to move on Ulster and offered their resignations.

He forced the British government, Churchill included, to back down. With a European war on the horizon, the Army warned that more than a third of its entire officer corps stood to resign in sympathy with Brodhead.

It was a blackmail that Churchill, for one, never forgot.

Brodhead was subsequently promoted and, along with Churchill, joined together as architects of the disaster at Gallipoli. It is to be noted he did not like the expedition from the onset but once given the Anzac Corps to command, carried on like the good soldier he was.

General Sir Llewelyn Brodhead's judgment in battle proved deplorable. Although the ax fell on many high-ranking officers, Brodhead merely suffered humiliation. He managed to save himself from dismissal by giving some highly questionable testimony at the initial inquiries.

Nevertheless, he was denied a field command in France, which could only be considered a disgrace, a sort of left-handed slap on the wrist.

Brodhead's sudden assignment to Ireland on the heels of the Rising was looked upon as a chance to redeem himself in the eyes of the War Office and the General Staff. With carte blanche to keep the Irish under control at any cost, the General was suddenly in his divine element.

After being shut out of all information, it was a relief for me finally to be summoned to Dublin Castle. Perhaps I could get a fix on what they intended to do with over two thousand Irishmen rounded up and stashed away. Some had been fighters in the Rising. Others were citizens simply swept up without arrest warrants and held without charges or legal counsel.

"So you are the son of Desmond and Atty Fitzpatrick?"

I owned up to my tainted parentage. I've seen those dull blue eyes spelling hatred before from many a bench, from many peacocks wearing Sam Browne belts, from more than one lady at a garden tea. Llewelyn Brodhead's hatred burned through the centuries, burned through my jacket and flushed my skin. I must not be lured into an argument I could not possibly win. The best I could hope for was to fence around a little bit, hoping he was playing like a cat with a cornered, wounded mouse, to enable me to glean some kind of information.

"Well, you've bagged the lot of us," I said. "Am I to get an inkling of our status?"

Oh, that wicked little slash-mouthed smile! He folded his hands and kept looking, penetrating me until I had to look away rather than get into a staring contest.

"I am administering martial law. All prisoners are barred from access to the British legal system."

"What are your intentions, sir?"

Oh God, he smiled again. "We have already held secret court-martials. We have sentenced ninety-six perpetrators of this so-called Rising to death. The rest are being held as prisoners of war."

I nearly passed out, pleasuring Brodhead with my perspiration and dizziness.

"Where? On what charges?" I managed to ask.

"We have endless laws on the books dating back for a century to take care of the Irish and sedition and treason."

"But they must have a chance to defend themselves."

"Perhaps you didn't hear me, Fitzpatrick, they have been tried and sentenced to death."

"Ninety-six people tried and given death sentences in a week? It is a sham, General Brodhead, this prisoner-of-war status. Does that not, in itself, imply you have captured enemy troops? Isn't that, in itself, an admission by the Crown that the Irish are different people? Sir, you don't take German prisoners of war out and shoot them, and they don't put British prisoners before the firing squad."

"Save your clever Irish tongue. We can do what we wish to do."

"Does that not imply that you have always had in mind a separate standard of justice for the Irish?"

Brodhead slammed both hands on the sides of his leather chair. "Let me tell you why you are here, Fitzpatrick. Our fifteen hundred Fenians in custody are *hostages* to assure us that Ireland remains passive. If you go on ranting, you shall be responsible for minimum sentences doled out to these men of twenty years in penal colonies."

He rose from his seat, leaned over his desk, his face reddening. "As for those death sentences, they shall be carried out at my pleasure. The louder you protest, and the more trouble you stir up, the more people we will execute. I suggest you and your mother keep your big mouths shut or you shall become directly responsible for the executions of those condemned. You may go, Fitzpatrick."

"Haven't you learned anything in your entire experience in Ireland? Your loathing of us as inferiors is so inbred you see nothing wrong in what you are doing."

"Neither does the American press and public. Our ambassador in Washington reports outrage at you in editorials across the entire country."

I dimly heard him say . . . "Don't bother to attempt to contact us again. Dublin Castle is closed to you."

I got back to my office as quickly as I could, locked myself in, and tried to find reason. There was no doubt now why Llewelyn Brodhead had been sent to bless us.

Why should England have reacted in such a manner? The Rising posed no threat to their rule in Ireland. It was not carried out by trained soldiers. It was done and over within a week and punishment should have been meted out to fit the crime.

In their stampede to keep us silent, had they entirely lost sight of their own glorious history of democracy and justice? Not when it came to the Irish. The lengths that England would go to in Ireland had already been established in the great famine.

Down through the ages they knew but one way to rule us . . . by intimidation. When trouble stirred they'd overpower us with their armed forces, impose martial law, suspend justice, spy, murder . . . BULLY.

Bullying had always put the Irish in their place. Why not bully now? In the sordid British experience here, what did the execution of another ninety-six Irishmen matter?

They lost focus that these were ordinary citizens in their own country protesting for their freedom. The men they intended to kill were dreamers and intellectuals. Dear Lord, when do you line up poets against a firing wall and shoot them down?

May 3, 1916

I was folded up in three halves so I could fit on my office couch and avoid the springs when a distant crackle made me unglue my eyes. Maybe my hearing was playing tricks on me.

My old partner, Robert Emmet McAloon, likewise bedded down in his office, flung open my door.

"Did you hear it?" he cried.

"Aye, are you sure it was rifle shots?"

We spent the next hours frantic until our fears were confirmed: we finally found Kathleen Clarke, just after being advised to come to Kilmainham Prison and remove Tom's body.

It was she, God love her, who kept me together. I had to wait outside the gates while she went in and fetched him in the funeral wagon. Kathleen had married Tom after he had served fifteen years hard labor for Fenian activities. Old Tom, the tobacconist, led the Brotherhood. His lady was pregnant with their fourth child. He was dead now, gunned down by a firing squad.

and

As he was leaving Kilmainham, another funeral wagon passed us. I went from one to the other. Damned, it was Tom MacDonagh. No place for him to be shot dead. He was Brotherhood, sure enough, but he was an educator, a poet, a critic, a founder of the Irish Theatre, the editor of a periodical. I loved the nights at his cottage, which was the intellectual hub of the Gaelic revival. This battle-hardened, failed painter, who tried and lost in Paris, had commanded Jacob's Biscuit Factory.

and

The fear that stabbed me. Shooting down the first president of the Irish Republic on this day was shoving it in our face. A year ago he had stirred the nation with an awakening eulogy over the grave of an old Fenian sent back from America.

Padraic Pearse was taken to the wall in Stonebraker's Yard and only then saw Tom Clarke's and MacDonagh's bodies, still and lifeless at the foot of the wall.

Down he went in a volley: the mystic Gael, the writer of excellent verse, the Royal University graduate, the lifelong educator.

A short and terse announcement came at the end of the day from Dublin Castle that Pearse, Clare, and MacDonagh had been found guilty of treason by a military tribunal and executed by a firing squad.

Ah, you can envision what went on now with so many others under death sentence, can ye not? Irishmen doing their Irish thing, that last writing of defiance ... or simply expressing the love they were leaving for their family ... visits, not knowing if they were last visits ... priests intoning ... other priests daring to speak out from the pulpit for the first time in protest ...

Dawn came with chilled hearts and breaths held ... and then, the crackling volley of gunfire ... again.

May 4, 1916

That's the day they killed Joe Plunkett, another academic, born of aristocracy. Joe Mary Plunkett had been dying of tuberculosis but left his hospital bed to join the Rising and do whatever a man in his condition could do.

He married the sister of Tom MacDonagh's wife in Kilmainham just prior to their shooting him.

and

Ned Daly who commanded so well at Four Courts but had the misfortune of being Tom Clarke's brother-in-law.

and

Willie Pearse, similarly afflicted with the curse of being Padraic Pearse's brother.

and

Michael O'Hanrahan, a literary man. His will and sole possession, the copyright of his first published book.

May 5, 1916

John MacBride had his very own day. He was a symbol of long-standing hatred, selected for revenge.

Old John was on no one's war council, just an Irish rover with a drinking problem who had somehow won and wed one of Ireland's great beauties, Maud Gonne, an actress like my mother. They had separated.

In his earlier rovings, John MacBride had fought on the side of the Boers against the British and was given the rank of major.

The British had never forgotten or forgiven that he had taken up arms against them a decade earlier. He went to his maker with bravado, snarling that he had looked into British rifle barrels before. His death was particularly pointless and nasty.

For a moment the executions stopped. They were creating a foul stench on the face of sweet justice. Asquith, the British prime minister, assured the ineffective John Redmond that he himself was shocked at the carnage; he promised to slow things down.

The Irish playwright George Bernard Shaw wrote a scathing article in England that the Irishmen recently shot had been killed in cold blood after surrender.

The first stirrings of outside resentment.

May 8, 1916

The British executed Eamonn Ceannt, a handsome Irish lad who loved and lived his Irishness by speaking the ancient language, playing the pipes, and dancing the jigs and reels. His exclusive military background was that of working in the City Treasurer's office.

and

Michael Mallin, a silk weaver with four kids and another on the way who had once drummed in the British Army in India. He was second in command to the Countess Markievicz at St. Stephen's Green and the College of Surgeons.

and

Con Colbert, a bakery clerk and one of eleven children. He was a proud drill instructor in the Home Army who didn't have the worst of it during the Rising, seizing and commanding Watkin's Brewery.

and

Sean Heuston, a twenty-five-year-old lad from Limerick whose religious family proudly included a nun and a priest. He had captured the Mendacity Hospital.

May 9, 1916

To give things a nationwide caution, Thomas Kent was executed in Cork, where his three brothers and eighty-four-year-old mom resisted till their ammunition ran out.

A nightmarish aspect began to grip Ireland, and curious journalists from abroad were finding their way in. General Brodhead proved so intransigent that, at last, Asquith arrived. Yet, he arrived cleverly, not in time to stop the killings. . . .

May 12, 1916

Sean McDermott, a jolly Irish barman of thirty, crippled by polio, who also had the misfortune of being Tom Clarke's best friend.

and

James Connolly, a man of stature and a powerful symbol of the Rising. Connolly, a Scottish-born, self-educated labor leader and father of seven living children, was a tough man in a dangerous profession in perilous times, a no-nonsense, dedicated republican and socialist.

At the General Post Office Connolly had been twice wounded, receiving a smashed left ankle and a fractured shinbone, but he continued to direct the battle from a cot.

Unable to walk, he was removed from his cell on a stretcher and strapped into a chair, then shot by the firing squad as he sat there. The manner of Connolly's execution, killed in truth for the crime of being a union organizer, made a most indelible mark on the public.

Asquith slipped back to England later that night. With Connolly as the cherry on the cake, the prime minister called a temporary halt to the executions and shifted focus to England's very own traitor, Sir Roger Casement.

Had England's statement overreached its purpose in those days following the Rising? I think there now stands a small but possible chance that this is the case. As your man here said before, you just don't go around shooting poets.

SIR ROGER CASEMENT IS IN THE TOWER OF LONDON

Dublin, Mid-May, 1916

Rory was welcomed into Dublin Castle in a manner fit for royalty. General Brodhead personally met him at the door in a velvet smoking jacket of hunting-coat red trimmed with black satin collar and pockets.

"Landers! By Jove, it's good to see you again," he said, extending his hand. Rory was unable to reach him with his own stiffened arm in gloved fingers.

"Oh sorry," the General said, "how is that, anyhow?"

"Not bad at all," Rory said, wiggling his arm. "They've been doing a lot of patchwork surgery on it. I'll possibly get forty to fifty percent use of it back. The doctors feel they've done as much as they can do for now. They want to make a judgment in a few months after I do a routine of exercises."

"Bad luck," Brodhead said.

"Well, it's pretty good for holding things. A whiskey glass or a beer bottle fits right in. I can hold a book and turn the pages with the other hand . . . I did discover I was a right-handed toilet paper user, very awkward, that switch-over."

Damn, he liked the lad's spirit! "How about the eyes?"

"The doctors call my condition concussive injury to the optic nerve. I can see fairly well. I can get around, even ride a horse, which is most important. My sight will suddenly come clear for periods, but I can't do detail work. Eventually I'll be fitted with special glasses."

"You certainly look more chipper than the last time I saw you in Wandsworth Hospital in London and pinned the Victoria Cross on you. Too bad about the lad who got you back to the beach."

"Flynn."

"Died on the launch out."

"I suppose we stopped the last grenade the Turks threw."

"I must say," Brodhead puffed up, "the evacuation was a masterpiece, without casualty. The Turks had their minds on the mules you ran up the gully. Too bad about the mules."

"Yes," Rory whispered, "too bad about the mules."

"Have a seat, Lieutenant. Let's see if we have anything here better than navy grog."

Rory studied the room he could only see in images. Like most of Anglo Dublin, it displayed a tattered elegance. The General rang for his batsman who returned with a pair of stiff Irish whiskeys. Although it was May, the fire was good stuff to cut the chill off the Castle's stones.

"Cheers."

"Cheers, sir."

"Obviously I was hoping for a command on the Western Front," Brodhead said, "but once I understood my mission here, I realized that this is precisely where I was destined to be. As an Ulsterman, I've been dealing with these Irish scoundrels all my life, and I believe I am in place to help clear up this condition for all time. This island is part and parcel of Great Britain. Their treacherous attempt at secession makes it clear that the Irish must be made to accept their status as British. By the way, you're not of Irish descent, are you?"

"Not that I know of, sir. My mother's parents are both English. Dad is Swedish, German, New Zealand, one of those mongrel mixes."

"Catholic?"

Rory shrugged. "Not seriously," he said.

"Any political feelings about the so-called Rising here last month?"

"I'm a New Zealander, sir. The business over here didn't

make a lot of sense to me. Didn't we have Irish troops, Dubliners, down at Cape Helles?"

"Indeed we did and we have Irish in the trenches in France. We are all British, wot?"

Rory smiled in agreement.

"You missed a hell of a show. I personally attended the execution of all sixteen of the blighters. Bloody interesting. Unfortunately, a temporary suspension has been called in the executions ... against my strong objections ... but ... we still hold eighty of them under sentence of death."

"Are you going to resume the executions?" Rory asked. "I'd like to see one."

"God knows what the politicians are up to, but I think for now we are going to have a wait and see how they behave. If they stir things up with their editorials, streetcorner rabble-rousing and rioting, we can always resume the firing squads. . . ." He paced and lectured. "For the moment there is only one traitor who matters. Sir Roger Casement. He's in the Tower of London, where he belongs. He will be given a good English trial, then we'll hang him. It is imperative. Casement must be the one public showcase."

"Sorry, sir, but you'll have to excuse my ignorance. Can't read a newspaper without a magnifying glass."

"That son of a bitch, Casement. An Ulsterman, yet! After he was knighted, mind you, that son of a bitch conspired with the Germans against us. He's a fucking queer, you know. We're going to get him the same way Edward Carson got that other Irish queer, Oscar Wilde. Runs in the race."

Brodhead was quick to refill both glasses, warming up to the principal gist of his invitation for Landers to come to Ireland.

"Landers, the Gallipoli Commission of Inquiry is still open-ended, apt to keep digging up what is past. I think everyone knows what they have to know about a very dicey military situation. The only purpose now for further inquiry comes from those Liberals who are trying to pin a black eye on our military. You might be called to testify."

"Me, sir? I certainly have no qualifications to render opinions."

"Don't be too modest. You were privy to a great many planning meetings. That Victoria Cross makes your word extremely important in their eyes. Specifically, I am told, you may be wanted to testify on what took place atop Chunuk Bair."

Rory sensed that he had fallen into a situation of splendid serendipity. Brodhead would owe him a great deal if he played the General's game now.

"I don't know how to answer that, sir."

"There's talk that when Colonel Markham arrived from headquarters, he placed Colonel Malone under arrest on my orders. Furthermore, Major Hubble is alleged to have refused to carry out the arrest."

"I can't help you on that, General. I wasn't anywhere near them at the time."

"You heard nothing between Markham and Malone?"

"No sir."

"You've heard nothing since?"

"Christ, I hear all sorts of things every day. Rumors fly, you know. If the two colonels were in disagreement, I just didn't know."

Brodhead took his seat and edged forward. "They are looking for a scapegoat, you see. And I'll tell you why. After the war, they want to stand the Army down to nothing. The more upper echelon staff they can discredit, the greater the argument to cut off our funds. Do you realize we may not end up with an army large enough to defend the Empire? They have destroyed Churchill. Well, Churchill wasn't exactly one of my favorites, but he *did* bloody well have the Navy ready for war and his father *was* Lord Randolph Churchill. . . . Excuse me . . . just thinking out loud. The Aussies, in particular, are out to get me. A journalist by the name of Keith Murdoch thinks the Nek attack was unnecessary, when common sense shows that it had to be done to protect the Suvla Bay Corps. . . . One last thing— Colonels Malone and Markham were killed by Turkish fire, were they not?"

Rory picked up the General's concern, clearly. "Yes, sir. The Turks were hitting us with mortar fire prior to their charge to retake Chunuk Bair. Major Hubble and Jeremy went out to the perimeter to stop them."

"Well then, and this is hypothetical . . . suppose, for argument's sake . . . you *were* present but did not hear Colonel Markham give orders to arrest Malone. Suppose Colonel Malone wanted to stay on Chunuk Bair and you heard Colonel Markham say that he was representing General Brodhead and, after looking over the situation, thought it would be best to get off Chunuk Bair. . . . Hypothetical, of course."

Rory had no trouble buying into Brodhead's lies because it could continue to give him access to the General and to Dublin Castle. For what purpose, he did not yet know, but he was in Ireland to find out.

"I'd say that was about the way it went," Rory said.

"Suppose you could manage that if you're called?"

"You're my general, sir," Rory answered.

The General's butler arrived and announced dinner. Brodhead led Rory to the dining room with his arm about the young man's shoulders. "I think you'll find this a tad better than what we were eating at Anzac Cove."

Indeed it was, from venison down to an extravagant trifle. Chitchat and remembrances of a pair of good fellows wove through the courses. When the decanter of Napoleon was opened, warmed by flame in its great bubble glasses and swished about, Brodhead returned to serious matters once more.

"What is your status vis-à-vis the Army?"

"Your invitation for me to come to Ireland was just perfect, sir. As I said, the medical staff feels I've gone as far as I can for now and really don't need hospital control. I opted for an open-ended furlough and I'm free for three months. I could return to New Zealand for a discharge. Or, I could stay in England after a final medical evaluation. It's rather up to me."

"Do you have anything to do in Ireland?"

"I want very much to see Countess Caroline Hubble."

"Yes, of course."

"Flynn, the chap who got me to the beach, has grandparents and other relatives here. Two of the other men in the battalion also had Irish relations. I'll call on them."

"After that?"

"Little meditation somewhere. When I'm meditated out, I'll probably try to wipe out London."

Brodhead chuckled.

"You might like it here in Ireland, Landers. It has some rather decent places. Splendid boating at Kinsale. I could lay that on for you. Also, some marvelous private trout streams in Ulster. Horses, they are good with horses, the Irish—about the only thing they're good at. Some of the scenery in the west is worth taking in. The people are strange but harmless. They are awful liars. You'll find that out the first time you ask for directions."

"Never thought about staying in Ireland for any time."

"Landers, I've done something naughty."

"You, sir?"

"Sometimes when an exceptional officer is up for medical discharge, the War Office will make an exception, if . . . a ranking officer requests him for special duty."

GLORY! "Sorry, General, I don't follow you."

"I am convinced that what I am doing here in Ireland will do as much to preserve the British Empire as our army in France. It is vital to our continued imperial existence that we silence the Irish. We can't have Irish ale house politicians pounding on the peace table, now, can we. They'll set off unrest through our entire colonies."

"I think I understand what you're saying, sir."

Brodhead reached into the pocket of his smoking jacket and withdrew a handful of officer's pips. "I wore these when I was promoted to captain, more years ago than I'd like to think about. The War Ministry is willing to grant exception if you remain in Ireland on my personal staff."

Rory seemed bewildered.

"I'll tell you why, Landers. I'm putting together a small but unique team of officers, directly reporting only to me, to see and hear and know everything that is happening in this country. You are one of the most ingenious young men I've come across. You get things done, if by the rule or not. I know how you smuggled Dr. Norman off Gallipoli. I also know how many Turks you killed during their counterattack. Stick with the Army for a few more years. I see nothing but a brilliant career for you . . . and, I need you."

"I'm a New Zealander, sir."

"Well, New Zealanders are British! You signed up for the duration."

"In actual fact, I'm not all that anxious to return home this way, and particularly after what you've offered me."

"Well, good enough. If I may indulge in a moment of sentimentality, you would be taking Christopher Hubble's place. How say you?"

"Pretty heady stuff, sir. Let me make my rounds here in Ireland and report back to you. Let me think it through."

"And I'll hold these for you," he said putting the pips back in his pocket. "So, where do you head for first?"

"I've been in contact by phone and mail with Countess Hubble. She was unable to travel to London to see me. Seems that her father has had a severe stroke and is completely paralyzed."

Brodhead rested his head on his chin, sadly. "Beastly time for that great family," he murmured. "Lord Roger, a most, most wonderful human being simply sailed off into eternity, God rest his soul. Sir Frederick! What an Ulsterman that was! Caroline told me he was stricken over the boys."

"How will I find her?"

"The most exquisite creature who ever graced Ulster," Brodhead said. "She's not a child any longer, in her mid-fifties, but she is still the queen of Ulster in my book. When I paid her my sympathy call, it was she who was worried about me rather than about herself."

"I'm anxious to see her."

Brodhead took a long sip of the potent cognac and his eyes showed the first glaze of intoxication. "Shall I let you in on a secret?"

"Please don't tell me anything you'll regret tomorrow."

"Oh, you'll know what I mean when you lay eyes on her. I have adored that woman, from afar, for three decades. Of course, I've never been so much as a ha'penny out of line. Lord Roger and I were thick chums. With him gone, so tragically . . . and my own marriage rather . . . well . . . stale . . . Beatrice and I have had separate bedrooms for years. Good Lord, what am I prattling on about?"

"Sounds very understandable to me, General."

"Caroline is a bit of a wild one, wrong politics, and all that—a *carefree* youth in Paris. She's got this Irish clown Galloway hanging around her—for the money, no doubt—but he's off in London, producing a play or something. Lord Roger kept her in hand, made a great woman out of her. Now, by God, she's doing the right thing, staying in Belfast at her father's side." He stopped to see how this was going down with Landers. Yes, Landers was showing loyalty incarnate.

"General Brodhead, I am honored by your trust."

Sir Llewelyn cleared his throat.

"She is best handled by a strong person like Lord Roger. It would seem that she's ready for a real man to comfort her now."

"Lady Caroline will certainly know of my own feelings toward you, sir."

Brodhead grinned broadly. "Do think it over and come back as one of my aides."

"Thank you, sir. I'll return in a fortnight with my answer."

Late May, 1916

"Lieutenant Landers, you're most welcome!"

"Thank you, Countess Hubble."

"Please call me Caroline," she said, signaling the butler. "Take the Lieutenant's bags up to Jeremy's apartment."

They stared at each other curiously, then came together for a shyish peck on the cheek.

"Jeremy was right," Rory said, "you must be the most beautiful woman in Ireland."

"Twenty years removed, at least," she said. His voice, strange, a recollection flashed through her.

"Something wrong, ma'am?"

"What?"

"You're staring at me," Rory said.

"Oh, I'm sorry. You hit me with a startling family resemblance to someone. Even the voice."

"Everyone says that. I guess I've got a very common face."

"And I'd say that with your blarney, you're a once-removed Irishman."

"I've not a drop of Irish blood, I'm afraid. A New Zealand mongrel."

"Now, what are you staring at?" she asked.

"I've never seen a place like this."

"I'll give you the tour later." She took his arm, guiding him past the entry. "We've a rare day of sunshine. Why don't we get acquainted in the garden."

The garden, fountain, and view to the museum was likewise stunning, quite beyond belief that Jeremy, or for that matter, any human being could live in such a place.

Caroline ordered refreshments. Rory remained enchanted with everything, and herself as well. She was dressed in lavender and was lightly scented, but the darkness beneath her eyes told him that she had gotten herself up for the occasion. Caroline's hair was half-gray now but she still cut a figure that would have tempted any man a generation younger.

"How long can I have you?" she asked.

"As long as you can stand me," he answered. "I do plan a trip in the south and west to call on the relatives of some lads from our battalion."

The maid came with a tray, followed by the butler with an ice bucket.

"How did you know I wanted a beer?"

"Every New Zealander wants beer. You're much younger than I envisioned."

"Well, the one thing a place like Gallipoli does, is offer rapid advancement."

"I'm terribly sorry I was unable to visit you at the hospital in London. My father has had several strokes and the last one, when the bad news came, was rather severe. Are you going to end up in London?"

"Probably, sooner or later."

"My gentleman, Gorman Galloway, well, he's not exactly my gentleman. He's my guy. Gorman is producing a play in London. Sorry he isn't here to meet you, but he's the man to do up London with . . . if you like actresses."

Rory laughed. She was splendid. "I read most of Jeremy's letters and he read mine. Gorman Galloway is a very funny fellow. I look forward to meeting him."

"He's been the rock. He's kept things together for us. How are you coming along, Rory?"

Rory explained his medical condition; rest, then reappraisal.

Probably more surgery on his hand and wrist up to the elbow. The eyes? Well, one could live with it.

Rory played with the beer glass, set it down. "How goes it with you, Lady Caroline?"

"Lousy, thank you. As you can see by the surroundings, at least I get to suffer in comfort. I've reached that point where I put ha'pennies in the little fortune machines on the boardwalk of the amusement park. There has to be a reason one just does not die with her sons. I'm on a day-to-day basis to try to find that reason. I can't tell you how I've been looking forward to your visit."

"How much do you really want to know?" Rory asked.

"You're very wise and very sensitive for your age, Rory. I want to know everything."

"Some of it is going to be very painful."

"Of course it will be, but at least I'm sharing with them. I know we'll have occasion to laugh. I think it will be most comforting."

"I'm looking for a tad of comfort, myself," Rory said. "Right off, Jeremy . . . well, I'll never have another friend like him."

"Here I am pitying myself so much I didn't stop to realize how much you've suffered."

"It's been a bitch, lady," Rory said.

"I'm so glad you're here," she said.

"Jeremy transformed himself into a most splendid human being. I wish you'd seen the character and competence of this man. He handled the news of his baby's death like a champion."

"Molly died in childbirth, at the same time. I thought it was too much to hit him with both deaths at the same time. I was going to wait until, at least, he got off Gallipoli."

"We'd figured that might be the case with Molly. He had one determination. He was going to come out of it as a man even if he had lost her."

"You don't know how wonderful that makes me feel. He was a wreck when he left Ireland."

"Lovely man . . . we were all crazy about him."

"And Christopher?"

Rory scratched his head. "Old Major Chris."

"Somewhat of a horse's ass, I take it," Caroline said.

"In Egypt, till he got news of his wife, he was a shyte of major proportions. What can I say? But he turned into very much of a human being. Chris was funny with all his Brit crap. He found out something the hard way about the loyalty and love men can give each other."

"Chris? Jeremy told me he had changed to an all-right fellow, but . . . "

"What about that wife of his?"

"She's living a middling life in Canada. I can't fault her for leaving, but she's not worth the bother."

"I'm going to tell you something you might not believe, but it's true. Chris also realized why she left him, and he never once wished her ill."

"Are you telling me the truth, Rory?"

"Yes, ma'am."

"That's hard to believe," she said softly.

"I know. But seeing both those lads grow into fine men was a revelation to me, and the experience of them has been important to my own life. It told me I could also rise above my own sorrows."

"And I can as well?" she asked.

"You're going to find the reasons that will make the rest of your way worth the while."

Sir Frederick Weed was wheeled out to the veranda a short distance away. His chair was set so he could look down the slope of the hills and see the stacks of Weed Ship & Iron. His nurse took up a magazine beside him.

"My father is nearly totally paralyzed. He cannot speak, but he hears and comprehends everything. His mind is as keen as it ever was. We've worked out a language by blinking his eyes and some small movement of a couple of fingers. Come, let's meet him. He'll enjoy your rowdy stories, if you have any."

"I'm afraid I do."

They made to the veranda, where she greeted her father with a kiss and set his lap robe straight, then took a chair in front of him.

"Freddie, this is Rory Landers. You know him from Chris and Jeremy's letters."

Rory could detect a smile through Weed's watery eyes.

"I've heard a lot about you, sir," Rory said.

"Rory is going to visit for a while. He's going to tell us all about his year with the boys."

Weed blinked.

"He said that you're most welcome."

When Caroline and Rory had retired from the veranda, she turned and watched her father for ever so long. "He just sits there, day after day, looking down at the empire he created. He is trying to will his grandsons back to life and himself to the man he once was. He refuses to accept that those things are gone. He fights to no avail, wondering why his willpower can't remake the past."

"Is there anything I can do or say to help him?"

"Yes."

"What is that?"

"It will have to wait, but there is something we both need to know. Now, how about letting you have a stretch and a cleanup before dinner."

She took him up the great winding stairs in the foyer and down a hall with walls filled with paintings and indentations holding statuary. She opened the door to Jeremy's apartment.

"Are you sure you want me to stay in there?"

"Jeremy would be livid if I put you up anywhere else. And Rory, this is not going to end up a sad experience."

"I know that."

As he entered the room, Caroline took his arm and turned him around to her. "Are we going to be able to get their bodies back?"

Rory shook his head.

"Why?"

"Please don't."

"I must know. I have to put it to rest."

"There are ... thousands of unidentifiable skeletons ... thousands and thousands, ours and the Turks. They're all bleached white and lie in piles . . . everywhere. . . . Is that what you wanted to know earlier, for your father and yourself?"

"No," she said. "It is something quite different."

There was joy in Rathweed Hall in the next days as Rory recounted the boisterous scene in Cairo. It was right to tell these two. They could now have Chris and Jeremy's happy days to be part of the memory. You could fair feel the old man laughing inside him.

But what was it they really wanted to know? It seemed that would have to come later, when fuller trust had been built.

Rory was sketchy about his own past. He did speak of Georgia and his hope he would find her, but nothing was said of Calvin Norman. For the most part he stuck to his Landers story, that he was a lad at odds with his father.

Caroline was much taken by Rory, but she was nobody's fool. Running the vast operations as she did, and being raised and living in an atmosphere of constant conspiracy, she got the scent of Rory's hiding something. What it probably was, in her mind, was a childhood pain of some sort he didn't care to be open about. It was something, though. Whatever it was, Caroline decided to let the days pile up without probing.

On the other hand, Caroline had intimated from the beginning that there was something about Gallipoli she and her father needed to know.

At the end of a week, Rory told Caroline he was going to make his little round of the country. He promised to return to Rathweed Hall, of a certainty.

She gave him a set of keys to her townhouse on Merrion Square in Dublin. "Bachelor officers' quarters can be a bit stuffy and confining. Now, I want you to take these keys and feel it is your home, like you and my lads were cousins. Come and go as you want, Rory. And have yourself a party or two, girls welcome."

Rory blushed. Imagine his mom ever saying anything like that to him. "You're like my Georgia," he said. He went up to pack after promising to phone her regularly, and to return.

As he threw the last of his gear in his bag, Caroline came to his parlor. "Can we have an up-front talk before you leave?"

"Of course."

"I mean, up-front."

Oh hell. What did she already know? What did she suspect?

"I'll tell you what's on my mind," she said before he could chart a course. "You have alluded to the fact that you may be here in Ireland for some time. I know, firsthand, how General Brodhead feels about you. We went through the same experience with Chris. Are you going on his staff?"

"Jesus Christ, Caroline. I didn't want to bring the General into too much of the conversation this week because I didn't know if it was the right or wrong thing to do. Yes, he's asked me to join his staff and part of my wandering about now is to think it over. You'd certainly be the first to know if I did."

Caroline stared at him without comment.

"All right," he said, "he and your late husband were cronies, I gather?"

"Yes, very much so, identical twins—one in a factory owner's cutaway and the other in military uniform."

"Knowing from Jeremy of your unhappy marriage, I didn't feel right in bringing up anything of that nature."

"That's very good of you, Rory. But what has Llewelyn Brodhead to do with Roger Hubble?"

"He's got the hots for you."

Rory was fairly shocked that Caroline didn't so much as blink an eye.

"I was once very beautiful . . . "

"You still are."

"Cut it out. Anyhow, I've had lads in heat sniffing around me all my life, Rory. Even though Llewelyn was close to my husband and always proper, I have long ago picked up on his ardor. He has a shipwreck of a wife and, beyond Ireland, a penchant for whores."

"Brodhead? Whores? Do you know that or are you just saying it?"

"Weed Ship & Iron is into so goddamned many bedrooms,

I've lost count. Espionage, industrial and otherwise, was a way of life. We once had a retired Brigadier running our intelligence service—fortunately he is deceased—who had the goods on everyone in the British Isles, and particularly Ulster."

Rory held up his hands. "I'll never try to lie to you again, Caroline. I should have told you I may be going to work for him. I'm sorry about that. It was just a bad call on my part. The rest of it. He's hot for you. He told me to slip in the good word for him. I figured you already had that all figured out. The rest of it is your business."

"Thank you, Rory," she said, then dropped the other shoe: "We're almost finished. My father and I want you to tell us about Brodhead at Gallipoli."

"What about him?"

"We analyzed his testimony and reports to the commission. He lied to cover his ass, and don't tell me you were only a lieutenant."

"No, I won't tell you that. He's my general."

"Good old boys club?"

"Whatever I say, good, bad or otherwise isn't going to bring Jeremy and Major Chris back to life."

"You don't know us, Rory. We are ancient Gaels, ourselves. We are as we are, and we must know. You don't have to tell us much. Just confirm what we already believe."

"Why?"

"Don't let my surroundings here fool you. I know what's going on in this country and I believe Jeremy was intending to make a declaration to become a republican. He always had the soul of a republican, and he had a mentor who opened his eyes to terrible realities. As far as I'm concerned, Llewelyn Brodhead is harmless. He may not be so harmless as far as Ireland is concerned. As for what happened at Gallipoli . . . my father and I are haunted . . . I told you—we are ancient Gaels."

Rory felt a rage from her he'd never seen in a woman before. There was no use trying to quarrel with her, with the strange look in her eyes. Lord, what to do? The open wounds of these two people might only be closed by vengeance. And what of himself? Rory thought. Would not his own vengeance be the end of his search in Ireland?

"Will it matter between you and me if I join his staff?"

Caroline's face flushed. He was a tough lad, all right. No wonder Jeremy adored him. "I want you to go back to Brodhead's command, Rory. If it means we take him off our slate, so be it."

"I'm not a very sophisticated lad, Caroline. It would be better if we leave the General out of it. I just don't understand all the in-fighting."

"Like hell you don't," she said. "For the sake of appearances," she continued, totally switching tones, "if you go on Llewelyn's staff and if he should ask, tell him you relayed his interest to me, and let him know I was quite flattered by his attention. No harm in that, is there, Rory, making the old boy feel good?"

"I'll tell him I caught a light in your eye at the mention of his name."

"Welcome to our dirty little games, Lieutenant."

He put his arms about her and gave her a tight squeeze. Jaysus, what a woman, he thought. Everything was falling into place so damned well he could fairly believe it.

Although they still held their secrets, they felt a bonding, like mother and son.

It had been a restless night until it suddenly struck her! Caroline bolted upright in bed, flung her covers off and paced, then howled with discovery!

It was nothing that Rory Landers had said that gave him away, so much as the manner he said it. He claimed no Irish ancestry, but certainly one of his parents was Irish. There was too much of a Donegal lilt unconsciously weaving in and out of his conversation.

Good Lord, she had spotted the Larkin face the moment he entered Rathweed Hall and even a similarity of voice. At first she wondered if she hadn't unconsciously expected Conor to come through that door for the last ten years.

Landers had many of Conor's moves: his knowing stare, his startling candor, the laugh, the mystery of his travels in Ireland. Of course Rory was aware of Jeremy's republican leanings. Jeremy knew who Rory really was and never gave him away but left little hints throughout his correspondence to her.

Caroline's personal assistant, Tony Pimm, was at Rathweed Hall within the hour.

"We need to lift some Army records of a colonial, a New Zealander. I want them duplicated. Lieutenant Rory Landers. Canterbury district or county, Christchurch area, the South Island."

"Landers? I thought you and Freddie were very taken by him. What's our man up to?"

"I don't think he's Landers. He's somebody else."

"I see. Some soldier who knew Jeremy and Chris enough to get into Rathweed Hall and work a swindle on you."

"No, that's not his game. The relationship with my sons is genuine and I adore him. I need information out of New Zealand. Is our office in Wellington properly connected?"

Tony Pimm nodded that it was.

"I think he enlisted under the name of Landers because he didn't want to carry his real identity into Ireland. Have Overcash in Wellington round up the names of all the stations, owners, and transfers, and the like, and see if anything Irish pops up."

"Like what?"

"Larkin."

"Holy Christ."

"I'd wager he's Conor Larkin's nephew and, hang on, Tony, he's been offered a post inside Dublin Castle by Sir Llewelyn himself."

CHAPTER
77

"Sixmilecross! Sixmilecross!"

Rory's heart leapt as the train slowed. He pressed his head against the window of his compartment trying to focus his eyes. The train eased into the lay-by to take on water at the tower. Down the line a conductor helped a woman and little girl off the train to a waiting buckboard and husband.

Rory knew from Jeremy's description that he was on the exact site of the ambush. British troops had been riding the train, Conor and his party were strung out along the rail and at the crossroads, horses and wagons tied just beyond the bridge in the trees.

His compartment door opened. It was a different conductor. He leaned over Rory, reading the patch on his shoulder.

"New Zealand, is it?"

Rory nodded.

"Me partner sez to me there is a Victoria Cross lad in the military car. And where might you have been to exact this distinction?"

"Gallipoli."

"Ah, tanks to Mary you're alive, then. Me own son was wounded at Ypres. Gassed."

"Sorry to hear that."

"Irish relatives, have you?"

"No, I'm just on leave, touring about."

"You couldn't have found a grander place. Er ... and what persuasion might you be?"

"I'm an R.C."

The conductor smiled. "You're sitting on sacred Irish ground. A very famous encounter took place here. It was some years ago, but the Irish Republican Brotherhood ... You've heard of them?"

"Sorry, no."

"Our lads. Anyhow, they laid a terrible defeat on the British."

"I'll be damned."

"Well, best of luck to you, Lieutenant, and it's an honor and a pleasure to be shaking the hand of a V.C. winner."

Forty minutes later the first conductor slid the door open. "Rodale Bridge," he said, "with transfer to Flynn, Crew, Spamount, *and* Castlederg. This is your stop, sir ... here, here, you let me help you with your bag."

Rory debarked to a hero's salute from the two conductors. A dozen or so passengers made for a waiting shuttle. As both trains moved on, Rory looked about. He could make out the black-on-black of a priest coming over the roadway toward him.

"Uncle Dary?"

"Rory lad, oh, Rory lad!" Dary sniffed as they embraced. "You gave me a chill just now. I thought for an instant it was Conor walking toward me. You've the same manner. God, you've Larkin written all over your face, you're that handsome. Now, did you get to see anything of the countryside?"

"It was a bit fuzzy flashing past the window, but it did remind me more than a little of New Zealand. It's so green."

"All the lads who emigrated to New Zealand wrote home the same thing you're saying."

They walked to the proverbial Model T Ford. "Compliments of Bishop Mooney," Dary said. In a moment they were on the road to Londonderry.

"We've a million years to catch up on. First, tell me how you're feeling."

"At this moment, I feel great." Rory went over his wounds and prognosis.

"Are you free for a while?"

"Yes."

"That's grand," Dary said. "The bishop has a fishing cottage up in the hills, about ninety minutes' drive. It's out of sight and well stocked. It's ours for as long as we want it."

"That's just great. Sounds like your bishop is a right fair chap."

"Mooney is a dear, dear man. I've been at his side since my ordination. He was sent to Derry because they needed a soft churchman then, and frankly, the Cardinal didn't expect him to last too long. The Bishop has a bad heart, but he's fooled everyone. I, uh, run a good part of the diocese routine for him, as well as the schools and orphanage. When he passes on I expect I'll be transferred into a more . . . traditional situation. In Bogside, you must have Bogside priests, it's that miserable. We are a mite too liberal, I'm afraid."

What was not to like about Father Dary? Rory felt the comfort of one who had known him for a thousand years. He felt the first uncanny and unexpected sheer glow of the warmth of family he'd known since he left home. He was taken by the wonderment of it. There was so much to tell and hear and he smiled inwardly at the prospect of the coming days.

"I've a notion," Rory said, "of why you wanted me off the train before Londonderry."

"*Derry,*" Dary corrected. "Well, there's been trouble in Dublin and the Brits are rounding up anyone who blows his nose in a green handkerchief. With you gallivanting around in British uniform with a false name, best not to take a chance. You see, we're heading into Larkin country. If we were so much as to set foot in Derry, much less Bogside, you'd be spotted as a Larkin in a blink."

"That's what I figured. I must be able to get to Ballyutogue, though."

"Our cottage is fairly close by. Most of the village men will be droving cattle into the Derry pens and the women will be selling their lacework there as well. I've arranged for us to slip in by dark one night. Your Aunt Brigid is dying to see you."

*　　*　　*

They prepared their catch. Dary smoothed the turf fire as Rory pan-fried the trout.

"I've heard about the turf fires," Rory said. "It does smell like angel's breath." Rory reckoned the fish was as well cooked as it was going to be. "Well now, wee Dary," he said, showing the pan, "Jaysus, forgive me, Uncle. I've heard you referred to as 'wee Dary' all my life, by Conor in particular. I'll mind my manners. And you're not that short. We had troops half your size," and on that mention Rory bit his lip as Chester Goodwood flashed through his mind. Wouldn't the gaffer squad have loved to have been here now!

"I've not heard myself called wee Dary for so many years. Would you continue to call me that?"

"Are you sure?"

"I felt it down to my toes."

"Wee Dary it is, then."

Their contentment ultimately found its way into Rory's officer's bag and a gift bottle of cognac from Caroline Hubble.

"Mary," Dary said, "we only see this at Christmas about every fifth year."

A restless silence fell, which both of them recognized as a prelude to family business. Dary went to his satchel and produced a letter.

"This letter came to me about four months ago from Liam."

Rory scanned it and handed it back. "I couldn't read the Squire's writing with two good eyes. You'll have to do the honors."

"Aye," Dary said. He wet his lips, then his whistle, with a taste of the magnificent velvet of the cognac.

"My son Rory," Dary began, "it has taken this long to find the courage to write to you. I am sending it to Dary knowing that in time you will find your way to Ireland.

"Perhaps wee Dary, better than anyone, can explain the meaning of my tears of guilt and personal misery. From that terrible moment you left us, I found myself in the grip of great pain that I knew intimately from my own boyhood. I wore that pain from childhood into manhood. I realize that I have laid on you the same kind of pain.

"I don't deserve your forgiveness, but I can never rest again until I ask for it and I can never be entirely whole again until I win it. Ballyutogue Station, like its namesake in Ireland, has become a place of sorrow. You haunt the land, my son, every whispering leaf on every whispering tree. Bless you for keeping your letters coming to your mother and sisters and brother. You are ten feet tall in Tommy's eyes. He worships you.

"We had to put RumRunner down. I wanted the old boy to hold on until you came back but he just laid down one night and refused to get up.

"If prayers will help you, you've a powerful amount of them from me, and us.

"I'm so sorry for what I did. Please come back when your roving is done. I love you, son. . . . Your father, Liam."

It was a new moon, barely a sliver, just right for a pair of men down from the hills, skimming over the land, unseen. A tad of moonbeams flitted in and out of the rapidly moving clouds. Dary as well as all the kids in Ballyutogue, knew the route, which for generations had held hideaways and a passage for republicans on the run.

Father Cluny, an out-and-out republican dressed in peasant's attire, warmly welcomed Dary and Rory. First they went to the forge, which was always unlocked. It was dark until Father Cluny got the lantern working. Rory went from bench to bench, anvil to bellows, feeling the tools, ancient enough to have once been held by Conor. The fires in the pit softly glowed, setting off the sweet smell, and outside he found the stone fence and the well. Everything seemed so small.

"We'd better get to the cottage before Brigid has a stroke," Father Cluny said.

At the crossroads the hanging tree outlined itself. "Up there is our fields," Dary said. Rory could near see his da and Tomas coming down the road and Conor, in smithy apron, all meeting and slipping into Dooley's for a quick one to face the missus with.

Rory's knees gave to trembling as he stood before the Larkin cottage. It sprang open and Aunt Brigid, penny-plain as Rory had envisioned, clutched him as a steady stream of tears cascaded down her face.

The meal, of course, had been days in preparation. Rory related Liam's fine life in New Zealand and what each of his sisters and his brother was about and he assured Brigid the home was devoutly Catholic.

"You know my beloved da, Tomas, and Kilty were not exactly holy men, but they made their peace with God. Conor never did, but you might for yourself, and in his behalf, might you not?" she inquired.

Brigid rattled on about her late husband Colm, finer in death and memory than he had been in life, what with his smelly pipe and smellier dog . . . God rest his soul . . . a good man with his acres . . . but never much for intimacy.

Rory's poor eyes tried to find every inch of the cottage, the room where they had all been born, up the ladder to the loft where Conor and his da bedded down until they left home.

Rory was overcome, just like so. He needed to be left alone for a half-hour of pure trembling, having no idea how overwhelming the experience would be, or why.

At last the four of them made to the graveyard. Dary held a torch and pointed to each stone.

The first stones were very old, with lettering in Gaelic, and worn flat. Rory ran his hand over one of them and crust crumbled in his fingers.

"That's your great-great grandfather Ronen, about 1800, between Wolfe Tone and Robert Emmet," Dary said.

"God, can you imagine. Conor told me about Ronen's brothers taking him down from the whipping post and spiriting him to Donegal, his bones poking through the flesh from the flogging. . . . "

"Aye," Brigid said, "he is the patriarch of the Larkins of Ballyutogue along with his wife, Nellanne."

"The next two are memorials to the families of Cathal and

Aidan. Unfortunately none of their bodies made it back here, except Aidan's."

"Cathal," Rory said from memory, "and his wife Siobhan and their four girls all boarded a death ship in 1848 on their way to America. The two youngest girls died a horrible death aboard ship. The others called America their final home, except Cathal, who made his way back here to die. And Aidan was killed fighting to save his cottage and fields. His wife Jenny died in the workhouse and their six kids disappeared forever in a foundling home."

"You know it well," Brigid said. "In '47."

Reading with his fingers, Rory lit up. "Jaysus, does this say Kilty?"

"Indeed it does," Brigid said.

"Then this must be his wife Mary and their three wanes."

"They died of the hunger, and your grandfar, Tomas, dug them under and awaited his own demise only to be saved by Kilty's miraculous return," she went on.

"Tomas . . . Finola . . . "

"The fine stones and all the restoration work was done through the generosity of your father, Liam, God bless him."

Brigid's voice faded into the background. "This is the best-kept plot in Donegal . . . I put fresh flowers on it from my garden . . . people come from all over to see these graves. . . . "

Rory took the torch from Dary's hand as he came to the final stone. Dary led the other two away, retreating to the church.

Rory played the light close, then ran his fingers over the carving, again and again and again.

CONOR LARKIN
SON OF TOMAS AND FINOLA
BORN 1873–DIED 1914
PATRIOT

"I'm here now, Uncle Conor. You knew I'd be. I was too late for the Rising, but there wasn't much I could have done. It didn't go too well at first, but memory of it refused to dim. They're trying to clean the country out and intimidate us one more time.

"So much to tell you about Jeremy and Caroline and me and even Major Chris.

"It's like a miracle took place. Liam wrote and asked for forgiveness. I never heard music so beautiful as the sound of wee Dary reading me his words. Dary says you and Tomas got things turned around. It wasn't all Liam's fault, our troubles. I want so badly to make things right at home. . . .

"Uncle Conor, I think I know why I am here in Ireland. I'm in a position to strike a blow. I think I know what I am going to be called upon to do. You've got to help me now and give me a sign that what I'm intending to do is the right thing. It's a right and a wrong too big for me to figure out alone. Send me a message, man. . . . "

Dear Da,

Wee Dary must write this for me until I am fitted with special glasses.

I forgive you. I need forgiveness as well. I have been a shyte of a son trying my best to always torment you. I cannot think of what is better in life now than coming back to New Zealand and dreaming of the grand days we are going to share.

You do realize I have to stay where I am, for I've a task. It's the Larkin fate and I hope I am equal to it.

I cannot write much more except to say I came through Gallipoli much better than many others.

There is one great thing you can try to do for me. I realize that Georgia Norman did not believe I loved her and that I would eventually want to be free of obligations to her. That is why she broke it off, to set me free. But she didn't tell the truth. She was already divorced from Calvin Norman, but she told me the divorce was not final and she was going to give him another chance after the war.

In actual fact, I met Dr. Norman in Gallipoli only to learn that they were already divorced and he had remarried. He was a great man and tragically has been in and out of mental institutions, but there is hope for his recovery. Mom will be happy to know that I pray every once in a while these days, and I pray for Dr. Norman first.

Da, please find Georgia for me if she is to be found. My love for her is no less great than life itself.

Dary tells me this letter will be personally delivered to you by a priest going to New Zealand aboard a hospital ship in the next few weeks. You will have to do a lot of reading between the lines, but once I'm home we've a lifetime to catch up.

I love you, too, Da.

Rory

Time was winding down at the fishing cottage. All bridges had been crossed, except the big one. Dary wasted no time in getting to it.

"What are your plans, Rory?" he asked.

"Probably head back to Belfast and Lady Caroline. Maybe I'll take her up on the use of her house in Dublin. Hit the pubs. Make a dent in Dublin. I plan to go to the west. Everyone says it's beautiful."

"You're lying in your teeth, Rory Larkin."

"Me?"

"When you've heard as many Bogside confessions as I have, you become fine-tuned to the modulations in a liar's voice. You're going to join Brodhead's staff, isn't that what?"

"Maybe."

"Ho, I'll say a big 'maybe' for you."

"I don't want to appear too anxious. What I think is that I'll ask for a trial period so I can back out. It's easy enough to use my medical situation as an excuse to leave. Maybe I'll have some more surgery on the hand. The eyes may have to wait. Just so I can ride a horse. Maybe, I'll find a lass to read to me."

"I'm talking about Larkin parading around as Landers inside Dublin Castle. You'd be doing a balancing act on the sharp side of a knife."

It is family, Rory thought. The man is a priest. Should he

know or not? So far, Rory had been able to hold it to himself alone. A secret happens when two or more people know and then it's not apt to be a secret anymore.

"Let me help you, Rory," Dary said. "You've kept republican matters out of our lovely new friendship. I have not been sympathetic unless it pertained to a family member. Did you know I organized Conor's escape from Portlaoise Prison?"

"You . . . what!"

"Of course, you've had no way of knowing. I'm serving a beautiful bishop who desperately needs my help. But I'm starting to see things differently—first, since Conor's death, and in more recent days, in revulsion over the executions."

"Ah, wee Dary . . ."

"I still keep my distance from the Brotherhood, but I've never closed the door on a man on the run." Dary's mouth tightened. "I am a Larkin."

"Something else you think you'd like to tell me, Father?"

"You're clever, just like your uncle. Rory lad, a priest is really a core of a man papered over with layers and layers of dogma, like the skin of an onion. An enlightened bishop and the Larkin name has compelled me to peel layer after layer off me to find if a real man exists in there."

Dary stopped and closed his eyes and turned his back.

"Hey, man, what's going on?"

Rory turned Dary around. Yeah . . . they could tell one another. Dary's voice wobbled. . . . "I know a terrible truth. Ireland is never going to be free unless Irishmen spill blood for it. It does not make me a Brotherhood man, but it makes me understand those who are."

"So, what goes on now with the layers coming off? Half-man, half-priest?"

"More than you know," Dary whispered.

"And you know that I came to Ireland to find the Brotherhood. Is there anything left of it since the Rising?"

"Aye," Dary said, "I'll take you there."

78

A small phalanx of guards briskly entered the dining room of the Russell Hotel, examined and okayed it. General Sir Llewelyn Brodhead fumed in and was ushered to the prime private booth on the corner window as his men took up their stations around him.

Brodhead was in a snit. There had been two days of solid argument between himself and London until, at last, he had to give in to orders to cease executions of the Rising leaders until further notice.

Just when we had the Irish on the run, Brodhead thought. Damned American editorials were now chastising the British! This was an internal affair, damnit! Putting the Irish down was the question, not winning a popularity contest in the United States. Well, he thought, 10 Downing Street will see. They'll resume the executions within the fortnight, he told himself.

Whiskey arrived. Brodhead stared down to the street. Another squad of guards had cordoned off the General's car, escorting vehicles and passage to the Russell Hotel.

Suddenly the mood turned from gray to gold as Caroline Hubble showed at the dining room door. She never failed to lift eyebrows wherever she appeared.

It was her suggestion that they meet openly and in a public place. Caroline was often seen in men's lairs with high government officials, industrial leaders, and luminaries in the worlds of art and theater. And, lest we forget, it was risky to gossip about her. Since she had been a young lady, she had won the reputation of coming right on at a gossiper and filleting them in public.

Caroline toured the room, stopping at table after table for chitchat, so when the curtain closed her in with Sir Llewelyn, it caused no turned heads or wagging tongues.

Over sherry . . . his second whiskey . . . she unpinned her hat and laid it aside.

"I have to say," she said, "I was delightfully surprised when Lieutenant Landers said . . . well, you found me. . . . well, he said some lovely things."

Brodhead blanched and cleared his throat. "I trust it was all proper," he said.

"Good Lord, yes. After all, Llewelyn, we've been good friends for what? A quarter of a century, anyhow. When one becomes a widow, old relationships can take a turn."

"I certainly didn't mean to be leading a cavalry charge," he said.

"Just putting your big toe in the water to test it out?" she said, taking control of the conversation. "Well, here's to Landers, who delivered me with great skill and aplomb."

They clinked glasses.

"Did Landers mention to you that the War Office has agreed to make an exception regarding his injuries if he goes on staff with me?"

"Well, I think he'd make a superior officer," Caroline said.

"Agreed," Brodhead nodded. "He's not all that refined, backwoodsman and all that, but he has 'future colonel' written all over him. He is shrewd, resourceful, gets things done. And men are willing to follow him as, thank God, they are willing to follow me."

"He told me he was going to think hard about staying in the Army," Caroline said.

"Like all young men coming out of battle and hospital, Landers needs a bit of time for procrastination. He'll come in. Loves danger. Hard charger. In his blood."

"Both Freddie and I have taken a fancy to him. He makes us feel almost like, well, Jeremy and Chris are still here. I expect to see him before you do and I'm going to put the good word in for you."

He ordered quail. She opted for salmon, off the bone.

Over nibbling they lowered and lifted eyes and smiled and she blinked hers and he staunchly held his level until they were staring at one another, bang-on.

"Is my interest in you in any way being encouraged?" he ventured.

"Well, what do you think, Llewelyn?"

"There is a possibility, then?"

"There's always a possibility."

He felt warm. He stifled his desire smartly by staring down to St. Stephen's Green and mumbling that it hardly seemed the place of a recent battle. He mentioned how fortunate for Countess Markievicz and her rabble that he had not been commanding the opposition troops.

Having restored himself to the task ahead, he mellowed his way into the next phase with utter sincerity. "So long as Roger was alive, despite your unhappy separation, I'd never have dreamed of doing anything out of line. Alas, my own marriage has been virtually nonexistent ... for more years than I can remember. Beatrice is a ... decent sort."

You bet, Caroline thought, decent and extremely well situated politically, socially, and economically.

"I still have utmost respect for Lady Beatrice as the mother of my daughters, though I had to finally reconcile not having sons ... not that my daughters aren't lovely women ... but a man should have a son. ..."

"Yes, Freddie had the same problem with my being a girl."

"But you've overcome it. Being a woman, I mean. Oh dear, I've just put my foot in my mouth."

"I admire you coming right out with what everyone thinks."

"Caroline, there are ten thousand men in the British Isles who would cut off their right arms just to be sitting here with you."

Like the ten thousand arms that floated from Gallipoli to North Africa, she thought.

"May I ask. What about this Galloway fellow?"

"Gorman? He has been a devoted companion. He's terribly amusing."

And would like at your treasury, Brodhead thought.

"We have loads of the same friends in the theater and among the writers. We share a great number of political feelings, to be frank."

"Well, you were always your own man, so to speak, when it came to politics. Freddie and Roger learned to live with it. I rather admire that in you. Fair play, that's what we're all about. And, uh, the quiet moments of your relationship with Galloway."

Caroline hedged, allowing herself a moment to reflect. "Shall I say that I would not have been so taken by your attention if Gorman and I had more suitable intimate relations?"

"I take it, then . . . "

Salad arrived. He mumbled that it was too vinegary. Suddenly her hands were on his. "I'm hungry for a real man," she said, and looked away quickly.

Dessert was wordless. She assisted him quietly in getting his cigar lit.

"I didn't intend to be so forward," she said.

"You are delicious," he said, taking a long draw. "Can't get enough of these Havanas since Gallipoli."

"Too bad Freddie can't smoke them anymore."

"What do you suggest we do, Caroline," he came out with, at last.

Caroline shook her head and shook it again. "I think we ought to retreat to our individual domains and give it some good hard thought."

"My dear, don't ask me to cut it off entirely."

"Certainly there are numerous social occasions where we can see each other. I'll bring Gorman along and you arrive with Lady Beatrice. I think no private contact for now. If we continue to have the same feelings, we'll have to arrange to discuss it."

"Nothing is going to change with me," he said.

"It came on so suddenly," Caroline said. "It must have been hiding there somewhere for years. I know I am with a very strong and trusted friend. And I know you will never betray me."

"Caroline, hush up."

I trust you, Llewelyn, she thought, because you love that uniform more than anything in your life, and in any scandal, dear Beatrice will have you reduced to the rank of private.

"Having said all this," Caroline said, "this brazen hussy here feels very shaky."

"Will you be at the Officers' Ball at Dublin Castle?" he asked.

"I never pass up the chance to dance with young men."

"Grand," he said, "lovely."

As the curtain opened his troops doubled their alert.

Father Dary crossed the Gratton Bridge over the river Liffey onto Ormond Quay Upper, the recent locale of gun and cannon fire. Rubble-cleaning crews compelled him to take a zigzag path. He climbed the stairs to the law offices of McAloon and Fitzpatrick and wedged his way into Theo's cluttered mash of a room.

"Father Dary," Theo greeted him, "are you down in Dublin to offer condolences on the Rising? Rachael will be delighted."

"Theo, you're a bona fide ass. How did you all come through?"

"We're reeling about. Look at the center of the city, would you. You might have thought we had ten divisions inside the GPO rather than a hundred misplaced clerks, bartenders, and bookies."

"Have the executions really stopped?" Dary asked.

"For the moment, thanks to your prayers and those of others."

"Your mother?"

"Somehow she slipped through the cracks. Countess Markievicz is under sentence of death. Maybe one lady per Rising is sufficient. Mom hasn't been active since Lettershambo. She still represents a great figure in Irish eyes. A weird dust is settling all over this. The British reaction has been insane, just plain insane, against everything they say they stand for."

"I think everyone knows what they're saying to us," Dary said.

"Yes, but . . . " Theo began, unfolding himself from his seat, standing, and trying to find pacing room but finding none.

"But what?"

"Have some priests in your diocese, who never breathed a republican breath in their lives, started to whistle a different tune? Are they a little pissed about shooting Irishmen against the wall with impunity?"

"Well, as a matter of fact, I've heard some damned hard remarks."

Theo tickled the tip of his nose. "My nose itches. I can smell it. Not much, Father, but a drift of anger is on the wind. Know what I heard secondhand out of the Castle? The British Ambassador in Washington sent an urgent cable to the Foreign Ministry in London to stop the executions. Seems that the editorials straight across America are now asking hard questions about what really happened here. Tidbits, only tidbits, but Jesus, wouldn't it be lovely to have it all boomerang on them? It's about time something decent fell our way. Meanwhile, I've still got eighty people under death sentence, and a British prison ship carrying four hundred of our lads left Kingstown today. No one has been publicly charged with anything."

"So, how's it going to play out?"

"Maybe further executions will be suspended. Maybe some of them will be commuted to life in prison or something shorter. Maybe, maybe, can't be sure. The one thing that *is* certain, Sir Roger Casement is in the Tower of London and they must get him in a show trial, to justify their behavior."

"I've had an interesting visitor," Dary said suddenly.

"Oh?"

"Rory Larkin. Conor's nephew from New Zealand."

That engaged Theo's attention.

"He enlisted about a year and a half ago under the name of Landers. He intended to make his way to Ireland and he didn't want to carry the Larkin name in."

"Bright fellow."

"Very bright. He won a field commission, survived Gallipoli, and has won a Victoria Cross. He and Jeremy Hubble became very close. Through Jeremy he learned about Conor and your mother. He wants to meet her."

"That would be lovely. Anything else he wants?"

"The Brotherhood," Dary said bluntly. "He wonders if there's still a Brotherhood?"

"Of course there is. Since the Rising more men about the country have wanted to join than we have room for. It's a case of gaining our senses and forming a new leadership. The Brits have done a pretty fair job in rounding up our top people."

"There is still a central authority, then?"

Theo nodded.

"And you and Atty are in contact with them?"

Theo was about to hedge, but that was nonsense. He was talking to Conor Larkin's brother, the man who engineered a most illegal prison break. He also sensed that Dary had his own sense of outrage over the executions.

"Yes," Theo said. "What is this . . . "

"Rory Landers."

"What's his story, Dary?"

"He's very young, early twenties. A lot of things remind me of Conor. He feels overwhelmed, obsessed with a need to do something in Ireland, especially now."

"Why?"

"It's the Larkin fate."

"He's in uniform?"

"More than that. General Brodhead wants him on his staff in Dublin Castle."

"Ah Father, it's far too early in the day for you to be drinking."

"As Christ is my savior," Dary said.

Rory, Father Dary, and Theo were at their buoyant best, as were two of the most delightful ladies in Dublin. Dinner was a lark, the first without awful tension since the Rising and killings. Long misplaced laughter covered the coming serious intent of the meeting.

Theo, a man who saw everything, saw Dary and Rachael

eagerly volunteer to do the dishes for the lack of wanting further conversation with anyone besides themselves.

As Atty and Theo took Rory up to the library on the top floor she remembered the first time she had taken Conor there. They gathered close to the turf fire.

Theo also saw the unmistakable shock of electricity that blew off the instant his mother and Rory Larkin shook hands. Atty was more than twice the young man's age but had suffered little loss in her regal manner, her great presence, and still had more than her share of beauty. Theo hoped that Mom was merely startled for the moment. Lord Almighty, those Larkin men have a thing about wanting to get into the Fitzpatrick women's knickers. It was hell being the head of this family.

Theo repeated his feeling that sands were shifting in Ireland. "If it keeps running this way," he said, "we're going to vote Sinn Fein in in two years and Sinn Fein will pull out of the British Parliament and declare recognition of the Declaration of Independence."

"And?"

"Ah, the real fun starts when the Irish try to rule themselves. Well, Mom," Theo said with a sigh, "it's time to drop the bomb."

"Rory's a Larkin and he's looking for the Brotherhood," Atty said.

"I am," Rory said.

"What about this British uniform . . . and your arm?"

"I've been invited, not commanded but invited, to go on General Brodhead's staff in the Castle."

Silence. Atty was looking at a young Conor, was she not? Daring like Conor, who dared to go inside Weed Ship & Iron and doctor Sir Frederick's private train to run guns. Conor at Lettershambo . . . himself over there with a Victoria Cross for gallantry. She began to shake. Theo held her.

"Now, Mom," he said strongly.

"Are you his ghost, or what? This isn't true."

"I'm not Conor. I never will be Conor. But there is something I can do. I know that. Ireland's really bleeding now. I've got to make my mark."

"Playing the Landers game inside Dublin Castle," she murmured, "is going to get you into the cell next to Roger Casement in the Tower of London. If they don't get you soon, they'll get you, maybe by a slip of the tongue or just being in the wrong place for a moment. No, I'll not have it."

"Here's my thinking," Rory said, ignoring her entreaty. "I can pull out cleanly any time I want. All I have to do is say my eyes are worse and I'm off to England the next day. The minute I go into Dublin Castle, I'm looking to plan something that can be accomplished. Soon as that is in order, I'm out of Ireland."

Atty was unable to make a decision. She groused with herself. It was all the tension, all the nightmares coming back again in this lad's form. Why the hell did he come to Ireland! All that was left of the high council were threads. Any action now would have to be approved by one of the survivors like herself.

She and Rory locked eyes, as they were prone to do for semi-instants, half-seconds. Theo, still not missing a thing, finally spoke up.

"Rory is in a position too important for us to pass over. I agree that he can't stay too long. No matter the risk, he goes in," Theo said.

"Good," Rory said.

"I won't agree," Atty said.

"It's my responsibility, Mom. You'll have to come around."

CHAPTER
80

"Rachael, when you touch me like that I think I'm going to melt and die," Dary whispered.

"Then melt and die," she answered. "I'll touch you again and again, here and here and here."

He held her hands, then drew them to his lips. Her arms went about his head, with strength, and drew his head to her breasts. Dary felt bosom against his cheek.

"Nothing is this good," he said.

"It gets better," she whispered, "much, much better."

Dary separated from her abruptly. "How would you be knowing that?"

Well, he had to know and now was the time. "I'm not chaste," she said, in the direct manner of a Fitzpatrick.

Why should that annoy him, indeed! After all, he'd been hearing confessions for over a decade from women he'd never believe would have indulged. Why had he always thought of Rachael and virginity in the same breath? He was going to ask something stupid like "Did you confess?" or "You were forced upon?" Oh, the damnableness of wanting all women pure!

"I want no secrets between us," Rachael said. "I think you ought to know about it."

And then what, he thought. Would he ask her to do penance or chastise her? Wouldn't that be rather hypocritical under the circumstances? He and Rachael were not exactly priest to penitent.

"I don't need to know," he pouted with plain old male pride.

"On the other hand, in that we are in a close family friendship and so forth, my understanding of the situation . . . yes, I want to know."

"I was in my sixth form at school, just ready to graduate. My history teacher, Ned Finch, was a very decent lad from an Anglo family. Despite the disparity in our ages and the fact I was his pupil, we had a strong attraction to each other."

Dary found himself all quivery with a dry lump spreading through his throat to his chest; his hands were a bit shaky. An emotion he had never felt or known of welled up inside him. Jealousy? Is this jealousy? It's a bloody monster, if that's what it is. He got together an outward show to cover himself and demonstrated that it was all in a day's work for a priest.

"Dary, maybe that's enough."

"Indeed, no. Do go on."

"We were like great chums more than anything. Ned was into reading poetry and going to theatre and we liked to ride in Phoenix Park. Being as there were no other lads who caught my fancy, I really looked forward to Sundays with him. We *were* entirely discreet."

"Entirely?"

"Sort of. If you want to keep seeing a fellow and enjoy his companionship, you fool around a little, you know, a little."

"I don't know." But he did. From confessions. Kisses, kisses with the use of tongues, breasts . . . breasts were the first very major target. Then rolling about so that parts accidentally rub against each other, entirely innocent . . . bah!

"I didn't feel sensual toward him, but we were pals and the boys my age were real dullards."

Well, that eased Dary up a bit. The Virgin had been *his* woman for over thirty years and Mary's virginity was Her gift to all women. He knew that virginity was not a reality, but now that he felt "that way" about a girl, virginity seemed its old awesome self. He wanted Rachael's story to end that way *for her sake*. What the hell was he thinking about? It didn't make tuppence difference if she was or she wasn't so long as Mary was. And Rachael wasn't Mary. Besides, they'd have to cut out what they were doing, anyhow. It could only be a short-lived dalliance.

"Ned enlisted in the Royal Irish artillery a month after the war started," Rachael went on. "He was going to fight in France and he pleaded with me to do it."

The old demon leapt into Dary's throat again!

"I went to Mom and we talked it over."

"You and your mother?"

"Of course, my mom, who else? I already know what a priest would tell me. I wanted to hear the truth and not a lecture. Dary, I'm sorry."

"What did Atty tell you?"

"She asked if I loved him and I told her I didn't love him in a sexual way but he was my dearest friend and I was terribly emotional about him leaving for war and he *did* love me desperately. I thought I ought to make him happy.

"Mom said she understood. She told me how to be careful and also said, for God's sake, be joyous, laugh a lot at yourselves and be very, very glad afterward."

"She told you that!"

"Of course. Once Mom had broken down the barriers of pain and sorrow for Conor, it was a wonderment watching the two of them rush toward each other down a path. They could make each other out a mile away and Conor would always whisk her off her feet ... and she's no little lamb ... and twirl her around. Sometimes they'd throw off all their clothing and leap into the icy lake screaming and howling for joy. It might have been a day when ten Brotherhood men were captured or some other disaster was on their necks ... but when they saw each other, oh, did they go for each other. So, when she told me it was all right to be with Ned that way, she said ... 'Make it be happy.'"

Dary stopped his own pouting and studied her. For the first time he realized a woman's love was not a one-time gift ... an ultimate sacrifice to be borne with regret that she would never be the same. Love from a woman like Rachael could be given over and over to a man, with great wonderment.

She took his hands. "Ned was happy. He went away happy. He was killed in the first month. I'm glad he went away happy."

The stranger had been sitting, sitting, sitting in his threshold for a score of years, and him holding in his powerful habitude, and now it was seeking a way out and the stranger was seeking its way in with the rush of feelings of an ordinary man.

"Did you enjoy it?" Dary asked the most pedantic question of all.

"Truth?"

He said, "Of course," but he didn't really mean it.

"It was clumsy and painful. But it was joyous."

"Oh."

He felt her soft fingers touch his face, then her lips. "Dary, Dary," she whispered, "I was waiting for you."

As they held each other she whispered meekly, "I was hoping you'd get jealous."

"Well, you hoped correctly, lass."

"What are we going to do, Dary?"

"I was about to ask the same question."

"Are those tears, Dary?" she asked.

"Only tears of joy," he said.

"Mine as well. I was waiting for you, mon, I was waiting for you . . . I was waiting for you."

81

Clonlicky Crossroad, Near Baltimore—June 1916

Ireland, as an island, has ninety-four corners to it where you can go no farther without getting wet. Clonlicky Crossroad was one of them. It serviced farms nearby and had a milk collection station, a provisions store, a pub on the left side of the road, and a church on the right.

It was never known as a dangerous place insofar as republican activity went. However, to it fell the dubious distinction of being made an example, in the post-Rising order of things.

Quinn's Pub, a meager hard-assed Guinness bar, was owned by the Widow Quinn and boasted the normal bent of a lot of republican talk but very little action.

Like every woebegone public house, republican oratory and song was part of the menu for Saturday night and after Sunday Mass. Well, some fecking informer, the bane of Irish life, had reported to the Royal Irish Constabulary that the Widow Quinn was hiding a Brotherhood lad in her cellar. He'd been on the run since the Rising. The Constabulary turned the informer over to the local Army barracks.

No less than General Llewelyn Brodhead drove all the way from Dublin to observe the new order of things. A full-scale attack was made on Quinn's Pub, loaded with drinkers of a Saturday night. The Brits came in as though they were attacking Gibraltar.

The Brotherhood lad was nabbed in the cellar, taken to the barracks and, after a ten-minute court-martial, put against the wall and shot by a firing squad.

The next day as the parishioners were leaving church after Mass, the British leveled every building at Clonlicky Crossroad, save the church.

The tumbling was done by a pair of tractors driving parallel about thirty feet apart dragging a chain and steel beam. One went on the right side of the building, the other went on the left side, and the chain and beam went through the middle, chopping it to the ground, furniture and all.

General Brodhead noted that it was more efficient than eight horse teams dragging logs as they had had to do during the famine.

As though the executions in Dublin had not caused enough of an early chill, the news of the tumbling of Clonlicky Crossroad spread like the plague of the Dark Ages. Impact of the tumbling threw the Irish people right back into the potato famine of the last century.

General Brodhead had delivered a potent message that no further nonsense from the Irish would be brooked.

Dublin Castle, One Week Later—The Officers' Ball

"My goodness, Erma, who is that gorgeous young officer behind Sir Llewelyn in the receiving line."

"New staff man."

"My daughter will be livid she didn't come tonight."

"He's a frontiersman from the colonies. V.C. winner."

"I hear he wears a glove over his right hand all the time. Isn't that romantic?"

Rory sensed Caroline Hubble was close, and she was.

"Hello, handsome," she said to him. "It looks like you're the belle—or the beau—of the ball."

"I can't dance these things," Rory said.

"Oh, that won't matter. There's a lovely balcony for chatting, outside." Caroline fluttered her eyes in mock awe. "While

I've got you," she said, "I've put you down for dances numbers, let's see, ten and fifteen on my card," she said.

Caroline moved on down the receiving line to where Sir Llewelyn stood ramrod and bemedaled, and Lady Beatrice stood wide. Caroline and Beatrice bussed cheeks.

"Ah, Caroline, good to see you about," Brodhead said. "Do save me a dance before your card is filled."

"Oh dear, Llewelyn," Caroline said dismayed, "let me look. Look what I went and did. I'm afraid you're out of luck."

"Has a general no rights here?" he mumbled.

"I'll surrender one of my dances with Countess Hubble to you, General," Rory said.

"Good lad! I told you this was a resourceful young man!" Brodhead beamed.

"Number ten is yours, sir," Rory said.

"The gavotte, cropper!"

"Beatrice, I'll catch up with you in a moment. I've yards and yards of news," Caroline said.

The ballroom, used on the odd occasion as a Throne Room, had a jaunty air tonight. A note of victory prevailed. Marble, gilt, great Waterford chandeliers, and no lack of upholstered silk tapestry could almost make one feel one was not even in Ireland. Dublin, no matter how polished, was still provincial. It had been taken as far as it could go tonight, for a colony.

Caroline and Beatrice had their heads glued together like a pair of Siamese twins during the intermission. The General's wife's conversation, alas, matched her looks. As the music started up, Sir Llewelyn offered his wife his arm.

"Do this one with Caroline, dear," she said. "I've trampled on the feet of every junior officer in the room and I'm pooped."

"Caroline?" the General asked.

"You're too kind, Beatrice," Caroline demurred.

'Round and 'round in the oblong hall they waltzed until the ends of the room grew smaller as dancers retired and circled the dozen remaining couples, now in the center.

"You've been on my mind constantly," he managed.

"Myself as well. I can't tell you how lovely it feels to have a strong arm holding me. Let us lilt and fly and show these young puppies a thing or two."

"I want to see you badly"—as they whirled.

"And I, you," she said. "I'm holding a conference with some of my subcontractors from the south up in Belfast shortly. We'll have lunch in my private dining room."

"Yes," he confirmed, and held her a tad closer to feel that bosom press against him.

"Llewelyn," she said breathlessly, playing her fingers deftly over his neck.

Lady Caroline and the General modestly accepted the applause as the music stopped and they returned to Lady Beatrice.

"Lovely, lovely," Beatrice said. "I used to dance that way once," she said in her singsong voice.

Like hell you did, Brodhead thought.

A glowering light colonel demonstrated all teeth as he bowed to Caroline.

"Martin!" Caroline cried with joy. "I've been waiting for you. Best dancer in the Fusiliers."

Martin hacked out a silly nasal laugh as he arched his body back.

Caroline looked at her dance card at the same instant Lieutenant Landers bowed before her.

"Why don't we take our dance out on the balcony," she suggested.

An unusually decent night greeted them. Over the way stood the Protestant cathedral, smaller than the real ones in France and England. Everything in Dublin was half-sized, except for the Guinness Brewery.

"Give us a hug," Caroline said. "I know how difficult it is for you to write notes, but thank you for the telephone calls. It can be maddening trying to get through from the west."

"Ah, it's not much better in New Zealand."

"How was your journey, Rory?"

"The west of Ireland is magnificent."

"We try to keep anything of worth in Ireland a secret so we Anglos can have it for ourselves."

"It was a good place to go, for many reasons. I found I hadn't spent all my tears over Gallipoli. I miss my pals fiercely. Jeremy, beyond fiercely. I suppose given time I'll be able to control things enough to carry on with my life."

"I see you're wearing captain's pips. Does that mean you're staying in Ireland?"

"The General has agreed I can leave when I feel I must. He's trying to lure me, inch by inch."

"Which one of the lovely ladies has captured your heart, Lieutenant Landers?" Caroline asked.

"You," Rory said.

"Good, then you see us home," she said.

"Caroline, you've been too magnanimous about the town-house. I was planning to bunk in at the barracks."

"Indeed you will not!"

"I appreciate everything, but I don't want to be a nuisance."

"I promise you I won't attack you in the middle of the night."

"Well, I mean, suppose you're having company or a dinner or something?"

"Rory. Will you treat it exactly as Jeremy and Christopher did?"

"You really mean that, don't you?"

"I do. Gorman will be over for the weekend. The three of us will do up Dublin, if you're off-duty."

"Grand. Caroline, tell me it's none of my business, but are you the least bit interested in Llewelyn Brodhead?"

"Yes, I am," she said, "interested and serious. Dead serious."

CHAPTER 82

Caroline Hubble never came down from her bedroom without looking the best she could look on that given day. She was attired in a pale blue dressing gown and wore her hair long. She poked through a stack of legal and business work in the solarium of the Merrion Square townhouse as Rory made a late morning appearance.

"Good morning, Prince Charming," she greeted him.

"I didn't realize that dancing was so much exercise."

Caroline rang for the butler. She smiled as Rory laid on a sheepman's breakfast for himself. ". . . And a rasher of bacon, Adam." Turning to Rory, she said, "It's unnatural to simply sit down, ring a bell, give an order, and there it is."

Rory sensed a very subtle shift in Caroline's demeanor, a bit of firmness, a new aspect to her otherwise constant sweet nature. She poured herself a cup of tea, chewed into her toast, and adjusted her glasses.

"I say if it looks like a kiwi, runs like a kiwi, quacks like a kiwi, and lays eggs, then it's a kiwi."

"I'm a kiwi all right. Question is, have I laid an egg?"

She found the paper she wanted. "Canterbury District, the South Island between Oxford and Kowai Bush. The Landers farm was purchased by Liam Larkin, proprietor of Ballyutogue Station in 1907."

Be cool, lad, he told himself. Across the table sat someone who could be as dangerous as a hangman.

"Am I under arrest?" he said at last.

"If you want to know how I got this, Jeremy wrote to me. I've known from the minute you walked into Rathweed Hall."

"That's not true, Caroline. Jeremy would not break a trust."

"You believe that?"

"I know it," Rory said. "You might not like the next line, Caroline. Jeremy intended to become a republican."

It confirmed her suspicions. Jeremy was born with that soft Irish nature and Conor Larkin was his god. His disaster with Molly, his hatred for his father, his inability to set in comfortably with his own caste all pointed to it. Still, on hearing it, it rocked her, even though she had suspected as much.

"What's your story, Mr. Larkin?"

"I was underage, pissed at my father, and passionate to get to Ireland from the instant I learned of Conor's death. A funny thing happened along the way called . . . Gallipoli. You sort out your troubles in a hurry in a place like that. I almost made the terrible mistake of not writing to my father to forgive him. Thank God, I didn't die and leave him with that hanging around his neck. Maybe Ireland was none of my business then. It is now."

"Conor played my father for a fool and that's what you did to me," she continued.

"All depends on how you look at it, about who is playing who for what. That's a mighty fine organization you run. A hell of a lot better than British intelligence. How are you playing this now, Caroline?"

"That all depends on whether you give me straight answers or not."

"Seeing that the situation is highly in your favor, I'll do my best."

"Are you certain that Llewelyn Brodhead isn't setting you up so he can make you spill the name of every Brotherhood man left in Ireland when they get you on the torture rack?"

"It's crossed me mind. However, I've got to go with instinct. I don't think he's that smart."

"How smart was he commanding seven divisions of infantry?"

"From the beginning?"

She nodded.

"In Egypt it seemed that he was a little less uppity than most career pommy officers. We were *his* Anzacs and we were going to be the best troops in the expedition. He demonstrated, on numerous occasions, he'd go to bat for us. He got us the equipment and animals we needed by taking on the theatre commander. He overlooked a lot of . . . naughty adventures, say, in Cairo, including Chris at the Aida Hotel.

"He was a brutal disciplinarian in getting the troops ready. Some medical people say he put as many men into the hospital with his training as he left standing.

"In my opinion, considering what we were going into, I think he did the right thing. A lot of men wouldn't have survived Gallipoli otherwise. But that was just good standard British Army training. Well, you know his history with Chris before the war," Rory said.

"You mean the gunrunning and the mutiny at Camp Bushy?"

"Aye. Chris had to really swallow ten tons of crap to get that mule corps shaped up. What Chris did with our battalion was to make something work. It would have been a disaster without the mules. Brodhead knew it. Chris was all man about it. In fairness to the General, he went on record with the War Office against the entire Gallipoli expedition. Once assigned to the Anzacs, however, he played the good soldier. He lived and moved among the men, shared our hardships. Maybe he got a better brand of booze than we were stilling and had better rations, but his hole and my hole looked pretty much the same. He was fairly popular with the officers and men."

"So, you don't fault him," Caroline said.

"I didn't say that. The rest of it is fucking sad."

"All right, once again, how smart was he in commanding seven divisions of infantry?"

"Bearing in mind Napoleon and Caesar wouldn't have had a chance—"

"I'm speaking about Llewelyn Brodhead," she demanded.

Rory's voice dipped low. "He was a lousy general. The planning for this campaign guaranteed a disaster. On those things he had say, he was somewhat less than no good. Nothing worked, from the landing site to the most simple communications. Naval gunfire was a disaster, and in six months they couldn't get it straightened out. We were badly underequipped, underfed. Evacuation plans were nonexistent. Medical facilities were beyond primitive ... but that wasn't the half of it, Caroline. ... "

Rory hung his head and took time to get control of himself. "War is war and any man who aspires to be a general must steel himself against losses. He was from some century long ago," Rory said harshly. "He thought he owned the Anzacs. He made blunders that were real pissers, but the worst of it was, he didn't give a big rat's ass. I was with the man time and again after we'd taken terrible casualties and never once saw him blink an eye. He had no conscience. Troops were his for the slaughter, no more, no less. His tactics were archaic, often mad ... he was born without tears to shed."

Some of the iron had drained from Caroline. Fear of her next question hung over both of them.

"All right," she said, eyes tearing, "you know what I want to know."

"The short version or the long version? The Aussie charge over the Nek was a suicide mission with no tactical purpose. Llewelyn Brodhead simply lost his head."

"You did not read the Commission of Inquiry's first report, did you?" she asked.

"One of those nice blue ladies in the hospital read it to me."

"Well?"

"Brodhead lied to cover his ass. As one incompetent general in a pot of a dozen other incompetent generals, he was able to ooze his way past the bitter truth."

"And Chunuk Bair?" Caroline asked.

"We arrived at the top at daybreak after a most dangerous all-night march and climb. Shortly thereafter the Suvla Corps landed but stopped on the beach without even attempting to make contact with us. We were only a battalion strong with no chance to thwart a Turkish counterattack. Some forty to fifty thousand British soldiers just sat there on the beach.

"Brodhead should have ordered us off Chunuk Bair immediately. Instead, he did the opposite. He sent Colonel Markham up to us with orders to remain there seven hours after we should have evacuated. The New Zealander, Colonel Malone, refused to stay any longer and he and Markham got into an argument.

"Brodhead, by phone, ordered Chris to arrest Colonel Malone. Chris refused. Brodhead was expecting eight hundred of us on totally exposed ground to stand off thirty to fifty thousand Turks.

"Anyhow, Malone ordered the evacuation. As it started, he and Markham were killed by a shell."

"Where were my sons?"

"The Turks were inching up on us. Chris and Jeremy went out to our perimeter and charged into several nests of machine guns to try to buy us time to get off the hill."

"You heard all of this between Malone and Markham?"

"Yes."

"Do you know that Brodhead has testified that it was he who ordered the evacuation?"

"Yes, he lied . . . and he's asked me to lie as well."

They sat there, chalk-faced.

"How did my sons die?"

Rory wept a bit and continued shaking his head.

"How did my sons die?"

"By British naval gunfire!" Rory said. "Now fucking leave me alone!"

"What are your intentions now, son?"

"When I know yours," Rory answered. He dried his tears and gave a hardy blow of the nose.

"Brotherhood?" she asked.

"Maybe."

"They'll want you to stay in Dublin Castle. You can't carry that off for too long."

"We all know that."

"How far will you go?" she asked.

"How far will *you* go?" he retorted.

"How many more villages does he plan to tumble?" she asked.

"As many as it takes to crush the Irish spirit. . . . Your flirtation with Brodhead?"

"I wasn't positive. I am now."

"Lure him?"

"To his death. Seems that we've been thrown together, Rory. Of course, you have no choice but to trust me,."

"I do trust you."

"I've been wondering all along if I could really do it," she said. "Even as a general in battle, he killed my sons needlessly through his incompetence and panic. Is that right?"

"Yes," Rory said.

"I am the daughter of Freddie Weed and all that inplies. Father and daughter are a paradox. Freddie longs to die but he cannot die until Brodhead is assassinated. I long to live but I cannot live until the same thing happens. He killed my sons and now he plans to kill Ireland. I'm not a republican, Rory, but I have learned from the executions that I am an Irishwoman . . . and I love hearing myself say it. You can't take out Brodhead by yourself, Rory. Suspicion will fall immediately on his staff, and you can't stand too much scrutiny. On the other hand, I can do it, but I need an ally, be it the Brotherhood or yourself, alone."

"There's some talk about making a move if they sentence Roger Casement to death."

"I've always adored Roger Casement," Caroline said. "Is vengeance wrong? It would be wrong knowing what Llewelyn Brodhead will do to Ireland, having the means to stop him, and not doing it—that would be wrong. Sometimes a man or woman has to stand up and take responsibility for thousands who can't. Is it wrong to kill a killer to stop him from further killing?" she cried.

"I came here wondering what I could possibly do in Ireland. . . . Now I know," Rory said.

CHAPTER
83

When the Tara Street Railroad Station was planned and built in the last century, two sets of architects had worked on it. The firm in London engineered the tunnel and tracks from the central depot, while a firm in Dublin produced the blueprints for the terminal building.

Only problem was, either the tracks or the building was on the wrong side of Tara Street. After due discussion, arbitration, and court action, the net result was seventy-five feet of abandoned tunnel, which was boarded up on both ends.

The Brotherhood gained secret access to this abandoned stretch of line and, using it as a starting point, charted a labyrinth of sealed rooms, hidden ladders, movable sections of flooring and roofing, over rooftops that ultimately led to a garret three stories up over Poolbeg Street, an area of general commerce near the river.

If you were looking for the safest hideaway in Ireland, look no further. It had been crafted over a six-month period by Conor Larkin, took a half-hour to reach once one entered the tunnel, and it never came close to coughing up its final destination.

Furthermore, it was airtight because the location was known only to Conor, Dan Sweeney, Seamus O'Neill, and Atty. Only Atty survived the Lettershambo Raid and only then shared the secret with Theo.

Over time its larder was stocked with nonperishable food including essential liquids. It sported a small turf fire and a

secure phone line. It was now reopened as the rendezvous for
Rory, Theo, and Atty.

Rory followed Theo down from the roof, remarking about
the incredibility of the place. Theo removed the ladder and, with
a long handle, slid the roof shut.

"Hello, Mother."

Atty Fitzpatrick was waiting on a well-worn settee.

"Hello, Rory lad," Atty said. "This is where we meet from
now on. There will only be the three of us. Needs a bit of dust-
ing and some new supplies. I'll bring them up. The telephone
still works. Never pick it up until you hear five full rings, a stop,
then a redial."

Rory surveyed the place. A small dormer brought up sounds
and smells of steel-ringed wheels on cobblestones and the
omnipresent Dublin aroma of ales from no lack of nearby public
houses.

As the sky darkened and the town blinked on in waves of
twinkling lights, low roofs made a fairyland silhouette. Even
curtains, Rory thought. He let them fall together.

"Kind of rare up here," Rory said.

Atty had a bittersweet reaction to the place. She checked the
cupboards, stopped here and again by returning memories.

Theo trailed after her, shaking empty bottles and chucking
them. At last! A keeper.

Atty became all business. "Theo and I will be your only con-
tacts. No one else in Ireland knows we're getting information
out of the Castle. Your name is nonexistent. We still have a
Supreme Council, although, as you can imagine, communicating
and meeting is a very dicey proposition these days. Theo and I
are gong to take much of the responsibility and make plans and
decisions until we can form a cohesive group again. Is that all
right with you?"

"Yes, that's fine with me."

"How is it going in the Castle?" Theo asked.

"Some of the security is really sloppy," Rory said. "I might
have a crack at some informers' lists."

"That's good, but we have to be very careful. First of all, you aren't the only Brotherhood man working inside the Castle. Secondly, there are double agents playing both sides. Thirdly, they may plant a list with several false names on it to trap someone like you in their midst. Anything you touch, do it with suspicion," Atty instructed.

Rory blew a breath and nodded, acknowledging her years and skills at the game and also realizing the thin ice he himself was skating on.

"I've got one thing," Rory said. "Brodhead is planning a series of setups. The Army or the Constabulary is going to plant a few cases of rifles or bombs in various locations around the country, then go through the pretense of a raid, find the arms, and tumble the building as they did at Clonlicky. Kilorglin is first, during the Puck Fair in August."

"Bastards," Theo said. "If we alert anyone in Kilorglin the Brits will suspect someone in the Castle tipped them off." He smacked his fist into his palm. "We might just have to let them level the place to keep our source secure."

"Bad show," Rory said.

"August," Atty said. "That's about the time we'll be getting a decision on Sir Roger Casement. Brodhead's subtle way of turning the screws."

"So?" Rory asked.

"So?" Atty echoed.

"So," Theo said, "it all seems to add up to one thing, doesn't it?"

"Brodhead has to be assassinated," Rory said.

"So say we all," Theo said.

"No," Atty said, "I'm afraid of British reprisals."

"Mother, he's going to murder countless Irishmen and rip down all of the country he can get his hands on. Will reprisals be that much worse?"

"On the other hand, Brodhead's being killed or disappearing just might cause the British to reflect for a moment or two. It could have the opposite effect. It could just put a stop to the wanton destruction and killing," Rory said.

"Rory might be right, Mom. It's a calculated risk we have to take."

"Jesus, I hate assassinations," Atty said.

"If there is any such thing as a righteous one, Brodhead is it," Theo said.

"If Brodhead is killed, suspicion comes your way very quickly, Rory. You are Conor Larkin's blood," she said. "He was the most courageous man I've ever known, but he had a terminal problem about not being able to execute anybody, one on one. It's one thing to kill Turks in battle. Have you ever put a pistol to a man's head and shot him?"

Rory's mind went back to a hot day in a dry stream bed in Gallipoli . . . reaching for his pistol as Dr. Calvin Norman lay prostrate from the heat . . . leveling the gun at the man's temple. His Uncle Conor had come to him in that instant and told him not to do it.

"You see, Rory, close as you are to Brodhead, you can't do it without walking to the gallows, yourself. The only alternative is life on the run for the rest of your days. In fact, I'm on edge every day you stay in the Castle."

They sipped their tea, Rory and Theo loudly, and Atty as though drinking from an empty cup on the stage, ladylike.

"Get a grip," Rory said, abruptly coming to his feet. "We've an ally who knows who I am and is just as anxious to see Brodhead dead—in fact, even more anxious. She has access to him, can get him alone, anywhere. She will be the shooter. She needs an ally to dispose of the body. This will give us the opportunity of having Brodhead simply disappear from the face of the earth, making it more difficult for the British to justify reprisals."

"Who is she?" Atty asked, expecting a spurned mistress out for revenge. Too much could go wrong with that sort of person.

"It's Caroline Hubble," Rory said.

"Are you mad?" Atty cried. "She can't be trusted!"

"If she can't be trusted, why hasn't she picked up the telephone and turned me in?" Rory said. "She had me cold from our first meeting."

"Because she wants to set you up to force you to give the entire Brotherhood away."

"Mom . . . now, Mom . . . you are being emotional, and ridiculous," Theo said softly.

"Me? Ridiculous? Weed and Hubble are ridiculous."

"Mom, she wants Brodhead dead for some very obvious reasons."

"And some not so obvious, Atty," Rory said. "This woman is not her husband or her father."

"Are you telling me she has become a republican?"

"She has always been politically independent of both her father and her late husband. She did extraordinary work on behalf of Catholic education in Derry. She lives with an Irish rogue, Gorman Galloway. She's turned Weed Ship & Iron into a public company, recognized the union, and she is now giving away large tracts of the Earldom to her peasant farmers ... just like you did, Mom. Mom ... love ... we may have struck gold."

"Vengeance for her sons?" Atty asked.

"It's killing her," Rory said. "You can believe this or not, Atty, but she is convinced Brodhead will return Ireland to the Middle Ages. The Brits can't send anyone worse, but they can sure send someone better. The risk is worth taking."

"I can't bring myself to making an alliance with the daughter of Frederick Weed."

"Conor never made love to her!" Rory shot out, hard and abruptly. The effect was resounding. When the silence had settled down into the tattered rug, eyes were no longer meeting eyes.

"You make the call, Mother," Theo said. "I'm overdue for a meeting with Lord Cornelius. He may have a message on some of our prisoners."

Theo, not the most graceful of men, stumbled up the ladder onto the roof. Instead of roaring with excitement over the budding plans, Atty seemed almost mean-spirited.

"How would you know about Conor and Caroline Hubble?" she asked.

"Conor told me the first part of their story when he was in New Zealand. Jeremy told me the rest of it, including the rumors about yourself and Conor."

Rory was in the shadows near the window frame. It was a sight she'd relished and longed for, and it startled her. For that instant it was Conor standing there. This had been their place for over four years. Oh, the lovings and free-flowing danger of it all! And young Rory, his head working like Conor's, a master of the game.

Rory peered down to the street, brain dinnlin', same courage, same daring. Like Conor, he was now fixed on his mission. In this gray world things could go wrong so quickly. One day in Dublin Castle and the next on the run and all that that rotten life entails.

"Don't do it, Rory," she said. "Once you're in you never get out. After a time you lose count of all the bombings and knee-cappings and killings and years of rotting behind bars."

"You two found a world, right in this room," Rory said. "Would you change any of that?"

"This is *our* country. You've a land of your own."

"I'll go when it's my time to go," he said.

"Goddamn you, you didn't hear a word I said," she spouted angrily.

"I need to be here," Rory said. "Don't ask me to go again. I didn't swim all the way from New Zealand to this safe room to slink off. You seem to forget, Brodhead killed my brother Jeremy with his fucking stupidity. Think I can live a rich full life by tucking tail and fleeing? I've got to finish this, Atty, I've got to finish this."

Atty was fumbling her lines and her thoughts. Seeing him up here had derailed her mourning, sparked a springtime. She never thought it would come again. And Lord, she didn't want it from him.

They stood on either side of the bed until the mattress became a third party. Don't even think about it, you bastard, she thought.

"We seem to have a real talent for antagonizing each other. Either mutual repulsion or mutual attraction."

"And a silver tongue to go with it," she said. "I've seen that leer from the lads all my life. You do it better than most."

"By God, Atty, you're afraid of me," Rory said. "Or is it that you're afraid of yourself? Don't count yourself totally innocent. I know the look, too."

"I'm old enough to be your mother."

"You're afraid of me, Atty. You're afraid I'm going to make you enjoy it. You don't want to enjoy it. You want to live forever wrapped in martyrdom."

"God, Rory, you're a real bastard, aren't you? Am I not allowed to be shocked by your resemblance? Are you that damned arrogant?"

"Arrogant to what? Give me one more come-on and I'll forget I'm a British officer and a gentleman."

Yes or no, Atty girl? He looks through you the same way Conor did. It's highly unlikely he doesn't know how to take care of a woman.

Atty played her next lines to slice his throat. "I don't want an imitation Conor Larkin. I had the real thing, and one dead Conor is worth a dozen live Rorys."

Rory reflexively grabbed her arm with unquestioned power and shook her.

"Well," she said, "excuse me for making any comparison. The difference between you and Conor is already quite clear."

He let her go. "I'll be back here Sunday at three o'clock. Make your decision. If you have any fucking brains you'll put your claws in and make an alliance with Caroline Hubble. I can make the way out without help."

Atty lit another candle and held on, then flung herself on the bed, pounding the pillows with her fists and cursing Rory Larkin for arousing her. Oh, he was the Larkin, all right; she was totally intimidated by him. Her lifelong game of wilting men before her eyes didn't work on a few of them, and he and Conor were two.

How dirty wrong would it be to have one more breath of Conor? How scummy would I feel afterward? But, to hell! I'm not a widow! I'm not lying alongside him in Ballyutogue! Did not Conor find a life with me after Shelley's death? Am I forbidden? Conor! Conor, lad, what should I do, now? What should I do?

CHAPTER
84

In that it was wartime, the southern part of Ireland was suddenly in a manufacturing posture. Their usual donkey-and-cart methods needed to be speeded up considerably. Weed Ship & Iron, for one, had a dozen subcontractors in Cork, Galway, and Dublin.

An entire new line of defensive security items were on the planning board and a meeting at the Belfast yard had been called with Weed's engineers and the Army's engineers working up a full shopping list of items to protect constabulary stations and barracks, mesh window coverings, and the like.

General Brodhead pounced on the conference as a viable reason to make the trip. Of course, he'd review the troops and constabulary in Belfast as well.

Rory was in charge of security en route to Belfast and back. Brodhead had an armored military train car, which was kept in a locked shed. The general's quarters were in the center of the car with guard details on either end. Movements of the car were kept hush-hush, usually hitching on to a train at the last moment. After the undercarriages were inspected, a sweep engine was sent fifteen minutes ahead to make certain the tracks were clean.

At Weed Ship & Iron, Lieutenant Landers joined the military group and the subcontractors for an indoctrination tour.

Sir Llewelyn saw them off, after which he joined Lady Caroline in an exquisite small private dining room attached to her father's office.

"No calls during lunch. The General and I will join the meeting at the conference center afterward."

As she put the phone in the cradle, Sir Llewelyn touched her shoulder as soft as he was able, but rougher than he should have. Caroline had adjusted herself to the proposition that she was enjoying what she was deploring.

"I hope you haven't regretted our last conversation," he said.

"Not the thought of you and me, my dear," Caroline said. "But it's what we have to go through to arrange a forty-minute lunch alone. I'm getting qualms about the whole thing."

"I don't want to let go of this," he said. "I realize looking back on my life, I've never come close to anyone like you. It was never part of my game. Now, I find myself absolutely struck and sleepless."

"Llewelyn, we've known each other a long time. I say what is on my mind," she said sending an unusual sensation of fright through him.

"Indeed," he said.

"Maybe what we are trying to do is simply not on," she said, watching the color drain from his face. "No less than ten thousand people know you are on the premises here. The truth is, there is probably no one in Ireland who doesn't know either your face or mine. There are always a half-dozen people around me and God knows how many around you, all the time. Slipping away for a rendezvous is a puzzle for the gods. It's probably dangerous for you to be unguarded, and virtually impossible for me. It's not like Gorman and me, who are accepted as a couple. We can't risk a chance that someone, obscure, might see us accidentally."

"There has to be a way and we're going to find it," he said. "Listen, if you will. I was born into a breed that dictated things from the beginning, that being an Ulsterman of class means one has to be super-British to maintain his standing. The military, and no option, was clear-cut to me from childhood. A woman like Lady Beatrice was clear-cut. We have slept in separate bedrooms for almost seven years, and before that I wasn't all that bully."

She put her hands on his. "I'm so sorry."

He stuffed his pipe and grunted in dismay as he brought it to a light. "Am I boring you?"

"Of course not."

"If you are in the military, ambitious, and an Ulsterman, certain holy commandments govern your life. Your life is the regiment. Lust was not considered a sensible option."

"Yes, poor Roger used to say that growing up in men's clubs, men's schools, the Army, that hard sport and a cold shower took care of one's urges."

"Problem is, that's no joke," Llewelyn answered. "Our other holy commandment is the sovereignty of the empire. To govern what we were endowed to govern, we produced the kind of officers who held our mission sacred. Therefore, I never became a rounded man, a scholar of other than field marshals, or a cultured man, or a political man, or even one who gives a damn about his rose garden. Out in the colonies one has a little leverage for sport with a mistress, or whatever."

"And in Ulster it's a no-go," Caroline said. "You're the most important man in Ireland and I won't be responsible for seeing a brilliant career go up in smoke. Once upon a time when I was an improper young lady, I adored this kind of intrigue. Freddie always caught me because I wanted him to, to make him angry. My situation with Gorman is that we're improperly proper. No one even bothers to gossip about us anymore."

The mention of her constant companion annoyed him.

"I used to watch a promising colonel or brigadier toss it all away over some woman beneath him, and I simply could not understand it. God, I envied Roger Hubble when you two were married, and every time I've seen you since."

"Seems like we're star-crossed," she said. "With this situation there is absolutely no one I can confide in," she said.

"A general is even lonelier," Brodhead opined. "Well, we surely can't run off to the continent these days," he said, with a sting of black humor. "I'm so tied to my command I can't even take off a long weekend to do a little fishing. I've been dying to go to Donegal for a shot at the salmon. I'm told they're running in the thousands."

"Wait a moment. What did you just say?" Caroline asked.

"A fishing holiday without a dozen staff climbing up my back."

Caroline became intense as *discovery* worked its way up through her. "Of course. How stupid of me. Strange how you turn things inside out to find a solution that has been in front of your face, all the time."

Lord, is this true! he wondered.

Caroline let out a little squeal of delight then reached over and gave him a lingering kiss, and quickly wiped the lip rouge from him.

"The hunting lodge," she said. "It hasn't been used since I left Hubble Manor. It's completely removed."

"I've been there time and again with Roger. He showed it to me after you did it over. Rather ... exciting ... but what about the gamekeeper and his wife?" he asked.

"They retired several months ago and I sent them to America for a year to visit relatives. I've not appointed a new warden."

His heart was racing at the possibility of a woman of Caroline's stature. No one before her remotely gave him cause to toy with regulations.

"No matter how we plan it, it still carries some risk," Caroline said.

"Maybe not," he replied, turning on the "battle" plans.

"Will you be able to get there by yourself?" she asked.

"Let me think about that," he answered. "Of course, I can take a weekend at Brodhead Abbey. At that point, send staff to Londonderry Barracks and tell them I'm going fishing alone. I might mention I'm heading south, in the opposite direction, to throw them off."

"Well now," Caroline said, showing outward nervousness, "shall we do it?"

"Yes."

"My, this is exciting. I could go up ahead and tidy things up and get a turf fire going and lay in some necessities. Here's the number of my private phone at Rathweed Hall ... tell me when, I'll be there waiting."

"We don't want to go in by horseback?"

"Do it the simple way. Drive to the north gate of the earldom.

I'll have unlocked it. Drive in for about nine miles. There is an unmistakable path at the foot of the big hill with a stand of birch trees. You'll see my car parked in there. It's only a quarter of a mile up the path to the lodge, but it's narrow to drive. Park beside my car and hike in. The lodge is about a fifteen-minute walk."

He closed his eyes to remember. . . . "Yes, it's completely hidden."

"Nothing within a radius of ten miles."

Their hands were wet with anticipation as they held them clasped together.

"Try not to make it too long. It doesn't have to be a week-end, either."

"Caroline . . . "

"Let's do it," she said.

As the conference broke up, Brodhead's armored car was taken out of the shed where it had been under guard. The Dublin mail train had been diverted into the yard to pick it up.

Rory Landers had been one of the hits of the conference. He roughed out ideas of extremely thin metal covering to fit over light civilian vehicles to make them semi-armored.

Llewelyn Brodhead saluted and said cheerio to the gathering and boarded.

"It's on," Caroline said, bussing Lieutenant Landers as he boarded.

The general took off his Sam Browne belt and unbuttoned his jacket and invited Rory to do likewise. Watching the scenery flit by outside the train window cooled his high state of emotion.

"I'd say the big meeting went extremely well, sir," Rory said.

"We have to button up in our fortresses in the countryside, and when we do come out, we're not going to be suckered into ambushes. A lot of good ideas passed back and forth today. I'd say a drink is in order. Help yourself. . . . Got a lot of compliments on you today, Landers."

"Cheers."

"Cheers, sir."

As Brodhead seemed to have a permanent cat-that-swallowed-the-mouse grin, Rory lay back and waited for him to either open up or shut up. He feared it was too much for Llewelyn Brodhead to conceal a conquest like Caroline Hubble. That would end the hunting lodge and maybe her participation entirely. Brodhead must not reveal a planned tryst.

The grin remained on Brodhead's face as they talked about this and that.

"Oh, Lady Caroline requested that I give you a little furlough. She's anxious for a visit," Brodhead said.

"I'd like to visit with her, soonest," Rory said.

"Caroline confided in me," Brodhead said. "You bring her a great deal of comfort, Landers. I think she feels that you are a surrogate son, in a manner of speaking."

"In a manner of speaking, I love her dearly," Rory said. "I've met one woman like her but also unlike her—my Georgia . . . if I ever find her. You know what Caroline does, sir? She fills me with a kind of confidence in myself that makes me feel like a king. After seeing her great loss, firsthand, she has taught me how one should behave in the face of ultimate tragedy."

"Too bad you didn't know Sir Frederick in his day."

"I enjoy his company, too, as a matter of fact. You can feel his power and joy without his even moving. He must have been a wild fellow in his time."

"You don't know the half of Freddie Weed," Brodhead said, laughing to himself. "Better not cross that one."

"I haven't met this Galloway chap, but I've seen photographs and heard quite a bit about him. I wonder why someone like Lady Caroline would be taken by him."

Brodhead grumbled, shrugged, and belted his whiskey. "Caroline has an artsy side to her. She is right at home in the bohemian crowd. Odd bunch, that. Actually, that's part of her allure. But, I must tell you she was also the most perfect aristocratic wife a man could have."

"Sir, may I be so bold as to ask about . . . uh . . . "

"Caroline and myself?"

"You have asked me to put in the good word," Rory said.

"Frankly, Landers, it's a no-go situation. I've decided not to press the issue. It's simply the wrong thing to do."

"Sorry to hear about that, sir. What I mean is, well, Lady Caroline is rather . . . not to be believed . . . and I was secretly hoping for you . . . if I could be of service . . . maybe put in another good word next week."

"No, it's a dead issue. Duty before pleasure, you know."

Rory felt fairly comfortable that Brodhead was going to remain silent on this matter. Too much at risk, otherwise. Now, Rory told himself, was time to spring the news.

"Sir, I've an unpleasant matter. I particularly waited until our return to Dublin so we could be alone. General, it's my eyes. They've gotten worse."

"Oh, my dear chap."

"I tried to carry on before bringing this up, but I'm afraid the way it's going, I won't be able to carry out my duties much longer."

"This is a bloody blow, Landers!"

"When the old vision started getting more blurry, I conferred with Wandsworth Hospital in London. My doctor there tells me there are two medical facilities the Army has, as well as a very fine civilian surgeon in Scotland, who specializes in concussive optic nerve damage. It appears that medical advances are coming forth by leaps and bounds, as they are apt to do in a war. I'm afraid I'm going to ask to be released from your command as soon as it is convenient."

"Hell, it never will be convenient, but we can't have you walking around with a cane."

"Thank you, sir."

"Sign off with Colonel Hunt and get to England as soon as you can."

"God bless you, General. I thought I'd travel to England via Belfast after I visit Lady Caroline."

"Does she know?"

"No, sir. I couldn't tell her this time. She's had so much grief. I hope she finds some real happiness soon."

"Yes," the General said, "so do I."

The sliding section of the roof opened.

"Are you down there?" Atty called.

"Aye, I'll send the ladder up," Rory said.

He set it into position, then he realized he had a clear look up her skirt. He satisfied himself with a quick glimpse, then turned his head away and steadied the ladder with his good hand. Atty caught the by-play and she smiled to herself.

How many times had she come down the ladder to Conor that he ran his hand clear up her leg or she leapt into his arms and pushed him over on the bed.

"Been waiting long?" she asked.

"Not to bother," Rory said.

"The trouble with safe-house life is the waiting. I thought I spotted a couple of detectives canvassing the Tara Street Station. It took a while before I could get into the tunnel."

They sized one another up with an unspoken overlay from the previous meeting. They knew that personal animus had to be set aside.

"We're in," Atty said.

Rory shook his head and let the built-up anxiety ebb. "Let me catch my breath."

"Aye."

"We're not moving any too soon on this. Brodhead and staff are starting to draw up a master plan for the pacification of Ireland by the numbers . . . and it's ugly."

Atty automatically made tea. Making tea in hideaways was a

way of life returned. Once she could follow Long Dan Sweeney by his trail of dirty teacups.

"I have to know, Atty, if this decision comes from you and Theo alone or if it has the approval of the Brotherhood."

"I have been able to contact eight people, the highest-ranking survivors of the Rising, and the ones who will most likely make up at least part of the Supreme Council. It is as official as I can get."

"How did you put the proposition to them?"

"I didn't name Brodhead. I said we've a fair whack at an important British official. Yea or nay. The vote was ten to nothing, including Theo and myself."

"Caroline came to the Merrion Square townhouse last night, saw me for a few hours, and returned to Belfast after midnight. We went over it hard to make certain she was making the right decision. She's a contained woman, much like yourself, but, as the reality of Brodhead gets closer, the rage is unlike anything I've ever known before."

Rory paced, so much like Conor, clarifying his thoughts.

"From the moment of the Gallipoli Commission of Inquiry when she knew Brodhead was lying, she began to set out her snares. When he came to call on her after Gallipoli, she held him blameless, which took a bit of doing. Bit by bit she's been putting . . . shall I say *delicious* moves on him. The stars are lined up right. She's been a long-standing fantasy of his. His own marriage is a shipwreck."

"I can't believe that Brodhead isn't suspicious."

"Why? His past experience with women shows him using Asian girls as concubines, mistresses, or whores, sort of par for the course out in the colonies. I don't think he has any respect for women, thinks of them as inferiors, the same way he looks down on the Irish. Caroline would be the ultimate score of his life, his Holy Grail."

"You're talking from both sides of your mouth, Rory."

"Women have been trained objects. He is vain beyond vain. Enough for him to believe he is some kind of magnificent dashing figure. Caroline, on the other hand, is the unattainable woman. He's now vain enough to think he can win her. What I'm trying to say is that, in actual fact, he's naive about women, but he's never been in the ring with anyone even close to Caroline."

"And you think he'll rendezvous with her, unguarded?"

"He has to. If they're seen together by so much as a grocery store clerk or a maid or any of his own guards . . . his career goes up in smoke. So, if he *is* suspicious he simply won't show up. If he does show up, it will be by himself. Moreover, we can watch to see if he has been followed."

"Aye, aye, aye," Atty said. "Where do they meet?"

"An abandoned hunting lodge in the hills, deep in the Earldom. Years ago she changed it from a hunting lodge to her personal hideaway and studio."

Atty stiffened, realizing that Caroline had lured Conor there years before. Her cheeks reddened. Caroline had turned it into an exotic little playground . . . only for her husband and herself, Atty hoped.

"What about the gamekeeper?" she asked.

"She retired him a month ago. He and his wife are on an extended trip to America. I think she retired them the minute Brodhead lied to the Commission of Inquiry. Caroline has been planning this for a long time."

"Go on."

"Time is yet to be arranged. She gets there first and gets the fire going, carries an envelope of happy powder, lots of booze. Brodhead doesn't hold whiskey too well, he'd never make an Aussie."

"Or an Irishman."

"She's opting for a three-night party."

"If she plays around, he's going to get suspicious in a hurry."

"Atty, Caroline is going to romance him, take him to bed and make love to him and gain his confidence. Having completely relaxed him, she'll pick the right time."

"She will be the shooter?" Atty asked.

Rory nodded. "She's going to be the shooter."

Atty was struck by Caroline's daring and her sacrifice. "I'm deeply moved, Rory. The fact that she's willing to go to bed with that bastard."

"So am I," Rory said. "She's going to have him so tired, he won't have enough strength to spit."

"Well now, that's quite a woman," Atty said. "What about the weapon?"

"She's going to use a little double-barreled Italian Lenetti. Three inches long, fits in the palm of the hand. It holds two 44-caliber slugs with soft lead noses. We tested the pistol in her basement. At close range it could blow a hole in a cruiser."

"Backup weapon?" Atty asked.

"Kitchen knife."

"What about tire tracks?"

"Too much rain."

Atty became a little queasy but used her acting skills to display a professional manner. "We've a dead general," she went on, "in a remote hunting lodge and I hope no one in Ireland on his side has a clue where he went. Now what?"

"Caroline leaves the lodge, ties a ribbon on the gate to signal that the deed has been done. She returns to Hubble Manor in her car. Two of our lads, who have been waiting in a duck blind about five hundred yards from the house, see the ribbon, come in, remove the body and clean the place up, then put him in the trunk of his car and drive fifty, a hundred miles south and give him a cement suit, either at the bottom of a dry well or a lake. Car goes in the lake."

"Charming," Atty said. "What can go wrong?"

"Just about anything," Rory answered.

"And you'll be long out of Ireland, in England or Scotland."

"That's the idea," he said. "The plan is rough now, but you start hanging out at the Abbey Theatre. She attends every new play. Good contact point. The two of you are going to have to keep refining things."

"I am terrified that I'm going to end up liking her," Atty said.

"It's not hard to do. . . . Sorry, I meant nothing nasty," Rory said.

"Well, I am happy you'll be out of Ireland."

"Aye," he whispered, "so you'll not have me to contend with anymore?"

He had deliberately pushed the button.

"That's right," she said angrily.

"But when I'm gone, Atty, let me say you're going to be sorry as hell."

"You know, you're a real bastard. You know I'm afraid of you."

"Yeah, you're scared as hell you'd find me flying you to the moon."

"That's right," she said.

"So, have it your way," he said sliding the roof open.

"You'd love it my way, sonny boy," she retorted.

"And you mine, darlin'."

"I'll go up the ladder first so you won't have to worry about me looking up your leg."

"You know I'm in torment, Rory! What the hell are you trying to do to me! You're out of bounds!"

"Are you all that innocent, Atty? I know when I'm being worked." He set the ladder into place.

"Good luck, now," she gasped.

As he looked at her she backed away. "Do you want me to come to you, or not?" he demanded.

Atty was stopped by the wall, teary-eyed, wild-eyed. She was desperate for him! She wanted him to go!

"All right," Atty cried, ripping the top of her blouse open then pulling her straps and freeing her breasts. "You want to see them. Here, have a look, Rory boy. Come on, lad! Feel them! Put them in your mouth. I'll lie down for you!"

"God Almighty!" Rory cried. "What am I doing! Oh God, God, God, I'm so ashamed." He plunged to his knees with his face in his hands in an eruption of self-hatred. "I'm not fit to live ..." He pawed out with his good hand, keeping his face turned from her. "Please, cover yourself. Please, try to forgive me."

The river that had backed up against the dam now burst uncontrolled. He groveled and cursed himself. Rory felt something on his head. It was Atty's fingers softly running through his hair. "Can you hear me, Rory?"

"I'm so ashamed. It's the worst thing I've ever done in my life."

"Listen to me, Rory. We've been on a mad ride since the moment we laid eyes on each other. I was trying to re-create a moment of something dead and gone. And you, insanely, wanted something that belonged to Conor."

"Yes," he sobbed.

"You'll find love again and I'll find the comfort of a good man, but it can't be with each other."

"I know . . . I know . . . I'm so ashamed."

"Of what?"

"Of deliberately tormenting you. This lust was devouring me, Atty. Even when I first loved Georgia, I was a wild colonial boy looking for sport. Georgia and I found real love that grew by itself over time. But you, Atty Fitzpatrick! Bells, cannons went off, madness engulfed me. You're right, I wanted Conor Larkin's woman. I wanted to feel once what Conor felt. I've worshiped him. In death his power brought me halfway around the world. But can't you see, living under the shade of this enormous tree, I wanted to be as tall as himself for only a minute . . . and ended up covering myself with disgust."

"You're very much forgiven. And the truth is that you are very much like Conor."

"Atty! Why doesn't he let go of us!"

"Ah, don't you know? It isn't Conor afraid of letting us go. It's always been us, afraid of letting *him* go."

CHAPTER

86

Father Dary Larkin and Rachael Fitzpatrick walked a quay of the river Liffey as a priest would with a family member, envying the soldier boys and their girls, affectionately entangled.

They took a bench, probably not far from where Molly O'Rafferty had once bade farewell to Jeremy Hubble. They were still shattered that she had had an early miscarriage of their child.

Yet, it served to awaken them from their short, forbidden excursion into dream places. It was the medieval year of 1916 and they were now face to face with a firestorm of hard truths.

Truth was that Dary, in a moment of madness, grasped white hot iron and nearly burned himself up. He was again in the clutches of his vow, a vow as strong as Conor's had been to the Brotherhood. Rachael's tender years and his putting her on the edge of disaster drove home the impossibility of their situation.

"What did Bishop Mooney tell you?"

"He told me that there is no greater blood sport in Ireland, more vicious, than destroying a defrocked priest."

"It sounds like the same kind of intimidation you've had all your life, first from your mother, now from everyone else. Can't you see now how she passed her sexual agony on to you? Women are not images of the Virgin Mary," Rachael said softly.

"We've problems that won't be solved by telling the Church to go to hell," he said. "We're in love, Rachael, like Conor was in love with Shelley. Shelley knew Conor could not live outside Ireland, and I'm not certain I can or want to be a fleeing coward.

The price they paid is in my mind all the time, us being lepers, you being savaged."

"And can you go on serving a church that will bring something like that on us?"

"It's not only the Church, it's the nation. I'd be doing you the favor of your life if I give you up."

"Are you filled with guilt now?"

"No, but I'm so frustrated. All my days I've been stuffed, saturated with the sin of man and woman. I loved so many things the Church stood for. In our middling way, we provided some kind of faith for the Irish people so they wouldn't give up. Without us, Ireland would be a land of beaten curs. Rachael, I have believed with all my strength in the love of Jesus. Yet from the beginning, in seminary, the novices were stealing looks at girlie magazines we found hidden in the cells of the Christian Brothers. For some priests, chastity is a suitable way of life. So be it. But I've seen the best of our breed become drunks and worse . . . what has bloody torn me up is that a priest can be an alcoholic, he can play with little boys, but God forbid he touches a woman. That is our ultimate sin. And the bloody hypocrisy of the Church's covering it up and even turning on our victims.

"When you touched me, Rachael, it was the most powerful truth of my life. And the truth was, THEY HAVE LIED TO ME. It cannot be God's will that man be celibate. God tells me that you and I are right. The love of a man and a woman is the highest order of giving praise to God.

"Each probe to each question I ever made was met with dogma that I must accept without question. But God kept rattling me, telling me, 'Dary Larkin, they are perpetuating a lie.' They turned us into neuters so the Church would own us, body and soul, and we could not have families to share our lives because it would take time away from the Church.

"They have stolen God's most precious gift . . . you, Rachael . . . in order to keep me in total servitude. Well, seeing this for the lie it is . . . a lot of other things began to unravel in me. Still, I cannot come to terms that I've wasted my life. I cannot believe that my work as a priest has not made things better. I want to be a priest—but to be the best priest I can be, I need you as my wife. We can't bear another pregnancy, Rachael."

"What are you telling me, now?"

"You're young. In time you'll get over me. The other way out is a road not worth taking."

"Dary, you're lying to yourself. You've never given in to them, totally. You've had the scent of freedom and, with me or without me, you're going to have to stand up and face all their inquisitions and black magic and damnations and whatever else they throw at you. But don't do it for me. Do it for Dary Larkin. This is what has been dealt you. If you can't be the priest they want, then get out before they make you into a priest you'll hate. I'll take all the rotten garbage they'll throw at me, because I know what God means for us. Otherwise I want to walk in the sunlight with you. No more of the hiding and shame."

"Don't curse me as well, Rachael."

"Did you learn nothing from Conor and my mother? Or Conor with that Shelley girl? Don't you believe God smiled on them?"

"Then you'll wait for me?" Dary asked.

Rachael was her mother's girl. She knew instantly what he meant. But now, her fright was in common with every woman. She could not bring herself to ask the question.

He took her hands in daylight. "Look at me, Rachael, now there's my girl. I want to go to France because this is the best my church has to give. The trenches are filled with Irish lads who desperately need me. I'm not trying to play the Lord's game from both sides. I am not guilty about one minute with you. I know God approves of our love. Yet my own heart needs healing and I must earn my passage in the trenches."

"You're right, Dary. We need to stake our claim. It's pretty clear, isn't it? I'll be waiting."

"And when I come back, I'll take on anything they throw on us. I love you so, my Rachael."

"I take it you'll be leaving shortly?"

"I need no further training for my job except to harden up a little. I'm off to England and have been promised a newly formed Irish unit."

"When?"

"Three days."

"Oh, thank God. I was terrified you were going to leave right now."

"Saying good-bye to Rory was very hard. But I feel a contentment, a happiness in knowing that I'm a Larkin. I'm happy that we have already been united."

"Don't you think we ought to go to our room?"

"I was wondering about that. I'm worried about getting you pregnant again."

She leaned up and whispered into his ear. "Mom told me there are lots of ways we can do it without actual, well, you know, official fornication."

CHAPTER

87

August 1916

Roger Casement was an off-horse in the republican movement. His role in the Easter Rising, as his role in life, had been one of a loner.

Born to an Ulster Protestant family, this brilliant and compassionate soul joined the British Consular Service where he won international renown as a humanitarian and was ultimately knighted as a Commander of St. Michael and Knight of the Realm.

Casement's struggle was to break through bureaucratic bulwarks to expose conditions in the Belgian Congo Free State. Native workers on the rubber plantations were starved, killed, or had their ears cut off. Women and children were punished by amputation of their limbs.

Casement found more of the same in British-owned plantations in Brazil, where a common punishment was fire-branding the genital openings of both men and women.

Like many good Irish missionaries who went into places that only Irish missionaries would dare, Sir Roger finally wrecked his health and returned to Ireland and retired.

Having fought the cruel treatment of colonials all his career, he was inexorably drawn to protest the centuries of bondage of his own country. Casement joined a long list of Anglo-Protestants from Wolfe Tone to Charles Stewart Parnell who took up the cause of republicanism.

The Brotherhood took advantage of his years as a skilled diplomat and assigned him a number of overseas missions. As the time for the Rising drew near, Casement was dispatched to America to obtain Irish-American support and money. The mission was a failure.

He was then sent to Germany to obtain arms. The Germans had been supplying vast numbers of arms to the Ulster Volunteers before the war and at the same time, keeping an open line to the Brotherhood, their main purpose to embarrass the British.

To test the waters now, the German Staff came up with a clever plan. They had captured a few thousand Irishmen on the Western Front. Casement was given the offer to try to form an Irish Brigade for the German army from these prisoners.

Casement was only able to enlist fifty-two men to fight the British, and some of those were of questionable background.

The bloom was off the rose. Instead of the hundred thousand rifles that Casement insisted were necessary to support the Rising in the countryside, the Germans agreed to send one shipload of twenty thousand, just to keep their hand in.

These arms on the converted freighter *Aud* ended up at the bottom of Tralee Bay due to missed signals. Casement had been returned by submarine and was turned in to the Constabulary by an informer from the "Irish-German" volunteers.

As the Easter Rising was bombarded into submission, the countryside failed to join in. Sir Roger Casement was whisked away to London to be separated from the run-of-the-mill Catholic rebels. Here, indeed, the British had bagged the traitor's traitor, one of their own who could be tried in London and held aloft as a name to be reviled for all times.

He had been a man of six feet, greatly handsome, bearded and with extraordinary, seeking dark eyes. His imprisonment singled him out for humiliation. Without a belt and losing weight rapidly, keeping his pants up had become a major problem. Symbol of symbols, the Tower of London was his final internment place. No one could miss the point. What was left of Casement's health deteriorated rapidly.

The British added the acid of homophobia. Casement had lived quietly with his homosexuality, rendering harm to no one. Yet how lovely to be able to make a link to the case of another Irish homosexual, Oscar Wilde, who had been imprisoned after a withering prosecution by Edward Carson, the leader of the Ulster loyalists. Could not a case be drawn that Wilde and Casement were afflicted with the same diseased flaw in the Irish race?

Casement was refused a trial in his own country; he was denied access to bathing facilities, and his broken body became scaled with open sores. With his energy bled dry and in a deep depression, Casement yet managed to keep the great Irish weapon, *words*, and indeed, he had the last word.

Unlike the rebels of Dublin whose crimes were not clear and who were tried and killed in secret, Roger Casement had committed treason under British law. The showcase trial was staged to vindicate British justice.

Yet it was the words, piercing from the lips and pen of Roger Casement, that were to immortalize the affair and ring out to a world of small peoples who were listening intently.

> Loyalty is a sentiment, not a law. It rests on love, not on restraint. The governing of Ireland by England rests on restraint and not on love; and since it demands no love, it can evoke no loyalty.

The dead martyrs of Stonebraker's Yard in Kilmainham Prison reached out from their graves, crying out in concise measure that no other armies nor leaders of wars nor rebellions in all of England's history were taken out and executed.

> Judicial assassination is reserved only for only one race of the King's subjects, for Irishmen. . . .

The Irish legacy threading from generation to generation was not much more than the grace of words from the dock, and few were more profound than those of Sir Roger Casement.

In Ireland alone in this twentieth century is loyalty held to be a crime. If we are to be indicted as criminals, to be shot as murderers, to be imprisoned as convicts because our offense is that we love Ireland more than we value our lives, then I know not what virtue resides in any offer of self-government held out to brave men on such terms. . . .

Self-government is our right, a thing given to us at birth; a thing no more doled out to us or withheld from us by another people than the right to life itself. . . .

It is only from the convict these things are withheld for crimes committed or proven . . . *and Ireland*, that has wronged no man, that has injured no land, that has sought no domination over others . . . Ireland is treated today among the nations of the world as if it were a convicted criminal. . . .

If it be treason to fight against such an unnatural fate as this, then I am proud to be a rebel. . . .

Irishmen, who yesterday seemed content with the status quo, awakened these days to view their national personality that ranged from compliance to cowardice. The most legal of all the Easter Rising trials now clearly seemed the instrument of British revenge. But open public trials have their risks, and even in the end when he was sentenced to be executed by hanging, Casement was granted the "fair play" of the last word:

Let me pass from myself and my own fate to a far more pressing, as it is a far more urgent theme—not the fate of the individual Irishman who may have tried and failed, but the claims and the fate of the country that has *not* failed. Ireland has outlived the failure of all her hopes—and yet she still hopes. Ireland has seen her sons—aye, and her daughters, too—suffer from generation to generation always for the same cause, meeting always the same fate, and always at the hands of the same power; and always a fresh generation has come forward to withstand the same oppression. For if English authority be so omnipotent a power, as Mr. Gladstone phrased it, that reaches to the very ends of the earth—Irish hope exceeds the dimensions of that power, excels its authority and, with each generation, the claims of the last. The cause that begets this indomitable persistence, the faculty of preserving through centuries of misery the remembrance of lost liberty, this, surely, is the noblest cause men ever strove for, ever lived for, ever died for. If this be the cause I stand here today, indicted for the convicted and sustaining, then I stand in goodly company with a right to noble succession.

The British Cabinet floundered. If they could only convince Casement to say his real purpose in returning to Ireland was to stop the Rising, then they'd have an out to reducing the death sentence to a prison term without losing face. He wouldn't hear of it. Casement's compassion for humanity was what emerged from that courtroom, above the charges, above the sentence itself. The smears of his homosexuality were lost in the man's eloquence.

Casement smashed his glasses in his cell, cut his wrist, and tried to rub in a poison powder he had hidden in his jacket. He was found, rushed to the hospital, and saved for another day.

Sir Roger Casement was hanged at Pentonville Prison on August 3, 1916.

In Ireland there was a nationwide introspection and facing up to centuries of denial. In truth, as a people, they had not shown the stuff of free men. The moment had come in their history to redeem themselves as a people.

An answer had to be forthcoming quickly to the death of the Easter Rising martyrs.

88

Brisbane, Queensland, Australia

Squire Liam Larkin stepped outside the Prince of Wales Hotel facing the lush, semitropic, splendiferous greenery of Albert Park over the way.

Jaysus, he thought, the fecking heat here could fecking melt fecking rocks. To a man acclimatized by the all-pervading dampness of Ireland and even greater wetness of the South Island, Brisbane held the furnaces of hell. It was easy to envision exiled convicts busting rock in this place.

He made to the taxi rank and showed the driver a slip of paper.

"Eh, let's see here now, 32 Kangaroo Lane . . . 32 Kangaroo Lane." He scratched his jaw. "Aha, the new estate of houses near the Royal Australian Army Rehabilitation Center."

Liam chose to sit in the front, not particularly comfortable in the back seat of an automobile.

"Where you from, cobber?" the driver asked.

"New Zealand. South Islander."

"How 'as the war treated you?"

"Son in Gallipoli. He got out with some wounds."

"My lad is in the trenches in France," the driver said.

"I'll pray for him."

Over Victoria Bridge, the taxi made toward the sea and the budding Gold Coast.

All Anzac conversation these days got around to wondering

how they ever got caught up in such a war. When it had first begun, the enthusiasm was for King, Empire, and all that was bombastic. Gallipoli had tarnished all visions of glory. The long haul was agonizing.

A large sign designated the hospital. It was a hot and sunny day. One could smell the ocean close by. A huge lawn was filled with patients mostly in pajamas or robes, many in wheelchairs, being tended by nurses and orderlies, others on crutches with missing limbs.

"These are the worst cases," the taxi driver said, "the ones they couldn't recycle back to combat in France."

Liam asked the driver to slow down, as though he were expecting to find Rory among them. All those lads like that . . . hard go . . . terrible.

They turned off into a cozy street of palm trees and wooden two-story homes where many of the staff were housed.

"Here we are, cobber, 32 Kangaroo Lane. Would you like me to wait for you?"

Liam pondered. "I don't know," he said.

"Well, there's a taxi rank at the main entrance to the hospital. The number is 2-2-2-2."

"I think I can remember that."

"Good luck to you, Kiwi."

The taxi drove off. Liam felt parched and sweaty and a little shaky. He knocked on the door. No reply. He spotted an outside garden spigot, drank, and splashed his face. A porch swing in the shade lured him and he eased into it and set it into motion, soon picking up the sound of the swish-boom of the surf and letting his face go blank. He sat stone-still, like a shepherd, until the heels of a woman's shoe tapped out a rhythm in quick step down the lane.

Liam, immobile, latched on to Georgia Norman as she came into view. She was pretty enough but her movement and pride of gender in her walk said *woman*.

Georgia came on the porch, made for the front door, dove into her bottomless purse as women are apt to do, then sensed another being there and looked over to Liam.

She was startled, but wordless.

"I'm here in peace," Liam said softly.

"Rory!" she cried, "Rory!"

Georgia came close to fainting, grabbing the porch post and starting to slip when Liam steadied her and led her to a wicker chair.

"Is he all right?"

"He was wounded at Gallipoli. I don't have too much information. Some loss of use in his right hand and a clouded vision that comes and goes."

She thanked God several times as a bit of color returned to her cheeks.

"He's in Ireland and under his enlistment name, so contact isn't too easy. He's a captain, you know, won the Victoria Cross."

Georgia bit her lip, then used Liam's shoulder for a short, sweet sob. "I'll get you a cool drink," she said quickly. "Hard or soft?"

"A beer would be the end of the earth."

She returned. "No need to ask how you ran me down?" she asked.

"I'm a sheepman. I've a lot of experience in finding stray lambs, although you did give me quite a runaround."

"Actually this rehabilitation center was on the planning boards before the war started," she said. "Even back in New Zealand I felt I'd be coming here once my husband left. I'm the Head Matron of one of the departments. I deal with the shell-shocked lads."

"Oh God," Liam whispered. "Where do you find the strength?"

"Don't make me cry again, Liam. It's hard enough in there."

"Rory always wrote to his mother and brother and sisters until he left Gallipoli. After that, only a few letters, written by nurse's aides. I always knew he'd find his way to Ireland so I wrote to my brother, Father Dary—he's a priest."

"I know."

"I wrote it months ago. I wanted it waiting when Rory got

there. I couldn't live any longer with what I'd done to him. He got the letter," Liam said shakily, "and he wrote me back."

"What did he say?"

"He forgave me. And don't you know he asked me to forgive him as well."

"I'm so glad."

"Thank God he misses New Zealand. He's coming back one of these days. We're going to make it now. . . ."

"You've suffered, haven't you, man?" she asked.

"Aye. Rory asked one favor, to find you. He met your husband on Gallipoli and holds him in great esteem. He also knows that the two of you were divorced long before the war and only stayed together for the sake of his career."

"Calvin has a good wife and a chance for recovery, although he still occasionally plunges into despair."

"Father Dary wrote me how great Rory thought he was. Georgia, Rory pleaded with you from Gallipoli. He said he knew why you sent him off empty, so as not to saddle him with something he'd be sorry for after the war. He loves you more than ever, lass, like it would take half of forever to get over you. . . ."

"Rory was equally unfair," Georgia said. "We both knew he'd get mixed up in Ireland. He had every right to ask me to wait till the end of the war. He had no right to ask me to wait forever, without contact, only to wake up one morning and get a letter from Father Dary saying he'd been shot by a firing squad or hanged. So, I made the break clean for both of us, he not burdened by me and me the same."

"But you are burdened by him," Liam said. "You bore his child. I want to see my granddaughter."

Georgia walked away.

"I want to see my granddaughter," he repeated. He handed her his great handkerchief to dry and blow, dry and blow. "You loved him that much."

"Ah Squire, don't you know that after Rory Larkin gets his hands on you, you're not much good for anyone else. It started as a lark, but by the time he went off to war I knew there'd never

be the likes of him again, and I had to have something of his, forever."

"You love him that much," Liam repeated.

"Wars and deaths and boys enlisting under false names and
divorced husbands who may or may not be divorced, you can be
certain that the record offices are in a shambles, so many dead,
so many unidentified. So, coming to Brisbane as a pregnant war
widow was no trick at all. I'm entirely accepted here, and as for
our child, it was the most beautiful decision of my life."

Liam caught sight of a pram being rolled up Kangaroo Lane
by a nanny, with a wee head sprouting over the top. Liam stumbled off the porch. He picked up the wane with a tenderness
sometimes needed in his profession, like holding a stray lamb.

"Her grandda," Georgia said to the nanny.

"What did you name her, now?" Liam asked.

"Rory," Georgia said.

"Rory? But that's a boy's name."

"Not anymore, Squire. The boys will have to share it."

"Well, come to think of it, Rory O'Moore was a great Celtic
King. The Chieftain of the Chiefs. Rory. That's grand . . . Rory."
He edged his cheek to his granddaughter's cheek as he held off
the tears. The wee lass approved of him, and he breathed air
from a sweet-scented place beyond all altars, all sky, beyond all
mortal pleasure.

CHAPTER

89

Sir Llewelyn checked the gear in at the rear of the utility lorry used for hauling and odd jobs at Brodhead Abbey. Fishing poles, boots, creel, fishing box, extra flies, lantern, stove, etcetera, etcetera, etcetera.

"Everything appears to be here," he said to his caretaker, Mr. Mufflin.

"My missus packed the refreshments in this case."

"Jolly good."

"In the event of an emergency, may I say where the General has gone?"

Sir Llewelyn thought about it. Part of the game was taking the small risk that an emergency doesn't come up. "Actually I'm driving south near Carrick-on-Shannon," he said giving the opposite direction of where he was going. "I've a retired pal with a very secluded cabin—and Mufflin, I'm in desperate need of absolute quiet."

"I quite understand, sir."

"Brigadier Cushman has things well in hand at Dublin Castle. If someone calls, Mr. Mufflin, I will be here at Brodhead Abbey Sunday late afternoon and will be at Dublin Castle for Monday parade. Now crank me up."

The van engine clug-clugged alive and in a moment he drove through the gates of Brodhead Abbey on down to the main road, where he turned north for the short trip up Inishowen Peninsula.

An hour later Brodhead turned onto a dirt road before

Carrowkeel, satisfied he had not been spotted or followed wearing fishing clothing in an old utility lorry. He came to a halt before the pillars of the big iron north gate of the Earldom of Foyle.

As he emerged from the vehicle, Sir Llewelyn stiffened himself for the possibility of rejection, walking gingerly to the gate. Cheers! The lock was open and the chain down.

He shut the gate behind him and drove with the daylight to make it in before it grew dark, his mind now opened to a delirium of flesh-borne illusions. He pressed the throttle down, glimpsing occasionally about and behind him to see if anyone else were around. Clear, all clear. Clear sailing. There? The hillock and stand of birches. Yes! Yes! There was her automobile.

Brodhead parked next to her vehicle, just as the sun dipped behind the hill shading the surroundings. He walked briskly up the path still scanning for the unwelcome watcher.

"Hello!"

By George! There she was, waving and coming to him at a run. Powerful sighs of relief as they embraced hard. The magnificent smell of the peat smoke wisped to them as they made up the pathway, arms about the other's waists.

Inside the main lodge room he set down his kit and they embraced and kissed. "I was beginning to get into a snit," she said, "I was afraid you'd decided not to come."

As she left to make herself comfortable, his eyes played over the rafters, he quickly opened and shut closet doors, poked back curtains, and otherwise looked for any sign of another person. There had been no shoe tracks on the path outside, and thus far, the place seemed alone to the two of them.

She came out as sheer and open as could be considered decent and seemed totally comfortable in a dressing gown that fell to and fro, just so.

Brodhead had peeked at some of her famous nudes at Rathweed Hall, although they were now out of public eye.

Brodhead wrestled with the top of a champagne bottle, and

its blast spilled on him. Caroline assured him there was plenty
more and suggested he, too, make himself comfortable. He
returned in a silk brocade bathrobe of Asian design. Between
mentally undressing her and continuing his suspicions, his
unease became apparent.

"How did you manage to get all the supplies in?" he asked.

"There's a large-wheeled pushcart in the barn for just that
purpose."

"Of course, how stupid of me."

"I don't blame you for being suspicious—" she began.

"Blast," he interrupted. "This is all a bit new to me. It doesn't
feel quite natural without a platoon of guards."

"I quite understand. Cheers, this will help settle things."

About three-quarters through the bottle, a second one was
uncorked and Llewelyn promenaded before the fire, hands
clasped behind him, up on his toes, down and up on his toes
again. On the sofa nearby, Caroline played her cleavage and
bared leg to perfection and his attention became riveted.

If there was one thing Caroline Hubble was the master of, it
was making her company feel at home. Comfortable he became.
Two and a half decades of wondering about her would soon be
realized.

The meal was exquisite.

He made a grope or two and she countered with an ethereal
quality to touch in a way that he never had felt before or knew
existed.

"I'm a dullard, Caroline, a bit unsure of myself."

"You won't be when we're through, General, we're on my
battlefield now," she said, "and stopping time slowly is what
we're going to do."

"Woman, you are magnificent. Why me, or is that not to
ask?"

"It wouldn't have been proper of me to let my years of affection be known to you. I've always been amazed by your
strength and single purpose, and you're straightforward, as a
British officer should be. I've always loved those things about
you. Alas, dear Roger, along with his decent side, was a very

devious human being. And alas, Gorman is certainly not all that much of a man beside you."

"Why do you keep him around?"

"There aren't many men I care to be with. And those I might want, I can't have. Gorman is soft and entertaining, knows a lot of mutual jolly people."

"I want to do this job here in Ireland with such finality, the War Council must give me a command in France," he said suddenly. "I am going to return a field marshal." He caught his breath. "I want to be able to come to you on an equal basis, and as the strongest and most gallant man you've ever met."

"Maybe I can help, quietly, of course."

"Would you?"

"Llewelyn, what do you want me to say? I don't give myself easily. I am very taken by the thought of the power we could share."

"May I sit beside you, Caroline?"

"First, pour us a little Irish, something with a bit more snap to it."

Much of her lovemaking with Roger depended on her ability to fantasize, mostly to herself. Toward the end of their relationship, she found him disgusting but played a role of feigning enjoyment. Can't take that away from a man. It is his basis of existence. Brodhead believed his uniform was the basis of his existence. Nonsense, he was no different. All of them were the same . . . except . . . Conor Larkin.

The slug of Irish whiskey helped a bit. Her revulsion toward Llewelyn Brodhead turned to hatred. You son of a bitch, she said to herself as she smiled and looked lovingly, while he reached inside her robe and grabbed a breast.

She slowed him down with sweet kisses and whispers and he was awed into understanding that the game had a rhythm. Thank God, Caroline knew what was on his platter soon. The thought of it allowed her to translate his nauseating touches into an ecstasy. She ran her fingers through his hair and repeated, "Slowly, darling, softly," as his lips searched her neck and shoulders like a hungry hyena.

Another grand jolt of Irish whiskey. Rory was right. Sir Llewelyn could not hold his booze. It was difficult to keep him in a gentle manner when his basic existence was heading for explosion.

Better not let him make a mistake now, she thought. It would probably humiliate him into impotence. Lovely thought, but she had to play the game this night to the letter . . . and she played him like a Stradivarius, quitting at just the proper instant.

"If you'll excuse me for a moment, my darling," he said, breaking and calling on himself not to muck it up in front of her.

"Why don't you slip under the sheets," she said. "I'll bring the refreshments in."

Sir Llewelyn's relief came just as he closed the bathroom door behind him. He gasped, arrayed himself, now dizzy with expectation and a lot more controlled.

He got into the bed. There was a fire and uh . . . well . . . mirrors about and the place was filled with incense and there she came. . . .

He sat up, his eyes nearly flying off his face as she slowly disrobed at the foot of the bed. All that could be heard was the heaviness of his breathing.

"Hello, there," she said, coming over the bed to him.

The rest of it was like a magnificent cavalry charge in slow motion . . . her words always reassuring as her hands played Chopin and Mozart over his body, including a theme or two from *The Magic Flute*. Distrust was gone now.

Caroline mastered him, bringing him alive, over and again until his collapse made him nigh onto immovable.

"Where are you going?" he rasped.

"A lady has to do her thing," she said. "I won't be long, darling, and darling, you are beyond wonderful. . . ."

The pistol was in her purse, in a hidden compartment. Over there, by the dresser. Now? Think, Caroline. Don't take him too lightly. He is a trained beast. Too easy to foul up now. She was queasy and felt ravaged . . . violated . . . but to keep her head, that's what counted.

She got from the bedroom into a tub that had been heating

and poured in a few buckets of water to get it right, then immersed herself and let the water's curative powers take over. From there she went to the rear porch and vomited over the railing, then under an icy shower.

She made just enough noise closing the bedroom door to find out his state. Sure enough, the bastard was not full asleep. She cuddled up alongside him and kissed him and played with him until he groaned himself asleep. Not tonight, Caroline, not tonight. Each time she turned, he seemed alert to awaken, as though he were a wolf sleeping with one eye open. Play it smart, Caroline, play it smart.

The smell of bacon drifted into the bedroom. Llewelyn popped an eye open, remembered, and groaned with a sudden, new happiness.

"There's my warrior."

He lifted his head off the pillow . . . slowly. Caroline, looking fresh as the morning smiled in the doorway and entered with a tray in her hands, set it on the nightstand and sat beside him. He made it to a sitting position and she kissed him.

"Caroline," he whispered.

"Here," she said, handing him the tumbler with cognac and bitters. "Take this for the tummy wobbles."

He emoted an "Ahhh," then she handed him the second glass, "A little hair that bit the dog," and she cuddled up next to him.

"Gin and tonic. Oh my. Good thing we don't have a twenty-mile forced march today." He held her strongly with one hand and held the glass with the other. "Caroline, was I, you know, all right?"

"You don't have to worry about a thing, Llewelyn," she said.

"I've never had an experience approaching this," he said.

"You're quite a man," she whispered, and touched him to see if things were alive and well. They were. "I'd like to slip into the sheets with you, but I think I'd better attend to the kitchen."

"Do I have time to shower and shave?"

"Yes," she said, "I lit the boiler. There should be plenty of hot water. Take your time, darling."

As she stood, he took her hand, and his eyes misted up. He kissed her fingers. "Can we become lovers?" he asked.

"I've been thinking about it," she said. "If you get out of Ireland and back to England, there's a lot more maneuvering room."

He watched her leave, a smitten man. Getting his legs under him took a bit of doing. He laughed and in a state of euphoria gloried in a singing shower, then lathered up to shave admiring the good-looking, virile chap in the mirror. He sipped his gin and tonic and groped around for a cigarette.

He found his smokes in the bedroom. Damned. No matches. Caroline's purse. He called but caught a glimpse of her standing outside getting a breath of air.

Oh, what the devil. The purse was double normal size and he fished about, running his fingers over the bottom. As though magnetized, his hand felt something hard through the cloth. He traced it with his fingers.

Brodhead quickly closed the door and dumped the contents of the purse on the bed. The hard object was still there but not to be seen. He turned the purse over, studying its stiff bottom. There, a secret compartment.

Llewelyn quickly solved its riddle and stared at the Lenetti pistol.

"Well, it's certainly good for one's appetite," he said, devouring a hunter's breakfast.

"Beautiful day out," she said.

"Well then, maybe we can take a little stroll?"

"I don't want to get you too tired, too early," she replied. "Ready for tea?"

"Yes, thank you." He topped his breakfast with a pastry and a second cup. "You know, Caroline," he said, rapping his fist impatiently on the table. "When we sadly have to part, I'm having it out with London. I say we resume the executions of the Easter Rising people. What do you think?"

"Oh, I think we'd better make a rule about politics."

"In our class, isn't it rather traditional to share a similar view?" he said.

"Freddie and Roger got along quite well with our differences."

"So you think we should stop it."

"It's not making us look very good to the rest of the world, in that we've stated some very noble purposes for being in this war," she said.

"To hell with what the world thinks! Did we care about world opinion when we went into India . . . or South Africa? Now the Turks, my late honorable enemy, there's a crowd who knows how to keep traitors in their place. Armenia sided with Russia against the Turks, and by God, they've lived to regret it."

Caroline was confused at his sudden turn. Word was just filtering out that the Turks had all but razed Armenia to the ground, killed all men of fighting age, and took old people, women, and children onto a death march all the way to Syria, guarded by the Turkish Kurds.

"The rumors of the death march are true?" she asked.

"Indeed. Those who survived the hunger, heat, rape, and beatings and got there alive were sent into huge caves in the mountainsides, hundreds of thousands of them, and the Turks sealed the openings."

"Llewelyn, what has gotten you so irritated?"

"Traitors," he answered. "Let me tell you something, Caroline. In Gallipoli, when I ordered the Australian Brigades over the Nek and the slaughter started, I had but one regret. I regretted that it was not Irish troops I was sending over. We'd have that fewer to contend with after the war."

"That's ghastly."

"That's how to put traitors down, and I daresay the world won't give a piss in hell what the Turks are doing to the Armenians. Of course, we British are a bit too civilized for that, aren't we?"

"Were we all that much better during the great famine!" she snapped. Your lousy crowd, she thought, had better get used to people winning their freedom. That's what this country is going to be all about.

She stood up and started clearing the table testily.

He reached in his jacket pocket and tossed the pistol and its six rounds on the table.

"Sit down! Over there!" he commanded.

As she attempted to speak he repeated the command with a raging voice.

Caroline sank into the sofa while he took up a chair opposite her. He had a small revolver trained on her.

"Don't move a hair. I'm a crack shot with this."

"It would have been very much nicer if you simply inquired about the pistol. I've carried it for personal protection for twenty-five years. Roger gave it to me."

"Six rounds of ammunition for two round chambers . . . hidden in a secret pocket . . . you see," he said, breaking into a sob but still holding the weapon at her. "I thought last night was real! You were toying with me all the time! You're a dirty Irish traitor! You're a whore! You are no better than those wanton Eurasian sluts!" He snarled and wheezed, the sweat near boiling from the red anger of his face. "You know who has her lover boy in London! I'll tell you. Your whore slut sister, Lady Beatrice . . . and I thought . . . I had . . . the one woman in the world . . . who was not a pig. All right, pig! Dance for me . . . I mean dance for me! Now!"

"Sorry, General, I will not dance for you."

"Well, we'll see. We'll see how close I can come to that lovely face of yours, before I blow it to pieces. You'll notice my pistol is also what a lady would carry. I'll put it in your hand after I split your head in half. When they find you . . . simple case of suicide . . . mother's grief . . . "

"Brodhead!" a man's voice boomed out.

The shock diverted him with its roaring suddenness. He turned about, looking, and in that instant Caroline was able to duck behind the stone fireplace.

Three shots boomed out from the direction of the staircase to the balcony. Brodhead fired back at a figure moving down the stairs. Rory was hit and tumbled down to the bottom of the steps.

Brodhead staggered up from his chair, screamed, then slipped to the floor, his pistol sliding out of reach and blood gushing from his chest.

Caroline came into the center of the room. Brodhead reached for his pistol. Caroline quickly picked up Rory's and aimed. Her hand was solid as steel. As Brodhead's fingers touched his pistol, Caroline fired, and she was dead true.

"Rory! Rory!"

He propped his back against the steps. "Listen up—no time for panic or discussions . . . ask only easy questions . . . move quickly . . . "

"Hit? Where?"

"Shoulder . . . neck . . . see if bullet passed through . . . "

She leaned him forward, ripped his shirt open, and felt his back. Blood and a hole. "Yes, it went through. There's blood on your back."

"He dead?"

"Very."

"Get his pistol."

He examined it and nodded. "Good. Small caliber. He meant to do your face in up close. . . . Vodka . . . poteen . . . "

"I've got it."

Rory pointed to his own mouth and she fed him several large gulps. "Give me something to bite on . . . then pour vodka in wound. . . ."

Caroline grabbed a towel, folded it, and slipped a corner of it into his mouth. He nodded and clamped down. In went the vodka. Rory bordered on fainting . . . his eyes rolled back, but he brought himself to bite down one more time. Caroline filled a second towel with the remains of the vodka and sponged his face and tears and snot.

"Ice?" he groaned.

"Yes, there was some in the ice shed. I brought it in last night."

"Pillow case, fill in ice . . . front . . . back . . . then wrap it on . . . immobilized arm."

"Iodine first?"

"No . . . vodka is fine . . . bullet probably cauterized wound."

Rory drank in great deep gulps while she quickly cut up sheets, packed the ice, and with his directions bandaged his arm against his body.

"Tighter . . . more booze . . . drink . . . watch bleeding . . . "

Calm, thank God. The blood color of the wound was lightening. Good.

"Are you going to go into shock?"

"Fuck no!"

"Oh, my baby, my baby," she let herself go, "make it for me, baby."

"Aye . . . do my best . . . the plan is fucked . . . we have to think smart."

"The pain?"

"Bad . . . upstairs . . . balcony . . . medical kit . . . morphine."

As Caroline found it she looked up to the rafter and saw where he had been hiding. God only knows, he might have been there for days.

"Easy on the morphine . . . about third of syringe . . . don't want to go under . . . "

In good time the morphine took hold, and although woozy, he was comfortable. The bleeding slowed further. Shoulder blade, collarbone, dislocated? Jesus, what?

"I can talk better."

"How long have you been hiding up there?"

"When I left you in Belfast, I reported to a hospital and private doctor in Scotland, then doubled back to Ireland. Almost four days in that crawlspace."

"Oh my darling!" Caroline cried, holding his head to her. "I love you so, Rory. The moment you walked in my house and told me I'd find a path to take to make life worth living, I was already walking on it. You are my path to life, Rory. I asked God . . . I asked God . . . if it were wrong of me to start feeling alive again, as though my sons were still living through you . . . as though Conor Larkin were still alive."

"I love you that way, too, Caroline."

"It can't be wrong then. I see Chris coming down off his high horse and Jeremy rising to manhood, and you are the two

of them wrapped into one. Are you going to make me a grandmother, are you?" and she wept unabashedly. "You might have
gotten killed too."

"No way I was going to leave you alone. You hurting over
last night?"

"It's all right," she whispered. "It was the right way to go
about it and the right thing to do."

"Dry your tears, huh ... and let's figure a way out of this
mess ... let's see if I can stand."

He fought to his feet then sank to his knees again. "Can you
drive the car in?"

"No, the path is too narrow. I've a large-wheeled pushcart."

"I'm too heavy for you to handle, darling. Here's what we'll
do. You pack and clear out and tie the ribbon on the gate. When
you're clear, there's a pair of Brotherhood lads in the duck blind
nearby. They'll see the ribbon and come and tidy up, deal with
me, and remove the body."

"I'm not leaving you," she said.

"They'll see your face."

"I'm not leaving you," she repeated.

"I think it's quite safe. Only other men I saw in Ballyutogue
were these two, Boyd McCracken and his son, Barry. Boyd was
with Conor at Lettershambo."

"I trust them," she said without hesitation.

"Then get them in here."

In ten minutes Boyd and Barry were in the lodge and sized
up the situation. Rory was made comfortable on a makeshift bed
on the rear seat. Every constable and soldier knew Countess
Hubble and would pass her through automatically.

Caroline hugged Boyd and his son with compassion and
affection they would remember all their days. They started her
car and moved back to the lodge to clean things up and remove
Brodhead's body.

"Here's what we do," Rory said. "Full syringe of morphine.
Every twenty minutes stop and see if my pulse and heart are
steady. If I begin to lose pulse, there's a couple vials of smelling
salts to pick up the old heartbeat. . . . Use back roads around

Derry to clear it . . . then find a telephone . . . Atty is waiting in a
safe house in Belfast. . . . She's to give you the name of a safe
doctor as soon past Derry as possible. I can't make it all the way
to Belfast."

She gave him the shot, tucked him in, and kissed his cheek.
As his eyes fluttered shut she said, "Don't worry, son, I'll bring
you through."

CHAPTER 90

"My dear, dear, dear Caroline," Churchill said, leaping from behind his desk, holding her hand and kissing it. He took a look at her from arm's length and his eyes misted up. "It's been so long since you were in London. How is Sir Frederick?"

"About the same. Unfortunately he is a cat who has used up eight and a half of his lives. You, dear Winston, are only making your third comeback."

"Minister for Munitions isn't exactly First Lord of the Admiralty, but I feel I have a use and even perhaps a future."

"And I predict that your future will make your failures very small potatoes."

"Dear Caroline, loyal comrade. Your affection and support have been a pillar of my strength. You know, I still feel faulty in your presence."

"Quite honestly, Clementine has told me how you have suffered over our losses at Gallipoli."

"She shouldn't have. I don't believe in public displays of grief."

"You have suffered," she said.

"I'm doing my all to mold my agony into a determination to make something of my life that will make those wrongs palatable. I cannot still my prodigious will to be a leader. I may not be able to come to peace with the reality that my hold over the life and death of others must always be a part of it."

When they were seated, Winston saw that Caroline bore her

look of unusual power that spelled a conversation demanding absolute candor.

"We are going to have to talk about Gallipoli and some other unpleasant matters, and I am going to do most of the talking."

"In that case, I'll do most of the listening," he said.

"I have analyzed the Commission of Inquiry reports and your own testimony, syllable by syllable. You were the chief architect of a blunder. We need not go over what was wrong. The bottom line was that even if we had the Greek and Italian armies, the success of the venture would still have been very much in question."

His eyes chilled on her.

"I adore you for accepting the role of scapegoat with grace and dignity. You have never pointed the finger at anyone else. You have heard lies and cover-ups of the generals and admirals and kept your silence. You alone, Winston, have been humiliated. Most of it was due to the incompetent generalship of men you had no power to control. You had the War Council and the nation behind you in the beginning. They all deserted when things went wrong. I know you've suffered for me and my loss. I like your stuff, Winston."

"I am most humbled by your words, Caroline."

"I am aware that Asquith is quietly bringing you in as a consultant to him on the Irish situation."

"You know correctly, as usual."

"May I speak to you from here on out as an Irishwoman."

Winston Churchill was stunned.

"The executions in Dublin are fast becoming one of the great political blunders in the history of the British nation. It has fingered England for acts of terror and injustice. This blunder has ennobled the Irish cause and through it you have done what the Irish were incapable of doing by themselves. You have united them."

Well, that was the damned truth if it was ever spoken.

"Anglos always loved it in Ireland, but now, man, you're going to get voted out."

Churchill drew on the comfort of a cigar, but her eyes went right through the smoke.

"Casement, though legally tried and executed, was the worst miscarriage of justice in our times. By hanging a great humanitarian, you not only spat on the Irish people, but you have told future generations they have no legitimate aspirations. You have said, as never before, 'We British think you Irish are pigs.'"

He started to speak out, but she banged her fist on the desk, un-Caroline-like.

"You have a problem," she continued. "In two years the Irish people will vote in a party to recognize the provisional government of the Easter Rising and pull out of the British Parliament. You have two thousand Irish prisoners of war in Fronach in Wales. You have eighty people under death penalty who say they are Irish citizens and not British. Well, what will you give them, Winston? The right to become British again?"

"When we do have women's suffrage and you win your seat in Westminster, Caroline, I suggest you will be the most troublesome backbencher in our history."

"You're frightened half to death to have the Irish at the peace table because when they win a measure of freedom, it will go off like a chain reaction throughout the Empire."

Churchill's affectionate regard for this woman was equal to his respect for her as a skilled adversary.

"I have heard very little from you that I would disagree with. Of course, I'd only agree in private. I'd deny it in public," he said.

"Asquith wants the Irish on the back burner until he gets his peace treaty. Then you can deal with the colony. You know that once you get them at the conference table, you'll negotiate them out of their socks and underwear."

"Well, thank God I won't have you to face across the table, Madam Countess."

"In Ulster we'll end up being British. The rest of Ireland will become something like the Belgian Congo Free State."

"Not all that bad, Caroline. You have very well established your foundation for something. Now, what is it?"

"Knowing that some measure of Irish freedom is inevitable, why the hell did you and Asquith send Llewelyn Brodhead over with a scorched earth policy?"

"The Easter Rising was a bolt from the blue. We knew we had to clamp a lid on until we were ready. We feel now that Brodhead was the wrong man to send, but once sent, it would be too much of a loss of face to recall him. Speaking of the devil, he hasn't reported to the Castle for several days. He's overdue from a fishing retreat."

Caroline had won stage one.

"Brodhead or no, there will be no more executions at this time."

"Brodhead blundered at Gallipoli, at the Nek, and Chunuk Bair," Caroline said suddenly and bluntly.

Winston, thrown totally off balance, reddened.

"My sons' deaths were a direct result of his incompetence and sheer panic—right or wrong, Winston?"

"For God's sake, Caroline!"

"You owe me two, said Aladdin to the genie, yes or no? You owe me two, and I'm collecting if either one of us is ever to have a decent night's sleep again."

"Llewelyn Brodhead lied at the inquiry. The Nek was butchery. He should have evacuated Chunuk Bair seven hours earlier and he would not have evacuated at all if Colonel Malone had not disobeyed orders. Anything else before I am granted my leave?" he asked.

"We're about halfway there, Winston."

"What is your point! I demand to know your point!"

"Brodhead mutinied on the eve of war, threatening the Crown with losing half its officer corps. He helped us win world denunciation in the Boer War. How would you rate him as a British general?"

"I shall not now or ever denounce the magnificent role England has played in world civilization. This little people of ours has been the light of mankind for centuries, opening a world to trade, to the instillation of a culture and system of justice and government second to none. We have done for the world many times over what the world has not been able to do for itself. When one is burdened with such an enterprise, mistakes are made. In the producing of men to hold and enshrine our noble works, yes, there are going to be foul mutations. The system is so large and so powerful, incapable men suddenly find themselves in mighty positions because of war. Llewelyn Brodhead is a beastly mistake."

"And you shouldn't have sent him to Ireland?"

"No."

"And you can't recall him."

"No."

'You still owe me one, Winston. Yes or no?"

"Caroline . . . "

"*You owe me one.* Yes or no?"

She was tenacious and had him boxed in, cleverly. He dreaded what that debt was going to be.

"I owe you one," he said, "but I am not certain if I am prepared to pay the debt off now."

"Are we sworn to secrecy?" she asked.

"Of course."

"I killed Llewelyn Brodhead."

No further conversation was possible until a bit of whiskey opened the passages.

"I lured him to his death in the most ancient of ways and I shot him. My confederates removed his body and dispensed with it and his vehicle in such a manner he may never be found."

"Your confederates?"

"The Irish Republican Brotherhood. Well, Winston, is it the Tower of London or are you going to pay me the one you owe me?"

"This is dreadful!"

"Let me put it this way, Winston. I am at peace with the assurance that God will dispense me better justice than England has the Irish. Llewelyn Brodhead was going to make a Gallipoli out of Ireland."

This was a battlefield kind of decision he was required to make, a fast and smart one. England would be shaken, half to the ground, over a scandal like this. The well of sympathy for Caroline Hubble could conquer the bloody world! Mere word of the assassination would create the kind of furor that would bring Ireland to the peace table.

But what of the other parts of it? Is it a greater evil to destroy a known evil? Oh my dear Winston . . . he told himself . . . how many foul deeds had he buried for the sake of England? He, himself, had ordered assassinations. That, too, was part of the business of running a government. Just another secret in a lifetime that would gather many more.

And the final part of it. He had adored this woman since childhood. She was worth a hundred Llewelyn Brodheads. She had to do this to stop her own dark and depressed descent to death. Maybe, just maybe, he too would lose his own nightmares of Gallipoli.

"I am prepared to settle our account," he said.

"No one knows that I have contacted you on this. It is our secret to the death."

He nodded.

"I blundered my assassination attempt, wounding him badly. He still had enough left to come after me with his pistol. A young British officer, secretly in the Brotherhood, saved my life and in doing so was grievously wounded."

"Please go on."

"This young man, Lieutenant Landers, was one of the heroes of Gallipoli. He and Jeremy were like brothers. He won the Victoria Cross."

"I know who Captain Landers is," Churchill said.

"Give me his life."

Winston stood and a lot ran through him. "I owe Landers as well," he whispered. "What must I do?"

"He's in a safe house in Belfast. As you are aware, ships are now able to travel to New Zealand unescorted and without convoys. Several regular troopships have been partly converted to hold a hospital facility."

Oh, this woman, this glorious woman. She was playing like a chess master now.

"So, we'll put him aboard in a hospital cabin," Winston said.

"First things first," she answered. "There are tens of thousands of records of killed in action, missing, prisoners that are in turmoil, unaccounted for, a general mess . . . right?"

"Right, as usual."

"Find the records of Lieutenant Rory Landers, New Zealand. He enlisted under that name. Make a final entry in the Landers record that he died aboard ship en route to New Zealand after emergency surgery and was buried at sea with full honors."

Winston understood perfectly.

"But before you do, make a duplicate of the Landers record, only the party's name will be Rory Larkin. His record should be changed to read that he was evacuated from Gallipoli and taken to the base hospital in Alexandria where he spent several months; was sent back to New Zealand and discharged."

"So, Landers is dead."

"And Rory Larkin was never in England or Ireland."

Damned shame, he thought, that he didn't have her planning some of the campaigns. "You are entirely correct, Caroline. Thousands of war records will never be unscrambled. As long as I am engaging in something disgraceful, I'm glad it's for you."

"Us," she said.

"Yes, us. Tell me, Caroline, is he one of *those* Larkins?"

"Yes."

"I take it he's a good chap."

"Aye, mon, that he is."

Weather seems to be the one thing everyone has in common everywhere in the world, hot or cold, good or bad, wet or dry, it comes up first thing every morning and is our last worry at night.

In the South Island we get a pot full of rain so that sunny days ... or hours ... are revered like a blessing from a saint, although I don't know if there is a saint assigned to spreading sunshine in the South Island. If there is, he's doing a lousy job.

Today is a little bit of everything, mist, fleeting darkening clouds, chill, wind, and some nice periods of complete calm and the almighty feeling of sun. I guess weather is pretty much like life itself.

Whatever the elements, I still love most to climb to the crown of my hill over my land by my tree and the best trout stream in New Zealand, which is also mine. From up here the world down there seems understandable and manageable. These days when I meditate I seem to come up with a lot better answers.

The latest on Ireland was explained to me up here. It went like this. Sir Roger Casement was hanged. A few days later the British general in Ireland disappeared and has never been found. The executions stopped and those under death sentence were commuted to prison terms. A year later everyone was freed on amnesty including seventeen hundred republicans from the prisoner of war camp in Wales.

In 1918 the Irish voted in the Sinn Fein Party, which recognized the Republic that was declared at the General Post Office in the Easter Rising of 1916. This compelled the British to sit down and talk things over, but they came kicking and screaming all the way.

Whatever the fate of the conferences, Ireland is bound to get the shaft and no doubt will have to gird up for another round of troubles. Nonetheless, we are moving in the right direction.

As for my family, things are in good order, relatively speaking. There are family quarrels, some sickness, misunderstood children, and all the disasters that befall every family in every lifetime. However, the view from the crown of the hill says that the Larkins have come through in grand fashion. From the moment Rory and I declared our love, I got around to seeing my kids differently.

Like Tommy, for example. I had him slated as the minor partner in the ranch, never stopping to think that Tommy might have a few plans of his own. So, one day his teacher calls me in and shows me some of Tommy's paintings of scenery and Maoris and the animals and says, "Liam Larkin, this boy is an artist, a gem who will go as far as his ambition will carry him. He needs training."

Well, shyte, what does a South Island schoolmaster know? Then Mildred showed me Tommy's hidden trove of drawings and paintings. There were sketches of me that spoke off the paper, they were that fine. And one of his mother like to brought me to weeping. See, he never showed me his art because he was afraid I'd be disappointed by him not wanting to be a rancher.

Christ, I hope a person can make a living by painting pictures. My position was real clear. I was going to do everything to encourage and support him and I'd be there if, God forbid, he fell on his ass.

So Tommy Larkin is in Paris. I don't know how much art he's learning yet but he sure is getting an education on women and having a hell of a time.

Madge, my oldest girl, was the only one to fulfill her mother's dreams. She married a nice boy, Donnie, who got through the war in one piece. The government gave out veterans' homesteads and he's doing very well on a good section of land. I've a grandson from them, already.

My major problem with Madge and Donnie is to try not to give them too much too soon. Anyhow, Donnie is a proud kid, up from poverty and determined to make it on his own.

I might add that I showed extraordinary tolerance by making no fuss over him not being a member of the true faith. He's a good hunting partner. He used to have to bag a rabbit when he was a kid, or go hungry. I kind of hope they raise their kids as Catholics, but on the other hand, it doesn't really make much difference now, does it?

If Tommy fooled the old Squire here, Spring totally flabbergasted me. She got into a group of anthropologists who were studying Maori origins and customs and became completely taken with that sort of work. She wants to spend her life learning the various native tribes and peoples of the South Pacific islands.

Now I can't honestly figure out the value of such a profession. Well maybe, if she spent her time tracing Irish roots, that would be different. But, mind you, my daughter Spring is the first accepted and only female anthropology student in the London School of Economics.

Spring is no beauty but well endowed, and she has a way with the lads, and although she likes them and they like her, her anthropology comes first ... so she writes. She and Tommy exchange London and Paris visits often and apparently know how to have a good old time. Mind you, these kids never ... hardly ever ... ask for extra money. You know how good it makes me feel that I can provide this life for them?

I suppose the Larkin of us all is Father Dary. He's not "Father" any more except that he's an expectant father. He fell desperately in love with a magnificent creature, I'm told. Her name is Rachael and she's the daughter of Atty Fitzpatrick. Rachael is the fancy spelling for Rachel.

When he returned from the war and resigned the priesthood we figured there would be hell to pay, but his Bishop, Mooney, made a powerful stand on his behalf on his right side and the Countess Caroline Hubble made an equally powerful stand on his left.

Dary had given years of devoted service in the Bogside, working the bottom of the pit. Powerful support arose for him from the people.

The Larkin name in Derry and Donegal is not to be underestimated, and I suppose his Rachael girl is able to charm the devil's grandmother.

Caroline Hubble helped sponsor his founding of an institute of advanced study and personal tutoring for exceptional students from all over Ireland.

In his last letter Dary said he was seriously considering running for the late Kevin O'Garvey's seat, be it in the British Parliament or an Irish Parliament.

Brigid . . . well nothing much will change there. She remains the keeper of the ashes.

Like I said, things are in pretty good order, relatively speaking. I've got a special love for Georgia. I have signed over a hundred acres of land and with my help and government help built a rehabilitation facility large enough to hold twenty war veterans at a time.

It is not that she and her staff can restore them to full physical or mental health, but she can do enough so that when they leave, they can carry on a useful and independent life. Three of her lads are excellent hands on the ranch. For our little country of a million people, our losses were terrible . . . just terrible.

Hey! Hey! Hey! By God, there's sunshine for you! Not from that lazy saint up in the sky but sunshine coming up the hill on horseback through the mist.

Rory and Georgia. They are so hot for each other I swear that one of these days they're going to get into bed and fry each other to crisps.

And would you ever look at little Rory sitting in the front of her daddy's saddle and Georgia riding with their son . . . my grandson. He's a real thumper, that boy. Do you know what they named him? They named him Liam, after me.

Can you ever imagine something like that?